SHADOWORLD

D1522028

SHADOWORLD

Book 4 of the Colorworld Series

Rachel E Kelly

Published by Colorworld Books, Williston, North Dakota, USA

Shadoworld. Copyright © 2015 Rachel E Kelly

Published by Colorworld Books, Williston, North Dakota, USA.

Web Site: http://colorworldbooks.com

ISBN-13: 978-1517271664

Cover Photograph by Richard J Heeks

Cover Design by Beth Weatherly

For Darkness and Winter
-who birthed Shadoworld.

The Allegory of the Cave

Within a cave are men who have been prisoners there since birth. Their legs and necks are fastened so that they can only look straight ahead at a wall where shadows are cast from a fire and puppet show taking place behind them.

Tell me, could our prisoners see anything of themselves or their fellows other than shadows? Would they not assume that the shadows they saw were the real things?

Suppose one of them were let loose and compelled to stand up and turn his head. He would have a hard time understanding how the puppets are truer than the shadows.

Suppose he is then forcibly drug up and out of the cave and into the real sunlight. He would be frightened, unable to properly perceive a single one of the things he was now told were real because of the glaring light.

At first, he would find it easiest to look at shadows. Then he might observe reflections. Finally he would be able to look upon and understand the objects themselves. The last thing he would be able to do would be to gaze upon the sun itself.

He would come to understand that the sun is responsible for allowing him to see anything at all.

What would then happen if he went back to sit in his old seat in the cave? His eyes would be blinded by the comparative darkness because he had come in so suddenly out of such brilliance.

As he learns to perceive the shadows again, he would likely make a fool of himself. Especially if he tried to describe what he saw outside the cave to his fellow prisoners.

But knowing that the light is responsible for all, and having seen it in its truest form himself, he would eventually discern all that is right and valuable in anything—even the shadows.

Thus we see that the eyes may be unsighted in two ways: transitioning from light to darkness or from darkness to light. The same applies to the mind.

-The Republic, by Plato

One

Closing the lid of the industrial dishwasher, I push a button to start it. I carry a tray of freshly washed mugs and plates I unloaded out to the front, catching a glimpse of the clock as I pass. Twenty minutes to closing and there are still almost twenty people in here. The chilly January night must have enticed more customers than usual into the warmth of the coffee shop.

"We're not getting out of here until midnight," James mumbles as he wipes down one of the espresso machines.

"Hot date?" I tease, stacking the mugs carefully on the counter next to the machine he's working on.

James sighs wistfully. "I thought that hottie in the corner was interested because he's been looking over here all night. But I've been watching and he only looks over here when you're in the picture." James shakes his head disappointedly, his light brown, sweeping bangs falling into his eyes. "Flash that wedding ring more often, sweetie. You're cramping my style." He throws his bangs back with a toss of his head.

I look briefly to the man in the corner bent over a cup of coffee and holding a book. He's wearing a beanie and a distinct pair of square-rimmed glasses; I don't remember serving him, so James must have. I turn back to the clean dishes. "Please. I'm almost nine months pregnant. If that doesn't send the 'taken' message, I doubt a ring will make any difference."

"I need gaydar classes," James laments. "All I see is hot and not hot."

I laugh, placing the last mug on the stack. "Maybe if you'd try for more than looks, your gaydar would kick in."

"Says the woman married to Rico Suave."

I swat him in the butt with my empty tray.

"Excuse me," says a female voice from the counter. "Can I get this in a to-go cup?"

"Yep," I answer, reaching for a Styrofoam cup and lid.

"Thanks," she says enthusiastically as her friend comes up beside her. The two become locked in conversation about the band they went to see earlier as they turn in unison for the door. For a fleeting moment I begrudge them their carefree evening, wishing I'd had a little more time after recovering from leukemia to just live and enjoy life a little bit. Instead I'm about to be a mother. I'm working at the coffee shop as a way to integrate myself with a normal life. It's a lot harder than it sounds, because I've found that losing superhuman abilities is like losing a limb, or one of your five senses.

"He's looking at you again," James says out of the corner of his mouth as he leans against the counter.

"Still don't care, James," I sing-song. "Go clean something."

He complains about me stealing all the testosterone in the room as he saunters off to the back. My curiosity has gotten the better of me, and when I peek at the corner again I can see that the guy over there is indeed staring at me. And interestingly, he doesn't look away when he catches my eye. He doesn't smile, and I look away first.

I do not want this guy hanging around until after closing, so I'm going to take this creep into my own hands. Maybe I can also encourage some of these people to the door at the same time. I grab a stack of disposable cups and lids and weave through the tables, asking people if they want their beverages to-go. When I get to his table, I offer him a friendly smile. "Would you like a to-go cup, sir?" But I don't wait for him to answer. I pick up his mug and dump it into the cup, fastening the lid and sliding it in front of him. "We close in ten minutes," I say before heading for the next table.

"When are you due?" the guy asks from behind me.

I turn around, caught off guard by the question. Our eyes connect for the second time and a wave of… something washes over me. Familiarity maybe? He's clean-shaven and his features have a nondescript roundness to them that would make it difficult to draw up his likeness in my head after the fact. So if he is, in fact, someone I have met before it's no wonder I can't remember. James said he was hot but the glasses and the hat define his 'look' more than anything else.

"Soon," I manage to reply, and it's one of the few times that my impending due-date doesn't stir me with anxiety, distracted as I am by the man's face. I can't tell how old he is.

He gives me barely a smile. "Boy or girl?"

"Boy," I reply. "I don't actually have ultrasound confirmation. My husband doesn't want to know the gender, but I have a feeling."

Why am I striking up a conversation? I catch my hand resting casually on the chair across from him, my weight shifted to one foot to get more comfortable.

"Congratulations," he says, sipping his coffee from the cup I gave him.

"On what?" I say. "Having sex?"

Oh my gosh. Did that come out of my mouth?

He clears his throat and adjusts his glasses with a thumb and forefinger.

"I mean—you know, people say that all the time and I'm not sure why," I blurt. "It's not like I had to work for it. It happened on accident. Well, not on accident. It just wasn't planned. I mean, I know how it happens, but I didn't think I could get pregnant at the time and—" I clamp my mouth shut. *What the crap was that, Wendy?*

A few seconds of weird silence pass. I'm less mortified than I'd expect, but no less surprised that something so brazen would come out of my mouth.

"I can see your point," he says. "But it's the thing people say."

I nod. "I know, it's just... small talk has always made me uncomfortable. I used to—" I stop, appalled that I was about to tell a stranger that I used to be an empath, capable of sensing people's emotions so distinctly that I'd been accused of being a telepath. Geez, I must be lonely or something. Or maybe it was the fight I had with Gabriel before I came to work today that has me wanting to commiserate with strangers. I step back. "Sorry. I just realized I need a life. Enjoy your evening." I turn to go before anything else falls out of my mouth.

"Is the baby healthy?" he asks.

Once again I hesitate and turn back. This time I resist the compulsion to stand at-ease. But unexpectedly I'm a little touched by what sounds like genuine interest.

"Yes," I reply.

"I think the congratulations still stands," he smiles. "Considering how difficult pregnancy can be, endurance is a feat."

He closes his book and tucks it into his backpack on the floor. He touches the side of his glasses with thumb and forefinger as if he's about to adjust them again, but catches himself in the action. I bet it's a nervous tell. Odd since I couldn't be more comfortable talking to him, which is in and of itself a miracle. Ever since losing my life force abilities I find conversation shallow and empty. So I don't invite it.

He scoots his chair out and scoops up his cup and slings his backpack over his shoulder at the same time. He holds a hand out to me after he stands. "It was nice to meet you, Mrs…?"

My eyes fall to his outstretched hand, and the usual part of me rebels. Where once I avoided touching people for fear of hurting them, now I avoid touching them for fear of hurting myself. Skin contact is a torturous reminder of what I don't have. I lived my whole life able to feel people through their skin, and later by being in their vicinity. Now I'm paralyzed, in a sense; I used to experience so much by comparison. "I'm Wendy," I reply.

His hand falls, and I could swear his face falls with it. "Take care, Wendy," he says.

"You too," I reply. I watch his back as he pushes through the glass door and into the street, wondering if I'll ever see him again. I'll probably give birth soon, which will put me out of commission. I'm not sure if I'll come back to work afterward. I don't even know the guy's name…

Confusion takes the place of disappointment. Why am I bothered about never seeing some random customer again?

Maybe it was because I actually *wanted* to talk to someone. Why to him, though?

I turn away from the door and find that the place has cleared out. "You dirty double-crosser," James scowls as he stacks dirty dishes from the empty tables into his bin. "You got his number, didn't you?"

"I did not," I say defensively, coming to help him, starting on a table behind him in order to hide my embarrassment. I can only imagine how that looked. "We were just talking."

"Talking is always how it starts," he says, turning around to hold the bin out for me to put the dishes in. "Are you going to give me the scoop or what? I need to live vicariously."

"I am happily married, James," I say, annoyed at his prying insistence, keeping my head down while moving to another table.

"Could have fooled me," James mumbles.

I stop and put my hands on my hips. "Excuse me? I'm not allowed to talk to people? I have a conversation with one guy and all of a sudden that means I have a crappy marriage?" Angry, I snatch a rag from the side of the tub and start scrubbing a table vigorously.

James has a quicker temper than I do, but this is the first time I've seen it directed at me. James likes to get in people's faces when he's mad, and he does so now, walking up to me and aggravating my personal space. "I'm not talking about that guy," he snaps. "But I've got two working eyes and it doesn't take a marriage therapist to see that there's tension between you and Gabe. Every time he comes in here after work to fawn over you, you act like you have a million things to do all of a sudden. You disappear in the back, washing dishes. You wipe down tables that are already clean. You sweep the floor. Damn, woman. You've got a vision of Latin perfection to warm your bed every night and you give him the cold shoulder like he beats you at home."

"You have no idea what you're talking about," I say, hands on my hips. "You have no idea what Gabriel and I have been through, what we're *going* through."

James' jaw drops and he drags out a chair all of a sudden, sitting down in one movement. "Oh hell, he does hit you, doesn't he?" he says in one horrified breath.

"What? Of course not!" I say, appalled. "Why would you think that?"

He pats the table for me to sit down. "It's okay, sweetie. This is a safe place. I'm sorry I lost my temper. I should have known—well, I *did* know. I just wanted to believe in fairy tales."

I refuse his invitation. "James," I say sternly. "Gabriel does *not* hit me. He's the most thoughtful, amazing man ever."

James doesn't look convinced. "Wendy, I swear I'm not going to tell anyone. You can talk to me. I know it's addictive to be with him. They say the abusers are usually the charming ones. But you're going to have a baby soon. You don't want him to grow up with that kind of example, do you?"

"Stop it, James!" I say. "Gabriel is everything in private that he is in public. That's why I married him. I swear to you, he does *not* abuse me!"

James sits back in his chair, squinting at me. Desperate for a way to make him believe me, it hits me that if James can so easily jump to believing the worst of Gabriel, then it's because I have *made* it that easy. I haven't looked at my behavior toward Gabriel from James' perspective before.

I plop down in the chair across from him. "James, I'm not lying. Gabriel is… He just… demands a lot." I search for a better way to put it, but anything more descriptive is not acceptable to tell. "And I—have issues I'm working through. He's impatient for me to do that, not to mention I'm a mess because I'm about to become a mother, so yeah, it stresses us both out. We've both been through major changes." I look James in the eye now to convey my seriousness. "But he does not abuse me in any way. We're just… normal married people trying to make it work."

Normal married people. That's the problem. I've spent my whole life cheating, reading people supernatually and never having to blindly trust anyone. And my inability to cope has poisoned every other aspect of my relationship. And I'm pregnant in the midst of it.

I stand up, determined not to go there tonight. "Let's hurry up. I want to see my pillow in an hour."

James doesn't pry further, which I think means he finally believes me. I consider it settled as I methodically go through the closing routine. Busy hands and an idle mind allow too much thinking though. James' words about how I treat Gabriel gnaw me with guilt. But I don't know how to change the lack of connection I feel whenever he is around. I hate it. I hate the chore it is to be around my own husband. I hate that he thinks he knows what's good for me better than I do. He says my problem is not my inability to cope with losing my abilities; it's my refusal to find a new passion and purpose. He tried to sign me up for an art class once, and I didn't take it well. He held his ground so firmly that, in an effort to prove my point, I finally confessed that intimacy felt so devoid of connection that I often felt used at the end of it.

I have never seen him so upset as I did that night. "Offering intimacy when you don't mean any of it appears to be a common pattern with you. And I keep falling for it," he had said angrily before spending two nights away from the house. When we spoke again, we agreed to not be intimate until I could offer myself honestly. It's been three months and that day has not yet come.

Since then, things between us have balanced out mostly, at least on the surface. The calm is ominous. And my pregnancy is a ticking time bomb. I don't want to be a mother right now, and I worry the added pressure on both me and Gabriel will break us entirely.

I stop winding the vacuum cleaner cord and swear under my breath. I said I wasn't going to go here tonight. My hands are cold and numb as I finish putting the vacuum away. I can't face Gabriel like this. I wish he wouldn't wait up for me after work. He says it's the only way he'll get to see me since he works in the mornings during the week and I always close at the coffee shop—that was what we argued about earlier today.

When James and I finish, I turn off the lights and we exit through the back, greeted by a short-lived, brisk wind. I'm jumpy and distracted, which causes me to forget to set the alarm. "Crap," I say as I pause with my key in the lock. "I forgot again."

"I'll get it," James says.

I shake my head, grateful for the opportunity to put off heading for home, even if it is only for a minute. "Go ahead. I got this," I say as I pull the door open again.

"Are you sure?" James says skeptically, huddled into his hoodie sweatshirt, hands buried in the front pocket.

"Yes. Go. I'm fine. You look like you're going to freeze."

He looks at me, unsure. I shoo him with a hand and go back inside without waiting for him to answer. Darkness envelopes me as I shut the door and my heart jumps like it always does in the dark. I count to ten before flipping the switch. I do that every time I go into a dark room. I'm hoping I can desensitize myself to it and it won't frighten me so much.

I open the door that leads to the store front, my eye catching on something falling past the front windows. I move forward to get a better look.

"Is that snow?" I ask the empty coffee shop. Sure enough, it is. Large blobs of white plummet to the ground steadily, especially visible against the yellow beam cast by the nearby streetlight. I didn't know it came down in clumps like that. I've only ever seen snow once before, and it was sparse flurries of tiny flakes then. I dig my phone out of my pocket, curious if snow is in the forecast. That's when I see the text from Gabriel:

Are you all right?

Irritation bubbles in me. He knows what time I get out. Why is he freaking out that I'm not home yet?

If I reply, I'll end up saying something snide, so I don't bother. I wipe a few tears from my eyes, disgusted with myself because I wish I could not be so angry at him over such a small thing. I tuck the phone back in my coat pocket, arm the security system, and exit through the back again. A cup of coffee in one hand, I fumble my key into the lock and turn the deadbolt with the other.

I drop the shop keys in my bag and shove my free hand deep into my coat pocket.

"Hey sweetie, how 'bout you gimme a coffee?" a gravelly voice says from nearby.

I jump and whip my head to the right. A dark figure emerges from the shadows by the dumpster across the alley. He's well-dressed but not wearing a coat. He probably wandered here from the bar the next block over; it wouldn't be the first time. He staggers a little bit as he comes toward me.

"Back off," I growl, holding my ground.

He sways to a stop, miffed. "Hey, I only wanna coffee."

"We're closed," I say.

"You got one in yer hand right there," he slurs, jutting his chin at my right hand.

I look from the coffee to him. "It's for someone else."

"Yer boyfriend? He won't mind." He shuffles a few steps closer to me.

Already upset over the events of the night so far, I make a split-second decision. "Fine," I say, taking the lid off the coffee. "You want this coffee? You can have it." I toss the contents of the cup at the man. The dark liquid hits him squarely in the chest and he jumps back. He calls me all sorts of ugly names as I toss both the lid and cup into a nearby dumpster. I'm sure I burned him pretty good. I know it was hot because I put it in the microwave right before I came out here, but to my surprise he doesn't retreat to nurse his wounds. Instead, he yanks his sweater off and launches himself at me.

Before I have time to react, a commanding, familiar voice from behind me says, "Stop where you are." It's Farlen, my bodyguard.

The man obeys, standing in the middle of the alley, shirtless with an angry red patch on his hairy chest.

"If you don't want me to turn you over to police for harassment, turn around and go back where you came from," Farlen says. I look over my shoulder to see his statuesque form holding a gun aimed at the lurker, his thin eyebrows drawn together sternly as he watches the man spew a few more insults and turn to walk a not-so-straight line back down the alley.

A bit shaken by my close call, I play off my nerves, burying my hands in my pockets and hunkering into my coat to escape the gentle but frigid wind. "Sorry I had to use your coffee in self-defense," I say. "Riding with me?"

Farlen nods as we walk toward my small car parked down a side-street.

"How about this snow? Weird, huh? How often does that happen? Once a decade?" I say, looking up at the white flakes falling more heavily.

"Mrs. Dumas, that wasn't very smart."

I give him a sour look. "Don't you start. It's bad enough I have to have protection still. At least let me fight my own battles when I can."

"What would you have done had I not been there?"

"Kicked him in the nads," I reply, searching for the right button on the key fob in my pocket to unlock the car doors.

Farlen walks around to the passenger-side. "That's effective only if you connect."

"Who says I wouldn't?" I say over the top of the car, pulling my door open.

"Drunk men tend to protect their family jewels better than you'd expect."

I ease behind the steering wheel of my car. With all of my layers on, my pregnant belly almost touches it. Hands numb again, but this time from the cold, I ignore Farlen and huddle in my seat, holding my fingers to my mouth to blow on them.

"You'd think someone who grew so accustomed to wearing gloves all the time would have a pair handy when they're obviously necessary," Farlen says, an uncommon smirk on his face.

I glance at him as I continue to blow warmth into my fingers. "Did you just make a funny, Mr. Spock?" I say, using my brother Ezra's moniker for Farlen. Jokes and sarcasm aren't really Farlen's style, but I could swear that ever since Ezra started calling him that, he purposely plays the logical, even-keeled Star Trek character even more. Of course, it probably only seems that way because I lack my emodar. It makes people seem flatter than they actually are on the inside.

Farlen isn't paying attention to me though. Instead, I can tell he's suddenly on high alert. He puts a hand on the dash as he peers through the windshield that's slowly becoming blanketed with snow. "Drive, Mrs. Dumas," he commands. "Immediately."

Having never been ordered so directly to do anything by Farlen before, I obey, backing out of my spot swiftly and calming my nerves. Something is wrong.

Two

*E*asy," Farlen says, his hand still on the dash. "No rush."

"But you said—"

"Mark has it under control. But you need to get moving in case."

Hands at two and ten, I accelerate nervously into the street and head toward home: my Uncle Moby's house. Glancing periodically at all of my mirrors, I don't see anything suspect, but I guess that's why Farlen has this job and not me.

"What's going on, Farlen?" I ask when I can't take the suspense any more.

"Who was the gentleman you were speaking with in the coffee shop?" Farlen asks.

"You know James—"

"No, the man in the corner," Farlen interrupts.

"Oh," I say. "I don't know. Some guy. I encouraged him to get lost." I furrow my brow. "Hey, how do you know that anyway? Were you hiding out in there? Geez, Farlen, you're sneaky. Where were you?"

Farlen shakes his head, checking my mirrors. "Same place I always am. Patrolling the perimeter. But we have other means…"

"Other means?" I demand. "Do you have someone spying on me inside? That is messed up. I don't need people stalking my every move," I whine. "It's a public place. What do you expect is going to happen?"

"We don't spy on you, Mrs. Dumas," Farlen says. "But our counter-surveillance revealed that someone was tapping into the camera feed inside the shop, so we got a look at what they were seeing."

"Let 'em see!" I say, throwing a hand up. "What do I care?"

"Your value is your knowledge. You know more about life forces than anyone," Farlen says coolly. We've had this conversation before.

"Not sure what watching me pour coffee is going to tell them," I grumble.

"Understood. We'll make a circuit until backup arrives," Farlen says into his communicator. Then to me, "Make a right at this light. We've cornered someone."

My eyes widen in surprise as I stop at the light before turning. "Who?" I say, excited.

"Carl," Farlen replies.

"No way!" We haven't been able to get in touch with my father since he called to give me a list of people he and Louise had done hypno-touch on—a list we later suspected was incomplete. "What was he doing?"

Farlen's face goes impassive, and it looks like he's listening to whoever is speaking in his ear.

"What!" I demand when Farlen's expression becomes pensive. I restrain myself from stomping the gas pedal. Except for the fact that Gabriel retained his astounding ability to be able to count outlandish quantities instantly and memorize books cover to cover, the supernatural chapter of my life is over. The memories of those months have faded like any other memory. The trauma of loss remains, though. Carl is… a connection to that world even though he lost his ability years ago. I can't help but be excited.

Farlen finally replies, "Mark believes Carl may have been trying to be caught."

That wasn't what I expected. "Trying to be caught… Like, he walked up to Mark with his hands up?"

"Not exactly. Turn here," Farlen indicates.

"How exactly?" I demand. "And you're going to let me talk to him, right?"

"Robert has ordered that we defer to you as to what to do with Carl. It looks like Mark rightly assumed that you'd want to see him. So as soon as the area is secure, we'll meet up there."

"Okay. And while we drive in circles, you can tell me how you came across Carl."

"Like I said, it was clear someone was tapping into the coffee shop security cameras remotely, so I called backup to have them keep a tighter perimeter in case someone got excited. Mark finally traced the signal to a nearby bar, and he found Carl there."

"What was he doing?"

"Sipping a beer from what I hear. Watching the camera feed from his mobile phone."

"Wait, if you guys were running a perimeter, how did that drunk guy end up getting anywhere near me?" I ask, making another turn.

Farlen gives me his second smile of the night. "Contrary to your opinion, we do let you handle your own battles if possible. I knew he was there before you emerged."

I glare at him. "Somehow that doesn't make me feel better about your spying. I think you just insulted me a little bit."

"On our way," Farlen says after touching his ear. Then to me, "We can head back."

Farlen directs me to the bar a block away from the coffee shop. The place must be clearing out because there are parking spots on the street right out front. I pull into one and send a quick text to Gabriel to let him know I'll be late. Farlen leads the way up the snow-covered walk. I'm full of nervous excitement as I open the front door. A gust of warmth hits me as I step into the dimly lit interior. A quick glance around reveals that there are maybe ten people left. It's a nice place, actually. It looks like it's been remodeled recently to have more contemporary furniture. Popular music emanates from overhead and the extensive liquor collection behind the bar is backlit, making the ambiance more like a club. I spot Mark and another man I recognize as part of the security detail flank a hunched figure at the bar.

As I approach, Mark stands up and offers me his stool. The hunched figure—presumably Carl—doesn't look up. When I take Mark's seat, however, my father's eyes shift my way. He's wearing a mustache now, hiding most of our family resemblance. "I told them I wanted to see Rob," he says.

"Could have fooled me," I reply, unzipping my coat because it's stifling in here. "Considering that if you wanted to see Robert you should have staked out *his* place of work instead of mine."

Carl lifts his mug and guzzles the remainder of his beer before dropping it back to the counter none too carefully. "One more," he calls out to the bartender.

"Robert's not coming unless I ask him to," I prod, propping an elbow on the bar. "And I'm not going to ask him if I don't have a good reason."

Carl turns in his stool to face me, his eyes bloodshot. I wonder how much he's had to drink. "Good reason," he says. "Like what?"

The bartender plunks another full mug down and then looks at me questioningly.

I wave her off. "I don't know. You tell me why you want to see him and I'll decide if it's good."

He laughs, turns back to his beer, and takes a swig before asking, "How far along are you?"

"I'm due in a week," I reply. "What do you want Robert for?"

He runs a finger over the edge of his glass. "Knew it," he murmurs. "Bastards."

I'm about to open my mouth to demand that he talk to me, but Carl says, "I need Rob. Get me my brother."

"Get him yourself. You know where he works," I say, frustrated. "You have his number."

"If it were that easy, I would have done it. This is my last chance."

"You're not making any sense."

He looks like he's calculating, still running his finger over the glass' edge and watching the bartender sweep behind the counter without actually seeing her. "Do you want your child to be safe?"

I put my hand on the bar and lean toward him. "Excuse me? Is that a threat?"

Carl turns to face me abruptly and I flinch. "Is it?" he says.

I narrow my eyes.

"I need Robert to help me disappear."

"Why?" I say. "Is this like the last time? People on your back over what you did to them?"

"Doesn't matter."

"Yes. It does." I cross my arms. "You're asking me for a favor. I'm entitled to information."

"You want information? Okay, here's the most useful information I can give you: stick tight with Rob. You'll be fine."

I'm not sure how to respond to that, but Carl preempts further questions by shooing me with his hand. "Call Rob. Tell him to make me disappear and I'll never darken your door again."

I glance up at Mark who stands behind Carl, at the ready. I've been under the impression that Carl is the one who has been instigating the times I've been followed in the last few months. That's why I still have protection. Whoever it is has resources, because most of what Mark does is sweep for surveillance on me and the rest of my family. But Carl is implying that he isn't the only threat.

SHADOWORLD

"Stick with Robert because?" Mark prompts.

Carl looks up at Mark now. "Like you don't know. Some of us go to church, trying to follow God. Some of us follow Rob. The difference is Rob delivers." Carl looks at me now and laughs, taking a swig. "Clever man, my brother. Wastes his talent, in my opinion, but even so he gets a helluva lot done, doesn't he?" He gulps down half his beer at once.

I bite my tongue against defending my uncle. Carl is beyond understanding what makes Robert so special. To me he is Uncle Moby, because he is a huge but little seen force. He spends most of his time beneath the surface. But when he reveals himself, it is always magnificent. "Tell me about the list you gave us," I try. "Names were missing, weren't they? Were they already dead?"

"What list?" Carl says disinterestedly.

"The hypno-touch people I cured?" I say. Carl can't have forgotten that he called me up and gave me that list.

He looks confused for a moment but then he sits up in recognition. "Oh. Sure. The list."

I wait expectantly.

"What did you want to know?" he says.

I puff impatiently. He really is drunk. "Why didn't you give us the whole list—why did you leave off some names? Kaylen says some were missing that she remembered from the compound—which means they can't have died from hypno-touch sickness already."

Carl guffaws. "You wanted the *whole* list? Good lord, Wendy. A bit too ambitious for your own good."

I pause, watching him peer into his beer, distracted. The more I watch him and turn his words over, the madder I get. He acts like the list was a hobby to kill time. "Carl," I say carefully, determined not to lose my temper with him. "How many names are on the *whole* list?"

His glazed-over eyes shift up to my face, but he doesn't answer. I doubt he's seeing me.

"Carl," I say, and then snap my fingers in front of his face. He blinks a few times. "How many people?" I repeat.

"Just me," Carl says. "Me, myself, and I." He looks around. "Where's my brother?"

I'm getting nowhere, and Carl is getting more drunk by the minute. I stand up and look at Mark. "Let Robert figure out what to do with him. I'm tired. I need to get home before Gabriel comes after me."

Carl leaves his half-finished beer on the counter and swivels around, holding his wrists out to Mark. "Cuff me, Sheriff."

Mark is already on the phone with Robert it looks like, and I follow Farlen toward the door. Before I get too far away, Carl says, "Wendy, a piece of advice: boats aren't very secure."

I look over my shoulder and say, "Carl, I lost my ability. No one wants me like this."

Carl's eyebrows lift, maybe in surprise, maybe in consideration. But he chuckles before holding up his hands and examining them. He chuckles. "So did I. Didn't stop it though."

"Stop what?" I say, having turned around again.

"How far along are you?" Carl asks, his eyes on my belly.

I roll my eyes and follow Farlen again. When we meet the outside air, Farlen says, "He has a point."

Holding my car door open, I say, "Carl? About what?"

"The boat is not secure."

"In case you hadn't noticed, I don't live on the boat. I haven't been anywhere near it in months." After I recovered from leukemia, Gabriel bought our first home—a boat. He wanted us to fix it up together. It was supposed to be a bonding experience. But we discovered I was pregnant and I told Gabriel I was not going to live on a boat with a newborn. We've been trying to sell it.

Farlen doesn't respond even when I look at him. He's trying to look busy with surveying our surroundings.

"Farlen, what?"

"Nothing." He opens his door and we both get in the car.

"Don't nothing me, Mr. Spock," I demand.

"I don't even know what that means," he says, putting on his seatbelt.

"It means that I know there is a reason you brought up the boat. You barely speak most of the time. So when you do, I know something's up—oh my gosh! The boat." A shock of realization hits me. "Gabriel," I say in a low voice, putting my hands on the wheel in irritation. "He's been working on it, hasn't he?"

Farlen looks straight ahead.

I face him. "Don't worry. I won't rat you out. But he is so going to get it." I start the car and pull into the street, furious.

Farlen sighs.

Three

*W*hat did you do today?" I ask from the bathroom, brushing my short bob of hair.

Gabriel's face appears in the doorway instantaneously. He leans against the jamb and pushes his nearly black bangs to the side. "Shouted. Paced. Demanded. Repeated myself. You know, everything involved in molding young minds. Teenagers are exceptionally hard-headed considering their youth. I'm going back to college-level instruction as soon as there's an opening."

"Anything else?" I place my brush in the drawer and reach for my toothbrush.

I catch his expression in the mirror. He looks delighted by my interest—not what I expected from him when I'm sure he's been keeping his afternoon activities from me. "Worried about you. You got in awfully late. Did you go out without me?" He looks nonchalant, but I have no doubt the idea bothers him.

"I know you worry," I say, squeezing the toothpaste. "That's why I texted you to say I'd be late."

"Late is something like thirty minutes. It's nearly two A.M."

"No. Late is anything after the usual time," I garble with the toothbrush in my mouth.

"I beg to differ," Gabriel says, crossing his arms. "That may be the denotative meaning, but in our culture, the connotative meaning implies a limited window of time."

As I brush back and forth, up and down, I use the reprieve to cut my temper down a notch. I spit toothpaste in the sink and turn around. "I know you check up on me through Farlen. So it's condescending to pick at me about what time I got home as if you didn't know how late I was going to be *and* what I was doing."

He raises an eyebrow slightly but doesn't move. "It would be nice if I didn't have to check with Farlen to find out where my wife is."

"It would be nice if my husband trusted me to get home without checking up on me all the time."

"That would be nice, wouldn't it?"

My mouth opens. "You don't trust me?"

"Why does that bother you?"

"Why does it bother me that you don't trust me?" I say incredulously. "Seriously?"

"You certainly don't trust *me*, so I don't know why that would be so appalling."

"I do too!" I say, my face turning red.

"No," he says. "You never share what's going on in your head. Secrecy is pretty difficult to trust. You should know."

"Secrecy?" I exclaim. "I'm not the only one not sharing things. How about you and the boat? Huh? How long have you been working on it and keeping it from me?"

He pushes off the door jamb and his hands fall to his sides. "It was going to be a surprise. And I had to do something with myself while you were at work!"

"Then read a book!" I yell. "Clean the bathroom! Organize the closet! Get a hobby! Don't work on a boat that we agreed to sell and then hide it from me! I said I didn't want it. Why would you surprise me with something I don't want?"

"I actually cleaned the bathroom yesterday," he says calmly. "And refinishing the boat is my hobby."

"Shut up!" I shrill. "You know what I'm saying!"

"Yes, fine. I'm fixing up the boat. For you—for us. I know you said you didn't want it, but that will be short-lived. When you see what I've done, you'll want to keep it. We don't have to live on it. We'll make it a weekend hobby."

"Our weekend hobby will be a newborn!" I say. "Not *boating*. If you've fixed it up, sell it. Maybe it will earn us a down payment on a house."

"Is that what this is about? That we live with your uncle?"

"Of course not! Living with my uncle was my idea. What this is about is that you hid it from me!"

He walks toward me. "No," he says, and I can tell he's controlling his voice. "What this is about is you not trusting me. I'm okay with that. Really. What I'm not okay with is you not giving me a chance to earn your trust. You shut me out every time I try. And I…" He puts his face in his hands and doesn't move.

Stepping back until the counter hits my back, I watch him, searching for his emotions, but it's like staring at a screen full of static and waiting for something to appear. There are a million miles between us, and I don't know how to cross. Torn between anger and guilt, my tears have already made it out of my eyes. Guilt wins. "I'm sorry," I whisper as I look over his shoulder for an escape route.

"What do I do?" he asks, looking up finally and locking me in place with his eyes. "You're picking a fight with me over the boat. Why?"

I shake my head and sink to the floor, closing my eyes.

"Don't do that," he pleads. "Don't close your eyes. They're all I have left."

"I'm sorry," I repeat.

"Please," he whispers. "Why won't you look at me?"

"I wish I'd stayed blind," I say, my voice cracked. "It would have been easier."

Silence.

"I hate this," I say, burying my palms in my eyes. "I don't want to keep pretending that I'm going to get better. It's been six months. How can I be a mother like this?"

I bring one knee up and count to five before continuing, "This body… It's half-alive. How do people live this way? How do they not shrivel up inside from the lack of feeling?"

He still doesn't speak.

"I'm going to let Uncle Moby figure out what to do with Carl because I need to—" I take a deep breath, cross my arms over my raised knee, unable to look at him still. "I finally understood what happened to him—why he's so broken. He lost his gift and he never recovered. He spent all those years fighting to get it back." Sobs build in my chest and I whisper, so softly I'm not sure if he can hear me, "I'm becoming him."

Several seconds of silence pass. I'm afraid to open my eyes so I lay my head on my arms. I can't bear to see his face. His disappointment will be too much to take. I can't expect him to want to keep reaching for me when I never reach back.

"I want to love you," I whisper, saying words I've thought hundreds of times but never had the guts to say because of how terrible they are. I don't know if he's still here, and something about not knowing has given me bravery.

When I am met with further silence, I say, "But I don't know how to."

Suddenly, a wave of exhaustion washes over me, dulling the edges of my despair. I suddenly desperately want to be alone, and I slump where I sit, seriously entertaining sleeping on the floor.

I hear the bedroom door close, and I open my eyes to an empty bathroom. I stumble out to the bed and bury myself, too tired to cry. In the haze before sleep, I am instinctively aware that tomorrow is going to be different. It has to be. Whatever different means, I'll take it.

ℿ

I've wet the bed. Embarrassment and irritation meet me at the same time. Pregnancy is so dumb. It's like your whole body malfunctions for months. It's completely dark, so Gabriel must have forgotten to turn the night light on for me. I'm scared of the dark. I reach out to wake him. Gosh, I hope it didn't reach his side. I'm met with surprise when I don't immediately touch him. I reach further and discover nothing but cold sheets.

A dull throbbing starts to envelope me from my lower back, leaching around to my middle that tightens in response, and I stop fumbling for Gabriel. That was a real contraction. Grogginess leaves me instantly. My heart thumps into overdrive at the possibility that it's time. Which means I didn't wet the bed; my water must have broken.

"Gabriel?" I croak, fumbling for him again, but my hand touches the edge of the bed. He is definitely not here. Memories of our argument surface and it seems so stupid now. I can't do this alone. I need Gabriel.

I heave myself over and reach for my lamp, knocking something off the nightstand in the process but managing to click the light on. I squint into the dimly lit room. We have a couch in here, but Gabriel is not there either.

"Oh no," I whisper, remembering my words to him. *I want to love you but I don't know how.*

Did he leave?

Another contraction grips my abdomen, tightening it like a rock. I curl up, losing myself to the sensation as it peaks and crashes to the other side. Afterward, I look for my phone but it's not on the nightstand. Where did I leave it? Bringing my legs over the side of the bed I spot it on the floor. I awkwardly reach down to pick it up and see from the time that I've only been asleep about an hour. I text Gabriel:

Where are you?

I don't know why but I'm afraid to call him. I'm in labor and I'm afraid to call my husband… I sit for a good minute, staring at the bright light of the screen, my finger hovering over his name. I am a big fat wimp.

"You are a big fat wimp," I repeat aloud, hoping it will egg me into calling him.

Nope. Still a wimp.

I'll get Kaylen. She and I have been pretty tight the last few months. She knows where I am and never prods. She's easy to be around, like always.

I push myself out of the bed and stumble toward the door only to reach it and remember that my pajama pants are wet. More water trickles down my legs.

"Uuuuuugh!" I cry out bitterly, turning around and heading for my dresser instead to get some new clothes. On the way, I stub my toe on the rocking chair ottoman. I curse several times, giving up and falling into the chair, enduring both the spasms in my back as well as the throbbing in my toe.

I lie there for a while through a couple more contractions, which are pretty mild. But I end up feeling sorry for myself and being stupidly angry at Gabriel for putting this new rocker here.

At the same time, however, my heart aches desperately for him. Kaylen is not Gabriel. What if I've pushed him too far? Why did I tell my husband I didn't love him? I clearly do; I'm about to have a nervous breakdown at the prospect of losing him.

I start to whimper, which then turns into sobs. More contractions. More crying. And I don't feel obliged to do anything but lie here. I've been planning on having the baby here at home anyway. Looks like I'm in the right place. But aren't I supposed to call the midwife?

No, Gabriel was supposed to do that.

"Where are you?" I ask the room. I might have gotten up the nerve to actually call him.

"I'm right here," Gabriel's voice says from the door.

"Where have you been?" I demand.

"Outside the door."

I give him a look. "Then what kept you?" I rub my abdomen as it contracts again.

"I was under the impression that you wanted me to stop forcing my way into your life," he says, still not having left his spot by the door.

"I can't do this with you right now," I say, cold because of my wet clothes. "I need new pants."

His eyes scan the length of me and recognition slowly moves over his face. He strides forward. "Are you—? Is this—?"

"My water broke," I say.

He practically leaps for the dresser. "Good heavens, Wendy! Why didn't you say so?"

I'm not sure how to answer that. Honestly it's because if I were him I wouldn't want to be anywhere near me after what I said to him. He's so excited now, and I don't want to ruin it by reminding him that I told him I didn't love him.

He doesn't seem to expect an answer as he shuts the drawer and brings me a pair of flannel pants. If this weren't Gabriel I was dealing with I'd swear he doesn't remember the conversation. He helps me peel off my old pants and step into the new ones.

While he's getting a towel to put on the dampened chair, I rub my belly during another contraction, thinking I need to say *something*. The air is so thick with the words I said I can't concentrate on laboring, and I'm going to need to.

He puts the towel down, but I notice he's especially careful not to touch me, holding the rocking chair still while I sit back down. And that's when I realize that Gabriel must feel the divide as much as I do. For once he's foregoing the conversation, and for once I wish he wouldn't. I'm afraid of silence but I'm also afraid of words...

The havoc in my head is so agonizing that I reach out suddenly, driven by my instinct to ground myself against the tempest. I put my hand on his. The movement shatters my composure and I grip his hand harder. "I need you," I sob.

He crouches next to me, his eyes instantly on my face. He squeezes back. "What do you need?" he asks, and I know he doesn't just mean this moment.

"Don't give up on me." I choke on the words a little. I swallow before saying, "I always need you. Even when I act like I don't."

His wide eyes question me for only a moment, and then he reaches up and cups my face in his hand. I reach for him, and he responds immediately, standing as he lifts me up from the chair and embracing me as if I'll change my mind at any moment.

"I will do anything for you," he whispers into my neck. And I know he means it without condition. If I ask, he will follow me into any hell—even a hell created by my own actions. He already has physically. He endured so much to give me time to figure out how to cure us from hypno-touch sickness last year—which I unwittingly caused. I watched him dragged down every day by suffering that should have broken his will. But he emerged from each day committed to staying the course.

I grip him harder, overcome with the love and affection for him that has escaped me for so many months. Of course he will stay by my side through this different kind of hell. How could I ever expect anything less? I only had to ask.

"I think… I don't know how you could still love me." I say into his chest.

Gabriel has relaxed into me, guiding me toward the bed. Unwilling to relinquish me when we reach it, he holds me close, resting his chin on my head. He shudders and then says, "This is like when we couldn't touch each other. You thought I wouldn't love you because we couldn't have the type of relationship we'd grown up expecting."

"I think you're right," I croak after another contraction. I *do* know what I'm missing. I know what it's like to connect so deeply that anything less seems shallow to the point of being superficial. I am now forced to wear gloves of a different kind. But Gabriel loved me even when I wore literal gloves. He showed me how to *be* loved and how it's not hindered by limitations if you're willing to go places you're afraid to go.

I lift my head to look at him. "I'm going to figure this out," I say determinedly, and then my expression falters. "What I said earlier… I didn't mean it. I'm sorry. I think sometimes that I don't love you like I did before because we can't… speak like we used to. But the thought of being without you… I don't know how I'd survive." I look down, frustrated by my own conflict of emotion.

He touches my cheek. "You did mean it. Don't apologize." He takes my hand in both of his and sighs. "I know how to keep my cool when you're angry. But when you are honest it always cuts me to the quick. I have not handled those times very well. I was afraid of what more you might say, and that created a cycle that drove us apart."

"But I *do* love you," I insist. I might have doubted before if it was true, but the last fifteen minutes have proven that the love I have for Gabriel is very much alive and well.

"I know," he says. "If you didn't love me, you would not have suffered so much the last few months."

"Then what—"

"By saying you *wanted* to love me, you were saying you didn't know how to anymore," Gabriel replies. "Love is an action. And you don't have the tools you used to use."

I consider it. "But why can't I accept what I can't do? Why does it still hurt as much today as it did six months ago?"

"You're trying to give more than you're capable of. Let it go. Wendy, I promise I don't need as much as you think. You smile at me and I get so happy inside that I'm invincible. You touch my hand and it reminds me of how lucky I am that you picked me."

"Seriously?" I say. "Gabriel, we used to be connected on so many levels all the time. How does a smile even begin to compare to that?"

"For me, it has *always* been about seeing you happy. That makes *me* happy. When you aren't happy, I'm miserable. When you aren't happy, I'm failing. I hate failing."

I lay against Gabriel's chest. "So you're saying all I have to do is be happy. Sounds a lot simpler than it actually is."

"That's the nuts and bolts," he says. "And when I'm *not* making you happy, I want to know what to do differently. I want to fix it, and I'm impatient to do it. The longer you stayed silent, the more convinced I was that you didn't care *what* I could offer. You were outright rejecting me. It wasn't until you said you wanted to love me but couldn't that I understood you felt as deficient as I did."

I tilt my face up, kiss his willing lips gently. "I love you," I say. "I really, really do."

"I know," he whispers, massaging his fingers into my hair. And then he chuckles. "Anytime you give me that 'I wish you would go away' look, I'll know that what it really means is, 'I love you so much that the language of mere mortals cannot express it.'"

"That's probably about right. But I'm going to find a way to live among the mortals again," I say as my belly tightens, this time with much more intensity than before. I cringe when it reaches its peak.

"Ah, Wendy," he says worriedly. "I am torn between continuing this conversation for as long as you'll allow it, and attending to the fact that you're in labor. Could you please direct me as to what I should be doing right now?"

I laugh, feeling immensely better about the fact that I'm about to give birth. "Calling the midwife," I say.

He jumps. "You're right!" He releases me gently and hops up, looking this way and that for his phone.

"Use mine." I point to the nightstand.

I keep my eyes on Gabriel bouncing around the room, phone to his ear, yanking the sheets off the bed and bringing me something to drink. Just like that, Gabriel is back to the enthusiastic force I love. Now if I can just get *myself* back to the confident person I once was, I can put this era of darkness behind me.

Four

They make hospitals and drugs for this kind of thing," Ezra says. Squatting, my arms are draped over the ottoman. I exhale through the latest contraction. I ignore Ezra. I've been at this for hours now, and I'm tired from not sleeping much last night. I'm out of clever come-backs.

Gabriel, seeing the contraction is over, massages my neck to relax me for the next onset, and says, "Drugs are intended to numb the pain, but they also numb everything else. Wendy wants to participate in the entirety of the experience."

"Oh my gosh, oh my *gosh*!" Kaylen squeals, bouncing from foot to foot, porcelain cheeks bright pink with excitement. She recently got thick bangs cut, making her look even more youthful than she normally does. "He's almost *here*! Perfect timing, Wendy! A Sunday! I don't even have to worry about missing it because of school!"

"If she starts howling you're going to wish you were at school," Ezra warns.

"Shut up, Ezra," I say groggily. "Don't throw your wet blanket of lameness on Kaylen's joy. I need her energy."

"Eeeek!" Kaylen says, squeezing fists in the air and then clapping ecstatically.

"You kids have fun," Ezra says. "I'm going to find somewhere to be. I love you but there is no way I am watching a baby come out of... my sister."

I chuckle, but another contraction interrupts me. Gosh, these things are getting a lot closer together.

"They're getting closer together," Gabriel says, mirroring my thoughts.

"If you want to use the pool, you'll probably want to get in now," Maria, my midwife, says from nearby. "You may not feel like moving later."

I nod, letting Gabriel lift me up.

"I'm out," Ezra says, turning on his heel. "Call me when the gross stuff's over."

Once he's gone and Gabriel has shut the door behind him, Kaylen says, "I know you told me before that I could be in the room but are you sure you're okay with it? I don't want you to be uncomfortable once you're undressed..."

"Kaylen," I say, shuffling like an old person to the bed so I can pull my clothes of. "At this point the Pope could walk in and see me naked and I wouldn't give a flip."

Gabriel chuckles as he helps me get my shirt off. "My mother would probably flog you for that sacrilegious comment. As well as offer penance for your lack of modesty."

"Which is why she's not here," I say. Maris was not a fan of the home birth idea either.

I wasn't at first until Kaylen and I had a conversation about the last time I gave birth. I was in a hospital that time, inviting every drug they'd give me. I wanted to separate from the whole thing because I knew what came afterward and I didn't want to endure it while fully aware. I wanted to find a way to drug myself out of bonding once my daughter was born, so I wouldn't fight with myself so much when I gave her up. I don't know if it worked at all.

Kaylen listened to my sad story and declared, "Wendy, you've got to do it completely different this time. Whatever you did that time, do the opposite this time. You don't want bad associations."

As soon as she said it, I was sold. The decision to birth in the water was also Kaylen's idea. She said after all that time of seeing so many people's life force strands react to water, getting tangled together in it, she knew water did something special beyond what we could see. I agreed.

So here I am, at home and in the oversize tub in my bathroom. The contractions grow stronger like the coming of the tide, rushing up closer and closer, stronger and stronger until I can't think past them. I fidget, searching for a better position in the tub to alleviate the ever-intensifying spasms of pain.

As the hours creep by, my body holds me captive. It hurts to move or think. My eyes stay closed because it even hurts to see.

Locked in the grip of the contractions, for the first time I am grateful that I don't have emodar—one less distraction. Between contractions I don't move either. But power slowly creeps into me. I'm feeling. And it's not breaking me.

It's invigorating, and I want more of it.

I get my wish, but when the pain becomes so sharp that I cry out, I change my mind. There is obviously a threshold that can't be passed without losing yourself.

"Let go as much as you can," Maria says. "Let the contractions work."

I struggle not to tense up, but I start flailing as pain consumes every part of me. It has me in its grip and won't let go. I clutch the sides of the tub for dear life, and when it passes all I can think of is that the next contraction will be coming soon, and how will I escape it? "I don't think I can do this," I whimper.

A hand is on my back and I look up blearily into Gabriel's face. "Don't be ridiculous," he says. "I've been watching you every moment, and I've never seen anything so raw and powerful. You are breathtaking."

"You look like a wild goddess," Kaylen says from behind Gabriel. "Fierce."

"The more you let go, the sooner it will be over," Maria says.

"I can't let go when it feels like that!" I snap.

Cool and calm, Maria instructs me to take a new position: squatting. She says to focus my energy downward.

As soon as I'm in position, another contraction moves in, grabbing my insides, wringing them out, and flapping them violently in the wind. I'm completely out of control of my own body, and I can't hold still. I convulse in the water, fighting for control of my arms and legs. By the end of it, it's all I can do to cling to the side of the tub to keep from slipping under the water.

Maria has me try a couple more positions in an effort to help me get through it, but with the same result. After a failed hands and knees position, I come back to a squat. My arms are like jelly from hanging one-armed to the tub every time I lose control of the rest of myself. I shift my weight from foot to foot nervously.

"I have an idea," Kaylen says, unsure.

I look at her sourly, tired of being an experiment. I'm about ready to get out of this tub and try my luck in the bed. At least I won't drown there. "Unless it's Morphine, I don't want it," I grumble.

"Uh, no. But, um, maybe Gabe should get in with you and hold you in place," she says. "Stay like you are right now, and Gabe can be behind you and keep you from thrashing."

I'm a bit delirious from so much effort to control my body that I can't find the wherewithal to decide if that's a good idea. But everyone is looking at me for an answer, especially Gabriel.

"Why the hell not," I say, waving a hand. "But hurry up. Another one is coming."

I place my forehead on the side of the tub that I grip with both hands. Gabriel splashes behind me and arms bar me on either side, hands rest next to mine, and his chest—which is bare so he must have at least gotten his shirt off—touches mine, somewhat hesitantly. We have not been this close in quite some time, but I don't care about anything but getting through this contraction.

It comes, and I grit my teeth, holding on. As it nears its peak my arms and legs flail, but I'm held in place with iron bars and a concrete wall at my back. I manage to gulp air in the middle of it this time. I find a sliver of purpose, enough to expel my energy downward where I'm supposed to rather than to my limbs.

"Good," Maria says.

Gabriel chuckles from behind me. "Bravo, Kaylee. I should have thought of that earlier. Wendy likes her walls."

"Shut up," I say. He's totally right, but I'm sick of all these people talking. "I'm trying to have a baby here."

I start off groaning as the next contraction proves worse than the last. I see stars and screech angrily. But Gabriel holds me in place, catching my arms as they escape from where he's caged me. We do this over and over, and the contractions move closer and closer together. I'm in a zone, focusing the pain down where it's supposed to go with more and more purpose each time.

After a hazy span of time, the contractions spread out. I have more time to catch my wind between them.

"Are they…" I gasp, "slowing?"

"Wendy, if you feel pressure, the timing indicates you're ready to push," Maria says quietly.

I look up at her with wild eyes. "Seriously?"

She smiles encouragingly. "Yes, whenever you're ready, exhale down and push with each contraction. Assume whatever position feels natural—although you're doing beautifully where you are."

Whenever I'm ready? Is she kidding? I was ready two hours ago!

With relief, I expel my pain through pushing as I squat with Gabriel holding me still. I feel ever more pressure and I instinctively know the baby must be close to making his appearance finally. So I instruct Gabriel that I want to brace myself between him and the tub wall.

Feet in place, I push again, and it's a blessed catharsis to do so. I plunge into it with renewed vigor. Each push is a sweet release. Excitement seizes me because I can actually feel the burning pressure of the baby's head.

"Gabriel," I pant after one push in which I'm certain I've made real progress. "You have to catch him."

He moves to the front of me.

Impatient, I push before the next contraction builds force. I think I growl; I'm not entirely aware of my own actions because I am focused on nothing more than expelling what feels like a giant bowling ball. I groan with strain, astonished by my own ability. I retreat a little, frightened that I might push my own organs out in the process.

"Don't be afraid of it," Maria says from somewhere nearby. "Don't force it. Use it to release."

I take her advice. *Release.* I think the word over and over. I think the word *release* through every fiber of my being. There is no torment anymore. Only release, only letting go. I have so much power I might be able to will anything into existence.

I open my eyes for Gabriel's face, and he glances up at me. "I see the head!" he exclaims. "Keep going. Oh my!"

Imagining my child so close to my arms fills me with a primal drive that reaches past reason. I release him in one grand exhale. He slips out and into Gabriel's waiting hands.

Gabriel lifts our baby boy out of the water. His spindly little legs extend in surprise as he hits the colder air. Then he sneezes, and it's the most adorable sound I've ever heard. I watch in stunned wonder as Gabriel holds his slippery little body to his own bare chest. "Oh my," Gabriel shudders, clutching him. "Oh my." He repeats it over and over, his voice trembling with awe. I'm crying, especially when Maria suctions the baby's nose and a loud cry escapes his tiny mouth—the sound of life.

Gabriel scoots over to me, edging our son's squirmy little body into my arms. "A boy," he whispers. Gabriel places one arm around me and one hand on our son's mass of dark hair.

I can't find the words to reply. A smile finds my face without effort, however, and I look at our son in a silence so full of meaning and power that it seems to pause the passage of time. Drinking in the sight of his face against my chest, wet and squashy, he is possibly the most dazzling thing I have ever seen in or out of the colorworld. In my mind's eye I can see his life force wound with ours in the water. I can see the energy vapor pulsing heavily from us as this moment changes all of us internally. Forever. I can't see it, but I swear I can perceive it with some other sense.

I look up to see Kaylen leaning over the edge of the tub, her cheeks streaked with tears. "You should see your faces," she blubbers. "Oh my gosh... Oh my gosh, he's perfect. What are you going to name him?"

I look down at the face of our baby boy. I've tried to broach names with Gabriel before today, but he told me he didn't believe in naming someone before you've met them. "You can't possibly know what suits a person until you see their face," he'd said.

I laugh softly, remembering.

"Any ideas?" Gabriel says. "I have none. How can you place something as ordinary as a name on something so extraordinary?"

"What are you going to say when you call for him then?" Kaylen giggles. "Extraordinary is kind of weird. You could call him Extra or X for short." She laughs again.

I roll my eyes. "We are not calling him Extraordinary." I look down at my son. It's hard to imagine this helpless individual all grown up and having a full-blown personality. Even hazarding a guess as to what he'll be like when he's older is daunting. But if choosing a particular name can encourage him to become a certain way, I know what name I would choose.

"Robert Gabriel Dumas," I say.

"Well that sounds just right," Gabriel replies.

"Perfect," Kaylen breathes. "Can I call him Robbie? It's going to be a while before he can fill Robert's shoes."

"You're probably right about that," I say, lost in helpless adoration, imagining all of the stories I will tell Robbie about his great uncle as he grows.

This feeling is familiar: I'm hooked. Just like the last time. After my daughter Elena was born, I didn't have her for more than a couple of hours, but the strings of my heart wound firmly around her anyway, like Robbie right now. My heart expands effortlessly to make room for him. My past fears over how I would love him enough when he came were so unfounded. Maternal love. It's easy. It breaks through the barriers I've unwittingly built these last months, reminding me of what it feels like to give yourself away so fully. I have no emodar or enhanced senses that make me experience this moment so powerfully. Realizing that makes me believe that I can rediscover how to love Gabriel with the same energy I used to.

Robbie came to me at this time in my life for exactly this reason. He will teach me how to love again, how to live again.

Five

Pacing the grand entryway of Uncle Moby's home with Robbie in my arms, I keep glancing at the time on the five-foot wall clock. Maris, Gabriel's mother, is scheduled to arrive within the next hour. I'm looking forward to the relief of an extra set of hands; I'm dead on my feet.

This shouldn't be so hard. Robbie is only one baby. And I do get breaks. Gabriel insists on taking the nightshift most of the time. But I have to wake up anyway and pump. Kaylen takes Robbie after school while I cook dinner. At first, I started cooking again because I felt like a useless, lactating couch potato. But the first day Gabriel came home to the smell of a citrus-infused Gumbo and a homemade baguette, his eyes lit up like I'd given him a million bucks. Aside from right after giving birth, and when we would fawn over Robbie together, I couldn't remember the last time he'd looked at me that way. I wanted to see it again the next day, and then the next. So cooking dinner became a sort of silent expression of intimacy, and I began to speak to him through food, even using spinach and artichokes once. He immediately got what I was saying: I'm held back from expressing love in all the ways available, but it doesn't mean I don't want him and what we do share.

That night after dinner was one of the best I have had with Gabriel in too long; we talked extensively about how our physical intimacy has changed. Whenever we find a comfortable place with each other, we're thrown for a loop, and we have to relearn physical love. Somehow, merely acknowledging that made the adjustment seem less daunting. And it made me feel less inadequate.

I look down at Robbie, feeling oddly normal, like the bizarre situations of my past life have been washed away by a predictable tide of feeding, changing, and rocking. Life has acquired a certain simplicity, even if it is hard and tiring. He's four weeks old, and despite the uneventful monotony of motherhood, Robbie's sleeping face still has me under an unexplained power. Seeing it causes my heart to brim over with a love that dissolves the trying moments of the day into nothing. I am in love with him. Some kind of helpless, mindless, senseless love. He doesn't do much more than eat, sleep, cry, and poop, but it doesn't affect my love for him one way or another, or my desire to be at his beck and call no matter how onerous the work.

"He's got me under some kind of spell," I told Gabriel one day. "I wish I could see it in the colorworld."

Gabriel was holding Robbie in his arms, rocking him gently. "Did you hear that Robbie? Your mother thinks you've been philtering her. What cantrap is this? It must run in the family since she has me under the same incantation. You'll have to teach it to me some day so I can ensure she doesn't run off with another thaumaturge with draughts stronger than my meager attempts at gallantry to woo her. You'll help your papa out, won't you?"

I leaned against his arm, warming at hearing Gabriel use his full range of vocabulary. It has always risen and fallen with his happiness.

He kissed me on the forehead then, and a thrill moved through me unexpectedly. Overcome with the implications of that sensation, I ran to the bathroom and had a silent cry, finally one that wasn't from sadness. My skin wasn't dead. It could make me feel. I *would* feel again, and I was on the right track.

The doorbell breaks past my thoughts, and I almost leap to the door, careful to keep Robbie asleep as I fling it open.

"Maris!" I whisper excitedly, taking in the sight of the short Hispanic woman responsible for the uniquely wonderful man I married.

"Hola, Wendy! Oh, mi, mire usted poco mamá!" she says, grinning brightly. I think Maris is trying to influence me to learn Spanish. When I first met her, she spoke in English all the time, but I find more and more that she speaks English mixed with Spanish. At least I know she says hello.

"It's so good to see you!" I exclaim as quietly as possible, bringing her into a hug, trying not to squeeze Robbie between us.

"Yes, and your bed will enjoy seeing you, too. Give me my grandson, and you go reacquaint yourself with your pillow. Voy a manejarlo," she says, making no further small talk and reaching for Robbie.

I relinquish him without complaint, grateful for Maris' unapologetic demands. She doesn't ask to help; she just does it. I am so *lucky* to have her... and Gabriel, and my Uncle Moby, my brother Ezra, and my adopted sister Kaylen. I have so much. Guilt creeps up on me from the shame of the last six months I've spent dissatisfied. Why do I *still* struggle when I have so much around me?

Baby steps, I remind myself again, climbing the stairs. It's okay to take baby steps.

₪

When I wake I'm so groggy that I can't bring myself to get out of bed. I don't know why I woke up if I'm still this tired, but when my breasts throb, I realize I'm engorged. I need to go pump or feed Robbie or I'm going to be really uncomfortable soon.

Rolling out of bed, I shove my feet into a pair of slippers and check my blood sugar. Low, but not worrisome. As usual. After I fully recovered from leukemia, my diabetes appeared to be gone as well. But about three months later, I developed symptoms again. Gabriel guessed that we had temporarily cured my diabetes when we reinserted all my life force strands, but my disease caught up to me and displaced my strands once more. Nevertheless, when it came back, it stayed as manageable as it had been when I was growing up. But since breastfeeding, I now only inject about once a day. Making sure I get enough calories is the only thing I have to be diligent about.

I make my way downstairs, but before I reach the kitchen, I hear voices: Gabriel and Maris. They are speaking in low, vigorous tones, compelling me to stop and listen before making myself known.

"There's no harm in having it done now. I thought that was why you chose not to get an amniocentesis... so it would be safer after he was born," Maris says.

I creep closer until I'm right outside the archway to the kitchen, curious about Gabriel's thoughts on the subject.

"I know Mamá, but Wendy has been somewhat depressed since the pregnancy started. She's finally making progress recovering, and I don't want her getting stressed out unnecessarily. It can wait until he's gained a few more months at least," Gabriel replies.

Maris sighs. "Mijo, bless us that the Lord provided a miracle in our time of need, but that's not the case for everyone. If I could have known early that something was wrong with you, I could have kept you that much healthier… taken preventative measures against complications. I would expect you'd want some peace of mind after all you've been through. You have no idea what kind of damage might have occurred during the treatments. You ought not put off what you need to do. You may regret it later."

Confusion drives me forward.

I walk into the kitchen. "What miracle? What was wrong with you?" I ask severely, my hands on my hips.

I regret my tone immediately. Upon seeing me, an expression flashes across Gabriel's face that I haven't seen since I was dying of leukemia: the stony rigidity of emotional control. It sends me into a panic, because I'm sure I'm not going to like what lies beneath.

The silence that strikes the room suddenly goes on forever, as if we are all simultaneously paralyzed, but for different reasons. I want him to stop looking that way, and unable to take the tense air, I stride forward and take Gabriel in an embrace I know he wasn't expecting.

"Sorry," I say, "How was *your* day?"

He puts his arms around me in response. "Terrible. I had to break up a fight, and I was reprimanded by the principal for having threatened to fail one of my students, regardless of grades, if he didn't stop speaking foully and bullying other students during the lunch hour. And I missed you and Robbie. But nevermind that. I'm more interested in your day and answering your question."

When Gabriel loosens his hold, expecting me to want to relinquish him, I don't. I hold on to him because hugs have a way of maturing into something more meaningful when you let them. I may not be able to feel that shift like I used to, but I know it happens.

To my surprise though, I *do* feel the shift: my own. Gabriel's obvious unease over answering my question overwhelms me with compassion, and the desire to express my love creeps up on me suddenly. Not wanting to let the sensation pass me by, I reach up and pull his face to mine, kissing him firmly on the lips.

When I come away to reveal his dazed and delighted expression I say, "No matter how my day was, I shouldn't demand answers from you as if you were hiding something. I know better."

I look around then. Maris is rolling tortillas, and Gabriel's hands are free, so where is Robbie?

"Sleeping, Love," Gabriel replies, translating my expression.

"By himself?" I ask.

"It would appear so."

I turn to Maris. "Where?"

"In his crib of course," she replies.

Robbie's crib is in the room that adjoins ours that used to be the lab when Gabriel and I were sick. To surprise us, Kaylen got with Robert about remodeling it into a nursery one weekend while we were away visiting Gabriel's parents before Robbie was born. I haven't used the crib at all yet because he won't stay asleep there. If he sleeps away from me at all, it's in the bassinet next to my bed.

"But... how? How long has he been asleep?" I say.

Maris glances at the microwave clock. "Oh probably a couple of hours."

I turn back to Gabriel. "We need to adopt your mother."

Gabriel chuckles. "It is rather impressive. I say she drugged him. My mother has a reputation for unconventional 'home remedies.' But she denies it, and I have no way to prove it."

Maris tosses a finished tortilla on a pile she's been accumulating. "Lying is a sin," she says. "I don't do it."

"About our conversation, Love," Gabriel says. His eyes dart around the room before he continues, "We were just talking about having genetic testing done on Robbie, to be sure he's as healthy as he has been from day one. I'm sure you remember we discussed it during the pregnancy, but opted not to at the time. My mother is of the opinion that we should have it done forthwith."

"Yes, I gathered that. That's not what I asked though," I say. He very well *knows* he didn't answer my question. Gabriel doesn't ever miss my words. He catches *everything*. So he's trying to divert me—and after I gave him the benefit of the doubt. I'm not going to like this...

Gabriel sits down and sighs. "I know, but it's not unrelated."

I find a chair nearby and sort of fall into it, trying to look unconcerned and natural, not like I'm totally terrified inside.

Gabriel watches me carefully as he talks. "When I was a few months old I was diagnosed with Spinal Muscular Atrophy, type I. It's a genetic disease characterized by degenerating motor neurons due to the body's inability to produce a particular protein. Type I is almost the worst form of the disease, and the prognosis for living beyond the age of two is rare. And if one manages to live past that age, their prognosis increases to possibly living into adolescence. They require all manner of therapy during that time and are rendered basically immobile. I managed to live beyond the normal life expectancy until age six when my health took quite a turn. I contracted the flu, and SMA causes complications with the respiratory system, so any kind of infection can be deadly."

Gabriel looks hesitantly at his mother. I can tell he doesn't want to share the rest. I'm leaning forward, bewildered. How has he never told me this before? I look him up and down, wondering how he sits here in front of me. He seems perfectly healthy. He had lung cancer and survived for goodness sake! Talk about respiratory problems to complicate your condition! What am I missing?

"And?" I demand.

Gabriel looks at me again. "I recovered."

I hear a loud smack of a utensil on the counter, and we both turn to Maris who holds a spoon in her hand, looking severely at Gabriel.

"Gabriel Daniel Dumas. You ought to have a little more gratitude toward your maker who preserved your life, who answered our prayers and the prayers of everyone who dedicated so much time and energy in supplication for your life. Your impertinence ought to induce God to drive you to humility. Fortunately our Father is just and loving and looks past your constant neglect of his mercies."

Gabriel rolls his eyes. "Mamá, if I have a different explanation, it doesn't make me any less grateful."

Then he turns to me. "I recovered miraculously and suddenly. In fact, whereas before the doctor tested me and found the autosomal recessive genes proof positive of SMA, my genes after the recovery showed me only as a carrier, not infected. My mother claims it was divine intervention. But I claim it was a faulty diagnosis."

Maris takes out her grievances on the tortillas, rolling them more roughly. She mutters something in Spanish, and then stops to cross herself. She is a devoted Catholic, so the sight isn't unusual for her.

Gabriel looks upward before leaning forward and propping his elbows on his knees. "My mother claims I'll be going to hell if I don't acknowledge divine intervention."

I know Gabriel's opinion of religion. In fact, most people would probably call him an atheist because his idea of God is a lot less mysterious and miraculous. But I'm curious what Maris thinks; I want more details.

"So you think it was prayer that cured him?" I ask her.

Maris seems to appreciate that *someone* wants to know her version of the truth and she purposely avoids Gabriel's face when she looks at me.

"I know it was," she says, pausing her rolling. "When he took a turn for the worse, our church held vigil just for him. Two hours of prayer over my boy. Pleading with the Father to spare his life. I don't suppose we expected such a miraculous cure. But we prayed for his recovery nonetheless. A day later he woke up recovered from the flu. A week later he stopped having symptoms of his disease. Atrophy disappeared as he began to use his limbs. He learned how to walk. The doctors were stunned. They tested him and couldn't believe that his genes revealed him as only a carrier." Maris huffs. "They labeled him misdiagnosed. Ignorant lot. We knew better."

I turn to Gabriel. "That is the craziest story I ever heard."

Gabriel crosses his arms. "Crazier than recovering from leukemia or Small Cell Carcinoma in only a few weeks? Or ALS like our friend Randy?"

"Gabriel—not that I'm arguing for divine intervention or anything—but surely it has occurred to you how… miraculous it was? Unlikely? Coincidental? What do you think was wrong with you for six years?"

He shrugs. "Of course I've considered that. I think it's more likely that I had some kind of viral infection that was overlooked that invaded my nervous system. It's also not unheard of for carriers to exhibit symptoms for a time, albeit not nearly so drastic. I don't know, Wendy. How would you explain it?"

"I haven't got a clue. Explanations are your area. So what's this got to do with Robbie and genetic testing?"

"For peace of mind, Mija," Maris says. "Gabriel is a carrier, so you should have Robbie tested for that reason if not for the nature of the pregnancy."

"What are the chances that Robbie would be more than a carrier?" I ask.

"If you aren't a carrier, there's no chance," Gabriel says. "If you *are*, fifty percent."

"What are the chances I am?"

"Extremely unlikely. I don't think it's worth testing *you*. My mother's main concern is the circumstances surrounding Robbie's conception."

This is far less dire than I feared, so although it wrings my sanity a bit to entertain the possibility, Maris is right. I was full of toxic drugs when I got pregnant with Robbie. It is in everyone's best interest to be sure Robbie wasn't affected. I have no idea why

Gabriel's initial reaction was so dramatic. "I don't have a problem with it," I say. "My fragile and overprotective nerves will survive."

"I didn't mean to imply you aren't strong enough to handle the uncertainty," Gabriel says. "I just didn't want you to have to endure it if it's not absolutely necessary."

I look at him critically. This is not like him, sparing feelings. He's known for taking difficult conversations head-on. There's more to this, but I'll bring it up later when we're alone. Instead, I change the subject, "Gabriel, maybe it *was* a result of prayer. You know what good intentions look like in the colorworld."

"At least one of you has some sense," Maris says. "Gabriel, your continual obstinacy toward God is going to send me to an early grave... which is fortunate since someone has to beseech the Father on your behalf before *you* get there."

"I find it hard to believe that a divine being would condemn my doubts when evidence of such a being's existence is both circumstantial and disputed over so heavily," Gabriel sighs. "It doesn't seem very fair to me."

Maris smiles at Gabriel lovingly in a way that only a mother can. "I know cariño. No God would deny *your* goodness."

"The illogical theism that governs your devout sacrosanct practices will forever confuse me, Mamá," Gabriel says.

Maris just laughs.

I hear Robbie's cries from the baby monitor Maris brought into the kitchen. I hop up and motion to Gabriel to come with me. I think he's grateful for the escape as he jumps up to follow.

As we head up the stairs, I say, "Tell me what you're not telling me."

Gabriel is silent for a bit before saying, "What are you referring to?"

I glance back at him as I walk into Robbie's room. "Your weird behavior and your 'I wanted to spare you the stress' BS explanation back there."

I scoop Robbie up and go into our room to sit on the rocking chair to feed him. "Waiting," I say as Gabriel sits on the bed and removes his shoes. He lays back on it and I can no longer see his face.

"I'm afraid, all right?" he says, annoyed. Both his tone and choice of words are unusual for him.

"Of what exactly? Me losing it over a little genetic testing?"

I don't know what he's doing over there. His breathing sounds heavy. "No. I'm afraid of what the tests will reveal."

"Gabriel," I say, looking down at a happily suckling Robbie, "he's the picture of health. His development has been normal from start to finish."

"That doesn't mean anything where genetic diseases are concerned," Gabriel says. "Would you like me to make a list of all the side-effects of the various drugs you had? It won't be pretty. I'm surprised we both didn't become permanently infertile."

To hear Gabriel so genuinely worried, fear pounds in my head, and I start to imagine all of the ugly possibilities. Dammit, I shouldn't have asked. Now I'm going to be freaking out until Robbie gets a clean bill of health.

"Have you been worrying over this since we found out I was pregnant?" I ask, horrified at the possibility.

Gabriel brings his knees up. I can't see his face, and I think he wants it that way. "No. Right after Robbie was born I went to Robert to ask him what had become of Carl. Robert said he did as Carl asked and helped him get out of town, which was fine, but Robert asked Carl if he had any parting words for you, and Carl said, 'Tell them to be vigilant about the child.'"

"That could mean anything," I say, confused at what he finds so cryptic about that statement.

He sits up and puts his arms on top of his knees, his face careworn. "I know it could. But..." Gabriel's expression turns harrowed. "In light of our history I've become somewhat... paranoid about your safety. And now that Robbie is born, that wariness is doubled. I see monsters around every corner."

"That's not like you," I say.

"I know," Gabriel says. "Our strained relationship of late has put me in a fix. I've become more and more insecure about myself and everything around me. Everything is so... fragile." He looks at me with haunted eyes. "I fear that losing it all is a much more feasible possibility than I had ever considered."

I look down at Robbie, not really seeing him as I let that sink in, ashamed at the struggle I've caused Gabriel. But how could I have known?

"This isn't a criticism," Gabriel says, reading my expression. "I never mentioned it because I didn't want you burdened with my problems. But I've come to realize my happiness and confidence is drastically dependent on you. Perhaps it's a byproduct of the loss of your abilities as well. I surmise I, too, was affected psychologically by the loss of connection. It was exacerbated by estrangement."

"I'd say you should have told me, but I should have told you what I was feeling sooner as well," I say, looking up. "Let's stop this thing where we spare each other's feelings."

"I agree," Gabriel says. "And let's get Robbie's tests taken care of. Then we can all sleep better."

Six

With careful movements, I make sure Robbie's blanket is tightly swaddled around him before gingerly lowering him into the crib. Holding back triumph over keeping him asleep for the transition from my arms to his bed, I wait a couple minutes to be sure it's going to stick. I've celebrated prematurely before.

I'm about to turn around to leave when my phone rings from my jeans. Holding back a litany of curses, I snatch it out of my back pocket to silence it. And then I hold my breath and watch Robbie for signs of waking.

The kid hasn't moved a muscle. His fingers rest against his bottom lip like he's pondering his dreams. It's absolutely precious. I shake my head, wondering for probably the hundredth time if Robbie even cares about loud noises or being jostled. He never reacts consistently.

Closing his door to a crack, I kick off my shoes and flop back on my bed, looking at my phone. As soon as I see who it was, a great lump of foreboding stops up my throat. It's Robbie's geneticist. We've been waiting a month and a half for this call. Or maybe I should say we've *dreaded* this day for a month and a half.

My finger hovers over the number, and I'm paralyzed with terror so all-consuming that I can't think straight.

My phone dings loudly at that moment, startling me, and I almost drop it. I have a new voicemail.

I put the phone down on my stomach and rub my face. I don't think I can do this. I might be on the verge of having a heart attack, as loud and irregular as my heartbeats are right now.

"Don't be a wimp, Wendy," I say aloud, snatching up my phone again, and seizing the momentum to tap the button to listen to the message before I can change my mind.

"Hello, Mrs. Dumas," a practiced female voice says. "This is Doctor Demelin's office. We'd like to schedule an appointment with you and your husband to discuss Robert Dumas' test results." I barely hear the rest of the message. My pulse is now pounding in my ears.

"Something is wrong with him," I say out loud, testing the words. And a sob escapes my throat at how right they sound.

"Stop it, Wendy," I chide myself as I wipe my leaking eyes. "You don't know anything."

But I think I do. I don't know why, but ever since Gabriel confessed his concern over Robbie, I've moved from being a basketcase about my marriage to a basketcase about Robbie. I just... know this isn't over. It's naïve to believe that there will be no consequences to the miracle that saved me. My throat burns with gathering tears. I press my lips together and pinch my eyes. But sound is forcing its way out. I'm not going to be able to hold it together. I need Gabriel. I need him right now.

I tap on his number, not expecting him to answer because he's teaching.

"Wendy? Is everything alright?" he answers after the second ring, surprising me. The sound of his voice is a life line.

"No," I croak, breathing through my nose. "I need you. They called."

"Heavens. I'm on my way. What did they say?" he demands.

"Don't know," I say, keeping the sobs from escaping with the words. "It was a voicemail. I couldn't bring myself to call back."

"One moment," he says. I hear him murmur to someone away from the phone.

I close my eyes and hang on to my composure.

After several unbearable minutes, he says, "I'm walking to my car now. I'll see you in about fifteen minutes."

"Don't hang up," I blurt, afraid to be alone with the silence.

"I won't," he assures me. I hear a car door slam and an engine start. "Where is Robbie?" he asks.

"Sleeping," I say. "In his crib."

"He's coming along, isn't he?" he says conversationally. "Third day in a row napping on his own."

"Don't," I say. "I don't want to pretend that everything is normal."

"Then what do you want to talk about?"

My mind is jumping in several directions at once at a million miles an hour. "Don't know," I blurt. "I just can't be alone right now."

"Alright," he says calmly. "I'll stay on the line with you."

I hear the sounds of road noise for several minutes before I say, "Gabriel."

"Yes, Love," he replies.

"Do you think they call you to set up an appointment if it's good news?"

His answering sigh is laden with the sound of dread.

"They said they want to *discuss* Robbie's results. That's bad, right?" I say. "If it was good news there wouldn't be anything to discuss."

"I'm inclined to agree, but conjecturing isn't going to make the unknown any more bearable."

Our conversation continues like this for the remainder of his commute. I keep guessing at the news while Gabriel repeats that we can't possibly know. We finally agree that we're going to insist on speaking directly to the doctor rather than waiting on an appointment. We need to know one way or the other.

When Gabriel turns into the driveway, I am already through the front door. I throw myself into his arms, and suddenly it becomes easier to breathe.

He wastes no time in leading me upstairs to our room where we sit on the couch while he makes the call. I let Gabriel do the talking, hanging on to his hand tightly, afraid of falling apart. I pull my legs into his lap and cling to his arm. The closer I get, the more in control I feel.

Gabriel calmly and politely tells the secretary his request, and she tells him that she can have the doctor call us as soon as he's available. Her estimate is between one and two hours. It sounds like a lifetime, but unless I want to go down to the man's office and break down the door, I'm just going to have to endure some uncertainty.

When Gabriel hangs up, neither of us speaks. There is really nothing to be said until we know something more. The seconds tick by, and when I'm tired of staring at the floor I close my eyes and focus on the shape of Gabriel next to me. He's holding me with both arms, his cheek resting against the top of my head.

I inhale his scent, which is not nearly as poignant as it was when I could smell better, but it still smells like him. And it occupies one more of my senses so that I have less room to fret over how our lives will change in the next couple hours. In light of this eventuality, I have the sudden urge to preserve this moment. I want to remember what it was like to live before… whatever is about to happen.

I find Gabriel's lips, which react with surprise at first, but it does not take much prodding to get them to respond. Reaching up to put my arms around his neck and straddling his lap, I make my intentions known overtly by unbuttoning his shirt.

Gabriel pulls away for a moment, though I can see the hopefulness in his eyes. "Are you sure?" he asks.

"I need you." My eyes are wet as I reach out. "I need you close."

He draws me to him, and we pass the time rediscovering one another for the first time in nearly six months. While his skin lacks the magnetism of our past experiences together, and my mind and body lack the presence of his emotions, my need for him grows more powerful each moment. I cannot get enough of him, and it infuses the passion of the moment with much more than physical want. As our breaths and movements fall into a kind of synchrony, I know instinctively that Gabriel is feeling exactly as I do. Without emodar and the colorworld, we have managed to meld ourselves anyway. And we've done it without the supernatural.

A moment of desperation becomes a moment of intimacy so powerful it brings tears to my eyes. My body remembers this, and my senses come alive as if awakened from a deep sleep. My nerves respond. My skin responds. My *heart* responds. I cling to him all the more.

"I love you," I whisper in his ear. But it doesn't feel like enough. I whisper it again. And then again. Over and over because my feelings for him cannot find enough of an outlet.

He holds me tightly, responding with more intensity every time I say it.

"I love you," I say, crying now. I feel... full in a way I'd forgotten I *could* feel. I didn't experience the same sensations I used to, but I get that the message is the same as it has been every other time I've been intimate with Gabriel: I'm not alone. And how grateful I am for that. To not be alone. So simple, yet it makes all the difference to living.

"Mi encantadora doncella," Gabriel whispers as he runs his fingers through my hair. "My Wendy. You are my everything."

"I've missed you," I say, burying my face in his neck. "So much."

He sighs contentedly.

Robbie's cry breaks through the serenity of the moment. Remembering what brought Gabriel and me together right now jerks my heart like a choke chain. I tense in Gabriel's arms for a few counts, thinking I would give everything to reverse time so I can experience the last twenty minutes over again.

"Wendy, we can do this," Gabriel says. "We can. I know it."

I can't respond, lost as I am in fighting off the dread that's threatening to consume me again. I sit up, keeping in contact with Gabriel's skin for comfort as I get dressed. It sounds like Robbie might be putting himself back to sleep; his cries are not very insistent.

Once Gabriel and I are dressed, however, we creep into his room anyway. We both want to see Robbie's face.

He's awake, but not crying, looking around.

Gabriel reaches for him, bringing him to his chest and bouncing him as he places his cheek against Robbie's downy, dark hair.

And then the phone rings from the nightstand.

Gabriel and I look at each other.

Legs like Jell-O, I sit on the edge of the couch and pick up the phone. I put it on speaker as Gabriel comes to sit next to me.

"This is Wendy," I say.

"Hello, Mrs. Dumas," a male voice replies. "This is Dr. Demelin. I understand you'd like the results to Robert's tests. I've got his file here. Is this a good time?"

"Yes," I say in a small voice. "My husband is here as well. We're eager to have the results. It's been an excruciating wait."

"I understand," Dr. Demelin says.

A pause.

"What we found, I'm afraid, is not good news," he continues. "He has a mutation on his dystrophin gene indicating a form of Muscular Dystrophy."

"Which one?" Gabriel demands.

"Duchenne Muscular Dystrophy," Dr. Demelin says. "Are you familiar with it?"

Gabriel groans and sits back, Robbie on his shoulder.

I look down at the phone and then Gabriel again. I don't know anything about this disease. How upset am I supposed to be?

"You should feel fortunate the diagnosis was made so early," Dr. Demelin says when neither of us answers. "Robert likely would not have exhibited noticeable symptoms for a few years. But he's going to get a jump on treatment now and that's going to keep him healthier longer."

My mouth has gone dry and Gabriel doesn't look inclined to speak. He's staring ahead, patting Robbie gently on the back, his expression stony.

"What's the prognosis?" I croak. It's the only question that really matters. What else are you supposed to ask in a situation like this? 'How long will my child live?' seems to me to be the *only* pertinent question.

I hear Dr. Demelin take a decided breath. "DMD is the most severe form of Muscular Dystrophy. Currently, the average age of death is mid-twenties. But you should have every reason to hope for the best case scenario with Robert. With diligent care and therapy, his decline can be put off. New medical interventions are being developed all the time."

I say nothing, only absorb that answer, trying to picture my sweet little Robbie leaving me when he's not much older than I am now. I begin down the path of counting all the things he'll miss, about how that day will feel, but I can't imagine it.

Gabriel's face is still hard and empty.

"How does it progress?" I ask. *Also known as, what will it look like as my child approaches his death too soon?*

"It varies, but generally muscles weaken and fatigue will be common," Dr. Demelin says. "He'll face motor skill problems and lung issues. He'll eventually lose his ability to walk. His heart will also suffer so he'll be medicated early to keep it from working too hard. Because of the several different systems involved, Robert will have regular consults with several different doctors. He will be monitored closely in the coming years. I'm afraid I can only speak in general terms at this point. He'll have several physical assessments with specialists to give a more accurate idea of the state of his disease. And you'll work with one primary doctor to come up with a game plan for his treatment."

To my surprise I don't experience a moment's disbelief. I guess months of facing a terminal illness myself has impressed upon me the fragility of life and the inevitability of death. Or maybe I am in shock.

"Are there any other questions I can answer for you?" the doctor asks.

I look over at Gabriel again. But he has hidden his face behind Robbie. It looks like he has no intention of participating in the conversation.

"Probably," I say tiredly. "But I can't think of any right now."

"I understand. Feel free to contact me directly if you think of any between now and when you meet with the specialist. But expect to be contacted in the next couple days about those assessments."

"Okay," I say barely above a whisper, wanting to get off the phone probably as badly as the doctor does.

I am about to dismiss him but a question occurs to me. "How is the disease passed?" I ask.

"Usually it is passed from the carrier mother," he replies. "I don't know if you are a carrier, but if you've never had a history of any muscular problems, and no other males in your family have had the disease, it was likely a spontaneous mutation that occurred either within the egg or the fetus in-utero."

"Okay. Thank you for the call. I appreciate it," I say quietly.

The doctor wishes us well before I hang up, and once the room submerses back into silence, I lean forward, elbows on my knees. "How am I supposed to feel?" I ask, unsure if I'm asking Gabriel or myself.

Gabriel finally looks at me, and his eyes look dead. He lowers Robbie to his knees and we both look down at him. He's sucking on his fist, indicating that he's soon going to be upset that it's not satiating his hunger.

Oh God. How is this happening? I reach out for Robbie's hand, its warmth and softness making it hard to imagine that his body is working against him right now, both developing and declining at the same time.

Gabriel continues to say nothing as he fixates on Robbie. Maybe, like me, he's imagining Robbie grown but immobile and helpless. And it occurs to me suddenly that Gabriel must know exactly what that's like. He has personal experience because of his mysterious childhood illness.

"Gabriel…" I say, reaching out for him now.

He pushes Robbie into my arms instead. And then he gets up and leaves the room.

Whatever control I have managed to hang on to shatters as he disappears. I hold Robbie close to me, and as his scent filters into my nose I sob, in the gall of bitterness. I see the faces of the people we tried to help who had hypno-touch. I bet if I'd chosen to skip all those ungrateful people that I felt so moved to save from Louise's and Carl's hypno-touch, Robbie would be a child with a happy and healthy life ahead of him. Instead I drugged up, keeping myself alive long enough to beg every last one of them to let me help them. If I had cured Gabriel and Kaylen and myself from the very beginning,

Robbie would have no genetic abnormalities. I let out one sickened laugh at the disgusting irony of it. I sacrificed my *child* for a bunch of nameless strangers.

I fluctuate between outrage and sorrow, and with every passing moment I lose all of the progress I have made in the last couple months. Confidence and happiness and assurance and faith drain away like water. But I don't care. I hate everything and everyone. This is so stupidly unfair. What the hell have I done to deserve a life that continues to knock me down whenever I begin to stand up?

As fury burns through my veins, I am eventually left raw and aching. And empty. I keep looking down at Robbie, waiting for something to fill me up. I need a plan. I need some kind of determination. Or a conviction to hold me together. But what kind of plans can I possibly make? Imagining the barest inkling of the future is suffocating. I want time to stop so I can catch my breath. Putting Robbie over my shoulder, I pat his back to burp him.

"I don't want to do this," I whisper, but it took all the air in my lungs to say it out loud. "I *can't* do this."

I scramble away from the vision of the future, completely unprepared to face the darkness that lies ahead.

I'd rather die.

I have never felt such things so strongly before, even when Gabriel and I were sick. Even when Elena died. Her death was sudden and there was no dread of the agony to come. There was only guilt. So maybe it's because I know sorrow, or maybe it's the likelihood of facing *years* of such sorrow, but I don't want to do life anymore. There is nothing but suffering in it for me.

I lay Robbie down gently on my knees, watching him and hating my every breath that brings me closer to his demise. His innocence of the future that awaits him fills me with the most profound conflict. I am embittered by the fact that even if I were to find the guts to end my own life, I couldn't. What would he think when he got older and found that his mother committed suicide because she couldn't stand the idea of a future with him? And with all he is slated to endure, how could I possibly inflict more on him?

I can't. Which makes trashing my own life completely out of the question. But it doesn't mean I don't wish I could. I'm being drowned slowly. But these waters will never bring the sweet relief of death. I am cursed with the living kind.

Seven

This doesn't look like Robert's office. Have I walked into the wrong place? Scanning the unfamiliar interior, my eye falls on Robert seated on the other side of a desk, so this must be right. The most obvious change is the windows. The shades in Robert's corner office have always been drawn two-thirds of the way closed, the sunlight only coming in near the floor of the wall-to-wall windows. But today they are open wide and the room feels huge and could at first be mistaken for being outside. Robert has moved his desk so that it faces the west windows and his back is to the north ones. The orange light of approaching sunset frames the Monterey skyline spectacularly. The two remaining walls have been painted a rich dark blue, accented with a large white leather couch flanked by rough-hewn wooden end-tables, giving the space a nautical vibe.

"Wow, Uncle Moby," I say, turning to my uncle who is now standing and watching me. "When did you redecorate?"

"Six months ago," Robert replies. "Kaylen's doing."

"Kaylen did this?" I say, turning around to see if I can spot Kaylen's hand in the details. That's when I notice a collection of photos near a small conference table. I laugh when I see what they are: whales, both under the water as well as coming out of it. Kaylen knows why I call Robert "Uncle Moby." It's because he reminds me of Moby-Dick, the whale in Herman Melville's novel that ends up being much more than anyone expects. Kaylen has started calling Robert Uncle Moby as well, so I know the whale photos are a tribute to him, and the design choices reflect that, too.

"I think she was right," Robert says, looking around the space. That's when I notice the windows are framed with gauzy linen curtains. They won't shield any light, but lend softness to the space.

"I do like it better this way. The natural light makes a difference in my mood, I've found."

"No kidding," I say. "It might also blind you when the sun sets."

Robert chuckles. "Kaylen said that was the point of taking the shades away. She said, 'Uncle Moby, when you feel the urge to pull the shades, you know it's too late in the day to be working. So come home.'"

My heart melts as I imagine Kaylen saying that. She has adopted Robert just like the rest of us have, even though she's not biologically related, nor did she grow up knowing Robert. But I love seeing signs that she's integrating herself, because I know that's been a challenge for her in the past. I have no doubt that Robert allowed her to redecorate his office for just this reason.

My eyes finally make their way back to Robert. "I came because I wanted to ask if you know where Carl is."

Robert sits back down in his chair, lacing his fingers in his lap, giving me one of those penetrating but knowing looks he is exceptionally good at. We regard each other for a while, and his silence very clearly asks me to be sure I want to ask this question. I know the answer to it has to be yes. By the same token, my uncle knows that I'm exceptionally careful about asking him for help because I know the hazard of requesting even the simplest things.

"I don't know," Robert says when I hold my ground.

My brow wrinkles in confusion, and then irritation. Why is he lying to me? Robert knows the future. Or at least some of it. How much, I doubt I will ever know. But enough to be able to figure out where Carl is if he chooses.

"I want to talk to Carl. Where is he?" I repeat, this time more insistently.

"I don't know where Carl is, Wendy," Robert says quietly.

"Are you saying you don't want to figure it out?" I ask, annoyed. Okay, so Robert doesn't know off the top of his head where Carl is. But he knows what I'm asking.

"I'm saying I don't know where he is. And I'd like to keep it that way."

"Fine. Then isn't there some way you can point me in the right direction and let *me* figure out where he is?" Robert can get visions for other people. He doesn't have to be involved. Why is he being so difficult? It's not like I'm asking him for a cure for Robbie. I've certainly thought about it, but I know better.

"Yes," he replies, and then his eyes drop to his hands. More quietly he says, "But I don't want to."

My lips part. He doesn't *want* to? What is that supposed to mean? I stride forward and slump into a chair across from his desk. I cross my arms and look at the floor, wishing there was some way for me to find Carl *without* my uncle.

"Why?" I ask when no ideas come to mind. "I just want to talk to him. Why is that such a problem?"

"Because I promised to help Carl disappear," he replies quickly.

"You made Carl a *promise*?" I say, aggravated with myself for allowing Carl to talk to my uncle at all. "He doesn't deserve promises."

"What *does* he deserve, Wendy?" Robert asks, avoiding my face. It's an odd moment. Robert is not a standoffish guy. And he always speaks definitively. This is... weird.

I'm about to reply that Carl deserves suffering, but he already has that in a lot of ways. I sigh and prop my elbow on the arm of the chair, resting my cheek on my hand. "He deserves to be around to watch Robbie die." The words stop up my throat. I manage to swallow a few times before saying, "He deserves to feel guilt for the rest of his life for what he's done. And I deserve to get answers to my questions. I deserve to know the truth about everything without evasion and cryptic warnings." I shift my eyes up from the floor to my uncle's face, which is now crossed with lines of grief. He's finally looking at me directly. "I don't know much, but I know I don't deserve this."

"No, you don't," Robert agrees, his own voice quavering now. His eyes, which are becoming red, go distant again. He sniffs a few times, his jaw quivering, and I know he is fighting tears of his own. I hate to see him so broken up and I know by coming in here and saying what I've said, I've thrust my beloved Uncle Moby into a place he doesn't want to be mentally. And it will mean a struggle for him that I can only imagine. Robert has to fight against knowing the future all the time. And when someone he loves is hurting, the struggle is torturous.

I am rotten. I knew this before I came here. It's *why* I came here demanding for access to Carl only a few weeks after Robbie's diagnosis. It's a long shot, but he is the one person that might be able to help me save my son. I couldn't say exactly why, but my last conversation with Carl has been rubbing the back of my mind. Plus, Carl has proven to have access to medical care that regular people don't. Robert's no dummy. He knows the only reason I would care about Carl is because of Robbie. I attempted to manipulate my uncle, whom I look up to more than anyone else.

"I'm sorry," I sob, hopping up, weighed down with guilt, especially when I see that Robert is overcome, his tears flowing freely. "I shouldn't have come." I want to run and hug him while at the same time wishing to run away.

Robert holds up a hand, his face now drenched. "Wait," he croaks, and he yanks open a drawer. I watch him fumble for a pen. His movements are frantic and he sways as if drunk. He rips a piece of paper from somewhere, leans over it, and scribbles something quickly.

He folds it several times until it's the size of a spitball. He clenches it in his hand, glaring down at his fist for several seconds as if it offends him. I watch his shoulders shake and am filled with unspeakable terror at seeing my uncle fall apart this way. Robert often exudes a power that cannot be fully articulated. I have cowered from it before, some part of me knowing that I am in the presence of a force that demands attention and respect. At this moment I sense that power, but in the face of such visible grief, I am struck with the thought that this is what it must look like when a god cries. And if a god is crying, there must be much to fear.

Full of awesome dread, I'm frozen in place even though Robert's presence is terrible to endure. A cold sweat moves over me.

Robert holds his shaking fist out toward me but does not look up.

When I don't move, he closes his eyes. "Here," he says, his brows drawing together as if he is in pain.

I leap forward even though it didn't sound like a command at all. Rather, it was beseeching, as if the paper is literally burning his hand and he needs someone to relieve him.

As soon as my open hand is beneath his, he opens his fist. The bit of paper falls into my palm and he withdraws his hand, tucking it into his lap.

"Start there," Robert says, still not looking my direction, and I'm kind of glad he's not.

Paralyzed, I don't know what to do.

Robert turns his chair back toward me, facing the window where the light of sunset is starting to blind me. So softly that I barely hear him, he says, "Where it begins." He slumps visibly, as if completely exhausted suddenly. "Go please," he says more loudly but still gently.

Not needing further invitation, I run from the room, fist wound tightly around the tiny folded paper that is too light to be as scary as Robert made it seem. I expected it to feel like lead. For all I know, it's not in my hand at all. I make a beeline for the stairs and then burst outside, gulping the brisk, early-May air as if I have escaped sudden death.

"What—" I pant, hands on my knees. "What?" I open my hand, staring at the paper, afraid of it, as if the information it contains is akin to Pandora's box. It must contain some secret that will release darkness, the likes of which I have never before seen.

I make my way to a bench near a bus stop, wrapping my coat more tightly around me. I stare at the paper, wondering what to do. Robert seemed like he'd rather die than give it to me. But he *did* give it to me. So does that mean I'm *supposed* to look at it? Or did Robert bend his own rules and I should burn the paper so I won't be tempted to look at it? Whatever the paper contains, I'm convinced that looking at it is going to change the future, drastically enough that I will look back on this day and... I'm not sure.

I recall Robert's look of dread. I replay every word he said, searching for a hidden message. But I only become more confused. The problem is, I don't know if Robert giving me the paper was the right thing or the wrong thing. Was it a test? He's done that to me before... Did he plan to give it to me all along or was it on a whim? I vacillate, unable to settle on one or the other.

I look up, immediately distracted by the bustle of the street. It's rush hour, so the babble of voices and footsteps and cars has meshed into a pulse of city life. As I watch the coming and going for a while, I calm a little, and instead of the paper still clutched in my hand, I picture my uncle. I love him. So much. With tears of a different kind now in my eyes, I know I would do anything he asked. Even give my own life. I would follow Robert into hell if he said it was the right thing.

After my encounter with him just now, enduring his look of sorrow, I am desperate to know what he *wants* me to do. I don't care about Carl anymore. I don't care about whatever future this paper will bring if I look at it. I just want to do what my uncle would have me do. The problem is I don't know what that is.

I put the paper into my pocket. Now is probably not the time to ask. I'll give him time. For now, the paper will stay folded.

Eight

"*W*en, did you steal my Magic shirt?" Ezra demands, coming into the kitchen where I'm stirring pasta sauce. He leans over the pot to see inside.

I swat him away. "No idea what you're talking about."

Kaylen walks in then, carrying Robbie, her finger pulling back an edge of Robbie's collar. "Wendy, have you seen this rash on his chest? I think you should get it checked out."

"What?!" Ezra yells, facing Kaylen now. "You too?"

Kaylen stops and looks at Ezra with surprise. "What is your problem?"

Ezra holds his hands out toward Kaylen, palms up.

"No," Kaylen says, eying his open hands with annoyance and holding Robbie away from him. "You can hold him later."

"Not Robbie," Ezra says. "Your shirt." Then he throws up his hands and groans loudly. "Now *both* of you are stealing my clothes?"

I look at Kaylen's shirt. It's a black T-shirt with a circle containing the letter 'M' at the center, hedged by five symbols on it: a tree, a sun, a water droplet, a skull, and a fireball. "Ohhhhh," I say. "Magic shirt. As in that card game you play? It looks better on Kaylen."

"Of course it looks better on her. She has *boobs*," Ezra says. "I can't help that I'm a dude. But it's tournament night. And I wanted to wear *my* shirt."

"What am I supposed to wear?" Kaylen complains. "I won't fit in."

"You're going?" I ask. I had no idea Kaylen was into nerdy card games.

She nods. "Ezra's been teaching me. He says I'm ready."

I start chuckling and turn back to my sauce. "Kaylen, it doesn't matter what you wear. Fitting in is not something you should worry about."

"What is that supposed to mean?" she asks, bouncing Robbie on her left shoulder.

"Calm down," I say, dragging the pot off the stove and bringing it to the island. "All I'm saying is that Magic the Gathering tournaments aren't frequented by many… girls." I laugh again as I picture it. I've driven Ezra to tournaments before, which is why I know what I'm talking about.

"That's quite a stereotype," Kaylen chides.

Sniggering under my breath, I say, "Sure. But if it fits, it fits."

Ezra, I notice, has remained uncharacteristically silent. "Are you bringing Kaylen to elevate your status among the nerds?"

Ezra gives me a dirty look as he scoots into a barstool. "Wen, you've been out of school too long. It's no longer uncool to be a geek."

"Yeah right," I snort. "High school doesn't change. And nerds will always be at the bottom of the adolescent food chain. Not sayin' it's right. Just sayin' it is."

"It's called Geek Chic, Wendy," Kaylen says.

"Sure, superheroes are getting their fifteen minutes of fame. But late night comic book store get-togethers are still reserved for the most nerdy among us—primarily dudes. Any dude that brings a girl to one gets instant cool nerd cred."

Kaylen turns to Ezra. "Are you using me to look good in front of your friends?"

Ezra slumps in his stool. "No. It's this one girl there. She just… hangs all over me. I'm hoping you being there is going to… ward her off."

"Sounds like a recipe for disaster," I mumble, testing the pasta to see if it's done.

"You jerk," Kaylen complains. "You taught me Magic so you could use me?"

"It's not that," Ezra says defensively. "I really want you to play. It's fun. Why does it matter if I also need you to keep Bertie off of me? You'll still go, won't you?"

"Bertie?" I ask. "Is that seriously her name?"

"Oh, I'm going," Kaylen warns. "You're going to regret this, Ezra Whitley."

"Uh oh," I mumble, pulling out pasta bowls.

"Wendy, seriously, have you seen this rash?" Kaylen asks, changing gears and peeking under Robbie's onesie again.

"Yes," I reply, standing on tiptoes in search of the salad plates. "It's nothing."

"How do you know?" Kaylen demands, laying Robbie on a blanket on the counter so she can take his onesie off and make a full-body exam. I hate when she becomes overbearing. If anyone deserves the overprotective parenting award, it's Kaylen, and she's not even a parent.

"Geez, Kaylen. You're worse than me," I say. "Babies get rashes. It's a thing. And even if it weren't, Robbie has been to see three separate doctors this week who would have told me if he had a flesh-eating bacteria. I'm a little more concerned about how much stress his respiratory system is under or how long he's going to be able to walk—something he hasn't even learned to do yet."

Kaylen's face is screwed up when I turn around, and her cheeks are red, giving away that she's close to tears. I shouldn't have said that. Kaylen took Robbie's diagnosis as badly as I did, maybe worse—if that's possible.

"Sorry," I sigh, standing at the counter across from her.

"No, I am," she says. "I know you're on top of it. I just…" She looks down at Robbie's face. "I'm just still freaked out. I see the boogeyman everywhere. I sometimes wonder if you're cursed."

"I wish I could say that," I reply. "Instead everything that happens to me can be traced back to Carl and his stupid ambitions. Looks like I'm enticed by similar ambition. And Robbie is paying for it."

"Aw, Wen, don't do that," Ezra says, hopping up to sit on the island now so he can pick penne out of one of the bowls I've portioned. "Besides, how do you know it wasn't passed genetically?"

"Why would it be?" I ask, knocking the spoon I'm using a little too violently against the edge of the bowl to get the last of the pasta off. "After all the drugs I had? And besides, I'm sure Uncle Moby would have mentioned it after the diagnosis if someone in the family had had muscular dystrophy."

"Why would Uncle Rob know his genetic history?" Ezra says. "He's adopted."

I drop the spoon in the pot of pasta and gawk at Ezra. "Are you serious?"

"Yeah," Ezra says, and from his tone I can tell he's surprised I don't know. "When you lived at the compound and I lived with Uncle Rob I asked him if any other family was around for me to meet. He said he and Carl were adopted by an older couple that had died years ago."

Why this piece of information should turn my world so fully upside-down is beyond me at the moment, but reality is now slightly off-kilter. "Is that all?" I ask. "I mean to the story? He and Carl were adopted; that's it? No reason why his biological parents gave them both up?"

"Carl was a baby and Rob was four or five, so he doesn't remember much. But he was told by his adoptive parents that his biological parents had died. It was a closed adoption so he never got access to records."

I fall into the other barstool, lost in imagining my uncle and my father being taken in by a family not their own. The both of them had supernatural abilities... Where did they get them? It has to be more than random coincidence since both boys possessed abilities. What if... it's genetic?

If it is, why do I not have abilities? Unless Carl and Robert's abilities aren't natural... Then how did they get them?

The more I guess, the more possibilities there are, and the more lost I become.

"What am I missing?" Ezra says, watching my expression fluctuate.

"Two brothers with superpowers," I say. "Two parents who died from who knows what. Ezra, we have explanations for how people come to have supernatural abilities through hypno-touch, but we still don't have a clue how Robert and Carl came to have the abilities *they* did. Shoot, we don't even know how... Gabriel... can... count..." I stop midsentence and put my hand over my mouth as the connection is made with the force of a wrecking ball.

I prop my elbow on the counter, chin in hand. "Gabriel was sick as a kid... on his deathbed even. And then he got well... miraculously. And he can count billions of strands... that's not a coincidence. Neither are Robert and Carl... Not the same circumstance... But still far too coincidental..." I shake my head. "I'm missing something." I look between Kaylen and Ezra. "But I sure as heck am going to find out what it is."

"I have no clue what any of that meant, do you?" Ezra says to Kaylen as I walk over to where my jacket is resting over the back of a chair. I dig in the pocket for the folded paper Robert gave me yesterday. For some reason, I feel like I got my answer about whether I should look at it because I'm suddenly confident. I have no idea why precisely, but I'm going to strike while the choice feels right.

I undo each fold, smoothing out the wrinkles against the table's surface.

It's an address, located in a suburb of Los Angeles. I don't recognize it.

"What is it?" Kaylen asks from over my shoulder.

"Where it begins…" I murmur, echoing Robert's words although I'm not sure what they mean.

"What?" Kaylen says as I refold the paper and stick it back in my pocket.

"I don't know," I say quickly, wishing I'd waited until I was by myself before looking at the paper. I don't know why, but it feels like I'm violating Uncle Moby's confidence by showing it to someone else. "Just something Robert gave me when I asked about Carl. Haven't figured out what it means."

"You're trying to find Carl?" Ezra says, grabbing a bowl of pasta and spooning sauce over it. "Why? Didn't you talk to him a couple months ago?"

"Yes. But Carl was drunk at the time," I say, wanting this conversation to be over. "I shouldn't be thinking about it. Forget it." I take Robbie from Kaylen's arms as I hear the back door open. I'm pretty sure it's Gabriel. Thank goodness. I am definitely not ready to talk about my conversation with Robert with anyone. I'm still working through what it all means.

I do know, however, that whatever this address is, I'm going there. I'm not sure when exactly, but I will.

Nine

When Gabriel and I are alone later that night, I feel bad about keeping my conversation with Robert from him. To appease my guilt, I instead tell him about my conversation with Ezra, the one in which I found out that Robert and Carl were adopted.

"That's certainly not something I ever would have suspected," Gabriel remarks.

I wait, watching him put together an outfit for work the next day, but he says nothing more. I rock in my chair while Robbie nurses and, trying not to sound too eager, I say, "Yeah... But it might be something that explains where their supernatural abilities came from."

Gabriel's head pokes around the bathroom doorway, "What is the purpose of this information?"

"You're not curious?" I say, perplexed that Gabriel hasn't latched on to this new tidbit with more interest.

"Of course I'm curious," he replies. "But I'm curious about everything. You, on the other hand, are curious only when it serves a specific purpose."

I frown at him. "Ouch."

He rolls his eyes at me before grabbing his shoes that are near the door and putting them in the bathroom as well. "It's not an insult. It's an observation meant to serve my own purpose, which is to find out what prompted such an inquiry into Robert's background."

"Robert's background is *my* background," I say defensively. I'm trying to have a conversation with him. Why is he being so difficult?

"Is this about Robbie?" Gabriel says suddenly, sitting on the edge of the bed to face me.

"No," I answer, and I know it was too quick so I say, "I don't know. Ezra brought it up and I just thought it was… noteworthy. I don't know if it serves any purpose. But I wonder about it. Seems like if both Carl and Robert were born with abilities, it might have been a genetic inheritance. And that got me thinking about you—where *your* abilities came from—" I throw my free hand up. "I don't know. I'm not good at connections. That's why I'm telling you, so you can tell me what it all means."

He watches me pensively, making an attempt to read me. Then he says, "You're hoping this will lead to a way to help Robbie, isn't that right?"

"No!" I protest. "What does any of what I just said have to do with Robbie?"

"It's written in your hesitation. And it doesn't take a genius to figure that if you had the ability to continually push a person's wayward strands back into their body, you might be able to permanently stave off their illness. You want your ability back, so you're trying to figure out if there's a way to do it."

My mouth opens in outrage. "Where do you get these things? I wasn't thinking that at all!"

"You know it won't work," Gabriel says, ignoring my reaction. "Robbie's illness is biologically driven. Ours was life force driven. What are you going to do? Reverse death? Don't you remember what that did to Carl?"

Livid, it takes every ounce of willpower not to raise my voice again as I hiss, "Don't you patronize me, Gabriel. There is *no one* more aware of how Carl's obsession has twisted the lives of so many, ours and Robbie's included. How dare you accuse me of following in his footsteps. You know what I think? I think you don't trust me. I think you refuse to look at the situation with Robert and Carl, not to mention *your* mysterious abilities, for the blatant coincidences that they are because you believe it will force me down some damning path."

"So you don't deny it then," Gabriel states, again ignoring my accusation.

Furious, I stand up with a now-sleeping Robbie and go into his room. It's less dramatic an exit than I'd like since I can't stomp out while keeping Robbie asleep.

Standing over Robbie's crib with him bundled tightly in my arms, I stick my nose in his neck and inhale. I love his new smell.

It reminds me of the colorworld smell: clean and pure. I place him down gently, my fingers lingering against his feathery, dark locks.

Now that I'm out of Gabriel's scrutinizing gaze, however, I become irritated with myself for letting him push my buttons so easily. He's not exactly wrong. My reasons for going to see Robert yesterday about Carl did stem from pondering my ability and how to get it back. But I hadn't taken the logic as far as Gabriel apparently has. Go figure.

"I'm sorry," Gabriel says softly, coming up beside me.

"You were thinking the exact same things as me," I accuse, turning to look at him. "Why did you make it seem like *I* was the bad guy?"

Gabriel rubs his face. "Because you tried to hide that you were thinking it."

"That's a dumb reason to interrogate me and make me feel like crap."

"Wendy, the last few weeks have been... terrible. Since we received Robbie's diagnosis, you've not shared any of what's been going on in your head. I spend all my time searching for a way out for Robbie. My head is going to so many awful places and I am terrified that I'm going to be tempted to do something ill-advised. I only... wanted you to admit that you were struggling with similar things. I could have gone about it differently, I admit. And for that I am sorry."

My shoulders fall as my temper deescalates. "Me too. Yeah. My head has gone places—not as much as yours has, though. But enough."

"For the first time I've been grateful that you can't feel my emotions," he says. "The weight is like being held just under the surface of the water by an invisible force. Unbearable. My students have been exceptionally good the last few weeks, afraid I'm going to explode at them—which I have many times."

"I know the feeling," I whisper, staring at Robbie's chest rising and falling in rhythm. It lulls me further. So peaceful. Innocent. And ignorant of the future that awaits him...

"What I wouldn't give to take his illness upon me..." Gabriel says longingly. He laces his fingers over the top of mine that rest on the edge of Robbie's crib.

After some hesitation, unsure if I want to bring up more heavy things, I say, "You've been where he will be, haven't you?"

A tremulous sigh escapes Gabriel's chest and I know the answer is yes. When he doesn't elaborate I lean gently against the side of Robbie's crib and face him. "It's not like you to hold back."

"You don't really want to know more."

"How do you know?"

He gives me a sidelong glance. "You want me to tell you what it's like to have an illness render you incapable of using your own body?"

"No," I sigh, leading us out of the room and sitting on our couch. Gabriel sits next to me. "But... remember the times since I lost my abilities that I've been honest with you about where I stood in our relationship?"

"You mean the time you told me you felt like you'd been violated when we made love and then that other time you told me you didn't love me?" he says, propping his arm on the back of the couch as he faces me. "How sweet of you to remind me."

I roll my eyes. "Oh stop it. I'm *reminding* you because I want you to tell me if you regret that I told you those things."

He frowns. "Okay I get it. You're saying that even though something hurts to hear doesn't mean it shouldn't be said."

I give him a half smile.

"Alright," he says wistfully. "I guess it's my turn to rip *your* heart out."

I wince. "Lay it on me. Tell me the worst part first."

Gabriel leans more heavily against the back of the couch. "The worst part for me was being unable to speak. People assume you are unintelligent if you can't talk back to them. If they talk to you at all they speak to you like they would a toddler just learning to use words. And they don't focus on your face let alone your eyes because it makes them uncomfortable. So every time you encounter someone new, you never actually get to connect with them. When you don't have the ability to speak, or even move your hands to gesture, your eyes are the only way to communicate. And when people refuse to give you that, it's like being ignored. And it happens all the time. Every day. Until you see yourself as completely isolated from the rest of humanity."

"That's awful..." I say sadly. Maybe I should take notes on this so I can school people on how to act around Robbie as he gets older. But on second thought, Gabriel is probably going to make absolutely sure that doesn't happen to Robbie. Gabriel is going to be a huge asset in this...

"Hey, that's why you've always looked at me in the eye..." I muse. "It makes it hard to look away. I can still remember what it was like to feel you watching me from across the kitchen at the compound. It was like you were speaking to me with your eyes…"

He nods slowly. "I'd never thought about that, but I suppose you're right. I used to stare at people until they'd look at me. I got a kick out of making them uncomfortable. And I guess I never lost that habit. I like people to fully engage. Eyes and all."

"That sounds exactly right," I say. "And it looks like as soon as you were able to talk again, you learned every language you could to communicate in."

"I was learning languages before I could speak. My body might have been idle but my mind wasn't. Which leads me to the next most horrible thing: being unable to move," Gabriel says. "Lock a man in a dungeon or chain them up. It will never be as terrible as being stuck in a body that doesn't do what you ask it to. Trying so hard all the time and failing makes you retreat into yourself until you don't fully experience what's going on around you. I lived in my head. I read voraciously to escape as much and as often as possible. I spent my childhood half-dead to the sensations of the world."

"You clearly benefitted intellectually," I ponder. "I have no idea what that's like exactly, but I do know that losing my abilities has been a similar loss. I was used to experiencing life more fully, and when I couldn't, I felt like a large part of me was dead. I'm a house with a thousand windows but every window is blacked out from the outside. It's hard to adjust to that."

He squeezes my arm. "I suppose we all have our losses to adapt to, but I guess it's harder when you know exactly what another will experience. If Robbie were going to face something I had never experienced, it would be easier to deal with. The unknown is sometimes welcome."

"Speaking of," I say. "We need to talk about this Carl thing."

"Wendy, I'm afraid to know more than we already do about the connection between life forces and illness. This is a path Carl went down. And I don't know if you or I are ready to face the same choices."

I close my eyes and nod. "I absolutely want what I used to have. I'm fighting every day to find peace with what I am now. And yes, I'm dying for there to be some kind of loophole to save Robbie. I know it's a path that could lead to dark and scary places. It may place us before two paths in which the wrong one is incredibly enticing. I don't know what our limits are. But we can't hide from it just because the possibility of being too tempted scares us."

"Carl wasn't ready. How do you know we are?" he implores, shaking my hand a little for emphasis.

Good question. How *do* we know? Can we know? Is it possible to ignore information like Carl and Robert's adoption without wanting to know more? This isn't just about them. This is about me, too. How can I live without uncovering all the facts possible?

Uncle Moby is my go-to example for moral dilemmas. He is faced with knowing too much all the time. How does *he* know when to stop searching for an answer?

Rules.

"Life and death," I say, looking up at Gabriel. "Uncle Moby has rules. And so should we. We don't question how what we learn can affect life and death. And Uncle Moby says basic information is always a safe bet. So let's make our goal understanding the origin of natural abilities. Yours and Robert's and Carl's. We start there. And when we've figured that out, we can decide what our next question to answer will be. You agree?"

Gabriel considers it for several seconds before nodding. "Agreed."

"Plus, we have an advantage over Carl," I point out.

Gabriel tilts his head questioningly.

"We have each other. Carl never had anyone around to tell him to not kill people."

"One would think people shouldn't need anyone to tell them that," Gabriel says, grimacing. "But as history proves, that's sadly not the case." He looks at me seriously. "Wendy, do not kill anyone."

I laugh but raise my arm to the square. "I promise. No matter who it is."

Ten

Why haven't you ever dug deeper into your miraculous recovery as a child?" I ask, fiddling with the vent so it will point more to the back of the car where Robbie is. Gabriel and I are on our way for a weekend visit to his parents. Our plan is to get as much information from them as we can about his childhood illness and recovery.

Gabriel taps the wheel. He looks nervous. He's been so quiet since we left Monterey. And he doesn't answer now.

"I can't read minds anymore," I say, "but I think you don't want to do this."

He glances at me. "An accurate deduction."

"Hmm," I say. "Mister Dumas, I haven't seen you this nervous since you asked me to marry you in a shotgun wedding planned by you and your mother. What gives?"

After several moments of silence, Gabriel sniffs. "As you know, my mother is a devout Catholic. We argue incessantly about everything from my choice in clothing to how she prepares her chiles rellenos, but religion is the one thing my mother clings to more tenaciously than she does anything else, including me and my brother. We ardently disagree over the particulars. She refused to speak to me for an entire two years while I was in college because she felt I insulted her bible-study group when I came home for a visit. The whole argument was based on my recovery as a child. When we finally made up, I promised her I wouldn't ever address the basis of that particular 'miracle' again."

"Okay... but you didn't want to discover the truth for yourself?"

"I don't function that way. If I were to search for the truth, I daresay I'd find it. And when I found it I'd be obliged to inform her of her error."

"Why is that? You could find out and then keep your mouth shut about it."

He looks at me skeptically. "Wendy, I cannot let ignorance prevail if it's in my power to dispel it."

"Seriously?" I say, in disbelief myself now. "You can't just let people be wrong if it makes them happy?"

"No. It's like an itch. I have to scratch it. So I promised my mother that I would accept the incident as she said it was, and not tear down the one thing she felt was blatant confirmation of her religious faith. You don't wonder why I've never brought it up, even to you? You would ask questions and I'd be compelled to find the answer for you. It's how I'm built. So I've put it out of my head entirely, out of necessity. There was no other way to keep my promise."

I hear him, but I'm having a hard time wrapping my head around his oddly-functioning brain. But then, that's Gabriel. He's wired differently. I *can* understand his desire to maintain a relationship with his mother though, even if he was restrained from being true to himself. He only goes against his nature if he has a lot of love and respect for the person. He did that for me once, too, when he promised to let go of his theories surrounding my death touch. Gabriel has clearly always operated in extremes.

"Oh Gabriel…" I say softly. "I didn't know… I'm sorry. I didn't realize doing this might drive a wedge between the two of you. I'm sure there's another way…"

Gabriel shakes his head. "There's no other way. As I said, I can't go behind her back and unearth the truth. If I'm going to break my promise to her, I have to do it honestly."

I feel awful about what I've asked of him. Gabriel has never broken a promise to me, probably never to anyone. I have always, even in the direst circumstances, been able to trust a promise from Gabriel. And now I am asking him to break one with his own mother. Would I want someone coming between Robbie and me that way?

He won't live long enough to face that kind of moral dilemma.

I take several breaths to ward against the pressure building up in my chest. I reach up to take one of Gabriel's hands and lean my head against his arm for good measure. I close my eyes, find my center as I have with Gabriel in one way or another so many times since Robbie's diagnosis. I can't imagine going through this without Gabriel. When Robbie was born, I said he would teach me to love again and I was right. The warped irony is that it has come through sharing the sorrow of Robbie's horrific fate.

So much of what we're having to do is twisted. Robbie shouldn't be dying because I wanted to save people. I shouldn't be looking into the same dark possibilities Carl once explored. Gabriel shouldn't be going against a promise to his mother. I hope these aren't omens. Gabriel breaking a promise is about as likely as Armageddon... which is apparently far more likely now that Gabriel is going to go against every instinct in his nature.

ℸℸ

"That was delicious, Maris," I say cordially, after Gabriel leaves the room. He told me to broach the dreaded topic with his mother. He says I'll have a gentler touch; he's probably right.

Meanwhile, he's going to see what he can get from his dad. Gabriel's father, Daniel Dumas, the quiet man I've had little interaction with, intimidated me when I first met him because his personality is so vastly different from Gabriel and Maris', but I've come to accept him as a quiet observer. Despite his aloof exterior, however, I once sensed with my emodar that he is extremely intelligent. I don't think he misses a thing. He simply reserves commentary most of the time. And in fact, on my wedding day I danced with him and he assured me of Gabriel's devotion to me in a moment when the walls were crumbling down. He knew exactly what to say because he is always watching.

Maris doesn't seem to have heard me as she digs through a cabinet for a container to put the leftovers in. I wonder at her demeanor. Since we've arrived, she's been as distracted as Gabriel was in the car.

"What's kept you so silent today?" I ask, rinsing the dirty dishes and stacking them for the dishwasher.

Maris smiles brightly at me, and it may be the first time she has really acknowledged me. "Oh nothing, Wendy." She wipes her hands with a towel, but I notice they weren't wet in the first place. She puts her hands on her hips, looks around the kitchen. "I'm going to leave the rest of the cleanup to you tonight," she says. "I just want to get my hands on my precious grandson. Are you okay with that?"

"Of course," I reply. I don't need emodar to know that her response of 'nothing' was definitely *something*. "Why don't you go get him and come talk to me? I've had a rough couple of weeks."

After a few moments she returns with Robbie, and it's nice to see her genuine smile as she gazes down at him. I know that look. My week has been full of appointments for Robbie's disease, Duchenne Muscular Dystrophy, or DMD for short. I have seen so many doctors I can't keep them all straight. When it feels like it's choking me, I hold Robbie and wonder at him. Love overwhelms me and I don't care if I meet a new doctor every day for the rest of my life.

"Anti-depressant for any occasion," I say.

Maris wipes her eye and I wonder if it was a tear. Maybe her preoccupation has been because of Robbie's diagnosis. Gabriel said she didn't take it well at all when he told her over the phone. I bet for someone such as her who watched her own child waste away, this predicament hits all kinds of hot buttons.

When Maris remains silent, I say, "The doctors are pretty hopeful you know. There are several promising clinical trials. It may be years before we see any symptoms because he's being monitored so early. I have to say, it could be a lot worse." I load the last of the plates into the dishwasher and rummage under the sink for the detergent.

I wait for her to speak, hoping that she'll start to draw parallels between Robbie and Gabriel and open up about her own experience.

"Yes it could," she replies, encouraging her finger into Robbie's hand as she takes a seat at the kitchen table. He grips it in a tiny fist, bringing it to his mouth. "I have no doubt that you two will handle it with the strength and grace I know you both possess. The Lord has prepared you exceptionally well for this challenge."

That didn't go as planned. She sounds self-possessed where Robbie is concerned. Maybe her melancholy is for another reason.

"What's bothering you, Maris?" I ask, starting the dishwasher and turning directly toward her so she can't dismiss me again.

Maris glances at me before sighing. "Just my Michael. I have not heard from him in a while. And he won't take my calls. That's not like him, and I worry."

That was unexpected. Ugh. *Mike*. Maris may think it's odd for her other son to be such a jerk, but a jerk is all my brother-in-law has ever been to *me*. I'm having a hard time considering avoidance a cause for alarm. I haven't spoken to Mike since he called to thank me for curing Gabriel. He probably only did it because we all expected me to die.

Mike is either a personal trainer of famous people like he says or he runs some kind of underground business. Either way, he knows a lot of people. He was set to give Gabriel and me fake papers while we were on the run once. Then he offered to get me into a clinical trial for leukemia. And another time he provided me with experimental diabetes monitoring. But I've since gone back to traditional testing and injecting because of how little I have to do it. Mike is… a giant mystery. I wouldn't be surprised at all if he was involved in illegal activities.

He is so much that Gabriel is not… The two don't look much alike. Mike's features lean more heavily to his Hispanic side. Gabriel, who is only a year older than Mike, is more intellectual, more mentally organized. Mike is more volatile and just… angry. In light of learning about Gabriel's childhood illness, I now find their closeness in age odd. Gabriel was diagnosed with Spinal Muscular Atrophy at three months old. It required rigorous therapy and attention. I wonder why Maris decided to have another child so close in age. I can't imagine having another child right now, especially when I run the risk of all my eggs carrying the mutated gene. SMA is genetic, too. Didn't she worry that she would have another child with the same problem?

"Maris, it must have been difficult to raise Gabriel, given his condition, but to have two boys so young? That must have been exhausting."

"It was," she replies. "But I had to do what I had to do. Michael needed a family. As heartbreaking as my sister's death was, the Lord knew better. I needed him. Being able to raise another child eased much of the loss of deciding not to have more children. They would have had a twenty-five percent chance of being born with the disease. I couldn't do that."

"Wait. Are you saying Michael is not your biological son?" I ask, stunned that I never knew this. Geez. Why am I suddenly finding out everyone is adopted?

Maris looks up. "No. Gabriel never told you?"

I shake my head, leaning over the island and crossing my arms.

"Ah well, that's just as well. Gabriel has never thought him any less than a brother although they're technically only cousins. I took custody of Michael when he was one year old and he took to Gabriel right away. He followed him everywhere as soon as we brought him home to live with us." Maris looks lost in memory as she rocks back and forth with Robbie. "Gabe went through a rough patch about that time and developed pneumonia from a cold right after we adopted Michael and nearly died. That was years before his recovery. And even as young as Michael was, he would cry whenever we tried to take him away from Gabriel's room. He would curl up in a little ball at the end of Gabe's bed and sleep there. The cutest thing you've ever seen. I could swear the two could talk to each other the way they would look at one another without moving or making a sound. It was really something. Gabe persevered through that, of course, and as Michael got older he was such a help to me. The two of them were so close. It was such a blessing for Gabriel to have a loyal companion. It's probably why he survived so long, always having Michael around to entertain him."

"That is so sweet," I say, trying to imagine the Mike I know doing something like that. The way he pesters Gabriel… Mike has a chip on his shoulder where Gabriel is concerned. Gabriel once told me, in so many words, that Mike hates me because I came between Gabriel and him. "What happened to Mike's parents?"

"I don't know anything about his father. Probably some deadbeat Alma met. She had a rough life. And breast cancer cut her time short. She was diagnosed right after Michael was born. She didn't come to me until the very end. My dear sister… She fell out of touch with the rest of us for years, so it was out of the blue. I was thankful God allowed me to be a mother to more than Gabriel and that Michael could have a family to love him."

I wonder why Gabriel has never told me this before. And if what Maris says about their relationship is true, why has Gabriel allowed the silence between him and his brother to prevail? And is Mike still stuck on hating me? "What does Gabriel think?" I ask. "About Mike's avoidance?"

Maris looks uncomfortable. "I haven't brought it up to him."

"Why not?" I take a chair across from her.

"Because it's not his business."

I pause, translating what she's saying. She and Mike must have had a fight. Why would she care if Gabriel knew about that? I have a lot of things I'd *like* to say, like what a jerk Mike is and how she should let him come beg for forgiveness when he finally comes around, but that probably won't go over well.

I sit back in my chair. "Mike must have something going on that he's not sharing with you all."

Maris looks up, eyes wide. "What makes you say so?"

I shrug. "I just—well—you and Gabe both talk about this wonderful version of Mike, but since I've known you all, all I've seen is him do is make you miserable. If he's really the person you say he is, that's gotta mean he's got something going on that's making him… not so nice."

"He is speaking to Gabriel, isn't he?" Maris says, her eyes slightly pinched with worry and she rocks Robbie back and forth a little faster.

"I don't *think* so. I haven't seen Gabriel talking to him since we were sick. But then we aren't always together."

Maris' slight concern turns to alarm. She stands up, walks over to me, and eases Robbie into my arms. She turns briskly on her heel, her blue linen skirt flapping behind her, and leaves the room.

At a loss, I gape at the empty doorway for several seconds until I hear her voice echo from the hall, "Gabriel Daniel Dumas! Where are you? You come speak to me this moment!"

Crap. This is not at all what I had planned. With Maris now rankled, there is no way I can bring up Gabriel's recovery.

I hop up with Robbie and follow the raised voices I hear from Dan's study, ready to do what I can to mitigate what looks like a possible major confrontation between Gabriel and his mother. I find the three of them where I expect, but I hang back in the doorway, intimidated by distinct tension in the air.

"Gabriel!" Maris yells. "Lying is any form of deception, including omission! You intended to deceive me, therefore you lied!"

"I never intended to deceive you, Mamá," Gabriel says from the couch, one ankle crossed casually over the other knee, hands clasped behind his head. "I simply avoided the subject."

Dan sits in an armchair across from him, looking like the lawyer he is, but dressed down somewhat in a sport coat and slacks. His raised eyebrows are the only indication that he is disturbed by the confrontation going on. I guess lawyers make it their business not to get riled in an argument.

"Avoided the subject?" Maris shrieks, hands on her hips and looking down at him menacingly, all five feet of her. She catches her eye on me and lowers her voice a little as she continues, "The number of times we have spoken and you didn't *once* mention that you two weren't on speaking terms? Lies!"

"You never asked," Gabriel says nonchalantly.

Maris makes a frustrated sound. "Dan, I can't speak to this boy. He makes his own rules. He'd claim the sky wasn't blue if it suited him. It's a wonder Wendy puts up with him at all!"

Dan smiles just barely. Gabriel glances at me before saying, "Actually Mamá, that's partly true. Wendy and I can both attest that the sky is not any one color at all, but rather a menagerie of fluctuating color given the time of day. Although in the common visible world, it is indeed blue, so I suppose technically the claim may still stand given—"

"That's enough, Gabe," Dan interrupts in a commanding voice when Maris stamps her foot. Her face glows bright red.

Gabriel looks flustered now as he lowers his hands to his knees and sits up. "Mamá, you always take Mike's side." He holds his hands out, palms up in surrender. "I wasn't going to invite the opportunity to hear you berate me about how it's *my* fault Mike doesn't talk to me anymore. If Mike wanted you to know, *he* could tell you. And I'd say that given the fact he hasn't mentioned it to you even once in the past six months means he knows it's his fault. So why don't you go ask him yourself what his problem is? Because I never could get a straight answer. He has never once returned my calls about Robbie's birth, so he obviously doesn't care. Our lack of communication is certainly not from lack of effort on my part."

"We haven't heard from Mike in months," Dan says in his quiet French cadence. "Your mother and I assumed you had been communicating with him. So we have not worried so much."

Gabriel leans forward, clasping his hands. "I haven't been. Why on earth didn't you say anything?"

"Because, son, you tell us every time you and Mike so much as argue over what kind of oil to put in your car," Dan says, his brow now plunged into a 'V'. "We never would have imagined you wouldn't tell us if you had gone months without speaking to him."

Gabriel looks from his mom to his dad, his face slowly taking on a skeptical frown. "I have an idea as to why Mike won't speak to *me*. But you must enlighten me as to why he is also not speaking to *you*."

Dan glances at me and opens his mouth to speak, but Maris interrupts, "It's a private matter."

Gabriel, taken aback, turns to his dad. "A private matter? What does that mean?"

Dan and Maris pass a look between them before Dan says, "It means that we argued with Mike over something that he spoke to us about in confidence. Telling you would betray his trust."

Gabriel's mouth is hanging open as he leans forward ever more. It's a wonder he doesn't fall right off the couch, his head swiveling between his parents again, flabbergasted. This is clearly not something he has ever encountered from them. Then he sits back suddenly, crosses his arms, and says, "Very well. In that case, the subject is moot. I have no idea why you are asking *me* why I haven't been speaking to my brother when you are guilty of the same thing. You see what your own deception has cost you? If you were concerned, you could have asked me at any time and I would have told you the truth. Yet still I am reprimanded for choosing not to mention it for my own sake even though it is Mike's childish behavior that has alienated all of us."

Maris explodes in rapid Spanish, her face growing even redder. Dan watches her with his brow wrinkled pensively. Gabriel looks like he's ignoring her entirely. I stand stock still, alternating my attention between the three of them, wondering if I should interject and what I might say. But I don't have a dog in this fight.

A minute or so in, Gabriel shakes his head in exasperation and stands up. "Your upset is misdirected, Mamá, and therefore useless to me." He walks over to me and puts his hand on the small of my back, guiding me out.

"Gabriel," says Dan in a booming voice before we reach the door.

Gabriel stops, and as I look back at him, his eyes move to the ceiling, petitioning patience. I can see Dan over his shoulder, standing beside Maris who is now weeping. Her rapid change from anger to tears is impressive.

"No matter how much knowledge you gain, no matter how old you become, this woman is still your mother. And as such she deserves your respect and your bridled tongue," Dan says.

Gabriel whirls around. "*My* bridled tongue? What of hers? She came in here on the attack, calling me a liar and then getting more upset when I explained the misunderstanding. You want me to take her verbal abuse without comment?"

Dan's shoulders slump slightly as he puts a hand on Maris' arm when she looks like she is about to leave. She has stopped crying and now watches Gabriel with a forlorn look, as if apologizing. Maybe. I don't know her that well.

"Yes, I do," Dan says. "Consideration is a skill you could use more of. What better situation to practice than with your mother, who will love you unconditionally no matter what proceeds out of your mouth?"

Gabriel looks down at the floor, bristling and obviously biting his tongue so it doesn't dig him deeper.

Dan, who must know that Gabriel is better at staying silent than saying the right thing in situations like this, guides Maris to a chair, whispering something in her ear. She lets him, clearly comfortable being treated as the queen in her castle. But in watching Dan interact gently with his wife, I understand where Gabriel learned the way he treats me. I can't help but appreciate it even if I think Maris is being manipulative.

Gabriel chooses to stand where he is. He watches his parents, and I can tell he is dying to be dismissed. If the room weren't so heavy with hard feelings, it'd be funnier to see him behaving like a child being reprimanded, waiting to dart to his room to sulk.

"From this point," Dan says, "we need to determine who is best suited to find and speak to Mike. I know he still has that apartment in LA, so I have every reason to believe he still lives there."

"You should make that determination," Gabriel says, "seeing as I don't have a clue whether your disagreement with him was more or less serious than my own."

"It's quite serious," Dan says. "We'd hoped to give him some time and then attempt to speak with him again. But he hasn't been returning correspondence."

Gabriel rolls his eyes. "Very well. I'll see what I can do. I believe his refusal to see his own nephew was meant to rile me. My guess is he *intends* you to worry."

"There would be no need," Dan says. "We have worried all along. Why do you think we allowed our disagreement to escalate the way it did?"

"You can be sure I'll be getting whatever you argued about out of him," Gabriel adds, disgruntled. "Why would he go to you and not me?"

Dan and Maris glance at one another before Maris, who has calmed down quite a bit, says, "I suppose you'll find out when you speak to him." Maris stands up then and takes Robbie from me once more. "I'll be outside." She looks at me purposefully. "Wendy, good luck, Mija." Then she walks from the room, head held high.

Taking me by the hand, Gabriel makes a beeline for the couch. "You see why I have chosen not to engage her on the subject, Wendy?"

Dan sighs as he returns to his own chair. "Back to that, Gabe. There is nothing your mother knows about what happened to you that would be remotely helpful. In her mind, she went to church, she prayed, her friends prayed, and God healed her son. I heavily discourage you from speaking to her about it. The two of you clash far too easily, as you can see."

"I suppose I could pull my medical records," Gabriel says.

"I'll save you the trouble," Dan says, standing and going over to his giant walnut desk. He opens a drawer, takes out a thick file, and brings it to Gabriel. "There is nothing to see though. Misdiagnosis and spontaneous recovery. I've spent enough time with it myself."

Gabriel's brow furrows as he flips through it.

"What about Gabriel's counting ability?" I ask, sitting next to Gabriel. "When did you notice it? Does anyone else have such an odd ability like that in your family?"

Dan shakes his head, removing his coat and draping it over the back of the chair before sitting down. "We never wanted him exploited for it. It was just an incessant need to count everything in sight. No one would know whether or not he was right, so we never pushed it. He couldn't talk when he had SMA, so we weren't aware if he was capable of it then. It's been catalogued that children with SMA usually have above average intelligence though, which we obviously noted after he recovered. He talked nonstop, like he'd been saving it up in the six years he spent immobile and unable to speak."

"I couldn't do it before the cure," Gabriel says, coming up for air from his furious memorization. I'm sure that's what he's doing with his medical file.

"Really? But you had the languages ability, right?" I say.

"Oh yes," Gabriel says, replacing the last page of the file and shutting the folder. "Dad, did Mike ever say anything to you about why he took issue with Wendy?"

Dan sits on the edge of his desk. "Mike never spoke to us about it. I suppose if he'd ever disrespected Wendy in front of us, we might have chosen to bring it up, but your mother and I agreed to let the two of you work it out. I take it this was the reason you two fell out of contact?"

"I can't say for sure. I can only guess. And in my estimation, there are two possibilities. The first has to do with my stay at the compound. He's the one that told me about it, you know."

"Oh yeah, he had a friend stay there, right?" I say.

Gabriel nods. "I got into the compound because of my counting ability, but Mike had no chance. He wanted me to share what I learned there, but it was clear pretty quickly that it wasn't going to happen. I signed that agreement you know, to protect their research and patents and such. So when Mike wanted details, I couldn't divulge them. He got angry with me, of course. I don't know why he was so perturbed about the whole thing. I thought he was over it until our confrontation at the wedding. I can't be sure, but I've wondered if perhaps he still holds—"

"What confrontation at the wedding?" I ask.

Gabriel recoils, revealing a definite hesitancy. "Mike made some offensive accusations. He said I had kept the information about the compound not out of principle like I'd claimed, but that it was my way of keeping *you* from him. He told me I was afraid he would have stolen you if he'd been given any opportunity. Can you believe that load of rubbish? I don't believe I have ever fought so hard not to punch him. I told him not to bother calling me anymore. And that was that. Until my illness, of course. But I suspect I only put off his anger for the time. In the time we had contact I never could get him to come clean. He hasn't bothered calling me since, even though I've called him a few times. Ridiculous to spend so much time on such triviality."

I cross my arms and sit back, confused. On the one hand Mike absolutely loathes me. On the other, Maris told me on my wedding day, when I asked about Gabriel and Mike not getting along, that they fought over women all the time and that Mike might have actually threatened to steal me, just to bug Gabriel. It sounds like that was true. But why would something that silly drive such a huge wedge?

Dan clears his throat. "Gabe, you and Mike have been at odds over women since you were in third grade. How many times have you taunted each other about this or that girl, and you both knew not to take the other seriously? Why would you allow that to get to you? You know he wasn't serious."

Gabriel sits back and clasps his hands behind his head again. "We had a rule. Whoever won, won fairly. We wouldn't step on the other's feet if a girl chose the other brother. And he always won. I wasn't going to take the chance that he'd think that rule applied with Wendy."

"Gabe," Dan says, holding the bridge of his nose, and it's the first time I've ever seen Dan rattled, "I realize that you follow agreements to the T, that you would assume such rules applied even after marriage, but Mike doesn't. He tends to follow common sense more than that kind of logic. And he has enough love and respect for you to not follow through on such an agreement, even if he threatens as much."

"Whether or not he was serious, I wasn't going to take the chance," Gabriel says. "Furthermore, he was so sensitive about the compound nonsense that I didn't put it past him to stoop to that level to get back at me."

Dan looks pensive, but I am completely floored. Whoever heard of brothers having a weird rule like 'whoever gets the girl first wins?' While it's not surprising that Gabriel would stand by any agreement, Dan's right. Mike is a lot more practical, even if he is a jerk. And what's this about Mike usually winning? He must have a dual personality. I don't see anyone, let alone Mike, beating Gabriel at charming the pants off of anyone.

"This has to be about the compound," I say. "Mike has to have been pushing your buttons to get you to talk."

"I agree," Dan says. "The two of you can get past this, if you can just get in front of him."

"And if he demands to know the ins and outs of life forces and hypno-touch?" Gabriel asks, raising an eyebrow at me.

I throw my hands up. "I don't know, Gabriel. Surely he can see the importance of keeping the things we learned about life forces as secret as possible."

Gabriel looks at his dad now. "Do you have any suggestions? Surely our respective disagreements with Mike are not mutually exclusive."

"Most likely not," Dan says. "I'm hoping that when you speak to him, he'll feel at liberty to tell you."

Eleven

"*Ugh,* Wen. This family gets more freak show by the day. Before you know it, Robbie's going to start climbing walls like Spider-Man," Ezra says.

I plop down on the couch next to Gabriel. We've just finished cleaning up after dinner where we told Kaylen and Ezra about Gabriel's childhood recovery from SMA. "That would be awesome," I say.

Gabriel strokes his chin. "I wonder if Robbie will possess any supernatural abilities given his parentage. Excellent cogitating, Ezra."

"Cogitate? It's called thinking," Ezra scoffs. "You know, Gabe, I've been *thinking* about signing you up for ESL classes at the local community college. If I did that, would you go?"

Gabriel's mouth turns into a bit of a smirk. "And I've been *cogitating* about signing you up for my physics class. If I did that, would *you* go? It would give you a better grip on reality over comic books."

Kaylen's eyes go distant as she interrupts Gabriel and Ezra's sparring, "You develop super counting ability after you are cured miraculously from a terminal illness. And you survive terminal illness a second time? You sure have gotten lucky, Gabe. *Someone* wants to keep you around."

Gabriel sighs. "It does sound uncomfortably coincidental, doesn't it? After my recent recovery, I was surprised my mother didn't call in the archbishop to examine me for stigmata or something equally ludicrous. I took her lack of comment to mean she desires peace between us as much as I do."

"Okay, okay," says Ezra, who hasn't sat down yet. He puts his hands on his hips. "There's a simple explanation for this."

"Yeah, probably," I say, stretching my feet out on the ottoman. "But simple is usually pretty obscure."

"Not this time," Ezra says. "Are you guys totally forgetting Gabe's freaky life force strand count? Forty-nine billion. Remember? That's sixty-one percent more than anyone else we encountered. In math world, that kind of variance will skew an entire plot. It's off the charts."

"We assumed that was because of his natural ability," Kaylen says, placing Robbie in his swing and turning it on.

"Yeah, which we now know isn't entirely natural since it developed *after* his first cure," Ezra says. "Considering a correlation now exists for super high strand count, freaky counting ability, and spontaneous illness recovery, you can connect the dots."

"Okay so how does that get us any closer to an explanation?" I ask.

"Because you can stop wondering *why* he recovered," Ezra says impatiently. "You know why. Somehow he managed to have nineteen billion extra strands shoved into him. Obviously that's the cure."

Silence moves among us as we turn over the logic of that. Kaylen is the first to speak up, "That actually makes sense." She looks at Gabriel and tilts her head. "Is it weird to think you're supposed to be dead twice over?"

"*Supposed* to be?" Gabriel says, scowling. "As if death at six years old from a viral infection was supposed to be my destiny? Please don't tell me you buy into such nonsense, Kaylee."

My head, on the other hand, has leapt somewhere else altogether: Robbie's predicament. If Ezra is right, does that mean that Robbie can be cured by gaining extra strands? Can a person donate strands like they would a kidney?

Don't go there, Wendy.

"The question we have to ask is how did they get there?" Ezra continues, interrupting my intriguing and terrifying thoughts. "Who did it? Because someone did. I don't know whether it was God, an angel, or some crazy energy voodoo, but they got there somehow. Kaylen said it, didn't she? *Someone* wants you alive?"

Gabriel throws his hands in the air and stands up. He paces with purposeful steps. "Bloody religion! You see what that agreement with my mother has done? Kept me from understanding my own welfare and history. Kept me from exercising my own thoughts! Confound it! Religion does nothing but dampen common sense, judgment, and mental enlightenment. It forces compliance to a system dependent on self-imposed ignorance! I hate it!" He pounds a fist in the air.

"Relax," I say. "The point is we now have a direction to look."

The front door opens then and Robert comes through. "Sorry I'm late," he says. "Got caught up at the office."

"No problem," I say, jumping up. "I made you a plate. Let me heat it up for you."

He follows me into the kitchen, and I nervously consider what to say. I haven't had a chance to be alone with Robert since he gave me the paper with the address on it. I want to ask him about getting to LA in the next couple weeks. And after learning that he was adopted, I've wanted to approach him about it. For some reason I feel like it's important to know as much as possible about his and Carl's background, should I get a chance to speak to Carl again... which I'm confident will happen if I follow through on going to the address Uncle Moby gave me.

"How was your day?" I ask, as Robert sits at the bar and thumbs through his tablet. He apparently hasn't mentally left work yet.

Robert stops and looks up at me. "It was productive. Thank you." And then he stares at me expectantly.

The microwave beeps, breaking the silence, and I take his plate out. I place it in front of him, and to my surprise he puts his hand on mine. It melts my nerves away instantly. There is no need to be apprehensive around Uncle Moby. He is a lot of things, but most of all kind and careful with people's feelings.

I look from his hand to his face, which bears a look of encouragement. "How was *your* day?" he asks, removing his hand from mine and picking up his fork.

I pull up a stool. "Pretty much the same as usual. But I had a question for you."

Robert blows on a forkful of quiche before putting it in his mouth, and I think he's waiting for me to continue, but as soon as he swallows, he says, "I scheduled a flight for you next week. Farlen and Mark will accompany you."

"A flight?" Crap, he must have already known what I was going to ask!

"To Los Angeles."

"Los Angeles?" I say, although I don't know why I'm playing dumb. I think it's because sometimes I hate when he preempts me like that. It always gets me to wondering what else my uncle knows that he doesn't say. Imagining the possibilities is kind of torturous.

"Yes," he says slowly. "I pushed your application through for the UCLA clinical trial you've been wanting for young Robbie. He has an appointment with them on Wednesday." He says the words purposefully as if we've talked about it already. Except I'm sure I haven't mentioned it before.

"Gabe asked me if I would," Robert explains after watching my expression.

"Um, thanks," I say finally, "Sorry, Gabriel didn't mention he was going to ask you." That bothers me. I've made a concerted effort not to involve my uncle in Robbie's illness much if at all. I don't want to burden Uncle Moby with that kind of temptation. And I don't want to tempt myself either.

"You're welcome," Robert says. He puts his hand briefly on mine again. "Don't worry. A specific request like that is within my ability and within my control. Gabe had obviously thought it through. Don't be too hard on him." He then looks intently into my eyes as he says, "LA holds a lot more promise than Monterey."

I lean back as he pulls his hand away and begins eating once more. Did he just encourage me to go to LA for *another* reason? That was way cryptic. "You want me to—" I start.

"Was there something else?" Robert interrupts, and it seems to me he doesn't want me asking the question I was about to ask.

I sit back and cross my arms. "You're saying you don't know already?"

Robert sets his fork down and strokes his goatee. I count five times before he says, "As I told Ezra, I don't remember much of my parents and the adoption was closed."

My mouth opens. "Can't you just let a person *think* you don't foresee their questions? You always freak me out."

He chuckles and picks up his fork again. "Wendy, I have so few people that know the scope of my ability that I like to take advantage of some measure of honesty. Plus, it's fun to 'freak you out.'" He smiles widely, eyes sparkling with amusement before he takes another bite.

I roll my eyes and step to the floor. "Fine. But one of these days I'm going to get you back."

"I can't imagine how. I'm sure I'll see it coming," he says, slightly taunting.

I put my hands on my hips, and I warm at seeing him so lighthearted. "I'll figure out a way. You'll see."

"I'm looking forward to it," he says.

His phone rings so I excuse myself and wonder over how few words transpired between us yet how much was spoken anyway. It looks like I'm going to LA in a week and a half.

₪

"What a lousy prannet!" Gabriel shouts. "When I get my hands on him I'm going to scrag him! What's he up to? Poncing about?" Gabriel scowls at the phone in his hand.

I roll my eyes. His insults have become more and more foreign. Since our visit to his parents' house a week ago, Gabriel decided that calling Mike fifteen times a day would be the most effective means of getting a hold of him. I doubt Gabriel expected Mike's complete lack of response.

"Are you worried?" I say, patting Robbie's back to burp him.

"Heavens no. His voicemail has changed twice. He's taunting me. Confound it! Now his impertinence is going to cost me a weekend to go down there and throttle him in person!"

"Taunting you?" I say skeptically, wondering if this is one of the few times Gabriel isn't being honest with himself. "How?"

"In a language only I would understand," he says. "Never mind it. I'll give him the audience he's requesting, but he'll regret it."

I carry Robbie into his darkened room and put him into his crib, resting my hand on his chest for a few counts and then raising my hand to hover close to him. I slowly stroke the air above him from his face down to his feet several times. In the past couple weeks I've rediscovered my energy therapy roots a little. I decided it was silly of me to not utilize what I know about life forces. When I touch Robbie this way, I know in the colorworld it's making a lovely sound and it's melding our life forces subtly and beautifully. It's calming to hear and experience it there, and even if I can't use my senses to do so anymore, I believe some part of us knows. And Robbie seems to not only calm when I do it, but also drifts to sleep more easily. I don't want to forget that life forces are real, and they are doing things even though we aren't aware.

"Speaking of LA," I say, emerging from Robbie's room and shutting his door quietly. "I'm flying down there the day after tomorrow. Uncle Moby got Robbie an appointment with that clinical trial at UCLA. Maybe you can give me Mike's address and I can check it out."

Gabriel, who has been removing his watch and emptying his pockets onto the dresser, spins around in alarm. "Wednesday? When were you planning on telling me this?"

I glare at him, aggravated at his attack. "You're lucky it was today. Because I had planned on telling you the same day you decided to tell me *you* asked Robert about pushing the application through. But it didn't look like *that* was ever going to happen."

He looks at me incredulously. "I did tell you."

"No you didn't," I reply clippingly as I cross my arms.

"Wendy. Yes, I did."

"When?" I demand.

"A week before we went to my parents' house last week."

"Um. No," I say. "Maybe you thought you did. But I remember no such thing."

His eyes glaze over and he looks a little flustered. "El cielo. On second thought, I had every intention of telling you, but we got in that argument." He looks up. "You remember? I was so grateful we reconciled that it must have slipped my mind. My apologies." He goes into the bathroom, leaving the door open.

I sigh, guilty about not telling Gabriel about my other reason for going to LA. "It's okay," I call after him. "Things have been crazy busy. Which reminds me of the other thing I need to do in LA."

"Wendy, you don't have to go see my brother," he says from the bathroom. "Leave Mike to me. You have enough to do with Robbie. Furthermore, I have every reason to believe he's going to be as belligerent with you as he was the last time. I'd rather him not rack up more slights against you before I've had a chance to talk some sense into him."

"I can handle him," I say, kicking my slippers off and sitting on the bed. "I'm going to be there already. Isn't it worth the effort to try?"

"Not if you make the situation worse," Gabriel says, coming to stand at the doorway of the bathroom, toothbrush in hand.

I purse my lips. "You think I'll screw it up?"

"You're not exactly skilled at tempering yourself."

"I resent that!" I protest.

Gabriel rolls his eyes. "Wendy, you and Mike are like gasoline to each other's fires. I'm not saying you are without self-control. But both of you seem unable to be around one another without casting offense."

When I look back at him challengingly, he continues, "Mike and I understand each other. I am the most equipped to speak to him and get honest answers. Mike has a lot of pride where you are concerned and the likelihood that he will open up to you is slim to none. Surely you can agree with that?"

I lay back on the bed. "Fine. But for the record, when I said I had other business in LA, I wasn't talking about Mike anyway. I was talking about this thing with Uncle Moby's and Carl's biological parents. He gave me an address to get me started."

"Really?" Gabriel says. "Address to where?"

"A graveyard in the city of Orange," I say, turning my head to see Gabriel. I looked up the address right after my uncle encouraged me in a roundabout way to go there. It was a bit anticlimactic to find out it was an address to a graveyard, but I've learned not to underestimate Robert's ability even a little bit.

"His parents' burial site perhaps?" Gabriel says, sitting on the end of the bed.

"That was my initial thought," I say.

"Sounds like you'll have an interesting day," Gabriel says. "I'm disappointed I won't be able to accompany you, especially to Robbie's appointment, but I'm guessing he'll need regular visits there from now on... Should allow me ample opportunity to regularly haunt my brother."

I'm not entirely sold on Gabriel's insistence that I can't be of use in the Mike situation. It's been a while, I'll have Robbie with me, and maybe Mike will feel more at ease with me in his own space. I have to find out from Robert what time my flight is. Maybe it will allow me an hour to swing by Mike's place to feel things out.

Twelve

Robbie screams almost the entire flight to Los Angeles, which, thankfully, is short. When we land, however, he falls asleep almost immediately, not stirring as I strap his carrier into the sedan my uncle arranged. Mark and Farlen are with me. When I asked my uncle why I still needed protection if Carl is now out of the picture, he gave me a blank look that has always translated as 'don't ask questions.' I know better than to argue when Uncle Moby gets decisive about something. I'm used to always having Farlen trail me wherever I go anyway.

When we're all loaded in the car, Mark says in his raspy voice from the front seat, "Robbie's appointment isn't until three and it's only ten. How about shopping?"

"What am I? The queen of England?" I say to the back of his shiny, bald head. "No, I don't want to go *shopping*. My husband is a high school science teacher. And changing diapers doesn't pay money."

"True, but your uncle is a billionaire," Mark says, turning to me and smirking. He bobs his grey, bushy eyebrows tauntingly. "Robert always tells us, 'Wendy has an unlimited budget. Do whatever she asks.' Come on. I love shopping. All these months I've been on protection detail for a woman—figured I would have gotten some mall time."

I wrinkle my nose. "Mark, are you jerking my chain?" I turn to Farlen who is in reserved silence on the other side of Robbie. "Is he joking?"

One corner of Farlen's mouth lifts, the only change in his stately countenance. "No," he says.

I turn back to Mark who's now grinning weirdly at me. I half-expect him to start panting like a bulldog. That's the animal he has always reminded me of, jowly and aggressive except when he's casting a joke my way... and when he's hoping to go shopping? "Wow," I say. "Sorry, you got the wrong girl."

Mark's face scrunches up in disappointment. "Don't you ever have the urge to do normal people things? Like blow some money? You could use the stress relief."

"Since when are you so interested in how I spend my time?" I ask.

"Since I'm sure we're here for more than an appointment with a doctor. You've had that look since we left."

"What look?"

"The look. The one you wore for months while you were dying. It always said you had something to do."

"Wow, Mark," I say. "You're supposed to be my protection detail, not my psychologist."

He twists around to face me. "Knowing how your brain works is part of my job. Gotta be able to predict your moves."

I roll my eyes. "Fine. For your information, I *do* have something to do. Here's the address." I hand up my phone to show him.

"Mike Dumas?" Mark frowns, shooting me a look before giving the address to the driver. "Didn't see that one coming," he mumbles. "Never liked that guy..."

"I take it he wasn't your fan either?" I say.

"You could say that," Mark grunts. "He always saw himself as above our security protocol when he came to visit."

Wow. Maybe Mike isn't angry with *me*, but with the world in general. "Who are you really, Mike?" I mumble to myself as I settle back in my seat. I practice different conversations with him in my head. I'm determined not to react to Mike's insults this time. Although chances are good I won't get to try them out since Mike most likely works during the day. My plan is to leave a note to let him know I was here and I'm available this evening after Robbie's appointment to get together. I doubt he'll take me up on it, but the point is to make it clear that I'm extending an olive branch.

After a while we come to a stop in front of a four-story apartment building. Cars are crammed bumper-to-bumper along the streets and down every alley. This is definitely Los Angeles.

"Just let me and Farlen out here," I say. "I'm leaving Robbie for now so he can sleep. Mark, I guess that puts you on babysitting duty." I grin at him.

"Nope," Mark says, unlatching his door. "See, Wendy, I'm the boss. Which means I get to delegate if I want to." He nods at Farlen, who remains seated.

"Don't like kids?" I say to Mark as I shut the door behind me and we head up the walk.

"Nah, I like 'em. But they don't like me. I guarantee if I'd stayed back there Robbie would've woken up squalling as soon as you shut the door."

The exterior door of the building is locked so I examine the buzzer system. I find the apartment number on it, push the button, and wait.

To my surprise, a male voice comes over the intercom almost immediately, "Hello?"

"Is this Mike?" I say, although I'm pretty sure it is.

"Yes. And this is?"

"Wendy," I reply. "You know, your favorite sister-in-law? Can I come up?"

I expect a pause of surprise, but he jovially replies, "Just who I was hoping to see today! Come on up."

I roll my eyes as the door buzzes. He sure is laying the sarcasm on thick. Mark and I walk into the foyer where a remodel is going on. The plaster walls have been patched but not yet sanded. Several huge crates take up the center of the room, which might contain new furniture. The carpet was recently ripped up, leaving behind aged, yellow glue spots on the cement beneath. The elevator has a sign that says, 'Under Maintenance. Use Stairs.'

My nerves make themselves known as we ascend the stairs to the third floor. The only way I'm going to get out of being rebuked by Gabriel for doing this behind his back is if I can get Mike to come around. My history with Mike tells me that's incredibly unlikely. Which means I just threw a wrench in my already delicate relationship with Gabriel. Why did I feel so compelled to do this? Maybe I want my buttons pushed. Or I want an excuse to be really snarky and take my life's frustrations out on someone. Yeah, that's probably it.

It looks like the remodel has already made its way through this upper floor. The doors and casings are all freshly painted, new wood flooring put down, and globe light fixtures installed above. I find Mike's door and knock. I square my shoulders and paste a friendly look on my face as I hear the lock and chain move on the opposite side of the door.

Mike looks exactly like the last time I saw him. He has a white compression shirt on—apparently the only thing he ever wears. But instead of shorts like last time, he has blue warm up pants on. His eyes rest only briefly on my face before they settle on Mark who is standing behind me.

"Still needing a babysitter I see," Mike says.

Part of my plan to keep my cool is to count to three before I answer any of Mike's brash comments. I do so now, and a brilliant idea occurs to me. I hold out my arms for a hug and step toward him. "Oh Mike. Thank goodness you're alright," I say with exaggerated relief. "We've been so worried."

He leaps back, eyes wide.

I drop my arms to my sides. Then I burst out laughing. "Oh my gosh, you should have seen the look on your face just now." I turn to shut the door behind me, catching Mark's subtle smirk. He'll stay outside the door like Farlen always does when I'm away from home.

Mike is scowling at me when I turn back to him. "Cute," he says, brows drawn together in irritation.

I laugh again, satisfied that I took him *completely* off-guard. "Don't worry, I'm not lethal anymore," I say, standing in the middle of his living room, hands behind my back as I take it in. There isn't much, actually. It's pretty sparse as far as personal touches. Mike plops down on the end of his grey sectional sofa, as far away from me as possible.

"How's life?" I ask, looking at a small lineup of sports memorabilia on a shelf above the television. Mike is a soccer fan. The Mexico National Football Team. I move in for a closer look at all of the shelves of the massive entertainment center where all of Mike's personal effects are kept. He has a lot of photos, several of him and Gabriel. He also has a few books and lots of CDs on a bottom shelf so I plop down on the floor to examine the titles. I don't recognize a whole lot of them. Most of it's rap.

"What are you doing?" Mike asks.

I ignore him, hopping up and moving into the kitchen. He has a small dining room table where a laptop is sitting next to a stack of manila folders. They have names on them. His clients maybe?

His kitchen counters are somewhat cluttered with appliances, but clean. No dirty dishes in the sink except an empty glass. Hanging under the cabinet over the sink are three coffee mugs: red, white, and green, to match the chevron-striped rug under the table. I guess he and Gabriel also share an appreciation for the colors of their heritage. A pair of running shoes is against one wall, and a large Ficus tree is next to the one window in the dining area. It lives in a huge red pot.

As I take in the essence of Mike through his personal space, I have an unfounded sense of comfort, like it's exactly how I imagined it would be, although I can't say I ever stopped to guess what Mike's apartment would look like. I also feel like the space is... incomplete. It's missing something and I'm not sure what or why.

As I turn to leave the kitchen, Mike is standing in the archway, his trunk-sized arms crossed menacingly. "Can I help you find something?"

I give him a once-over. "Yep. Your phone."

His face slackens with confusion for a moment. "My phone?"

I look over his shoulder and to the right. The far wall is adorned with a framed vintage Batman poster. I look back at Mike. "Oh you thought I was here to see you? No, no. I'm here on an errand from your family to make sure your phone works. You have one, right? Did you change your number?"

"Pfft." He brushes past me to the fridge. "Do you want something to drink?"

"Sure do," I say, walking over to the cabinet next to the fridge and taking two glasses out.

Mike has stopped to watch me with veiled disbelief, his hand on the open fridge door.

"What?" I say, plunking the glasses on the counter.

"How did you know which cabinet?" he asks, eyes slightly tightened.

I look from the glasses to the cabinet, finally recognizing what I just did—got glasses out like I knew exactly where they were. I have no explanation but luck. But, deciding to have some fun with Mike, I say with as straight a face as I can, "I had one of my bodyguards break into your place one night to make sure you were still alive— since you don't answer your phone."

Mike's eyebrow raises a tiny bit, and I could swear a smile moves in the background of his features, even though his face doesn't move. "That's not possible," he says, opening the freezer and taking out a bin of ice cubes.

"Keep tellin' yourself that," I say, leaning against the counter. "My uncle develops surveillance technology. I can sneak in anywhere I want."

Mike looks out from under his heavy brows like he's deciding whether to believe me. He silently takes a bottle of tonic water from the fridge and a few things from the cupboard, including some kind of syrup—one of a line of several different flavors I notice.

"None for me," I say as he pours tonic water into one of the glasses. "I'll just take water."

Mike shakes his head and fills both glasses with his back toward me. "Don't you know it's rude to be picky in someone else's home?"

I debate whether to point out to him that I'm diabetic, but decide I'm actually interested in whatever this drink concoction is. So far he has grated ginger into each glass, added the syrup, and is sprinkling something from a spice jar. I watch him, struck by how normal this feels. He's usually so uptight around me, but here he is, making me a drink like we're old friends.

He grabs two swizzle sticks from a cabinet and gives each glass a stir before handing one to me. Then he picks up his own, and heads back into the living room, resuming his place on the couch.

I take a sip, walking slowly, analyzing the taste. "Lavender," I say. "Interesting."

"What brings you to LA?" Mike asks, setting his now half-empty glass on a coaster on the end table next to him.

That sounded really genuine. Are we getting along right now?

"Appointment for Robbie," I say, almost sitting on the couch, but at the last minute, sitting on the floor instead. "But I'm also here for you."

He tilts his head. "I bet you are."

I squint at him. "Your mom had a conniption fit the other day when she found out you and Gabriel weren't talking."

"She does that."

"She also said you were ignoring her phone calls."

"I was." Mike stretches his legs out on the length of the couch.

"What's the matter?" I say. "Vying for attention?"

"Oh sure. Because causing a ruckus to get attention is the adult thing to do," Mike says, setting his mouth in a sarcastic line.

I shrug and give him a mischievous grin. "Why not? Your mom can be a total drama queen. It's so impressive it's actually entertaining."

"Oh I know," Mike says, shaking his head. "She and Gabe in the same room and disagreeing about anything is like fighting pit bulls that can suddenly and randomly transform into kittens."

"My favorite part is when she breaks out the towel," I say, smiling. "For Christmas I had one embroidered with the words: 'Maris' Beat Stick.' Below that in fine print was: 'For best results, wet towel before whoopin' delivery. For additional insult, leave towel sopping.'"

"Argh!" Mike groans, throwing his head back. "You're not supposed to *encourage* her!"

I giggle. "She smacked my brother with it once, too. One of the freakin' funniest things I've ever seen. Ezra called Gabriel a name using a bad word and Maris came at him from behind. Smacked him three times with a towel like he was a toddler. She even chased him to get in the third smack. Shoulda' seen the look on Ezra's face."

Mike's shaking his head and laughing.

"Ezra had no idea how to act. Gabriel put an arm around him and said, 'Sorry, chap. The day has come that you and I need to have The Towel Talk so as to prevent further incursions when my mother is around. Here are the things that will earn you one towel smack.'" I even lower my voice when I repeat Gabriel's words and try to copy his overly proper cadence. "Gabriel went through a whole list and then went on to two smacks and then three. At the end of it, he said, 'But I have to warn you, the margin of error only lends about seventy-five percent accuracy, so keep that in mind.'"

Mike guffaws and slaps the arm of the couch. "He and Mom once had an argument about 'Towel Smack Inconsistencies.' She'd given him a different number of smacks from the last time he'd done something similar. He told her that consistency was the key to good discipline. He offered to write out the right number of smacks next to the behavior so she could remember and do it right next time." Mike continues in a falsetto voice, "'Oh sure, Mijo,' she said, 'you do that. And make one for each room and two for the hallway for quick reference. Then make three more to keep in the car to have on hand while traveling.' Gabe grinned and ran off like he'd won a good behavior medal. Totally oblivious."

"Oh my gosh," I gasp, laughing so hard my eyes are leaking. "That is so him."

When we stop our chorus of chuckles, I pause to realize that I'm actually enjoying myself. With Mike. Who may or may not still hate me for no reason. Mike seems to recognize this at the same time as me, and we glance at each other awkwardly. The moment of ease leaves as quickly as it came.

I clear my throat, take another sip of my weird lavender-ginger tonic and then set it on the coffee table, three-quarters full. "So," I say, "here we are. Being friends or something."

Mike looks away. "Seems that way, doesn't it?"

"How long 'til we go back to the other way?"

He looks like he's in a discussion with himself. "I'd say not long."

I purse my lips to one side, pensive. "I did enjoy yelling at you without guilt. And threatening you with my bodyguards." I tilt my head and watch him, considering whether to keep this conversation as shallow as it currently is or try for something of substance.

My thoughts flash to Gabriel again, his possible reaction to the betrayal of my being here... Determined to make this right and in a burst of courage, I add, "Probably because I knew you never really meant any of it."

Where did that idea come from? What a weird, complicated relationship Mike and I have if insulting one another is merely a show...

Mike is staring at me as if he can't believe that either. Or maybe he's considering whether or not he *has* meant all the things he has said to me. I don't know. I don't have emodar anymore, and his face has been slowly hardening. "One day that optimism of yours is going to bite you in the ass in a big way."

I peer through the side of my glass in front of me, wondering what to say next. Something quick-witted? Or sensitive?

"Guardian sister. Loyal friend. Beloved daughter..." Mike says, pondering. "The woman who chose to not only stay with Gabe, but actually... backed him down more than once. Saved everyone's life while she wasted toward death... You've been exalted to Sainthood in my mother's eyes. And an angel in my father's." He looks at me, his eyes a bit too intense for my taste. "Do you actually believe you're as fantastic as everyone says you are?"

"Is that what bothers you? That people like me?"

He shrugs, picks up his glass again and downs the rest of it in a few gulps. He notices my own glass on the table. "You didn't like it?"

"It was a little odd. But okay," I reply, not missing that he didn't answer *my* question. "I'm diabetic. I try not to drink sugary stuff."

He looks annoyed, although I don't know why he would be. I *did* ask him for water. There is no pleasing him. I sigh.

"I don't like you because I don't trust you with my brother," Mike says. "As smart as he is, Gabe is one of the most desperate and naïve people I know when it comes to his heart. He wants acceptance so badly that he'll throw himself at wherever he finds a particle of interest."

Mike places both feet flat on the floor and leans toward me. "You think you're the first girl he's confessed undying love to? You think you're special to him for any other reason than that you stuck around? Then you're just as naïve as he is." Mike sits back, puts his feet on the coffee table again. "They all leave him eventually. Every single one. Gabe's only saving grace is that he always bounces back."

One… two… three… four… five… six… Counting to three is not going to work this time. And I'm having a devil of a time holding back tears. Stupid Mike. I stand up, walk over to the window so I don't have to look at him. I pin my lips together. My head is spinning, consumed as I am with anger and hurt. Perhaps if Gabriel and I weren't on such shaky ground it wouldn't be so easy to fall victim to Mike's venom-laced words. But fall I do, struggling as I have been to accept that my efforts to love Gabriel are enough.

And here I am… Causing further strife by visiting his brother. Why? Because I want to push Gabriel away when I have finally allowed him closer?

Confusion circles me, blurry words and memories threatening to prove Mike right. Most pointedly, a memory I have held sacred but that Mike has now sullied. I asked Gabriel once why he loved me. He said, "Because you chose me." At the time, while I watched him kneel at my feet and wrap me in blankets, I felt like his queen, his beloved. I felt in his emotions what I had continually seen in his actions: giving up of self. But now it looks like a mark against me. Proof that everything Mike is saying about me is true.

I put my palms to my temples. Who is Mike that I should trust anything he says? What has he ever done to me but find my wounds and salt them? I don't know why he does it or why it continues to afflict me each time, but I will *not* lose myself now. I clear the uncertainty from my throat and turn around.

"Say what you will," I reply, evening out my voice. I take a few steps toward him and raise my voice. "I know who Gabriel is on a level you will never understand. And I know that he loves you. I know you feel betrayed by him, and even if I don't understand the whys, I understand that you need someone to blame." I hold out my hands. "Here I am, Michael. Take your best shot. Throw your darts and then let me know if you feel better at the end of it. I will never make hating me easy for you."

Mike still hasn't looked my direction. I'd almost guess he didn't hear me. But then, in a faraway voice, he says, "Give it time." His eyes are lost in some memory.

I sit on the edge of the coffee table, quite close to him, watching, and waiting, wondering if this experiment is over, when I should leave, whether I will make any progress today… So far nothing has been accomplished. Mike, though he occasionally speaks to me without malice, does not seem capable of letting go of his disgust for long.

"So," Mike says, shifting gears with a lighter tone, as if the exchange we just had didn't happen. He props his elbow on the back of the couch casually. "I gotta know, if my brother and my mother are concerned about my not talking to them, why are *you* the one that shows up? Not that I'm complaining. I prefer your company to theirs." He does that odd background smile thing again.

Maybe Mike has a mental illness…

"Since when?" I taunt, crossing my legs and arms to indicate I'll be staying right here next to him whether he likes it or not.

He shrugs. "Since now." He gives me a once-over and tilts his head slightly. "For a limited time only. So, why *did* Gabe send you instead of coming himself?"

I pause, figuring out how to answer.

Mike puts his feet on the floor, now only inches from me, and sniggers. "Because you came without telling him, huh?"

I dislike how quickly Mike figured that out. "I was already coming down here, so it was stupid not to at least knock on your door to make sure you weren't dead." I bob my foot, unable to contain my nerves otherwise.

"But Gabe told you not to, right?" Mike says, leaning toward me, his dark brown eyes piercing.

"Why would you assume that?"

Mike smirks. "Why did you come without telling him?"

"I never said I didn't tell him."

Mike guffaws and puts his feet on the coffee table inches from me, his knees bent to form a V. We are closer than we have ever been, and I'd say he's trying to physically intimidate me. If I move from my seat, he wins. But then he points a finger at me and says, "Look, Wendy, let me give *you* a piece of advice: stop assuming I don't know my brother. I know him better than you do, and don't you forget it. I bet he said you'd make it worse—our relationship—right?"

I try to be cool, but my mouth opens a little before I catch it.

Satisfied, he leans back against the couch but keeps his legs in my personal bubble, now crossing an ankle over his raised knee. He leans back, clasps his hands behind his head like Gabriel often does, except this pose has a slightly more provocative flavor to it. Abs and biceps flexed, Mike is extending himself into my space just to irk me, and putting on a show of his brawn as well. His pose screams that he knows he's a sight well worth seeing, and he's skilled at using this to his advantage.

But cocky men who use their breadth to influence their agenda were once my specialty. I may not have emodar, but the game hasn't changed.

Casually, I prop my feet one-by-one on the couch next to him, showing that I'm not going to be physically intimidated. I rest my hands on the coffee table on either side of me until my arm is touching the fabric of his pants. "Oh is that right?" I say, leaning forward and into his protruding knee. "Well look here, Playboy. Let me give you a piece of advice: you may know Gabriel, but you don't know me. Guys like you don't scare me, and when I decide I'm going to do something, I don't give up."

"Playboy?" Mike winces. "Here we were finally having a nice conversation and you have to start name-calling." I notice he tries to be inconspicuous about moving his leg out from under me.

"Michael Dumas," I say, swatting his leg because it's now obvious to me he's uncomfortable with the idea of me touching him. Sure enough he flinches a little but doesn't move. "Your attempts at distraction are pathetic."

"What am I trying to distract you from?"

"My purpose for coming here."

"I'm trying to distract you alright, but you should let me. You won't like the truth."

I push his legs off the table, scoot until I'm in front of him, leaning as close to him as I can reach. "I can handle it," I say, forcing him to look me in the eye.

He does, but glances away almost as quickly. I can tell I've rattled him. He slides out from under my gaze and stands up, making a show of collecting both our glasses. I cross my arms and smirk. I win.

"What's next?" I say to his back as he goes into the kitchen, understanding now that our entire series of bizarre interactions thus far have been his attempts to dominate the situation. For what purpose, I can't say. "Do you want me to leave now?" I call after him.

"You'll wish you had," he replies, opening the dishwasher and depositing the glasses. He then stands with his hands braced on the side of the sink, head drooped. With his back to me I have no idea what his face is doing. And what does he mean?

As the silence stretches longer, I can't take it anymore. He's moodier than a three year-old. It seems like he's done trying to get a rise out of me, so maybe it's my turn. "Give me a chance to earn your trust. We can be friends. Can't you at least try?"

He turns around, but his eyes are on the floor. "You have plenty of friends, Wendy. It's time you had an enemy."

I bang my fist on the coffee table, frustrated and continually confused by the things Mike says. None of it makes sense. "Stop it!" I demand. I leap to my feet and come around the couch and into the kitchen until I am face-to-face with him. He can't help but look at me when I move back into his space. "You are arrogant and hateful and have never said one honest word to me. You're hiding something. I know you are, because I have never done a *thing* to you."

"Stop being so damn likable," he replies.

I throw my hands up. "What does that even mean? You hate me because people like me? That's the dumbest thing I've ever heard."

"My life would be far easier if you were less liked, yes," he replies matter-of-factly. "Not to mention the day you married my brother was the worst to happen to me since... well I can't remember anything worse."

I look at him with disbelief. Is he serious? He sure looks serious. I close my eyes and count to three.

"*Why?*" I plead.

"Because of who you are!" he yells, pushing past me to the window. "You've ruined everything. I have nothing because of you."

I hold my hands up. "You have nothing because you *chose* to have nothing! Everyone wants you to come back. They're all scared for you! Just pick up the damn phone. Why is that so hard?"

He faces the window in silence.

"What are you hoping to accomplish by avoiding everyone anyway? A pity party?" I heave with aggravation.

He turns around, the acrimony gone from his expression that now looks aged ten years. "I accomplished exactly what I set out to do," he replies softly.

"What does that mean?" I demand.

"You should've left," he says just above a whisper, turning around again.

"Left when?" I say. "Why?"

"Too late," he says.

The silence that follows is interrupted by a muffled grunt from somewhere behind me, beyond the front door. I turn around in time to hear something bang heavily against the wood.

"What was that?" I exclaim, heading for the door. As I near it, the more certain I am that a furious struggle is happening on the other side of it.

Thirteen

I pause with my hand on the knob. What do I do? Has Carl found me? Is Mark alright? Robbie and Farlen come to mind, and I fling the door open without further thought.

Mark is grappling with someone on the ground. Before I can figure out if he's winning, several black-clad figures materialize out of nowhere. They converge on Mark, who meets their attack with new strength, barreling his head into the gut of the nearest one while dragging another attacker who has his arms wrapped around Mark's waist. I take a step backward instinctively but can't decide between fight or flight.

Mark catches sight of me as he hits the floor, many arms and bodies on top of him. "Get out, Wendy," he grunts before his face disappears under the pile.

I'm being pulled backward by a hand on my wrist. When the apartment door shuts in front of me, I figure out that it's Mike. I turn to him, about to ask him to help Mark but remember Robbie in the same instant. It refuels my adrenaline, and I rip my wrist from Mike's grasp. I push past him toward the nearest window. I yank the cord to lift the blinds and fumble with the latch. Somewhere between the latch giving way and actually pushing the window up, my frantic concern for Robbie gives way to a realization: Mike is behind this. His last words were too cryptic to think otherwise.

I pause with my hands on the window frame but don't get a chance to react before thick arms are around me in a bear hug, affixing my own arms to my sides.

"Let go!" I screech. But the arms hold fast, immovable as iron. They lift me off my feet and I start kicking backward, hoping to connect, but I can't make contact. The wall is right in front of me though, giving me an idea. I place both my feet against it and shove as hard as I can.

Success. We fall back, and as we hit the floor Mike's arms loosen enough that I get free of them, and I roll off of him, coming to my hands and knees, looking this way and that for something to grab on to that I can fight with.

Mike launches himself at me, throwing me on my back. He grabs my wrists, bringing them over my head and pinning them with one hand. His reflexes are quicker than my brain, because by the time I think to kick, he has already immobilized my legs as well.

"What the hell are you doing?" I scream at him, arching my back to twist out from his grasp, but I can't find leverage. Panting from the effort, I stop.

To my surprise and sudden horror, he moves his face toward me, bringing his cheek close to mine and his mouth right next to my ear. When his lips touch my ear lobe, I turn my face away from him, tuck my chin in, and then jerk my head back, slamming it into his face with as much force as I can.

"Shit!" he exclaims, holding his nose in his free hand.

I sneer at him.

"Stop fighting me for a second!" he hisses.

"Oh I'm sorry," I spit. "Please, allow me to make assaulting me easier for you, asshole."

He reaches over my head with his free hand, and I feel and hear something tighten around my wrists—a zip-tie, I think. "I'm not assaulting you," he says matter-of-factly.

"Is that right? What do you call this then? Fifty Shades of Magic Mike?"

He stops and gapes at me for a second before exploding with laughter. "Damn, you're funny," he says. "I told you to stop being so likeable, didn't I? Fail." He puts his hand on my forehead to hold it down as he leans in again. Whispering so quietly there's no way I'd hear it if his mouth weren't right on my ear, he says, "Where we're going? Do not trust *anyone* you meet no matter how much you like them."

I furrow my brow in consternation just as the door flies open. I turn my head toward it. The doorway frames a woman, hair tucked into a black cap, dressed in black cargos and uniform shirt. She looks like part of a sting operation from the combat boots on her feet to the gun held in her hand. She takes one look at me and Mike and sniggers, "Enjoying your job a little too much, Dumas?"

"That smart mouth is going to cost you, Johnson," Mike barks at her. He then demonstrates his strength by standing and lifting me by one of my upper arms until I'm dangling above the floor.

"You aren't my superior this time, Dumas," she says.

Not to be outdone, I kick at Mike again, but no sooner have I done so than he drops me. I fall to the floor in heap. The woman laughs.

Infuriated, I leap up as fast as my bound hands will let me and make a rush at her instead of Mike. I'm thrown to the floor before I reach her though. Mike is on top of me again, this time with his knee in my back.

"I can give you some more alone time if you need it," the woman called Johnson says. "For heaven's sake, stop playing with her and subdue her already."

"I am warning you, Johnson," Mike growls, "I've seen enough today to have you demoted. Of course, your botched operation will probably sink you without my help. Your men are pathetic. All that banging around like it's the WWF."

"Should have let me at her," I say, my cheek pressed into the floor and GI Jane's boot inches from my face.

"You didn't tell us there was a bodyguard in the hall," Johnson says defensively, her hand on her hip. Beyond her I see two sets of combat boots pass the doorway—more men in black.

"There is *always* a bodyguard, you idiot!" Mike almost yells. "It's noted and highlighted on the first page of her file!"

"She probably can't read," I mumble.

GI Jane glares at me, brings her leg back to kick me, but I'm jerked upward and onto my feet before she makes contact.

"Here's the deal, Whitley," Mike says, shaking me by the arm as I spit hair out of my face, "you can either come quietly or I will hog tie you and carry you out."

"My *name* is Wendy Dumas," I say, trying to make eye-contact with him over my shoulder. "Or did the fact that I'm your *sister-in-law* slip your memory?"

He comes around to my front, his eyes blazing, and gets in my face. "No, it's not," he growls, shaking my arm again, this time more violently. "I don't care what you or anyone else says. Everything you have now, it's because of *me*. You're *mine*, Whitley. Your marriage certificate is nothing but a *mistake* that will soon be corrected. We are *not* related. Not now. Not *ever*."

He then throws me toward the doorway by the arm and I have to catch myself on the frame with my bound hands. "Why are you still here?" Mike snaps at Johnson. "You've got witnesses to deal with. Two minutes to sweep. And then your men have twenty seconds after that to be out the front door and loaded up or I'll make sure every single one of you loses your job."

The hallway is swarming with men in black now. And they all have vests that say SWAT on the back. Crap. Are these people government or is this a cover? Mark is nowhere to be found. And Robbie...

"You're right about one thing," I say, holding back tears of worry for my child whose fate I don't know any better than my own. "We're not related. When Gabriel and your parents find out what you've done, they're going to disown you."

Mike doesn't reply. He guides me by the arm past the two sentinels at the head of the stairs and we descend. The stairwell is empty, and we're halfway down when Mike says from behind me quietly, "You say I have never said an honest word to you. Well now's your chance. One question if you ask it before we reach the lobby. I swear to answer honestly."

Pausing in my step, I don't know what to make of the offer. It gives me a whole new list of questions. But time runs short with each step, and with no time to weigh possibilities, I ask the only question that really matters to me at the moment: "Did Robbie and Farlen get away?"

"Sure did," he chortles. "Farlen doesn't play around. Neither does Robert with his tech. They got away in plenty of time." We take five more steps, and I'm dying to ask more questions, but before anything can come out of my mouth, Mike pauses at the bottom with his hand holding my wrists. "Huh," he says thoughtfully. "You might have escaped if Farlen had been with you. I have mad respect for that guy."

"Then I'm glad he was with Robbie instead of me," I say as Mike opens the door to the lobby. I only see one SWAT guy here.

Even though I've already drawn the conclusion that Mike is with these people, all I can feel is incredulity. It's not like Mike has ever expressed any kind of familial loyalty to me, but I guess my feelings are for what Mike has done to Gabriel and his parents. He's going to pay for this. One way or another, I'm going to make Mike's life hell, and he's going to regret ever getting involved with these people.

When we break into the sun outside, the car I arrived in is nowhere I can see, and a navy blue van is waiting with the rear doors open wide. Mike leads me over to it and I step up into its dark mouth. Mike takes the bench across from me, and then someone shuts the doors, enveloping the two of us in sudden darkness.

For once, the blackness doesn't frighten me.

Fourteen

My thoughts have been on Carl since the van doors shut on me in LA. Things he hinted at... looks he and Louise passed to one another... his last words to me before Robert helped him disappear... He kept talking about someone else who was worse than him. Is that who has me now?

Has to be. Despite Mike's claim of a 'botched operation,' these people have some serious manpower. I still can't decide if they're government , but that matters little. From what I've seen so far, their pockets won't be emptying anytime soon.

The drive over is short, and when we stop I emerge into what looks like a regular underground parking deck. Only two men in black are waiting, and they flank Mike and me on our way to a glass-enclosed room with two elevator doors. We enter one of them, and the buttons indicate it only accesses basement floors. I have no idea which floor I end up on.

After walking through nondescript, maze-like, underground hallways, we end up in a bizarre white room. That's actually the only thing I can say about it at first glance. White walls, white floors, white ceiling. All seemingly the same texture and shade of white. Craning my neck in every direction when we stop in the middle of it, I suspect it is a perfect cube, maybe twenty feet square. In front of me, almost lost in the white space, are two curvy plastic chairs separated by a cube-shaped coffee table—all white. Somewhat blinded by all the white, I turn around to see the hallway I just came from, but I can't find the door. I look on every wall, suddenly disoriented because I can't remember from what direction I came in. The door must have shut flush with the wall.

Hysteria threatens until I see Mike sitting on one of the chairs, watching my reaction with interest. I have never been happier to see him. To have been shut in this doorless, white room alone would have been torture. I take the other seat, periodically scanning the walls as if I have simply missed the outline of the door amid all the white.

Maybe ten silent minutes into my stay, I abruptly discover another oddity to the room: no light source. I stand up and walk the perimeter, lift up my chair and sweep the ceiling with my eyes. I cannot spot the hint of a shadow anywhere, which leads me to the conclusion that every surface must be emanating light. These people obviously have a flare for the dramatic, and my guess is it's a psychological tactic. Pretty sure it's working.

Having given the room a thorough inspection, I collapse into the chair, avoiding looking at Mike although I want to. But no sooner do I sit down than Mike leans forward and sets something on the table in front of me: a small black bag. I open it and find a test kit, an insulin pen, and a small bottle of juice. Wanting to escape the glare of the walls, I get to work, taking my time testing. Blood sugar in normal range, I put everything back in the bag and place it in my lap, in need of something to hold on to that's *not* white. Out of the corner of my eye I can see Mike twirling a yellow pencil between his thumb and forefinger while he stares at me.

Seconds and then minutes pass until they all blend into one another. I have no idea how many. I have never been so bored in my life. Mike, on the other hand, seems to find my every move fascinating, but he has said nothing. I've gotten pretty good at ignoring him, although I have to say, this room is really getting to me. I wish I at least knew where the door was.

Eventually boredom escalates into agitation and I fight to keep still so as not to betray my discomfort. And then, because the coffee table is also losing its distinction amid the whiteness, I set the bag Mike gave me on the table, staring at it just to look at something new.

But still, panic chills me gradually, and a black vinyl bag on an invisible table is not going to stave it off. The suffocation in my chest snags on a memory that jerks into the front and center of my thoughts: what it felt like when someone died from my death-touch. It was the sensation of completely losing perception. It was becoming nothing. A lot like this room.

I've got to do something. With my options limited, and committed to not interacting with Mike if it kills me, I begin to hum the melody that has been shoving its way into my brain, desperate to fill the empty spaces caused by the stark whiteness. My mom was a fan of oldies, Simon & Garfunkel among her favorites. This one is called *The Sounds of Silence*. No mystery there.

After testing the melody, I sing:

"Hello darkness, my old friend...
I've come to talk with you again.
Because a vision softly creeping...
Left its seeds while I was sleeping...
And the vision that was planted in my brain... Still remains...
Within the sound... of silence.
In restless dreams I walked alone...
Narrow streets of cobblestone...
Neath the halo of a streetlamp...
I turned my collar to the cold and damp...
When my eyes were stabbed by the flash of a neon light...
That split the night...
And touched the sound... of silence."

I don't expect that I'll be able to remember all the lyrics; I have always known the first verse best. But I run all the way through the song without a problem. It's as if the lack of external stimulation has sharpened my memory. When I finish, I start over, propping my feet on the cube and laying my head back. By the third repetition, I'm tapping out the rhythm with my hand on the side of my chair and belting the song out at the top of my lungs.

I have no idea what Mike makes of my serenade. I've forced myself not to look at him even though I'm desperate to engage my eyes. But at least that awful anxiety in my stomach is gone.

Toward the end of my third go, I'm tired of the song and am ready to move on to another one. But as if summoned by my musical number, a hiss emanates from my right not five seconds after I conclude. I turn my head to see the long-lost door open. A man appears there, but my eyes are drawn not to him, but hungrily to the hallway beyond. As grey and industrial as it is, it's not white. And it's a welcome reminder that the world hasn't shrunken to the size of this box in the time I've been stuck here.

The door closes behind him, though, dissolving into the wall again, and I realize I'm sitting on the edge of my seat, leaning toward the doorway.

Settling back into my weird chair and propping my feet back up, I keep my eyes on the new person. He's blonde. Clean-shaven. He's probably around the same age as my uncle. His hands are in the pockets of his khaki slacks, and his light blue polo shirt is tucked in neatly. He could have just stepped off the golf course. Or maybe his tee time is right after this little appointment with me.

I notice he's not looking at me though. He's looking at Mike with a bit of a scowl.

I may have determined not to interact with Mike, but I have a snarky remark just dying to come out, and heaven knows I need to hear the sound of another voice in here.

"Who are you?" I ask the new guy.

He immediately turns his attention to me and smiles, his lips spreading widely over perfectly aligned teeth. He reminds me of the Cheshire Cat. He steps forward and holds out a hand. "My name's Andre. It's nice to make your acquaintance finally, Wendy. I've heard so much about you."

I eye his hand, not moving from my lounged pose, and then shift my eyes to his face. "Andre?" I say. "No. I'm here to see Morpheus."

Mike makes a wheezing sound, which turns into choking as he holds back laughter.

The man is facing Mike now, who looks up, his face starting to go red with restraint. "Sorry Sir," Mike says hoarsely before clearing his throat. "It's been a long day."

Andre shifts his eyes slowly back to me, confusion written all over his face.

I can see Mike out of the corner of my eye, biting his lip to keep from laughing.

"Morpheus…" Andre says slowly, his eyes slightly unfocused, trying to place the name.

"Yeah. He gave me the red pill and said he would explain everything."

This could not be going better. I can hardly believe it, but Andre has no idea what I'm talking about. Isn't he old enough to have been an adult when the movie came out? I wasn't, but Gabriel made me watch it because it's one of his favorites.

Mike can't contain his sniggering and tries to hide it behind a fit of coughing, sounding like a cat with a hairball. Andre certainly isn't buying it, because he's glaring at Mike again.

"I'm not speaking to anyone but Morpheus," I say, crossing my arms.

"What is this about, Dumas?" Andre demands, now furious at Mike. "What did you promise her?"

"That I could see Morpheus!" I say, putting my feet to the floor and sitting up. "He's supposed to explain how I ended up being your chosen one."

"Nothing, Sir," Mike says, holding up a hand. "She's talking about a movie. The Matrix. The white room scene?"

Andre gives Mike a blank look.

"Ah, trust me," Mike says nervously, obviously as surprised as I am that the man hasn't seen the movie, and now concerned that he's going to be the one to pay for the wrath of Andre's ignorance.

Getting Mike in trouble: check. I smile to myself.

Andre must have said something with his look because Mike gets up with a sigh. Andre turns his disgusting plastic grin on me once more. I catch Mike's face before he shows me his back, and he looks decidedly unhappy. Perfect. I love ruining his day. He heads for the wall where the door was. I watch with interest as he approaches it, and another hiss emanates from that direction as the outline of the door appears and opens without any effort on Mike's part.

Andre takes Mike's chair, leans across the table, and extends his hand toward me once more. "Let's try this again," he says.

What is the deal with this guy wanting to shake my hand? Is this another incarnation of Louise or some other more sinister psychopath intended to blend into the masses as a country-club-going philanthropist?

I eye his hand with disgust and put my feet up again.

"Can I get you anything?" Andre asks, withdrawing his hand.

"The blue pill," I say, rubbing my temples tiredly. Being clever really takes it out of me. And being abducted... And Matrix room psychological torture...

"Enough of that," Andre says sharply. He leans forward again and raps on the table between us. "Alright, Ms. Whitley. Tell me how you lost your ability."

"I don't feel like it," I reply, laying my head back and closing my eyes.

"I thought you wanted to know why you were chosen?" Andre says. "Or was that more movie nonsense?"

"You're nothing like Morpheus," I say, still from behind closed eyes. "He didn't demand information right off the bat, because Neo was the victim, and he also knew how freaky a white room would be. And at least his room had real furniture and a TV—sort of. And you could will anything into existence." I keep babbling, "Let me tell you, this is *quite* the introduction to your fancy outfit. Kinda campy and overdramatic. But my gosh, well-executed. A few more hours in this room and I might have performed an entire musical."

"Ms. Whitley!" Andre says. "You're getting nowhere this way."

"Me?" I say, head still reclined as I turn to face Andre. "*You* brought *me* here. It's *you* that wants something. You need *me*. A freaky white room won't change that. And considering I will *never* tell you *anything* about my abilities, my history with them, or anything remotely related, you better get used to being in the dark. Goodbye, Andre." I lay back again and close my eyes.

"As time passes, you'll come to understand how much you *do* need us," he says pleasantly, and I hear the brush of his clothing as he stands up. "Poor Robbie…" he says from further away, tsk-tsking. "With how little time he has left, it's a shame he won't get to spend it with his mother."

Footsteps retreat and I hear the hiss of the door. It takes every bit of my energy to not move. I hadn't considered it until this exact moment, but I am terrified of being in this white box alone.

I keep my eyes closed, searching to recall anything but what the room looks like beyond my eyelids. I think about my uncle's house, my room there, Robbie's room. I imagine him sleeping, his two little fingers resting against his lips as he ponders his dreams. I imagine the texture of my favorite green knit cotton blanket that I use to swaddle him in. He looks like a little burrito, all wrapped up tightly.

Robbie smiled at me the other day, purposefully, not like the usual dazed grins he wears. I can see it in my mind's eye and I can feel the pressure of his feet against my palms as I move his legs in a bicycle pattern and beam down into his face.

"Ugh," I say aloud as my breasts respond to the memory of nursing, and I put my hands to my chest, hoping I'm not going to start leaking through my shirt. I start crying as because being stuck here is probably inevitable. I'm going to dry up and never get to nurse again. Fury at Mike bubbles up mixed with anguish over missing my child. Memories of Robbie are clearly not a good idea.

I think of Uncle Moby then. He can find me, right?

I suppose he can… but will he? From what I've seen, Robert will definitely be outgunned if he makes a move. In that case, I hope he doesn't. I'm going to need to figure out how to get out of here on my own.

I open my eyes, immediately blinded by white once more. I can't decide what's worse: the unending white that brings the most profound boredom imaginable or the frightening memories that take on new color when I close my eyes.

Pulse quickened, I jump up and attempt to shake out my nerves. It doesn't work. I pace the length of the room, hum a few songs, run in place. When I close my eyes, Robbie and Gabriel leap to memory in full clarity. I think about what I was supposed to do today. The doctor's appointment. And then the trip to the mysterious graveyard this afternoon. If I had avoided Mike like Gabriel told me to, I wouldn't be in this situation... I miss Robbie. I hug my arms about myself and try not to cry. Who knows how long I'll be here? Weeks? Years? What if Robbie forgets me? It doesn't seem to matter that I know what a good father Gabriel is and how he will meet Robbie's every need while I'm gone; Robbie is going to think I abandoned him. Just like Elena.

I've got to get out of here.

I look around deliriously, the blank walls as empty as ever. I am completely isolated with no way out. I bang on the wall where I guess the door is. But I'm unsure if it's the right wall. The furniture could be shifting and I'd never know. I turn around and around, begging that the door might appear, or even the outline of one. I bang again and sob, sinking down to the floor finally.

Gravity makes its presence known, pressing me down. So I crawl on hands and knees to the nearest corner and curl up into it. I close my eyes and press my cheek to the floor, and I pray that the next time I open my eyes, I will no longer be here.

Fifteen

Sighing contentedly, I turn over in bed, hunkering down into the covers. Instinctively I listen for Robbie before falling back to sleep. My breasts respond by aching, and reaching down, I realize how long it's been since I fed Robbie. It propels me out of bed. I have to go make sure he's still breathing. But as soon as my feet hit the floor I can tell that something's not right.

The first indication is that I'm wearing socks. I never wear socks to bed. And I have jeans on. I fell asleep fully-clothed? It's almost completely dark in here but for a dim yellow light emanating from the crack of a door nearby. I don't recognize the layout of the room.

Adrenaline surges into me as I suddenly remember. The white room. Mike's apartment. I have no idea where I am now or how I got here…

Unable to spot a light switch quick enough, I head for the light. It's a nightlight in a bathroom. I flip the main switch, shielding my eyes from the sudden glare. A shower and a toilet. Taupe walls. Sea foam green towels. Matching floor mats. Several pieces of starfish art line one wall. The counter has toothbrush holder with a toothbrush in it. I gawk at it a moment, baffled at finding something so ordinary here.

I turn around, flinging the bathroom door wide open so the light can flood into the room. There's another bed in there. Someone is sleeping in it.

Heart pounding, I flick the switch I find next to me and the room bursts into shapes and colors. It looks like a college dorm room but with more square footage. The figure in the other bed sits up, kinky hair escaping from a long thick braid, eyes squinty from the light. It's a young woman, maybe my age. She rubs her eyes. "Oh.

You're awake," she says, an excited edge to her voice. She sounds a lot younger than she looks.

I gape at her, dumfounded.

She slides her legs out from under the blankets, turquoise blue nail polish standing out markedly from dark mocha skin. She's so short that her feet don't quite touch the floor. "They brought you in earlier today," she explains, smiling like being 'brought in' is some kind of sorority hazing. "I think you were sedated because you slept all evening and half the night. Don't sweat it. I hear activation can be kinda traumatic for some. I guess we're roomies!"

"I guess so," I say, unsure. Since when do abductees get ocean-themed bathrooms and bubbly roommates? What is this activation she's talking about? I edge back to the bed I woke up in, sitting on the corner. "I'm Wendy."

"Shawn," she says, jumping to the floor and holding out her hand with a friendly-eyed smile. She's a little chunky, but totally cute with dimples and wide eyes and curvaceously fun hips. I take her hand, liking her instantly. Her movements carry an innocence that makes me want to look out for her.

"Where am I?" I ask as she hops onto my bed and sits cross-legged like this is a middle school sleepover.

"Who knows!" she says excitedly, throwing her hands up and wiggling her fingers.

Her reaction renders me speechless.

"So where'd you come from?" she asks with unveiled interest.

"I was abducted from LA by my brother-in-law and then brought to a white room and interrogated by someone who was definitely *not* Morpheus who didn't tell me anything about what I was doing there. The room had its way with me, and then I woke up here."

Her laugh sounds cherubic, and I halfway wonder if I'm dreaming right now, and Shawn is merely a figment of my vision. I feel sort of loose with the tongue like a dream, like I can confess all my secrets to this angelic creature named Shawn and they'll be safely locked away in my subconscious. "Wendy, stop messing with me," she says, reaching out and placing her hand on my knee. "If we're going to make this dyad work we are gonna have to be honest."

"Dyad?" I say, although incidentally I'm racking my brain for what the word means, embarrassed that I don't know for some reason.

She tilts her head, staring at me quizzically before saying, "You think this is something else? Activation always starts with dyads."

"Shawn, I have no idea *what* this is. I'd like to hear what you think though. Because you clearly know more than me."

Shawn slaps her fist into her other palm determinedly. "You're right. There's a reason they don't tell you anything about Guild unification beforehand."

"Guild unification?" I say, lost in all the foreign terminology.

She jumps to her feet. "Omigosh, you're already in? I've heard that happens sometimes, but it's more like a rumor. How did you do it?" She leans forward conspiratorially.

I rub my temples tiredly, my body letting me know that even though there are no windows it is definitely the middle of the night. And holy crud, what I wouldn't give to relieve the pressure building in my breasts. "I have no idea what you're talking about, Shawn."

She draws in the corner of her mouth and sits back down. I swear I can see her thoughts engaging as she puts pieces I know nothing about together. She holds out an index finger suddenly. "I got it," she says, nodding. "Okay. I see."

"See what?"

"You're my first task."

"Which is what?"

"Who knows?" she shrugs. "Why don't you tell me your story and I'll figure it out." She props her chin on her hand, her elbow on her knee, and waits expectantly as her light brown eyes rest on me.

There is a definite magnetism in her attention. I want to earn her trust. I want to get her out of here because whatever she believes is going on here is a lie she has fallen for. "Shawn, I told you. I was abducted while in LA."

"Why?" she asks, though I can't tell if she believes me this time. I'm not sure it matters. She *wants* to listen to me and doesn't seem to care about the truthfulness of it.

"I once could give people superpowers," I explain, wondering what Shawn will make of the idea of life force abilities. "I'm guessing they want to know how." As soon as the words leave my mouth, I feel definite relief, as if sharing the secret with her was a big load off of my conscience. "But I can't anymore because I cured myself of leukemia."

Instead of confused, Shawn looks pensive. Then she puts her attention on me again, her innocent eyes begging for more.

"I don't know what these people want from me other than information," I say. "But Mike—that's my brother-in-law—is with them. He is the biggest asswipe I've ever met. He hates me because…well I actually have no idea. It's like he enjoys hating me, so he does it as much as possible." I purse my lips. "Actually, I kind of like disliking him, too. It's like we have a rivalry to see who can do a better job irritating the other one." I sigh heavily. "But he betrayed all of us. And Gabriel…" I close my eyes to an awful pang of guilt. "I should have listened to him," I say softly.

I open my eyes to find Shawn still watching me with inviting compassion. I love talking to her, I realize. And not just talk, but *confide*. I want to be her best friend. I want to tell her all about what it was like to love Gabriel back when I could share my abilities. I want to tell her how much I hate being alive most days. Robbie has been my primary reason for getting up each day. He has no expectations I can't handle. I want to tell her about what his cheek feels like against my lips and how imagining his disease is enough to strip the air from my lungs, how it collapses the earth so small that I can't find room to worry about anything else.

As I long to tell Shawn these things, it hits me suddenly that I'm speaking aloud. Everything I thought about saying actually came out of my mouth. Shawn has been absorbing my words with so much sympathetic silence that it has felt as if I have spoken aloud to myself in a dark room all alone. I look around the sparse room, wondering once more if this is a dream or if I'm running off at the mouth because I'm hazy from lack of sleep.

"Wow," Shawn breathes, toying with her braid. She kind of resembles Kaylen the way she plays with her hair like that. "That's incredible."

Kaylen… Somehow, seeing pieces of Kaylen in this person cautions me that Shawn is actually a stranger. I just confided some of my deepest thoughts to a stranger. After being kidnapped. Psychologically tortured. Locked away from my family in this room. What have I done? I stand up and back away from her a few steps.

I turn to look around the room, realizing I haven't tried to find a way out. I go over to the door but predictably find it locked.

Shawn is watching me, but doesn't seem bothered by the locked door.

"Who is it you work for?" I ask her.

She looks confused by the question, and for several silent moments I watch her mentally drawing more conclusions. I think she's as confused by our situation now as I was when I first woke up.

She obviously knows more about it than I do, but she's starting to get that I am not on the same team as her. Why did they put her in this room with me? This situation is becoming stranger by the moment.

I check out the room more closely. It looks like I have a dresser, a closet, a writing desk. The clock on the wall shows a little after four AM. Gabriel must have freaked out when I didn't return. What is Robert going to do about getting me out of here? I find it hard to believe he won't do anything. Will he use a vision?

At that moment, a realization slams into me. The address... The graveyard... I had asked Uncle Moby about finding Carl. And then when I was figuring out when to visit the address, Robert conveniently got Robbie an appointment in LA for Wednesday. He basically picked *the day* I would travel to the place he told me about. Time and place. That's what Robert's visions offer. I have no idea what the goal was but it has to do with something really important, something that scared even Robert. But here I am instead, having been kidnapped because I inserted a trip to Mike's apartment into my agenda.

Mike ruins everything.

"So this is a test," Shawn says, the hint of a question in the words.

I turn around, suddenly overcome once more with the need to sit down and have another pow-wow with her, desirous that I might purge the memories of all the ways Mike has screwed up my life. Perhaps it is Robert's powerful ability fresh in my memory, but I suddenly recognize that Shawn is no ordinary girl. Her effect on me is not normal. I am not a naïve, trusting person in the best circumstances, and this is possibly the worst. Shawn should have zero chance of winning me over, yet here I am, hating the mere idea of rejecting her advances for friendship and confidence. I shouldn't trust her one bit even though I desperately want to. I *hope* I'm wrong about her.

But I shouldn't trust anyone.

Whoa... In his apartment, when he was holding my head down so I wouldn't head butt him again, Mike said that where we were going I shouldn't trust anyone I met. Of course, that includes him, right? Why would Mike tell me that?

Does that mean I should do the opposite?

Shawn mirrors my yawn back to me and hops up from my bed. It looks like she has concluded whatever it was she was pondering. "I'm beat," she says. "We'll talk more tomorrow."

I'm both disappointed and relieved she's going back to bed, which puts me more on edge. I turn off the light and settle back in bed, trying to ignore my engorged breasts. I'm going to have to take a shower in the morning and see if the hot water can help me out. I feel like I have two melon-sized zits on my chest. Gross. It's so distracting that I can't properly think about this Shawn problem. Maybe I should take a shower now. But I can hardly keep my eyes open.

After several rounds of this argument with myself, my eyes win.

Sixteen

It's a good thing I have so much personal experience with life force abilities and their subtle but occasionally powerful scope or I'd be putty in Shawn's hands. Her ability is remarkable for how well it can infiltrate without me realizing until after the fact. This morning, after I took a shower and relieved a good deal of my engorgement, she asked me more about Robbie's illness. Since I had just finished flushing the milk reserved for him, he was heavily on my mind, and her question was such a natural progression after my depression in the shower. It was another of those instances when I told her about something without realizing I was actually speaking. I can't even think about talking to her or it *will* come out.

I don't think I've ever encountered anyone with such a powerful, mentally manipulative ability before. It's not mind-control exactly, but darn close. I have to be constantly vigilant, or she'll entice me under her spell and I won't realize it until after I've spilled my guts.

Many times I've pondered telling her I know what she's doing and she better stop it. But for some reason I can't find it in me. Usually I end up questioning myself and whether what I believe she's doing to me is simply my imagination. She's just so darn nice. She made my bed while I was in the shower, told me all about her family who sound like delightful people, and kept reassuring me that we would find a way to make our dyad work. I have no idea what that is, but I can't afford to start talking. It does things to my head and I lose control of my mouth. Even so, I feel like a low-life even thinking about accusing her of manipulating me.

We're brought a late breakfast by a silent young man, and for a moment I get a look past him into the hall beyond, which doesn't offer much to see. Before eating I check my blood sugar and prepare my insulin. Shawn watches this with much curiosity, as if she has never seen someone prick their finger before. I can tell she wants to ask questions, but resists. I'm not about to open my mouth again.

After eating, I look for something to do to prevent my mind from straying to anything important like my family or my experience with life forces or my own missing abilities. I discover a small collection of books on the bottom shelf of my nightstand and look through them. They're all classics, and one of them is a worn paperback of *Moby-Dick*. I smile and pick that one immediately, taking it for a sign that Uncle Moby is looking out for me in ways nobody else can. I make myself comfortable on my bed, and begin reading aloud.

Shawn takes up a place at my feet, lying on her back, seemingly content to be read to, again striking me as more of a child than someone guilty of having a part in my imprisonment. And this is how our day continues for the next several hours. If Shawn has designs to make me talk, she's patient about it, because she doesn't interrupt as I read but sometimes makes comments at the end of a chapter or asks questions about the story. I don't say a word outside of what Herman Melville has to say in his book. I can't afford to.

I take another shower before bed, and when I'm finally alone I expect to feel differently about Shawn and the events of the day. But I still don't feel quite like myself, as if Shawn's influence still clings to me even though I'm not in the same room. Without her in front of me, I am not likely to start blabbing, but I'm subdued still. And logic tells me this isn't normal. But I have no course but to continue to fortify my guard against her.

The next day I continue my reading, but it gets harder and harder to not let my mind wander in the middle of it. I'm getting bored and so is Shawn. I think she's starting to work harder on me, although I'm not sure how exactly. I go to the bathroom a lot to escape her, take two more showers, and spend some time going through each and every drawer and closet in the room. Shawn and I both appear to be outfitted with the same wardrobe. Underwear, socks, khakis, jeans, T-shirts, tennis shoes. Standard stuff.

When we go to bed that night, and darkness takes away the welcome distractions, Robbie and Gabriel push their way into my head despite fighting against them. I know I can't afford to think about them, though I desperately want to.

In a desperate attempt to avoid the onslaught of memories, I reach down and pinch my leg, hoping the pain will steal my wandering attention. When it's not enough, I also bite my free hand, bearing down harder and harder when the pain doesn't do its job.

But it's not working. I'm going to have to either draw blood or try something else. So I sing. I start with the song I sang for Mike, *The Sounds of Silence*. Then I move on to other Simon & Garfunkel songs that have seared their lyrics on my brain from all the times my mom played them. Eventually though, I stop momentarily to listen and discover that Shawn's breaths are further apart. She's asleep. And the pressure to speak has subsided quite a bit.

Shedding a few tears of relief, I turn over in bed and search for my long-suppressed thoughts. I've got to decide now what I'm going to do tomorrow or I'm toast.

Suddenly, something moves in the shadows in front of me by the door and I nearly jump out of my skin. Sitting ramrod straight in bed now, I don't make a sound, more desperate not to wake up Shawn than to worry about an intruder in my prison room. I don't doubt that I completely missed their entrance into the room, as desperate as I was to distract myself.

I wait for the figure to speak, and it doesn't. Instead it opens the door a crack and enough light from the hallway illuminates his face: Mike's face.

"Put some running gear on quickly," he whispers. "Don't turn on any lights. And don't wake her."

I sit there for about ten seconds, haggling with myself over how to handle the request.

"So you'd rather stay in here," his dark form says quietly. He turns for the door.

"No wait!" I hiss, not needing further convincing. I hop out of bed lightly, and since I made an event of examining each article of clothing in my drawers today, I know exactly where everything is. I dress quickly in the bathroom and bound soundlessly to Mike's side.

He shuts the door gently behind us, punches something on a reader near the knob, and leads me down a dimly lit hallway. I don't ask questions, because I only care about getting away from Shawn. And every step takes me further.

Incidentally, as I continue walking, the claws of influence loosen millimeter by millimeter. I return to myself a little bit at a time, and what I find is fury. I've been a caged animal, the parts of me that would have been fighting back all this time were suppressed by her. I should have been interrogating Shawn about her involvement, where she came from, what her imperative is. But instead Shawn has been like a tumor, steadily growing and taking over my mind.

I stop in the hall behind Mike, and he seems to know instantly that I'm no longer right behind him. He stops as well but doesn't turn around. "You follow me or you can go back to your room," he says.

But I'm too angry to listen. "Go to hell, Michael. Tell me what all this is about. Right now. That… That *girl* is—is some kind of *demon*. I'm not going back there. I'll slit my wrists if it means not talking—"

Mike's in front of me suddenly, his hand across my mouth, his eyes blazing. "Whitley, get your *ass* behind me and walk. I swear, if you make one more *sound*, I will sedate you and carry you back to that room." He holds my mouth for three more seconds, eyes boring into mine as he searches for signs of defiance. Then he lets go and continues walking briskly again.

Unwilling to tempt his threats, I rub my jaw and follow, stewing the whole way, wondering if I'll be going back to my room at some point and desperately hoping I won't. But in preparation for the worst, I weigh my options for dealing with Shawn. Knocking her out is probably the best possibility, and the mere idea puts a vindictive smile on my face. But remembering the state she puts me in even when she's asleep is enough to dissuade me from the possibility.

This raises a new question. That is no hypno-touch-produced life force ability Shawn has. It would take someone with life force manipulation skills like I used to have to create such a powerful talent in someone. How did she get it and is she going to die soon because of it? I flirt with all kinds of explanations, like Carl having gained his ability back and returning to the visuo-touch business, but it doesn't sound plausible. I don't get close to any likely conclusions.

Mike has finally stopped in front of a set of aged double-doors. I wish I'd paid more attention to my surroundings as we walked. All I know is it took a while to get here. This place is an underground city.

An empty gymnasium is beyond the doors: a standard-sized basketball court with a running track around it. I want to ask Mike if we are still underground, but he hasn't given the okay to speak. I do know that he told me to get running gear on, so without warning I take off at an even pace on the track, taking note of peeling paint on the cement block walls and the dust on some benches we pass.

Mike catches up to me easily, falling into step a couple feet to my right. I notice he wears a weapon. It's on the same side as me and I ponder for a moment whether I'm quick enough to get my hands on it. Mike has demonstrated his lightning reflexes before though, so I'll save my attempts to steal it for another time.

After the first circuit around the track, my lack of fitness shows. But I keep up a slow jog, worrying that if I stop, Mike will take me back to my room. I don't know what this is about, this midnight jog around an abandoned track, but after two strange interrogation tactics—the white room and then Shawn—I'm not going to assume this is anything less than yet another attempt to get information from me. So I keep my mouth shut. So does Mike.

I take the opportunity to think about all the things I've been suppressing, namely memories of my family, especially Robbie. I can honestly say I have no idea what Gabriel's doing except that it involves a plan to get me back. I wouldn't put it past him to pester Robert into getting a vision to rescue me. And I can see Kaylen and Ezra after the same thing. I trust Robert more than they do though and will heed his instructions without the need to question. So I hope Robert stands his ground in whatever course he has chosen to take concerning me. I think I miss him most of all right now, the order and peace his presence always brought to my life. There was something about knowing he was always near and aware of me even if we didn't spend a lot of time in heart-to-heart talks.

My legs finally refuse to take another jogging step and I fall into a walk, heaving, sweat pouring off of me. The air in this room is pretty stagnant. I glance at Mike, who has been following my pace, and he doesn't look winded at all. I also can't read his expression. What I wouldn't give to know Mike's honest thoughts just once…

"Ready to go back?" he says when he sees me looking at him.

My eyes grow wide. "Hell no," I say. "I'm serious, Mike. I will hurt myself before I give that girl any information."

We both stop and face each other synchronously. "Don't be so dramatic," he says, rolling his eyes.

"I'm not! Don't take me back there. I'm telling you. I can't take her anymore. I'm losing my mind in that room."

"Doesn't look that way to me," he says, lifting an eyebrow, the remnants of a smile moving in the background of his otherwise stern expression.

I squint at him. "Have you been *watching* me?" I say, trying to recall ever seeing a camera in the room.

He rolls his eyes again and crosses his arms. "I told you not to trust anyone. I was impressed that you listened."

"'Anyone' includes you, you know," I say, mirroring his stance.

"Of course it does. I abducted you. Why the hell would you trust me?" He turns his back to me and heads for the door. "Come on. Time for you to go back."

"I'm not going back," I say, unmoving.

He turns around. "Don't be juvenile. Let's go. Unless you'd like sedation and a trip back on my shoulder."

I don't doubt he's serious. But he brought me here with no explanation, and is now taking me back to the evil cherub's lair?

Desperate, I don't hold back. "Please, Mike. I'm serious. Unless you want me dead, I can't go back! She takes over my brain." I take a step forward. "The things I know are worth dying to keep secret. I know how to die, Mike. I would have done it before. Is that what you and the people you work for want?"

He looks at me pointedly. "Why do you think I brought you here?" He turns back around, striding again for the door. "Come on," he yells over his shoulder.

Confused, I take a few tentative steps after him, wondering how to get him to say more. He brought me here because he knew I'd die before I'd talk?

"Here are the rules, Whitley," he says, having stopped with his hand on the exit. "You don't speak of these runs to anyone, including Shawn. You do not speak in the hall at all and when you return to your room, you change back into what you were wearing, putting your running clothes back in the drawer where you found them. I will provide you with clean ones every few days to switch out. If you keep these rules, I will come get you each night, and you will have no problem during the day with Shawn."

I've caught up to him, and he waits for my answer, his hand still paused on the door handle.

"Okay," I whisper.

Seventeen

*M*ike keeps his promise, and so do I. He was right about having no problem with Shawn. I think her power and influence is dependent on prolonged, uninterrupted contact. When I get an hour or so away from her at night, I reset. I remember who I am and what I'm doing. I build up my commitment to silence. I come up with new ways to distract myself during the day. After finishing *Moby-Dick*, I write out a programming glossary. I rack my brain for all the computer programming terms I can remember from my time as a student and write them down neatly along with their definitions. And at night I stay up after Shawn goes to sleep, waiting for Mike to come get me. And then we run in silence side-by-side. I spend that time wondering why he's doing this. Why is he sabotaging his own interrogation attempts?

The only conclusion I have is that he's hoping to gain my trust, knowing that getting information from me won't happen any other way. I'm not falling for it though. My lips are sealed no matter what.

My silence, however, hasn't earned me any information about the place I'm staying. Shawn doesn't volunteer anything, instead always asking me personal and invasive questions that I don't answer. And Mike runs beside me silently, his mind elsewhere before depositing me back in my room.

The routine is getting old though, and I'm desperate for change. One night, while lying in bed and waiting for Mike, I calculate that it's been two weeks that I've been away from Robbie and Gabriel and the rest of my family. I don't want to do this anymore, which sounds pathetic, but resistance to Shawn's mental presence is exhausting after so long. I spend all day not being myself, and an hour each night remembering who I am again. I'm slowly losing my sense of purpose. How long is this going to go on?

Mike shows up finally, and I'm ready. I follow him wordlessly through the halls. I know the way now, having taken careful note of each turn through this labyrinth. I have begun to suspect that the route Mike takes me is not the most direct. I've also learned that the gym Mike takes me to is not the only gym. I've seen signs pointing the way to different recreational areas, and I think Mike takes me to this older one precisely because it's never used.

Especially sullen about my situation tonight, I impulsively decide I'm going to make a go of getting my hands on Mike's weapon. I'm feeling crazy enough. Afraid that Mike's going to somehow know I'm plotting, I act immediately, darting forward and reaching for his gun.

My hand touches the butt of it, but only for a moment, because before I can jerk it away from the holster, Mike's hand is on top of mine, holding it in place, and we are standing, his back to my chest, in the hallway. The whisper of our breathing sounds louder than normal, and we stand still for several seconds while I consider my error and wonder what it's going to cost me. Is he going to take me back to my room without our nightly run? Will he stop coming to get me altogether?

I don't move a muscle, wanting to explain to him how it's been a rough day realizing how long I've been gone from Robbie. I know the only reason I am aware of the day is because Mike gets me out of that room.

I battle with myself though. That I feel the need to apologize is preposterous! He kidnapped *me*. I don't owe him an explanation for my behavior. Especially when I know his job must be to get me to talk.

Mike pulls me around finally, not roughly, but silently. He puts a finger to his lips and pushes me against a wall, flattening himself next to me.

That's when I hear voices, followed by two figures crossing the end of the hall. Locked in conversation, they don't look our way. We're safe. But in that moment I figure something out: Mike is not supposed to be doing this. Why else would he be hiding from the people he supposedly works with? That must be why we take this long route to get to the gym, so we don't run into people.

Mike makes no comment about my attempt to take his weapon. He motions for me to follow him again, and then doesn't even keep a hand on his gun as a precaution. I've got to give it to him for his confidence and skill. If I'd actually gotten his gun away from him, it would not have been for long. I doubt I've got it in me to shoot him anyway. And even if I did, then what? I bet this place is teeming with people ready to take me down. No, I went after Mike's gun because I was bored, and fighting with Mike is something to pass the time.

Once we are in the gym, and I'm running alongside Mike, I say, "What does Shawn think she's doing in that room with me?"

Mike doesn't answer.

"What's a dyad?"

He just puffs away next to me.

"Some kind of induction thing? Into your secret society?"

I catch the corner of his mouth quirk.

I turn around and run backwards so I can see his face. "Did she believe me when I told her I was kidnapped?"

No reaction. But he's watching me run backwards.

"How did she get her ability?"

"You're going to trip," Mike says.

"Does this bother you?" I ask, noting that Mike's eyes haven't left me since I turned around. "If I trip and get a concussion will I get to see another part of this place? Maybe an overnight stay in a place that *doesn't* include Shawn?"

"You're not going to get a concussion."

"I could. If I wanted to," I point out.

"No, you couldn't," Mike says matter-of-factly. "I plan on keeping my job. And returning you to your room with an unexplained concussion is out of the question."

I turn back around to run beside him. "So what you're saying is, I could totally rat you out about these midnight runs and make you lose your job."

"Sure," Mike says. "If that's what you *want* to do. But then who would get you out of that room at night?"

"Touché, Mr. Dumas," I say. "But surely there's *some* way I can make your life miserable that won't ruin my own agenda."

He chuckles. "You have an agenda, do you?"

"Don't patronize me. You think you've got me against a wall, but that's only because you think you know what lengths I'll go to."

"You must think pretty highly of yourself to assume I would allow you to blackmail me with something as ridiculous as slitting your wrists."

I stop and put my hands on my hips. "Why am I here?"

"Information."

"No. I mean *why am I here*? With you in this gym in the middle of the night? You've interfered with your own objective by giving me a break from Shawn. So if my threats are so ridiculous, why would you do that? It's like you're being *nice* to me or something."

He mirrors my stance. "Whitley, excluding the things I've said, when have I *not* been nice to you?"

I hold out my hands to our surroundings and lift my brow expectantly.

He scowls. "Oh come on. You're fed three meals a day, have a nice place to stay, a nice girl to room with, and I even take you for a run every night. This does *not* count as something not nice."

I clasp my hands over my head. "So kidnapping is what you do to win all the girls over, huh? Drives them wild?"

He bobs his eyebrows. "They love surprise retreats."

I'm getting nowhere. "Stop it. Kidnapping a person falls under the 'not nice' category and you know it!"

My words trigger something, because he comes closer to me and glares down at me, heaving. "If it wasn't me, it would have been someone else! And if it was someone else, your people would have been put down, and you probably would have had a boot in your face that very first day, and then you would have been stuck in that white room by yourself for a *minimum* of three hours. When you finally met Shawn, you would have sung like a teakettle, grateful to finally be talking to another human being. I *should* have let it go exactly that way. But I didn't because I was trying to honor my brother in *some* way. You can't stand what Shawn does to you? Well guess what, that's what *you* are to *me*. You have been a *plague* on my life ever since you met my brother, forcing me to choose between the job and the cause I love and believe in, and my own family. Forcing me to balance the two in a way that lets me live with myself! So don't tell me about how hard your sorry life is, especially when I've done everything in my power to make it easier for you!" He throws his hands up. "Don't tell me," he roars. "I don't care anymore!"

He turns on his heel and strides briskly for the door. "Time's up," he says over his shoulder.

Held speechless, it takes me a few seconds to engage my legs to trot after him. I don't want to feel like a jerk for complaining, but I do. I don't want to feel sorry for him, but I do. I want to make it up to him, although I feel like a pushover for wanting to.

"Mike, wait," I say, when he puts his hand on the door.

"Let's go," he growls, holding it open for me.

"But we haven't been here that long," I say, slowing my pace, hoping I'm not pushing my luck.

"I told you I don't care."

My shoulders fall in disappointment. "Mike," I say. "I'm sorry you've had to choose."

He sneers at me. "Oh that makes it all better. *Thank you* for that."

"If this is so hard for you, why were you assigned to my case— that's what this is right? Your job is to get me talking?"

"It's been my job to find you for the last seven years."

My jaw drops. "*Seven years*? Holy crap, seriously?"

"Getting you to talk is not my job anymore. Now it's Andre's turn."

"Then... why are you still here?"

"Were you not listening?" he snaps. "I only put up with you because of my brother."

"But... Mike," I say, flummoxed. "I'm not saying I'm not grateful that you didn't let me rot in there with Shawn. But for you, the damage is done. You already abducted me." I say the next part more gently, "Help me understand. What are you hoping to salvage at this point?"

He refuses to look at me, and with his jaw taut and his eyes narrowed, I can't tell a sliver of what he may be thinking. "When you put it that way, I have no clue." He nods toward the door. "Move it. I'm taking you back."

I take two steps backward and cross my arms, steeling myself for Mike's probable reaction. "No."

He lets his hand fall from the door again, his expression intimidating. "No? No what?"

"I'm not done."

"So you'd like to be carried back then."

"Sure," I shrug. "But I can't promise I'll be quiet."

"If I sedate you, you will be."

"You didn't come prepared to do that."

"You think I won't?"

"No. I think you truly do not have a needle and syringe of whatever drug you keep threatening me with. After all, I've been pliant enough the last couple weeks, haven't I? You've gotten soft."

He gives me a dirty look. "Well I don't think you'll kick and scream," he mocks. "After all, if you get me in trouble, who will come save you every night?"

"Maybe I like Shawn. Maybe I'm ready to talk."

He smiles with half his mouth. "What happened to 'I'll slit my wrists before I talk'?"

I shrug. "Maybe after what you've done for me the last two weeks, I sort of trust you. You like these people and what they're doing, right? Persuade me."

He regards me critically, and I can tell he doesn't know if he believes me or not. I don't know if I meant what I said. I just want Mike to keep talking.

"Don't do that," he says finally, somewhat angrily.

"Do what?" I say, taking a step toward him finally. "Trust you?"

"Among other things," he says, holding his ground.

"Why can't you just… let me go? That would fix it, you know. They'd forgive you."

"You're kidding, right?"

I shake my head. "Why not?"

"Like you said. It's already done."

"They'd forgive you. I'd make sure of it."

He bows with his hands held out in mock worship. "The great Whitley extends her power to benefit lowly me? How have I deserved such grace?"

I frown. "You *don't* deserve it."

His expression turns ugly. "I don't want *anything* from you."

"Don't be such a baby. I can help you."

"Seven years," he says. "You want me to take seven years of work and throw it out. Not happening."

"Seven years," I breathe. "That's nuts. I guess it was kinda crazy that Gabriel ended up meeting me first at the compound then," I say, starting to think Mike's bark is worse than his bite.

Mike laughs mirthlessly and crosses his crazy huge arms. "Want to know how Gabe ended up meeting you first? I'd already sent one guy in, but his cover was blown and Louise tried to have him killed." Mike takes a step toward me. "I sent Gabe because he had no cover to blow, a blind spy completely oblivious to my purpose, so he'd be safe. Louise would be all over his counting ability, so he'd get in, no problem. And low and behold you turned up there. I didn't even know it until my brother so *graciously* informed me he was marrying a girl with lethal skin and I knew you were who I was looking for. You call it crazy, I call it a lot of other words."

I don't know what to say. And why do I feel so bad for him? Why do I want to help him?

"And you have given me nothing but hell since," he continues, glaring at me from under heavy brows. "An overzealous uncle, cancer, and then a child. It's like you had a list of ways to make my job harder and you checked them off one by one."

"I've just been living my life, Mike," I say.

"Me too," he says. "Try to remember that." He walks back to the door and opens it. "*Now* we're going."

My shoulders deflate, but I follow, afraid of pushing him too far. I've won something tonight, although I'm not sure what. I do know that my perception of Mike has shifted. Seven years dedicated to a task takes a great deal of commitment. He didn't say he did this for money. He said it was for a cause he believes in. With a few more nights of running, I might be able to find out what that cause is. Then maybe I can make this right for *both* of us.

Eighteen

Mike shows up in my room around mid-morning, worrying me since other than the guy that brings our meals and my insulin, I haven't had a daytime visitor since I arrived here. And if Mike is here in the middle of the day, that has to mean he's here officially and not secretly. Shawn stares at him, and I can see the questions forming behind her wide eyes, but she remains obediently silent.

"Someone wants to see you," Mike says to me, his face giving no indication of his purpose. "Let's go."

Yanking my shoes on, I fall into step behind him, the hallway unfamiliarly well-lit. This time he makes me walk in front of him like a prisoner. We pass a couple of people that glance my way but say nothing. Then, because I don't want anyone watching to think we are too friendly, I goad Mike over my shoulder, "Where are we going? Please tell me you're finally going to interrogate me. I need someone to insult, because Shawn is too innocent-looking. Give me a big burly dude with a bad attitude. Kinda like you…" I turn around and begin walking backward. "Hey, Mike, are you going to do it? That would be awesome. I've been saving all these insults up just for you."

Mike is stone-faced, looking over my shoulder to the way ahead. I'm having fun with this, so I make another attempt to take his gun. To my surprise, I actually get it out of the holster this time. But Mike grabs my hand before I can do anything with it. The gun drops to the floor. He slams me into a wall, the sound echoing down the hall, which is mostly empty but for a couple of people having a conversation down at the end. I expect the impact to hurt and I pinch my eyes shut instinctively. But no pain follows.

"You're getting quicker," his voice whispers close to my ear. "You actually had me worried for half a second that time." I perceive his hand on the back of my head; it must have cushioned me from the wall.

But when I open my eyes, Mike is picking up his gun and re-holstering it. I reach up for the back of my head, still expecting it to start smarting. Shaken up and bewildered, I gawp at him dumbly. He did an awfully good job of making that look and sound like it hurt. But he didn't even bruise me.

"Get moving, Whitley," Mike barks. I glimpse the back of his hand as I turn. It's an angry red. Like he just slammed it into a wall...

I turn around and obey, puzzled. Mike could have let me hit my head. It would have made my act that much better and I would have survived with a bump or two. Why spare me? Who is Mike, really?

Gabriel has never said an ill word about his brother. He once told me he and Mike were best friends *and* brothers. Even when Mike insulted me over and over, Gabriel never lashed out like I would have expected. He seemed to understand where Mike was coming from, even defended him. And Maris... she told me how Mike and Gabriel were inseparable. Gabriel believes in Mike's character, and Gabriel has higher standards than anyone I know. Which means Mike is everything I have discovered him to be, and more. It's just not possible that Mike is a lowlife that goes around abducting women from their families, not thinking twice about betraying his own. What he's doing here must be really something if he has gone to these lengths.

We stop in front of a half-open door, which halts my ponderings. Mike knocks twice before pushing the door open and nudging me in the back.

I step into a brightly-lit office with pale green walls and potted plants next to a curtained window. I appraise the window, perplexed because I thought we were underground... I can't see beyond the curtains, so maybe it's made to look like a window. Plush, white couches line the perimeter, and on the adjacent wall is a white desk. These people sure have a thing for the color white.

More disconcerting is that Andre is standing behind the white desk with that awful synthetic smile. "Hello, Wendy," he says in a silken voice, coming around to face me. "It's so nice to see you." He holds his hand out again.

I give it a look of disgust, instinctively backing up and running into Mike, who steadies me with a hand on the small of my back.

"I hear you've been thriving during your stay," Andre says conversationally. "Is there anything else we can do to make your room more comfortable?"

"I wasn't under the impression this was a hotel," I reply. "But in that case, I'd prefer to not have a roommate. And I need a key card."

Andre chuckles, revealing his set of perfectly straight teeth again. They'd probably be nice on anyone else, but on Andre, who already gives me a bad feeling whenever he's around, it's maniacal. "No, it's not exactly a hotel. But it could be if we can get your cooperation."

"You will never have my cooperation," I reply plainly, examining my fingernails like they are far more interesting than what he has to say. I see Mike out of the corner of my eye, standing near the door.

"Everyone has a price."

"I have no doubt you believe that," I say, collapsing into one of the couches. Andre worries me. I get the impression that his tactics will become more aggressive the longer I don't cooperate. Mike's implication that he should not have been in that white room with me when I first got here tells me that Andre intended to use whatever means necessary from the start to get me talking. How long can I reasonably expect Mike to protect me from that?

"We want your ability returned to you," Andre says, backing up to sit on the corner of his desk.

My hand drops to my lap and my eyes go to Andre; I am immediately interested in this unexpected line of conversation. "Return my ability to me? You're kidding, right?"

"I don't kid."

"Well you're an idiot. I don't want my ability back."

Okay, that was a lie. I *do* want my ability back. But I wouldn't need to go to these people for it. Hypno-touch would theoretically return at least part of my ability, but that's the same as exchanging years of my life for a life force ability. No, thank you.

"You misunderstand me. We want your ability returned to you in exchange for something you *do* want."

Even more bewildered, I stare at him for a few seconds before saying, "Am *I* missing something or are *you*? You *do* know what you're asking me to do, right?"

Andre's brows lift, and the beginnings of confusion move across his eyes, which he tries to hide.

"Wait, I see," I laugh. "You *don't* know what you're asking. Seriously, Andre, you need to get all the facts before you start *negotiating*. Otherwise you'll look stupid."

Andre composes his face. "Mrs. Dumas, if I knew everything you did about life forces, I wouldn't need you, would I? But it turns out I do, and I am willing to offer you a cure for your son in exchange for your full cooperation. You're telling me that doesn't appeal to you?"

My face blanches. My mouth opens. "I don't believe you," I say quietly.

"You should," Andre says. "We have extremely talented doctors working for us. We have access to technology you thought only existed in sci-fi movies. We have such brilliant minds within our organization that something like DMD doesn't present much of a challenge."

"Prove it."

"I thought you might ask," Andre says and stands up. "Follow me, please." He moves toward the door, which Mike has already opened.

I follow. My head is spinning, caught between fear and excitement that everything Andre says is true.

Mike's face reveals nothing, just the usual dour expression. Andre walks in front of us and Mike walks behind me, which I find strangely comforting—probably because compared to Andre, I see Mike as my guardian.

We don't go far before we reach a solid-looking door at the end of the hall. It looks like it leads into another wing entirely. There's a device on the wall next to it where Andre places his hand. Within moments the door opens with a click. The hallway beyond is at least twice as wide as the one we were just in. The floors are wood laminate and inviting, and the ceiling is much higher. There are pieces of art on the walls and an occasional couch or chair.

"This is our newest residential wing," Andre explains as we walk. "The one you are staying in is much older. This is not our research facility, otherwise I would be able to show you our technology more extensively. This will make my point for now."

He stops in front of a wooden door, holds his thumb to a sensor by the knob, and it opens. He holds out a hand. "Go see for yourself."

I walk into an apartment. It looks ordinary at first glance but when I step inside, the floor feels odd. It's carpeted but there's a spring to it when I walk. I want to look more closely but it's dark in here and I look around for a light switch.

"Lights on," Andre says, stepping in behind me.

The apartment brightens and I crouch down to look at the carpet, which seems normal as far as I can tell.

"It uses a special kind of air-capsule technology similar to foam but with more flexibility and durability," Andre explains. "All recycled materials... although you'll have to take my word on that. It's hardly the most interesting thing about the place."

The living room furniture feels like the carpet, and the couch and two chairs are each one molded piece, making them look very futuristic. There's no television that I can see, but Andre says, "Screen," and a holographic image appears in the middle of the room. I walk near it, impressed by how it's suspended in the air.

"It's made for true three-dimensional imagery, but obviously satellite channels aren't quite up to par. That limits its use, but entertainment will catch up," Andre says. "In the meantime, we have other, more important tasks to expend our resources on."

I look up to see Mike standing near the door like a sentry. He's watching me, his face annoyingly impassive. I move on to the kitchen and Andre shows me the sink, which is dual-purposed. "We believe that clean water is the most precious commodity there is, the most in jeopardy, so our goal with these apartments is to use as little water as possible." Andre pushes a button next to the faucet. It makes a low humming sound. "Put your hand under," he instructs.

I do as he asks, and what I feel is similar to a high-speed hand drier, but quieter and it works over my whole hand at the same time.

"It breaks up residue through sound wave technology and sanitizes with light wave technology. You can use it for washing dishes or washing your hands. The toilet and the shower both use the same waterless technology. Go ahead, see for yourself."

I take him up on it. After weeks stuck in the same room, I welcome the opportunity to see a different set of walls. Plus, it's fascinating. There are windows here, and I walk over to check them out. Beyond the curtains is a skyline view of Los Angeles. I can even see cars moving down below. Having assumed for weeks that I've been underground, I'm a bit dizzy with the shift in perception. Maybe I was moved up above ground after the white room...

Andre chuckles, startling me because of how close he's gotten. "No, it's not real. It uses the same three dimensional technology as the television, though. And it's a live feed."

Speechless, I look for indications that he's right. The only clue I find is that the light from the window doesn't filter into the room the same way real sunlight would. I'm tempted to open the window to verify. But there's no latch.

Moving back into the kitchen, the fridge is another impressive feat of technology. It's far less bulky than a regular fridge and I learn it's insulated with a material that's practically non-conductive, so once the door is closed, it loses virtually no cold air. The stove looks normal at first, but I learn that the surface has no defined elements, and Andre explains that the entire stovetop is an element that customizes itself to the pot or pan being used. The cookware it comes with, he explains, is specially engineered to only transmit heat internally, not externally, making it highly efficient. He demonstrates, holding his hand on the outside of a covered pot of water. He counts to 15 and I can see through the glass top that the water is boiling, yet the outside of the pot is cool to the touch. I also don't feel any heat emanating from anywhere else on the stove itself.

"We call it target-conductive technology," Andre says. "We use it in much more than stoves. As someone with a computer engineering background, you can appreciate the impact of being able to better control radiant heat in all sorts of technology."

I can. That's ground-breaking. It would improve hardware life and allow for ridiculously small components.

"This apartment is one of hundreds at this facility," Andre says, leading us out to the hall and closing the door behind us. "As I said, the most impressive technology we have is not found here but elsewhere. Nevertheless, we have one final stop that I believe will convince you of our capability if you aren't already."

I follow wordlessly, Mike at my shoulder. As is usual for me, I wish I had emodar right now to ascertain Mike's thoughts. I wish I could read Andre's mind. I'm having trouble wrapping my head around what I've just seen and I'm wondering if it's some kind of elaborate fraud to make me believe they have technology they really don't. We pass several people on our way to wherever we're going and they all greet Andre cordially like he's out for an afternoon stroll, not escorting a top-security prisoner. It's unnerving. With every step we take, my questions grow.

What in the world is this place?

We reach a busier hallway intersection and Andre leads me through a set of double-doors into what looks like a waiting room.

"Good afternoon, Amelia," Andre says to the girl at the window. "Kurt is expecting us, so we'll head on back."

Amelia replies with a smile and Andre leads me through another door and into what is definitely a doctor's office.

"This is our infirmary," Andre explains.

A man, Kurt presumably, follows behind us after a few moments. "Hello, Andre," says the tall, mustached man. "How nice to see you today. So this is her?"

"Yes, this is Wendy," Andre replies, stepping aside so Kurt can get a look at me.

"Perfect," Kurt says. "Oh Wendy, just wait. You're going to be amazed! Just a little injection. It'll have that diabetes under control." He looks at Andre. "I was told you only wanted the temporary injection?"

"Yes," Andre replies. "We want to be sure she doesn't have any adverse reactions."

At this point, my eyes are wide and I'm having trouble keeping quiet. I look around for Mike but he's nowhere to be seen. I have no idea where we lost him. I hold my arms behind me, backing up to the wall. These people can't be serious. And Andre expects me to let this guy inject me with something *willingly*?

Andre looks exasperated when he says, "Kurt is going to give you an injection that will foster insulin production. It's targeted immunotherapy. And it stimulates your thyroid."

I look from Andre to Kurt, undecided about how to act. Andre eyeballs me threateningly. Kurt looks sympathetic. "Really," Kurt insists, "it's not a big deal. You don't have a thing to worry about!"

"You'll have the injection," Andre says calmly. "Either willingly or unwillingly. But let's make this easier for both of us."

I take another step back until I hit a chair. "I'll take unwillingly," I snarl. "You think I care about making things *easy* for you?"

"Kurt, could you give us a moment? And send Dumas in," Andre says, and I can tell he's suppressing his temper.

Kurt gives me a bewildered smile before exiting the room.

Mike replaces him only moments later and looks blankly at Andre, feet spread, hands militantly behind his back.

"Wendy has decided she'd rather be strong-armed to get her injection," Andre says. "I believe that's your area."

Mike sighs and looks at me. "Do you remember the glucose-monitoring eyewear and intravenous pump I had you outfitted with when you had leukemia?"

I can't help my eyes from widening a tiny bit.

"That was nothing more than a highly specialized delivery system of this same drug," Mike says. "It was simply made to look like an old-fashioned insulin pump. You never once had to worry about your diabetes, even on your deathbed, did you?"

I draw back.

"Right," Mike says. "And while we're at it, remember the top-secret autograft procedure you received in the Nevada desert?"

I open my mouth. No way.

"Yep," Mike says. "That was us, too. You'd be dead already if it weren't for our technology."

"But... Carl..." I start.

"Your biological mother had a similar procedure, yes," Mike says. "Carl's insistence. Both for her *and* you. We too had a stake in your recovery, so giving him what he wanted was a no-brainer. As you can see, we have a vested interest in keeping you alive. So shut up and get your injection."

I cross my arms, unable to argue with that. Besides, I trust Mike's word far more than Andre's. Perhaps it's foolish, but I take Mike sneaking me out at night very seriously. That's trust. And it makes me want to return it. Plus, if it makes Andre look dumb, I'm in. "Fine," I grumble.

Mike looks at Andre. "Will you be needing any more strong-arming?" I can hear the slight mocking in his voice.

Andre smiles thinly. "Thank you, Dumas." It strikes me then that Andre has been using Mike's last name although going by first names seems to be standard protocol around here. There must be a good bit of tension between them.

Mike leaves. Kurt reenters and I hold out my arm. Kurt disinfects a spot and takes a needle from a waiting tray on the counter. I have injected myself so many times that I don't flinch when he inserts it.

"That's all," Kurt says reassuringly, as if I am a needle-squeamish patient. I wonder if he has any idea how I ended up here. "Hopefully I'll see you in a week and we can give you the permanent fix," Kurt adds. "It's brand new! We've perfected it in the last few months!"

I open my mouth to ask what he's talking about, but Andre interrupts, "Thank you, Kurt." And then he takes my arm to lead me out of the office. I shake him off as we enter the waiting area though. Mike is there and takes his former place right behind my shoulder.

When we reach the main hall intersection again, Andre stops and turns around, fists on hips. "That was the three-day injection. But as Kurt mentioned, we do have the full cure. I would have given it to you today, but seeing as I don't know the status of your ability, how you corrected yourself to begin with... well I don't want to upset what is obviously a delicate balance." He shrugs and winks at me. "As you said, I don't know much about life forces, do I?"

Absentmindedly, I rub my arm where I received the injection. Could he be telling the truth? Robbie can be cured? Why do they want my ability back? It looks like they're doing just fine without life force abilities.

"We can help you with your son," Andre says. "Think about it. What you've seen today is only the tip of the iceberg."

He turns around and walks down the hall.

"Let's go," Mike says, nudging me the other direction.

I obey, hardly seeing the floor in front of me as we head back to the wing we came from. I ponder a hundred questions, a hundred possibilities, and most of all, I'm wondering, hoping, dreaming, that what Andre says is true, that they really can cure Robbie. What if they can? What do I do then?

When we are through to the other wing, and Mike latches the door behind us, I can't take it anymore. "Mike, is he serious?"

"Completely," Mike replies.

When we get back to my room, Shawn is gone. It looks like Andre finally got wise and realized it wasn't working. But to my chagrin, he was right about something: everyone has a price.

Nineteen

Mike hasn't come to see me in two days, not that I'm surprised. With Shawn gone I don't need an escape from her. I could use an outlet though. During those two days I have not administered a single insulin injection. Every time I've checked, I've been torn. I want Andre to be right while at the same time dreading the decision that will ultimately result.

But it turns out Andre wasn't lying. About my diabetes at least. The more I acclimate to this fact, the more anxious I become. I've practically worn a path across the floor from where I've been pacing, biting my nails, and fretting over the decision that has no clear answer.

I miss Gabriel. I've been living two weeks suppressing my feelings about being apart from my family out of necessity. But with Shawn gone I am free to think about them. And I wish I could see Gabriel for a moment, have him kiss my forehead and hold me close. He would listen to me, and then he would say something that would make me look at this in a way that would leave only one clear answer. I'm half a mind without him around. I spend about an hour of the day feeling sorry for myself, hugging my pillow and crying over him and Robbie. I'm lonely and miserable, and getting back to them consumes my every thought.

On the third day, I'm lying in bed at midnight, wide awake, imagining Gabriel lying next to me and holding my palm to his lips, telling me it will all be okay, that we'll get through this together, when the door cracks open.

"You look like you could use a run, Whitley." It's Mike's silhouette.

Relief overwhelms me. "Hell yes," I say, leaping out of bed and changing in the bathroom in record time.

I follow Mike as wordlessly as always. When we reach the gym, I sprint around the track twice before settling into a more comfortable jog. Mike has kept pace with me the whole time, and all the while I've been wondering why having his stone-faced presence around is so comforting. I don't figure it out.

"Andre will be paying you a visit tomorrow morning," Mike says suddenly.

"Yeah. I figured I'd be seeing him soon."

"What are you going to do?"

The question makes me angry. I don't know what I expected Mike to say, but it wasn't that. Since when does Mike have questions? He's just supposed to stare ahead all unreadable and surly while I goad him and bounce insults off of him. Who does he think he is, asking me, his prisoner, questions like we're pals ruminating over our life problems?

"Why do you care?" I say tightly.

Silence prevails for a while. I build up all the reasons I dislike Mike, not the least of which is that he's as much at fault as Andre for putting me in this impossible place. The walls are closing in, and walls make me lash out. And with Gabriel fresh on my mind, I'm mad at Mike again for betraying him this way. I'm mad at Mike for being such a confusing mix of clashing words and actions. I hate that I don't know where he stands on *anything*.

"I have a question," Mike says.

He sure picked a grand time to start voicing all these queries. What I'd really like to do is slap him. "You already asked one," I say.

"Well I have more than the one, believe it or not."

"How does *that* feel?" I snap.

He thinks about it. "I feel like shit all the time. You complicate everything."

"Go ahead and roll in it then," I say, picking up my pace to relieve the choler burning through me. Mike is such a selfish jackass.

We make one more circuit before Mike says, "Wendy."

I stop and put my hands on my hips to glare at him. "What?" I bark.

"Do you really no longer have your ability?"

"No, Mike. I do not."

His brow furrows. "Not even a little?"

"No," I say impatiently, wondering why I'm answering Mike's questions at all.

"Do you have a way to get it back?"

His ignorance is beyond aggravating. "Maybe."

"Maybe? What does that mean? Does it involve having hypno-touch again?"

"There is no other way to get life force abilities that I know of. Other than being born with them. So yes. If I want any part of my ability back, I have to undergo hypno-touch again. Which will put me six feet under in about fifteen years, give or take."

"But I don't get it. You *were* born with them."

"No, I wasn't."

"Yes, you were," he insists.

"You are as stupid as Andre," I say. "I have no abilities anymore because I *reversed* my hypno-touch. If I had been born with my abilities, I would have kept them like Gabriel did his."

Mike looks perplexed, staring down at the floor. "That can't be."

"Well it is." I come closer to him and get in his face. "You and everyone you work for are idiots. You know nothing. It's my life-span you're asking me to screw with, and as you know, Gabriel has a vested interest in it. And my brother. And my sister. And my uncle. I'm sorry people have to care about me, Mike. I'm sorry my life can't be more *expendable* to you. I'm so sorry that every morning you wake up and have to agonize over the moral implications of your actions all because I became someone who matters to your family."

"Will you shut up, Whitley," Mike says, waving his hand decisively in front of me. "I'm telling you, it's just not possible that you don't have a natural-born ability."

I throw up my hands. "Oh get over it! Your life's work is a big fat letdown. Sorry. Go find a new hobby. What you think you know is wrong."

Mike shakes his head in frustration. "Dammit, *why* do you waste so much time being pissed at me? I'm the guy that kidnapped you and I'm a jerk, so get over it and stop acting like I *owe* you courtesy. You spend all this time getting up in arms instead of using your head!"

"Oh now you're giving me advice?!" I yell. "You expect me to listen to you but then not care if you're a jerk? Everything you say is a freaking contradiction!"

Mike crosses his arms and exhales deliberately, yet his words still come out in a rush, "This isn't about me. Let's say you're right about not having a natural ability. What are you going to do about Andre's offer?"

I glare at him and mirror his stance. "Seriously, Mike. *Why. Do. You. Care?*"

"Because Gabe is my brother!" Mike yells, throwing his hands up.

"Why does that matter at this point?!"

"That's not for you to worry about. All I'm saying is if getting your ability back means killing yourself, don't do it. Not even for Robbie. I'll find a way to help you out with that."

"Oh is that right," I snap. "You're going to *help* me while I'm here locked up until I agree to chop years off my life with hypno-touch? You need to open your eyes to what you're doing! You think you can walk this line of morality, doing whatever it takes to help some greater good you imagine, all while picking and choosing the collateral damage to ease your conscience. That's exactly what my father did, and look what happened to him? You're going down, Michael Dumas. Straight down to your own personally-created hell. Blame me all you want. My dad did the same thing. Blaming my adopted mom for everything that went wrong after she took me away from him. It was his *life's work*, he said. The risk to my life was *worth* it. And you've been singing the same tune."

I take off running again, wishing I knew how to run myself right out of this place.

"So what are you going to do?" Mike says, catching up to me effortlessly, unperturbed by my tirade.

I groan loudly. "Shut up, Mike. *Shut up!* I hate you so much right now that all I can think about is shoving your face into the wall as soon as the opportunity presents itself. Does that answer your question?"

Mike finally stays quiet, jogging wordlessly beside me for a couple more circuits. Having eased a little of my fury through yelling at Mike, and expending my energy through my legs, I feel a bit more level-headed. Mike has made it clear that he doesn't want me to give in to Andre's demands. I think Mike got me out of bed tonight for the express purpose of convincing me. I'd like to say I'm touched by Mike's concern for my life, but Mike's concern apparently has a *lot* of conditions. Instead I'm scheming. Slowly, a plan forms, and as it takes shape, the more perfect it is. Mike has shown some of his cards, and it might be enough to get me out of here.

"I'm going to accept Andre's offer," I say finally.

"No, you're not," Mike says, but I can hear the edge of a question in his voice.

"Yes, I am. You don't understand because you don't have kids. I've already lost one. I'm not going to lose another."

"Wait, what?" Mike says, putting a hand on my shoulder to stop me.

I jerk out from under his hand. "I said I'm not going to lose Robbie, too."

"What other child?"

I tilt my head curiously, because it truly seems like Mike may not know about Elena. "Looks like you don't know everything," I say. "But it's none of your business anyway. I'm getting Andre's help, because I don't give a damn anymore. I keep helping everyone else, and that's how Robbie ended up with DMD."

"You sure have put in a lot of wrench time resisting Andre's interrogation to suddenly flip sides."

I cross my arms and stare at Mike decidedly. "Well it turns out I haven't been idle the last couple days. I've finally had my head back, and you know what I decided? Whatever is going on here, this cause you told me you believe in, it must be big. Because if there is one thing I've learned about you, it's that you put a lot of value on your loyalty to Gabriel. You wouldn't be doing this if you didn't *really* believe in it. I may not trust Andre. But I trust you. And whatever happens from here on out, I put it all on you." I hold up my hands. "Have this your way. Maybe I can help you instead of plaguing your life and in the meantime add years to my son's."

"Hold up," Mike says, waving his hands. "You were just telling me I'm a moral scumbag, and now you're telling me you trust me? How does that line of reasoning make any sense?"

"I've always trusted you," I say, and this time I don't have to fib. Mike is the friend I have loved to hate. "I may not see things the way you do, but I believe you try your best. It's the same thing I've always done, too. And like you, I've gotten screwed, too." I rub my face. "Look, it's been a rough day. I miss Gabriel. I miss Robbie. And I am realizing more and more that this thing with life forces is going to keep following me. I might as well get something out of it for Robbie while I'm at it. I was ready to die last year, and I'm ready to do it now also, especially for Robbie."

Mike is at a loss for a response. He ogles my face, looking for an indication that I'm screwing with him. While I may not be serious about satisfying *Andre's* agenda, I'm serious about getting my ability back. I'm serious about curing my son. So my words are honest in that respect. I don't have to act, which makes Mike believe it. I can see it in his face.

"Gabe's going to lose it if you come back with a screwed-up life force," Mike says.

"Probably. But once it's done, he's going to respect my choice and do everything to help me. That's what he does. He's always been in my corner. And he wants Robbie cured as badly as I do."

"You're playing it down. What you're talking about is suicide. Maybe in fifteen years, but Gabe would never respect the choice to kill yourself. You're his world. Why would you do that to him?"

"Why are you fighting so hard against me? I thought this was what you wanted," I say. "So what if I get hypno-touch? It's my choice. You don't have to bear any of the blame. Gabriel's not going to hate you for something I chose to do."

"That's not the point," he groans. "It's not just keeping Gabe from hating me. It's seeing him happy. Like you said, I love my brother. Probably more than anyone. A dead Wendy makes a very unhappy Gabe. I'm not interested in living with the guilt."

Mike is so oblivious. He is also totally transparent.

"That's between the two of you. This is about Robbie," I say.

Mike shakes his head and backs away from me. "You're crazy. Gabe would never support this. You know he wouldn't. What about your uncle? What would he say?"

"He'd tell me death happens to everyone and I should accept it how it falls."

"Right?!"

"And I'd reply, 'Yep. Everyone dies. I'm giving my life for Robbie's. At least I can have a say in how it all goes down.'"

Mike clasps his hands on top of his head. "You're serious."

I frown at him. "You are so ridiculous. Pick a side already, Mike. You've spent seven years tracking me down for these people, so own it already."

"Whitley, I didn't invest that kind of time for Andre to screw it up. Just turn him down. You can renegotiate for your son with someone who isn't interested in the next promotion. This place is full of *good* people. Andre just... has something to prove. His career depends on your compliance so he's willing to go places other people aren't. He's an overzealous bad egg. Asking you to get hypno-touch is out of line, but he's in a hurry for results."

I shake my head. "It's not about Andre. Hypno-touch is the *only* way to get results. You people want me to have my ability? Then this is how."

Mike has bewilderment written all over his face, but it makes me like this plan more and more. "I swear, it's like you were put on this earth to provoke me at every turn," he says. "I can't win."

"*You* can't win?" I scoff. "You're kidding right? You managed to kidnap me, and now I'm doing what you want. Please, explain to me how you would *like* this to go, since I'm cooperating wrong."

He gives me a withering look.

"You don't even know, do you?" I say.

"I just told you. Turn Andre down."

"Why? To buy time for what, exactly?"

"To figure out a better way than hypno-touch."

I laugh. "Man, you sure don't have unrealistic expectations."

"Look," he says, "if you share what you know, some smart people can put their heads together. I mean, you've seen a little bit of what these people are capable of, so it can't be that far off the mark to assume there are other ways."

I cross my arms. "I'm done arguing with you, Mike. It's *because* of what I know that I realize there *isn't* another way. And besides, I may be agreeing to get my ability back, but I never said it would include telling you people all of my trade secrets. I'm done with putting *worthy causes* above Robbie. So this is about him. Now take me back to my room."

He grumbles something about regretting ever knowing me, but leads me out of the gym. Our walk back to my room is silent, but before he opens the door, he looks at me. Mike hasn't ever *really* looked at me much. He's always too busy being morose or professional. Whenever he has put his eyes on my face, it's because he's yelling at me and telling me how I've ruined his life. But this time he's looking at me like he wants to understand. I wouldn't call it pleasant, but at least it's not like I'm the scum of the earth.

"I don't believe you," he growls finally.

That was not what I expected. I manage to keep my cool though as I say, "You assume I care whether or not you believe me."

I open the door to my room and let myself in. "Goodnight, Mike," I say, closing the door.

As I undress in the bathroom and get ready for bed, I hope and pray that Mike wasn't serious when he said he didn't believe me. I don't know how long it's going to take Mike to act in the way I expect, but I'm willing to take this to the line and tell Andre tomorrow that I accept his offer.

It's a pretty big bet. Mike needs to not only believe that I'm willing to go where Andre wants, but he also needs to be so disturbed by it that he'll get me out of here before I can carry it out.

Do I believe that Mike will risk his job in order to save my life?

I think so. Mike operates on a scale of morality I am starting to learn. Besides, I don't have much to lose. Whether I get my ability back here or with Carl, both will lead in the direction I want.

Twenty

*W*hitley," a voice says, rousing me from sleep. "Wake up." I open my eyes, and in the partial light from the bathroom I find Mike crouching in front of my bed.

Bingo.

"What are you doing in my room?" I grumble, turning over.

"Talking to you. Look at me, will you?" He shakes my shoulder.

"No," I say, glad I'm facing away from him so I can hide my smile. "If this is about Andre, I'm not interested."

"I've got a proposition." He turns on the light.

"On pins and needles," I say, pulling the covers over my head. I'm actually grinning outright, and I seriously need to get my face under control before Mike sees it and figures out I've totally hoodwinked him.

"You're nuts, woman. You act like this is a hotel rather than a prison. I come in here at four AM and you roll over like I've interrupted your beauty sleep. I have seriously done a terrible job putting some fear into you. Kidnapper fail."

"My, my, aren't we chipper this morning," I say from under my blankets. "A happy Mike is uncharted territory." I turn over. "*Now* you have my attention."

"Well it turns out I'm not going to let you accept Andre's offer."

I make a face. "*Let* me? Mike, you shouldn't use that word if you want to stay on my good side."

"Here's my proposition," he says. "I'll get you out of here, but I want something in exchange."

"Mike, why would I take your offer to get me out of here when I already have a way to do that *and* save my son? *And* you want something? This is a bad deal."

"Because I'm going to tell you something that will make you hate Andre. You'll want to get as far away as possible."

"Don't the two of you work for the same people?"

"Sure. You'll hate me as well, but that won't be anything new."

"How will I know you're telling the truth?"

"Because you trust me, remember? You said so yourself."

I rub my eyes tiredly. "I trust you, but I hate you. You want something from me in exchange for me *not* cooperating with the people you work for. This is making more and more sense. Fine. What."

"The organization I work for is responsible for Robbie's illness."

I sit up abruptly, eyes wide. "What? How?"

Mike remains squatting on the floor, and calmly says, "Your meds were spiked while you were sick. Not just for diabetes, but for preserving your reproductive system. See, they've never had a way to cure hypno-touch sickness—never seen it done, so the expectation was that you would die. They wanted to be sure your reproductive cells would remain viable. After you were dead. So they could be harvested."

My mouth drops open. The way he said that... like I was a faceless scientific experiment...

"The drug does occasionally cause spontaneous mutation though," Mike continues. "But it's never been a problem before because mutated ones are always separated out before preservation. Only the normal cells are kept. Robbie's conception was not supposed to happen."

"Not supposed to..." I whisper, testing his words to see if they are as heartless and cruel coming from me as they sound out of his mouth. Who am I talking to? Surely not the man who rescued me from Shawn's mind-control lair every night... My whole world shifts suddenly and dizzyingly. I put my hands on my head, flabbergasted. Mike's vendetta against me has cost Robbie his life?

I look up, on the verge of angry tears. I can't cry. Not in front of Mike. How could he do this? Kidnapping me is one thing. But hurting Robbie? What kind of person...? I was a fool to think I ever knew who he was.

Sick to my stomach, and with my internal rage needing an outlet, I bring my hand back and slap Mike's horrible face as hard as I can, but like some kind of ridiculous ninja, he catches my wrist before I touch his face.

"We aren't friends and we aren't family," he rumbles threateningly. "You don't get to act like I betrayed you, because we never had a relationship to begin with." He tosses my hand away and stands up.

Heaving with unspent fury now, I stand up as well, walking around to the other side of the bed where I wrap my arms around my middle, turn my back to him, and bite my lip. I want to make him writhe. But I'm supposed to be carrying out a plan here that requires Mike. He said he wants to get me out of here, but I don't believe him. He is full of lies. And I can't stand the idea of going *anywhere* with him. I want him to leave. I want to never see him again. No. I want to forget I ever knew him.

"I hate you," I say, my eyes finally sprouting tears I can't contain. "And Gabriel will hate you." I still don't look at him. "Get me out of here. But it will earn you nothing. You're a lost cause, Michael Dumas. And you deserve every bit of what's coming to you." I rub my eyes, pushing determined tears away.

I turn around when he doesn't respond. He's watching me with that stupid, blank look.

"You know nothing," he snaps, throwing a small, black backpack on the bed between us. "And I don't have time for your pity party."

"You're right," I seethe. "I know nothing about being a selfish son-of-a-bitch. But you and my dad would get along great."

"Tomorrow, you're going to take out the guy that brings you breakfast," Mike says, ignoring my comment. "It'll be someone different. Younger. More inexperienced. He'll be armed, but if you take him by surprise, it shouldn't present a problem. Can manage that?"

"Sure, I'll just picture your face when I do it," I say caustically.

"That's not a good idea. You wouldn't have chance in hell of taking me down and you know it," Mike says, mirroring my crossed arms but looking a lot more intimidating than I do. "Confidence is the most important ingredient. Use the tray. Don't approach him. Be sitting on the bed and hold your hand out. He'll come further into the room to give it to you, and as soon as you get your hands on the tray, use it quickly and decisively. And then take his key card. You'll need it to get out of the facility. Lock him in this room behind you."

"Then what? I have no idea how to get out of here and I'm sure to run into more people."

"Not tomorrow. There's a big meeting going on during that time, so it will be virtually clear. There's a map and money in the bag. After I leave, put the map in your pocket, and only take it out in the bathroom with the door closed. Read it thoroughly to familiarize yourself. Follow the instructions on the map *exactly*. It will give you a clear route to the surface, and then the first thing you will do is hail a cab, which is what the money's for."

"Place sure isn't very heavily guarded if I someone can just *walk out*," I say.

"You can't. There is a perimeter patrol and heavy-duty surveillance. But I'm sending you out at the weakest point. And I've got a distraction in the works, so they should be occupied when you break their line. But don't dawdle. You're going to trigger the perimeter sensors, but you should be able to get a taxi before they have time to leave my distraction and converge on the breach."

I catch my mouth open. This sounds ludicrous.

"Once I leave the room, you will have exactly five minutes to pack what you need, (no more than what will fit in the bag), turn off the light, and get back in bed before I reactivate the cameras. You'll put the bag in the bathroom. It's the only place the cameras don't pick up."

"Ok…"

"And this last thing is the most important. Once you get outside of this building, the only thing you care about is getting at *least* twenty miles outside of the center of Los Angeles. And *stay* outside of it. No matter how out of the way you have to travel to avoid that radius. Do you understand?"

"Sure."

"You don't look sure. You look scared."

"I do not. But I don't have the best confidence in your plan."

He chuckles, lightening the tense air an octave. "Whitley, subterfuge is what I specialize in. Follow my instructions to a T. The plan will go off without a hitch."

He turns to go, but before he leaves the room, he turns around. "Follow them *exactly*, Whitley. If you don't, you'll sacrifice your freedom. Don't screw it up. You won't get another chance."

Twenty-one

*Y*ou gotta be kidding me," I whisper to myself as I look at the grate in front of me. It's about three foot square, and this is supposedly the route that will cut through to another part of this underground fortress. It should put me only ten feet away from the exit Mike told me to take to the surface. It will bypass a lot of hallways where I might run into people. But I'm going to have to crawl for a hundred yards.

I loosen the latches and the grate swings out on hinges. Squeezing inside, I close the grate behind me and check the watch that Mike included in the backpack he gave me. I have four minutes to reach the end of this veritable tunnel. Mike's instructions have this planned out minute by minute like some kind of Navy Seal operation. It's nuts, and to my chagrin, quite humorous:

Fifteen paces.
Look to your right.
Open grate by lifting latches on top and bottom.
Close behind you.
Shimmy skinny ass one hundred and three yards without clanking around. Think like Catwoman. Be Catwoman.
At precisely 9:34, and no sooner, open grate and exit vent.
Close it immediately, latching both top and bottom.

On the one hand is Mike and his unending belligerence. On the other hand is stuff like this list of instructions clearly meant to make me laugh.

I crawl down the vent and worry again about the kid back in my room. I hope I didn't seriously hurt him. Anticipating the confrontation with the guy who would bring me breakfast this morning kept me up for what was left of the night, but it turned out to be anticlimactic. I must have really taken him by surprise, because I whacked him with the breakfast tray once in the face and once on the back of the head and he collapsed. It was too easy. And what I'm doing right now, crawling down a vent to escape, sounds too cliché to be real.

And I hate that I'm picturing being a graceful, leather-clad Catwoman right now...

When I reach the end of the vent, I check my watch. One and a half minutes ahead of schedule. So I wait.

It occurs to me that I have no way to unlatch the grate from this side. And I don't see anything in my instructions. Did Mike seriously forget I'd have to get the grate open?

I reach out to test it. The other grate took a good deal of force to yank open, so I expect this one to be the same. I grab the edge to jiggle it a little, but I've barely put any pressure on it when in swings open suddenly, all the way.

"Shoot!" I hiss, grabbing for it as it flies away from me. I lose my balance and fall forward, right out of the vent and onto the floor. Rolling over quickly, I look this way and that, relieved to find that the hallway is empty.

I decide to wait the thirty-seven seconds left outside of the vent and then proceed left like the instructions say. I find the door Mike indicates and tap the key card I stole from the kid.

The light flashes red. That's not what happened at the last door I used this on...

I try again. Flashing red.

I turn the handle, but it's definitely locked.

My heart bangs at my ribcage. Key card again. Red light. Try the handle. Nothing works. Look right. Look left. I'm alone. Why isn't this card working? I try it again with the same result.

Plan B? I don't have one. And Mike's map doesn't tell me anything about where any other exits are. I can't just stand here...

I turn right and head down the hall, passing several doors on the way. I try a couple but they all require a key card. I try mine, but it does not work. Breathing rapidly, I'm in full flight mode, looking for anywhere I can hide and compose myself.

I finally discover a bathroom, and though it's not the most ideal hiding place, at least it's not a hallway with no cover.

Finding a stall, I close the door and lean against it, taking deliberate breaths. *Think, Wendy.*

I look through the bag to see if by some chance Mike gave me something to defend myself with. Nothing. And I didn't even look for the weapon on the kid I knocked out in my room. *Stupid, Wendy, following Mike's stupid instructions so literally.*

I put the bag back over my shoulders. Someone had to have discovered the guy on the floor in my room. Which means they deactivated the card. So I need a new card. Which means I need to find a person and use force again. But with what?

Having just taken someone out with a breakfast tray, I feel enough confidence to leave the bathroom stall. Then I crack open the door and peek out into the hall, listening as hard as I can. But I might as well be deaf. The hallway looks empty, and this seems like as good a place as any to ambush someone. So I wait.

After quite a bit of time, I begin to wonder if I'm ever going to see another person. It looks like every soul in this wing is at the meeting Mike told me about. Is it a monthly morale meeting? Sexual harassment seminar? Should I keep going down the hall until I hit pay dirt?

As I'm deliberating, a furious, brown face suddenly appears in front of me.

I let out an abbreviated shriek, leaping away until the sink hits my back.

It's Mike.

I put my hand to my chest to calm my pounding heart. "Gosh, you scared me!" He's dressed in crisp blue jeans; a white, button-up shirt; and dressy brown loafers—none are things I have ever seen him wear.

Having come all the way into the bathroom, he stands with his arms crossed, feet splayed, his face livid. "The women's *bathroom*, Whitley?" he says, his voice strained with aggravation. "Nobody would *ever* look *there*."

"Where else was I supposed to hide?" I hiss. "My key card wouldn't work! I couldn't open a single door! It was this or the hallway!"

"Yes! Because that idiotic move with the air vent activated emergency lockdown. The instructions said to wait until 9:34!"

"But—" I start, hardly believing that such a minor error would cause such a thing. "Why didn't you tell me not to touch it!"

Mike holds his hands up in exasperated disbelief. "You saw mind-blowing technology only three days ago. And you thought you could drop one person, swipe his key card, and crawl through a vent to be home free? I gave you exact times for a reason! What do you think this place is? A boarding school?"

"I don't know *what* it is!" I yell. "That's the point!"

He has his hands on his head now, and he looks like he's going to pull his hair out. He stands there looking at the floor for about ten excrutiating seconds. He looks up at the ceiling, then down again, clearly torn about something. Then he strides past me briskly and kicks one of the bathroom stall doors. I nearly jump out of my skin at how loud and violent it is. He kicks it a second time with so much force that it's hanging by only one hinge. He walks three steps away from it, but stops and turns around again and kicks the last hinge. The door topples all the way. He keeps his back to me, his hands on his hips. I hear him utter a low groan. I can't read the tone of it. Angry? Frustrated? Pained?

Stunned by this sudden, savage show, I don't move, but gape at his back, afraid of what he'll do next. I glance at the bathroom door, wondering if I should make a run for it.

"Did you do this on purpose?" Mike asks finally without turning around.

"Do what? Screw up the plan?" I say, cold suddenly. I wrap my arms around myself, uncertain whether I should be afraid. "Why would I do that?"

He's silent.

"Um, aren't we wasting time?"

"It's too late," he says quietly.

Panic of a different kind fills my lungs as I imagine being locked in an even more secure hole forever. Robbie, who has grown closer by the hour, is suddenly snatched away from my imaginings. "No," I say. "I need to get out of here." I make for the door. I'm not going down like this.

Mike's hand is on the door before I even reach it. Geez, he's fast.

"Out of the way, Mike," I order. "I don't need you."

Mike's expression has gone back to that blank emptiness. "You don't want to need me. But you do. I don't *want* to help you, but I have to now."

"Why do you have to?"

"Because you just cost me my whole career. Everything I've worked for. I now need to get out of here as much as you do."

"That doesn't mean you have to help me."

"Oh but it does. Because I hate failing. And I'm not going two for two today."

"Whatever," I say, crossing my arms. "I'm not going to apologize for screwing up your life. Ruining your career is not even close to getting you back for what you've done to me."

"Go cry in a corner," Mike says flippantly. "For real. Stay out of the way." He then stands behind the door, his hand reaching out and resting lightly on the handle. It looks like he's waiting for someone to come in.

"I thought you said the bathroom was a terrible place to hide."

"It is. But it's a great place to fight. Go find another place to be useless. But if I tell you to do something, don't give me lip. Do it. And I promise I'll get us out of here."

Rolling my eyes, I saunter to a bathroom stall, but keep the door open enough to give me a good vantage point.

Mike has incredible timing, because as soon as I find my place, the first person coming to check out the bathroom makes his appearance. He pushes the door open cautiously, but Mike yanks the door open the rest of the way, grabs the guy by the shirt or head or something too quick for me to see, and yanks him inside. In the same motion, he slams the door shut and leans against it. He takes the man and, with only the strength of one arm, flings him against the wall, much like he did me that one day, except without protecting the guy's head, which lolls over after impact. Mike flings the now-unconscious man as far away from the door as he can, to my feet to be exact.

I've barely had time to recover the alarm when Mike cracks the door open a second time. Then, without looking, as if Mike knows where the second guy has hidden, he reaches into the hall, past the edge of the doorway, and yanks in his next victim. Wedging the door shut with one foot, he delivers the same skull-crushing treatment as the first guy, knowing exactly where to hit them that will knock them out in one blow. I've never seen anything like it except in movies. Mike doesn't even get winded because of how quick and decisive he is.

He shuts the door again, waits for a few beats like he's counting, and then flings it open again to reveal another perpetrator. This one has a gun held out, but Mike seems to have already expected this, because he goes for the weapon first, knocking it easily from the man's hand before hauling him inside to do him damage. At this rate, he's going to quickly fill this small bathroom with bodies. So I start dragging the nearest one further into the bathroom, dropping him into the stall at the very end before going to get another one, almost getting knocked down by Mike's latest flying victim.

As I'm pulling the next guy to the end, I catch Mike finally engaged with someone. It looks like he's close to losing control of the door, struggling to keep his foot planted while getting enough leverage on the guy he's holding. This latest guy is fighting back, straining in Mike's grasp while reaching for his weapon that has fallen to the floor. He gives up on that and instead turns to drive his shoulder into Mike to throw him back against the door. I think Mike was banking on that because he does a subtle shift to the side, and the guy drives his own head into the door while Mike twists the man's arms behind him and gains the upper hand.

Having seen enough people coming in here with guns, I decide I ought to get one of my own, so I leap over a body and pluck one off the floor in time for another body to slam into me.

Thrown to my butt by an unconscious man in black who is now lying across my lap, I look at Mike with annoyance. "You totally did that on purpose."

Mike shrugs and smirks at me. "I told you to stay out of the way."

I look around at the bodies strewn about. "Freak of nature, Mike."

"This should be the last two, Whitley. Hurry up and get out of the way. And be ready to move."

"Last two?" I say, grunting as I push the guy off of me. "How do you know?"

Mike taps his ear, and then flings the door open. The scene is nothing but fists and feet and grunts. Mike knocks one guy on his butt while holding the other guy in a headlock. He plucks a weapon off of one of them and to my utter surprise, fires a shot at each at extremely close range. They fall to the floor.

My mouth drops open. "You just—" But I stop because I don't see any blood. Lodged at the point of impact for each, though, is what looks like a staple.

"Neurotoxin," Mike says. "Paralyzes them instantly. But can only be used at short-range."

"Why didn't you do that to begin with?" I say, stepping over bodies to come to his side.

"The other way was more fun."

"Show off," I say as he opens the bathroom door.

"I enjoy putting my physical superiority on display as frequently as possible."

"Eew," I say as I tuck one of those fancy guns into my waistband.

"You know you liked watching."

"I was referring to your ego. It's starting to show."

"So you liked watching."

"Oh my gosh. Shut up."

"Stay right behind me," Mike orders. "We're going to be taking the fun way out."

"You are enjoying defecting way too much," I say, following on his heels as we jog down the hall.

We don't travel far when suddenly Mike stops and pushes me into a wall. He twists my hands behind my back, and something fastens around them. Another zip tie?

"What are you *doing*?" I demand, struggling.

"Mike Dumas here. Subject located. Sector thirty-three," he says, and I don't think he's speaking to me. He shakes me a little and pulls me off the wall none too carefully.

"Mike?" says a voice belonging to a huge guy with an impressive red mustache coming our way around a corner. He's wearing the same black pants and combat boots as the other guys, but his shirt is white with a black tie. And his hat is different from the standard cap. "What the hell has been going on? I've lost contact with eight guys in the east wing. Cameras are out, too." Two men in the standard black dress come up to flank him.

"She had help from one of the kitchen staff," Mike says. "I've been talking to Drew, and her uncle's the one that's been scrambling our systems. Had to be him today."

"Son of a bitch," the red-haired giant says. "How the hell does he do it?" And then he presses something behind his ear and says, "M here. Subject located. Verified."

"He's a Prime," Mike replies, shoving me forward.

"No shit," Mustache man says, walking with us down the hall. Everybody seems to know where we're going but me. "No wonder Andre's been chasin' his tail so long."

We reach a door, and Mustache man taps his key card. Then he goes through some kind of voice authentication process before the door unlocks.

As soon as we're through, I hear the sound of three shots from the special gun in rapid succession, and Mustache and the two other guys with him drop within the same second.

"Time to move," Mike says, holstering his weapon. He then cuts the restraints on my wrist with something else he produces from his person.

He takes off ahead of me, and I follow, but not without looking over my shoulder at the three bodies, daunted by Mike's deliberate and calculated use of force.

Mike uses a key card to tap us through several doors, eventually ending up in a stairwell. He takes the steps two at a time while I try to keep up.

I lose count of how many stories up we ascend. My legs are Jell-O. Just before I'm about to beg Mike for a break, we reach the end. There are no more stairs. Mike motions me through the door impatiently, and I find that we are on the roof of a tall building. The sudden shift in perception is disorienting.

Before I notice there *are* people up here on the roof, Mike has already engaged one of them. Mike knocks the air out of the guy with a punch to the gut. Then he brings his fists down on the back of his neck until the guy collapses on the asphalt. And then Mike darts across the roof toward a giant black man who has come around the side of one of the massive roof air conditioning units. This new guy rivals Mike in muscle mass and is at least six inches taller, like Mustache man down below. Rather than going for the direct attack, Mike puts up his fists, and the two dance around each other. The black behemoth smiles like a fist fight on the roof is the excitement he's been looking for all day. I don't know what's going on here. They both have guns, but neither of them is drawing.

"So this is how you wanna go down, eh, Mike D?" Behemoth says right before he throws a fist. Mike ducks and offers one of his own, which misses, too. Behemoth tries for an upper cut, which catches the end of Mike's chin. Mike jumps back. He doesn't take recovery time though, as behemoth expects. Instead Mike dives for the ground at Behemoth's legs, grabbing them in both his arms, locking his fists, and yanking them out from under the guy, all while lying on his stomach. He wastes no time once he's felled the man. He leaps onto Behemoth, punches him once in the face before he catches a blunt fist to the ear. Mike returns in kind, right in the guy's nose, which spurts blood. Mike then plucks his two guns, tossing one of them to the other side of the roof and then shooting the guy in the chest with the other—one of those stun gun things.

Standing up, Mike looks down at Behemoth. "Sorry, man. Don't forget you gotta be willing to sacrifice some skin if the other guy matches you for strength. That was one helluva hit to the ear though. I'm gonna be feeling that one tomorrow."

He motions for me to follow him as he heads for the side of the building. I can't do a thing but as he asks. What he's capable of doing with his body may be the most impressive set of skills I've ever seen in person. "I doubt he's interested in your combat lessons," I say.

"Sure he is," Mike says. "Cade and I go way back. We kick each others' asses for sport. And practice."

I shake my head in disbelief as we circuit the roof, looking over each side of the building. I'd guess we're about eight stories up. There are no fire escapes, and no conceivable way down other than the stairs we just took. Why did Mike bring us to the roof with no way off?

Twenty-two

How do you feel about jumping?" Mike asks.

My face pales. "You're kidding, right?"

"No."

"Mike, the closest gap between buildings is over the alley, and it's like twenty feet."

He laughs. "You are hilarious. I must have really impressed you for you to think that's in the realm of possibility. Either that or you've taken episodes of Batman way too seriously in your life."

I smile wryly. "As far as physical skill is concerned, you have done nothing but impress me for the last half hour. I wasn't willing to make a call on your boundaries. As for Batman, he always uses those cable shooty things, of which we have none."

He laughs and then grins at me, maybe the first look of its kind that I've seen directed at me. "Well, leaping over twenty-foot gaps is not in my skillset. But for your vote of confidence I might have to add it. Anyway, for this particular exercise, we're going for something closer to Batman's cable 'shooty' method."

He walks over to a shed that's toward the middle of the roof, rummages about, and comes out with a length of poly-coated cable.

"Where's the shooty part?" I ask nervously.

"No shooties," he laughs, walking over to the side of the roof. "Jumping. Down to that balcony there." He points below us, two stories away.

I peek over the edge. It looks tiny. I step back, dizzy. "Why couldn't we just go back down the stairs to that floor?"

"Because we won't be able to get into the room where the balcony is. Now stop being a sissy. I'll go first. Then you jump and I'll catch you."

"A sissy? This isn't grade school. We're talking about jumping twenty feet down, not seeing who can swing the highest."

Mike tosses the cable down and it lands on the floor of the balcony. Then he lowers himself over the side carefully until he's hanging. He's going to drop down two stories? My head spins. I want to reach out and hold on to Mike, but he's got his eyes closed like he's concentrating. I settle for holding my breath. He places his feet against the exterior wall, gives a little shove, and then lets go.

I watch him fall, and I put my hand to my mouth to suppress a little scream. He lands squarely in the center of the balcony, knees bent, arms out as if dismounting from the balance beam in a gymnastics routine.

He stands up straight and looks up. "Move to your right," he calls up to me.

"Get it together, Wendy," I mumble as I move to the side he directs, but all I can think is that I'm going to die. I'm going to totally miss and fall to my death on the concrete eight stories below. I'm embarrassed to say I'm actually crying with fright. And I'm starting to hyperventilate. I need to get this over with before I need a paper bag and ten minutes to calm down.

"Hands straight out," Mike instructs. "Aim for right here." He marks the center of the balcony. "Tuck your knees as much as you can though, so I can buffer your fall as much as possible."

"What!?" I squeak. "I'm not doing that!"

"You have to. They're sending backups to the roof since Cade and Ryan aren't responding. You want to stay up there with them?"

Mike has started climbing on to the balcony railing and I gape at him. "Mike!" I say. "What are you doing? This is insane!"

"Whitley, get a grip," he says, balancing on the railing as he looks up at me. "I'm just getting some height so I can better cushion you. I've done this before."

"Well I haven't!"

"You're going to have to trust me," he says, holding his hands out. "Stop thinking about it and psyching yourself out. Focus on the spot you want to aim for and do it. I'll do all the work."

Trust Mike? What on earth has Mike done to earn that kind of blind trust?

He doesn't want you dead.

Okay, that's marginally comforting. And Mike has already demonstrated his incredible skill.

"NOW, Whitley!" Mike yells.

I focus on the spot below. I figure it's like sports. You have to watch the ball in baseball right up until you catch it, and you have to watch the basket the whole time you're shooting for the hoop.

Hands out, I jump, keeping my legs up when I do, since that's as good as 'tucking my legs' is going to get. The wind lifts my short hair away from my ears. And since I've kept my eyes open, I see Mike's hands reach for me. But expecting an impact forces my eyes shut before I reach him. But none of the expected sensations come. I jar my head a little bit against Mike's chest, and his arms tighten around me enough to be uncomfortable, but I don't feel my feet touch the ground. As soon as I open my eyes, Mike sets me down, and I gawk at him. "How did you do that?"

"Practice," he replies, grabbing the length of cable, crouching down, and winding it around two rails of the balcony.

"You practice jumping from buildings? And then catching *other* people who jump from buildings?"

"Among other things," he says, feeding the cable down.

"I'd love to get a look at your job description."

"It only has one word on it."

"What's that?" I say, leaning over to see another balcony below us, and one on each floor all the way to the bottom where there is a grassy courtyard shared by three of the buildings here.

"Badass."

I snort. "I'd like to say you're full of yourself, but it's the truth."

"Was that a compliment?" Mike says, smiling at me before climbing over the railing and gripping the cables tightly as he lowers himself. A second smile. Mike must live for this ninja stuff, because I have never seen him in such a good mood. Which is weird since his hopes and dreams supposedly just crashed in burning flames.

"It was a statement of fact," I say. "I know lots of other facts about you. You wouldn't like those ones as much."

Mike hops down to the next balcony. "Your turn. I'll hold the cables still for you down here, but you need to do this quickly. We've got to get to the bottom before they see where we've gone and beat us down."

I bring my legs over, holding one cable in each hand tightly, but I don't descend as gracefully as I'd like. As soon as my legs reach Mike, he tells me to let go and catches me. Then he pulls the cable through the railing and loops it around the next one. We continue this process five more times, quickly establishing a rhythm. I learn exactly how to hold the cables most effectively, how to lock the cable between my ankles as I go down, and when to drop without Mike having to tell me.

As I'm climbing over the final balcony railing to descend to the courtyard, Mike yells, "Not catching you. Take it all the way."

I steal a look below and see him near the corner of the building fending off a horde of guys pouring around the side. They've found us. I huff because he's still not using his stun gun even though he is clearly engaged in close-range combat. The other guys aren't holding back though, and Mike is spending a lot of the time disarming them and dodging their shots. He uses one guy's body to block shots before throwing him at the shooter and knocking two people down in the process.

"What are you waiting for?" Mike yells up at me.

I grumble and start my descent, dropping when I'm halfway to the ground.

Running over to Mike, I pull my own stun gun out, but it looks like Mike has already downed all six of the guys and is now delivering them each a shot to keep them down. He then tosses all but one of his weapons and motions for me to follow. "Throw that out," he says, indicating the weapon in my hand. "It's not going to work."

I look at the fancy gun in my hands, shrug, and toss it into a bush as Mike leads me through the courtyard, an alley, and then the street. Mike's head is oscillating in every direction, on high alert. I find it hard to believe that they're going to ambush us in the street, since there are pedestrians everywhere, but Mike would know better than me I guess.

He has great timing as usual though, because we arrive at a bus stop exactly when a bus pulls up. We board and Mike takes a seat. I sit next to him. "We're going to get off at the next stop," he instructs.

"Why?" I say. "That won't put us very far from where we started."

"I told you the most important thing is getting twenty miles outside of LA. The fastest form of travel is a car. The next stop should have what I'm looking for."

"What are you looking for?"

Mike doesn't answer, so I spend the time watching the four or five other passengers. One kid has ear buds in, staring out the window. An older woman across from me offers me a smile. I smile back. "Where are you headed?" she asks once we make eye contact.

I'm not sure how to answer that at first and almost say something ordinary like the grocery store, but I change my mind. "I'm going to a place that will help me find my father."

"He's missing?" she asks, concerned.

"Sort of. More like trying not to be found."

"Here's our stop," Mike says, nudging my arm.

"See you later," I say, standing and waving at the woman.

"Take care, dear," she says. "Good luck."

"Thanks," I say, following Mike off the bus.

Mike remains silent as he makes a beeline for a parking lot. We weave through rows of cars and Mike stops at one. Then, from somewhere on his person, he produces a hooked rod and shoves it down the side of the window.

"You're stealing a car?" I say, horrified. "Why can't we take the bus? You gave me like a hundred bucks. That should give us enough to get far away and make a call."

He ignores me, catching his hook on something and tugging. The lock pops up and he opens the door. He reaches over the seats and unlocks my side and then his head disappears under the dash.

"You're like a human Swiss army knife," I say to the back of his head. "Is there anything you *can't* do?"

After another minute, the car roars to life and Mike's head reappears. I can see from his stony expression that nice Mike is gone again. With no more opportunities to physically get out his frustrations, the whole crashing and burning career thing is probably back at the forefront of his thoughts.

I sigh and look out my window as Mike backs out of the spot and heads for the street. It looks like a regular sunny day in Los Angeles. But inside this car, a storm is brewing.

ℼ

Where are we going?" I say, seeing we're in Santa Monica and headed north rather than south. I need to be southeast of Los Angeles to check out the graveyard address my uncle gave me, and Mike obviously has his own agenda, one he hasn't offered to share.

He stares straight ahead.

"Let me out," I say.

"No."

"Are we being followed?" I ask, looking in the side-view mirror.

"Yes and no."

"What does that mean?"

"It means we need to get way outside of LA before we're safe."

"Where are you going then?"

"We are going north. I'm taking you to Gabe."

"Let me out," I say, raising my voice an octave. "I have something I need to do before that."

"I told you that I wasn't failing at two things today. I'm taking you back to Gabe, and that's that."

I watch him, calculating, practicing sending daggers from my eyes. But really, I'm waiting. And when the car comes to a stop at a light, I throw my door open and hop out, slamming it behind me. I take off jogging, looking around for a good place to lose Mike, because I'm sure he's going to come after me.

This street is lined with apartment buildings, which isn't all that helpful for hiding, but I dart across the front lawn and around the side of one building to the back where I find a line of detached garages and not a single place to hide.

I turn around to try another direction and run right into Mike. He grabs on to one of my arms. "You are going back to Gabe. It's stupid to keep fighting me."

I twist my arm to get it out of his grip. "Hands off of me!" I stomp my heel into his foot, but he moves it, holding me at arm's length with little effort.

"You're going to have to drag me, kicking and screaming, back to that car," I threaten.

"Fine with me," he says, pulling me.

I dig my heels in. I know I can't possibly win, but I'm not going to go willingly. He half-drags, half-carries me around one side of the building, so I crane my neck and bite his arm as hard as I can through his shirt.

"Dammit!" he says, letting go of me. I make a run for it, but he grabs me again, this time holding me in a bear hug, my arms down at my sides.

I kick and wiggle in his grasp, but it's fruitless. Mike's going to carry me all the way back to the car and zip-tie me in the back seat.

"So this is who you really are then," I snarl. "You don't abduct women just for some stupid organization with a higher calling. You do it when it suits you personally as well."

He keeps walking. I can't see his face, only the grass as we pass because I'm tucked under his arm.

"You're nothing but a bully, Michael Dumas," I say. "You think you can get away with forcing people to do what you want because you're bigger and stronger. But take away all those muscles, and then what are you?"

He stops and lets go of me. I fall to the ground, but I don't try to run this time. I look up at him, because I must have struck a nerve. He's glaring down at me. "I'm trying to do the right thing. Why won't you let me? Ruining my life wasn't enough? *Please*, get in the car. We're out of time. I'll get you back to Gabe. Then you and he can argue about whatever you want to do next."

"I'm not asking for your help, Mike. I'm asking you to walk away."

"And what am I supposed to tell my brother? I let you go after your criminal of a father to get your life force screwed up?"

So that's what this is about… my conversation with the lady on the bus. "Mike!" I insist. "It's done! What are you saving now?"

"You!" he booms.

"I am not your responsibility!"

"Until you're safely back with my brother, you are!"

"I'm not a child! I'm not Gabriel's responsibility or anyone else's but my own! The only person in this situation who needs protection is my son! So stop keeping me from doing the one thing that matters!"

Chest heaving, eyes wild, he thinks for several tedious seconds. "I can't let you go on your own. You'll never manage to avoid the Guild. And we need to get out of here before we're *both* found."

"The *Guild*?" I ask. "Shawn mentioned that. Is that who you work for?"

Mike nods absentmindedly and then says, "Can you at least get in the car so we can get outside the radius? We *really* need to get out of here. I'm dead serious. They'll be here any minute."

"If you promise to go south instead of north."

He waves his hands wildly. "Fine. Whatever. At this point all I care about is getting us out of the hot zone."

I follow him and we take off at a jog toward the car. I'm relieved that he can be reasoned with. I have no idea what this 20 mile radius 'hot zone' is, but he's on edge enough about it that I believe him.

"Why is it you think you can find Carl?" he says once we're in the car. He whips it around and goes back the direction we came, this time heading south.

"Because I have an address."

"An address for Carl?"

"Not exactly."

"What does that mean?"

"It's where I'm supposed to start. My uncle told me. That's where I need to go first."

"Robert Haricott told you how to find Carl…" Mike says, clarifying.

"He told me where to *start*. And I'm going."

"No wonder you were ready to jump on Andre's bandwagon…" he muses. "You were already planning on screwing with your life force. Where's this address? Because I'm serious, you can't go anywhere within twenty miles of LA, or they'll find you."

"City of Orange. Should be far enough."

"Whitley—" He cracks his knuckles, irritated.

"If you are about to tell me what a piece of crap I've turned your life into, I don't want to hear it. I haven't ever done anything *to* you. I just live my life. And currently, you are getting in the way."

"That's what I'm saying. You do your own thing, and somehow, that thing you pick throws a wrench into what I'm trying to do *every single time*. I have *tried* to give you the benefit of the doubt, but it keeps happening. How can I not think you do it on purpose?"

I look at him skeptically. "Mike, you made finding me your sole task for seven years. Maybe you should go get a life and stop focusing on mine." Okay, so I *did* trick him into breaking me out of that underground Guild place, causing him to betray his employers, but I wouldn't have needed him to if he hadn't abducted me in the first place.

He drums the steering wheel and his expression turns back into his usual detachment. "You're stupid if you think you don't need my help."

I roll my eyes. "For someone so fed up with me, you sure are set on convincing me I need you around."

"Have it your way. But I'm going to be taking my money back," Mike says, swerving around a car and running a red light.

I wasn't expecting that... Is he serious? I'm going to have to figure out how to find my way around with no money, but that seems an easier task than fighting Mike. I bring the pack around to my front and dig into it. When I don't immediately find the money, I dump out the contents at my feet, suppressing worry over only having a few units of insulin left in my pen, and no ID to access my prescription. I haven't needed any since my three-day injection, and my blood sugar was fine this morning before breakfast, but according to Andre, today it should be wearing off.

The money is nowhere to be found. "It's not in here," I say, looking up at Mike.

"You lost my money?" he says, though his tone is not even slightly upset.

"Yep. Must have fallen out."

Mike chuckles, which is unexpected. "Forget it, Whitley. I have the money already. I took it so you wouldn't get far if you managed to run away. Wanted to see if you were going to put up a stink about giving it back."

"Why?" I say, annoyed as I throw things back into the backpack. I'm also bothered that I can't remember any point in which Mike was in my pack. He's a pickpocket, too?

"I guess I like to poke you to see how you'll react. I'm also nosy, so I'm going to help you find Carl."

I zip my pack, indecisive. I don't want to bring Mike with me. And why is he all of a sudden willing to help me do something he is vehemently against?

"It also looks like you're going to be in trouble with your insulin soon. I can help you with that," he tempts.

"Why are you helping me?"

"If you get taken by the Guild again, which is going to happen if you do this by yourself, my brother is going to kill me. There's no way I'll be able to break you out a second time, not to mention from the outside like I am now."

I sigh, holding my pack between my knees and crossing my arms. "You have the weirdest priorities. You kidnap me. Then sabotage your own efforts to get information from me. Then you help me escape. I screw up the escape plan, getting you fired. Then you offer to help me do the thing you busted me out to avoid in the first place. And all of this in the name of your familial relationships that are now so ruined that it's going to take divine intervention to fix them. Why did you even take me in the first place? You should have resigned this assignment as soon as it started crossing into your personal life."

He shrugs, and I notice he's slowed down quite a bit. We're on a freeway, and we must be outside of the radius he was ranting about earlier. "I'm a complicated guy, Whitley." He grins at me mischievously. "My job was more complex than you imagine, and with your uncle in the picture, I was the only chance of getting past him to get to you. And Gabe and I have a bond you wouldn't understand. Don't bother trying."

"Whatever. I'll just ask Gabriel when I see him," I say, sitting back and crossing my arms.

"He's not told you anything in the past about me?"

"That he didn't get why you were such an ass. You have more facets?"

"None that you need to know," Mike says. "So where are we going, boss?"

"I can't remember the address. It was in my phone. But it's New Hope Cemetery. We'll have to look it up or ask for directions."

"New Hope Cemetery?" he says skeptically.

"Yeah. I also have a plot number."

"So Carl is hiding out by a grave stone?"

"I very much doubt it," I say. "That's not how my uncle works. And he said it was the starting place."

"To finding Carl," Mike questions.

"That's my understanding."

"We don't need to look it up," Mike says. "I know where it is." He looks perplexed by something, but he doesn't voice it. I have a lot of questions where Mike is concerned, not the least of which are about where we have been for the last two weeks. What exactly is this *Guild* organization and what are they after? But I've blocked off my curiosity in favor of my mission for Robbie. We're on our way to the cemetery I should have visited weeks ago, and I'm not going to poke the bear.

Twenty-three

New Hope Cemetery is old and Catholic, so the mortuary is a stunning piece of architecture with lots of domes and arches and sculptures. But I'm on a mission so I don't stop to admire any of the monuments. On the way here I got a piece of paper and racked my brain for the plot number. I'm pretty sure I remember it but I wrote it down to verify that it looked right visually.

In the mausoleum, I get a map from the information desk and examine it. This place is huge, so I'm pretty sure we're going to want to drive to the plot.

Mike hovers annoyingly, standing at my shoulder, watching me trace my finger on the route we need to take.

"I need to ask them how these graves are numbered," I say. "I can get to the right section, but I'll have no idea which grave it is."

"Let me see that plot number," he says impatiently, snatching the scrap of paper from my hand.

Ugh. Like *he's* the expert on grave numbering… I turn around to go back inside and ask someone.

"Whose grave is this?" he asks, not budging from his spot on the steps, his voice commanding.

"I have no idea," I say. "That's how Uncle Moby works. He gives hints and it's up to you to figure it out. I'm going to go ask about finding plot numbers."

"Wait a minute," Mike demands, holding a hand up before staring at the paper again. "This is crazy…" The paper now tightly in his grip, his eyes bore into it as if he's willing it to spontaneously combust. Then he looks up at me again, accusation in his expression. "You swear you have no idea whose grave this is?"

"No," I say, aggravated but intrigued because it seems like Mike might know something. "Are you saying you do?"

Mike shoves the paper back at me. "I know where it is. Come on."

He jogs down the steps while I rush to keep up. I climb in the car, and he takes off at a reckless speed.

We wind through the grounds and come to an abrupt stop in front of a section of graves with impressive statues as headstones. Mike hops out of the car and heads into the cemetery without waiting for me.

Determined to not be bothered by Mike's abrasiveness, I jog to catch up. We pass six or seven rows of graves, and end up right in front of one whose monument is a stone angel hovering over a child.

"This is it," Mike says, his hands on his hips, his eyes piercing me.

Alma Rivera Fuentes

December 23, 1965 – April 16, 1988

"Alma…" I mouth, looking from the grave to Mike's expectant face.

No way. But then…1988. Maris said Mike came to live with them after his mom died, which was when he was only one year old. He's one year younger than Gabriel, who would have been two at the time.

I don't remember any of Maris' family surnames to verify, but the date adds up, and Mike's face says my assumptions are correct.

"Your mom?" I whisper, hardly believing it.

"Why would your uncle tell you to go to my mother's grave?" Mike demands.

I sink to the grass. Uncle Moby has definitely delivered a doozy this time. I can never predict that man's moves… What does he want me to do with this?

"Whitley!" Mike says. "Tell me what this means!"

I lift my shoulders and let them fall. "That your mom is step one to finding Carl."

"How is my dead mother supposed to help you find Carl?"

I sit cross-legged and pat the ground in front of me. "You need to tell me everything you know about her."

Mike doesn't move. "All you need to know about her is she had hypno-touch done by your father. That's how she died."

The words knock the air out of me. "Wh—what? Does Gabriel know about this?"

Mike clears his throat. "Gabe doesn't know anything. In fact, I didn't even know it until you all told me hypno-touch was lethal last year. That's when I pieced it all together."

I put my chin on my fist. "What else?"

"That's it."

I tilt my head at him. "Oh come on. No it's not."

He perches on a nearby headstone and crosses his arms. "You first. I ask you a question. And then you get to ask me one."

I purse my lips. "Fine."

"Why don't you still have your ability?"

"I already told you. I fixed the hypno-touch that was done to me. That meant I undid my abilities as well."

"That's not an answer. You have a natural-born ability. How do you *undo* natural?"

I throw my hands up. "I don't know. Why don't you tell me since you're the one that knows more about my abilities than I do?"

"Your father, Carl, was born with a natural ability. That means you are *guaranteed* to have one as well."

"If that's true, then why did Carl do hypno-touch on me so young?"

"My guess? To give you more than one ability."

That might actually be true. "I don't have an answer for you," I say. "As far as I know, both my emodar and my colorworld sight were given to me by hypno-touch."

"Colorworld sight?" Mike scoffs. "Is that what you call it?"

"What do *you* call it?"

"Energy world sight."

"That's dumb."

"And *colorworld* isn't? Sounds like a good name for a recreational drug."

I roll my eyes. "That was more than one question. It is *definitely* my turn."

"Shoot."

"What do you know about your mom's relationship with Carl?"

"*Relationship?* They didn't have one. She was just one of your scummy father's experiments."

"You don't have to say it like *I'm* the one that did it."

"I know I don't have to."

I take a cleansing breath. "They had to have known each other, obviously. How did they meet? Did your mom know my mom?"

"How the hell should I know?"

"Mike," I say, exasperated. "Why are you being so difficult?"

"I'm answering your questions. How is that being difficult?"

"It's the *way* you're answering them."

"Beggars can't be choosers. My turn," Mike says. "How did you control your ability?"

"I didn't."

"Then how—"

"My turn," I interrupt. "Was Shawn's ability natural?"

"Yes," he says, moving to sit on the ground. "How did you touch people if you didn't control your ability?"

"I could only touch certain people safely. How many people with natural abilities work for the Guild?"

"Tens of thousands."

My mouth opens in astonishment. "Where do they come from?"

"How did you know who you could touch?"

"By whether or not they were a good person. Mike, where do they come from?"

"They are either born from someone who already has a natural ability or from someone who has had hypno-touch. How did you figure that out—that you could only touch good people?"

"Gabriel's theory based on..." I stop. I don't want to go here and reveal information I shouldn't. But in reality, what harm could this particular fact do? "The literal brightness of someone's soul told me whether or not they were capable of withstanding my touch."

Mike looks puzzled. "How much *can* you see of the energy world?"

"Mike, so that means *you* have an ability, right?" I say.

"Yes-ish," Mike says.

"What kind of answer is that? Yes-ish? That's not an answer."

"Says you. Now *my* question."

I regard him shrewdly and then smirk and say, "I *can't* see any of the energy world."

He scowls. "You know what I meant."

I hold up a finger and tsk-tsk. "What is your life force ability?"

He finally sits on the ground, lays back, crosses an ankle over his bent knee. "Making things happen." He turns his head to give me a smug look. "Just think of it as getting my way."

I smirk. "How's that workin' out for ya?"

He scowls. "It's most effective short-range on very specific things. Long-range, big stuff, is like shooting in the dark. Only works if you have a lot of rounds. Sometimes things fall into my lap in the strangest ways. Sometimes they don't happen at all."

"Wow," I say dryly. "I have such a firm grasp on what you can do now."

"That's why I said yes-ish."

"Actually, it sounds more like normal life. Congratulations on being just like the rest of us, Mike!"

"You wish," he scoffs. "My turn. How much of the energy world *could* you see?"

"More than I'm going to tell you."

"Not an acceptable answer."

I cross my arms. "Sorry. Not gonna happen. Colorworld info is off-limits. Besides, you told me basically nothing about *your* ability."

"I guess we'll sit here and talk about nothing then." He clasps his hands under his head casually.

I know a lot more than I did before, so I don't consider this little exercise a failure. The question is, what am I doing here? Why this grave? How does this help me find Carl?

Right place, right time…

Mike's mom…

Maybe the question is what would I have done if I'd come here *before* going to see Mike that day I flew to LA. I would have figured out pretty quickly that this grave belonged to his mother…

I sit up straighter, realizing that my very next move would have been to go see Mike. I'm sure of it. Which means I would have ended up in this very same situation. *Mike* is the key. This grave is just supposed to make that unmistakable.

I look at him as he watches the sky, his mouth in an irritated line.

"I'm here for *you*," I say. "That's why Uncle Moby had me go to this grave. Either before I visited you or after, it was supposed to impress on me the significance of having you to help me find Carl."

Mike rolls his head toward me. I can't translate his expression, but I think he's processing that. "Whitley, I know jack squat about finding Carl."

I shrug. "That's what you may think. But either way I need you if I'm going to find him."

"Heh," he sniggers. "I have no doubt about that. But I'd rather take you to Gabe first."

I bite the inside of my cheek, pondering.

"Why are you so opposed to it?" Mike asks after a while. "Are you afraid of him?"

"No. I just… don't want to have the discussion."

"You're a wimp."

"I know. But he's going to try to talk me out of it. We're going to get into this huge fight, and I'm going to feel like crap."

"You *should* feel like crap. It's a stupid idea."

"Mike, my uncle's advice was to go to you about finding Carl. You must know something. Why won't you tell me?"

Mike lifts himself up on an elbow. "I'll make you a deal. You let me take you back to Gabe. Then I promise I'll tell all. Everything about the Guild. Everything I know about my mom. Because I can guarantee you I'm not telling you a thing until I accomplish *my* goal."

I can't really argue with that. What other reason would I need to see Mike but for information? As for Gabriel, I'll just come up with a really convincing argument…

"Deal," I say, holding out a hand.

Mike sits up and takes it. "Holy smokes. You're actually doing something that isn't working *against* me. I need to write this down." Then he pulls me up by the hand. "Let's go, Whitley. We gotta lot of miles to cover. And lots of Guild boots to avoid."

"Boots?"

"Slang for the military side of the Guild. The non-gifted ones. Easy enough to avoid them. But it's the gifted ones—we call them Primes—that will put a crimp in our plans."

When we get back to the car, I remember my blood sugar and the sad state of my insulin store. "Uh, Mike, how long before we reach Gabriel? Do you think he's in LA? He might be there looking for me."

"He's meeting us in San Francisco."

"What? How do you know that?"

"Because I sent him a message."

I groan. "Mike, is there any way you can answer my questions in more than a sentence or two? Why do you make me interrogate everything out of you?"

"Why do you have to ask so many questions? First things first: get you some insulin."

I draw in patience. I'm going to need a lot more of it before this road trip is over.

Mike drums the wheel silently, eventually turning on the radio and adjusting the dials to a station he likes. Popular music. He bobs his head and completely ignores me. Then he cracks his window. Then a song comes on that he knows the words to and he cranks it up.

Then he starts singing at the top of his lungs. In falsetto. I think it's Selena Gomez. I look out my window and press my lips together to keep from laughing at him. He can't sing for crap.

"You have a terrible voice," I say, once the song is over.

"Selena doesn't care."

"Yeah. Because she's not here. I'm just sayin'. You should uh, keep your day job." I bite my lip, sniggering.

He scowls at me.

"I guess you better freshen up your resume. Hey! You should apply to be Selena's bodyguard!"

"Great idea. Except for one thing."

"What's that?"

He gestures at himself. "She wouldn't be able to resist all of this. They say you shouldn't get involved with your help."

I roll my eyes. "Your ego is showing again."

"Hey, I'm used to resisting, but Selena is *hawt*."

"Oh my gosh."

"Girls like confidence."

"You're mixing up confidence with arrogance." The words ring with familiarity and I pause. "Funny. I had almost this exact conversation with Gabriel once. I guess you two have something in common after all."

"You're jealous."

"Of what?" I snort.

"Selena."

"Where do you get that?"

"You said it: Gabe thinks Selena's hot, too."

"No, I meant about arrogance versus confidence."

"When was this?" he asks curiously.

"When we met."

"Details?" he prods.

"Why would I give you details? You never return the favor."

"Oh come on. Humor me. Or I could find another song to sing…" He reaches for the dial.

I swat his hand away. "Fine. He basically told me he had a thing for me and then told me I was crushing on him and wouldn't admit it. When I rejected him, he got more smug and said he'd win me over because he had skill with women. I accused him of being arrogant. And he told me I was confusing arrogance with audacity. So yeah. Same conversation. You two obviously share inflated ego syndrome."

"Confidence, Whitley. Not arrogance. But we also share a hardcore crush on Selena Gomez."

"Gabriel does not have a crush on Selena Gomez."

Mike laughs loudly. "Yes, he does. But it looks like he's never told you."

"Fine. I'm sure he finds her attractive. Big deal. So what?"

"*Finds her attractive*?" Mike mocks. "Okay. If that makes you feel better."

"What are you trying to do?" I ask.

"Irritate you. Mission accomplished." He grins at me and then suddenly swerves into the parking lot of a fast food restaurant. "Hungry?"

"I thought we were getting insulin."

"Not until tonight. Too many people in drug stores during the day."

"What are you planning?" I accuse.

"Don't worry about it. You'll psych yourself out. And I'm going to need your help."

"Mike…" I say, an edge of whining to my voice. He must be planning on stealing it. "They can look up my prescription. We can pay for it."

He holds the door to the restaurant open for me. "First of all, no. Second of all, no. I told you. Stop thinking about it. Now, what do you like on your burger?"

"You mean after all those years of stalking me, you don't know?"

"I didn't stalk you for seven years. I *searched* for you for seven years."

"You know what I mean."

"Yep. And you're right. I do know what you like on your burger. But I didn't want to creep you out."

"I didn't realize you knew how to be considerate."

Mike just laughs.

Twenty-four

*B*ut if the *Guild* can track prescriptions and anything else, won't a drugstore holdup for insulin show up on their radar?" I argue, my last ditch effort to avoid doing this. Mike told me that everything about me is tracked, and we have to stay completely undetected or we'll never make it to San Francisco. But stealing is not something I want to add to my list of questionable deeds.

Mike scoffs. "Whitley, I am too good to end up on anyone's radar. You, on the other hand, are so sloppy you might trip the alarm going *in* to the store."

"Why am I even going in then?"

"Because stealing is a useful skill. It's about time you learned."

"Yeah, if you're a career thief."

"Or when you're a diabetic low on insulin. Stop being a baby."

"Mike," I whine. "I can't do this."

"Stop thinking of it as stealing. It's a job. I'm your commanding officer and I've briefed you on a mission. Focus on your part. That's all."

"*Fiiine*," I intone, reaching for the handle.

"Before you go," Mike says. "Fluff your hair or something—whatever it is girls do to look good last minute."

"*Why* am I trying to look good?"

"Because if the pharmacist is a dude, which is likely, you need to use all of your assets." He hands me a tube of lipstick.

"You keep car jacking tools *and* makeup on you?"

"Hey, sometimes I like to wear girly stuff. Don't judge."

I give him a look of disbelief.

He rolls his eyes. "It was left in the car. Put it on."

"Eew. No. Who knows what lips have been on that."

"Whitley. Insulin is more important than a few germs on a tube of lipstick. Do it."

I give an exaggerated sigh and run the pink pigment over my lips.

"Perfect," Mike says, giving me a once-over when I'm done.

We both get out of the car, and in spite of the chill in the late-night air, I feel deathly hot. And nauseated. But that's most likely due to my current high blood sugar from dinner earlier. I took the last of my insulin after the burger and fries at lunch, so my need for insulin may be the only thing propelling me forward. But the closer we get to the door, the more lightheaded I become. I think I'm going to faint. Mike takes one look at me before we go inside and says, "This is not going to work. You look like a thief, and you haven't even stolen anything yet. All you have to do is provide the distraction. Why are you so nervous?"

I shift from foot to foot. "I've not stolen anything since I was six when I took a pack of gum from the store. My mom made me sweep the entire sidewalk around the store in apology and payment for stealing. I guess the lesson stuck, okay?"

It looks like he's thinking. Hopefully it's a backup plan that involves me *not* entering the store at all.

A smile quirks his lips finally, and before I can ask him what the new plan is, he steps forward into my personal space, grabs my face, and kisses me full on the mouth. I'm so taken by surprise that I don't process what's happening at first. As he presses harder though, I come to and push him away. He holds me tight though, keeping his lips on mine. I'm so angry, I start trying to kick him, but he holds my face tightly, and I can't tell if I'm making any contact.

He finally releases me, and I leap away from him. "What the hell was that?" I shout.

"Times a'wasting, Whitley. Let's go." He reaches for my hand with his usual quickness before I can dart away and drags me toward the door.

I'm livid. I cannot believe he just *kissed* me! I hope Gabriel punches him right in the face when he sees him. I'd do it myself, but he'd probably get away before I could land one. The *nerve*! He's always *assaulting* me, throwing his muscles around to get what he wants… I need to put a stop to it. I need to figure out a way to send a *really* clear message.

I'm inside the drugstore at the moment though. And when I finally pay attention to what's around me, I spot Mike crouched behind an aisle, gesturing me to go on.

I glare at him and stalk toward the pharmacist's counter, thinking of all the things I'm going to say when this is over.

"I need some help with cough syrup," I snap at the pharmacist, a young, tired-looking man who sits on a stool behind the counter, holding a Car & Driver magazine.

"It's on aisle three," he says without looking up.

"I *know* where it is," I say, fighting to temper my voice. "I need help with it, you know, advice from a pharmacist, which is what you are, aren't you?"

The man looks up at me with annoyed boredom. He does not like his one A.M. magazine perusal interrupted.

I eyeball him expectantly. He heaves himself off the stool and follows me to the cough syrup section.

"So I have a two-year old," I explain once we arrive, "and he's pretty congested, but from what I can tell, none of these children's cough syrups contain anything for congestion. None of this cold stuff period has anything anti-congestion. So what's the deal? Two-year olds don't get snotty noses? That sounds like a bit of an oxymoron, doesn't it?"

The pharmacist starts pulling items off the shelf and examining the ingredients. I roll my eyes, although he can't see me do so. That a pharmacist doesn't know what's in cough syrup is just stupid. Didn't he learn over-the-counter ingredients in Pharmacy 101? I actually came up with the question on the fly rather than the line of questioning Mike told me to use. I don't want to take any of *Mike's* suggestions if I can help it. I was in a pharmacy not too long ago for Robbie for this exact thing anyway. Of course, he's not two, but being the naïve first-time mom, I had no idea you don't give anything like cold medicine to babies. You do give it to two-year olds apparently— sans congestion medication—which makes my question now worth asking.

"Hmm," he says after drawing the same conclusions I have. "I imagine they took it out to avoid overdose. Decongestants are pretty powerful and could easily be abused."

"Right, well that doesn't help a snotty nose. What do you suggest?"

"You could use a saline solution and an aspirator."

I let my mouth drop open slightly and prop an arm casually on one of the shelves. "Seriously? I'm supposed to squirt saltwater in his nose and then suction it out? On a two-year old? That's about as likely as getting child-support out of his deadbeat dad." I'm really pushing this distraction a little far. So sue me. Getting assaulted by my husband's brother has me feeling especially vindictive.

The pharmacist smiles a little, but he tries to hide it from me. I put my other hand on my hip and toss my short hair subtly.

"Fair enough," he says, "Well I can't make this recommendation officially, but get the children's version labeled for five and up; halve the dosage and he should be fine. But if he starts running a fever you should take him in."

"You are such a lifesaver," I gush, reaching out and squeezing his arm.

As I expected, he becomes uncomfortable with the physical contact. Time to reel him in.

"Oh sorry!" I say, holding my hands up. "I shouldn't have done that. I'm just so grateful to be treated like a person with a brain instead of an idiot who can't follow instructions outside a medicine label." I shrug. "I'm a hugger. Even with strangers." I smile and wink at him.

"Oh, no it's fine," he says, clearing his throat. "Anyway, it's a liability issue. Too many people *don't* follow instructions."

"Yeah I know," I sigh. "His dad tried to give him Advil once for teething when he was a baby. Geez. What an idiot, am I right?"

The pharmacist looks at me with a slight smile. "I'd say that would *not* be a good idea."

"Yeah really," I reply. "So while I have you here, if you don't mind—I know you want to get back to your magazine—but what's your opinion on Tylenol?"

"Sorry about earlier," he says a little sheepishly. "The late night crowd isn't usually so interesting."

I wave a hand. "Water under the bridge. Anyway, I was going to get something for my headache the other day, and I figured Tylenol was the safest. I don't like to take drugs much, but I've been seeing all these articles about Tylenol—how it's bad. Is that true?"

The pharmacist launches into the pros and cons of various pain relievers and how moderation is the most important aspect of over-the-counter drug use. We eventually move on to other topics, like pharmacy school and how this job wasn't what he envisioned. I lose track of time, but I want to be sure Mike has enough time. So I laugh and smile at all the right places, prompting new questions when the conversation lulls. I can do this in my sleep. I discover, as I talk, that the lessons I learned about people in my years with empathic ability haven't left me. I must have lacked confidence before today. I'm flying blind, but I've flown enough times that I know the drill.

When I think I've been at it long enough, I pay for the cough syrup and accept his number.

I go straight to the car, and find Mike behind in the driver's seat, tapping the steering wheel with a leering grin on his face. Not forgetting his actions before this started, I bring my hand back to slap him. He catches my hand again. "You can't possibly think I'm going to let you do that. Why do you keep trying?" he says, shaking his head and tsk-tsking.

"Because you deserve it," I spit.

"Oh come on. It was a tactic."

"A tactic?" I say, infuriated. Then I wave my hands and shake my head. "Nevermind, I don't care. Did you get it at least?"

He starts the car, putting it into reverse. "Of course I did. Twenty minutes ago. I was thinking about leaving you here and telling Gabe you ran off with a pharmacist." He tosses a bag at me. "At that rate, you probably could have batted your eyes at him and he would have given the insulin itself up freely without the stealing. When's the first date?"

"Shut up!" I yell, digging through the bag and yanking out a new insulin pen. "Gosh, you are the most irritating person I have *ever* met." I yank my sleeve up. "Look, I don't know what your boundaries are, whether you even *have* boundaries. But using your physical strength to get what you want is where I draw the line." I prick my hand to double-check my sugar level. "You're scum. And you're going to get what's coming to you. I swear, Mike, if you weren't Gabriel's brother..." I toss the meter violently into my backpack.

"If I weren't Gabe's brother, then what?" he demands, piercing me with his eyes again.

"I'd have nothing to do with you," I say, uncapping the pen with my mouth and speaking through it. "And if by some miracle we became acquainted, I definitely wouldn't try so hard to be nice to you."

"I didn't realize you were trying now."

I jab the pen in my arm, partly from relief that I'm finally getting my blood sugar under control, and partly to calm myself after Mike's blatant disrespect. I wonder at what I meant. I wouldn't say I've been *nice* per se. But I've been patient. I've been forgiving for reasons even I don't know. I've been understanding. He says the worst things to me and I bite my tongue. Every time I think I might be getting somewhere with him, he turns into this horrible person with a personal vendetta against me. It's completely backward. After all he's done to me—to *Robbie*—why do I bother? I cap the pen and toss it in my backpack.

"Well, I'm done trying with you, Mike," I say quietly. "Take me back to Gabriel." I cross my arms and look out the window, shaking inside.

A lead-heavy silence falls over the car. I stew. I wonder what's going on in Mike's head. Is he so oblivious that he really doesn't see how everything he says and does contradicts itself? What does he *really* think? And then I wonder what Gabriel will say. I know him pretty well, but I can't predict what his reaction will be. To any of this.

Once I calm down a little, exhaustion hits me. It's after three A.M., and I've had a heck of a day with practically no sleep last night. As if reading my mind, Mike pulls into an office complex and around the back. He parks the car and turns it off. Assuming he's stopping for the night, I recline my seat and avoid looking his direction.

I don't hear Mike move though, and I'm held entranced by the moment of stillness. I would bet money that Mike's unmoving silence means he's contemplating something heavy. I desperately wish I knew what. I just want to understand him. It hurts that he not only won't let me, but actively seeks to thwart any effort on my part.

"I'm sorry about the kiss," Mike says, breaking the silence. "I was just trying to—forget it. It was uncalled for."

I turn over to face him. "Trying to what?"

He hesitates, not looking my way. Hands at his sides, eyes lost in the darkness, he says. "Make you angry. You can't be nervous when you're angry."

I can't deny that he's right about that, and maybe if it weren't the umpteenth time that he's used his brute strength against me, it wouldn't make me so mad. But that's a dumb thing to get bent out of shape over, with his history with me in mind. It's like getting sad that your pet snapping turtle bit you. Snapping turtles bite. Gabriel's brother is a snapping turtle. But I'm treating him like a box turtle instead.

I don't know why I like to imagine he's somehow recovered, somehow repentant, somehow… a box turtle underneath. As I look at his outline in the darkness I think that whatever demons Mike has, they must really torment him. That's the only explanation I have for the mixed signals he constantly gives me. But then, maybe I'm confusing the things he does for me as being *for me*. In reality, Mike has only ever expressed loyalty and respect for Gabriel. If I see some personal benefit from Mike's actions, it's incidental, not intentional.

"Apology accepted," I say, turning back over. I wish Gabriel were here. I really miss him, and I'm glad Mike convinced me to go back now instead of after I find Carl. I'm exhausted with the ups and downs of being around him anyway.

It was stupid to think I could do this without Gabriel.

Twenty-five

I wake up to the sensation of a moving car, but I don't let Mike
know I'm awake yet. I have no ambition to speak to him. We can
make it all the way to San Francisco in silence for all I care.

About an hour and a half into it, I know I can't put off my
blood sugar any longer. So I sit up and dig in my backpack for the
test kit.

"I snagged some granola bars at the drugstore if you need
something to eat," Mike says. "Behind my seat in the bag you put the
cough syrup in."

I test first, finding my sugar heading toward low, so I reach
back and bring the plastic bag to my lap. I examine the box of granola
bars, but throw them back in the bag.

"Sorry, it's not a hot breakfast, princess," Mike goads as he
watches me.

I resist glaring at him, but can't help grinding my teeth. I open
the glove box, and look under the seat to see if there was any food left
behind by the person Mike stole this car from.

Not even a breath mint. I look out at the road ahead, but we're
in the middle of nowhere on the 5. Gabriel and I have driven this
way between Monterey and his parent's home in Bakersfield, so I
recognize it. I'd estimate we're about a hundred miles from Monterey.
Home.

"I'm allergic to tree nuts, Mike. The bars aren't allergy safe."

Mike looks over at me. "Shit. You're right."

"I wouldn't expect you to remember."

"Well I would," Mike says, more agitated than I would have
expected.

"Oh yeah, the stalker thing," I say.

"It's been my job to know everything about you," he says.

I can't decide if I prefer this overt confession over yesterday's effort to play dumb about knowing what I like on my burger. Both are bothersome, but in this case I don't like him assuming the essence of who I am can be diluted down to a single file of facts. "But you don't," I mumble, looking out the window.

"Can you make it to the next town?" he says. "We'll pick something up."

I remain quiet, determined to interact with Mike as little as possible. Instead I remember Gabriel's smile and Robbie's softness in my arms. Anticipation of our upcoming reunion electrifies me with excitement. This will all be over.

I notice that the traffic is becoming heavier, and then it slows to a crawl. There must be an accident ahead.

Mike cranes his neck to see around the car in front of us, and I decide to turn on the radio to see if there's a traffic report. I don't have to search for a station though.

"*—urging citizens to steer clear of the city so as not to hold up emergency vehicles trying to get through. And if you're just now tuning in, we've got breaking news of a massive earthquake that has just struck the San Francisco area. They're estimating a magnitude of at least nine that happened at six-fourteen this morning. It's too early to make any estimation of fatalities, but it's safe to say that the epicenter was at least close to downtown and extending clear down to San Jose, so the damage is devastating. Authorities have shut down the roads headed into the bay area, so if you're going that way, you'll soon run into blockades set up to redirect traffic away.*"

The breaking news notice starts to repeat, and I turn the radio down slightly, my chest pounding in panic. I look at Mike, dumbstruck. I cover my mouth, life sucked out of me.

Mike knows what I'm thinking. He heaves in a concerted breath. "No. They're not there. I gave Gabe instructions. They haven't left LA yet. They should be fine."

I'm not sure about his tone… "What instructions? Tell me exactly what you told him," I demand as I grip the side of the door, blood pounding into my ears, dread crushing my lungs.

"I sent a message that we'd be in San Francisco tomorrow morning. I told him we'd meet him right at the airport and that he was *not* to go to San Francisco any sooner or it would put us in danger of being caught."

"Why would he would listen to you? You kidnapped me. He's not going to trust anything you say! He's going to come up with his own plan. I know him. What if he went to San Francisco already to throw you off in case you were lying, in case—"

"Wendy, stop," Mike says firmly. "They're fine." He grips the back of his neck. "They're fine. Trust me. Gabe will listen."

"How do you know?" I plead. "Can't we call them at least? What's the harm in calling?"

"I just know, okay? It doesn't matter why. But Gabe will know. As for calling, even if I had a phone, that would be the very worst thing we could do right now."

"*Why?*"

Mike shakes his head solemnly. "Right now, the *only* thing on the Guild's radar will be you."

I open my mouth in confusion, having no idea what that means. "I don't understand. What do they want?"

Mike glances at me. "This," he says, turning up the radio to indicate he means the newscast, "is why they need you. And now that something this monumental has happened, they will spare no expense to find you." He opens his window now, leaning out as far as he can to see ahead.

"I don't understand," I say in a small voice, wanting to cry but too afraid to. I can't think straight. I need Gabriel here. I bet he would know right away what Mike is talking about. He would blow me away with his intellect, and together we'd come up with a plan. And this would all make sense. He'd be next to me, and I'd have Robbie in my arms, sure of his safety. And Ezra would make fun of everything. Kaylen would just be happy that we were all together. And Robert would be watching over us, doing odd things that end up changing everything. And right now I don't know if *any* of them are okay. They could all be dead. Just like that. Buried under tons of rubble. Fallen under a collapsed home. I have no way of knowing, and Mike's telling me that I can't get some assurance because some undercover organization will hunt me down to the ends of the earth?

"We have to get out," Mike says, bringing his head back into the car. "We can't go through a blockade. Get your things." And then he pulls over to the shoulder.

"What!?" I say, aggravated by Mike's lack of explanation.

"Your things!" Mike says loudly. "We have to get out now! We're going to head into that grove." He points to an orchard of young trees on the other side of an access road that runs next to the freeway.

Compelled simply by a need to move, if nothing else, I do as he asks, slinging my backpack over my shoulder and following Mike out of the car.

He motions for me to move faster, leading me through the thick brush that borders the freeway. We reach the trees, going further and further in until the freeway is out of sight.

"Stop," I heave, catching myself on the trunk of a tree. "I'm stopping until you explain to me what's going on! Or I'm heading straight back to the road to find someone who will let me borrow their phone."

Mike pauses a few yards ahead and turns around. He sighs and closes his eyes. "No phone calls. They will have your entire family watched, monitored. Every phone call and email traced. They have resources so vast that nothing is out of their reach. A simple call from a stranger's phone will have them falling on us in minutes."

"What are we supposed to do?" I cry. Fear for my family is so all-consuming that I can't contain it. My stomach hurts. My chest burns. My eyes sting. What if Robert saw this ahead of time? What if this is why he was so upset about giving me that address in LA? And it's a weekday, isn't it? What about Kaylen and Ezra? Their private school is in San Jose... If the earthquake was after six A.M. they would have been on their way...

"I can't take not knowing!" I say finally, pressing my back into the tree. We need to move. Go back. If the traffic was due to a blockade, the police will be able to let me contact my family safely...

Mike strides forward. He puts his hand on my shoulder, the most real and unguarded look on his face I have ever seen. It's declarative and certain. "Wendy," he says insistently, his eyes on mine, something else he has never done. "Gabe and I. We have an understanding. I may have abducted you. I may have stuck you in an underground hole with Shawn. But there is an unwritten, unbreakable trust between him and me. He knows I will keep my word to him. I told him no harm would come to you, that I would make sure you were back together if he would do exactly as I said. Why do you think I took you away from the Guild in the first place? Because I couldn't break my word to my brother. Even at the cost of years of work.

Whatever you believe about me, believe that. I can't... hurt him like that without hurting myself. He knows this. He trusts this. They are not in San Francisco. Believe me."

I want to. I need what he's saying to be true. But I've already built up so much tension in my head I can't possibly dissolve it. So I cry until my breaths can't keep up. I'm going to start hyperventilating if I don't find something to breathe into, quick.

Mike tugs on my arm, tentatively at first, but I resist, becoming more hysterical, so desperate for assurance that I can think of nothing else. So he pulls more firmly until I am against his chest and he's holding me tightly, his trunk-like arms like a vice. Against them I brace myself, finding control eventually.

"Slow down," he says, his hand on my back. Then he starts counting through my breaths to time them.

I think I believe him. But a chaos of emotion fights for a way out. Maybe I just need to cry, probably from the stress of all the ups and downs, from indefinite separation from my family, or from the constantly changing circumstances since.

As I find a center, I comprehend that Mike is holding me. He's compact but hard as a rock, and he smells like aged cologne and sweat, and cotton. Mike is holding me? What alternate universe have I dropped into?

I push away from him, hoping in vain that the moment doesn't become awkward.

"Thanks," I say, looking away, mortified for reasons beyond my comprehension.

"Okay, seriously, let's not make this weird," Mike says, looking anywhere but at me. "Insult me or something. Let's get back to normal."

"If you're wrong about Gabriel, I'm going to make your life hell."

"You already do, Whitley," he sighs.

"It's your own fault," I say. "Now you talk."

"I will if you walk," Mike says. "We're too close to the road."

"Where are we going anyway?" I say, tightening the straps on my backpack and following him, my worries over Gabriel and the rest of my family leaving quicker than I'd expect. I don't have a choice other than to believe Mike's assurances. What good would it do to entertain the opposite?

"To San Francisco," Mike replies.

"Uhhh... why? Gabriel's not going to be able to get there if they're shutting down every route into the city. We'll have to figure out a new rendezvous point."

Mike gives me a look over his shoulder. "I thought you knew my brother? He'll find a way to meet us there. Especially with Robert's resources. So we better do the same."

"On foot?" I say, running to catch up.

"For now. We've got to get to the next town to get you something to eat."

"I don't understand why we don't drive. They're too busy redirecting traffic to check if each car that passes is stolen." I finally fall into step with Mike's brisk pace.

"If redirecting is all they're doing, traffic wouldn't have slowed to a complete stop like it did. And we were five miles from the exit. That's a serious traffic backup. *Redirecting*? I bet they're talking to each person. A good excuse to look in every vehicle. And they're looking for *you*."

"How do you know that? You're saying every highway patrol dispatch is rigged? By these *Guild* people?"

"I'm not taking chances."

"Fine. So tell me why the Guild needs me."

"Because you are the only one with any hope of understanding what the hell is going on in the world right now. All the weird weather that has happened in recent years? Especially the last couple. People have looked past it, crying climate change. But it's not, not according to the scientists at the Guild. And nobody is smarter than them. Fires, floods, hurricanes... natural disasters cropping up everywhere with the frequency that has never before been seen. Something is happening. The Guild knows this, *has* known this for years. And it's been slowly building every year. It would be ten times worse right now if they weren't working tirelessly to prevent and mitigate disasters. But they're losing the war. They've got to figure out where it's coming from. An earthquake in their own backyard is going to scare the hell out of them. They want to know what's happening at any cost."

"What does this have to do with me?" I say. "I don't know anything that could help them understand it."

We reach a wide aqueduct at the edge of the orchard. Mike looks up and then down it. I worry for a moment that he's going to make us swim, but he begins walking alongside it instead.

"It's not about what you know," he says. "It's about what you can do. What you've *always* been able to do. You can see the other side. They call it the energy world, where energy is actually visible. And other than your father and his mother, you are the only one alive who has ever had the ability to see it."

"Why would seeing the colorworld help them understand natural disasters?" I say, scowling and scuffing the gravel with my feet as I walk. I am so over people thinking I can do more than I can. Louise, Carl, and now some secret *Guild*.

"Because everything that happens in this world is mirrored in that world. These disasters? They want to track their energy movement. You would know more than me. The only way to stop these disasters is to know what's causing them. And the only way to know that is to see who or what is pushing energy around like this."

"Who? They think a *person* is doing this?"

"What other explanation is there? They've kept tabs on just about everyone with abilities, but some have still slipped through the cracks. It's possible that someone is out there with an ability they haven't catalogued, causing disasters world-wide."

"That's ridiculous. Who on earth would have that kind of power, life force ability or not?"

"A third generation Prime. That's what we call someone born with natural abilities. And each generation is born with more powerful abilities than the last."

"You're saying all these people originated from hypno-touch?"

"Yes. Hypno-touch has been around since the sixties."

"So Carl and my uncle…"

"Their mother *and* father both had hypno-touch."

"So Louise didn't discover it."

"It was actually Louise's father, Eric Shelding, that discovered it."

"Whoa," I say.

"What I don't get is why you and Carl no longer have abilities."

"I already told you why I don't," I say. "But Carl lost his ability because he was evil. Life force light powers abilities. If you lose your light, you have nothing to power it. Ergo, no ability."

We finally see an access road that crosses the aqueduct. Mike comes to a stop, turning to look at me. "Are you serious?"

"Yes," I say wearily, starting to feel my lack of blood sugar. How far until we reach the supposed town Mike was talking about? I might have to chance one of the granola bars. I'm about to ask Mike if the bars have nuts as an actual ingredient when I catch a flash of orange in the trees on the other side of the aqueduct. It's an orange grove. Is there still fruit on the trees? Isn't it mid-June? I leave Mike behind and jog to the crossing. Making a beeline for the trees, I'm more sure that I'm seeing a few oranges still clinging stubbornly on the branches long past harvest. Looks like the universe has smiled on me. Picking up my pace, I find a tree that looks good for climbing and ascend.

High among the branches, I shake the ones that still have fruit, and a few oranges fall to the ground. I climb back down to find that Mike has gathered them up and is already eating one.

"I can't believe there are still oranges on the trees," I say, taking two, and sitting down nearby to test my glucose.

"Blood oranges," Mike says, showing me the ruby-colored inside of one. "Later harvest."

"How serendipitous to have actually found a blood orange grove then," I say. "Now that I'm not going to faint from lack of food, are we still headed for the nearest town?"

Mike nods.

"Why?"

"Transportation."

"Are you back to one-word communication?" I ask, annoyed.

"What can I say? I'm fickle."

"Fine. If you don't want to talk about your plans to get us to San Francisco, are you going to tell me what the Guild's mission statement is? How do they have abilities? Kidnapping women and inflicting psychological torture on people with a white room doesn't bode well for the health of their souls."

"World peace. Prosperity. Equality," Mike says. "Everything good people want. And I already told you. Andre's too ambitious for his own good. A bad egg. So are you saying that when people do immoral stuff, poof, their ability is gone?"

"I actually don't know. But my guess is it's more gradual. I saw Carl and Louise both in the colorworld though. They were like light vacuums. It was pretty clear to me why Carl lost what he could do. You couldn't look at the two of them and not... feel sorry for them."

Mike stares off pensively, and I hope this isn't the end of his talking. I'm finally getting some answers.

"You're telling me the Guild, with tens of thousands of people with abilities, doesn't know this?" I say when Mike remains silent. I start peeling my first orange with shaking hands. Thank goodness I found these before I passed out.

Mike hands me an orange he has already peeled before I can finish though. I can't help analyzing the gesture. I want it to be a kind one, but I'm sure he's just trying to keep me alive. "I'm sure they do," he says. "But I told you they don't tell me anything I don't need to know. That's the way they operate. But I'd be willing to bet most Primes don't know it."

"Sounds like a terrorist organization. Nobody knows fully what's going on. They all do their individual parts."

"It's not a terrorist organization."

"Whatever. So they're full of kittens and rainbows then? A bunch of do-gooders?"

"Yes."

"If that's true, why didn't they just, I don't know, knock on my door and ask for my help? Was kidnapping really necessary?"

"They tried that with Carl. And he ended up blackmailing them. And then faking his death. And then disappearing again, thanks to your uncle. They weren't going to make that mistake with you. Secrecy is something they value more highly than philanthropy. It's necessary to continue to grow their numbers without push-back from the huge number of people that would fear that kind of power."

"Grow their numbers... through hypno-touch? That kills people, you know." It suddenly makes sense to me why Carl laughed that night at the bar when I asked him about the list. He told me I was too ambitious. It's sickening to imagine how many people Carl might have *actually* done hypno-touch on if there are thousands of these Primes Mike is talking about.

"Yes. It does. But they do it ethically."

"Oh do tell."

"Remember what I told you about Robbie? That they medicated you to preserve your eggs? They do the same thing with other people who volunteer. They do hypno-touch on people who are terminal. Then they harvest their reproductive cells."

"Euthanasia," I say. "Because hypno-touch will kill them faster. Do they tell them that?"

"Yes. And they do get compensated. Their families are always taken care of. Scholarships. Life insurance. Medical bills paid."

"Bribery. To die sooner?"

"No. To parent a generation of individuals with abilities far more powerful than what hypno-touch can produce on its own. These people jump at the chance to leave a legacy. You should know what it's like to be them. You went around for months trying to fix people so you could die happy, right? Is it so hard to believe that other people would do the same thing?"

I purse my lips, still not liking this. But I have to admit that it's worlds better than what Louise and Carl were doing... Although why Carl was supposedly fighting against these people, I don't know. It sounds exactly like what he was telling me he wanted.

"Let's get moving," Mike says, standing.

I throw the remaining two oranges in my pack and follow suit.

Twenty-six

Mike sticks to the trees as we travel mostly east. A lot of helicopters have been passing overhead, headed north, probably part of the relief effort. Mike always pulls me beneath the low-hanging canopy of trees until they're out of sight, so it's been slow going. When a grove ends, Mike scans for the next closest one, even if it involves backtracking a little. Sometimes we can't help but traverse open fields, but Mike always makes us run.

"What kind of transportation are we going to find in this town we're headed for?" I ask after a while.

"A Guild vehicle."

"What am I missing?"

"I'm going to steal one."

"You're going to find a car owned by the Guild. In a town in the middle of nowhere. And it's going to be available to steal. Did I get that right?"

"Yep."

"You are the most irritating person to communicate with, you know that? One minute the mouth is on full-blast. The next minute you're clammed up."

"I only tell you what you need to know."

"I see they've brainwashed you to their ways," I say. "What's with the name anyway? The Guild? It's so campy. Like a secret illuminati cult. Or a terrorist organization…"

"It's not a terrorist organization."

"Still a dumb name."

"You have a better one?"

"In my head I just think 'those bastards' but I've also subconsciously named you the same thing. I don't want to confuse the two."

He gives me a sardonic glance over his shoulder.

"How about Gordon Bennett?" I suggest.

"What?"

"It's an expletive Gabriel uses sometimes."

He walks silently for a while, and I think he's decided to ignore my ramblings. But then he says, "How about 'Gordy' instead? Gordon Bennett is too long. And saying something like 'Son of a Gordon Bennett' loses the umph getting lost in all those syllables."

I smile. "Well if I see any of those Gordies, I'll tell them to go Gordy themselves."

Mike laughs, a raucous carefree laugh. His indulgence is surprising. He opens a granola bar and bites into it when we stop on the edge of the current orchard we've been walking through. I wish I could risk having one. Something more substantial than a couple oranges would be nice…

He scans the horizon for where to go next and catches me watching him chewing. "Sorry about the granola bars," he says, shattering his hardened persona once again with an actual *apology*.

"Sorry about your job," I reply.

He doesn't speak but points toward a massive grove on the other side of the field in front of us. It spans as far as I can see in both directions. The open field that separates us is also large, a bigger space than we have yet traversed, so Mike thoroughly scans the skies before sprinting over the field of new sprouts. It's recently been irrigated; my feet sink deeply as we run. I move more slowly than usual because of this, and Mike even comes back to help me along.

Reaching the tree cover on the other side, I pause, hands on my knees to catch my breath after such a strenuous run. I grimace at my muddy shoes but my eye catches immediately on something on the ground. A lot of somethings… The ground is littered with them. Almonds.

I blink and then look up, scanning the trees around me. They're all heavy with young, green almonds. Hands on my hips, I laugh.

"What?" Mike says, watching my face, but I'm looking up. So he does, too. Then he jumps, looks down, leaps back. Swears. And then he's grabbing on to me and pulling me back toward the field.

"Hijo de puta!" he exclaims. "This is mierda de toro! Are you kidding?"

But I can't stop laughing, and the more freaked out Mike becomes, the funnier it is.

He keeps tugging me and I don't resist, unable to contain my hysterics. Mike grumbles, more to himself than to me, "Seriously... We manage to stay out of the radar, and then fate sticks a condenado almond tree grove right smack dab in your maldita carretera... Like some kind of twisted joke... What the hell?"

"Chill, Mike," I say through my giggles. "It's not like fate is shoving them down my throat. It's fine."

Mike lets go of my arm and looks at me. "Are you sure?"

I shrug. "I think so. I mean I walk by them in the grocery store without going into anaphylaxis," I chuckle. "So yeah, I think I'll be good."

"Well a bin in a grocery store is a hell of a lot different than an entire grove of them." He has guided me between two rows, as far away from any of the branches as we can get. But we're surrounded anyway.

We stand a few rows away from the open field we came through to get here. I survey the pale-shelled almonds that litter the ground under my feet from last year's harvest. I actually don't know if it's just the nuts I'm allergic to or the trees and the shells also. Looking at all those almonds on the ground as well as overhead *does* make me a little nervous. I don't have an EpiPen with me should I... I don't know... trip and fall and inhale one as I hit the ground... That's unlikely as far as statistics are concerned, but for me, entirely probable. My life seems to be a constant string of events in which I fall in a grove of almond trees while one gets shoved in my mouth, so I can never be too careful.

Mike is expelling intermittent curses, having walked to the edge of the grove to look back over the field for an alternate route.

The longer I ponder it though, the more glaring the irony becomes and I can't let it go. This should not be ignored. And I've learned a thing or two about situations like this. There is no such thing as coincidence. And this is most definitely ironic to the point of being coincidental, which means it's meant to be more.

"It's a sign," I murmur pensively, crossing my arms and examining the grove as I contemplate it.

Mike comes back to my side. "There's no other way unless we walk through the open field. That's more perilous than walking through the grove. We'll be careful. But you need to tell me if you start to feel even a little bit off."

I shake my head slowly and hold my hands out. "It's a sign."

He grunts. "A sign of what exactly? It's more like a bad omen. My mother would probably be crossing herself right now."

"I don't believe in bad omens. I think bad omens only become that way when you see a sign like this and don't question your course. Because if you see a sign and you ignore it, the bad thing you're headed for is likely to happen... which is where people get the idea of bad omens."

"Okay, so what? The grove magically appeared here to influence us to alter our course?" Mike puts his hands on his hips and scoffs. "There are almond groves all over the central valley. It's not an unusual sight. Besides, you can't do the simplest things without the most ridiculous circumstances following you, causing you to implode the lives of everyone around you."

I appreciate Mike's push-back for once. It gives me more confidence that I'm right, because he sounds like my former self. He's me months right after I married Gabriel when veritable almond trees were put in front of me that I plowed through, nearly ruining everything I had with him. Because I saw things exactly like Mike is seeing this now. This is one of those moments. I'm sure of it.

"No," I say. "I don't think it magically appeared. But we've already had *two* conversations about my nut allergy today alone when most days it doesn't cross my mind. I think it's more likely *those* conversations were had so that this grove could become that much more ironic and therefore stand out the way it does."

Mike scrutinizes the grove as if proof of my theory will be spelled out in the trees. He crosses his arms, looking annoyed. He takes a long time, staring. Thinking, maybe.

"And the blood oranges was a warm-up," I say, my conviction gaining more steam. "We found the *one* fruit tree that would have something to eat this late in the season and we found it right before things got real dire with my blood sugar? I was even about to ask you if the bars had nuts in the ingredients right before I saw that grove. Come on, Mike. The universe was looking out for me then, using trees. And it's looking out for us now with these."

He looks at me and then away, his face stiffening. There goes his mood... triggered by who knows what, as usual. He walks up to a tree and rips a branch off, tossing it as far as he can.

"Sheesh, Mike. Why are you always taking your angst out on the wrong thing?"

He keeps his back to me, staring off into the grove. He crosses his arms, and I think I see his shoulders heaving.

I wait, flabbergasted by his reaction and wondering if I should say something. But I know better after all this time. So I opt to be silent and wait.

After another minute, he hangs his head and sighs.

Then he twists around to look at me, his face wiped clean of his earlier outburst. "What should we do now? Through it, around it, or backtrack?"

"Backtrack," I say. "This grove is huge. We should stop trying to get into town."

"Thing might as well be a wall," he grumbles to himself. Then louder, "And Gabe? I don't know how we're going to get there in time if we don't go through this grove."

"We'll go back to the road. Maybe take the other side of the freeway? Pretty sure there's not much agriculture on that side. We can head north on foot."

"If we're going to take so much risk being spotted, you need a weapon," he says, coming over to me. He lifts up the edge of his untucked, button-up shirt and reveals two guns. These look like the real kind. He grabs one, tucks it into the back of my waistband, and covers it with the edge of my T-shirt. He then lifts up the hem of his jeans to reveal a smaller pistol. He unfastens the holster, lifts up my pant leg, and attaches it to me. I'm not very excited about being loaded with weapons, but I'm not going to argue. Mike scares me when he gets violent and then quiet and decisive. Last time he did that, I ended up jumping into his arms from two stories up.

He rolls my jeans back over the gun, and pauses before standing. "Whitley," he says quietly, looking at the ground and not me. "I can take it when you insult me, when you hate me, when you yell at me. But don't be afraid of me. When have I ever shown that harming you is who I am?" He looks up at me finally, his expression accusing.

My breaths come short, and I feel frenzied for some reason. "I don't know *who* you are," I whisper.

He sighs and stands up. "I guess you don't," he mumbles. Then, more loudly to me, "Let's go. We've got almond trees to avoid." He walks out into the field.

I tug my backpack straps higher on my shoulders and catch up to him. We trudge through the deep earth. Mike takes a different route back toward the road, and we eventually come upon a group of huge sheet metal buildings with farm equipment parked nearby.

Suddenly, however, we spot a cloud of dust in the distance, evidence of an approaching vehicle. Mike reacts quickly, guiding me between two of the buildings, underneath a shelter, and tucking us between the wall and a tractor.

He seems to analyze our options for a moment before saying, "Stay here. I'm going to find out who it is. See if I can get us some help."

"What kind of help?"

He doesn't answer, instead standing up and squeezing out from behind the tractor where I am. Before he disappears from view, he looks at me. "Stay put," he warns. "Don't come out until I get back. And don't hesitate to use your weapon if you have to."

He turns to go but hesitates, turns back around. "You have that sweatshirt you brought?"

I nod.

"Put it on. Put the gun in the front pocket instead. It'll be easier to hide in case…"

I don't like this. "Splitting up is never a good idea in the movies," I point out as I dig the sweatshirt out.

"This isn't the movies."

"Except it is. We're getting chased down by a secret society and you're the Mexican Jackie Chan. And I'm packing way too much heat," I say as I put the gun where he asked.

Mike smiles and tries to suppress his laugh so it comes out as a wheeze instead. "I can't believe you just said you were packing heat." He shakes his head. "Stay put, okay?"

Twenty-seven

This is the first time I've been completely alone since before I was abducted. I come to realize this several minutes after Mike has gone. Even after Shawn left and I had the room at the Guild facility to myself, I knew the cameras were always rolling in my room. With the solitude now, my brain sort of vomits on me with all the things I haven't had a chance to think about for more than thirty seconds: Robert and Gabriel and what they might be up to, the Guild and what they want from me, Kaylen and Ezra. And Robbie… Does he remember me? Anxiety squeezes my lungs at the possibility that Robbie may have the impression that I abandoned him. I can't let my head go there though. It's not going to do anything but put me under the weight of guilt.

As for Robert, he never reacts. He plans. He puts things in motion. The best thing for me to do is act like Robert isn't out there. Attempting to align my actions with his would be impossible. And Gabriel… All I know is he's going to find me. Mike's right. No earthquake will stop him. He'll find a way to get to me. And Mike is going to be working toward the same thing.

What I need to do is decide what I'm going to do about the Guild. According to Mike, they believe I can figure out the cause of the more frequent natural disasters. When Mike brought it up, I wasn't convinced of the problem. But if I really consider it, it's not always the events themselves that are so noteworthy, but how frequently they've occurred. The mountain west, California specifically, has seen a record number of wildfires in the last few years. There has been a severe drought in Russia for two years now. Several devastating tsunamis and earthquakes around the world have made the news recently. Last year when I was in Florida, trying to get home to Monterey, there was a hurricane that was particularly vicious, not to mention out of season. This past winter the northeastern part of the country had two blizzards that dropped several feet of snow in a couple days. Record low temperatures in Europe... I think I remember reading something about that. And oh yeah! Snow in Monterey. I found out that the snow extended all the way down to LA. That was bizarre. And well over a year ago... the lightning storm in San Francisco over the ocean.

So there's a problem, obviously. I haven't acknowledged it until now because the issues in my own life are always the kind that consume every moment.

But do I have a responsibility here? The colorworld is nothing but a memory. The only way I know to get it back is through hypno-touch, which may only grant me abilities at partial strength. And what if they aren't the *same* abilities? So much of a gamble...

Stumped for what to do now, I sigh. These are things I chose not to think about in favor of the possibility of saving Robbie. I'd like to think that if it came down to it, and I was lying on the table, I would not have gone through with it. I just... wanted options. I think that's what I've been after. I don't like how Robbie's condition has nailed all of us down to a future of tests and therapy and drugs. I hate that Robbie will be so limited. I hate that *his* limitations will be borne not just by him but by everyone.

But this is no longer only about Robbie...

As time passes and I mull over the same impossible questions, I calculate how long Mike has been gone, and I begin to worry.

Something is wrong.

My body tenses, and I hunker down further behind the big wheel of the tractor. I reach for my ankle to be sure I remember which side the pistol's on.

I take the other weapon out of my front pocket and test its weight in my hand. I have never held a real gun before, let alone used one. The stun gun was a lot lighter than this. I examine the parts, figuring out how I *would* use it if the eventuality were to arise. In fact, it feels like the eventuality might be now. I have to go find Mike.

I examine all the moving parts. I know what the trigger is, but I'll probably mess something up if I fiddle with anything else. Mike said the safety was on when he put the gun on me. So does that mean I flip that little lever to take it off? Sure, why not.

Once I've got the thing figured out, I hold it out like I've seen people do on TV and feel immediately foolish. I wonder if anyone would take me seriously. I'm more concerned about shooting myself than an offender.

I search for confidence, remembering what it was like to con the pharmacist, how easy that was. I picture some Gordy militia-man taking Robbie, and anger swells. I hold the gun with confidence, thinking this isn't so bad. I crouch further onto the ground and aim underneath the tractor at a tire laying against the wall of the building across from this one, looking through the sights, lining them up.

When I feel like the gun is under *my* control and not the other way around, I put it back in my pocket. I stand up, scooting out from behind the tractor and plastering myself against the sheet metal wall of the warehouse. There is nothing to see here except a bunch of farm equipment—plows and sprayers and a combine. I listen but don't hear anything. So I move toward the closest corner to peek around it.

I see an open field of crops on this side. So I edge along *that* side of the building for the next corner. When I reach it, heart pounding in my ears, I peek around the edge. A black SUV is parked about fifty yards away, and I immediately flash back to the time I was running from several ominous black SUVs at the airport and Cannery Row. I thought they were Robert's, and later Carl's. But it was the Guild.

Coming back to the present, I see two men loading a limp body into the back seat. I recognize the dark skin and white shirt: Mike. Dread funnels into my stomach.

Crap. I lay my head back against the building, fighting to breathe normally. But it's not working. I rub my face with both hands in exhausted fright. If Mike has been seriously hurt… I don't know what to think about that. I *won't* think that. Besides, I never heard a gunshot… Oh please let him have been shot with one of those stun guns…

I stare down at the ground, the seconds passing at lightning speed. I'm losing the opportunity to act.

"What do I do? What do I do?" I whisper.

I put a hand to my chest, close my eyes, try not to let the situation get blow out of proportion in my head. Searching for ideas, however, Mike's last words to me keep bombarding my thoughts on repeat, "Stay put." It brings me no closer to a solution and only makes me more aggravated with him. Did I not tell him it was a bad idea to separate?

"Stay put?" I say in a low voice as if Mike is standing in front of me again. "Sure, I'll stay put. While your sorry behind gets shot by Gordies. Idiot."

Fear is subdued by irritation at Mike. I peek ever so slightly around the corner a couple more times, the second time noticing that the two men have begun approaching the buildings where I'm hiding, no doubt searching for me.

One of them heads my direction, and I pin myself to the wall again. Staying put is not an option. As I imagine what pattern of search they'll make and how I can avoid them, a brilliant idea comes to me: if they're both looking for me, that means they've left their vehicle unattended. With Mike already in it.

I don't think any further. I dash back to the corridor between the buildings where I started among all the farm equipment. I hope the other guy went around the far side of the building next door, because if he didn't, it means I'll run into him in this corridor. I pull the gun from my pocket and stick to the wall of the building, moving as quickly as possible over and around piles of tires, pallets, and unrecognizable farm equipment parts.

I don't spend much time checking around me, partly because I'm too afraid, and partly because it will slow me down. I want to get to their vehicle so I can get out of here.

I reach the other end of the corridor, and the SUV is only about twenty-five yards away. I stop at the corner, look right, spotting a second SUV that direction, near the corner of the warehouse opposite the one I'm next to. Two bodies lie on the ground. Mike's work before he was downed? Oh please let the two men I've seen lurking be the only ones I need to worry about…

I make a mad dash for the SUV where Mike is. I yank the driver's side door open and hop in, pulling it shut behind me.

Still afraid to see if they're hot on my heels, as well as choosing to believe Mike is fine, I fumble for the ignition, my heart sinking when I find it empty. I glance around, but don't see the keys anywhere.

"Shit, shit, shit," I say, slamming my hands on the steering wheel. "Stupid, Wendy!" I don't know why I assumed they'd actually leave the keys behind. They're professionals!

I look up though, baffled that I still can't see them anywhere. They must have actually gone *inside* the warehouses to look.

Worry over Mike drives me to the back seat where he is. No blood… Thank God. Hands trembling, I lay one hand on his chest and search for his pulse with the other. My trembling hands make it hard to pick up the subtleties of vital signs though, so I put a finger under his nose. His warm breath hits my hand.

Putting both my hands on his barely stubbled cheeks, I bow my head, gasping with relief. "Oh thank God," I say. I feel my adrenaline exhaust itself at that moment, and I sob twice, not having recognized how much worry I've been accumulating since I first saw Mike unconscious.

I look out the window toward the warehouses again, and I duck down immediately, having caught sight of one of the men coming around the corner where I was hiding earlier.

My first idea is to conceal myself right here in the backseat. Maybe I can ambush them with my gun?

I don't think I can pull that off. Maybe if it were only one person, but these are two armed and trained Gordies. Between the two of them, they could probably easily beat my reflexes. Anyone who looks at me holding a gun would know I don't know what I'm doing and rightly guess that I don't have the guts to pull the trigger.

Desperate, and keeping my head below the windows, I put my gun back in my pocket. I look for the keys again. I open the center armrest, and my eyes fall on something that fills me with glee: a stun gun. I wouldn't have recognized it as one if I hadn't actually held one earlier because they look so similar to real guns.

I glance quickly to check on the approaching figure, and then, moving gingerly so as not to rock the vehicle, I squeeze down onto the floorboard behind the driver's seat to find the most advantageous position.

Once I'm in place, I expect one of the doors to open immediately, but it doesn't. My nerves at a fever pitch, I feel more idiotic by the moment. And then I hear mumbling outside, but it sounds like the receiving end of a conversation, so there's not much more than a few 'yes sirs.'

No sooner have I thought this than the back opens. I can't see anything from where I am crouched down, but I'm not going to move now. I wish I could blend into the seat indefinitely, rethinking whether this is a good idea.

"Backup's on the way. We sit tight," says a man.

"Dammit, Jim," says a more youthful voice with a southern accent. "I'm tellin' you, she's somewhere in them sheds. I saw two sets of prints coming outta that field. We ought to do another sweep." I listen hard, and it sounds like this voice is *approaching* Jim, the first voice. I'd give anything for them to be right next to each other at the back. But if I reveal myself and actually manage to shoot one while the other one isn't in range, I could really screw myself.

"We are not an extraction team," Jim says. "Those buildings are huge and full of places to hide. And Mike D likely hid her somewhere good. There's only two of us. When backup arrives, we'll find her."

The kid sighs and I hear gravel crunch under foot. I still can't tell if they're both in range. "But we took out *Mike D*. That's 99.9% of the threat. We go through 'em one-by-one. We're lookin' for a scared girl alone with no training."

"We're going to follow orders. Nothing more," Jim replies calmly.

"Try thinkin' for yourself once or twice. If you wanna be a yes-man, go back to the military."

"I believe we agreed I'd take alpha on this mission. Your suggestion has been noted and considered," Jim says authoritatively. "This job is too important to get wrong. Furthermore, we've got grid tech here to protect. We *cannot* leave it unattended."

The young guy grumbles something, but this time I'm sure he's closer to the back. I hear and feel them take something out of the back of the vehicle.

Afraid this might be my only chance, I grip the stun gun in both hands, pop up, aiming over the back seat at the first person I see: a gangly blonde in a black uniform. I wish I had something clever to say before I shoot, but the truth is I'm terrified, and aiming takes my full attention.

I pull the trigger.

It doesn't give to the pressure of my finger though. Nothing happens.

I try again. Nothing. But I sure as heck have taken the young man by surprise. But only for a second. He smiles. "Hello there."

He walks casually around the car while I clamber over Mike's body to the other side to make a run for it, dropping the stun gun to the floor. But when I open the door, Jim is there. Crap.

I strongly consider the real gun in my pocket for a moment, almost moved to reach for it. My fingers twitch, but being confronted with the real possibility of shooting them, I don't think I have it in me.

Jim grabs my arm and removes me from the car, not roughly, but forcefully. He has a gentle face, and he looks at me pityingly. "Don't be afraid," he says, cuffing my hands with one of those zip-tie things Mike used before and holding me against the side of the SUV. "Nobody here wants you harmed."

I have the innate sense that I shouldn't put up a fight. For a second I worry that this uncharacteristic idea isn't my own, that one of these guys has a life force ability that he's using on me. But now that I'm thinking instead of fighting, I realize that docility will keep their guard down, and it might offer an opportunity. Besides, I might end up like Mike if I pin myself as aggressive.

I have no idea what my plan to escape might be, but I wish in earnest that they won't wonder why I'm wearing a sweatshirt in June, that Mike was somehow inspired to make me put it on for this reason, and that they won't search me and discover that I have two guns on me. If I can psych myself up enough, I might be able to use them.

"Team 4 here," the kid says from behind me on the other side of the vehicle. "Target found and neutralized. Awaiting orders."

"Confirmed," Jim, who's standing in front of me, says. There's a pause, and Jim appears to be listening, so I assume he's got a radio in his ear.

"Understood," Jim says, looking over my shoulder.

"I'd like to say this was an exciting take, but that was so easy I probably won't remember it next week," the kid says.

Jim gives him a disapproving look over my shoulder. "This is the way missions should always go. Wishing for gunfire and fistfights is not our way."

The kid stays silent, but I hear him turn in the gravel, and in my peripheral vision I see him lean against the hood. "I guess I should go wake up Nathan and Sahid."

"I don't think it's an NTG," Jim says. "Mike Dumas prides himself on taking people out without weapons when he can. They probably have concussions."

"Arrogant bastard," the kid says.

Jim opens the door next to me, chuckling. "You're just jealous you don't have the same skill. We got real lucky taking him out like we did." He holds me by the arm and pushes Mike's feet off the seat. He nudges me to sit on the edge. I'm in disbelief that the guns are still on me, and I sit down carefully, afraid of letting Jim see the visible lump at my front.

He leans over and picks up the stun gun I dropped on the floor. "It's palm-print-activated," he explains, smiling genuinely at me. Gosh, I hope I don't have to shoot him. "Only works if you're approved in the system."

This is the moment I've been waiting for. The idea is so contrary to the nice things I was just thinking about Jim that I hesitate... But it's now or never. With confidence surging forward that I didn't know I had, I dig my bound hands into my pocket, bring out my gun, press it to Jim's chest.

"You seem like a nice guy," I say in a low voice so that the kid doesn't hear, "but I am *not* going to be separated from my family anymore. I *will* use this on you. If you don't want to lose an organ, you will take that stun gun and shoot blondie. Do it. Now." I shove the gun at his chest, pushing him to the left, closer to the hood, and closer to the kid.

Jim, to his credit, keeps his cool, assessing the situation in a few short seconds. I look him in the eye for good measure, and for the first time I think I might be able to go through with shooting Jim here if he makes the wrong move. Not a lethal shot. But an arm or a kneecap is fair game. And he's close enough I won't miss.

Jim appears to come to this same conclusion, stepping to the side to get a better shot at blondie. He raises the stun gun over the hood of the SUV, and the ping of the shot followed by the sound of something large hitting the gravel behind me indicates he met his target.

I press my gun into him again, forcing him to back up. "Now shoot yourself. Because I'm not leaving you awake to call for help right away."

Jim opens his mouth, but I shake my head and press the gun at his chest again. "No talking. We don't need anyone hearing on the other end, do we? And move that gun slowly so I don't have to wonder if you're going to aim it at me."

Jim nods, eyes pinched as he brings the gun to his hip. He fires.

Jim drops at my feet.

I gawk at him for a few seconds, disbelieving what I just did.

I back up until I feel the vehicle behind me.

"Holy. Crap," I whisper.

My concern shifts to Mike. I turn around, climbing into the back seat with him. I wonder if the 'NTG' Jim was talking about means the stun gun? If so, the kid said he was going to wake up the other two guys... Does that mean that a person shot with one doesn't have to wait for it to wear off? Maybe I can wake Mike up. This area must be crawling with Gordies, and I need Mike to take the best route out so we don't run into more.

I scan Mike's body for the staple-shaped device that I know the stun gun delivers. I lift up his shirt, searching the curves of his chest to his waist. I lift each of his arms, which are really heavy, looking on the undersides of them for where he was shot.

I examine his jeans-clad legs briefly, and then grab on to him to get him rolled over. "Gosh, you are freaking heavy," I say, grunting as I try to roll his shoulders so I can flip him over. It's not working. So instead I move to the top of his head. I bring it into my lap, hook both of my arms under his, and lift with all my might to get him into a sitting position. It works, but I'm sweating as I prop him up with my own back once he's upright. Exhaling a few times to gather my strength, I twist around and hold him up with my hands while I look at his back. "Gosh, you're built like a tank. Do you take steroids? My brother says that's why you have a bad attitude. I think he might be right."

I see nothing on his back.

"Dangit, Mike," I huff. "Where did you get hit?"

Only one last place to look, so I hook my arms under his again, his back to my chest. I take a few breaths to prepare myself while scooting him as close to the edge of the seat as possible. And then, as swiftly as I can manage, I twist his torso as I let him fall back to the seat, this time face-down. But with my arms hooked around him, I fall too. Disentangling myself and pulling my sleeves back, I look at his back again, from his shoulders down to his jeans. And that's when I spot it. I burst out laughing. Mike took a neurotoxin staple right in the behind. Oh my gosh, I can't believe I'm about to dig a staple out of Mike's *butt*.

Giggling as I get my fingernails under the end of it, I pull. It takes a lot more force than I would have expected, but it comes out. I sit back and look closely at it. If I still had superior eyesight, I bet I'd see a lot more than a really sharp staple.

"'njoying yuself back dere, Whit?" a familiar gruff voice garbles.

I jump, nearly poking myself with the staple, which I promptly throw outside. "Holy crap, Mike. You scared me. That wore off fast."

Mike turns his head, his eyes a bit bloodshot. His hand that hangs down to the floor twitches, and I move to sit more out of his way, on the center armrest of the front seat, facing the back. I notice a rack in the cargo area, full of oblong black cases, sort of like the kind that hold musical instruments, all identical, about 24 inches in length.

I turn my attention to the windows though, scanning for anyone that might be approaching. So far so good.

"Are you okay?" I ask him.

"Y'shoved my'eye in the buckle when yuh flipped me over." He brings a hand up next to his face, pressing it into the seat for several seconds before making an effort to sit up. "Damn, I hate that stuff. Feels like lead in my veins."

"Sorry about your eye," I say. "You're as *heavy* as lead. I was lucky I got you flipped over. I never would have found the, uh, staple in your butt otherwise." I laugh again. "I am never going to let you live that down."

He gets into a sitting position, taking concerted breaths. "And I'll never let you live down having to massage my butt to get it to come out."

"I did not massage your butt!" I protest.

"Your word against mine. And I say it takes a little massage to get those suckers out. What would *you* know about Guild technology?"

I glare at him.

He mocks my expression and then brings his knees up one-by-one to stretch them. "And I do *not* take steroids. If you ever imply bullshit like that again I'm going to tell Gabe you made out with the pharmacist to get insulin."

I open my mouth. "He would never believe you."

"Wanna test that theory?"

"If I were you I'd stick with the steroid story. At least then you'll have an excuse as to why you're an asshole." And then something occurs to me. "So you heard me say that while you were knocked out?"

"I told you the NTG only paralyzes. I heard and felt everything." Mike edges out of the vehicle, swaying a little but staying upright.

I spend a few seconds cringing that he was aware the entire time I was searching his chest and then manhandling him to get him turned over.

"Get the keys off Jim, will you?" Mike says, bending down to touch his toes.

I do as he asks, exiting through the front passenger door and finding the keys in Jim's pants pocket. "Are you okay to drive?"

"Yep." He walks gingerly over to me and snatches the keys from my hand.

I frown at his back as I hop in the passenger side. Mike goes around to the other side, but instead of getting in, he bends down and starts messing with something under the steering column. His hand reemerges with a small black box connected to the vehicle with lots of wires. He turns it over in his hands for a moment. A GPS-enabled device of some sort? I expect him to rip it out, but he doesn't. He leaves it hanging and hops in the driver's seat.

"What is it?" I ask.

"Tracker," he replies, pulling the door closed and turning the key.

"You're not going to leave it behind?" I ask as he puts the vehicle in drive.

"Nope," he says, going only as far as the second SUV, where he stops. He backs our vehicle up until its hatch aligns with the other vehicle's.

He opens both hatches and I notice the second SUV also has a rack of identical black cases. What *are* those?

He begins loading all the cases into our vehicle. They don't look light, shaking the car as he throws them in, but he manages. He doesn't offer an explanation.

"Why do we need those?" I ask after he shuts the hatch and gets back in the driver's seat.

"Insurance," he replies.

Aggravated that he's back to communicating the bare minimum, after all I did to get us out of there, I cross my arms and stare out the window.

Snapping turtle, Wendy, I remind myself.

Twenty-eight

Mike drives until we reach a two-lane road, which is actually pretty congested for a country road. People headed away from San Francisco maybe? He stops the car and produces a knife from somewhere. Leaning down, he cuts the wires from the box he called a tracker earlier and tosses it outside. He gets out of the car, lays down on the ground and scoots underneath, leaving only his feet in my view. After a couple minutes, he reappears. But other than a filthy shirt and greasy hands, I have no idea what he was doing under there.

Instead of driving on the paved road, he crosses over it and punches the gas. We drive strictly east over more dirt roads at a frightening speed. I brace my feet and grip the armrest of my door, praying Mike knows what he's doing. We cross over a canal and through several orchards and fields. As if traveling at such a high speed weren't terrifying enough, Mike keeps looking right and then left, like he's searching for something. I bite my tongue, hanging on to patience by a thread. But it's slowly turning into fury. I want to know that Mike has a good reason for driving like this. I want to know what to expect in the next twenty-four hours because it's becoming obvious that we are *not* headed to San Francisco, having been travelling either east or south since we got in the car.

Mike finds what he's looking for rather suddenly, slamming on his breaks. We slide to a stop on the gravel, and I silently thank the inventor of seat belts. Mike turns into an overgrown access road toward a dilapidated, clapboard building. He backs the vehicle up to it once we reach it, and hops out. He opens the hatch and unloads the cases from the rack, carrying two at a time through tall, thick brush and into the abandoned building. Two of its walls are leaning inward precariously, and the other two are half-gone. Mike returns after a minute and grabs two more cases. After three of these trips, I get out and follow him to see what he's doing. Inside the darkness of what looks like it used to be a barn, Mike stacks the cases in a dusty corner next to a couple of rusty fifty-gallon drums. He unloads every single one while I watch with my arms crossed. I see more red with each silent pass. He treats me like those cases: as if I'm cargo that needs to be deposited somewhere instead of a person that has a right to know what's going on.

After shutting the back of the SUV, he drags a bunch of wood over to his pile of black cases until it's completely concealed.

He dusts his hands off and stops in front of me, observing my expression as if it's a curiosity. Then he grins. "I hope you don't think that face is going to work on me. You should save the stank-eye for Gabe, someone who might actually care about your complaints."

He turns for the SUV.

Furious, I look down at the ground, pick up a fist-sized rock, and throw it at him as hard as I can.

"Ow!" He rubs his shoulder where I hit him as he turns around. "What the hell is wrong with you?" he glares.

I stomp around to the other side of the car and hop in, yanking the door closed.

"A rock?" he says disdainfully as he gets in the driver's seat and starts the car. "You actually threw a rock at me..." He says that part to himself, disbelievingly. He pulls back out to the road we were just on and continues east at the same breakneck speed.

"Why?" I ask after a couple minutes, staring at the blur of passing fields from my window.

"We're not going to be able to get into the city. I'd planned to sneak past their lines using their own vehicle, but now that they know that's where you're headed..." Mike replies, not answering the question I meant, but surprising me with more than a one-word answer.

I wait, wondering if I should press for more. I feel his eyes on me so I face him.

"Do you want to know what the cases were?" he asks before I can speak.

Does he seriously need to ask?

I guess he translates my expression, because he says, "It's part of technology called the Grid. It's allows them to scan anyone within a twenty-mile radius they choose."

"Scan?" I ask. "Like facial recognition?"

"Far more complex and accurate than that. But that's why I was adamant about getting twenty miles outside of LA. Think of it as a long-range, heat-seeking scanner. They can see anyone within the radius—create a three-dimensional schematic of the people in the area within the Grid. The program can match your height, body type, movement signatures, silhouette, any data the Grid accumulates to known data. It can find you in the grid area in seconds once it's set up."

Gosh, that was a lot of words all of a sudden. Mike's talk function seems to have an on-off switch. I need to figure out what it is... Rock-throwing maybe?

"So they're in the habit of hunting people down then," I say.

"The intended applications are far more complex."

"Spying?"

"Pfft. From a simple-minded perspective. But no. It predicts natural disasters."

"Sooo, you went from finding people within a twenty mile radius to disaster prediction. Explain how these two things are related?"

"Its development was based on animal behavior. They react to disasters before they hit. Storms, earthquakes, that kind of thing. Tracking the patterns of animal movement would alert them to erratic behavior, warning of an impending event. But they discovered that the technology was too short-range. Setting the Grid up in Florida, for instance, would only allow for event prediction within a few hundred miles of the Grid center. It would never help with predicting things anywhere else. So that use became obsolete. But they discovered that humans within the Grid radius also operate in patterns. And human behavior could predict disasters even thousands of miles away. When animals change their behavior due to an incoming event, they still stay within a range of home. People, on the other hand, have a much farther reach. Their influence can move like a domino effect over the whole globe. With the internet and speed of travel, people in California can have an effect on people not only in the next state over, but across the ocean."

"People don't act weird like animals do," I point out.

"But they do. It's just more subtle. Enough that the Grid picks up on it.

"People are affected by a lot of things though. How do they know if they're acting weird from an impending natural disaster, a murder down the street, or something they read on the internet?"

"They map how those changes in behavior progress over the Grid. If the changes in behavior are sporadic and non-directional, chances are it's something they all encountered via the media. No disaster. If something moves *across* the Grid, directionally, it's not media-driven. It's more likely an impending disaster. Crime events can obviously be ruled out easily enough. It's all highly calibrated. I'm not the guy that translates the data."

"This sounds awfully theoretical," I say. "And way too complicated."

"Only because neither of us are mathematicians. What I told you was a very dumbed-down, rudimentary explanation. It's all about spotting when patterns are broken. Ask your brother. He would totally get it. He's a Prime."

"Ezra? Oh because Carl was his dad and his mom had hypnotouch."

"Yep."

"So if this stuff is moving directionally, it has a source, right?"

"Now you're getting it. That's exactly what it means. That's why they believe a person is causing all of the events."

"So they can use this Grid then, can't they? Maybe set up a bunch of them and triangulate?"

He looks at me appreciatively. "Yes. That's the hope. The Grid technology is the Guild's heart and soul right now."

"Holy cow," I say. "That's intense. In that case, why would they need me?"

"Because the technology isn't being perfected fast enough. And they're concerned the threat is more than one person. The directionality is always changing from one incident to the next, making it difficult to triangulate. Setting up and taking down a Grid is no quick task. They want you to see what they can't."

"Mike... even if I *could* see the colorworld again, what you're talking about needing me to do... that's not how it works. The colorworld is just as senseless as *this* world. It might as well be an alternate reality with its own rules. It would take more than a lifetime to understand it."

Mike sniffs. "To be honest, I don't get it either. Not anymore. When you couldn't tell me why exactly you lost your ability... well it's obvious you don't understand enough about it to do what they need. They've overestimated your capability."

"No kidding," I say, relieved. Worldwide natural disasters are way beyond my colorworld job description. "So this Grid... that's their crowning achievement? Thousands of these Primes and that's all they've done?"

"Of course not. But stopping the disasters is their focus right now. All hands on deck. Developing other technology that will reshape human experience is simply a matter of human resources and priorities. Right now those priorities are making sure there's an actual world left to reshape."

"Got it. And you hid part of their world-saving Grid in a shed, why?"

"I told you. Insurance. Besides, I'm pretty sure they were using it to find you. Couldn't let *that* happen, could we?"

"How do you know? Maybe they were setting it up there because of the earthquake."

"First of all, it doesn't help to set it up *after* the disaster. Second, it wouldn't work for its intended purpose here in the valley because there aren't enough people. It's suited to heavily-populated areas like LA. It takes that much human data to map patterns and spot disturbances. And finally, it's a guess. Based on listening to Jim. Sounds like the spokes can be set up in smaller clusters that have a much shorter range, and they guessed you'd be traveling north. That would allow them to make a pretty good guess about where you'd cross the spokes' radar."

"How'd they know we'd be going north?"

"Ben," Mike says darkly.

"Who is that?"

"Remember the guy who shook your hand in the coffee shop you worked at?"

It takes me a moment. I'd all but forgotten the guy I met the same night I spoke to Carl the last time. But once I draw up the scene, I remember. He had a beanie, glasses, and a nondescript face. He asked about my pregnancy... "What about him?"

"He can track people he's made an emotional connection with."

"We made an emotional connection? I barely remember him."

"It's part of his ability. People naturally like to talk to him. His talent is remembering people's... flavor and being able to sniff it out. Think of him as an emotional bloodhound. But only directionally, generally."

"You didn't take this into consideration when you snuck me out? That one of your Primes could track me?"

"First of all, he doesn't usually remember scents that long. That was what? Four months ago? And second, the plan was to get you to Gabe too quickly for anyone to have time to track you down. I was literally going to drop you off at the airport and get you into Robert's circle of protection immediately."

"Why would this guy remember my scent for so long?"

"Maybe he didn't really. We might have been unlucky enough to pass close to him at some point and he picked up our direction, so even if he only had partial recollection, our closer distance made up the difference. Or maybe you made quite the impression. Were you especially emotional the night you met?"

"I was pregnant, Mike. It's part of the package."

"Hm. That's a good point…"

"I was also depressed the night I met him," I say, remembering the night more clearly now. "Gabriel and I were fighting."

"Fighting?" Mike says curiously. "I thought you guys were perfect for each other or something. Love at first sight and true love and soul mates and all that."

I listen for the hint of sarcasm in his tone that I expect, but I don't hear it. "You don't stay married and in love without effort, Mike," I say. "And besides, I was having a hard time… adjusting. After losing my abilities."

He nods pensively.

"So does this mean we're screwed?" I say. "With Ben out there tracking me."

"All abilities have their limits," Mike says. Then he grins and waves toward the back, indicating the road behind us. "So does the Grid. They can't activate the full Grid without all the spokes."

"They don't have extras?"

"They probably have a few backups, but they're outrageously expensive and time-intensive to produce. We took fourteen spokes. Two sector's worth. And a Grid requires seven sectors. They now only have five. They can't set up the Grid without most of what we hid in that barn."

"They only have one Grid in operation?"

"There are seven total around the world, near the largest populations. They've been up and running for a few years now. Disassembling one is not something they'd do lightly because of the constant stream of data one produces, and with things like they are, they need to be on top of these disasters every moment. I'm still floored that they moved the one in LA just to find you. Years of meticulous data collecting and they tossed it to locate you in the central valley. I'd bet money that's why they didn't see that earthquake coming. That being said, we have a bargaining chip now. They're going to want those spokes back. I can still hardly believe that of all the places we could end up, we ended up at the spot where they planned to set up a sector. And not only was there one sector's-worth to take, there were *two*. Somebody in charge of Grid security is going to lose their job. Blows my mind."

"It was the almond trees, Mike," I say, propping a foot on the dash. "They got us a Gordy car like you wanted. And a way to squeeze the Gordies. That's what happens when you stop working against the universe."

He glances at me, entertaining that idea. About a minute more passes and he says, "You're right about the almond trees."

"Did you just say I was right?" I wrinkle my nose. "That neurotoxin did something to your head."

"Shut up. It wasn't just your almond trees, so you know. My ability made it all come together."

"Your ability? You mean the mysterious Yes-ish? The one that gets you what you want, but only sometimes, maybe if the stars align, but you have no control over it. Or are you talking about another imaginary ability?"

Mike rolls his eyes. "Forget it." He reaches for the buttons on the radio.

"No, no," I insist, swatting his hand away from the radio. "Tell me. I want to know."

"No, you don't."

"Miiike," I beg, tugging on his arm, which causes him to flinch away. "I really do want to know. I was messing with you."

"No."

"Stop being such a baby," I frown.

"What are you going to give me in return?" he asks scornfully.

"What do you *want*?" I ask skeptically.

"Information."

"You told me the intimate details of Gordy's pet project and didn't ask for anything in return then. This reeks of an ulterior motive."

"Oh I already collected payment on that information. You dug an NTG staple out of my ass. That kind of favor demands payment."

About time I got a thank you for that. "What kind of information are you after now?"

"Well… I'll be telling you about my ability. So you'll have to tell me something about yours. But it has to be something big."

I purse my lips. "Not sure if that's such a good idea."

"I'll go first. Then you decide what the information is worth on your end."

I narrow my eyes suspiciously. "That's awfully *trusting* of you. What if I decide your information sucks and not worth anything I know?"

"I trust your judgment. You operate fairly, even if you *are* a pain in my ass."

I scowl. "Fine. Go for it."

"I influence people," Mike says. "Put ideas in their head. Even over long distances, but it becomes unpredictable, especially if the person I'm trying to reach is someone I haven't met personally. Then things can happen in the strangest ways. I've perfected using it one-on-one though. In hand-to-hand combat, for example, I can influence people to move their body a certain way while I'm fighting them and counter their moves before they've begun."

"*That's* why you look like a Mexican Jackie Chan when you fight…" I say, having a revelatory moment. "You choreograph it. Cheater. I bet you're an amazing dancer, too."

"I am," he says, chin in the air. "I can make *anyone* look good while dancing with them, too. And it is *not* cheating. I've trained for years. Hours each day. And I can't do the things I do without being really fit and having excellent reflexes."

I roll my eyes.

"Don't give me that face. I know you enjoyed getting your hands on me earlier. It's okay." He smirks at me.

"Yes, Mike. You're the god of big muscles, and you should star in your own Ninja movie and grace the cover of every romance novel ever. Hell, you're Batman. But with more muscles. Women faint and men hide in shame when you take your shirt off. Do you have a Facebook fan page or something that you need to check periodically in order to satisfy your addiction for daily compliments on your physique? Because being on call all the time for stroking your ego is exhausting."

Mike chokes on his laughter once, twice, trying to stifle it but gives up finally, chortling loudly. "Who needs a fan page? You're doing a great job. Tomorrow, you can tell me more about being Batman."

I smile. "So. I'm waiting to hear more about how Yes-ish saved the day."

"First of all, you have to get that I am always using what I can do. Getting you to Gabe has been my goal since..." He makes a face, hesitates. "Just know it took all kinds of mental influence on my colleagues to do what I did at the Guild. I got too confident at the warehouses, though, and I got shot in the ass—"

"How did *that* happen anyway? I've seen you fight off twenty guys before. And this time you couldn't handle four?"

"Took me by surprise. It was only supposed to be one car. Two showing up as randomly as I needed seemed outside possibility. So I didn't turn around to see someone coming up on me. My ability *delivered* though, because all this time I've been trying to come up with a good bargaining chip, just in case. Had no idea I was getting a two for one on my goals. The SUVs that showed were the last two vehicles in a caravan sent out to set up the Grid."

"*You* brought them? How is that?"

"Sent out the bat signal. The universe answered."

I give him a look.

He shrugs. "Hey, that's how it works long-distance without a particular person in mind. No telling how it'll come back, which is why I miss the mark occasionally. It worked this time because you were paying attention to almond trees. That's the part I suck at when it comes to the bigger stuff. Making the catch. I gotta start looking out for almond trees. That's actually why I told you about the Grid. Figured I owed you something for teaching me that."

"So that's it? You brought two Gordy cars our way with your Yes-ish ability?"

"Oh! I'm sorry. I got us fourteen multi-billion dollar bargaining chips and a getaway vehicle with my mind. What did you do?"

I shrug. "Saved your butt when you got tagged. Literally."

"Ha! Please. You actually think that was all you? You don't have the skill or guts to do what you did on your own."

My mouth falls open. "Ohmigosh. Tell me you were not in my head."

He bobs his eyebrows at me. "Oh yeah, baby. I was all up in your head like Jason Derulo."

"Eeew," I make a face.

"*You'll be screaming moooore, in my head. I can see it going down, going down. In my head,*" Mike sings loudly. "*I see you all over me in my head!*"

"Aaagh! Stop!" I say, covering my face.

He chuckles. "As soon as they downed me I got you to stay put until they started looking for you. I wanted you to get to the car so you could ambush them. Which you did. Except you wimped out or something, and then I heard you excited over that useless NTG when you had an actual working gun in your pocket." Mike shakes his head at me.

"Maybe, if you'd *told* me how those guns work back when I first saw one, I wouldn't have made that mistake," I complain.

"Whatever. You *should* be thanking me. I worked on Jim to keep him from searching you. I practically begged you not to bite and kick him like you did me that one time. And then when I heard him telling you how the NTG worked, I thought, 'if this stupid girl doesn't use that gun in her pocket, we are *screwed*.' The best way for me to influence people is suddenly and in the heat of a moment. So that's what I did with you. Betcha were pretty impressed with yourself, weren't you?"

I remember all the times Mike is talking about. I even remember wondering if someone was using their ability on me. I recoil, not liking the possibilities Mike's ability offers. "So you can make people do things…" I say, testing the ugly words.

"No. I can put the idea in their head. It's their choice whether they take it. You clearly did not take my suggestions all the time."

I'm not sure if I like that better or not… Discomfort slithers down my spine. Mike was in my head… Getting me to do things…

"Your turn," Mike interrupts.

"Is your ability why you were assigned to finding me all those years ago?" I ask, not done with this topic.

Mike seems bothered by the question at first, but after a considerable pause he says, "Yes. Fat lot of good it did me though. Took so damn long. And remember how I told you sometimes things will fall into my lap in the strangest ways?"

I'm rooted to my seat, already knowing where he's going, but hoping I'm wrong.

"You fell into my lap with an engagement ring on your finger," he finishes, saying exactly what I guessed. I don't like the idea that I might have met Gabriel because Mike was manipulating me.

Everything you have now, it's because of me. That's what Mike screamed at me when he abducted me in LA.

"You came to me *through my brother*," Mike says, gripping the wheel harder, his face clouded over.

I clutch my stomach. *You brought me to Gabriel.* That is so messed up. I don't know what to do with information like that.

Mike, however, doesn't hold back now, "I brought you to the compound with my mind. I brought you to your husband, your child, your best friend, your uncle. I kept you from dying of diabetes, stayed in yours and Carl's heads every day to get you to talk to each other, hoping he'd tell you about your biological mom's unconventional autograft treatment... I was the cheerleading voice in your head. Then, when I tried to get you to go to your uncle for help—use his ability—you wouldn't listen. I had to physically *visit* you to get you to go see him. All because the Guild needed *you* alive and I needed my brother. I'm your fairy-freaking godmother, Whitley."

Oh God... How much of the last two years was me, and how much was Mike?

"Mike," I say timidly, afraid. "You remember when you called me that one morning, and I told you Gabriel was in the hospital? And you hung up on me?"

"Of course. It was the first time one of my phone calls actually got through. Your uncle had been running interference for you for weeks. We couldn't touch you. I was so pissed. And then you told me Gabe was in the hospital. I was so sure you'd put him in a coma by touching him. Almost lost it with you and blew my whole cover. That's why I hung up."

"Uncle Moby knew we—?" I stop and shake my head. I have got to stop being surprised about what my uncle has known, and what he probably still knows that he won't say. And the things he has done for me that I'm still finding out about... He knew where we were the whole time we thought we were 'off grid' but he didn't interfere. He wanted us to have some peace... Because he knew what was coming maybe? God love that man. I miss him.

"I ended up using the Guild's resources to see what Gabe was in the hospital for," Mike says, more subdued, staring straight at the road ahead, "because I knew it had to be major. Gabe would never go to the hospital for anything less. When I found out, I wanted to come down right then, but with you having popped up on the radar, I had an emergency meeting in Kansas City to be briefed on my new assignment. But I told them about my brother, that I needed to be there, that I *would* be there whether they wanted me to or not, so they let me go in undercover, try to extract information that way. That's also when I learned about how your version of hypno-touch was lethal. They said that was probably what was wrong with Gabe. They told me you were the only hope for him."

Mike runs a hand through his hair. "I've never hated anyone as much as I hated you at that moment."

His statement should probably sting, but I'm beyond relieved. If Mike was busy hating me, he couldn't have been in my head that night when I found the iron-clad conviction to search for a cure.

"But on the red eye back to California that night, I knew I needed you if I was going to save him," Mike says.

My heart drops. *No.*

"So I started telling you not to give up. If you could break it, you could fix it." He glances at me. "Guess it worked since you were so full of *positivity* the next morning."

Tears are in my eyes and I look away. Dammit. Why does the moment in my life that I felt the greatest strength have to be because of Mike's freaky mind games? The light that consumed me that night… so tangible that I thought I might burst… That was *Mike*? I want that moment to myself. He should not have been there. It's wrong. Have any moments of strength ever actually been my own?

I take several shaking breaths.

"So did you… mentally help me when I was in the white room?" I ask quietly, looking down at my hands.

"With the singing idea, yep."

"And when I was with Shawn?"

"Reading is a sure-fire way to ward off mental influences. I put those books in there, too."

I can't look at Mike. I hate him. I feel like I've been violated. And for the last seven years, apparently I *have* been.

"Why are you telling me this?" I ask acerbically. I want to not believe him. I want this to be another one of Mike's jerk moves where he purposely tries to make me feel bad about myself.

There is silence in the car though. We're travelling on a paved road again, this one as abandoned as I would have expected for the farmland in the central valley. I don't remember when we turned. I can tell by the sunset blazing in my window that we're headed south. But I have no idea where to. I don't care, transfixed as I am by my own despair.

"Because I feel bad about getting physical with you so many times," Mike says out of the blue, and his sudden reply is an indication that he's been deciding whether or not to answer since I posed the question ten minutes ago.

But I don't understand what his answer has to do with my question. He felt bad so he decided to make me feel *worse*?

But then I get it suddenly. Warmth washes over me, and though I fight against it, I can't help losing myself to what I now understand as Mike's first effort at vulnerability with me, at making amends.

He's giving me power back. He's saying he's done hunting me. He told me his ability works best when he catches people off-guard, when they don't stop to question the ideas he puts in their heads. By telling me, he's given me back that power.

"Thank you," I say softly, still unable to look at him. But I mean it. And maybe I don't hate him. But I don't know who I am, who I've been all this time, unaware of how much of my actions in the past couple years were my idea or Mike's.

Yanked too many directions at once, and lost for a purpose as I struggle to make sense of my recent past, I can't find conviction or reason to continue to guard the secrets I've sworn I'd keep until death.

"I used to be able to share my abilities with other people," I say without a hint of remorse for saying so.

"Share your abilities...?" Mike questions.

"Yeah, super-sight, super-smell, super-hearing. That's what allowed me to see the colorworld. I also shared my emodar. I could share those abilities with people who could touch me without dying. They could experience the colorworld, too."

Mike slams on the brakes, eyes bulging and wild. He blinks. He does it five more times before he says, "Are you telling me the truth?"

I nod.

His mouth falls open. "Holy... Holy mierda."

"So. Does the Guild already knows this? Because Carl could do it, too?"

"I am positive they know it," he replies. "I had no idea either of you could ever do that. But it finally clicks why they're stopping at nothing to find you. You're the Holy Grail of life force abilities."

I roll my eyes. "Holy Grail? Oh spare me. They've got crazy Grids that can spy on everyone in a twenty-mile radius and predict major geological events. I see pretty colors. And I can show other people pretty colors. Big deal."

"It's gotta be more than that," he says. "You're playing down what you can do. *Carl* could see pretty colors. You're a second-generation Prime. You had to have seen more. I mean hell, you explained to me why Carl lost his ability. You can tell how bright someone's soul is. And you managed to save over a hundred people by fixing their life force. How did you do that? How? It can't be just seeing pretty colors."

"Life forces are made up of strands. Billions. Hypno-touch yanks them out of place. Gabriel counted them. Kaylen used her telekinesis to put them back in place."

Mike is staggered. "And the pool trips?"

"Water is the only thing in this world that can affect life forces. It separated the strands enough that we could work with them."

Mike lays his head back. "Holy mierda. Whitley, you are seriously underestimating your value."

"You said not half an hour ago that the Guild *over*estimated my ability."

"I was wrong."

"Mike, I didn't do anything by myself." The words are heavy. "I didn't have any mental breakthroughs except for figuring out that Kaylen's telekinesis worked on life forces. I just saw stuff…"

"That other people translated," Mike finishes insistently. We are still at a full stop in the middle of the road. "Are you listening to yourself? Get some of the Primes like the people who actually engineered the Grid in your colorworld with you, and tell me they couldn't figure out how to track these natural disasters back to their source. You got together with a couple talented people and figured out how to fix a life force made up of billions of strands. With ten thousand various Prime abilities at your disposal analyzing the makeup of the energy world, then anything can be done." He looks ahead and begins driving again, more slowly. "Man, I can't believe—I mean I can. But damn, I'm ignorant. All this time, I knew you were important. But I didn't even conceive this."

I sigh, unconvinced. "Doesn't matter. I can't do it anymore anyway."

"Thank God," Mike says.

I look over at him. "Why do you say that?"

"Because I'd be obligated to take you back."

"You keep a strange set of rules."

"You have no idea."

Twenty-nine

The view when I wake up is gorgeous. A blue lake stretches out from the rocky shore where we're parked to touch the gentle slopes of the mountains in the distance. The sun behind me kisses the ripples of the lake, and a soft breeze brings the scent of it through the crack in my window.

It's a view that should bring contentment, but I remain uninspired. And we've officially missed our rendezvous with Gabriel. What now?

Mike is outside the car already, skipping rocks across the surface. He looks happy. I can't see his face, but it looks like something someone would do if they were happy. We haven't spoken much since his confession last night. I didn't feel much like talking. And Mike was focused on stealing a new car, one less conspicuous than our Guild SUV now that we're not going to San Francisco. We are now the proud car thieves of a junky minivan.

I open the door of the van and step out, stretching my arms toward the cobalt sky.

"Show me how to do that," I say, coming up behind him.

"I am. You're watching, aren't you?"

"So if I watch you I'll become a rock-skipping expert. Is that what you're saying?"

"No guarantees."

"Isn't that the truth," I mumble, picking up a rock that looks as flat as the one he chose.

I watch the way he moves, leaning over, holding his left arm out while he holds his right elbow close to his waist, his wrist the source of power as he flicks the stone like a discus.

I take a couple steps closer to the lake and copy him.

I fail miserably. My rock flops.

"Takes practice," Mike says, his rock bouncing over the surface six times before sinking.

I try again. And again. Each time the rock sinks as soon as it hits. But I have to admit, it's a satisfying sound—the plunk as it contacts the water's surface.

So I pick up a handful of stones and chuck them, one by one, into the water, relishing the sound that's slightly different each time if I really listen.

Plonk.

Plunk.

Ploink.

PluUNK.

Mike glances at me a few times, and finally says, "Show me how to do that."

"It can't be duplicated," I say, throwing another rock in.

"Is that right?"

"Listen." I throw a particularly large stone in. It makes two sounds. A smack as it hits and then a plunk as it sinks in.

I throw a much smaller stone in. It makes a higher-pitched splash.

"No rocks are created equal," I explain. "Can't duplicate the sound."

"My, aren't you reflective this morning."

I stop throwing and look at him. "My, aren't you nice this morning."

He sits down on the ground, facing the lake. "Probably shouldn't get used to it."

I pick up another handful of rocks and keep throwing. "Where are we?"

"Lake Isabella. It's northeast of Bakersfield."

"Kind of out of the way, aren't we?"

"That's the point. We sure weren't going to make camp in Bakersfield."

"I mean, you're practically parked *in* the lake. How did you get down here?"

"I drove here a lot when I was a teenager so I know my way around, and I wanted to get as close to the water as possible."

"Uh, okay. You were... thinking about dumping my body here?"

He gives me a look over his shoulder. "Remember I told you all abilities have limits? Water scrambles Ben's. Being close to it makes it hard for him to smell you out. Actually, water does that for a lot of abilities. So it's usually a good rule of thumb to stick close to it if you want to avoid Primes who might be using their abilities on you."

I pause in throwing the rock I have ready, instead turning it over in my hands. Kaylen's ability was limited by water as well... I look at the lake, pensive.

"His ability must detect energy vapor trails somehow," I say, throwing my rock in. "They dissipate when they hit water."

"Energy vapor?" Mike says, twisting around to face me.

I throw the rock in. "It's related to emotions. Powers some abilities. I don't know much more than that."

Mike shakes his head. "There you go again. Underestimating your ability. Energy vapor trails? Sounds exactly like what they're hoping you can track with your sight."

I toss the rest of the rocks in my hand into the water and wipe my hands on my jeans. "Doesn't matter. I can't see it anymore."

Mike faces the lake again. "What's bugging you?"

I grit my teeth. So now he's my therapist?

"Nothing, Mike," I say. "So what's the plan today?"

He's silent for a moment, and I'd like to imagine that he's thinking about pressing me, that he might actually care a little bit about what's bugging me. But I've been bitten enough times by Michael Dumas that I don't fool myself for long.

"We need to contact Gabe," Mike says. "I've been racking my brain for someone the Guild won't already be watching who can deliver a message. But I'm drawing a blank."

"Ask a stranger."

"Won't work. As soon as they contacted Gabe, the Guild would find them and start interrogating. It needs to be someone that the Guild isn't watching that'll keep a secret no matter what."

"So everyone I have ever known is under surveillance?"

"Guarantee it."

"But my uncle specializes in *counter*-surveillance. You don't think he's taken into consideration that people are going to monitor him?"

"If anyone can avoid Guild surveillance tech, it's your uncle. But I don't know for sure. And with what I know about your ability now, they'll spare no effort. They get their hands on you, you disappear. Your uncle won't have a prayer of finding you."

"Are you sure they know about *everyone* I've known?"

"Try me. After seven years, I have your file memorized. If it's in there, I'll be able to tell you."

"Quinn Reese."

He twists around to look at me again. "Who is that?"

I smile. "Guess you shouldn't have made that guarantee after all. He's an ex-boyfriend."

"From when?" Mike says, disbelieving.

"High school."

Mike keeps silent for a moment. "And you have enough rapport with this guy still to ask for this kind of favor?"

"Oh yeah. Quinn and I go way back." Although I could *not* have predicted I would be needing him for a first time, let alone a second.

"Where does he live?"

"Watsonville, last I knew."

"That's less than ideal," Mike says. "Watsonville is too close to Monterey. And San Francisco. I did all that driving to get away from there."

"We can't just call him and ask? I don't know his number, but give me some time on a computer and I can find it."

"No," Mike scoffs. "Do you hear what you're suggesting? 'Hi, Quinn. It's Wendy. Your ex-girlfriend. Look, I need you to get a super-secret message to Gabriel. Write this down.' We need to see him in *person*. Phone calls can be recorded. Scanned. Flagged. If you think they don't have their ear to the ground to find out if you contact someone they don't know about, you need to start thinking more like a movie. Assume they have capability you never thought you'd see outside the silver screen."

"Fine," I grumble, crossing my arms. "So you're saying he's got to *deliver* the message in person, too?"

"Oh yeah. Your husband and your ex need to get together. I'm sorry I'm going to miss it, because Gabe is a jealous SOB."

"Actually, Gabriel loves Quinn."

Mike gapes at me. "You gotta be joking. When did they meet?"

"Right after that time Kaylen creamed the Gordies that were trying to corner us at the mall," I smirk. "That was you guys, right?"

"The Del Monte mall? Yes," Mike grimaces. "That was a bad day. We lost four guys. We didn't know she was a Prime. Underestimated what she could do."

"Kaylen's a Prime? But I thought she had hypno-touch at a young age."

Mike gives me a sidelong glance. "She can uproot trees and throw cars around and you assume that's a *hypno-touch* ability? There's no way."

I shrug. We don't actually know who Kaylen's real parents were, so there's no reason to argue. Her ability is scary powerful, which brings me to the other part of Mike's statement. "You lost four?" I ask, not really wanting the answer.

Mike nods.

"Sorry," I say quietly. "We were just... trying to get away. And I knew by listening that we were surrounded. And Kaylen's ability *isn't* usually that beastly. She, ah, touched me and I kept her going longer."

Mike twists around to look at me critically. "You did what you had to do. Why are you apologizing?"

I shrug. "I don't like the idea that Kaylen killed people or that I helped her."

"It happens," Mike says. "You can't expect to keep your hands clean when you're fighting for what you think is right."

I lean against the car. "I can see that line of reasoning helps *you* sleep at night."

He growls something that sounds like, "You just don't have enough enemies yet."

"You already fed me that line at your apartment," I say. "You guys have been doing a fine job giving me enemies. For the last two years, looking over my shoulder is all I've done."

"Speaking of which, can you explain to me how the hell Robert's men took down three of ours in the pitch dark in the woods that night you were converging on Louise's compound?"

I'd forgotten about that... So I was right. It wasn't Carl or Louise that tried to take us in the woods. It was the Guild. "I gave Sam and Farlen my sight so they could see your guys in the darkness. Life forces can't hide."

"Oh look, *more* blood on your hands," Mike muses, slightly taunting. "Squeaky clean Wendy... How does it feel to have disposed of six people's lives?"

So only one of the people Sam shot lived... I cross my arms tightly, not looking at Mike. I admit I feel a lot less than I would have expected. But that doesn't sit well, because somewhere along the way

I have detached myself from those people I had a hand in killing. They were faceless threats. I never once paused to imagine who they left behind or what impact they left on the world. I hate that simply by threatening me, I discounted them as people.

"The difference between me and you, Mike," I say, "is that I'm not okay with it."

"You are such a saint," Mike gushes. "Oh Wendy, how can I ever compare!"

"You can't," I say. "Don't even try."

Mike throws his head back and makes a gurgling sound. "You can't possibly get anything done second-guessing yourself constantly like that."

"Says you."

He shakes his head. "So. *My brother* loves your ex-boyfriend. That's bullshit. I can't wait to meet this guy."

"Let's go. I'm hungry."

"We need to do something about our appearance before we go out on the town. My parents live here. I'm sure the Guild has people here, watching. I'm actually nervous as hell about it."

I hadn't thought about that... "People? You mean they don't actually have facial recognition? They can't use the millions of cameras out there to spy on people instead?"

"Sure they do. But the number of cameras that are actually networked to an online system is pretty small. If it's not online, it can't be hacked. And even if it is, most don't have continuous feeds. They can gain control of a camera if they know where to look. They can even watch out for you in an entire city if they know you're there. But they can't process data from the millions of cameras out there continuously."

"They have it in movies. I thought you said all that stuff was real."

"One day soon, it will be."

"So are we dying our hair or something?"

Mike grimaces as he comes to his feet. "I do *not* dye my hair. A baseball cap and new clothes will work."

"You and Gabriel are a couple of pretty boys," I chortle as I get in the car and shut the door.

"No. We both have really great hair," he says, turning the key. "You can't mess up what God blessed you with. It's ungrateful."

"So you're not an atheist like Gabriel, I take it."

"No, I am not."

I guess that's that. Mike doesn't offer anything more, and I'm not pressing. Instead, I find my test kit to check my glucose while deciding what color I want my hair to be. I have the urge to do something drastic.

Thirty

Mike looks at me like I've sprouted horns. "You can't be serious."

I don't reply as I plug the clippers into the wall of the gas station bathroom. He'll have the answer to that soon enough. I look at my chin-length hair one last time. I turn this way and that, thinking as I have so often the last few months that my hair is more red since the chemo. And less curly.

"Why?" Mike says.

"You said we needed to disguise ourselves."

"We need to *blend* in, not look like weirdoes."

"If we look anything like *us* we're not going to blend in. What we want is to look nothing like ourselves so they overlook us." I eye the bundle Mike has tucked under his arm that I know contains jeans and a T-shirt. "You might as well raise a flag saying 'Here I am' with those clothes."

"What's wrong with them?"

"It looks exactly like something you'd pick out."

"Because I did."

I roll my eyes and check the setting on the clippers. I turn them on and lean over the trash can I've positioned in the sink as I start moving them over my head, back to front. I did this once before when my hair was falling out during chemo. I remember feeling disheartened at first. But when I was done, I looked in the mirror and felt oddly liberated. Having one less thing to worry about, I felt more focused. Dedicated. When I finally began curing people I wore my purple scarf most of the time, but the few times it was nothing but my bald head I felt proud of it.

I want to feel proud of myself again.

I check the mirror a few times to make sure I didn't miss anything, running my hand appreciatively over the texture. "How's the back?" I ask Mike, glancing behind me at him. His eyes are wide and he's rooted to the spot.

"Did I miss anything?" I repeat, turning my head again to give him a good view of it.

"Yeah, uh, right in the middle," he replies finally.

"Will you get it?" I shove the clippers at him. He fumbles them, and it's the first time I've seen his reflexes fail.

I turn around though and hold still, waiting. After a few moments I hear the click and the hum as he turns them on. The clippers move lightly against my head as he makes a few passes. Then he moves them further down my neck and I tuck my chin.

The clippers turn off, and I look in the mirror again. I run both hands over my head to brush away the cut hair and sigh at my reflection. I look different from the last time I was hairless, being a lot less healthy at the time, but it still stirs memories. Compared to now, it was a simpler time. There weren't any huge decisions looming over me like now. I was happy with who I was, unlike now. Recapturing the inner-peace of that time for a fleeting moment, I close my eyes and hold it close.

I feel Mike's eyes on me though, disturbing the moment. So I take the clippers from him, winding the cord up. It's probably true that there were other, less-dramatic means of disguise, but I need this reminder. The silence becomes awkward, so I say, "Seriously, Mike, you need to do something other than a T-shirt. You're going to jeopardize both of us."

"I am not. Everyone wears T-shirts. And jeans. *Not* everyone has a bald head."

I roll my eyes at him. "Mike, it's not about the T-shirt. There aren't a whole lot of guys with your amount of musculature. If you wear a T-shirt, *everyone* is going to be looking at you. Guild or otherwise."

"The *words* seem complimentary, but the *tone* is insulting."

I turn away from the mirror. "Mike, admit it. You're out of your element this time. Now turn around or get out of the bathroom so I can put on this awful dress."

He turns his back to me but crosses his arms. "What makes you say that?"

"It took you twenty minutes to pick out a pair of jeans," I say, lifting my shirt over my head.

"Because I don't buy jeans from thrift stores."

"Why would that matter? Jeans are jeans." I pull the blue dress I picked out over my head. It's long and flowy, and probably not as ugly as I imagine. It feels awkward. I look matronly in it, and I haven't gotten to the point where I feel like a woman instead of a girl. But it does its job, giving me a look I've never worn. It took some practical arm-twisting to persuade Mike to even enter the thrift store to buy clothes. He wanted to buy new, but he couldn't deny the need to save money. The clippers were an afterthought. I spotted them for five bucks in the appliance section and I knew immediately what I wanted to do with my hair.

"But these were *worn* by someone," he scoffs. "I don't know where they've been."

I can't help laughing this time as I pull my jeans off from under my dress. "Seriously? What's the worse-case scenario for where they've been?"

He turns and gives me a disgusted look.

I roll my eyes and shake my head. "Must be nice to have lived your pampered life. Never having to budget. Buy *used*."

"What would *you* have picked out for me to wear?" Mike asks.

"Something you're too much of a baby to be seen in."

His eyes narrow and he licks his lips. "Is that right? Challenge accepted."

I look at him doubtfully. "You're going to give me free reign to choose your wardrobe?"

He shrugs. "First, you assume your minimal life experience better qualifies you to disguise me. And second, you say I don't have the balls to wear something outside of my comfort zone. If someone calls me to the carpet, I don't shirk."

I give him a challenging smile and throw my hands up. "Back to the store then," I say, pushing open the bathroom door.

We walk a couple blocks back to the thrift store, Mike following me, his head on a swivel. I'm sure we *are* being watched, but not by Gordies. Mike is not someone people would overlook. His build is intimidating no matter who you are, and he seems to want to constantly keep it on display. The button-down shirt he left the Guild wearing is not only a fitted style, but he rolled the sleeves up as soon as we escaped the day before yesterday. If Mike would smile at people even a little bit it would go a long way to altering their perception of him as a weight-slinging junkie with an ego and a bad attitude.

Sliding men's shirts one-by-one over the rack rhythmically, I have my eye out for something in particular, and it doesn't take long to find it. I hold up the red-plaid, collared shirt for Mike to see.

His eyes widen a tiny bit, and he looks from the shirt to my face, back and forth several times. I can tell he is suppressing a reaction. I shove it in his hands and smirk after I turn around. Mike wants me to think he's an unflappable badass, but he's not as tough as he thinks if a lumberjack shirt can throw him off that much. I head over to the next row, which includes jeans. Having watched Mike thumb through them earlier, I know what his size is. And I also know which pair I want him to have.

I grab the faded pair of boot cut jeans with worn hems and knees and throw them at Mike. I catch his eyes narrow.

I go over to the accessories and grab the belt with the large brass buckle sporting a silver star and a black cowboy hat that I saw earlier. I also find several pairs of used cowboy boots. The one pair in his size is black, and although they look cheaply made, they're practically new. Leave it to Bakersfield, a more agriculture-oriented place complete with farms and cowboy attire.

"Perfect," I say, shoving the boots into Mike's chest and heading for the register. The cashier graciously lets us exchange the clothes Mike bought earlier for this slightly more expensive purchase, and we leave the store, me walking ahead and feeling smug.

Mike has not said a word since he told me to pick out his clothes, but the look on his face says he is *not* happy with this. I'm not entirely sure why he's letting me take control of his wardrobe, but it must be because he knows I'm right about the disguise, or maybe he just doesn't like backing out of a challenge.

We find a back alley lot and I turn my back while he gets dressed, biting my lip to suppress my grin. I'm not sure why I'm so giddy except that I feel like I've won a victory with Mike.

I hear a pause and the crunch of shifting feet after a couple minutes.

"You done?" I say.

When he doesn't reply I turn around. Mike is standing outside the driver's side door, so I come around to take a look.

He shifts his feet, his hands on his hips.

I bite the inside of my cheek and lift my eyebrows.

"Ready?" Mike says tightly, opening the driver's side door.

I'm content to watch him. He looks freakin' *good.*

He looks at me over the top of his door. "You coming? Or are you too much of a baby to be seen with me?"

Slightly confused by his statement, as well as embarrassed to be gawking at him, I go back to my side.

Once we're on our way to the FedEx office where I'll look up Quinn's information, the weird air in the car doesn't leave. Thinking the only cure is honesty, I say, "You look hella good, Mike."

He glances over at me, surprise on his face for a millisecond before it resumes its usual unapproachable surliness. It remains there for a few more silent moments. His mouth dissolves into a sly smile eventually. "Well damn. No one ever told me checkerboard flannel was white girl ambrosia. Going to have to get this shirt in a few more colors."

"White girl ambrosia?" I snigger. "Oh yeah. That shirt is to die for. Just don't tell anyone I told you that. It's an Aryan secret."

He laughs. "Sure thing. And by the way, you do pull off bald really well."

Looks like Mike is a little more box turtle today.

Thirty-one

I'll be damned," Mike mumbles as we both look at the computer screen. "USC. That's way better than him being in Watsonville. And with the Grid out of commission, we're free to go back to LA."

"Looks like he's on his way to medical school like he wanted," I say, hating that I still struggle to feel happy for Quinn.

"Dammit, it's June though… He's probably off for the summer."

I purse my lips. "Mmm, maybe. Quinn has worked really hard to be able to go to college. I bet he's taking summer classes. That's what I'd do."

Mike scrolls through what we can see of Quinn's Facebook feed, which isn't much, just a few pictures of him being tagged in campus events. Everything else must be private. Mike taps the screen on a photo of Quinn with another student. It looks like they're in a classroom lab. "This was posted two days ago," Mike says. "I think you're right. It's worth a shot."

My enthusiasm for this mission is sinking by degrees every moment, and though my minor victory with dressing Mike lifted my spirits, I now feel worse than I did this morning when I woke up to Mike skipping rocks. Quinn got into the University of Southern California and is going to be a doctor… And here I am… on the run again…

That gives me pause as I recognize that somehow I have been repeating a cycle and haven't been aware of it. In my experience, that's a bad thing.

"Why don't you have a Facebook account?" Mike asks, interrupting my ruminations. "That boggled me when I was, ah, keeping tabs on you."

I blink and come back to the present. "Um, because of my mom. She was paranoid about putting personal information online, so she never let us do stuff like that. Guess it rubbed off on me. Makes a lot more sense in retrospect though…" I look at Mike. "I never knew she was always running."

*And so am I…*More repeating cycles.

"She was one smart cookie," Mike says. "I have to give it to her for keeping you from being found all those years."

"Yeah…" I say, barely hearing him as I attempt to work out where in life I have taken another wrong turn.

"We've got what we need," Mike says, closing out our online session and pushing his chair away from the desk. "Let's get out of here. I swear I can feel Gordies closing in on us. And these jeans chafe. I'm ready for this to be over with."

In the car, Mike looks at me as he accelerates into the street. "What's up? You look like you've seen an almond tree."

I turn my attention to him, his words making more sense than I'd like to admit. In fact, my reaction to spotting the cycle was similar to when I saw the almond grove. Both were nothing but ironic happenstance until I thought about them beyond face value. As I contemplate my situation and how similar it is to the last time Quinn and I crossed paths, the more attention it demands. Repeating cycles are dangerous. Look at me and Carl. We lived practically the same life until I saved Gabriel.

"What makes you say that?" I ask, genuinely curious how Mike would draw such an accurate conclusion, one I didn't see until he suggested it.

"The look on your face. Exactly like your expression when you saw the almond grove. Not completely present but definitely not idle."

I furrow my brow. "I didn't realize you were paying attention. You kept pitching a fit about the grove putting a crimp in your plans…"

Mike doesn't answer for a moment, staring at the road ahead. "It's my job to be observant." Then he glances at me. "So I was right then… that you saw an almond tree?"

"Where would I have seen an almond tree?" I say. "We were inside."

He rolls his eyes. "You're stalling my question. I didn't mean a *literal* almond tree. Don't act like you didn't know that."

"It's not really any of your business," I say, crossing my arms and staring out the window.

He doesn't respond, and I use the silence between us to figure out what I'm missing this time, what I've done wrong to plunge myself so fully into a situation I've already been in. But I can't concentrate. My intellect has met a brick wall. All I know is that I'm here because Mike kidnapped me. The last time I was on my way to Quinn, it was because I was running from Mike and the Guild. I just didn't know it. Mike. That's the only common denominator I arrive at. And in fact, I fled north initially both times...

"I realized that the last time I saw Quinn was because of you and the Guild," I blurt. "I realized I've done this before—been on the run from you people. Mike—" I stop, feeling my voice rising. I crack my window to get some air. "Before now, you were just another guy. You were... Gabriel's brother that we rarely saw. You almost never crossed my mind. I never thought of you as anything more than an annoying asshole that occasionally came around to piss me off. And now I'm finding out that everything I've gone through and done and felt and struggled with... every moment that has been most wonderful and most terrible, you were always in the details. In my head. In my obstacles... In *Gabriel*. And I just... hate it. This whole Quinn thing has all the signs of an almond tree because of how similar the circumstances are to the last time I saw him, and I know I'm missing something. And I'm pissed off that you've been violating me all these years. I don't know who I really am because I don't know how much of my actions were you."

Mike is taken aback. "Wen, I only put ideas in people's heads. It's totally up to them if they take it. I don't make anyone do anything." Though I notice he used my actual name and that he said the words more gently than his usual tone, it doesn't erase my feelings even a little. If anything, his words are more infuriating because he just doesn't *get* it.

"Easy for you to say," I reply. "It's nothing to you because you've spent seven years obsessing over me and my life. You've been studying my every move. You probably profiled me. Tried to predict my actions. You know me on a level that most people don't, so to you that makes your actions toward me seem okay. It makes your mental violation seem *okay*. But I know *nothing* about you. I've been oblivious. I'm... I'm trying... I want... Agh!" I put my hands to either side of my head, discouraged with not being able to articulate my problem.

I roll my window the rest of the way down, closing my eyes as air blasts my face.

"If I…" Mike says after a few moments.

I wait, but he doesn't finish. I turn. "If you what?"

He doesn't look at me, but I can see that he's got the steering wheel in *both* hands rather than his usual, casual, one-handed grip. I've unsettled him, but if history is any testament, he's going to hold it all in. Familiar bitterness toward him creeps up on me, but I get now why I've tried so hard with Mike. I've just wanted him to come clean. To open up somehow and show me who he actually is. To maybe be a little *sorry*. Because if I felt like I knew him at all I would feel a lot less like I've been violated. There's a deficit between us that demands to be remedied.

When Mike refuses to answer, when he refuses to show any remorse as usual, I become livid, and the need to hurt him is so strong that I can't resist it. "I'm finally realizing what you are: A criminal—the worst kind. You've taken things from me without asking. You've forced me into situations I never consented to. What you've taken from me are things that money can't replace. All while I've been oblivious. I've been this huge part of your life and I never consented. That's what they say about thieves and rapists, Mike. That's what's so traumatizing about those kinds of things. You're a rapist. Maybe not of my body, but that's what you are in every other way imaginable."

Mike jerks the wheel and grinds to a halt on the side of the road, his eyes boring into me the entire time. I can feel them although I'm not looking his direction. Once we come to a complete stop though, I open my door and snatch up my bag at my feet. And I begin walking. I want to get away from him because I haven't felt this inclined toward violence since I found out Carl tricked me into harming Gabriel. I want to hurt Mike. I want to make him feel what I do. Like dirt. Like less than human because I've been used by him for so long. But I don't have those emotional tools anymore. I'm stuck alone inside my own head. But tears come to my eyes anyway, though I'm not exactly sure why. I feel far more vengeful than sad.

I cross the shallow ditch that runs next to the freeway and up a hill, headed toward some trees where I can scout out where to go next. I have not looked behind me to see if Mike is following, but if he were, he would have caught up to me and manhandled me back to the car already. I don't think he will this time though. I've made some grave accusations, and even Mike mentioned earlier how ready he is for all this to be over. He's *got* to be tired of this song and dance between us by now. I know I am. I want Gabriel so badly I can hardly breathe—I think that's what has prompted the tears.

As soon as I reach the top of the hill, I spot the town I was expecting and an extravagant-looking truck stop. I make a beeline for it, grateful that Mike hasn't pursued me. With Gabriel so weighty on my mind, I spend the walk convincing myself over and over that I *cannot* call him, no matter how desperate. I push him out of my mind, too close to the breaking point.

The truck stop is two stories, complete with convenience store, showers, two restaurants, and a hair salon. I walk up and down the aisles of candy and packaged snacks, my head too frazzled to know what I'm going to do next. I look for somewhere to hide out, but unless I want to pay twelve dollars for a shower room, a bathroom stall is as good as it gets.

It doesn't afford me the quiet I need to formulate a plan, however. People come in and out periodically, making me nervous and jumpy. Too fidgety to sit, I lean against the wall of the stall, arms crossed, but my hands keep shaking. I dig through my backpack to test my blood sugar, but it reveals normal levels. I don't know what's wrong with me other than raging emotions, so I squat down on the floor and wrap my arms around my knees, tucking my head into my lap in case this is the start of a fit of hyperventilation.

"I'm sorry," says Mike's voice.

I jump. My head snaps up, and at first I think I'm hearing things. But a grand sigh emanates from the stall behind me and I lean down to see underneath. That pair of cowboy boots is familiar.

Mike is in the women's bathroom?

I don't answer, mostly because I don't know what to say.

"God, I'm so sorry," he repeats. "I never saw it that way."

The main door to the bathroom opens at that moment, and the person takes the remaining stall. It gives me some time to process Mike's appearing here suddenly as well as his apology. I'm not sure what he's apologizing for exactly—he has a laundry list of slights against me—but I want to latch on to it anyway. It gives me a thrill of relief that I can't explain. The stranger washes their hands and exits, and I say the thing that's now bouncing around my head, "Why do I want to forgive you so easily?"

Mike doesn't have an answer, and I wonder if I *want* to forgive him because *he* wants me to, and he's got me under his spell again...

"You're a bad guy," I say. "Everything you've done to me should put you squarely in that category. I'm stupid for having trusted you even a little. I feel like… like one of those naïve girls that dates bad boys because she harbors some secret hope that she can tame them. You're arrogant as hell. Manipulative. You aren't that pleasant to be around. You almost never smile. Pretty much the only things you have going for you are muscles, good looks, and Jackie Chan moves. I've never been that girl, Mike. Instead I ate guys like you for breakfast once upon a time. I was never fooled by your type. So explain to me why it is that I can't seem to give up hope that one of these days I'm going to win you over? Because I should know better. I *do* know better. But then I get you to smile or laugh or say something even remotely personal, and I feel vindicated, like I've managed to prove all along that you are who I want you to be."

I hear him shift. I hate not having emodar so, *so* much. Whether Mike is going to come back with insults or more apologies, I couldn't say.

"You know what I've noticed about my ability?" Mike says finally. "Two things. The first thing is something I figured out yesterday. The people who are most susceptible to it are always the strongest ones. The ones who have their shit together, who know what they want out of life. It's like… being happy makes people more open-minded, which makes them more willing to entertain ideas that come into their heads that are outside of their usual habits. Because they aren't afraid of venturing beyond their comfort zone. And I think… they do a lot more listening. They notice a lot more than other people. Like you and those almond trees. Most people wouldn't spare more than a laugh over something like that. But you recognized that those trees were speaking to you. They were suggesting something to you and you know how to listen. Like when I influenced you to pull that gun on Jim. Wen, you're every bit the person you thought you were before I forced myself bodily into your life. More so, even."

I ponder that silently. His explanation makes sense. I want it to be true. And it's… nice. The nicest thing Mike has ever said to me.

"It's like my ability has a failsafe. I couldn't mind-control people if I tried. The mindless ones that you'd think would be perfect candidates for that kind of thing just don't hear anything anymore. I can shout at them for days, but they're deaf and blind to the world around them, even to their own thoughts. But you're neither. Ideas are a dime a dozen, Wen. Hearing and acting on them are the real skills. And those skills are all you. I had nothing to do with that. You own every bit of yourself."

I unclench my teeth. If Mike is making this up to appease me, he's doing an amazing job acting. "What's the second thing?" I ask.

"That I'm ridiculously effective in-person. If I'm in front of someone, they can't help but 'hear' me. People are better at acting on their ideas when they aren't alone. They're braver I guess. Even when I don't *really* want to influence someone, if I have a passing thought about them, it manages to influence their behavior anyway. I 'speak' to people even when I don't mean to. To be honest, it creeps me the hell out when that happens because it makes me feel out of control. I've found that the best way to keep from doing that is to be an asshole. Nobody feels brave or open-minded around an asshole."

My mouth opens as I get it. A wash of relief brings with it compassion, and I search for the right response.

"And Gabe..." Mike sighs. "Gabe neutralizes that part of my ability when he's around me. Not sure why, but I think it's because he's such a dominating force. I don't know. But when we were growing up I did whatever he wanted to do and didn't question why I wanted to follow him. He had grandiose plans and I was his side-kick. We were always together and I was content to take orders. It wasn't until college, when we stopped being around each other all that time, that I actually recognized what I could do. The influence I could have on people when I started actually having my own ideas away from Gabe. So when... when he married you and I realized I was going to be on my own even more, it was really... terrifying. Couple that with the fact that he put himself squarely in the way of me doing my job of getting you to the Guild... You get the idea."

"Does Gabriel know this?" I ask.

"I told you he doesn't know. I actually tried telling my parents about what I could do. In a roundabout way I told them about the Guild, how I'd found acceptance there. But my mom was convinced it was a cult and that I was under Satan's influence." Mike scoffs. "She believed I was practicing witchcraft and that's how I had these abilities."

"Seriously?" I say. "Is *that* what she was talking about when she refused to tell Gabriel why you weren't talking to them? Mike, I inexplicably killed people when I touched them for the entire first three months I knew her and *you* are the one that gets accused of witchcraft?"

RACHEL E KELLY

"Oh believe me, when Gabe first told all of us about you, she about lost her marbles. Accused Gabe of lying. My dad had to calm her down and remind her that Gabe couldn't maintain a lie like that to save his life. I still don't know if she entirely believed what you were capable of, whether she acted like she believed you just to keep the peace. But I know she didn't question Gabe about it again. After their falling out a few years ago, they each handle the other with kid gloves a lot of the time, believe it or not. Live and let be is pretty much how it is with them. But with Gabe recovering miraculously from things that should have killed him for the second time in his life, and Gabe telling her it was you that cured him, well she's got you elevated to some kind of angel incarnate, sent to protect her family."

"So you figured she could do the same for you," I say.

"I guess my mom has had supernatural overload, because she was not about to accept that I was endowed with a power to manipulate minds. And my dad…" Mike pauses, and I think if I had emodar I would experience spasms of rejection behind his words. "Let's just say he is and always has been wrapped up in my mom. He went along with her. At first I was too torqued at them to see it from their side. But I know now it's a lot of shit hitting the fan recently that's got Dad taking her side like he did. Gabe getting sick… and then Robbie… and all these things cropping up in her family that her Bible can't explain. She's gotta be a wreck if Dad's defending her narrow-minded views. But Dad's not doing anyone any favors, least of all me. So I distanced myself. I don't have room in my life for my mother thinking I need an exorcist. *She's* the one with problems."

My shoulders slump. That's awful. "But why ignore Gabriel? He's been trying to get up with you. You know *he* would accept it."

"Ignoring Gabe was an effort to bring you to *me* rather than the Guild breaking down your door. It was a last-ditch effort, actually, and it worked perfectly. As for telling Gabe, it wasn't an option with you in the picture."

"Oh," I whisper. "Right." No wonder Mike hates me. I took away his only confidant, the person that makes him feel safe and in control. Not that it's *really* my fault. Mike is the one that brought me to Gabriel in the first place, so he kind of created his own demise.

I shake my head. That's always how it works. We are our own worst enemy…

Another person comes into the bathroom again, which maintains the pondering silence between Mike and me for a little while. I feel a hundred times better than I did when I came in here. Mike's actions finally make sense. And I'm also relieved to know my instincts about him were right: he doesn't mean the terrible things he says, and all of it has been a way to cope with his demons. I'm confident again, and I realize that Mike has been the source of all of my angst the last few days. I guess it's possible to read people's distance without actually *reading* people. I guess I'm learning how to cope finally.

The stranger leaves the bathroom, and I say, "I'm sorry, Mike. For things I've done either intentionally or unintentionally to make your life hard."

I hear him pop his knuckles methodically. "You are kind of annoying when you're self-sacrificing, you know that? I don't want your pity. This is a once in a lifetime confession; don't get used to it. But at least you can be less confused. I've got to get you back to Gabe, and I can't do that if we keep going at each other like we have been."

I roll my eyes and open my stall door. "As long as I can still insult you. I'd hate to give that up."

Mike comes out of his stall, straightens his cowboy hat with a hand, looking ridiculously charming while doing it. He gives me a cocky, lopsided smile. "Hell, me too. All this sappy junk is Gabe's area."

I flick his hat off and trounce out of the bathroom. Once we're back in the car and headed toward LA again, I think about my bathroom conversation with Mike. I can't help but remember that the last conversation I had through a wall was with Gabriel when Louise had kidnapped me. It was the most real and honest conversation I'd ever had. Sure, this time it was a bathroom stall, but Mike just got completely and unexpectedly real for once, and I wonder if Mike and I will finally start to act like the family we are.

There has to be a way to manage and control his ability in a better, more constructive way. I bet Uncle Moby would be able to help. If anyone knows how to control powerful abilities with grace, that man does.

Thirty-two

*Y*ou're sure I look okay?" Mike says, tense lines forming around his mouth, and he's giving me what seems to be an accusatory look. "I'm going to need to talk to people and I don't want them preoccupied with... my clothes."

"You think people are going to be preoccupied with your *clothes*?" I scoff, shutting my door and coming around to his side.

He lifts his eyebrows expectantly like he's expecting me to know what he's thinking.

I cross my arms.

He mirrors me. "Back when you were in college, if you saw a guy like me on campus, what would you think? Be honest."

Given permission to look, I don't mind scanning the length of him, not bothering to hide an appreciative smile. "I'd think, dang, I never thought I needed a cowboy to take me away, but I've changed my mind. Must get number."

He looks skeptical.

"I told you. You look hella good."

He stares at me skeptically. "Whit, I'm asking seriously," he says.

"And I'm answering seriously."

He tilts his head slightly. He scratches his head. "You *do* realize I'm not white, right?"

"*No way*," I breathe, letting my jaw drop and my eyes widen. "I had no idea."

He scowls. "Smartass. What I mean is that I can't pull off the cowboy look you imagine like a white guy can. Especially in this fugly plaid."

"You look like you're pulling it off just fine to me," I say.

He shakes his head. "The ignorance of white people never disappoints."

I cross my arms. "I'm sorry my whiteness offends you. Like everything else you dislike about me, I can't help that."

"I don't dislike that you're white. I'm telling you that you're ignorant of what it's like to be *not* white, to be perceived with negative stereotypes. If a white guy puts on a pair of jeans, cowboy boots and hat, and a flannel shirt, then he gets seen as a heart-throbbing desperado or something equally alluring. If *I* put on the same thing, and I'm walking on a college campus, or anywhere else upscale for that matter, I get seen as one of the groundskeepers that can't speak English."

I gnaw the inside of my cheek, considering it. "I guess I could see that…"

He gawks at me. "You're telling me that really didn't occur to you when you picked this outfit out?"

"No."

"I assumed that was what you were going for. I figured it was a passive aggressive challenge to see if I was confident enough to put it on. And I was not about to wimp out."

"That would be pretty messed up of me."

"That's what I thought. But then I figured it was probably the thing the Guild would least expect to see me in, so I gave you the credit of being a genius for picking it."

"I was thinking it was more like a gaucho look. But I can see your point. You can take it off if you want."

"Whatever you need," he says, unbuttoning the flannel to reveal his white undershirt. "But I don't take singles. You better have some Benjamins on you."

I cross my arms again. "Nice try, Playboy. I said if *you* want to. And we all know you want to. It's like you can't stand it if any portion of your physique is covered up. You'll make any excuse to strip. Claiming your shirt is fugly and racist was probably more convenient than offensive."

"Maybe," he laughs, "but I have to say I'm a little disappointed this time. I like looking 'hella good.'"

"Is this my cue for your hourly ego massage?"

He glances at me through his eyelashes as he pulls his arms from the sleeves. "Why yes. Yes, it is."

I laugh and shake my head. "Oh please, Mike, stop!" I cover my eyes, looking shyly between my fingers. "Don't take the shirt off! It's the only thing keeping my hands off of you!"

He frowns at me, tossing the shirt inside the van and closing the door. "It doesn't work if it's not genuine."

"Sorry, Mike. I'm trying. It's just... the shirt. Ambrosial, y'know? I can't look at you the same without it."

He snorts as he walks past me.

"You're keeping the hat?" I call as he walks toward the campus. I'm supposed to hang back a little so we don't look like we came together. He says he needs to look *available*.

He turns around and walks backward for a second. "I like the hat," he calls back, bowing his head and touching the brim before turning his back to me.

Wow, he even knows how to use it. Whoever he is about to con into getting us Quinn's campus contact information probably won't know what hit them.

Mike seems to know where he's going, and I'm puzzled by this until I remember suddenly that Gabriel did his undergrad here at USC. I don't know if Mike went to college here, too, but if he and Gabriel are as close as I'm starting to understand, Mike must have visited him a lot at least.

The campus is nearly empty for the summer so we don't encounter many people. The sun has fully disappeared beyond the horizon by the time we arrive at a little coffee shop. Mike glances at me over his shoulder only once, confirming that I'm still with him. But then he goes inside. I wait a few more moments before following to make it look like I came separately.

It's surprisingly busy and loud inside; most seats in the place are occupied. Lots of laptop screens keep company with college students wearing earbuds to drown out neighboring groups caught up in raucous conversation. And then there are the more intimate gatherings: two kids bent over lattes and engrossed in their discussion. I find the edge of a couch in a corner with a good vantage point of Mike who is in line to order.

I glance around the shop, finding a stack of campus life magazines on a rack nearby that I can look occupied with. Sitting down with one, I glance at Mike periodically over the top of the pages, realizing that he actually *does* smile quite a bit. Just not at me evidently. The barista, a cute little brunette, is beaming and gabbing at him with big eyes already. He says something and flashes a grin at her, which sends her into a fit of laughter. She makes a flirtatious swipe at his hat, which he ducks. But he holds up both his hands in surrender while smiling charmingly.

No wonder he kept the hat. It's a convenient flirtation device.

"Look out, you're drooling," a voice says from next to me.

I turn to its source, an Asian girl with a short, spikey hairdo. She's got a hefty novel in one hand and a fountain drink in the other. She's chewing on the straw and looking in Mike's direction as well.

I almost hold up my left hand and show her that I'm married, but I'm supposed to be blending in as a college student. As inconspicuously as possible, I remove my rings and shove them in my bag. "Kind of hard not to look," I point out. "He's making a spectacle of himself."

"Oh look, she's going to give him a free coffee," the straw-chewer says, still staring. I don't think she really heard me.

I look to the register, and it appears that Mike has tried to pay the girl with a five and she's refusing, taking advantage of the opportunity to touch him as she pushes the bill back into his hand.

Watching Mike behaving so... not the Mike I know is unnerving, so I turn to the girl again. "So what's your major?" I ask conversationally, hoping it will steal her attention from Mike. As I take a quick scan of the room, it seems that Mike is drawing a few too many eyes. Doesn't matter what he wears. He's going to get attention of all kinds.

"Pre-med," the girl says, finally dragging her eyes off of Mike.

"Really?" I say, now very much interested in this girl. "Do you know someone named Quinn?"

Her eyes widen with obvious recognition. "Quinn Reese? Oh yeah, he's solid. We have like four classes together. How do you know him?"

"High school," I reply, astounded that I'm actually sitting next to someone that knows the person I came here to find. "Man, it's been forever since I saw him... I knew he was doing pre-med here, but I usually spend most of my time on the other campus. Been meaning to catch up with him..."

"Want me to text him?" she says, excited about connecting long-lost friends. "I think he plays racquetball on Wednesday nights. Not far from here."

"What a coincidence," I say. "That'd be perfect."

She digs her phone from the backpack by her feet.

"Hey, let me surprise him. Don't say who wants to see him."

She laughs. "No problem. You never told me your name anyway."

I glance up briefly, noticing Mike is now sitting at a table, the one with the largest group of students in the place. I look back at the girl and laugh. "Yeah, I guess you're right. My name's Whit."

"Short for Whitney?" she asks, furiously texting now.

"Yeah," I say, hoping she'll do as I asked and not use my name since it's fake and Quinn will have no idea who it is.

While she has her head buried in her phone, I look up again and see that Mike is now leaning into a girl whose back is toward me. She's messing with her phone, too. My guess is that Mike is having her look up Quinn. Looks like we're in a competition to see which of us can come up with Quinn's location first. But it also looks like the universe is making doubly sure we get what we came for. We're on the right track. A thrill exhilarates me.

"He says he just got done with racquetball. He's going to shower and then head over here," the girl next to me says.

I hold back laughter. I can't believe I have not only found someone that knows Quinn, but he's now coming *to* me. Mike can suck it with his fancy abilities and girl-schmoozing.

"That's so great," I beam. "Thanks! What's your name?"

"Faye," she says. "No problem. Kinda cool that you ended up sitting next to me and I knew your friend."

I'd like to point out to her that it's way more than cool, because I came here looking for Quinn, but she'd probably see that as more weird than cool. She's looking at Mike again anyway, and I wonder if I should figure out a way to let him know what's up.

"He's looking at you," Faye says.

"Yeah, because I know him," I admit, glancing up to see that she's right. I stick my tongue out at Mike, and I get the impression that he has accomplished what he came to do and he's ready to leave.

"Why didn't you say that before?" Faye says. "I'm like, over here checking him out something fierce and for all I know you're dating him. Could have spared me looking like an idiot."

"No, I'm not dating him," I reassure her with a smile. "Check him out all you want. Won't hurt my feelings. Or his. He's got an ego the size of Africa."

She lifts her chin. "Ahh, okay. So are you guys tight then?"

"You could say that. I'm uh, with his brother."

Her mouth opens with surprise. "Do egos run in the family?"

I don't get a chance to reply because Mike is in front of us, giving me one of those chin nods that I've always seen as rude and lazy. "Ready?" he says impatiently, solidifying that opinion.

"No," I say. "I'm gonna stick around. I found out Faye and I have a mutual friend that's going to meet us here." I give him a knowing look.

"How about that," he says, turning his attention to Faye, who looks like she's had a spotlight shined in her face. I'm glad to see I'm not the only one uncertain around Mike's physical girth and questionable attitude. Because now that he's in front of me, he's back to his usual obstinate temperament. Kind of blows my mind how quickly he transforms.

"You're scaring her, Mike. Go sit down and don't get your belt buckle in a bind. We'll go when I'm ready."

He glares at me for about two seconds before sitting on the edge of the coffee table in front of me, propping his ankle on his leg, his protruding knee dominating both mine and Faye's personal space. He takes a casual sip of his coffee, but he does it with recognizable swagger. It's true there are no open seats nearby, but I think he's sitting there and acting like that to play up the jerky demeanor.

Not willing to lay down to it, I lift up my foot and use it to push his knee out of our bubble. I give Faye a look. "I wasn't lying about the size of his ego. See?"

Mike scowls, and Faye glances from him to me, doe-eyed and silent.

At this point, I ignore Mike and focus on Faye, asking her about where she's from and about her classes. But Mike has stifled her ability to talk, and she gives only one or two-word answers. The air grows more awkward, and I'm pretty sure she's looking for an opportunity to run away. So it's a blessed relief when the front door opens and I recognize Quinn, who scans the café before his eyes rest on Faye and then me. He does a double-take.

Faye seems to have noticed him as soon as I do, and she hops up, running over to Quinn like he's come to save her.

I lean toward Mike. "Seriously, can you *not* do that so well? I need to get his trust and you're going to ruin it like that."

I don't wait for his answer. I stand up and skirt around Mike, approaching Quinn with a meek smile.

"Uh, hi," Quinn says, staring at me like I'm an apparition.

"Quinn, I've got studying to do," Faye says. "But looks like you and Whit have a lot of catching up. I'll see you in lab tomorrow?"

Quinn seems to have forgotten until that moment that she was there, and he looks at her for a few seconds before nodding. "Yeah. For sure."

"Thanks, Faye," I say, smiling at her.

"Really. No problem," Faye says, and I see her eyes nervously stray past me to Mike before she runs from the shop. Mike isn't *that* scary. I wonder if he's been influencing her to get lost.

"How are you?" I say, noticing Quinn's damp hair is more of a long mop now, like the picture we saw online. He's wearing tennis shoes, workout shorts, and a grey T-shirt with 'USC' on the front. He has a single-strap backpack and a racquet case slung over his back. He looks even more put together than the last time I saw him.

All good things, Wendy, I admonish myself when resentment bubbles up.

"Wen, every time I run into you it's under more bizarre circumstances than the last time," Quinn says, baffled.

"I know. But I really need to talk to you and it's too crowded in here. Mind if we go outside?"

"There's a small park nearby with some benches. Not usually occupied. Um, I take it you're not alone?" His eyes glance over my shoulder.

Glancing over my shoulder I see Mike standing where I left him, arms crossed and legs splayed, looking his usual intimidating self.

"Ignore my bodyguard. He's got anger issues. We think it's the juice," I say, waving a hand without looking at Mike, but I hear a low growl.

"Bodyguard?" Quinn mouths before turning for the door.

As Quinn and I, followed by Mike, walk silently to the park Quinn suggested, I think of how to broach the favor I need from him. I need to make him understand the desperate place I'm in and commit to keeping a secret.

This is a stupid idea.

Reaching a bench surrounded by a group of trees, Quinn turns around, his brow furrowed. He opens his mouth, but doesn't speak at first.

"I need a favor," I say suddenly before I lose my nerve.

Quinn's eyebrows lift now. "Yeah, um, I know."

"You do?"

"You have... an uncle. Right? Robert Haricott?"

"Yes..." I say, taking a step backward, suspicious of how Quinn knows that.

Mike, who either picks up on my concern or is worried himself, leaps forward and puts himself between us. "What do you know?" he growls at Quinn.

Quinn takes a step back as well, holding his hands up. "Nothing. I met him a week ago. On campus. It was an alumni talk. He pulled me aside afterward and said who he was. He told me..." Quinn looks at me. "You're not going to believe this, but he told me you were going to pay me a visit in a week and ask for help in contacting him. And when you did I needed to tell you, quote, 'Tell Wendy not to find us. We'll find *her*. Focus on the vision.'" Quinn's eyes dart between me and Mike, waiting for an explanation.

"Dang," I breathe. "How... When..." I look at Quinn. "I don't think I ever told Uncle Moby about you," I say, more to myself than to him. *How* does Robert do it?

Mike is speechless.

"And... he said to tell you to... not be afraid of who you are," Quinn says more quietly. "Wen, what is this about? I thought the guy was crazy at first. But... there was something about him, you know? It told me I should listen."

"He knew..." I shake my head in wonder. I unwittingly clench my hand against my chest. Knowing that my beloved uncle is so aware of me... Oh how I love him.

"Knew what?" Quinn asks.

"Exactly what you said," I reply. "That I'd come see you." I look at Quinn squarely. "My uncle knows some of the future. It's a skill of his. Thanks for the message. It's exactly what I needed."

"So..." Quinn starts. "Your uncle is a multi-billionaire who can... see the future, and you never mentioned it in all the time we knew each other?"

"I didn't know," I say. "I didn't meet him until after my mom died."

"Your mom died?" Quinn says, getting more confused.

"After I graduated high school," I say distractedly. Uncle Moby is telling me to stop trying to find him. I'm supposed to focus on the vision—which is about finding Carl.

"Seriously?" Quinn says. He puts his hands on his head. "Man, I'm so sorry."

"It was a while ago," I say, mentally changing my plans to what Robert's asking. I put my hands on my hips and turn away from Quinn, staring into the darkness. I miss Gabriel and Robbie so much I can hardly stand it. I want to be *home*. I want an end to the chaos.

But at the same time, I know I will do whatever my uncle says. I'll wait for him to find me. But he also told me to follow the vision and not to be afraid of who I am…but who is that?

I know how I've *felt*. I've *felt* like I've been thrust back into a situation I've lived before. Like then, I'm being told that I'm important and vital to some greater cause. Like then I find myself wishing for peace and simplicity again. I was blind to the importance of my abilities then… and I'm likely blind to it now. And maybe that's the message I need to finally get.

As for who I am, I'm starting to get that I'm someone who is supposed to be able to see the colorworld. And if I'm not supposed to be afraid of that person, then I need to go that direction. I need to find a way to get my abilities back.

"Okay, Uncle Moby," I say. "I'm not balking this time."

I turn back around. "Let's go, Mike. Time to fight back." I face Quinn. "Thanks for giving me the message."

"That's all?" Quinn says, holding his hands out.

"Well yeah. I was going to ask you to give Robert a message. But he preempted me. So there's only doing what he asks now."

"Why me?" Quinn asks. "Of all the people you've known, why would you come to *me*?"

There is a definite practical reason, namely that Quinn may be the one person I know well enough that the Guild doesn't actually know about. But other than that… "I really don't know," I say. "My guess is that one of us is supposed to learn something from continually running into each other like this."

"It's because I still owe you, isn't it?" Quinn says.

"Owe me?" I ask. "Believe it or not, I owe *you* a lot of who I am today. And every time I see you, I'm confronted with the parts of me that still need fixing. And I seem to need reminding of them at exactly the same time we cross paths."

Quinn's shoulders slump. "Maybe *you* don't think so, but I do." He rubs a hand through his hair uncomfortably. "Ever since last time… I wish I could make it up to you."

"You already have," I reply.

"Oh come on. Don't give me that."

"I'm being serious," I say. "I'm not saying you didn't screw up. So did I. But it's made me better. And if you'll let it, it will make *you* better."

"I had no idea you were into motivational speaking," Quinn smiles.

"Me neither," I sigh. "But I guess I don't want to see you beating yourself up. Take care."

I walk over to Mike, who has been watching silently, and link arms with him, leading him toward the main path.

"Wen," Quinn says to me, his tone uncertain.

I stop and look over my shoulder.

"I was too scared to know what I really wanted," he says, neither of us looking at each other. "My mom said you needed me gone. So I went because I'm not a fighter, you know that. I wanted to tell you last time... but... well you know it was weird then. But I wanted to tell you that if I'd been allowed to stick around, I would have done whatever you wanted. All this time... the thing I've suffered over the most was thinking that you believed..." He clears his throat. "Thinking that you believed I never loved you. That I used you." He looks up from his feet. "The things I told you when we were together, I meant them."

I let my eyes finally rest on Quinn. "I know."

He shakes his head at himself. "Gosh, I know this is awkward and weird, what with you being married now. But since this is the second time you've popped in my life like this, I figure I ought to get it off my chest finally."

"I'm glad you did," I say.

"Thanks," Quinn says. He looks up at the trees around us and then back down, shakes his head. "Don't even know what I'm thanking you for. Always understanding me I guess."

"You're welcome." I release Mike and walk over to Quinn. And then I take him in a hug, which he returns with emphasis.

"I'm happy that you're happy," Quinn says once I release him. "I'm glad you found someone that loves you like you deserve."

"Thanks," I say.

"You know, he contacted me a while back."

"Gabriel?" I ask.

"About your art."

"What about it?" I say, suddenly on guard.

"It was about six months ago. He wanted to know where he could find some of your pieces. Said you'd given up art, but you were pregnant and he wanted to retain something of your past for your child. You've had a kid?"

I nod, appalled at Gabriel's actions, but not surprised. "We named him Robbie." I look at Quinn squarely because I think he's not asking about Robbie so much as he is asking about my art. "I haven't done art since she died. Never felt right after that. Then my mom died and I couldn't have spent time on it even if I'd wanted to. I had my brother to take care of."

Quinn remains silent for several moments. He sighs. "Your mom was an amazing lady. I remember asking her which side of the family you'd inherited your artistic gene from. She said, 'From an angel.' I remember wishing my mom could be as proud of me about something as your mom was of you."

I nod. "I was lucky to have her."

"Congrats on the kid," Quinn says. "Don't be a stranger, okay?"

I nod again, once more linking arms with Mike who seems to be more on edge than normal. "We've got to get going. Thanks for everything."

Quinn and Mike exchange a dude nod, and Quinn heads a different way than we came in. Mike and I walk quickly to get back to the van, and after a full minute of silence, Mike loosens his arm from mine and says, "I haven't forgotten the steroid comment. I'll be getting you back. Expect it. And secondly, Gabe *likes* that guy?"

"Quinn is the reason Gabriel and I got back together."

"I find that hard to believe. That guy has it bad for you still. The only reason Gabe would like an ex who was mooning over you was if he could flaunt the fact that he had you and the other guy didn't. But *that* guy is obviously hoping for a way back into your life."

"This isn't some dumb TV drama, Mike," I scold. "This is real life, where people share parts of themselves with other people, and no amount of time and space can undo the impact those relationships had on the people involved."

"Yeah. Time has not undone *that* guy's crush on you."

"Quinn isn't looking to rekindle something. He's just mature about the past we *do* share. You can't *erase* the past. You can't look back on a time when you loved someone and claim that it was somehow not real because that person wasn't *the one*. That person became a permanent part of who you are whether you like it or not. So if you get a chance to hang on to the beautiful parts of it, you should."

"You make it sound like *you* still have feelings for him."

I consider that. It's silly to assume that I don't. And why shouldn't I? Especially when he continues to play an important part in my life? In fact, every time I get a chance to talk to Quinn, I'm more secure in the person I've become and in the choices I've made.

"You can't negate people and feelings, Mike," I say. "They never go away. They might manifest in unhealthy ways if we don't acknowledge them. You can deny past love, but you don't get to untie yourself from the people who were and are such a major part of you."

"Sure you can. You never talk to them again."

I shake my head. "My mom has been gone for three years. But that doesn't mean she no longer matters to me, that she no longer influences me."

"When you put it that way... Well it sounds like some idealist crap that would come out of Gabe's mouth."

I laugh. He's probably right. Gabriel's validation of Quinn's part in my life all those months ago that has had me seeing my past with him in a new way. If it weren't for Gabriel, I probably would have buried Quinn and everything to do with him. And with that, I would have buried the pieces of me that Quinn helped make. And then what a waste it all would have been...

"Thank you, Mike," I reply. "Gabriel is someone I try to emulate."

Thirty-three

I don't think Mike slept much last night. I didn't sleep so well myself even though I got the entire back seat to stretch out on. Every time I did wake up, Mike's breaths never sounded like sleeping. After we left Quinn, I expected Mike would lay into me about changing our plans, or at least have an opinion about what our new plans should be, but he stayed broodingly quiet. And in fact, we drove to Long Beach in silence, and then without explanation he parked at the city beach and started taking off his jeans, revealing that he's been wearing shorts under his pants this whole time. He also removed his white undershirt and his boots and went for a barefoot run on the beach. I stayed in the car to figure out my next move. But instead I worried about Mike, because he was gone for an hour.

When I saw his form take shape under the streetlights finally, I hopped in the back seat and pretended to be asleep. It was a while before he got into the car, and I kept peeking through pinched eyes at the windshield to find him leaning against the hood, staring into the darkness. Because I wasn't up to broaching the topic of a new mission with Mike, I didn't let on that I was still awake when he finally got in.

Mike is still shirtless when I open my eyes in the morning.

"Can I get an ego maintenance schedule?" I ask the back of his head. "This is getting excessive. Or did you give up on shirts?"

"It's dirty."

"So wear the lumberjack one."

"It's too tight on my arms."

"So cut the sleeves off."

"A flannel button-up with the sleeves ripped off? You've been educated on the awkwardness of racial stereotypes and *that's* what you suggest? You can't be serious."

I roll my eyes. "You are so high-maintenance."

"You're the one complaining, not me. It's not my fault my body makes you uncomfortable. I was just answering your question."

"It doesn't make me uncomfortable—Okay it does," I concede. "But you walking around shirtless is like a girl doing the same. There's obviously something to look at. But you feel guilty for looking... You wonder if they *want* you to look... Makes for awkward situations."

"If a girl walks around topless, she's obviously confident enough to do it," Mike says. "Nothing wrong with that. I have no problem being shirtless for the same reason. And if I catch someone looking, I take it as a compliment. And considering how much work I've put into looking like this, why can't I invite people to pay me the compliment of looking? It's like any other accomplishment. People like to be recognized for what they do."

"Good point. But nobody wants to be seen as just a hot body."

"And nobody really wants to be seen as just an Olympic gold medalist or *just* a famous actor. Or just anything else. If you're seeing someone's accomplishments as the sum-total of who they are, the fault is on you."

"Okay fine. But modesty is an important personality trait."

He chuckles softly, reaching for a bottle of water in the cup holder. "You might be right. But if people weren't so concerned with being modest about how amazing their God-given body is, we'd recognize that we all have one and we're all on the same playing field. Then it wouldn't be so scandalous when someone uncovers. Modesty is relative. If everyone were rich, then when someone spent their money on a Bentley, it wouldn't be seen as showing off."

"Fine, Mike," I say, sitting up. "You win. Flaunt it."

"About time I won *something*," he grumbles, downing the rest of his water in one swig. Putting the cap on, he says, "I know you're opposed to stealing, but you're either going to have to get over it or tell me where to find buried treasure. I've only got forty bucks left and less than half a tank of gas."

I stare at the back of his head, repeating his words in my head to be sure I'm understanding. "So... you're going to help me?"

"Help you? I don't even know what you're *doing*. But I don't actually *care* what you're doing. All I care about now is keeping you in one piece with your freedom intact. I'm done fighting you. Especially now that your uncle is... ahead of us. I think you should be with Gabe right now, but you are clearly set on some other course.

I've always been better at taking orders anyway. So I'm your bodyguard and underling. You say jump. I say how high."

That was entirely unexpected. And I'm not sure I *want* to have all the decisions on me. But this might be the best I'm going to get. And considering Mike's history and line of work, it makes sense. This is his comfort zone—taking orders. Mike's actually giving me his best for once. And that's touching.

To make the point that I accept his offer, but he'll never be just my yes-man, I reach my arms around the front seat's head rest and hug him through it, not letting his bare-chestedness stop me, resting my chin on his head.

He jumps slightly, but I don't let go. "Thanks, Mike," I say before releasing him and climbing into the passenger seat.

"So we need money..." I muse, grabbing my test kit out of my backpack, glad that this is the first order of business. It seems a far easier problem than figuring out where to find Carl. But if Robert thinks I can do it, then so do I. My eyes brighten suddenly and I sit up. "I've got it! Robert's home in Redlands. I know where he keeps his spare cash there."

"They've got it under surveillance."

I give him a look. "You're saying they have people watching it all hours of the day? No one lives there."

"I doubt there are actual bodies watching. But they've got ways of knowing as soon as someone goes onto the premises."

"What ways? How fast will they act?"

"I don't know exactly. Especially because your uncle has his own surveillance arsenal."

I think about that. I actually have no idea how much of his own security technology Robert uses. The only thing I *do* know is that somehow Robert is looking out for me. And I trust him. I trust him to know what I need even before I know I need it.

"We'll take the chance."

Mike sighs.

"You pick the lock and I'll get the cash, and then we'll jet. In and out of the house in less than two minutes."

"Pick the lock? What makes you think I can do that?"

"Is that my bodyguard playing dumb?" I reprimand. "Don't make me have to hire a replacement."

"I think I've made a mistake," Mike says, starting the car and backing out of the spot.

"Okay, all joking aside for a sec," I say. "Mike, I don't own you. We'll take it a day at a time. You don't want to do this anymore—help me—just say the word. I'm capable of staying out of sight on my own. You've trained me well." I grin at him.

He gives me an ugly look. "Don't flatter yourself. Following orders does *not* make me your slave. I'm volunteering for the job because it will make my life easier, not because I think I owe you a thing. So don't confuse this as some kind of favor."

I glare at him for a few seconds. He doesn't fool me. "Idiot," mumble, crossing my arms and sticking my nose up. "Have it your way." I put my feet on the dash and grab the last orange I have in my backpack. "We should have made this arrangement ages ago," I say, peeling the orange. "Welcome to your new life as my personal Mexican Jackie Chan slash Memphis Raines slash Jesse James slash Nathan Hale."

"Nathan Hale?"

"Yeah, the famous spy for the Continental Army? He's the guy that before he was hung said, 'I only regret that I have but one life to lose for my country.'"

"So I'm a spying, car-jacking, Ninja-thief?"

"Absolutely. And don't worry. My uncle will reward you handsomely for your service." I tilt my head. "Plus, if I'm going to take down Gordy, you can short some Gordy companies on the stock market and make a killing. So I gave you a terrific insider tip. You're welcome."

Mike shakes his head. "That escalated quickly."

"You forgot that because of you I have a lot of experience with bodyguards," I point out. "Ordering them around comes naturally. You only have yourself to blame."

He rolls his eyes and sighs.

Thirty-four

*Y*ou're going to stay right behind me, right?" Mike asks as we stand outside of my uncle's gated Redlands neighborhood.

"Yes, Mike," I say, catching my voice on the 'k.'

"And if I say we turn back, you turn back without arguing, right?"

"Yes, Mike," I say, rolling my eyes. "Please stop assuming I'm going to do something impetuous."

He purses his lips. "You do remember that the *last* time I gave you a step-by-step plan, you botched it so badly I had to trash my whole life to dig you out of it, right? So I'm *sliiightly* concerned that because I have now trashed my life, the only thing left is *losing* it if you mess this up."

"One thing, Mike!" I say, holding up one finger. "I messed up *one* thing! And only because you didn't fully explain everything!"

He holds up a hand and shakes his head. "Hey, taking orders doesn't require explanations. Did I ask *you* why you couldn't give me the location of the cash so I could do this more cleanly and safely by myself? Did I ask *you* why you chose to break into your closely-watched uncle's house instead of stealing a little bit of cash from someone temporarily? No. I follow orders even if they sound stupid."

"Bodyguards don't get to talk back, Mikey," I say. "And since you're into following orders, follow mine now and GO! I'll be *right behind you.*"

"I'm serious. If I catch one whiff of a Gordy, we are outta there," he says.

"Oh my gosh," I say through gritted teeth.

He stares me down for about five more exasperating seconds as I insert a finger under the edge of the black beanie I'm wearing to relieve an itch. In case I get caught on one of my uncle's surveillance cameras, I don't want Gordy knowing my head is bald so I can keep the disguise in public.

He nods curtly, and I could swear I can see him transforming back into his ninja-soldier role. He turns and starts jogging toward the fence.

I follow him through the darkness at an easy pace. We're both dressed in cheap black sweats and with plenty of vegetation around, we can stay out of the beam of streetlights. When we reach the fence surrounding the neighborhood, Mike gives me a boost and I'm up and over in seconds. It's another quarter-mile jog to my uncle's house. Mike decided we would not spend any time scouting the perimeter of either the neighborhood or my uncle's house. Whatever they may be watching with will be invisible, so our only goal is being as fast as possible. Should we run into trouble… well that was another thing Mike coached me on earlier—using a gun.

The wall around my uncle's yard is eight feet of cement and stucco. I worry that I'm not going to be able to scale it even with Mike's help, but he practically tosses me up like I'm nothing more than a beanbag. I catch on to the top with an arm and then a leg, scrambling up none too gracefully.

Straddling the top of the wall, I wait for him. He runs and jumps, grasping the top of the wall with one hand and then the other, pulling himself up as nimbly as a monkey. I watch in wide-eyed wonder. He leaps down as soundlessly as a cat. At the bottom he holds his arms out to me.

Having jumped into his arms before from a much greater height, I don't hesitate, and he catches me around my waist like last time. As we run toward the garage where I know the money is stashed, I double check my mental image of the inside. I've only been to my uncle's Redlands home a handful of times so I hope that everything is where I remember—including the money. I'm at least sure of the combination to the safe where it's kept. My uncle told me about it a long time ago and it's the same as his home safe in Monterey. I remember it because I stole *that* money once as well, the last time I went on the run.

When we reach the garage, Mike does his magic on the lock. As soon as the door is open, I'm startled by the tone of an alarm. A keypad is lit up just inside the door. Both of Robert's homes have commercial security systems installed, but he has never activated them that I know of, not when he owns his own surveillance technology. The systems were built into the homes before Robert bought them. So why is this one activated now?

The insistent trill sends me into a minor panic.

Mike nudges my arm. "Money," he mouths.

I run to the wall safe on the other side of the room. Out of the corner of my eye I see Mike try the button for the garage door. Nothing happens. *Crap.* Our plan was to take the car my uncle keeps here when we left because our car is far outside the neighborhood and we need to get to it quickly. But if the system isn't allowing us to open the garage, we won't be able to drive out as we'd planned. We'll have to get out on foot and that could give Gordy enough time to show up and sweep the area.

Desperate when I reach the safe, it takes incredible concentration to control my trembling fingers to turn the knob. I manage to get it open on the first attempt, revealing a stack of bills, credit cards, and a gun. I rake everything into the fanny pack at my waist. Mike comes to my side, and sweeps me toward the door. "Run," he whispers, pushing me ahead of himself. "Front wall."

I act immediately, sprinting across the front yard. The alarm moves into siren mode and the space around the house lights up, shooting me with adrenaline. Mike and I dart through the trees and reach the wall in less than thirty seconds. Once again, Mike boosts me up, nearly tossing me over the other side of the wall this time. He jumps up and over in one fluid motion, holds his arms out, and catches me when I jump down once again.

Mike leads the way and I stay right on his heels. On foot, it takes several minutes to traverse the neighborhood. He stops abruptly before we reach the community gate though, and I run into him. I nearly fall but he catches me and hauls me behind a bush. It's then that I see what he stopped for: a pair of headlights. Actually I count one, two, three sets. Larger vehicles. No flashing lights though.

"Gordy," Mike whispers, very close to my ear as he holds me down behind the bush. "Mierda!" he hisses to himself.

"What do we do?" I say in a frenzied, high-pitched whisper.

"They're going to sweep the area. I'm sure there are guys outside, waiting. Let me think a minute."

He squeezes my shoulders a little tighter as he falls silent. I wait, more antsy by the moment.

Finally, after what seems like forever, he says, "Okay, we're going to keep moving so we can get to the outside before they really fan out. They're going to station their vehicles in a grid, spread out enough that we don't have to take them all at once. Do exactly what I say. Stay right behind me. Do you understand?"

"Yes," I whisper. At that moment I hear a calamity of barking. "They have dogs?" I squeak.

"Yep, and they've caught our scent," Mike says, lifting me by the hand and moving quickly again. He darts from cover to cover, starting and stopping amongst the trees and shrubs. It's pretty sparse out here and I think we should make a straight-shot run for it, but I'm determined to trust that Mike knows what he's doing. I desperately hope we get out before the dogs reach us.

"Wen," Mike says over his shoulder as we duck behind a line of shrubs. "If you see a dog, don't hesitate. Shoot it."

I think my heart is going to beat right out of my chest. *Please, oh please, let us get outside this fence before the dogs catch up!*

In answer to my pleas, we reach the fence only moments later. But I finally catch sight of the first dog approaching too fast for me to react. I finally stop gawking at the dog when I perceive Mike hoisting me up. But I reach for the top of the wrought-iron fence a second too late. I flail. Mike reacts swiftly, pushing me up again. As my hands grip the railing, I hear a growl and a flash of fur out of the corner of my eye.

Screeching in terror, I scramble up, desperate to get my feet away from the snapping teeth. I fall over the other side like a sack of rocks, slamming to the ground and rolling once before looking up. My breath catches in my throat to see that Mike is grappling with the animal, a German Shepherd that has its teeth buried in Mike's arm while he struggles to reach his gun. But it's clear that every time Mike tries to, the dog bites down harder and Mike groans, instead trying to unlatch the dog's jaws from his arm.

Fury surges into me. "Stupid dog," I growl, snatching my gun from my waist. I stick it between the fence bars and take aim, "Hold still, Mike," I say, desperate that I not shoot Mike in the process. I ought to be able to get a bullet in the dog from only four feet away, but I've never shot a gun before.

The dog must notice me now because he grips Mike's arm harder, eliciting a higher-pitched moan from Mike who stands stock-still. That's all I need. I hold the weapon still by bracing my hand against the fence rail. With fierce concentration, I aim and force my eyes to stay open as I pull the trigger. I blink several times, recovering from the deafening sound. The dog whimpers, having dropped to the ground. Mike is already climbing the fence. Beyond him, two more dogs and several figures are moving in our direction. I fire two shots toward them just as Mike hops to the ground beside me.

"Let's go," he says, tugging my arm.

Mike leads me toward the road. There's an SUV parked there. "Mike!" I hiss.

"I know," he says, grabbing my hand and egging me to go faster.

The road is uphill from where we are, and as we get closer, Mike motions me to duck and we creep up the hill until we are right next to the SUV. Someone rounds the corner of it and stops abruptly, having spotted us. The Gordy reaches for his gun, but I can see that Mike already has his drawn. "Don't," he says to the guy, who hesitates.

At that moment, a second Gordy appears, aims his weapon at Mike. "Put it down, Mike," he says.

"No," Mike says, his eyes trained on the first guy, ignoring the gun pointing right at him only ten feet away. After seeing NTGs several times now, I can tell this one is a real gun.

I'm hiding behind Mike's back, and I have no idea what to do. My hand is on my own gun, but I'm not sure what to do with it. Aim it at the second Gordy who is aiming at Mike? That's a bad idea. I think for several beats and then move my gun to my back instead of my side where it can't be easily seen. Then I step out from behind Mike and walk directly into the aim of the second Gordy who is aiming at Mike.

"Wen—" Mike says for a split-second, but I think he realizes what I'm doing. Out of the corner of my eye I see him leap for the first guy—who was distracted by me moving—landing a swift kick to his gut and bringing the guy to his knees. Mike snatches his gun away, rounds a kick to the side of the Gordy's head and then turns for the second guy just as I reach him. Second guy's gun is only a foot from my chest.

"Drop your gun or I'll shoot her," the Gordy says.

I snatch the barrel so he won't adjust his aim for Mike. "No you won't. Your boss won't like you killing their prized asset."

"Maybe not, but he won't mind you injured. A paraplegic, maybe?" the guy says, sneering at me. But instead of choosing another place to aim on my person to make his point, he takes me by surprise by jerking his gun up and away from me. I hear the thunderous sound of a gunshot. I think for sure Mike's been hit until the guy in front of me collapses against the SUV at his back and slides to the ground. Something has spattered me in the face. When I look down, blood. Blood is everywhere. I can't find the guy's face. I stare, not really seeing.

"Let's go," Mike says, guiding me by the hand toward the vehicle. He scans the area over the top of the car as he opens the door and pushes me in. I climb over the driver's seat and armrest, shell-shocked that I have human remains stuck to me like confetti. I try not to think about what I just saw. I hold on tight to the handle above the door while Mike executes a hairpin turn and speeds away.

In mere seconds, he squeals to a stop in front of our stolen van that we previously stashed only a few blocks away. He hops out, comes around, opens my door, and gently helps me out. "Come on, Wendy," he says quietly. "Let's get out of here."

I let him guide me. Not until I see headlights in the distance do I have the sense to move faster. I hop in the car and slam the door shut as Mike leaps around the front of the vehicle for the driver's side. And then we're off again. I wonder what his plan is to get to our actual getaway vehicle without being tracked, but I'm too stunned at the moment to ask. Before our break-in, Mike stole yet another car, changed its plates, and we put all of our belongings in it, ready to make a quick escape.

I turn now to look behind us and see the headlights still. I look over at Mike but he's intent on the road and on controlling the vehicle at the breakneck speed we're travelling. Thankfully, one in the morning doesn't present many obstacles by way of traffic.

"Put your seatbelt on," Mike says, not looking at me. I do so quickly, noticing only now that blood is dripping down Mike's arm. I follow the trail of it up to a horrendous bite-mark left by the dog. It looks deep and *really* painful.

"I'm so sorry," I say, realizing I'm crying. I wipe the tears away only to come away with more blood on my arm. *Oh my gosh, my face is covered in blood. Don't throw up.*

"We may get out of this yet," Mike replies. "And then it will have all been worth it."

"Worth it?" I say shrilly. "You killed that guy, Mike!"

He glances at me only briefly with a look of confusion. "Would you rather him have shot me?"

"Of course not, but I didn't want anyone to get hurt. I only wanted to get some travel cash. I didn't want a gunfight. If I'd known people were going to be killed I wouldn't have done it."

Mike makes a quick left and I grab the handle again to brace myself. He makes a right, and then a left, and another right, zig-zagging through a residential neighborhood. All the while, his eyes dart this way and that. I'm not sure what he's looking for, but he continues to weave around blocks, but still heading in the same general direction.

Finally, he says, "Ah ha!" He all but slams the breaks, shuts off the lights, and turns carefully into a driveway that curves around the side of a house. I finally get what he's doing. He was looking for a place to hide the car quickly, and from where we're parked in front of a garage but behind a house, there's no way the van can be seen from the road.

He rolls down his window then, closes his eyes, and leans out. I think he's listening. After about ten seconds, he pulls his head back in, throws the car in reverse, and backs out the same way we came in. I have no idea how he manages getting around the curve with his lights off, let alone as quickly as he's managing, but Mike's skills appear to be endless. We're back into the street and are moving again in no time. He keeps the lights off and slows to a more careful pace. He avoids the main road, instead crossing over several to stay on residential streets. We encounter a few cars, but we don't appear to be followed anymore. Eventually we end up parked behind our getaway vehicle: a silver sedan.

"Come on," Mike says, opening his door. I follow suit.

Once we close the doors behind us in our new car, my panic dissipates quite a bit. Mike reaches behind the seat and brings out a rag, handing it to me.

I remember my face again and start wiping, avoiding looking at the rag as I do so.

Mike accelerates, this time moving at a more legal speed. He eases onto a freeway, headed west.

"Wen," Mike says finally, "if you thought going up against the Guild was going to be painless or easy, then you haven't been listening to anything I've told you. There are going to be casualties because it's going to start a war. And you're not going to like the cost. So you better be sure this is what you want. You better be sure that you can pull the trigger if it comes down to it. You can't hesitate in a situation like that. And I was sure we were going to get out of there; that meant protecting myself and you in whatever way was necessary."

I sigh, my hands shaking.

"I get it, Mike," I say, more calm. "I'm just a little freaked out that I have brains splattered all over me. I really thought that was going to be an easy job so I wasn't expecting to be chased by dogs *or* have a gun held to me. I've never seen anyone killed like that before so it's taking me a while to process it."

"Got it," Mike says. "Well you've learned lesson one in the Spy-Ninja-Carjacking-Thief Manual: Expect the worst and then you'll be ready for it."

"Ugh," I say, wiping more brain goop from my face, afraid to look in the mirror to see if I got it all. "My plan was to have my Mexican Jackie Chan do my dirty work, but it turns out I'm actually his *apprentice* instead."

"Well, young padawan, I'd say considering how *unprepared* you were for that, you're shaping up to be pretty badass. The way you took out that dog was impressive not to mention calling that guy's bluff about shooting you. Freaked me out for a second, but it gave me just enough distraction. Wasn't even my idea in your head, and it was perfect." He looks pensive for another moment. "I'm starting to think you don't need me after all."

"Maybe I don't," I smile, leaning over to take a closer look at the bloody mess of flesh on his arm where the dog bit him. I grimace. I want to clean it up, but I've got somebody else's brains on my rag. "You're dripping blood on the seat. Are you going to bleed out?"

"Probably," he says. "You better reach in the back seat and grab the fugly shirt and use it. I hate to ruin it but flannel is a superior bandaging material."

I laugh and reach behind him for the shirt. "How convenient."

Thirty-five

*W**hen* Mike finally gets off the freeway, I immediately recognize it as Pomona, my old stomping grounds. He drives into one of the dilapidated, historic neighborhoods and parks in an alley. He motions for me to follow. Peeking over fences into back yards, he finally finds one that meets his requirements and opens the gate.

It's not until he turns on the yard hose that I finally understand.

"They do make travel stops for this kind of thing," I whisper, putting my hands under the flow. I'm glad the darkness keeps me from seeing any pink-tinged water flowing off of my skin.

"Sure. But if you were hunting someone, where would you expect them stop and sleep and clean up when they have nowhere else to go?"

"Mm. A rest stop. Okay."

At that, I don't hold back. I stick my whole head under the water. If I'm not going to see a shower any time soon, I'm going to make every effort to get every bit of gore off of me.

"Screw it," I say, handing Mike the hose and then telling him to hold it above me. I strip off my shirt down to my bra and treat the hose like a shower. I'm shivering fiercely from the cold water, but if I can come away without wondering if people brains are still clinging to me somewhere I can't see, it will be worth it.

"You treat all of your bodyguards like personal shower assistants?" Mike asks. "Can I get you some complimentary shampoo?"

"Desperate times, Mike," I reply. "Did I get it all?" I turn around in a circle with my arms out.

"Yes, mistress. May I wash off my battle wounds now, ma'am?"

"Oh yeah, sorry," I say, stepping out of the flow. I've been so obsessed with getting the blood off me that I forgot about Mike's dog bite. He wouldn't let me bandage it earlier, saying he needed to clean it first. And in my defense, he hasn't let on that it's been hurting him.

Mike hisses a little though as the cold water hits his arm. The blood and dog slobber is dried and caked, and it's probably going to start gushing blood again once he gets it off. And we didn't bring the shirt with us...

I bound lightly over the grass back to the car to grab it along with a knife to cut it into strips.

I'm rummaging for the knife, thinking I remember seeing Mike put it under the armrest, when I hear, "Hey baby. You need some help?"

That is *not* Mike's voice.

I spin around, cursing myself for being dumb enough to not only be shirtless in a dark alley in one of the worst areas of Pomona, but alone as well. The person who owns the voice sure isn't alone. There are three of them, not Gordies, but probably even worse threats to come across late at night.

"No thanks," I say, trying not to look afraid. That's the key I learned when I lived here—to look confident and like you belong, but that's difficult with me being in my bra in an alley in the middle of the night. "I got it."

"Oh yeah, you got it," another one of them says, stepping forward to lean against the back end of the car, leering at me from under his hoodie. One of his friends goes around to the other side of the car and opens the back door, leaning down and rummaging through our things.

My eyes widen and I freeze when I see him find the gun and the wad of money I got from Robert's safe. He comes up, holding the gun and money on display for his two friends. "Yeah, she got it *all* under control," he says.

"Daaaamn," the third one, who has been silent until now, says. "How much she got there?"

"Somebody had a good night," the one fingering the money says.

Oh God... What do I do? Where is Mike? Do I yell for him? What if he runs up and gets shot?

"She a hooker," the first one says, jutting his chin at me and kissing the air.

Oh my gosh, they are totally right. I look exactly like a hooker. Be confident, Wen. Don't show them fear...

RACHEL E KELLY   273

I don't think it's working. I'm already holding my quaking breaths.

"You don't want to do that," I say, infusing my voice with as much confidence as I can, but I can hear it crack at the end. I cross my arms and lean against my open door. "My chulo is down the alley. If he finds you messing with his take, it won't be pretty."

The one holding the gun runs the barrel under his nose like he's smelling it, but I think he means it to be salacious.

"He won't mind if we take a piece," the first one says, edging directly in front of me, running his arm along mine. I can smell his sour breath and feel the heat of it on my face. And then he runs a finger down my front from my neck to my abdomen. By now I am visibly shaking and tears have come to my eyes. He leans into me, and my back is against the open car door. I close my eyes, unable to move, scared of what worse may happen if I run.

A loud bang sounds to my right, startling me and the guy assaulting me. We both look that direction and I almost collapse with relief to see Mike with his hand around the neck of the kid with the gun, having slammed his face into the top of the car.

Mike's expression is stony and so menacing that my hand involuntarily moves up to cover my mouth. He slams the kid's face into the car again. Then he picks the kid up in both hands over his head, his bare chest gleaming in the streetlight, and throws him over the car and into the third guy who has been standing near the trunk.

My attacker backed away from me at some point, and I watch his frightened eyes stay locked on Mike as he continues to step backward. He trips over the body of his fallen comrade and hits the ground.

Mike stalks around the car as the kid scrambles to get to his feet. Mike picks the kid up by his shirt and throws him against the trunk of the car. Then he punches him in the face. And then he does it again, the unique smacking sound of it reverberating in my ears. He does it five times until I come up behind him and touch his shoulder. "Mike," I whisper, afraid that I'm going to see Mike beat the kid to death. "Let them go."

Mike stands stock still, his bare back to me, his hand around the kid's neck, his arm oozing blood again from the bite. One of the goons has already found his feet and is running away. The other is still passed out—the one that had his face slammed into the car.

I put my hand on Mike's arm and tug lightly. "Come on, Mike."

He tosses the kid to the ground by the other one. Neither of them moves. I hope they're not dead, but I can't tell.

Mike shrugs off my hand and goes to the driver's side of the car. He picks up the money and the gun from the ground as I get in.

Mike throws everything in his hands at the back seat, starts the car, and peels off down the alley.

Relieved that I was able to stop Mike and that I'm... mostly intact, I hug my arms around myself, shivering both from cold and from the adrenaline seeping out of me.

I reach to turn the heat on and discover that I'm still clutching the lumberjack shirt in my hand. Staring at it for a moment, I remember what I had intended to do with it. I twist around and rummage in the back for the undershirt Mike claimed was dirty and slip it over my head. I also see the knife I was searching for on the floorboard and grab that, too.

Stabbing the knife into the fabric of the hated shirt, I yank it down the sleeve. I stab it again and discover that actually cutting another neat strip parallel to the first with a knife is not as easy as it seems. Not to be thwarted, I stab it again, this time on the other sleeve. I almost get it, but my line swerves to the left again, meeting the first line. When I hit the cuff, I hold the shirt in one hand and yank the knife through the cuff with the other.

Mike puts his hand on the shirt in my lap as he pulls the car over. "You're going to stab yourself," he says, trying to take the shirt from me.

"I've got it!" I snap, yanking it back. I stab the middle, and without a sleeve cuff to stop me, the knife glides through the fabric easily, all the way to the end in one swift motion.

Mike reaches over me and plucks the knife from my right hand.

"Hey!" I glare at him.

"Just..." he closes his eyes for a moment before opening them slowly. "Calm down."

"I *am* calm!" I snap.

"Wendy, you were jerking that knife around like a baton. You are *not* calm."

"Oh excuse me for not having ninja knife skills like you. It might not be pretty but I can get the job done! Give it back."

"No," he says. "You're not using your head and you're going to cut yourself. I'm not bleeding to death. Give it a minute."

I suck in an angry breath, knowing I can't actually overpower Mike—which makes me more upset. "You're being a bully again," I mumble. "I'm a grown woman. I don't need you monitoring my knife habits."

"Keeping you from hurting yourself is not being a bully."

I roll my shoulders without relief, shuddering. I cross my arms and look out the window. We're in the unlit parking lot of an office complex. I want to block the flashbacks, but sitting here with nothing to do isn't helping.

Why did I freeze?

Why did I let him touch me?

Why did I just *stand* there?

Why am I suddenly a target for goons in an alley? I was much better at this when it happened outside the coffee shop…

I shudder, remembering the weight of him against me.

Why did I stop Mike?

The weight of a hand rests on the back of my head and I realize I'm sobbing.

Recognition causes my body to fold with the weight of emotion: fear and anger and loathing writhing together. I cry out, slamming my fists over and over onto the dash, wishing with a vengeance that I could go back and have a redo. This time I wouldn't stand immobile. I would fight back. I would make them hurt. I picture it in my head, how it would go, how when he reached out to put his finger on my skin I would grab it and twist it until it broke. I envision all different scenarios, each time delivering them more pain and terror than the last.

When my imaginings run their course, I sit up, squeezing the last of the tears from my eyes with my palm. I sit back in the seat, looking up at the roof of the car, not able to look at Mike yet.

"Why did I stop you?" I ask, imagining how things might have gone had I still had my death-touch. Actually, I probably would have heard them before they ever saw me if I still had my abilities. This blind, deaf, *normal* body is helpless.

Mike clears his throat. But he doesn't answer right away. I imagine hearing and counting his heartbeats. "Because that's the difference between me and you," he replies.

I don't know what he's talking about. I can't conceive of that person right now. I can't remember what I was feeling as I watched Mike send his fist into the kid's face over and over.

"Thank you," I say. "It was stupid of me. To go into the alley alone like that. In a place like that."

"You're welcome."

"Can I bandage your arm now? I need to do something."

"If you let me show you how to safely cut strips with a knife."

"So you're a Boy Scout, too?" I ask, rolling my head over to see him smiling mildly. I'm tired suddenly but afraid to go to sleep yet.

Mike looks even more exhausted than I feel. Maybe it's the effect of the dash lights, but his eyes are slightly red and the lines of his face are more visible. He smiles back at me, but there is little emphasis in it and it easily falls into a frown. "I'm sorry I didn't get to you sooner."

I sit up and turn my whole body his direction. "Hey. You got there. I shouldn't have left by myself, practically topless. In Pomona."

"I'm not going to argue about this. I just want you to know I'm sorry. I failed. By my own standard. Not yours."

"Fine," I sigh. "How about them knife lessons?" I hold up the shirt.

Jumping on the new topic, he takes the shirt from me, showing me how to use the knife with more control. He holds the fabric over the blade, making small sawing motions and cutting across his front instead of toward himself or away. He cuts through only a couple inches at a time, keeping the two-inch-wide strip even. All of these are things I could have figured out on my own, but sharing the task is settling to both of us, and I think we're both sick of serious things like being chased by dogs, shooting people in the face, or turning juvenile delinquent faces into hamburger.

With the unused scraps and a bottle of water, I wipe away the dried blood from his forearm and gently wind the first strip around his arm. I take note of Mike's face as I do so, not wanting to cause him too much discomfort, but he appears mentally absent as I work. He's been more even-keeled in the last few hours since he was bitten than I have ever seen him—to me anyway. The fit of violence against the alleyway goons doesn't count.

"Do you like pain?" I ask, tying the ends of the first strip and grabbing another.

"It helps me think straight," he says, his eyes still distant.

"What are you thinking about?"

"What the hell I'm supposed to be doing."

"You said you'd be my bodyguard. Has that changed?"

"I did say that, didn't I…" Mike trails off.

I don't miss that he didn't answer my question. A shiver moves over me and I pause in wrapping his arm as sudden anxiety falls over me at the possibility that Mike might change his mind. If it weren't for him just now I would have gotten in serious trouble… What on earth was that about anyway? My life is this huge friggin' mess and I almost get raped in an alley in the wee hours of the morning on a Thursday? Am I cursed or something? Am I headed the wrong way? Or is this supposed to tell me something? The only thing I can think of is that it's telling me I need Mike. I *need* him. And if I have any ideas to the contrary, I need to drop them.

"What?" he says to my faraway expression.

I shake my head. "Just realizing how much I need your help."

He grunts. I don't know if it's affirmation or something else.

It's my turn. "What?" I say.

"Just… reminding myself why I'm not taking you back to Gabe yet."

"We've finally got plenty of money and the Gordies have no idea where we are. Why would you even be thinking about that? I'm *married* to Gabriel, I have a child that hasn't seen me in weeks, and even though I miss them like crazy, I don't agonize over not going back right away. It's the right thing to do."

He groans.

"What am I missing?" I ask, winding the next strip around his arm.

"My point of view," he replies.

"Why don't you tell me and then I can stop missing it."

"I'd rather find a liquor store and get wasted."

"Saying things out loud makes them easier to deal with," I say, tying the next strip tightly. "Alcohol only does that temporarily."

"Sounds like more Gabe nonsense."

"For someone who claims to love and respect his brother so much, you sure dog his ideas a lot."

Mike sighs, still staring off into the darkness beyond the car.

"Come *on*," I prod. "Let me be your friend for a minute and you just vent."

He doesn't reply. I'm about to give up, but he says, "In the past four days I've had to anticipate the reunion with my brother and my family. I'm constantly going over different conversations with them in my head… trying to explain my actions in a way they'll understand…"

"They will," I say, wrapping the last strip around his arm.

He groans, and I'm not sure if it's from the injury or dissent until he says, "I warned you about that optimism. No matter how *you* think it's going to go, I'm the one agonizing over it every single day. I keep imagining Gabe and how he must be wondering if I'll ever bring you back, becoming more and more convinced that I've irrevocably betrayed him. The further away I get from my life at the Guild, the more I realize all I have left is my family. Except I *don't* have them. Every day what I've done sinks in. Each day it looks more and more and more unforgivable. What you said to me keeps getting shoved in my face at every turn: what do I hope to salvage? There's nothing left. The anxiety..." He shakes his head. "Forget it."

I've paused in the middle of my job, my heart snagging on his words and obvious mental calamity. I don't know what to say. He's right that I've been completely blind to his perspective. In the heat of so many adrenaline-filled moments, I haven't paused to contemplate it.

"I'm so sorry," I whisper, nearly in tears over his plight.

"Don't do that," he says, catching sight of my face. "Please don't do that. And tie that last one. Tighter than you did the other. You're getting sloppy."

"I can't help it, Mike," I say as a few tears fall down my cheeks. I do as he asks, but I wish I had emodar so badly right now, not because I wonder how he feels, but because I know how he feels, and I want to experience it with him so that he isn't alone.

"Sure you can. Just remember all the horrible shit I've done to you and I guarantee the tears will dry quickly."

I grab on to his bicep in refusal, wrapping my arms around it tightly, laying my head against his shoulder. "Compassion is in my blood, life force ability or not. So no. I can't help it," I say, feeling this is perhaps the first time I have recognized this about myself, post-leukemia cure. In light of losing so much of what I could do, I'm immensely relieved that the compassionate person I became because of them is still alive and well.

His arm flexes under my grasp but I don't let go. "I've always been right about you, Michael Dumas. And they are all going to forgive you because they know the same thing I do."

"Dare I ask?"

"All you've ever cared about is doing the right thing. You were just confused about what that was for a while."

I swear I can hear him mulling that over. At least he's not arguing about it. I smile to myself, not exactly sure why until I realize that I'm happy. I look around for the origin, but all I have is Mike and the fact that we broke through barriers today. I'm certain that he doesn't hate me anymore. I think I can actually call him my friend.

Mike's breaths have deepened, and when he snores softly, I'm sure he is asleep. I stay melded to his arm, realizing that this moment of genuine friendship was something I accomplished because I didn't give up. In fact, in the past four days I have found my way back to the Wendy who is comfortable in her own skin, I'm filled with pride in what I have accomplished. Every bit of it was done without supernatural skills. No emodar, somatosense, telepathy, colorworld… Yet I have felt just as alive, just as purposeful as I once did.

I guess Gabriel was right; I just needed a purpose, a mission. God love that man. He knows me so well…

Carefully pulling my arm out from under Mike's, I recline my seat and curl up, beaming into the darkness, so grateful to have found my way back that tears fall from my eyes, this time happy tears. My chest feels full. Incidentally, I think of Gabriel, how I wish he were here share my triumph. But I'm content to be patient, excited that when I find my way back to him, I will be the Wendy he remembers.

Thirty-six

What do you know about Regina Walden?" I ask as soon as Mike's eyes finally open. I've been waiting for him to wake up for hours now.

He rubs his eyes, squinting into the daylight. "Your dead biological mother?" Mike yawns. "Why are you asking? And have you been watching me sleep? That's creepy."

"Do you know where she was from? Where did they meet?"

"Chicago. To both questions."

"Does she have any living family?"

"No immediate family. She had one older brother but he was killed in combat during the Gulf War. Her parents were older—early forties—when they had Gina. They're dead now. She has an aunt and two uncles. Some cousins."

"Did she go to college?"

"Art school in Chicago. She earned a bachelor's degree in Fine Arts with a concentration in art education. She ended up—"

"She was an artist?" I interrupt with interest. I don't know why that should surprise me. Why have I never wanted to look into my biological mother's life before now?

"Yeah. Even though it was in your file as a possible career, I didn't actually know you were into art until your ex mentioned it. Looks like that's where you got it from."

"An angel..." I say, shaking my head as I remember what Quinn said. He said my mom—Leena, my adopted mom—told him I inherited my skill with art from an angel. She must have meant from my biological mother, who was dead... Leena must have known a lot about Gina. I wonder if they were friends... "Sorry, what were you saying? She ended up what?"

He scratches his head. "Ahhh, right, she ended up working for a university in Chicago and that's where she got recruited for hypno-touch by Carl. She moved to San Diego with Carl not long after meeting him. She got a job there."

"San Diego?" I ask, furrowing my brow. "That's where my mom was from—my adoptive mom."

"Not surprising since he got with Leena pretty soon after Gina died."

"Yeah…" I say. We lived in San Diego for a couple years when I was in middle school. That was where I found my passion. I attended art camp the first two summers I was there. That's where I started doing frescos. I fell in love with them. They're like a cross between sculpture and paint. Two-dimensional like painting and permanent and lasting like sculpture. Most of my time was spent either perfecting my plaster pigmenting skills on small tablets or working with different mediums for sculpture. I honestly loved both and in an effort to combine both worlds, I developed a method of doing a relief fresco, and that's what got me accepted to a prestigious art program in high school, which I never attended because I got pregnant.

"Why the sudden interest in Gina?" Mike asks.

"I'm going to find Carl," I reply quickly, pondering what my nagging feeling about San Diego means.

"Wendy," Mike says, sitting up at full attention now. "Not this again. I can't help you find Carl."

"You told me you *aren't* helping me. You said I order you around and you do it."

He rubs his hands through his hair until it's disheveled and standing straight up. "I know I said I would do what you ask, and I will, but I would feel a lot better if you'd explain why you feel so strongly about this route all of a sudden."

"This morning I was thinking about our next move. I kept thinking about the Guild and how they're desperate for me to get my ability back, and you told me that everything I've described being able to do is exactly what they want. They're like, light-years ahead in technology, and they've bet the farm on me solving this. That's a lot of freaking chips, Mike. I have to believe that I actually *can* figure out what's going on. I don't have everything worked out, but I have a few theories about how I lost my abilities—I think we put my strands back in the wrong place. And I think if we get all the misplaced ones *out*, it would give me back every bit of what I could do before. And I think we can do that. But I need Carl's help. I need to see if he's recovered at all. If he is even a little bit, he has the best chance at that. Plus, I need to ask him about the Guild. He's been dealing with them the longest. So I've got to find him first. And if I know one thing about Carl, it's that everything he has ever done has been about Regina. And whatever he's doing now, it's *also* about Regina. If I know more about Regina, I know more about him. The more I know about him, the more likely I'll be able to find him." I puff conclusively and look at Mike.

He gapes at me dumbly. "Whoa, that was a lot of words. Did you take any breaths in there?"

"And last night I dreamed about the colorworld."

"That matters because…"

"I have *never* dreamed about the colorworld. And besides, this was like, so *clear*. I smelled it, felt it, saw it, heard it. Every sense was so clear. It's a sign that I'm ready to get it back."

"Ready? And you weren't before?"

"No. Because before I was doing it for the wrong reasons. I realized last night that I've actually figured out how to live without my abilities. I actually found peace with it. So after I dreamt about the colorworld, I knew it was because I was closer to being that person even without the supernatural skills. And you know how figuring out one thing puts everything else in this whole new light?"

"Uhhh… I guess?"

"Well I began to accept that you might be right about some of my abilities being natural. So that meant I started to actually ask why I lost them. That led me to questioning why Gabriel kept his abilities. It's because he was only missing strands from his chest. We *couldn't* screw up putting his strands in the wrong place because there was only one place for them to go. But for *me*, I had both head *and* chest strands missing. So I must have put some head strands in the chest and vice versa. It must have shorted out my ability. It was actually something we worried about when we figured out how to insert strands, but we were so desperate to get well that we agreed not to worry about it—after all, all strands look the same. But I am *sure* that like every other time I didn't know what I was doing, I'll be able to figure out how to differentiate them and put the right strands in the right place." I beam, excited to be able to share all of my new discoveries. I've been bouncing around in my own head, antsy all morning since I woke up.

Mike is overwhelmed and says, "Chest and head strands? Is this more life force business?"

I nod excitedly. "Now you get why I need to find Carl. So. Gina. Can you tell me *anything* else about her? What kind of artwork did Gina do?"

"Painting." He thinks for a moment. "Murals or something?"

"Frescos?" I ask excitedly.

"Yeah, yeah. That was it. I'm pretty sure she concentrated on fresco history in school."

A light bulb flashes to life as soon as he says that. "Oh my gosh, Mike. Take me to San Diego. Now."

"Wow. You are *really* hard to argue with when you're wired like that. It's kinda scary."

"Sorry. I told you. I've been dying for you to wake up."

"Why didn't you wake me?"

"Because you needed sleep. I can't have you bumbling around like a zombie. How did you sleep? You looked pretty comatose."

"Best sleep I've had in a while. So, why San Diego?" he asks, starting the car.

"A lead."

"Is there a more particular destination you have in mind?"

"I'll tell you when we get there."

"Hmm, a secret," he says, turning a corner. "I hope you aren't going to visit any old friends there. Hopefully the Redlands debacle told you what a bad idea *that* is."

I roll my eyes. "No. And it's not a secret. It's an eatery my mom used to take me to. I honestly don't remember the name. I just remember where it is."

Mike gives me a look of confusion. "So what does an eatery your mom used to take you to have to do with Carl?"

"Maybe nothing. Maybe everything," I reply. And then I eye his bare torso. "And by the way. It's a place of business. No shirt, no shoes, no service."

Thirty-seven

L'angolo?" Mike says, glancing up at the small sign. "Is that French? Or Italian?"

"Italian," I reply as we walk up to the little corner restaurant that's nestled in the downtown of one of San Diego's suburbs. My insides are twisting and untwisting for all kinds of reasons as I approach the front door.

Mike notices my nerves I guess, because right when we reach the door, he stops and looks at me. "Food that bad? You look like you're sick already."

I smile glumly, recognizing that he's trying to lighten my mood. "Actually, the lemonade is the only thing here that's terrible."

He smiles and opens the door for me.

I step through into the small, dimly-lit space and don't look around. I turn left and take a seat near one of the windows. Mike sits across from me, his questioning eyes on my face. All of a sudden, I don't know why I came here. To think that this would give me a lead on Carl is stupid. It's curiosity that drove me here over anything else. Curiosity about… an idea that seems too crazy to be real.

A short blond girl swoops in and offers us a wide grin. "Welcome to L'angolo. Can I get you a drink?"

"Italian soda, please," I reply quickly, already fidgeting with my napkin. "Apple."

"Lemonade," Mike says, smiling at the waitress before looking back at me.

"Sure thing," she says, heading behind the counter.

I give him a look. "I told you the lemonade was terrible."

"It can't be that bad. How can you screw up lemonade?"

"Trust me," I say, my stomach starting to contract uncomfortably and I worry I'm going to vomit if this keeps up. I put my elbows on the table and lean my forehead into my palms and close my eyes.

"What is wrong?" Mike whispers, poking my arm.

I don't answer; I move my palms down to my eyes to dam them up.

What is wrong with me? I should not have come here.

"Is it because your mom used to take you here?" Mike asks, now tugging on my arm.

"This was a stupid idea," I croak.

I hear a light clunk as the waitress sets the drinks down. "Need more time to decide?" she asks.

"Yes, please," Mike replies politely.

I hear Mike drag his glass across the table and take a sip.

"Well *that* explains everything," Mike says after a moment. "No wonder you're freaking out. This lemonade is awful. Why does it taste fermented?"

I look up and smile. "Some kind of probiotic thing. I can't believe they're still making it like that after all these years. You should have listened to me. I'm not paying for another drink."

He reaches out and drags my glass away. Watching my reaction, he takes a long pull from my straw.

"Now you can forget about dessert," I say.

The waitress shows up again and my stomach has calmed enough that I can eat something. "Do you still have the rosemary chicken Panini?" I ask her.

She smiles. "You've been here before then. That's one of our classics."

"Great. I'll have that and the micro green salad."

Mike's eyes scan the paper menu on the table and then looks at me and says, "Why don't you order for me since I'm on spending probation?"

I look at him critically, considering what he might choose. Mike comes across as a comfort food kind of guy so I say to the waitress. "The chicken parmesan hero. Can you add caramelized onions to that? And toast it." I glance down at the menu. "And the beet salad."

"That's pretty heavy," Mike says after the waitress leaves.

"Mike, why would you tell me to order for you if you're going to complain about—"

"Relax," Mike chuckles. "It was just an observation, not a complaint."

"Whatever," I sigh, looking up finally to see that we aren't the only ones here. The place is actually pretty busy since it's the lunch hour. It looks almost exactly the way I remember with random period pieces scattered about. None of the furniture matches and the fake plants are kind of chintzy but that adds to the charm. To me, the place has always been a hippie Italian grotto with some cheap American flare thrown in. Mismatched, unrefined, and perfectly wonderful.

"Why are we here?" Mike asks finally.

I close my eyes, remembering my mom's hands on my shoulders, shaking them. *Isn't it perfect, Wendy?* she gushes. *I knew you'd love it!*

I'm struck with a sudden worry of losing the most important piece of that memory. "There's still a fresco on the wall behind me on the other side of the restaurant, right?" I say.

Mike looks over my shoulder. "Oh yeah…" He gazes beyond me for a minute. "It's pretty nice, huh? Is it real?"

"What do you mean, *is it real?*" I ask, narrowing my eyes at him. "Of course it's real. What did you think it was? Spray-paint graffiti?"

Mike holds his hands up. "Wen, I am not art savvy. I wouldn't know Van Gogh or Picasso if I saw it and I *definitely* would not know a real fresco either. I thought it was the same as a mural."

I sigh in exasperation. "No, it is *not* the same. A fresco is like tattooing the wall. The pigments are infused into the surface permanently so that it becomes part of the wall. You can't scrub it off like a mural."

At that moment, the waitress shows up with our food.

Mike doesn't look at it but tilts his head at me. "You really are hardcore artsy fartsy. I never would have guessed."

I ignore the comment, although I do find it interesting that Gordy doesn't appear to know about my art. "That fresco is why we're here," I say, taking a bite of my sandwich. I close my eyes and sigh. It's as good as I remember, which is saying something since I don't have super senses anymore.

"We're here for a *painting*? Why?" Mike says. "And why did you not look at it when we walked in here?"

"It's not just a painting, Mike," I say between bites. Mike's indifference has my art-ignorance eradication instincts shifted into high gear so my internal battle has calmed. And it reminds me that I'm actually starving.

"This is really good," Mike says, looking at his sandwich after he takes a bite.

"Try the beet salad. It's to die for."

"I'm saving it for last. Beets are my favorite vegetable ever." I widen my eyes. "Really?"

"No," Mike laughs. "Kidding. I've actually never had them before. But it looks so good I don't want to ruin it. I want to admire it."

I reach over and punch his arm. "Jerk."

"So, are you planning on *looking* at the paint—er, fresco?" he says.

"Yes. I'm working up to it."

"Working up to it? Is this some kind of art appreciation thing? You take your time *anticipating* looking at it?"

"No, Mike. But that fresco has special meaning to me. It was the first *real* fresco I ever saw."

"Aaaand… that makes it hard to look at why?"

I don't answer until I finish my sandwich. I am going to have to tell him, but I'd like to get all my food down in case I start something ridiculous like sobbing.

Once our plates are clear and Mike has complimented the beet salad and claimed that beets might be his *new* favorite vegetable, I fold my arms on the table. "I was really into art growing up," I say as clinically as I can manage. "My mom was always taking me to places with neat local art to sample. San Diego is when I started really throwing myself into it, perfecting my techniques. She brought me here one day, saying she thought I would *love* the fresco that someone had done on the wall." I bite my lip and look at the renaissance-styled crown molding as I say, "I saw it and fell in love. I wanted to do something like it. The way the pigments were so sharp and smooth like a photograph—not textured like a painting. It made it seem like the wall itself had pushed the image out. It reminded me of sculpture, the way it *was* the wall."

A couple tears have managed to escape anyway and I sniff and brush them hastily away. "It inspired me. I obsessed over frescos from that day on. And I wanted to come here because… well because after you said Gina did frescos I was shocked that I'd never wondered where my artistic genes came from. My mom was really analytical-minded and Carl never struck me as into anything creative other than screwing with life forces. I have this suspicion… that maybe Gina did the fresco here. My mom... when she showed it to me, the look on her face was like she *expected* me to love it. She was always really encouraging of my art, but she was beaming ear-to-ear that day as I oohed and ahhed over it. I didn't think anything of it at the time but now I know she knew..."

"That she was showing you a part of your biological mother," Mike finishes. "She was reuniting the two of you."

"I don't know... Now that we're here I'm acting like a basket case and wondering why in the world I thought this would have anything to do with Carl. Instead I'm thinking of my mom and the fact that all that time she was encouraging me to hold on to the part of me that tied me to Gina, only I never knew. And I still have no idea if the fresco is even Gina's."

"Well let's go get a closer look," Mike says, standing up and pulling me by the hand.

I allow myself to be guided toward the other side of the tiny restaurant but I look at the floor the whole time, ashamed. Over the years I've blocked the image from memory because it has always made me too sad. I have stalwartly refused to recall it, so over the years I actually *have* forgotten what it looks like.

"I'll be damned," Mike says, stopping in front of the wall. "Look down at the very bottom corner behind that plant: '*R.W.*'"

I trail my eyes up to where he's indicated, catching only a tiny corner of the image. Sure enough Regina's initials are there in careful block letters. I put my hand over my mouth and shake my head in wonder, my heart aching for my mom—my adopted mom—who must have definitely been attempting to connect me to my past in the face of the heartache it must have caused her.

I wonder how it must have felt—raising another woman's child. I don't really know why Carl married Leena, but it could not have been out of love. Carl did hypno-touch on her even though he knew what would result. What kind of forgiveness and sacrifice it must have taken for my mom to dedicate her life to me the way she did. It wrenches my heart inside out that my mom spent so much time encouraging me to be who I was even though it meant something completely different from who *she* was.

I turn into Mike's shoulder because the tears won't let up. Just like when I learned why my mom had me give up Elena—so that she wouldn't one day be motherless—I shed tears of mourning and gratitude for the woman who didn't just save me, she went above and beyond. Even though she had no responsibility to do anything at all. She knew she would die. She rightfully thought *I* would die. She paved the way for me to make the most out of my life.

The weight of Mike's hand falls on my back, and once my tears have dried, I feel renewed, like the knowledge I've discovered has changed me internally. I step away from him and look at the fresco for the first time in over six years.

Seeing it brings the memory of it back into sharp focus. I step back.

"What is it?" Mike asks, worried. "Is it not the same?"

"No, it's the same," I reply in wonder. "But honestly I've blocked it from my memory until now so I forgot what it looked like. Now that I'm seeing it again after all these years... I can't believe... the significance is so obvious now."

"Significance? Why would you block it from memory if it inspired you?" Mike asks, confused.

I sigh. "Because I quit art after my daughter died. Cold turkey. I haven't picked up a brush, a piece of clay, or charcoal since."

"You had a daughter? *That's* what you meant by your *other* child?"

"Yeah. In high school."

"What the hell? Why didn't I know this? Or about any of your art? Once you surfaced at the compound, we looked at every piece of your history. We found none of this."

"My mom's doing. And it's all starting to make sense." I put my hands on my hips, staggered once more by my mom's foresight. She thought of *everything*. "I didn't use my real name on my art. In art world, my name was Gemma Rossi. My mom convinced me it was hip to have a pen name. She said when I was famous I'd want my real name private. But I remember now, when I had Elena, she had me sign the birth certificate as Gemma, saying it was a good way to leave that legacy with her if she ever searched out her birth mother. But in retrospect, it must have been two-fold. I bet she was making sure that if *I* was ever found, Elena wouldn't be. Wendy was my given name. Gina's middle name. Like you said, you've had feelers out for that name, and for artists because of Gina's background. Gemma was a way to protect me *and* Elena."

I blink back tears again and turn to look at Mike, whose face has blanched. "Gemma Rossi?" he whispers.

I'm confused by his reaction until I remember the Detritus Art Benefit. "The cloud sculpture in your parent's house that you and Gabriel picked out. Yeah, it's mine. I was there that night at the benefit. Freaky coincidence, huh?"

"Shit," he whispers, looking down at the floor. Then he looks back at my face like he's seeing it for the first time. He mouths something I can't make out.

"What? Do you remember us meeting? Gabriel says he doesn't. And most of the night was a blur to me. It was right after Elena had died... I was a mess. The cloud sculpture was the last piece of art I ever made."

Mike's chest is moving up and down rapidly. He looks over my shoulder at the fresco, eyes slightly wild. Clears his throat. "Tell me about the fresco. What's the significance?"

Concerned that Mike is blowing off my question, but knowing he's not the type to be pushed into talking, I turn around. "This is the colorworld," I say, roaming my eyes over the fresco. It's surreal to stand here after so many years and be able to see the work with entirely new eyes. Its meaning is obvious. I cannot believe I have forgotten it. I don't understand how I *could* forget it. The fresco is as beautiful as ever—more so—and it's clear that Gina saw the colorworld and pigmented it into this wall. "Carl must have shown it to her."

At the center of the fresco is a tree and it's a vivid blue-green—the trunk being darker than the leaves that are painted in such detail that I know it must have taken Gina days to complete just one branch. The grass is yellow, and from one side of the scene to the other, the grass color bleeds through different shades, sometimes as dark as burnt orange. The sky is a menagerie. So beautiful and sharp in color that it makes the image look like it's fluctuating even though it's frozen on plaster. I remember the first time I saw this, it looked like sunset. But I know better now. The real focus of the fresco is the figure sitting at the base of the tree. It's a woman holding a baby. And they are both purple. She wasn't trying to capture life forces precisely, but she conveyed that the essence of a person is purple. So they basically look like they have purple skin but it doesn't look weird since everything else is so off of its natural color as well. Again, I misinterpreted this at the time I first saw it as abstract and classic at the same time with the way the artist had played with colors. And I assumed that they chose the colors they did to brighten the inside of the restaurant, which is relatively dim.

"Wow," I say. No wonder this fresco touched my soul when I first saw it. I must have been capable of seeing some portion of the colorworld at the time without being aware of it. Aside from the overt symbolism here, I must have somehow intrinsically known that it was significant to me specifically.

Mike has remained silent behind my shoulder.

I turn abruptly then, walking up to the cashier who's ringing someone's bill. "What can you tell me about the fresco on the wall?" I ask her.

She smiles at me. "Pretty cool, huh? I don't know who painted it if that's what you're asking."

"Do you know any of its history? Like *when* it was done. Was it here before or after this restaurant was opened…? That kind of thing."

"Um, well I've only been working here for a year so I don't really know. It's been here as long as I have, but I bet the owner knows more about it. Do you want me to ask him?"

"He's here?" I ask excitedly.

She nods. "Yeah, give me a minute." She processes a payment for the customer she's helping while I wait, crossing my arms and trying not to look rudely impatient.

Mike comes up next to me. Still quiet. I want to ask him about Gemma Rossi and the Detritus Benefit, but this is more important right now.

I lean against the counter and look at the fresco again, drawing more meaning from it by the moment. "Look at it. A mother and a child? You pour all that you are into what you're art. There is a *ton* of meaning there. Look at the sun. It's setting in the distance. That symbolizes the end of something. See the leaves? They're speckled between shades of blue—exactly how they look during the fall in the colorworld. That would have been exactly when Gina was sick because she died in December. Look at the baby. It's a deeper shade of purple, much closer the actual color of a life force. And the mother is much lighter, almost like she's fading. Do you know what happens when a person dies? Their life force disappears. It doesn't go away, but it becomes invisible, even to me. The difference in the two figures indicates that her life is fading while the baby's is getting brighter. See the way she holds it? Like she's kissing the child goodbye? There's a tear running down her cheek." I choke out the words, tears nearly overcoming me again. I clear my throat. "I don't know if it will help me find Carl, but there is *nothing* more important to him than her. And anything she'd done—especially something as magnificent as this fresco—would be equally important to him. It would have kept her alive in his mind."

At that moment, the waitress emerges with a tall and placid-looking, middle-aged Italian man. "This is Mister Lombardi," the waitress says. "He owns this restaurant."

Lombardi holds out a long, lean hand and smiles pleasantly. "Hello. Jessica tells me you had some questions about our fresco."

I shake his hand and say, "Yes, I was just wondering if you could tell me anything about it—historically, I mean. How long has this restaurant been here?"

"About fifteen years. The fresco was here when we opened. It was perfect, actually, since it fit into the ambiance we were going for. I'm pretty sure the place was a restaurant before we moved in. I don't know who painted it though."

My countenance falls. "So who was here before you?"

"A Greek restaurant, I think."

"Do you know who owned it?"

Lombardi's eyebrows draw together a tiny bit. I think he's put off by my insistent interrogation. But he replies, "I don't know. But I'm glad you like it. I'm quite attached to it myself. It saved us quite a few years ago when we were struggling to stay open."

"Really?" I ask casually so my demanding questions don't freak him out further. "How's that?"

"Oh it was about ten years ago. We were more like a coffee shop at the time, struggling to stay open. One of our regular customers was particularly fond of the fresco and I remember he would sit right there." Lombardi points to a table that's in the middle of the space, directly in front of the fresco. "He would sit and admire that painting the whole time he was here as he sipped his latte. We got to talking one day and I admitted that I was probably going to be shutting down the place and I hoped the future owner would keep the beautiful painting so he could come visit it. The man told me that he'd be glad to invest with the stipulation that I never paint over the fresco and that I not ruin the integrity of it in any other way. It was written right into the investor's contract, actually. But it allowed us to expand to a full menu, saving the restaurant and keeping us going ever since. The man said he loved the coffee but the real reason he invested was because he loved the painting. So I've always thought of it as my good luck charm. It's the thing that keeps this place going." He smiles fondly, looking over at the wall where the fresco is.

I avoid letting my words come out in a torrent, "So this investor…" I say carefully. "Do you stay in touch with him?"

I think that was the wrong question. The man's eyes dip with suspicion. "I'm sorry," I say quickly. "That's none of my business. I just *really* like the fresco. I'm curious who did it and I'd think that if someone else loves it as much as I do, enough to throw money at a restaurant to save it, he might know more about its origins. If the artist is still alive, I'd love to find them and have them do something for me."

That does the trick. The man smiles. "No problem. I don't think he'd mind. Yes, I still stay in contact. He does own a portion of the restaurant after all. He doesn't live in San Diego anymore. He moved away years ago but I see him on occasion. I'd rather not give you his phone number, but I can give you an address. You can write him and ask about it."

"Thank you!" I gush.

Moments later, I'm clutching a slip of paper in my hand with the name *David Erlich* and an address which, lo and behold, is a post office box in Chicago. I can't believe what I just did… *without* supernatural abilities.

Mike and I exit the restaurant, and as soon as we hit the open air, I squeal and grab Mike in a tight bear hug. I kiss him on the cheek and dance all the way to the car.

Thirty-eight

alk to me," I say.

Mike ignores me, continuing to skip rocks, this time into a pond at our latest stop just north of San Diego. I've been sitting on the hood of the car, either lost in imagining having my abilities back once we find Carl, or worried about Mike's unbreachable silence since we left the restaurant. Unfortunately it's been more of the latter.

After the restaurant, I told Mike I wanted to go to the mall and buy us new clothes. He drove me without complaint, but he was barely there. And to my disappointment he made a beeline for a sportswear store. He picked up his usual black compression shirt, shorts, and tennis shoes. The look on his face when I protested that it wasn't a good disguise stopped me mid-sentence.

Determined to not let him rain on my parade, he sulked in one of the benches while I went into a Goth store to pick out my latest disguise. I had fun choosing from yet another style of clothing I have never worn before. I bought two entirely black outfits: one involving fishnets, a skirt, and a vest, and another more utilitarian one that included skinny jeans, a tank top, and a baggy overshirt made of some kind of see-through netting. And then I bought black combat boots, giggling at myself as I walked out of the store because it was the first time I ever *really* enjoyed shopping. But I think it's because I'm so *content* with myself finally that everyday things are actually *appealing.*

Mike strictly avoided my face when I asked if he was ready to go. He grumbled something about what a stupid question that was, so to spite him I made him stop with me at a wig kiosk on the way out. I took my time trying on every single wig, eventually settling on a platinum blond short do with sweeping bangs. I've been wearing it since then.

He's ruining everything though. I've been waiting patiently all day, thinking his funk since L'Angolo can't last that long, but it's been hours.

Since it worked last time, I hop off the hood of the car and pick up a small rock. I throw it at Mike's back.

"Stop it," he says, not turning around. "I have nothing to say."

"*That's* a lie. I know whatever it is has to do with Gemma Rossi and that art benefit."

"I don't owe you an explanation, Whitley," he says. He flings another rock.

That gets my attention. He hasn't stooped to using my maiden name since... days ago. Looks like I'm back to square one.

"So we met at the benefit..." I say.

Another rock. It skips six times.

"Gabriel says you both saw my sculpture and immediately knew your mom had to have it."

The next rock skips only three times.

"They gave out etched glasses at the benefit. Gabriel says you liked them so much that he gave you his, too."

Two skips.

"Somehow one of them ended up at Gabriel's apartment. That's where I found it."

"Just shut up," he says, turning toward me and stalking toward the car, yanking his door open.

I go around to my side and hop in. "Where are we going?"

"A hotel," he says, turning the engine over. "I'm tired of this sleeping in a car shit."

I can't argue with that, and I hope after some R&R, Mike will feel a bit more open to talking.

₪

Throwing my shoes off, I collapse on the bed in my room. I fold my hands over my chest, fighting to calm myself. Mike is back at it, making my life miserable just because I'm alive. Not only did he threaten to sleep in the car if I only got us one room with two queens, but before we parted ways to our own rooms I offered to take the slacks and button up he wore the first day we escaped the Guild and wash them in my sink. He cussed at me with words I have never heard him use, telling me to get out of his face and leave him alone the rest of the night if I knew what was good for me.

Blood now boiling, the only thing that might ease my anger is a hot shower. So I hop back up and spend a good thirty minutes under the stream of water, ridding myself of the evidence of the last forty-eight hours. When I get out, it's dark out but I'm not tired.

So I tuck my gun in my waistband, yank my T-shirt over it, and head for the door. Then, because I came here in my blond wig, I put that on before leaving as well. Once outside I take off at a brisk jog around the building, letting my footfalls set a more soothing tempo for my ponderings, which turn to Mike of course. Upon examining possible reasons for his new and improved hatefulness I come to one probability: at the time of the benefit, Mike would have already been working for the Guild, which means he ran into me and didn't know I was the one he was looking for. If he *had* known, he could have taken me then and prevented all this grief with his family. In fact, the happenstance of that meeting makes sense now. Mike must have been already using his ability in an effort to find me, and *that's* what drew our paths together that night, and not some faceless will of the universe.

I assumed Mike had gotten past the regrets of what might have been as far as his Guild mission is concerned, but I guess you can't let go of seven years of effort as cold turkey as I'd like to imagine. The question now is how I can help him. First order of business (after I find Carl), is making absolutely *sure* Gabriel is going to forgive him.

That's my plan. But dealing with Mike's ambivalence in the meantime is going to be tricky.

After about three circuits I slow to a walk, coming upon the entrance closest to my room once more, debating whether I will be able to sleep now that I've expended some of my energy. That's when I notice that the car we came in is missing. Thinking I must not be remembering where we parked, I turn this way and that, scanning the lot. But I don't see it. I dash into the building and knock on Mike's door.

No answer.

I knock again. Did he leave? Maybe he went out for a drink or something. Or maybe he left for real...

And I don't have a key to check his room.

I begin to panic a little. I'm not sure why exactly, whether it stems from worry for Mike or myself. But I know I need to find out if he really is gone. So I walk briskly but with controlled calm to the front desk where I hope to convince the clerk to give me a spare key.

"Excuse me," I say to the girl whose dark head is bent over a hefty book.

She looks up through her square-framed reading glasses and I put both hands on the counter and do a double-take. "Letty?!"

She tilts her head at me, her brow furrowing under her thick fringe of bangs as she peers more closely at my face. "Wen? Is that you? Geez Louise, when did you go blond? What are you doing here?"

"I have a room here," I say. "You *work* here?" *What in Hades is going on?*

"What a coincidence," she says, smiling and standing. "Let me give you a hug. It's been ages!"

I stand where I am in stunned confusion as she bounds around the counter. Whatever this is, I wouldn't call it mere coincidence.

She takes me in an embrace, which I return while my mind spins through possibilities. Is this Mike's doing? Why? How?

Mike. I came here to get his room key.

"Um, Letty. I locked my key cards in my room," I say. "Could you hook me up with a temporary one?"

"Abso-freakin'-lutely," she says, going back around the counter. "But you gotta dish on what you've been up to since… when was the last time we saw each other? Six months ago?"

"Yeah. Sure," I say, on guard for reasons I can't quite place. I did see Letty not long after I recovered from leukemia. It was Gabriel's doing, trying to get me to reconnect with people, and he and I were on a trip to San Diego to visit his grandparents, and we stopped by La Jolla, where Letty was attending a UC San Diego master's program. We had lunch and agreed to keep in touch—but we haven't. That's more my fault than hers.

She reveals a card from somewhere.

"I'm in 138," I reply. Come to think of it, we're not too far north of La Jolla now, so running into Letty isn't as much an impossibility as I first thought.

"I have a master key," she says. "Lead the way." She comes around and links arms with me. "Where is that hottie husband of yours, eh?"

"Not here," I say, struggling not only for what to say to her, but also what I should be *doing* right now. If Letty is here, and the Guild knows everyone I have ever known, then they know about Letty. Which means they're watching her. How? Cameras? Stakeout?

Bugs? I have no idea. I also have no clue if I should be worried about the happenstance of running into her. Does the Guild know?

Except I don't buy this as happenstance for a moment. This smells like supernatural skills in effect. And now that I'm thinking about it, the same must be true for the time I ran into Quinn at the gas station... Why have I never considered that possibility until now?

Too many coincidences to explain away...

Letty, I realize, has been chatting at me about her master's program and working nights at the hotel. She stops when we reach Mike's door.

"Wen, you look like you've seen a ghost," she says, sticking the key card in the slot. The light turns green and she turns the handle. "Tell me what's up, yeah?"

The lights are off, but Letty beats me to the switch.

The room is empty. And clean. No sign that anyone has been here at all...

"You sure this is your room?" Letty says. "No worries. People forget all the time. I can look it up."

"No," I shake my head. "This is his room."

"His?" she says. And then her eyes narrow. "Him who? Oh my gosh, Wen, who are you here with? Are you cheating on Gabe?" She squeaks and puts her hand over her mouth with her characteristic overly dramatic flair before continuing in rapid speed speech, "You trying to surprise your... whoever he is? He's meeting you here? That's messed up... Maldito, Wen. I mean, you two seemed off that time I saw you, but that's like, normal stuff, you know? Everybody schleps through relationship bull. My abuela always said you gotta work it out, you know? Who is he? Where's Gabe? Are you separated—wait. Oh my gosh... you were gravid that time I saw you! You have a kid? You have a kid! What's wrong with you?"

"Ugh, Letty!" I say, swatting at her arm. "Stop jumping to the worst conclusions. I'm not cheating on Gabriel. I'm here with his brother. This is his room. Mine is across the hall. He kind of hates me. Apparently so much that he abandoned me here with no car—oh shoot, I need to make sure I still have money." I dig my key card out of my back pocket and open the door to my room. Everything looks as I left it. I snatch up my backpack and unzip the pocket where I've been keeping the giant wad of cash I got from my uncle's. It's still there.

"His brother..." Letty says pensively. "What are you doing with his brother?"

I sit on the edge of my bed, at a loss for what to do now. I need to leave. But I'm not sure how other than to start walking. So I start packing up my things, which don't consist of much. I stuff my backpack full, and what's left fits into the plastic shopping bag I got from the mall earlier. "Where's the closest bus station?"

Letty has her hands on her hips, her expression stern. "You are the most frustrating person ever, Wen. I swear you live a double life. Every time I see you it's all secrets and rushing and crazy stories about your evil uncle and splitting with Gabe. Then you take it all back. You're here with your brother-in-law but he hates you... He left you here and now you need a bus in the middle of the night..." Then she curses loudly and jumps. "A *gun*, Wen? Who the hell are you? You hate guns."

Crap. I tug my T-shirt back down. "It's to protect myself."

"From *who*? You in a gang? That's gotta be it. You're in a gang. That's why you're always hiding stuff and blowing me off. He's in it too, then, huh? I mean, he doesn't look like he's in one, but then what do I know about that stuff. I'm just trying to go to grad school. You though, you're always up to something suspect."

"Letty," I put my hands on her shoulders. "I am *not* in a gang. I'm just... valuable to certain people because of what I know. They're hunting me. They're *always* hunting me. And they know about you, and I don't want to put you in danger because they're going to know I'm here with you, so I'm getting out of here so I don't cause you trouble, okay?"

"Whatever you say, Wen," Letty replies, and I can hear the disbelieving placation in her voice.

I walk with Letty back to the lobby, suddenly feeling very alone and afraid. I don't really know how to do this without Mike, but I guess I don't have a choice.

"Oh shoot, customers," Letty says at the same time I see the two individuals in the lobby about fifteen feet away. Letty tries breaking away from me, but I instinctively jerk her back around the corner by the arm.

"Hey!" she complains too loudly, and if the people I caught a glimpse of at the counter were paying any attention, they heard her. I only caught sight of them for a second, but that brief look has me certain they are Gordy. I can't put my finger on how I know that. Maybe it's their business casual dress, the fact that there are two of them—what I now know makes up a *dyad*, maybe the fact that they're at the hotel so late, or maybe I've learned to be sufficiently paranoid. But as I drag Letty around another corner leading to the stairwell, I put my finger to my lips, and peek my face around the edge, looking both up and down the hall. I see them, rounding from the lobby with purposeful strides. And there are two more with them. And these ones are dressed in black. Four total.

Gordy has found me. And Mike is not here.

Thirty-nine

I duck back, yank open the door to the stairwell and drag Letty with me.

"Wen!" she hisses as the door closes behind us and we climb the stairs. "What's going on?!"

"Do you have keys to your car?" I ask when we reach the second floor.

"I don't have a car," she says. "I take the bus. Grad student on a budget. Remember?"

"Crap," I say, racking my brain for plan B. I remember my gun then, and I pull it out.

Letty starts speaking in frenzied Spanish.

"Give me that master key card," I tell her.

Letty, while her nerves have her running off at the mouth about gangs and me owing her big for probably causing her to lose her job, has enough sense to do what I ask. And as soon as I have the card in my hands, I stop at a door and pray it's unoccupied as I stick the card in the slot.

The room is empty. I sigh with relief, shutting the door behind us, dead bolting and chaining it. Then, guessing that Letty will go for the light switch, I yank her hand toward me. "Leave it dark," I say.

"Are you ever going to explain what we're doing?" she demands in a whisper.

"I swear," I puff, sucking in frightened breaths, "I will tell you as soon as we're safe. But right now I need to figure out what to do because those guys in the lobby are here for me. I need you to do exactly as I say."

"Fiiine," she drawls.

"Do you have your phone on you?"

"No. I left it at the desk."

"Good," I say, guessing that a phone would be an excellent place to bug someone's location and conversations. I have no idea whether to worry if Letty has more bugs on her. But I'm assuming it would be a pretty inefficient way to track someone—bugging their shoes or clothes. People change them every day. But their phone is something they'd always keep close by.

"If you need a phone, you can use the one in here," Letty says, incorrectly assuming I was asking about her phone because I need to call someone.

"How does the sprinkler system work in this place?" I ask. "If I mess up the one in here, will it trigger more of them?"

"No. But it will call the fire department."

"Good enough," I say. "Where is the sprinkler head?"

"Right above us. You need a chair?"

"Please. And take this bag and set it as far away as possible so it doesn't get wet." I love Letty. She knows how to jump head-first into a plan. Once you get her to stop talking, that is. She has a weakness for anything exciting, so it's no surprise she'd be on board with a little adventure-filled vandalism.

I watch her shadow push the desk chair across the floor to me. "I need something to break the head off with," I say, stepping up onto the chair and steadying myself with one hand on the nearby wall.

With my eyes adjusted to the darkness somewhat, I see her looking around the room, eventually settling on something. She puts it in my hand: the TV remote.

"Perfect," I say, hacking at the sprinkler head with the remote. It's a lot sturdier than I expected. Letty has to hold the swiveling office chair still while I do my best to do damage to the stubborn piece of metal. Remembering what the sprinkler heads look like with the little glass vials of heat-responsive liquid, I stop and rethink my strategy.

"See anyone through the peephole?" I ask Letty.

She goes to the door and peers through it. "Nothing."

"Quickly. Open the door and see if anyone's in the hall yet."

She removes the chain, flips the deadbolt and cracks the door open. Her head disappears a moment before she pulls it back in. "Hall's empty."

"Okay, open the door all the way. Stand in the hall with the bags. Get ready to run."

Letty obeys, and in one violent blow to the vulnerable side of the sprinkler head rather than the metal fitting, I release a torrent of water. And an alarm begins blaring. I leap off the chair and take off running to the end of the hall, stopping a few doors short and again praying that this new room will also be empty.

No such luck. The door is dead bolted. In a split second decision, and in a flash of confidence, I run for the stairwell at the end of the hall opposite the one we came from, my gun leading the way, Letty picking up my rear. There's one more floor up, and that's where I intend to go. When I meet the stairs, there's someone waiting.

Having expected it, I immediately say, "Freeze," pointing my gun at the chest of dark-haired Gordy who is in the middle of raising his weapon, which I immediately recognize as an NTG. "Mine's real. Yours isn't. So lower it. Slowly."

He does until it's pointing at the floor.

"Hold it to your thigh. And pull the trigger," I command.

With a sigh first, he does what I say, collapsing at our feet.

"Holy mother," Letty exclaims, but I don't stop. I head for the stairs.

We reach the third floor. People are coming out of their rooms with the sound of the alarms, and I hold my gun out of sight. Some people look panicked, others are more aggravated, rightfully assuming a false alarm but not willing to make the bet by going back to bed. I search for the closest room that doesn't look like someone has come out of it. I try my key card, find it unbolted, and go in, Letty behind me.

I shut the door, deadbolt it. This time I turn on the light, because if anyone is watching from outside, they're sure to see every window lighting up. Ours won't stand out.

"Whoa," Letty says. "You are one crazy bruja, Wen."

I start digging through my bag. I pull out the black skinny jeans, tank top, and jacket. I take off my wig, which is now soaked, and start changing into my new, dry outfit.

"Daaaamn," Letty says. "Goth Sinéad O'Connor. I like it."

"You got something to put your hair up with?" I ask her, tugging one of my boots on. "And there's a black vest in there. You have black slacks on already, so that should work."

"Aye, Wen, you know my boobs are bigger than yours. I can't do the same size as you in a fitted top."

"Please. I was breastfeeding a month ago. My boobs went up at least a size. And the vest fits me perfect."

Letty unbuttons her white uniform blouse, puts her arms into the vest sleeves, buttoning it up. "This is cute," she says, admiring her cleavage, which testifies that she is still slightly bigger than me, breastfeeding or not. But at least it works. She winds her thick hair up into a bun and stabs a pen through it that she found in the nightstand. "How do I look?" she says, twisting this way and that. "I kinda dig this black. I feel like a classy gangsta, like I could do damage to someone if they look at me wrong. Do I get a gun, too?"

I laugh. "I've missed you, Letty. You even make danger fun. You have your reading glasses still?"

"Yup," she says, pulling them from her pocket and flipping them open with a flourish. She perches the black frames on the edge of her nose and gives me a duck face and sultry stare over the top of them.

"You make one *hawt* Goth librarian, Letty," I say, giggling at her and shoving all my wet things into the shopping bag, the dry things into my backpack. I toss the shopping bag into the bathroom, the backpack over my shoulders, and the gun in my waistband under my jacket.

"I'm ready to kick ass in this outfit," Letty says, taking up position behind me as I peer through the peephole. "What's next?"

"An opportunity," I say, watching a few dazed people pass in front of our door. The alarm is still going, and I'm betting the fire department is here by now. "We're going out there," I say. "And we're going to look like we just got in from one party, ready to head out to the next. We're buzzed and immature, and we don't take fire alarms seriously. In fact, this little hotel incident has given us something to talk about. And if there are any hot guys, we are all over that." I look back at her questioningly.

"The good old days," Letty says. "A coupla badass brujas out on the prowl. We got this. You're Mina. I'm Selena. 'K?"

I give her a sharp nod, sliding my game face into place as I open the door.

Letty and I link arms, headed for the stairs along with several others. But I don't look at anyone too hard. I'm so nervous I can hardly think straight. If I see a Gordy I'm going to be hard-pressed not to run, so I need to not look for one. I need to pretend like I'm part of the group that doesn't know what's going on.

Letty, however, is in her element. "Hey!" she gushes, "maybe we hang around a minute, see if any cute firemen to show up?" Letty grins mischievously.

"Window shopping?" I say, mimicking her energy and finding it easier than I expected. "I'm in."

We reach the stairs, and I keep my head down. Instead of looking at the people around us, I'm conversing with Letty about some guy named Freddie she dated who was a fireman. I have no idea if he's real or not, but I'm guessing a little of both. Letty has always been good at embellishing.

"No way!" I say when she's done with the scandalous tale. "He told you he was at a fire and he was really with another girl? I mean, *why*?" I say. "Why can't they just be straight, right? If you don't want a relationship, just say so!"

"It's always the same story," Letty laments. "Like a bad rerun."

Before we know it, we are outside, and I have no idea how we got away with it, because I am *sure* we passed some Gordy Boots on the way down. Actually, I *do* know. Letty is a freaking amazing actress. In fact, she continues the charade by gabbing about not remembering where we parked while I inconspicuously meander us through the milling crowd to reach the outskirts. There are two fire trucks, one only a few feet away. And several other vehicles, black SUVs. Fear catches in my throat and I struggle to get a hold of my nerves. We're outside. We're almost home free. I can't lose face now.

I glance around, looking for cover somewhere, but the parking lot isn't very full. Not enough cars to snake through unseen.

That fire truck is awfully close...

Near the front of it a fireman is interviewing a woman and a man. Witnesses? One of them mentions a blond girl with wet hair on the third floor...

Suddenly, I see three well-dressed figures moving through the crowd, observing, looking at faces.

They're combing the crowd for us.

My arm tightens around Letty's, and I do my best to move away from them, toward the edge of the crowd, but I know I'm going to have to act quickly if we're going to have any chance of getting away.

"We're hitting the ground as soon as we reach the back of the fire truck," I tell her in a low voice. "We'll roll under it and look for a shot to get away."

"Shoulda worn my leather pants tonight," is all Letty replies with.

Three seconds later, we reach the truck and Letty and I drop, rolling under the truck in synchronized motion.

Surely someone noticed. I expect to hear a "Hey! Someone is hiding under the truck!" But as we wait, watching the feet of the people in the group, I realize we totally got away with it!

"That was easy," I mumble.

"Duhhh-dudut-duhhh, dutdut-duhh," Letty starts singing the A-team theme song.

I only know it's from the A-Team because she's sung it before. I throw my hand over my mouth to contain my laughter. Letty has always been a huge fan of the A-Team. She used to watch it with her dad and brothers all the time growing up. Actually, she used to watch all kinds of campy action shows. Probably still does. She knows more about eighties pop culture than any nineties child ought to. And I'm only versed in it because of her.

"These women promptly escaped from a maximum security hotel to the San Diego, uh, *ground*," I say, improvising the opening narration of the A-Team show—something she and I would often do to accommodate whatever situation we were in just for fun. "Today, still wanted by the secret Gordy Initiative, they survive as..." I pause, thinking of a clever way to replace the ending.

"Goth queens of bad mother shut-yo-mouthery," Letty finishes. "If you have a broken sprinkler head, and no one else can help, don't call them. They probably did it. And if you can find which fire truck they're hiding out under, well, they're screwed."

I snort and cover my mouth again. "Bad mother shut-yo-mouthery?" I snigger.

She grins and shrugs. "Gotta trademark that."

I roll my eyes and look around at the numerous pairs of feet I see, guessing which ones might be Gordy. But that's probably a shot in the dark. I look on all sides of the truck, searching for a place we might be able to hide, an opportunity for escape before this truck moves. It's running already.

It appears that people are being ushered back into the hotel. I have my eye on what I'm sure is a Gordy SUV parked in the lot so as to be inconspicuous. Two Gordies are standing near it, talking to each other and probably into communicators. I wonder if I can manage two of them with my gun...

"Hey, what's going on over there?" Letty says, pointing the opposite direction, toward the front of the truck.

Three Gordies have their backs toward us and they're holding someone. A fourth comes in to help. I recognize the outfit...

"Mike," I say, scooting forward on my belly to get a better look.

Letty follows. "Isn't that—"

"Gabriel's brother that was staying here with me. Yeah," I reply as they shove Mike to the ground and two of the Gordies straddle him, tying his wrists. Mike's scuffle is not lost on the depleting crowd either, and it's clear that he's being conveniently implicated in the sprinkler vandalism.

"Daaaang," Letty says. "I guess he didn't abandon you after all?"

"I don't know," I say, indecisive about what to do.

"What are we going to do?" Letty asks, mirroring my thoughts.

I look right and then left, finding a couple of firemen's boots and maybe two other pairs of feet close by. "Letty, are you going to freak out on me if I shoot someone?"

"Um. Maybe I won't if you tell me why first," Letty says in an uncharacteristically timid voice.

"I was born an empath and able to see things that other people can't. These people are looking for me because they want what I could do. They kidnapped me and Mike got me out, but they're relentless. I can't leave Mike with them. And I can't be caught again because they have the resources to make me disappear and keep me from my family forever. Do you think it's worth shooting someone to prevent?"

"Hells to the yes!" Letty says, pounding a fist into the asphalt. "Let's *do* this!"

I remember at that moment that Letty is trained in using a gun. She used to go shooting with her dad and her brothers. I awkwardly pull my backpack off and dig through it to find the small ankle pistol and the knife. I hand both of them to her. "We're going to roll out to the right. We'll start shooting, back to back, but I don't have an extra clip so we've got to get to Mike as quickly as possible with as few bullets as possible. If we can get those guys off him, he can help us. Use the knife to cut the zip tie on his wrists while I cover you."

"They have a lot more guns than we do..." Letty says, trepidation in her voice once more, but she's keeping it together a lot better than I would have in her shoes.

"They're non-lethal. But don't get tagged, because then one of us will have to carry you out." I notice with excitement that the Gordies have convened in one place, having a pow-wow now that the most imminent threat—Mike—has been neutralized. I count ten of them. And the fireman boots are headed for the truck we're under. They're surely getting ready to load up and drive off. I wonder who they think the Gordies are? Law enforcement?

"Okay," Letty says and starts humming the A-Team theme song again, which I can barely hear over the thrum of the engine above us.

I do a quick check of shoes nearby as well as Mike's position where he's still plastered to the ground, I wait for the sound of the fire truck doors shutting. As soon as they do, I say, "Go," keep my arms close to my chest, and roll.

The Gordies don't see us at first, which is laughable. They're probably organizing a full-building search, but I'm a bit smug that they have *severely* underestimated me.

The first one to see us approaching is one of the guys holding Mike down. He lets out a yell about the same time one of the Gordies in the circle sees me. It's probably spineless, but I aim for the closest guy who happens to have his back to me. I tag him right in the butt. I don't plan on aiming for vital organs if I can help it.

They've all turned toward me at once, some more ready than others. But I can't afford to be choosey. I aim for another, shooting him in the leg as Letty and I stay close, walking toward Mike. I focus on the gun in my hands, keeping it steady and ready between shots. They're all so close together, and taken so fully by surprise at my overt assault, that I count eight shots between Letty and me before most of them find cover.

Letty has kept up a consistent position behind me. And out of the corner of my eye I see that Mike, true to form, has taken advantage of the moment of surprise and found his feet again, and is now kicking one of his captors in the face.

I keep edging toward him, moving my gun in a menacing arc around me, daring anyone to come out. I kick one NTG out of the range of one of the guys I already shot who is holding his injured leg.

Letty has made it to Mike with the knife finally, and appears to be having some trouble sawing through his bounds. But between his overwhelming strength and her sawing, he breaks free. And then, at that precise moment, something stings me in the shoulder blade.

I lose my legs. My eyes close as my head slams into the concrete. The gun flies from my fingers. For a second I teeter on the edge of consciousness. Everything is spinning even though I'm pretty sure I'm lying on the ground. As soon as I reorient myself, I attempt to move, but I can't feel my body. Crap. Did I get shot with one of those NTGs?

I hear grunting, indecipherable yelling, and the ping of non-lethal shots. Someone's hand comes to rest on my arm and then Letty's voice, "Wen! Wen, are you okay?"

I can't answer of course. And I can't open my eyes. They're glued shut.

Then I hear gunshots, the real kind. And then a great roar of anger. I could swear it's coming from Mike. What's happening?

"Holy mother…" I hear Letty say above me.

I hear a siren, engines, running feet…

And then, someone's arms are around me, picking me up. I'm sure they are Mike's. I recognize his smell.

He's running with me. He's silent, and I wonder if Letty is keeping up until I hear her panting with effort nearby. "Is she going to be okay?" she asks. "She said they were non-lethal, but…"

"She'll be fine," Mike answers gruffly, a tone I'm familiar with. It means he's not going to answer any questions in more than a few words. Oh boy, is he in for it with Letty.

We slow to a stop after a couple minutes, and a car door opens. Mike lays me on what feels like the back seat. My backpack strap is straining against one of my shoulders uncomfortably. I wish someone would take it off of me…

I hear doors shut, and the engine turn over, and then Mike peeling off at what I know is a breakneck speed. I'm sure I'm going to slide right off of the seat, but someone grips my arm firmly, holding me in place. Mike, I think. We make a few more turns before he releases me and I can tell we're on a freeway, traveling more smoothly.

Letty, who has admirably held all her questions in, now breaks the silence, "So, Michael Dumas, tell me what you're doing with my friend and what exactly I should be pissed at you for on her behalf."

Mike, of course, doesn't answer.

"Did you abandon her at the hotel?" Letty says, undeterred.

She is treated with more silence.

"Did you plan on coming back?"

Silence.

"Does Gabe know where she is?"

Silence.

"Who are the people after her?"

Silence.

"Are you staring at my boobs?"

I want to laugh, but I can't get it out in my state. It's kind of torturous, like my chest is expanding more quickly than my breaths can keep up. I listen hard for Mike's reaction, but he doesn't give one, at least not an audible one.

"How often do you work out? Those are some big guns. Can I touch them?"

"No," is the only response Mike gives.

"What's your favorite color?"

"Blue."

"Are you allergic to cats?"

"No." Looks like Letty is getting somewhere after all, though Mike's tone is emotionless and disinterested.

"Do you know how to use chopsticks?" Letty says.

"Yes."

"When's your birthday?"

"August."

"Boxers or briefs?"

"Boxers."

"Trucks or cars?"

"Cars."

"Boobs or butts?"

Mike pauses only briefly. "Both."

"Are you having an affair with Wen?"

If I could control my movement, I probably would have choked on my laughter.

"Violeta Gonzales," Mike says in a totally different voice from his other responses. This one is a silken tone he has *never* used with me around before. "I'm on my way to Chicago. Is there somewhere I can drop you off?"

"Oh lookit you, trying to impress me by knowing my name. That's creepy. You think I'm going to leave you alone with my friend passed out back there? I don't think so, Mr. Machismo," she replies, letting her usually light accent go heavier. "You better get used to me. Cos' I'm stuck to you like glue now. All the way to Chicago and wherever else you're taking my friend."

Mike replies in Spanish, to my aggravation. And Letty returns in kind. Back and forth they go, and I can't understand a word of it. If I'm judging tone though, I'd say Mike is flirting with her. And Letty is sticking to her guns and maintaining her overprotectiveness. I'm impressed with her resistance. But if anything can overpower Letty's ostentatious methods of copious flirtation with anyone—literally *anyone*—it's her protective instinct. She's fierce about friendship, and as evidenced by her behavior with me at the hotel, she is loyal no matter the circumstance. I really should have been better at being a friend to her over the years.

My shoulder has gone numb, and the cadence of the Spanish emanating from the front seat is soothing the rest of me to sleep. I don't wonder why Mike isn't telling Letty to pull the NTG staple from my back, because I think that's obvious: he doesn't *want* me capable of talking and asking questions. Bastard.

Forty

*S*o what's the story?" I say, watching Letty's back as she goes inside the gas station. I woke up in the morning with my shoulder aching, but the NTG staple was gone. Mike must have removed it while I was sleeping. It's just past sunrise, and I think he has been driving all night.

"What story?" Mike says, leaning against the car next to the pump.

I wait several moments. I know he's playing dumb. I lean next to him and cross my arms. "How we ended up at the hotel Letty was working at."

"How should I know?"

"Because that was way too much of a coincidence. Smells like the Yes-ish."

He sighs without looking at me. "Sometimes my ability sabotages me," he grumbles.

"How's that? Some part of you *wants* the Guild to have me?"

"No," he scoffs. "Some part of me wants to keep my word to help you. Apparently more than the part that wants to purge my life of you."

"So you *were* abandoning me."

"I told you I'd get you back for the steroid comment."

I roll my eyes. "You abandoned me."

"I was going to get Gabe."

"How'd you know to come back?"

"Passed the fire trucks headed the way I'd come from. Went back to check."

"So how long before you ditch me again? You know, so I can be prepared this time."

"Don't worry your pretty little bald head about it anymore. I'm going to be your slave labor until you accomplish your misguided mission and there's nothing I can do about it."

"I don't even know what you're talking about," I snap. "What is it with you? Always playing the victim? Always acting like you don't get a choice? If you want to leave, go! I'm not going to stop you."

"It's complicated."

"Then *uncomplicate* it."

"I did. I'm taking you to Chicago. To find your dad. So you can mess up your life force and save the world. I'm doing whatever the hell you tell me to."

Just to make him uncomfortable, I step closer to him, prop my hand on the car, other hand on my hip. "I don't get it."

He doesn't retreat. "Sometimes what you want and what you need to do are different."

"Which one is which? You *need* to help me? Why? Is this about the Gemma Rossi thing?"

"Whitley, if you say that name one more time I'm not going to speak one more word for the rest of this trip. Although that friend of yours can probably fill the hours just fine. Take your pick." I notice he avoids looking at me when he says it. What a baby.

Letty walks out from the gas station right then, grinning and holding up two bags of Haribo gummy bears in front of her chest. "Look what I found!" she says, squeezing them right in front of her breasts—intentionally, I'm sure.

I'm in the dark about the significance, but I'm guessing gummy bears were a topic of conversation last night. Mike says, "You *are* sharing those."

Letty gives him a look, hugging the bags more tightly. "Sorry Little Mickey. Hands off the merchandise. But I might share if you're a good boy."

"I was talking about the gummy bears," Mike says, smirking.

Letty narrows her eyes and purses her lips at him before turning to me. "Now that you're awake, you want front or back?"

"Depends on who's driving."

"Letty is," Mike says, screwing the cap back on the gas tank.

"Definitely front," I reply. "We don't need Mike ogling your gummy bears all the way to Illinois."

"Isn't that the truth," Letty says.

"I'm too tired to care about gummy bears right now. But make sure you save me some for when I wake up," Mike says, pulling open the door to the back seat. "The green ones are the best."

"No way," Letty says as we pile back into the car. "Orange."

"Whitley, come on," Mike says. "You're the tie-breaker."

"I'm out," I say, putting my seatbelt on. "I couldn't care less about gummy bears. I prefer caramels. Or chocolate."

"Ohhhh," Letty laughs, nudging me with an elbow. "I know you do."

"Are we still talking about candy?" Mike says, laying back on the seat.

"No. Chocolate is a confection," I point out.

"Don't worry, chica, I know what you like," Letty says, pulling a box of dark chocolate Raisinets out from behind her bags of gummy bears.

"Ahhh! You remembered! You are the *best*, Letty!" I say, taking them from her.

"Hey! What about me?" Mike says, sitting up again.

"What about you?" Letty says, looking at him over her shoulder.

"No love," Mike says, laying back down.

Letty laughs, throws one of her gummy bear bags at him.

"I knew I liked you," Mike says.

"Everyone likes Letty." Then, as we merge onto the freeway, I say, "Looks like we're in Arizona… That's pretty far from UCSD. Does this mean you're ditching grad school for a road trip?"

"You need me," she says nonchalantly.

I glance back at Mike, but he already has his eyes closed. What did he tell her? "I don't want you to flunk out of grad school because of my drama."

"Drama, Wen? Last night was serious business. I can't leave you to fight that off by yourself. Besides, it's summer break. And even if it weren't, you need friends."

I watch her as she tries different radio stations, amazed that she would drop her life like that for me.

"I can't disagree," I say. "Especially when those friends are as badass as you were last night. I had no idea you had that in you."

"Huh," she says blandly. "Says the woman who busted a sprinkler head to bring in the cavalry, hid under a truck, and then capped some bad guys with her glock. I was just trying to keep up with you."

"I think I've been around Mike too long." I open my box of Raisinets. "He's got crazy ninja skills. Makes it look so easy you want to try it at home."

"Oh I've seen Little Mickey in effect. Right after you got tagged. As I told him earlier, he is one scary mo-fo."

"You're telling me. I'm just glad he's not on the other side anymore."

"Oh yeah, he told me all about that."

"Did he now…"

"Little Mickey is a chatty Cathy."

I glance at Mike again. His eyes are still closed, and he's snoring softly already. "I have a different word for him, but I'm glad you two hit it off."

"He's not so bad. A giant poser. But it's so obvious that you feel sorry for him."

I expect Mike to react to that, but he either really is asleep already or doesn't care. "Yeah, but it gets old," I say, popping a Raisinet in my mouth. "You can only take fake so long."

"If memory serves me, stripping the fake out of people was your specialty once."

I look at her. "Pretty sure they just called it bitchiness."

Letty laughs. "Wen, whatever they called it, I guarantee they all appreciated it. Even if they wouldn't say. Like me. Remember?"

"Yeah…" I reply, recalling the time I told Letty she should stop pretending like she wasn't bisexual—of course I could only do that with such confidence because of my empathic ability. She blew up at me and then wouldn't talk to me for two weeks. That was really early in our friendship, and when she finally started talking to me again, she thanked me for calling her out, and I was the first person she had ever come out of the closet to. And we became inseparable after that.

"I owe you for that," she says. "That's why it was so easy to jump in to bat for you. I've always wanted to do for you what you did for me."

"Did you ever tell them?" I ask. "Your family?"

Her shoulders sag a little. "Yeah," she sighs. "I'm still pulling out the shrapnel from that one." She glances at me. "I haven't even been in a relationship with a girl, but apparently their daughter even *thinking* girls are pretty is a mortal sin in my family's eyes. Meanwhile my brother two-times his wife and my papá blames it on the overactive libido of the family line. What the hell?"

"Sorry," I say, cringing. "That's tough."

"Yeah, it is. But I don't regret telling them. All that time I didn't admit to a part of who I was, even to myself... that was way harder. Now I get to be me. If they struggle with it, that's their problem."

"I'm happy for you," I smile at her.

"After you told me about being an empath, I finally get how you knew. I was crushin' hard on you back then."

"Yeeeeah..." I say. "Me and everyone else." I laugh. "If sexuality is a spectrum you've got the whole range covered, in full force, all the time."

Letty grins and throws up a hand. "Hey, my papá did say my family has a healthy libido. There's a lot of hot people out there, you know?"

"You're the best. I don't know how I've survived without you around all this time." I pop another handful of Raisinets into my mouth.

"Me neither, Wen. But this time around, we're gonna stick together. I just feel it."

"I hope you realize what you've gotten yourself into. Because now that you've bought into my crazy life, as Mike will tell you, it will suck you into its crap whether you like it or not."

"In that case, I think I deserve to know all about it. Gotta prepare myself, y'know?"

"I'll start at the beginning," I say, immensely relieved to have someone to run interference between Mike and me. And besides, having Letty around feels right.

ᴎ

"How did you end up working for the Guild?" I ask, needing some conversation to keep me awake. Letty is napping in the back, and I'm determined to push through all night by having us switch off drivers. But since this was my crazy idea, I want to take on the bulk of the driving if I can.

"They found me," Mike says, ruffling his hair before putting his cowboy hat back on. He's really become attached to that thing.

"That's it? No induction ceremony? No official job offer?"

He gives me a derisive look out of the corner of his eye. "No. It's like a cross between fraternity hazing and bootcamp. It's called activation. You're assigned a partner and the two of you have a sequence of tasks. Each one becomes more difficult, and with each one you learn more about the Guild's purpose. Your Prime ability determines what those missions will be. They're wide-ranging. Anything from working in a hospital to teaching science to third-graders to pitching in on a security detail."

"That's why Shawn didn't care about us being locked up in that room…" I muse.

"Yes. Shawn was raised by Guild members though. She'd been looking forward to activation her whole life. They put her with you not just for her activation but also in hopes that she'd win you over."

"What was their pitch to get *you* interested in activation?"

"It was a slower process. I began training at a gym that was owned by someone in the Guild. I made friends. Found out things about them little-by-little. Became comfortable with them and said what I could do. They said they could help me. Mostly consisted of a lot of physical training. Within a year I had entered full-fledged activation because I saw all the good they were doing. Got assigned to the team responsible for locating unaccounted-for Primes. You were one of them. The rest is history."

"That sounds pretty normal."

"It is. The majority of what the Guild does is normal. Relief efforts. Philanthropy. Technological development. Until the recent dramatic increase in natural disasters their main focus has been finding a creative outlet for every single Prime human under their umbrella. They want people's talents utilized. No idle abilities."

"So what about Gabriel? His counting ability? It's got to be of the same caliber as what the Guild deals with. And his language capacity? He's not a Prime, is he?"

Mike shakes his head. "I have no idea where Gabe got his skills. None. The Guild is definitely interested in him, but they put his recruitment in my hands because of his personality. Gabe doesn't do secrecy so the usual methods of recruitment wouldn't work with him. Going through me would be the only way. But with finding you, things got weird. Scratched those plans."

"Well I can tell you that he has a life force unlike any other. Pretty sure that explains his abilities somehow."

I can feel Mike's eyes on me. "How's that?"

"Everyone has a life force strand count of around thirty billion," I explain. "Gabriel was the one and only person we ever saw that didn't fit that rule. He has forty-nine billion."

"You—*he* counted them?" Mike says, flabbergasted.

"In a few seconds. Craziest thing I've ever seen someone do." I tilt my head thoughtfully. "Although now that I'm thinking about strand counts again, I get something I didn't before…"

"He *counted* forty-nine billion life force strands…" Mike says incredulously. Then he looks up. "What do you get?"

"Prime humans… they have a head over chest ratio. Regular people have chest over head."

"What ratio?"

"The Golden Ratio. The proportion of head strand count to chest strand count is the Golden Ratio… It's swapped for regular people. Ezra, Robert, me… and Kaylen, just like you said. That's why her telekinesis was so powerful. And it disappeared when we fixed her strands. Like me."

"So that's what makes Primes different…" Mike says. "Their life forces are connected to their bodies differently."

"See, Mike? Talking is a *good* thing. You should do it more."

I think he rolls his eyes. "Fine. Let's talk. I have a question."

"Shoot."

"Why is it you chose Gabe?"

That was unexpected. But I have the answer immediately. "He's honest. Not regular honest. Absurdly honest."

Mike thinks about that. "I guess you'd pick up on that pretty quickly being an empath. Most people either don't get that about Gabe or don't believe it. It's been his downfall in so many situations."

"So I've heard. But if people grew up with a talent like mine, they'd value honesty more. I think people *like* to be lied to a lot of the time. They even like to lie to themselves. I never got to be ignorant to it." I shrug. "But it would drive anyone crazy to know a person *thinks* one thing but acts differently."

"It's all making sense finally."

"What is?"

"Your history with Gabe... Among other things."

I'm about to ask him what other things, but he says, "Now that you can't tell if people are lying or not, does honesty matter as much anymore?"

"Of course it does. Just because I can't test it doesn't mean I don't value the same things. Knowing that Gabriel would never lie to me brings me a lot of comfort and I trust him above anyone else."

"I have another question."

"Okay..."

"What was it like, being married without touching?"

"Where are these questions about my relationship coming from?"

"Curiosity. Who *wouldn't* be interested? It's a bizarre story."

"We were split up for most of it."

"Why would you even try? And so fast? Something like that is doomed for disaster."

"I guess it does sound pretty crazy..." I muse. "That's just it though. It *sounds* crazy. But at the time... it just seemed... right."

"That is so stupidly vague."

"I know. I wouldn't expect anyone else to get it. To understand, it'd have to be you going through it." I pause, bringing myself back to that time, searching for the answer. "I don't know if everyone is meant for one person, but I know that when I met Gabriel, it was more than being in love. I suddenly understood all these things about myself. I suddenly *wanted* things I hadn't considered wanting before. I'd never felt that with anyone else. And those things felt so important that the death-touch didn't seem like as big a deal. And Gabriel... well he makes overcoming anything sound possible. You just... want to believe."

When Mike doesn't respond, I fix my eyes on the dark road ahead that's mostly devoid of traffic at this hour.

After a while I laugh lightly, "I couldn't have explained all that back when I first met him. The feelings were so powerful that I would have been hard-pressed to separate any of them out. But now I can look back on it and see why. Kinda nice to do that."

"So... the touching. How did you manage that? I can't wrap my head around it. How can you be romantically involved with someone you can have no physical contact with?"

"There are a lot of other ways to connect. Lots of ways that create the same vulnerability. That's what physical intimacy is about anyway. Being vulnerable. Being an empath gave us an edge, too. Gabriel could be in my head in ways that regular people with no death-touch couldn't be. He was, ah, good at taking advantage of that talent."

I expect Mike to be uncomfortable, but he's pondering things silently.

Encouraged by his silence, I say, "The only reason he ever pressed to touch me was because I was unhappy with the limitations.

I was so hung up on thinking we'd never share the same closeness. Ignoring your physical desires is hard enough, but add in having to do that indefinitely... That's daunting. That was what was so suffocating. For me anyway. That's all I could see. It's all I could think about—the future of never touching instead of the connection we were sharing right then in other ways."

"So what made you... a couple then? Plenty of people have non-physical, close friendships with other people. It's like you were a couple in name only."

That's a good question. I have to mull it over a while to pinpoint what it is outside of physical intimacy that makes my relationship with Gabriel different from my other relationships.

"I mean, take out the physical aspect," Mike says, in line with my thoughts. "What's left that can't be found in other platonic relationships?"

"Commitment, I'd say. That's why I married him. I wanted the commitment he offered. If you're just friends with someone, you can have a fight about something and you can both agree to disagree. You can agree not to talk about it again. You can apologize and you can both accept that you function differently. You aren't bound by anything other than knowing each other and sharing some things in common. But when you're married, it's less about what you have in common and more about what you differ on. It's those things that actually change you and make you better. You have to hang on long enough to see it happen. That is definitely something I didn't get when I got married."

"You can do all those things with a friend."

"What point are you trying to make?"

"That what you and Gabe originally planned was to have a committed friendship."

"That's what we plan on *now*. Believe it or not, sex is a by-product of a committed friendship that's actually *working*."

"That's deep."

"Yeah... I just thought of that." I laugh. "Got me all introspective, Mike. Gabriel would call this right here G-rated intimacy."

"Whatever you call it, the lines between friendship and romantic relationships seem blurry."

"I think the commitment is the key. It's the only way to draw lines. Because obviously friendship could include sex without commitment. And everything in between."

"So why draw lines at all?"

That's a good question. I marinate on it for a while. I prop my arm next to the window. "I think…because people give up too easily. Before they get the returns." I glance at Mike. "People let themselves be ruled by emotions. Emotions say, 'This is hard. This hurts. This is no good for you. It's not worth it.' Commitment says, 'You promised. Just hang on.'"

"I don't get it," Mike says. "People break promises all the time. Why would 'I promise' in a relationship somehow change the dynamic?"

A sudden and penetrating ache takes up residence in my heart for Gabriel. "Some people don't break promises," I say softly. "So when they say it, you know they mean it."

"Gabe," Mike snorts, crossing his arms.

"Knowing someone will never leave you no matter how stupid you behave creates security. When you feel secure, you stop being afraid to show them who you really are. When you're honest about yourself out loud to another person… they reciprocate. And when you both do that, you allow the freedom for each other to change and become better."

"It sounds nice," Mike says. "But it's *your* reality."

"I guess it is," I reply. "But either Gabriel and I are the only people capable of having that kind of commitment and therefore commitment is a sham, or other people are just as capable and are just making excuses."

"My, aren't we confident after only two years of marriage."

"It's more like twenty years squeezed into two. Gabriel and I couldn't touch each other the first four months of our marriage. We separated for two months. Then we spent the next eight months being terminally ill. Right after that, we lost ninety percent of our ability to be intimate, just in a different way than before. Plus, I was pregnant that whole time. Then we found out our child will die as a teenager. Then, all *this*." I wave a hand at the inside of the car, primarily at Mike. "So yeah. I know what I'm talking about."

His only response is to scowl.

"So what about you, Mike? Why aren't you with someone?"

"Swore it off."

"Swore off what? Dating?"

"No. Relationships."

"Why?"

"It's complicated."

I suppress a groan over Mike's fragmented answers. "Mike, are we *ever* going to be for real friends?"

"Probably not."

It sounds like an honest answer, and I wish I didn't care. I don't know what to say, but I know I want to cry. How do you go through what Mike and I have been through together and be nothing more than acquaintances? Why does he feel at liberty to ask me personal questions but I'm not allowed to know anything about him?

I drum my fingers on the door in agitation. "Fine, Mike. I guess I'll wait until I have my abilities back to figure you out."

"Once I get you safely to Chicago, and you've found Carl, I'm leaving."

"Leaving?" I say, my hands automatically tightening on the wheel. "Leaving to go where?"

"You don't need to worry about it. But I'm telling you up front this time. Just like you asked."

Desperation winds its way into my chest. I almost tell him he can't. I almost tell him I'm not going to let him. I say ten different things to him in my head. But in the end I stay quiet, my worry over him growing. And with that worry blossoms determination. I'm going to win Mike over. I'm going to get him to confess whatever it is that holds him back from believing he will or should gain forgiveness from his family.

"Well that sucks," I say finally. "I'll miss you."

"You are such a liar," he grunts.

"I will," I insist. "You're a lot of fun, you know? We have the same brand of sarcasm and we operate on the same logic. You're insanely self-aware, and you're always fighting to do the right thing, like so hard. I know that life, and watching you try so hard sometimes hurts because it reminds me of myself."

"Whatever you're doing, it's not going to work," he says, looking out of his window.

"Okay."

"I want to drive," he demands.

"Okay." I veer over to the shoulder.

I've barely come to a stop before he unlatches his door and hops out.

We exchange places, and Mike pulls back onto the road.

"What are you going to do after you leave?" I ask.

"None of your business."

That's what he thinks.

"One more question and then I'll let you brood," I say.

He sighs, but that sounds more promising than silence.

"Why did you sabotage the Guild's plans with me?"

"You already know that," he says.

"I'm not talking about you not wanting me to screw up my life force. I'm talking about the very beginning. From the moment the Guild showed up at your apartment, you were... trying to help me in some way. Telling me Robbie was okay, being in the white room with me, getting me away from Shawn... it's not like they were physically hurting me."

I expect him to either not answer at all or to take his time considering *how* to answer. But instead he replies quickly, "I sabotaged *Andre*, not the Guild. I hate that bastard. If he had succeeded with you, I would have lost what little leverage I had in your case and he would have had his way with you and with a lot of others. I put nothing past that guy. Nothing. My goal from the moment we captured you was to take Andre down. I screwed it up when I tried to get you out though. Everything that went down with you is pinned on me. I'm Andre's scapegoat."

"I don't like him either, but what made you so sure about him?"

"I answered your question. Now go to sleep and leave me alone."

I buy his explanation only in part. Telling me as soon as he abducted me that Robbie was okay was not about taking Andre down. Keeping me from smashing my head against the wall when I went after his gun was not about Andre either. I grumble but I'm too tired to press further. Maybe tomorrow.

Forty-one

Why are you so sure this is him?" Letty asks, crouching beside me in the bushes of a one-story, dilapidated bungalow. We're in one of the many suburbs of Chicago, at an address Mike got by sneaking into a post office to use their system to look up the physical address associated with the post office box I got for David Erlich. I figured we'd hire an investigator, but Mike was set on a more aggressive campaign. He pulled it off flawlessly. Letty and I didn't even have to get out of the car.

"Long story," I reply. "But my mom left me a clue I didn't recognize until now. It helped me track down Carl."

"You got a lotta long stories, Wen," Letty says. "You make me feel like a kid with all your *life experience*."

"And you make me feel like a loser with all your education," I say, smiling.

Mike appears around the corner and crouches next to us. "Everything looks clear. But this place is rough. Carl's doing a pretty good job of living an invisible life in a piece of crap neighborhood."

"So what's the plan?" Letty asks.

"Knock?" I look at Mike.

He scowls. "Why am I suddenly your advisor?"

"Because I trust you to know what's best," I reply.

"What's best is not doing this at all, keeping your life force intact, and going back to Gabe."

"Why?"

"Because killing yourself is wrong."

"I'm not killing myself."

"Whit, you know where I stand on this. I'm not going to rehash it. Now what are we doing?"

I frown and sigh. "Fine. You sure the Guild doesn't know Carl's here?"

Mike shakes his head. "No way. They want him as much as they want you."

"Alright, you should hang out on the perimeter while Letty and I go to the door. We'll knock like polite, legitimate people and see if Carl's up for a chat. If something goes south, you'll be nearby."

He nods curtly and takes off around the corner again.

I look at Letty. "I don't know what to do about him. He says he's leaving after this, but I worry about him being on his own."

"Worry about *him*?" Letty chuffs. "He can handle himself, Wen. He's a black ops black belt."

"That's not what I mean—" I shake my head. "We'll talk later." I stand up.

"I know what you mean," she says. "Little Mickey is all steel on the outside, all conflict on the inside." She tilts her head thoughtfully. "I really like him. But he's not interested. I think he has a girlfriend or something."

"He told me he swore off dating."

She wrinkles her nose. "Why would he do that?"

"I don't know. You can ask him later and maybe he'll tell *you*. Come on," I say, linking arms with Letty and guiding her toward the front of the house.

I knock on the door, looking up at the peeling grey paint on the rotted eaves. I hope Carl actually lives here and it's not a decoy home. And in the hour or so we've been watching the house, we haven't seen any movement.

I wait with bated breath until I hear a lock turn on the other side of the door. It cracks open, and a bearded Carl appears. "Wendy?" he says through the opening, his eyes resting on Letty a moment before darting past me and around, looking for more people I bet.

I found him. For a moment I relish the fact that I found Carl when an entire legion of Gordies couldn't.

"Hey," I say, realizing I didn't plan how I wanted this conversation to go. "Do you mind if we come in? Kind of trying to stay out of sight as much as possible, y'know?"

Carl looks wary as he opens the door slowly. Letty thrusts out her hand. "Hi Mister Wendy's dad. I'm Letty."

I smile at her introduction. Carl's gone by Kevin Fowler, David Erlich, and Carl Haricott, so there's no way of knowing what name he *wants* to be called by.

"Carl," he says, shaking her hand slowly. He's wearing a blue T-shirt that looks like it's been washed a hundred times; I can barely make out the Chicago Cubs logo. He's thinner, his sandy hair lighter, His jeans are worn nearly through the knees. One of his toes is peeking through his black socks. He shuts door behind us and we stand in an arched entryway where nothing is on the walls and a pair of dingy tennis shoes near the door are the only thing to see here. "Is it just you?" Carl asks.

At some point in this visit he's likely going to find out Mike's here, and I want him to trust me so I should probably be truthful. No warning bells are going off. "My bodyguard is outside."

Carl freezes. "Robert brought you?"

I shake my head. "Me and Letty and my bodyguard. The *Guild* doesn't know I'm here." I give him a knowing look.

"How did you manage to evade them?" he asks over his shoulder, now leading us into the living room. He waves us to an orange and brown threadbare couch, but most of the room is taken up by two folding tables upon which he has an office of sorts set up. His desk chair is nothing more than a metal folding chair, which he brings around to face the couch. He walks over to the large front window and edges the curtain aside to peek beyond it.

"My bodyguard is skilled," I say, sitting down. "I promise we weren't followed."

"Nobody is as skilled as they are. And you found me, which means they can, too."

He begins pacing nervously.

"Carl, I found you because I know you. Not because I'm good at detective work."

He stops, his hands clasped behind his back. "How *did* you find me?"

"L'Angolo," I reply.

He moves a couple steps toward me, his eyes brightening. "You've seen it?"

I nod. "Mom used to take me there all the time. It's beautiful. I finally realized what it was. Who must have done it."

"Sara took you there?" he says, and I hear gentleness in his voice. Sara was my adoptive mother's real name—what Carl knew her by. But to me her name was Leena.

"When I was in middle school. She made sure I didn't lose Gina altogether. You ought to give her more credit."

Carl perches on the edge of the folding chair, a faraway look on his face. "Gina did it for you. I just never got a chance to show it to you." He shakes his head slowly. "You're right. I don't give Sara credit." He looks at me. "But how would you feel if someone kidnapped your child?"

I cross my arms. "I didn't come here to argue about my mom."

"Why *are* you here?" he asks.

"Because the Guild kidnapped me. And I found out what they want me for."

"It was Mike Dumas, wasn't it?" Carl says darkly. "I knew if Robert didn't hang on to you, he'd find an opportunity. Didn't realize he was with them until your illness. I warned Gabe in my email not to trust him. But he obviously didn't listen."

I open my mouth in surprise, but rather than get sidetracked, I say, "There's no reason Gabriel would have trusted your word over his own brother. But I'm not here to talk about my kidnapping either. I'm here because I know I wasn't supposed to lose my ability. And I need your help to get it back."

Carl's brow furrows. "You can no longer see? Wendy..." he says disappointedly, "After you lectured *me*?"

I count to three before answering with one of the many sarcastic remarks I want to let fly. "I lost my ability because I fixed my life force incorrectly."

"But you got well..."

"Yes. I fixed it enough to get well. But not to keep my natural ability. The same thing happened to Kaylen. She should still be telekinetic. But she's not anymore."

"Then thank your lucky stars," he says, sitting back in his chair and crossing his arms. "It means you are of no use to them."

"They would disagree with you."

"Stay away from them. They are the wrong side."

"I'm not picking sides. I'm only picking to solve the problem. I need to get my ability back so I can figure out who's *really* behind this, and I need your help to do that."

"Who is behind what?"

I put my hands out. "Everything! The tornados, the earthquakes, the crazy weather. Someone is behind it, and I need to figure out who."

Carl rolls his eyes. "An ever-changing earth, that's what's behind it. We're in a geological evolutionary jump. That's all."

"I beg your pardon, Carl," Letty interrupts. "But geological evolution does not occur this quickly. And it's a complex interplay of currents and meteorological changes and tectonic movement that has never been seen before. It's breaking records." Letty told me that when Mike brought up what the Guild wanted me for, she knew exactly what he was saying. Letty's grad program is focused on oceanography, which is closely linked to the problem.

Carl waves a hand dismissively. "I see the Guild has brainwashed you. Only *they* would be pompous enough to imagine that we can control the earth's meteorological and geological events, and convince you that *you* can take part in it. They don't want you for anything but access to the energy world. If they can discover its secrets, they can control everything. And everyone."

"This isn't about them," I say. "I can see with my own eyes that things are out of hand out there."

"Wendy," Carl says patiently, leaning forward and putting his elbows on his knees, "The Guild has grown so much in size and scope since their inception that they're getting too big to overlook. Their influence is too far reaching. They can't hide in the shadows and big corporate names anymore. They're preparing to reveal themselves before someone else can do it. The only way they're going to avoid persecution and bad press for controlling such a huge number of supernaturally talented people is if they find a problem and use their assets to solve it."

Carl crosses an ankle over a knee. "If there really *is* something to worry about in the world's weather patterns, the Guild is the one behind it. It would be just like them to create a problem they can solve to make themselves look like saviors."

Admittedly, Carl's arguments are pretty good, but not entirely sound. "You're forgetting one thing," I say. "Life force abilities don't work long if you're corrupt." I gesture at Carl. "You should know this better than anyone. If this is really the path they're on, they're going to run out of viable talent sooner or later."

"There are ways to exploit innocence," Carl says.

"You would know."

"Yes. I know exactly what I'm talking about," he says, brow furrowed. "Which is why you should listen to me. I *am* sorry for what I have done to you. It's been a hard road getting here, but I have, and

I'm admitting it to you now. *I was wrong*. But about much more than you. You can't fight them, Wendy. If you fight *with* them, they win. If you fight against them, they still win. The only course is to stay far away."

"I told you, I just want to figure out what's going on in the colorworld and fix it if I can."

He jabs a finger my direction. "Exactly what they want. Investing yourself in life force abilities, making you believe they are necessary. It's the same trap I was caught in, that made me do terrible things. Please, don't buy into their propaganda. Their high and mighty causes are a facade. What lies beneath is a mission to weight a portion of humanity with gifts... Either by default or on purpose they become the ones to control that power. Regardless of their stated mission, regardless of their *intentions*, absolute power corrupts absolutely."

I sit back on the couch. Carl is clearly solid in his belief. And I'm starting to feel like he might be right. And besides, Carl looks so... put together. As I've watched him speak and move, I've been trying to put my finger on what's different. He's more fit, that's for sure. But these humble circumstances suit him, or maybe it's that they reflect who he has become and I like that person. But at the same time... how do I deny the things I've been through that have pointed me to Carl, to getting my ability back?

I wish Uncle Moby were here.

"Why didn't you tell me about them?" I ask. "At least when you saw me at the compound that last time?"

"Given our current conversation, how is that not obvious?"

"You were afraid I'd jump on the Guild bandwagon?"

He throws his hands up.

"Carl, I have no intention of joining teams with people who kidnap me, who harmed my son. But I am *really* concerned about what's going on in the world. Are you saying you won't help me get my ability back?"

He looks at me with confusion for about three seconds before realization crosses his face. "You want me to do hypno-touch on you, is that it?" He shakes his head, bewildered. "You can't be serious. Please tell me I'm wrong."

"I have to get it back, Carl."

He scoots his chair closer. "No. You don't." He closes his eyes for several second, places his hands together. "I know it's hard to lose it. Believe me. I *know*. But you have to adapt. You don't need it."

I'm getting nowhere. Carl's not going to help me. "You always think you know the moral high road better than anyone else," I say quietly, close to tears. All this struggle to find Carl, and he's a dead end. What do I do now? Get someone else to do hypno-touch? Can I get the same results?

Theoretically. I don't know why I felt it had to be Carl doing it, except that I felt I needed to duplicate as much as possible to give myself a better chance of achieving what I had before.

"Wendy, I should have spent my life protecting you and what you could do. But I didn't. It's not about knowing what's best. It's about doing right by you for once."

I look at him, surprised by this new direction for Carl. He sounds really genuine and concerned. "I'm not a child anymore. I don't need protecting. I need you to trust me and have faith in me." I hold my palms out. "For once, can you please trust that I know what I'm doing?"

Carl's shoulders sag. His mouth moves, but he doesn't speak.

"Robert trusts me to do this, Carl. And he knows more than both of us combined."

"Rob told you to undergo hypno-touch again?"

"He told me to find you."

He sits back, crosses his arms, and purses his lips, glancing up at me a few times as he thinks. "You know plenty of people who know hypno-touch. You don't need me."

"It has to be you."

"Wendy, even if I had the full capacity of my ability as it once was, it still wouldn't be as precise as yours. I'd be digging at your life force blindly." His face tightens. "With you finally alive and well, how can you ask me to put your life on myself like that again?"

The petition in his voice takes me by surprise. Carl cares. He honestly cares about me... Here we are, having a moment. And it feels entirely natural.

"Because this time *I'm* choosing it," I say earnestly.

Carl rubs his eyes with his palms and then looks at me. "What made you so sure that finding *me* was the answer?"

"I told you, I asked Robert about finding you. He gave me an address to start. It was actually to a grave site. Mike Dumas' mom. It was because I needed him to help me find you. Without him, I would've been caught by—"

"Wait a minute," Carl interrupts. "I thought it was Mike who kidnapped you."

"He did. But then he busted me out."

"His mother's grave? Not the same mother as Gabe?"

"No. They're cousins. He was adopted by Dan and Maris."

Carl's face pales. "Who was his mother?"

"Alma Rivera Fuentes."

Carl pushes himself to his feet, placing his hands on his hips, a fiercely intent look on his face. "Mike Dumas is Alma's son?" he asks carefully.

"So you remember her."

He nods, still caught up in wonderment. He looks at me finally. "He helped you escape the Guild... Did he come here with you?"

"Yes. He's outside. He's my bodyguard."

"And he's *not* with the Guild?"

"Not anymore. He defected."

Carl falls in his chair once more, flabbergasted. "Mike Dumas is Alma's son."

"Yes..."

He looks at me again. "What can he do?"

"That's his business to tell. But if you know what his mom could do, that should tell you about him, right?"

He nods distractedly. "We discovered what Alma could do far too late." His voice grows quieter. "She would have saved them all. If she hadn't died." He rubs his hands over the tops of his thighs back and forth, nervously maybe? I can't tell. He looks up and around, discomfort written into the lines of his face. I'm not sure who he's talking to at this point "And she had a son?" He shakes his head, looking down at his feet again. "How blind you were, Carl. All that you wanted was kept from you, because you wanted to corrupt it. Just like them."

"What are you *saying*?" I prod. He seems to have forgotten that Letty and I are here.

"Is he outside?" Carl asks me. "I can show you."

"I told you he was my bodyguard, so yeah."

Carl goes to the door. I motion for Letty to stay and I follow him. He stands on the stoop, looks around. I push past him. "Mike?" I call.

He materializes from the side of the house. "You rang?" he says with a disingenuous smile.

"Carl needs you."

"Is he causing problems?" he says, not coming nearer.

"No," I say as Carl comes up next to me. "Something to do with your mom. Just get in here, okay?"

He rolls his eyes, crosses his arms, and walks toward us. "Woulda been a lot more fun if he was causing problems," he mumbles. Carl and I stand to the side to allow Mike's breadth through the foyer.

I shut the door and Carl says, "I wasn't expecting to ever meet you, Mike, certainly not accompanying my daughter, but it sounds like your help has been indispensable. Thank you for that."

"Carl," Mike acknowledges, turning into the living room and plopping down heavily next to Letty. "Looks like you found a dirty hole to hide in."

"Evidently it was not deep enough," Carl says, not sitting, instead clasping his hands behind his back, looking a lot like Robert. "But the truly baffling part is that when I finally stop chasing my life's work, even hiding from it, the things I previously wanted so badly for so long finally fall into my lap..."

Mike scowls and his eyes flit from me to Carl suspiciously.

"Cut to the chase, Carl," I say.

"Yes, one moment," he says, rubbing his hands together. "Wendy, would you mind being my subject?"

My eyes dart from Carl to Mike. I even look at Letty as if she might have a clue what Carl's up to. She shrugs with wide-eyed curiosity on her face. I turn back to Carl. "I'm not sure. *Should* I mind?"

Carl gestures at me impatiently. "I'm entering the energy world and I need a subject. You know how this works."

"Oh! Um. Wait. You have your ability back?"

Carl waves me again. "If I'm telling you I'm going into the energy world, that would be indicative."

I step next to him, hardly daring to believe it, and out of the corner of my eye, I see Mike flinch toward Carl, but he resists his protective urge and instead leans forward, elbows on knees, watching.

Carl puts his hand in mine and closes his eyes. I'm distracted by the gesture though. Carl has never touched me to my memory. Of course, there was always the likelihood of him dying, but he did it just now so casually. Hand-holding is not something you do with your long-lost deadbeat father whose negligence almost cost you your life along with countless others. I expect repulsion, or maybe that his hand should be cold or clammy. But it's warm and worn with age. It's astoundingly normal.

And he has his colorworld sight back? Who is this man next to me?

"Wendy..." Mike says in a warning but questioning voice.

I look up, and I see he is now standing, ready to leap into action at any moment. And worry is written on his face, his eyes honed in on the place where my hand joins Carl's.

I rejoice at this obvious show of concern. *And he used my real name again!*

But no sooner have I felt it than a brilliant light flashes before my eyes. I throw my free hand over them and step back.

"Wendy! Are you okay?" Mike says, his voice much closer to me now.

"I'm fine, I'm fine," I say, knowing immediately what's going on—I think. It's been so long since I've been in the colorworld, and I've never been taken here by someone else before. My eyes aren't accustomed.

"What on earth—?" Carl says. "It's far brighter... Where is that coming from?"

I'm trying desperately to adjust my eyes. Squinting between my fingers, blinking, one eye open. Nothing works. I'm gazing into the sun at noon, except the sun is right in front of me. "Let's turn around," I say, tugging Carl's hand so we can put our backs to Mike, who I suspect is the source.

Carl agrees and I can now see the colorworld that has been lost to me... some of it anyway. It's mostly lights and washed-out, colored blurs. It barely resembles the detail and vibrancy I'm used to. And it's bright. It's far too bright to look at for long without piercing my eyes. That's odd...

Nevertheless, I gaze at it, some part of me unclenching as I drink in the sights like a person starved of water. Except it's quite different still; I find myself trying to see more. And it's silent. I smell none of the characteristic scents. The lack of sense is a lot like the disappointment of a silent movie.

"I think it's Mike," Carl breaks into my ponderings. "Letty, would you mind moving to the other side of the room?"

I see Letty's purple life force move into my line of sight, a slightly purple blob that sort of blends into the surrounding pinks and greens of the room. I twist my head around a tiny bit to put Mike in my peripheral vision only to turn away.

"You're right," I say. "Mike's as bright as the sun. And he's making everything else in the room too bright to see."

To my disappointment, Carl releases my hand and the lights drop from my view. They are replaced with the dark and dingy interior of the living room.

I turn around to find Mike looking like he's about to pounce, legs spread, hands extended from his body slightly. Lithely he winds himself back to his brick wall bodyguard stance. "What is this about?" he demands.

I shake my head, at a loss.

"What does this mean?" Carl says, clearly expecting me to be the authority on this subject.

I do know what bright light usually means. But Mike's brilliance is so off the charts that he can't possibly fit that mold. "I don't know… I've never seen anyone even half as bright as him."

"Did he really just see the energy world?" Mike says.

I nod.

"And my life force is how bright?"

"So bright I can't see it."

"And that means?" he says, repeating Carl's question.

"It means I'm back to the drawing board. It rewrites everything I thought I knew."

Forty-two

The chirp of a phone electrifies everyone at once. My gut immediately twists with anxiety.

Carl, after startling, stands up and retrieves his phone from next to the computer, looks at it, and his brow knits.

"Terminal three. Four-forty PM," he recites.

"From who?" Mike asks, standing.

Carl shrugs. "Unknown number."

Mike walks over and takes the phone from him, but by his lack of comment, he seems to be as clueless as Carl.

"It's Robert," I say. "He's picking us up."

They both look at me.

"An airport terminal. And a time to be there."

"How do you know?" Mike says. "It could be the Guild. And terminal three could be anything."

"That makes no sense. If the Guild texted Carl's number, that means they know something about where he is. Which means they could find him. Why would they choose to take me in a populated place instead of some grungy neighborhood outside Chicago? And it's the airport. Trust me."

Mike wants to argue, but doesn't.

"Robert said I should stick to finding Carl, and he'd find *me*. So now that I've done that, he's going to stick to his part."

"I don't get it," Mike says, crossing his arms stubbornly. "How could he possibly know exactly when you'd be here? And even if he could find you so easily, that means he could find *Carl* easily. So why wouldn't he send you here in the first place? Why let me kidnap you and go through all of this crap?"

I cross my arms to mirror him. "Because he knows the crap is more important than the end-point."

"That is so stupid," Mike says.

"That's because you don't know how life really works," I shoot back.

"*I* don't know how life works? How old are you? Sixteen? I've seen more ugliness in this world than you'll *ever* see in your pampered, idealistic life. If you've got the power to save people suffering and grief, you have a duty to do it. Anything else makes you sadistic."

I stand up abruptly and walk toward him, balling my fists and gritting my teeth. "No, Mike," I say venomously. "What makes you sadistic is believing that people are expendable." I jab my finger at his chest. "What makes you sadistic is blaming all your problems on everyone but yourself. What makes you sadistic is believing in peace and love and unity but using secrecy and manipulation to get there. You are an *infant* when it comes to understanding how life works. Idiot," I huff. Then I look him straight in the eye and say low and threateningly, "And don't you *dare* imply words like that about my uncle ever again, Michael Dumas. You think I make your life hell *now*? You only know the *nice* me, the one that has put up with your infantile *crap* ever since I met you. And I can do it, too. Because I know what you really are. Scared. Scared of consequences. Scared of emotions. Scared of the truth. But you hide under all of this... this... *This!*" I gesture at the length of him. "So *back* off. I'm not scared of you. You're scared of *me*. You're not fooling anyone. So shut the hell up or get the hell out."

I don't wait for his reaction, I spin around and put my hands on my hips. "Four-forty is only like an hour away. So we need to move. You're coming, Carl. Do you have a car?"

Carl's eyes are bulging, and his mouth is slightly open, but he says, "I do."

Letty stands up. "Whew! Let's go. It's gettin' hot in here," she titters. "We better get outside so we can all cool off."

"I need to grab a few things," Carl says, eyes darting from me to Mike who is still behind me. "One moment."

After he leaves the room, I tug the ends of my light jacket down and turn around, avoiding Mike's face. "One of us needs to stay here with Carl while the other grabs the stuff out of the car."

"Letty can stay," Mike says, his eyes boring into me before snapping to Letty. He removes his gun and holds it out to her. "Violeta," he says, his voice returning to that purring cadence I've heard him use with her before. "Your file indicates you've been trained to use a firearm, not to mention your impressive show the other night."

"Si," she says, taking it from him and tucking it into her coat pocket. And then she looks at him challengingly. "And the rest of your family indicates you have been tr4ained on how to be a gentleman. You should put that into practice, Little Mickey."

"Whatever you say, Violeta." He holds a hand out for me to go ahead of him.

Once we are headed down the walk, Mike behind me, I say, "So are you leaving now?"

"No. I don't trust Carl."

I roll my eyes even though he can't see. We reach the car and I grab my trusty backpack along with the one we got Letty on our trip out here. I shut the door and look at him over the roof. "That's not the reason. I don't know why you stick around, Mike. I really don't. This isn't your fight. You don't want to be here. You tell me all the time that you're leaving, sometimes you *do* leave, but then you come back. I scream at you and call you scum, and now you're standing there, smiling at me like I paid you a compliment."

He tilts his head. "I like it when you yell at me."

"And that's a reason to change your plans all of a sudden?"

"It's a reason to stick around a little longer. See if I can get you to yell some more."

I balk at the lack of goading in his tone. "This sounds dangerously close to flirting."

He shrugs, throws his own pack over his shoulder, and slams the door. "I know you've been out of the game a little while, but that actually *was* flirting."

"Is this the new strategy?" I say, heading back up the walk. "Treating me like dirt isn't getting the reaction you want anymore, so you're switching to hitting on me? Why? To aggravate me? Make me uncomfortable?"

"We'll see, I guess."

I pause, my hand on the front door, finding myself exactly where I always end up with him. "Mike, I didn't think anyone could make me feel as many different emotions in such a short period of time as Gabriel has... but you might actually be a contender."

"Interesting," Mike says. "All this time, I've actually been a *contender* and I didn't even know it... If I'd known, I would have actually put *effort* in. But it looks like I can't help but own your emotions even without meaning to."

I grind my teeth and turn around, determined not to let him win this latest tactic. "You own no part of me. What you do is out of spite. What Gabriel does is out of love."

"If telling yourself that helps you sleep at night, be my guest," he smiles. "But the result is the same... Right? You get all hot and bothered and then you figure out how to handle whatever bugs you, right? I've watched you do that over and over with me, always testing a new method to deal with me. The patience you have... It is no longer a wonder to me now how it is you have managed to stay with Gabe. But guess what? I'm the Gabe you get to hate. And you never have to feel bad about it. I give you a punching bag. A cause. I expect nothing and I give nothing. It's the emotional workout without strings attached."

"They call those enemies, Mike," I reply.

He puts his hands on his hips and looks unapologetic. "I guess they do..." Then he looks at me and repeats himself, "But the result is the same, isn't it?"

I summon patience, but then catch myself. That's exactly what Mike said I do. And it bothers me that he knows that, that he uses that to come up with his next strategy. My head is now in knots and I don't know *how* to react that won't prove Mike's claims true...

Oh gosh, he's right. He is *really* good at getting in my head.

He's watching me, which is making me self-conscious. I feel like he can see my thoughts. I need to say something that will get him to stop looking at me like that. I remember the conversation Letty and I had earlier. "Why did you swear off dating?"

His eyebrows lift. "You need a date? My gosh, Wendy, we'll be back to Gabe soon. Keep your pants on."

I scowl and cross my arms. "Stop deflecting. Why aren't you dating?"

"Currently, I'm serving as your personal Mexican Jackie Chan. Kinda puts a damper on my social life."

"And if you weren't, you'd be dating?" I say, forcing myself not to get flustered.

"Nope."

I'm about to ask another question, but the door opens behind me. Carl's ready. Disappointed that I'll have to save this conversation for later, I trounce back down the steps, following Carl, trying to decide if I prefer this Mike to the previous ten or so versions of him.

Forty-three

*M*y heart has been pounding nervously ever since we stepped onto the pavement in front of the terminal at O'Hare airport. We had to assume it was O'Hare, since that's the largest airport near Chicago, but as we drove over I began to wonder if the whole thing is a hoax. It's hard for me to imagine that I may be reunited with Gabriel in a manner of minutes.

The four of us sit silently, side-by-side, scanning. It's a large terminal, and unsure of where exactly to be, we let the shuttle driver decide, and we found the closest bench.

"Wendy," Mike says.

"Let me guess. You've decided to leave again," I say, looking up and then down the road in front of the terminal. "Do whatever you want. You don't have to tell me anymore."

"No, I'm not leaving. It's just—"

I lean over to glance at Carl's watch again.

4:39

"What?" I demand impatiently.

He doesn't get a chance to answer because a line of three identical dark grey cars come to a stop at the curb about ten yards in front of us. I lean forward. Mike actually stands, taking a few steps forward to place himself in front of us. But I peek around him, see a familiar dark head.

"Farlen!" I squeal, leaping to my feet and pushing Mike out of the way. As I run for Farlen, he gets pushed aside, and another face appears, this one less familiar, but only because it's wearing a beard.

"Gabriel!" I shriek, my face breaking into a smile so big it hurts my cheeks. I close the distance between us in moments, throwing my arms around him and nearly knocking him over. I cling to his neck, pressing my face there, trembling as tears break forth. I drink in his scent so familiar that I can hardly believe it's real.

His arms are tentative at first, but when he embraces me finally he shudders. His arms tighten further, and he chokes on a sob.

"I can't believe... Gabriel, oh my gosh... You're here!" I squeal, leaning away to look at him—a *bearded* him. I touch his face, now unfamiliar, and his arms—which feel thinner. His eyes are wide, his mouth slightly open, and for once he may actually be speechless. I cling to him again, trying to get closer, hoping to squeeze the longing I've felt for him over the last few weeks out through my skin and into his.

He clutches me again, this time with more of himself, lifting me off my feet. I wrap my legs around him.

"Oh... Wendy," he says, his face now in *my* neck. He sobs a couple more times before he sets me back on my feet. "Is this real? Is it?"

I swat his arm. Then I grab his face to me, and press my lips to his—which is a different experience due to the extra hair on his face. I bite his lower lip suggestively and wind my hands behind his neck. I catch him entirely off-guard but he responds eagerly, his hands finding my back and my neck as he kisses me there, tugging me closer to him, sending shivers down my spine.

Someone clears their throat and we pull away to see Farlen nearby, keeping his smile mild, but I can tell he wants to laugh. Gabriel looks a little dazed for a moment, but then chuckles, "I plum forgot what I'm supposed to be doing. I think we're in a hurry. Heavens, not a thing else is coming to mind. Farlen, could you please direct me to the next task?"

"That would be getting into the car," Farlen says.

I turn to look for Letty and Carl and Mike, but Farlen says, "They're in the car ahead. The show's waiting on you two. Will you be needing a separate car? I can consult Robert."

"Uncle Moby?!" I squeak, crouching down to spy in the two other cars, which are too tinted to see inside. "He's here? Where?"

"Inside the car," Farlen replies. "Waiting for you."

"Mention of Robert definitely ruins my chances for a private car ride with my wife, Farlen," Gabriel grumbles from behind me.

I lunge for the open door of the car, spotting Robert smiling from the dark interior of what is definitely a limousine. I plop next to him, put my arms around him. "Uncle Moby. I have missed you so much." I sit back to find him looking dashing in a long overcoat, his goatee a bit more peppered than I remember.

He squeezes my hands. "The feeling was mutual. I've looked forward to this day with great anticipation."

"I have *so* much to ask you about, you have no idea," I say.

"Robert, if you weren't her uncle, I'd be a jealous mess over how excited she gets when she sees you," Gabriel complains, having taken the seat across from us. Then he startles. "Good gad, woman. You're brandishing a weapon? Criminy, what has my brother done to you? Inducted you into black ops?"

"I'm not brandishing it," I say, tugging my jacket down over it. "I'm concealing it on my person. There's a difference."

"Well I just espied it, so it is obviously *not* concealed. Besides, Robert's got enough men with roscoes, and I don't think they need your assistance."

"Roscoes?" I say and then scoot back to the other side of the car where he is, throwing my arms around Gabriel again. "You are so cute. Exactly how I dreamed you."

He relaxes under my hold, sighing again.

"Where's Robbie?" I say. "Kaylen and Ezra?"

"Everyone is safe," he says.

"And Mike? Did you talk to him? Oh I guess you couldn't have..."

"I have nothing to say to him."

I narrow my eyes at him, but before I can berate him, he says, "He hopped in that other car double-quick. It looks like my brother isn't man enough to come clean to me personally. Coward."

"He is not a coward!" I snap. "He gave up everything he'd worked for to get me away from the Guild! He did it for you. And he's so broken up he doesn't think he deserves your forgiveness."

"If any of that were true, he wouldn't have taken you in the first place. Everything since Del Monte is his doing. He's been causing us strife since we've been together."

"We are only together *because* of him!" I yell.

His eyes flash, and he's about to open his mouth, but Robert says, "Alright. It's been a stressful month for all of us. Let's take a step back and use our time productively."

"So where is Robbie?" I ask, settling back into my seat. "Kaylen and Ezra?"

"In Redlands, under protection, awaiting our arrival," Robert says.

"How secure is that?" I ask, sitting up, worried for a moment that Robert has no idea what he's up against.

"Extremely. If the Guild tries to take any of them, they will publicly expose themselves. Thanks to you I'm now confident my technology can't be beat. The Guild has obviously been spending their intellectual resources in areas other than surveillance."

"I sure had no problem breaking into your home in Redlands," I point out, not missing that Robert mentioned the Guild by name.

"You broke into Robert's home in Redlands?" Gabriel cuts in. And then to Robert, "Why didn't you tell me this? What happened?"

"She needed money," Robert says calmly. Then to me, "My apologies for my oversight on the alarm system."

"She—You—What?" Gabriel sputters.

"Yeah, that threw me a bit," I say. "I had no idea you had the system activated."

Robert chuckles. "I didn't. The Guild not only armed the system remotely but changed the code by hacking into the home security company's database. I hope I may one day shake the hand of and hire the person responsible for such an inventive idea. My company holds a long-standing reputation as the cutting edge in surveillance and counter-surveillance. The commercial security system linked into and required by the homeowner's association is laughable by comparison. I often forget the home was built with it.

"I do feel a bit foolish for overlooking something as simple as what security company I use and how it might be used against me, yet I still find it abundantly more humorous and satisfying that the Guild's only method of detecting your presence in my home was not high-tech perimeter monitoring, but a run-of the mill security system that would only go off if someone broke into the house—a long shot for them to assume. As stupid as I feel, it is not as stupid as they should feel. Because using such paltry technology reveals quite a bit of their hand: they do not have technology that can beat mine." Robert smirks, flooring me because I have never seen him do that.

"Ohhh *shoot*, Uncle Moby," I say, whistling. "Look at you, gettin' all uppity about your spy toys."

He laughs, leans forward, and pats my leg. "We've missed you, Wendy. It's been nothing but pacing, yelling, and hair-pulling since you left."

I frown at Gabriel next to me, certain that he's the one that did the yelling. I worried from the time I disappeared that he'd be all over Robert about using his ability to find me instead of letting things unfold more wisely. But knowing how much Gabriel must have been racked, not knowing what I might be enduring, I kiss his cheek and wrap my hand more tightly around his. "So guess what? Carl has his ability back."

"Wonderful news," Robert says. "And you'll have to tell us more, but we've arrived on the tarmac. Looks like the jet is prepped and ready. Everyone out!"

We scramble out of the car, and there are suits everywhere around the ramp to the plane. I see Mike approaching us.

"Gabe," he says, arms crossed, "I'm relieved to see you, brother."

Suddenly, a fist flies out from next to me faster than I can blink, and plants itself with a hard smack right into Mike's face.

I jump, Mike staggers back from the impact, falling on his butt. He wipes his bleeding lip and looks up at Gabriel as if being punched was exactly what he expected. I know for a fact Mike could have avoided that punch if he had really wanted to. And falling down is not something he does either.

Gabriel strides past Mike wordlessly. But Mike stops him by taunting, "That's it, huh? After all this, you only got one punch saved up for me? You going old man on me?"

Gabriel looks down at him, fists clenched. "This isn't a boyhood scuffle over a bet. It's not something that can be smoothed over by exhausting our testosterone in a tumble. You are a *liar*. You *took* my wife from me. You held her *captive*. I don't even *know* you."

Then he heads for the ramp. I glance from his back to Mike, unsure of what to do or say.

"I'll let you get one in this time if you want," Mike says, wiping blood on his shirt. "I'm feelin' generous."

I shake my head. "Physical pain only covers up emotional pain for so long. Maybe next time you should start off with, 'I'm sorry.'"

"Anything for you, Wendy," he says, spitting blood on the ground and standing up.

"All steel on the outside," Letty says, having come up next to me.

"All conflict on the inside," I finish before walking up the ramp and into the plane, Letty beside me.

Forty-four

Gabriel is doing something I have never seen him do: stroking his beard. It's not that long, but it gives him a whole new look, though overall he looks haggard: dark circles under his eyes, thinner... He looks like a man who has worried himself sick for weeks.

That's what's different about Robert, too. His face is slightly gaunt, and I think he really does have more grey hair. When he mentioned knowing I would be taking his cash in Redlands and had the safe already prepared for me, I assumed that meant he knew my kidnapping would end up all right in the end. My best guess is Gabriel was the source of his stress.

"I have a question, Wendy," Gabriel says.

"Only one?" I say. I've just finished telling him and Robert all that I've learned about the Guild.

"At the moment. I'm curious about this fertility preservation drug they've been using in order to create so many of these so called Prime Humans. Since Robbie should be one of these, it has me wondering if it's possible that you were *also* given this drug while you were ill. Seems that if they didn't expect you to live, they would have wanted to preserve your possible progeny. Would also make for a probable explanation for Robbie's unlikely conception."

I sit back in surprise, not having expected Gabriel to jump to that conclusion so quickly. I've been telling them only about the Guild so far, it being the most important information. I was going to jump into the rest as time allowed.

"Yes, they did," I say. "They are also responsible for the autograft transplant I received that worked so well. And the insulin pump I was given was actually a medication pump for the fertility drug but also for a drug that got me producing my own insulin."

He gawks at me.

That's when I realize I sounded like I was *defending* the Guild. But it was unintentional, a product of wanting to protect *Mike* by not implicating him in Robbie's illness.

"What are you holding back?" Gabriel asks, tilting his head.

I scowl. *How?* How does he do it? Always finding the *one* thing I don't want to share?

No use trying to talk my way out of this one. I sigh heavily. "It was that same fertility medication that caused Robbie's DMD. It causes mutations."

Gabriel's brow furrows. He pauses for a few seconds, processing that. "Why would you be reluctant to share—*Oh.*" His voice drops an octave. "*Mike,*" he seethes. "You're trying to protect him."

"We don't know if he actually *knew* the hazard involved when he hooked me up to that pump. And they didn't expect me to actually conceive…"

"Bloody hell," Gabriel seethes, his eyes flashing. "Now you're *defending* him?"

"No, I—"

"*Robbie,*" Gabriel interrupts, holding his hands out for emphasis. "Do you remember him? Our son who had five blood draws this past week alone? You're *defending* the person responsible for putting him in this place?"

His accusations take my breath away. Words escape me. My eyes shift to Robert who sits across from us. He doesn't interject, however, just watches us with his fingers steepled in front of his mouth.

Gabriel holds his head in his hands, but suddenly unbuckles his seatbelt.

Knowing exactly what he's doing, I grab him to hold him in his seat. Mike is at the back of the jet, sitting with Letty. "Gabriel, *no*. Just… calm down for a second."

"It's unconscionable," he growls. "He—he sat right across from me, didn't merely *offer* assistance, but *argued* for that insulin pump. And I *agreed*…" He pulls his hair. "I agreed because I trusted him. He lied. He lied to my *face*." Gabriel looks up at me, and his eyes are so empty that it's terrifying. I still haven't managed to inhale fully. I try to swallow but my mouth is dry. "He sentenced our son to a life of imprisonment in his own body. And you… you *pardon* that?"

He grips his arm rests and stands, shaking my hands off of him.

I frantically unbuckle my own seatbelt as Gabriel walks past me and turns for the back of the plane.

"Gabriel Dumas," Robert barks.

Gabriel stops, his hand on the back of my seat. I hear him sigh heavily, but he doesn't turn around.

"Not here," Robert says more quietly.

I expect Gabriel to sit back down next to me, but instead he changes direction and heads for the front of the plane. The cockpit is the only thing up there, so I don't know what he'll do. Memorize a flight manual?

I turn to Robert. "I... I didn't expect him to—to take it quite like that," I say quietly.

Robert lifts his brow.

"I had to, Uncle Moby," I say, blinking back tears. "Circumstances just... required me to trust him. How could I trust him if I couldn't forgive him?"

Robert unbuckles his seat belt and sits next to me, holding one of my hands and patting it. I lean my head on his shoulder, smelling ginger, the scent of kindness and understanding.

"You couldn't," Robert replies.

"Uncle Moby, has Gabriel... not been coping well?"

Robert sighs. "Something is deeply troubling Gabe. It took the daily efforts of three of us to keep him eating and sleeping. Robbie, I believe, was the only reason he managed to stay relatively grounded. Care of an infant is a consuming task as you know."

It sounds worse than I thought. "Did he pressure you? About a vision to find me?"

"Daily. But that part I expected. What I didn't expect was what happened after he received the phone call from Quinn. He became *more* volatile and demanding. And you became the enemy. He said you should have sought protection with us. He said you knew I could keep you safe, so there was only one reason you hadn't returned."

"Quinn called him?" I sit up.

"Yes. It was a kind deed. I've had him under protection ever since to prevent... interrogation."

"So did Gabriel figure out my plans...?"

"To reacquire your abilities?"

"How'd you guess?" I say, rolling my eyes.

He shrugs but smiles.

I frown though. "So Gabriel is that against it..."

"Oh I didn't say *Gabe* guessed your plans. No, he believed you took the excuse of kidnapping to permanently leave him and Robbie. Because the stress of 'normal' life and Robbie's illness was too much to bear."

I do a double take. "Are you serious?"

Robert quails. "Unfortunately. No amount of talking swayed him. He chose to believe it and began acting as if you didn't exist. At least outwardly. That's why I didn't tell him about your fly-by-night theft of the safe in Redlands. That was sure to provide him further ammunition to back his claim of your duplicity. Getting him to fly to Chicago with me took the lure of informing him I'd captured Carl— the person he previously blamed for Robbie's illness. I felt it prudent to not mention you'd be there or he likely would not have gone."

I balk. I never would have guessed this kind of behavior.

"I'd say your reception of him at the airport knocked quite a bit of that insanity out of him," Robert says. "But the trauma remains. Be mindful. Something has disturbed him, cut him deeply. I suspect it's the betrayal of his brother. It's clear the trust between them was so solid that Mike's treachery rocked his confidence in all his other relationships."

I look to the door of the cockpit, aching for Gabriel. Tears come to my eyes again and I put my fist to my mouth. Poor Gabriel. I *never* would have expected this from him. Never. And I think Uncle Moby is right: Mike wounded Gabriel in a way that will not easily be fixed.

Robert pats my arm. "Have faith, Wendy. You are not alone. You don't have to do this by yourself."

"Sounds like something Ezra would say," I sigh. "And if life were remotely normal right now, I might have more confidence. But things are about to get crazy. Hard decisions are going to have to be made. And I was hoping to have Gabriel's head in it. How can I give him the time he obviously needs if I'm running around, trying to save the world again?"

Robert laughs. "I love how you said that so casually. There is starting to be a pattern, isn't there?"

"Oh Uncle Moby, you and I both know you're just humoring us kiddies until we catch up to you. You know a lot more than you say. Like the Guild. You knew the name before I ever said it."

His eyes sparkle. "Can't get a thing past you, can I?"

"You get plenty past me and you know it," I say, elbowing him.

He crosses an ankle over a knee and sits back more casually, hands clasped over his stomach. "What I mean is that no one I have ever met has both grasped the scope of my ability as well as fully accepted that they are better off not knowing all that I know. You understood this even when you did not fully trust me. But now I cannot keep a secret without you already realizing I'm keeping it. Even in your depths of despair over Gabe and then Robbie... you did not falter in holding to that belief. And when I didn't fully trust myself to act in your best interest, *you* did. For me this has been liberating. I have been able to help you more because of it. You accept. You move forward. You don't stop to ask for directions all the time. And because of this, your destination has become more and more clear to me all the time, especially in the last few weeks alone."

I didn't think I could love Uncle Moby more than I already do. But I reach a new level of appreciation for him and gratitude that I was somehow lucky enough to have him in my life. "Thanks, Uncle Moby. I really needed to hear that right now." I smile at him. "But that's probably why you said it."

"It doesn't take supernatural powers to know that when you feel something strongly enough about a person, you should tell them."

"Well, I feel strongly that I need to tell you about my plans. I really need a listening ear. And Gabriel is apparently not in a good place to hear. Do you mind?"

"Wendy, at this particular moment in my life, there is no amount of information coming from you that I can't handle. Lay it on me."

I lift my eyebrows, but hold back questioning his confidence. Instead, I tell Robert about my experiences, the realizations I came to. When I get to my story about the fresco in L'Angolo, Robert puts a hand on my arm to stop me, "I never knew you had a child in high school. You're saying the child died?"

Considering that Robert kept up with me my whole life before we met, and what he just told me about knowing my future, I'm surprised at his claim. "Yes," I reply. "How do you not know that? I had my daughter under a different name. But I thought you were the guy who helped my mom out with stuff like that."

He looks equally perplexed by that, but only for a moment. "Leena was a very clever woman. And cunning. She followed through with everything she set out to do. We're overlooking that aspect of her by assuming she would not have found someone else to create an identity apart from me." Robert strokes his goatee. "She must have done it that way to be absolutely sure it would never be linked to your true identity, even through me." Robert shakes his head. "So thorough."

He looks at me. "I am so sorry about your daughter." His eyes become red and I worry he's going to cry, which in turn makes *me* feel like crying.

Robert manages to contain it though. He strokes his goatee again, and I notice his hand is trembling. "I have to confess something."

"What is it?" I ask, disliking the raw pain creeping into his features.

After an agonizing minute, his grey eyes clear and calm replaces the lines of uncertainty in his face. "As you know, I have kept a great many things from you over the course of our relationship, and all of them have been to protect your freedom to make your own future. But one thing I kept from you and most others out of shame… guilt... Pick your emotion. No one wants to appear weak. The reason I kept it from you most of all is because of the trust I know you place in me. I did not want to ruin your perception of me. I take that unquestioning confidence very seriously. I am realizing though, as we talk, that I have been missing the opportunity to bond more closely with you. I love you, Wendy. I consider you my daughter in every way. And I would hate…" Robert struggles for words, his eyes looking like they might tear up again. He clears his throat. "We approach perilous times and I would hate to have never given you the opportunity to really know me as I would like."

My pulse flutters. I don't like to see my stalwart Uncle Moby struggle so visibly when I know how much he already does internally. He's right though that it's frightening to me because I guess I have always considered my uncle larger than life. The figurehead of our family and the one person I admire more than anyone else. He's my rock. There for me in a different way than Gabriel is. And that's why I remain quiet, because when Robert speaks, the words are *always* important.

Robert analyzes his folded hands. "The most senseless question I can think to ask is whether my foresight is a curse or a blessing. Because I can't undo it. I can only manage it. Visions are threaded into every moment and every decision I make, both consciously and unconsciously. This is who I am. But I still ask that question every single day, because of the price I paid for the skill I now possess in utilizing it." He looks up. "I know you remember the main rule I live by when it comes to my ability."

"You don't mess with life and death," I reply.

"I told you at the time that I learned this lesson the hard way. I was married to a woman named Trisha. I met her because of a vision; I was already wealthy by then, and I wanted to find an honest woman who wasn't after me for the money, who could keep up with my busy life. Because of how easily I acquired more power and wealth, I also wanted someone who would help me remain humble, someone down to earth.

"Trisha was by no means what I expected," Robert chuckles, his eyes lost in memory. "I don't think *anyone* who knew me expected me to marry someone like her. She was a petite, blonde, quick-tongued, southern belle whose vernacular was riddled with 'sugar,' 'ya'll,' and 'bless your heart,' among other quaint phrases." Robert smiles fondly. "Probably her most endearing and exasperating quality was referring to me in front of whomever was around—family or high-powered executive—as 'Puddin'.' We'd be at a business dinner and she'd say something like, 'Puddin' is just tickled to have ya'll on board. Pleased as a peach pie.' Even if the deal hadn't been closed yet. Then she'd lean in really close to them like she was telling them a secret even though I was right next to her and say something like, 'He don't like people knowin' he takes favorites, but Puddin' lives and breathes for young energy like you.'" Robert laughs. "Of course, she said the same thing to the *old* energy, too. And then she'd tell them something that would absolutely embarrass me. But she was too charming for people to resist."

"She sounds like a hustler," I grin.

"Oh yes. She came across as naïve, but it was her strength because in reality she was as sharp as a tack and knew exactly what she was doing. Something about my pint-sized wife owning the dinner conversation with talk of peach pie and how often I left my socks on the floor always left an impression I couldn't have paid a publicist to reproduce."

"Sounds like a perfect match," I say, imagining Robert's placid demeanor next to such a vibrant, unapologetic fireball.

Robert swallows and leans his head back for several moments, staring at the ceiling of the cabin. Eventually, he clears his throat and quiets his voice, "We were going to have a little boy. But due to a developmental defect, the baby would likely die in the third trimester. You know better than anyone how devastated we were by that news. I went to work immediately, searching for a solution using my ability.

This was before I had learned that life and death are better left to fall as they may. I wanted to find someone who could help. And I did. No surgery like the one we were going to undertake had ever been done before. And the surgeon was brilliant and skilled, only just starting this particular procedure in which the fetus would be operated on in-utero. Our hopes were high. And with my ability having been the means to a solution, we had no reason to doubt that things would turn out okay."

He runs his hands over his thighs and then looks at me. "I wanted to tell you this story all those weeks ago when you asked about locating Carl."

"What stopped you?" I ask, remembering that day clearly. I have never seen Robert so distressed.

"It wasn't time," he says softly, almost to himself as he looks out the window. "Things did *not* go okay for Trisha and me. The surgery went well, but she got a severe infection and the pregnancy took a toll on her body so that the only way to have a chance to save *her* was deliver the baby early, prematurely. That comes with its own risks. By this time, Trisha was delirious and fevered and in a great deal of pain. I had to make the decision myself. So I decided to have the baby delivered. Gestation was far enough along that our son would have a good chance at survival. But in the end, Trisha died from infection and I lost my son to underdeveloped respiratory complications."

I catch my breath. Robert's eyes are red again and he doesn't look at me. He clears his throat a couple more times and says, "I cannot look back on that time without regret although I know I ought to let the guilt go. I know—I *knew* that if Trisha had been cognizant, she'd have not put the baby's life on the line. In the course of a pregnancy, a few days can make all the difference to development. My visions have never failed in their ultimate outcome if I stick to following them. And my goal had been saving the child. But I chose to interfere because I couldn't endure the price. If I'd allowed Trisha to carry him a little longer, he could have survived. I just didn't understand the cost of the miracle at the time. I was motivated by fear for Trisha's life. So I did the thing that I thought would save her. As a result, I lost them both."

I tuck my arm under Robert's, and I'm crying for him. "That's why you have the rule…" I whisper.

After several heavy moments, he looks at me intently. "I told you, I waver between curse and blessing. Because as much as I want to hate it and imagine how things might have gone differently, the longer I live, the more I can't deny the fruits of that hard lesson. I grasp that the goal I set when it came to finding Trisha in the first place was exactly the goal I achieved. Just not in the way I expected to achieve it. Were it not for Trisha and my son, who can guess what damage I might have caused along the way as I endeavored to overcome death in not only my life but others'? I had high aspirations… curing cancer, easing suffering, ending wars. I believed the possibilities were endless with my ability in effect. By my power I would *bring salvation* to people like a superhero. But this is an illusion that will inevitably crumble. No matter how well-intentioned you are, how ardently you crave happiness for others, nothing you achieve will last if you believe good acts are isolated, or that bad choices, mistakes, and even evil are exactly as they appear. Every *one* matters, Wendy. Every life. Every choice. Every act. Every thought. Every *one*. Trisha and my son died by my own foolishness. But they still affect every choice I have made. They have a claim in every accomplishment. They have a claim in every word I have ever said to you."

I cannot contain my tears. Rather than disappointment that Robert has now become more human, the strings of connection with my uncle tighten, and I find myself on the same plane as him. He pulled me up somehow; things look different here. *I* look different here.

Like Midas, Robert touched my soul with his own and changed it into something more valuable. I have often recited that I aspire to be like Robert. And though I meant it, I don't think I ever believed it was possible. It was more like a mantra. A nice motivational quote you spell out with cute fonts and frame on your wall. You do it not necessarily because you believe it, but because you *want* to believe it. And you hope that looking at it every day will help you one day do the thing that it says.

But today I have removed that quote from my wall. It's now written on my heart and soul. One day I *will* be like my uncle. Because he was once as lost as me.

"I love you, Uncle Moby," I say firmly as Robert disentangles his arm from mine and instead puts it around me. It makes me feel like a kid, tucked under his arm, but in a good way. Secure. With him near, I am hard-pressed to be afraid. I am hard-pressed to worry. After weeks of being on the run with Mike, the bi-polar moral mercenary, and despite Gabriel's scathing accusations, everything seems more doable. A bunch of Gordies can't touch me here.

Forty-five

Jet turbulence wakes me up from a heavy sleep. I rub my eyes groggily and discover that I'm reclined. I must have fallen asleep next to uncle Moby and he put my seat back. I turn to my left to look for him but instead find Gabriel sitting in his earlier seat, watching me.

"We need to talk," he says sternly before I can get a word out.

"Yes. I know. I wasn't the one that stormed off earlier."

He frowns. Gabriel looks more different every time I see him. I didn't notice it at first because I was just so excited about seeing him again, and the beard makes him look so different anyway. But now I can tell his eyes are more angry than lively. His shoulders more slumped. His hands, which are balled into fists, seem used to that position. Even when he was dragged down with cancer, Gabriel never lost his softness, especially toward me. He was never this haunted.

I reach out for his hand, but he flinches away.

"What happened to you?" I say.

His jaw flexes.

"How long are you planning to hate me for forgiving your brother?" I say.

"This isn't about my brother."

"Then what is it about?"

Gabriel looks like he has a hundred different thoughts going on in his head and he can't decide which one to voice first. But finally he says, "You asked about Robbie only one time. You've been apart from him for three weeks and you don't want to know how he's doing? His progress? His test results? Did you ever think of him while you were gone?"

I sit up. "Of course I did! Every day. But I didn't worry. I knew he was with *you*. I was so grateful Farlen got away with him, you have no idea."

"Our son has Duchenne Muscular Dystrophy and you didn't *worry*? How is that possible? I worried every day and I was *with* him."

I turn my head slightly, confused. "Gabriel, what is this really about? Is Robbie okay?"

"No he is not okay!" he shouts, throwing his hands up. "He has a terminal illness! He'll die before he's had a chance to really live! He'll be stripped of movement, of speech, and inevitably the air in his lungs! And you show up and not only *don't* ask about his state of well-being, but you *defend* the actions that brought this upon him!"

"I asked about him twice in the same paragraph!" I shout.

"You asked *where* he was, not *how* he was."

"I didn't realize I needed to clarify!"

"You do. One conveys an interest in one's location. The other conveys interest in one's well-being. The words that leave your mouth betray what you truly care about."

I put my feet on the floor and lean toward him, getting in his personal space and glaring up at him, my anger amassing. "Are you *really* accusing me of not caring about my own child?! *Really*? Because if that's *really* what you think, let me tell *you* something. Robbie was the whole reason I went to LA in the first place! I went because Robert gave me an address there when I asked him about finding Carl. And you know what I found at that address? Mike's *mom's* grave. And that's when I realized the key to finding Carl was Mike. And I was *so* concerned about Robbie that I chose to swallow my beef with Mike over that stupid fertility drug because not only was he my ticket out of that place, but he was the only way I stayed out of the Guild's clutches while I searched for Carl. And I found him when a whole legion of Guild Primes couldn't. And if you think I went a single *hour* without thinking of Robbie, then you must have completely forgotten who I am. And no. I *didn't* worry for Robbie while I was gone. Because I know who *you* are. And *you* would move heaven and earth for our child."

I wring my hands to calm down. But they keep shaking.

Gabriel sits there, glowering at me. But eventually his mouth softens little by little. So do his eyes, and he releases an exhale. He wrinkles his nose. "Actually, I don't have the ability to move heaven and earth, so I would never make such promises."

I watch him, trying to figure out if he's saying that to be obstinate or funny. But then I catch the twitch of his lip and I think it might be somewhere in the middle. "It's a saying," I reply, testing.

"It's a ridiculous, overused hyperbole."

We regard one another, measuring. I wish I could feel Gabriel. When I used to pick up on his emotions it was hard to stay defensive. But now I have no idea what he's feeling, and the unknown is scary, especially after his accusations. I want to believe he doesn't mean them, but Gabriel doesn't say things he doesn't mean... I want to hate him. But I want peace more.

It may only be his haggard look that softens me enough to rack my brain for something to say rather than the angry words that want to come out. I swallow twice for courage and then say, "There is only one person on earth who I think might actually be capable of moving heaven and earth, and that person is you."

The result is instantaneous. He clasps his hands around the back of his neck and bows his head. "I'm sorry," he breathes. "I know you love Robbie as much as I do."

I scoot closer to him and wrap my arms around him.

He shudders.

"Talk to me," I say.

He lifts his head finally, sits back, but keeps my hands gripped in his. "I've watched you sleep for a couple hours now. And I still don't know if you're really here."

"What do you mean?"

"I mean *you*. You're not the same woman that left me."

I'm more than a little concerned about his choice of words, but I keep my voice even when I say, "You're not the same man that I left behind either."

"You're probably right." I expect more, but he doesn't offer it.

Uncomfortable with the silence, I say, "Tell me about Robbie."

"Tell me about Mike."

I give him a critical look. "What do you want to know?"

"How much of this new you is he responsible for?"

I count to three in my head to keep from firing something snarky back to his accusatory tone. "I'm not sure how to measure the personal impact of being around an egomaniac twenty-four-seven. I'd say if I've increased at all in patience, that's due entirely to Mike."

It's his turn to be confused. "I don't understand," he says.

"Don't understand what?"

"Egomaniac... It sounds as if his behavior toward you has not changed."

"Oh it's changed alright. Now he's even more eccentric and unpredictable."

"Expound," he says, shifting in his seat to completely face me but refuses to relinquish my hand.

Grateful that Gabriel is not only talking rationally, but also taking an interest in Mike, I say, "Sometimes he was his usual, antagonistic self. But then he'd do nice things in the middle of it all. The weirdest part was that he was always looking out for me. He sabotaged the Guild's interrogation tactics, claiming it was about taking his partner, Andre, down. The times when he was beating guys up and doing crazy gymnastics with his body, he looked happy, in his element. He'd smile. We'd mess with each other. But then just as suddenly he'd start brooding again. He'd ignore my questions. He'd snap at me. He'd blame me for the entirety of his life's problems. And then he'd be a shoulder to cry on. When I thought you all were dead in the San Francisco earthquake, he hugged me and was adamant that you were fine. He started off trying to physically intimidate me a few times, but it didn't last long once I called him out on how messed up it was. Seems like whenever I would scream at him, he'd start being nice again. But then something would mysteriously set him off and he'd be on his hateful rampage again."

Gabriel looks surprised. "He never...? He didn't...? How about you start at the beginning, when you first went to his apartment, and give me the whole story?"

"Okay," I reply, and then launch into the tale, which, as I'm telling it, I realize it's chock full of relevant details. Gabriel is rooted to his spot except when he stops me to ask clarifying questions. His expression sort of twists when I talk about the offer Andre made and his demonstration of their ability to cure my diabetes. When I tell him about Mike's seven-year mission, he cuts in with, "*Seven years*? How did I not know? How is that possible?"

He grips my hand harder at the action-packed parts, particularly my experience with the goons in the alley. He frowns but remains silent when I talk about deciding to find Carl for getting my abilities back. And he repeats the phrase "Oh My" several times when I talk about L'Angolo. He asks a lot of questions about Letty's sudden appearance in the story, specifically what Mike's explanation was, since Letty showing up brought the Guild down on us. I get the impression that he suspects Mike did that on purpose and then at the last minute changed his mind about turning me over to them. I hadn't considered that. But with Mike's fragile state over the Gemma Rossi mystery in mind, it's entirely possible. In fact, the more I describe it out loud, the crazier Mike's behavior sounds.

"And then you found Carl…" Gabriel says after I gloss over the road trip to Chicago, which was mostly highlighted by fun reminiscing with Letty. The Mike in that part of the story spent the entire time being irritated with my existence and offended at my efforts to be extra nice.

"Yeah, which brings me to the *really* shocking parts of the story," I say.

"I feel like we missed an intermission. How can there possibly be more shocking information?"

"Shocker number one: Carl has his ability back. I mean, it's like looking at a really haphazard impressionist painting of the colorworld, but it's back."

"Good heavens, and he *showed* you?"

I nod. "Because he was trying to show me something about Mike, only shocker number two happened and he couldn't."

He sits there waiting with his mouth open before frowning at me. "You're really going to make me beg for it?"

I laugh. "Hey, you do the pregnant pause thing all the time."

"I'm going to change that about myself immediately."

I grin and then clear my throat, pasting a more serious look on my face when I say, "Mike's life force is so bright you can't look at it. I mean, it's basically like looking at the sun. I have no idea why."

Gabriel leans away from me, his brow furrowed in confusion.

"I know. It's mind-boggling. My only guess is it has something to do with his ability."

He thinks about that for a while. "What did Carl want to show you in the first place?" Gabriel asks finally.

"I don't know. We got the call from Robert about meeting you guys at the airport."

Gabriel groans quietly. "And all of this brings us to your actual mission. To rearrange your life force once more, right? Wendy, that would kill me. I've already got Robbie's fate weighing down the future. Don't ask me to endure this, too."

I don't know what to say. I hate that I have to be gentle with Gabriel. That leaves me at a loss for how to communicate how important this is. I don't know the best way to go about getting my ability back, and it would be nice if the one person who *can* weigh in on that actually *will*. Instead, it looks like I have to figure it out on my own.

Gabriel has been watching my expression. "Don't do that," he says. "You're shutting me down."

I rub my face and bring my knees up to sit cross-legged in my seat. He follows suit. "Me shutting *you* down? Gabriel, I have told you everything I have memory of since I went to LA weeks ago. But you haven't told me a thing. I know what you believed about me. I can't get into life and death questions with you when *we* aren't okay."

"I haven't told you anything because I haven't made sense of any of it," he says, an edge of defensiveness to his voice.

"Maybe, if you tell me the senseless details, we can make sense of it together."

He looks down at our hands. "Or you'll just recognize that I failed in my loyalty to you, that I did *not* have the trust in you I obviously should have."

"Been there. Just spit it out. I promise you'll feel better."

He turns my hand over, looks at my palm, and then brings it to his mouth. He kisses me there, and connection finally stirs between us. A little bit of him has come back with that familiar movement.

"I'm… *sorry*," he says. "*So* sorry. When you leapt at me at the airport, it shook everything loose. But still I thought, if I'm wrong, it's only about a few things. *Okay, I'll take her back, we'll work this out.* I didn't expect you to sit there and tell me everything that happened without hesitation, sparing no details. But you did, and I realize I was wrong about *everything*. And I have no idea how it was I got lost in the nightmares so thoroughly."

"What about Mike? What he did to you? It must have hurt. Pain colors things all wrong."

His face darkens. "I don't wish to talk about Mike."

"Doesn't matter what you *wish*," I say. "You *will* talk about it."

He recoils. "I will? Since when are you the one in this relationship that demands the other talk?"

"Gabriel, I was stuck for weeks with a guy that only spoke in singular, declarative sentences ninety percent of the time. I have never had to work so hard to get a straight answer out of someone, and I still don't know if I ever did. So I have new appreciation for being open and for doing someone the courtesy of answering a damn question. I have new appreciation for that part of *you*. And I'm not about to let you change that about yourself."

He smiles softly for a few moments. Then he holds his hands up. "Understood. I'll do my best." And then he deflates just as suddenly. "Yes, Mike's actions laid waste to our relationship. I can't seem to get off the merry-go-round in my head. The one where I fight to understand what happened, what motivated him to act as he did, how I should have spotted it. I have no answers. Whatever the truth is, it resides outside of what I believed possible. And when the impossible becomes possible, every other impossibility is up for reassessment."

"Why don't you ask him?"

He scoffs.

"Are you scared of something?"

"No," he says, affronted.

"You sure said *that* quick."

"Wendy, I have no guarantee he would answer truthfully. I can't trust a word he utters."

"You have to start somewhere."

"Or I can wash my hands of him."

I sit back and look at him doubtfully. "Gabriel, from my point of view, it's not so hard to imagine. He's got his own life. He found acceptance and support from a bunch of supernaturally talented people. He found friends and became indoctrinated little by little. You guys grew distant after our marriage, and meanwhile the pressure of his job to get to me increased. And he began to justify his actions, first a little, then a lot. To me, that's simple to understand. But based on your violent reaction to his actions, you know something I don't. I know next to nothing about your relationship with Mike except that it's such a huge part of who you are, how you think and act, that you can't simply walk away from it. You're going to bleed out that way. I'm not going to stand by and watch it."

He rolls his head back. "I can't do this right now, Wendy. I can't imagine when, but definitely not right now."

"You get a pass for now, because it looks like we're about to land," I say. "But this conversation is not over."

"I don't like this role reversal," he grumbles.

"I don't like it either. But I'm about to see Robbie and that trumps all." Then I look at him worriedly. "Do you think he's forgotten me?"

Gabriel sighs. "I showed him your picture every day. And videos on my phone. I'm pretty sure Kaylen did the same thing. I think she was worried I wasn't."

"Aww," I say, touched. "See, deep down you didn't actually think I'd left."

"Hope is a hard thing to crush," he replies.

"Thank God."

He gives me a look.

I laugh and shrug. "Someone needs to be thanked for that fact."

He smiles and looks me directly in the eye finally. "Wendy, I *am* sorry for everything I have said to you since the airport. For everything I thought *before* the airport. I was lashing out... I am a mess without you. I truly do love you."

"I love you, too. And I knew you didn't mean it," I say. "Besides, you're pretty mild to deal with when you're emotional compared to Mike. And I told you, I've earned a lot of patience from dealing with him."

"I can tell." And then he sighs. "And I had forgotten how beautiful you are."

"I did too for a while," I say. "I finally *feel* beautiful again."

Forty-six

*W*e've been redirected," Gabriel says, sitting down next to me.

"To where?" asks Letty.

"Los Angeles, Orange, and part of San Bernardino county have been designated as no-fly zones," Robert says, coming up to the small conference table on his jet where we've assembled. We've been circling about a hundred miles outside of LA Ontario airport for about twenty minutes, waiting for clearance to land. "Darren has informed me that riots have been sprouting up outside of LA and spiraling outward. News coverage is saying they're sporadic and unexplained, but they suspect some kind of chemical warfare. An act of terrorism."

Mike is on the outskirts, leaning against the wall. "Distraction tactic."

"The Guild is behind it?" I ask.

"It's a good guess," he replies. "Probably some Prime ability causing the riots. They're probably going to ambush us while heads are turned."

"Robbie…" I gasp. "Will they take him?"

"Maybe to get to you. They're past screwing around."

"Darren has been on high alert," Robert says. "We'll land at the Redlands airport. It's about five minutes away from my home."

"What about the no-fly?" I ask.

"It's on the outskirts. We'll slip in," he replies. "But they suggested Palm Springs as an alternate. I think that's where they're hoping we'll land."

"Your home is the backup plan," Mike says. "If they lose you at the airport, they're ready in Redlands. You need to get Robbie and the others out of there now to meet us somewhere. If we time it right, we can avoid a confrontation."

"And go where?" I say, throwing my hands up. "They'll just chase us down to the next stop. This is ridiculous. We need to actually *talk* to them. Negotiate or something? Or out them on the media? Can we do that?"

"No way. They'll be ready for that," Mike says. "Negotiation, maybe. You could give them Carl."

"We are not giving them *people*," I say, frowning at Mike.

Mike shrugs. "They'd probably take Robbie as a trade, too, but I figured you would like that idea least."

"Stop being an ass, Mike," I say.

"What about you?" Gabriel says to Mike cooly. "Will we get a reprieve if we give them *you*?"

I scowl at Gabriel. "Uncle Moby, what do you think?"

"I think we're making our stand in Redlands," he says with certainty.

"I hope you know what you're doing, Mr. Haricott," Mike says, pushing off the wall. "If Andre's in charge still, he's going to bring a battalion."

"Uncle Moby *always* knows what he's doing," I say.

"I always know *what* I'm doing, but I don't always know *why*," Robert clarifies.

"You don't know *why* you're landing us in Redlands and inviting a war?" Mike says.

"Oh, I definitely know why I'm doing *that*," Robert says as if it's a silly question. I know from experience that he's totally messing with Mike, and I hold back laughter as Mike's face screws up in confusion like he's sucking on something sour.

"Don't bother," Gabriel says to him drily. "Get those two together and you become certain they must be communicating telepathically. I've learned to go with it."

I look at Gabriel, surprised that he's not only speaking *to* Mike but that he's also sympathizing.

"Since when do you just *go* with anything?" Mike says.

"I'm not sure… Probably when you decided to steal my wife from me," Gabriel replies matter-of-factly. "Or it might have been before that… when you were poisoning my wife and unborn son." He throws his hands up. "You know, it might have been when you sent me to my death at the compound. Take your pick of any of my hardships and I'm sure you'll find I had to go with a lot of things, all of which were your fault."

"My bad," Mike says. "Here I was thinking that meeting the love of your life was the best thing to ever happen to you. All this *hardship* came after meeting *her*, you know. How about I return her to the Guild and you can go on with your life, trouble-free?"

Okaaay, nevermind. "Know what? How about you two take the conference room while we land," I say, standing.

"No, thank you," Gabriel says, coming to his feet beside me.

"Oh c'mon, Gabe. Just *go* with it," Mike says derisively.

Gabriel ignores him and exits the room. The others follow. I cross my arms and glare at Mike. He tries to scoot past me but I stand in his way. "*This* is your game plan to get Gabriel to forgive you? Pushing his buttons?" I step closer to him and lower my voice. "He's a freaking wreck because of you. Why can't you ever own up to anything? It would go a long way."

He gives me a lopsided grin and puts his hands on my shoulders. "You want me to own up? Being a jackass is just who I am."

"No it's not," I say as he catches his weight on my shoulders. I peer into his face. "Are you drunk?"

"Little bit. I'm thinkin' about staying this way. What do you think?"

I drag his hands off my shoulders and push him into a chair. "I think if being drunk actually made you nicer you should go for it. But it obviously doesn't."

"Aww, I *am* nicer. Watch." He clears his throat. "Wendy, you are the only one that puts up with me. You're right. You don't make hating you easy. In fact, I kinda think you're amazing." Then he wrinkles his nose. "Dangit. I guess they were all right after all." He looks up at me again. "How'd you do that? Make me like you?"

I groan. "Sober up, Mike. We need your A-game." But it's clear he's becoming more inebriated by the moment.

"I just complimented you. Supposed to say 'thank you.' Thought you wanted me to be nice."

I close my eyes a moment, mustering patience. Again. This is getting so old. Why do I put up with him? Why? "How long will it last this time, Mike?"

"Prolly until the alcohol wears off. Buuuut, being nice to you will tick my brother off, so I might stick with it if you're not gonna let me drink."

I want to shake him. Violently. I want to make him look at me and tell me why he acts this way. Instead I shake my hands out and say, "Mike, did you leave someone behind at the Guild? A girlfriend or crush or something? You said you swore off dating. Is that because you have someone?"

He looks pensive, as if he has to remember, and I'm not sure how drunk he is, whether I'm getting through. He's not really slurring, so...

"It's that obvious?" he says finally. "Yeah, I left someone behind. She's gone forever."

Burning curiosity falls over me then, and relief at getting somewhere with Mike finally. I crouch down in front of him. "Why forever? Never say never, Mike. This is all going to go *somewhere*, right? Maybe we'll bring her over to the dark side." I offer him a smile and squeeze his arm.

He bellows a laugh suddenly, and then looks at me. "I think never is a safer bet in this case. I got shit to do. Can't be mooning over a woman."

"We'll see about that," I say, patting his leg and standing. "If the woman can make you less... this," I gesture the length of him, "then I'm going to find a way to win her over."

Mike just laughs, sits back with his hands behind his head, puts his feet up on the conference table, and closes his eyes.

Forty-seven

Nothing noteworthy happens when we land at the Redlands airport. I can't see much from above because it's late, but as far as I can tell, no black vehicles are waiting for us, and the airport itself is operating on a skeleton staff since the no-fly order only a couple hours ago. We load up into waiting cars and head through the darkness to Robert's home. We don't appear to be followed, but this is too easy. Robbie is so close to my arms and I am convinced that we'll arrive to discover he's missing, along with Kaylen and Ezra, and the Guild is going to hold them hostage until I give myself up.

"It's gonna be okay, Wen," Letty says from next to me. "He's okay."

I would tell her that she can't possibly know that, but I'm afraid if I open my mouth I'm going to throw up.

Gabriel squeezes my hand, but that gesture feels empty, too. Robert rode in another vehicle with Mike so I don't have the benefit of his insight.

We come down a hill and the streetlights make everything look exactly like it did when I was here only a few days ago. I can see the tiled rooftops peeking up from the trees in Robert's neighborhood. When we pass a familiar section of road I flash back. I can hear the sound of gunfire next to me. I reach up and touch my face, remembering the warm splatter I found there after Mike killed that man. It was someone that knew Mike, I'm sure of it now. I think he didn't expect Mike to behave so ruthlessly, and frankly, neither did I. I've encountered a *lot* of things I didn't expect in the last few weeks. I've been capable of things I didn't expect. And I think I'm going to have to do a lot more of that if I'm going to keep my freedom.

We're through the back gate, and everything looks quiet. No one speaks a word, and I'm glad for the moment that I don't have emodar. We turn down the driveway and the gate opens for us. As soon as we reach the garage, suited guards start coming out of the woodwork.

I let go of Gabriel's hand, unlatch my door, and run for the garage, ignoring the thrum of voices erupting around me. "Robbie?" I say to Darren at the back door.

"Inside," he says.

I dart through the garage and explode into the kitchen, meeting a throng of people including Kaylen, Ezra, and Gabriel's parents. The room erupts into greetings and questions, but I have eyes only for Robbie, who I find locked in Maris' arms.

Tears spring forth at seeing him. I reach for him and Maris' relinquishes him to me in a lullaby of Spanish.

"Robbie," I gush, touching his cheek, his head, his hands, refamiliarizing myself with his softness. He's bigger and chunkier, which I expected, but what I didn't expect was what it would be like to look into his brown eyes, which are far more attentive and interested. He's more aware and interested than before.

I sink down into a chair, sitting him on my knees as we look at each other. I can't keep the smile off my face, and he offers one in return. A tooth barely peeks out from his bottom gum and it makes his smile absolutely adorable. I talk to him about how much I've missed him. I ask him what he and Dad have been up to, whether he's been learning more big words and if Kaylen has been hovering too much and if Ezra has been introducing him to comic books. I ask him if Uncle Moby has been hanging with him and telling him I'd be back soon. He gazes up at me, fading in and out of his toothy grin as if answering me.

I hear lots of hustle and bustle around me, but I close my eyes and hold him to my chest, inflating my lungs over and over with the scent of him, re-memorizing his shape. I can't believe how much I've been holding back when it came to missing Robbie. And I realize that the trepidation I felt on the way here was less about whether he'd actually be here and more about whether he'd start screaming as soon as I picked him up, that he'd see me as a stranger.

"He knows you," Kaylen says, the first voice I've really distinguished since I came here. "I can see it in his eyes."

I look up for the first time in probably ten minutes, realizing that the room has emptied but for her and Ezra. And Kaylen's hair is short, just above her shoulders.

"Either that or he's just happy about all that gas he let out right before you got here," Ezra says.

Kaylen smacks him. "Is not!"

I look down at Robbie to find his attention still on me. I'm with Kaylen. Even if he doesn't know who I am exactly, I think he perceives the connection enough to know that I'm special.

"Where did everyone go?" I ask, making faces at Robbie to see him grin again.

"Gabe was in here a second ago, looking like someone desecrated his prized dictionary, as usual," Ezra scoffs. "So I guess he still thinks you're a good-for-nothing doxy then?"

Kaylen cowers. "*Ezra*," she chides. Then to me, "He was just really worried about you."

"*Really worried*?" Ezra mocks. "Seriously, Kaylen, *really worrying* was what me and you did. About *Gabe*." Then he grins smartly at me. "It is good to have you back, Wen. I mean, not just because Gabe is a freaking psychopath when you aren't around, but you know, I was sometimes afraid I'd never see you again. But only sometimes. Robert was on top of it."

"Thanks. We're okay," I say, laying Robbie on my lap and putting his hands to my cheeks. "Gabriel's issue is not really with me. It's Mike."

"What else is new?" Mike says and I look up to find him leaning against the doorjamb. His jaw is pretty red, and the side of his lip is swollen from the hit he took earlier.

"Hey look, Robbie," I say, turning him on my lap to face Mike. "It's your Uncle Mickey."

I expect Mike to come closer, but when he doesn't, I say mockingly, "Are you scared of babies, Mike?"

"I think Gabe would slit my throat if I touched his precious son," he says, but I can see his eyes roaming curiously if not longingly over Robbie.

Well, well, does Mike have a soft spot for kids? Dying to find out, I say, "You let me worry about Gabriel. Come here."

"I'm not the best role model for a kid." But he takes a tentative step.

I roll my eyes. "I'm not asking you to teach him ethics, Mike. Just hold him. Fortunately for you, that doesn't require moral skill."

He shrugs and closes the distance. I put Robbie in his waiting hands. Mike tucks him in the crook of his arm and starts bouncing him. He looks down at him, and to my surprise, introduces himself as Uncle Mickey, but he says it in a Daffy Duck voice.

I snigger and put my hand over my mouth as he moves on to a Yoda voice, "A smart one you are, young Robbie. Your jackass uncle, they may call me, but more fun than your dad, am I."

"Michael?" says a quavering voice behind me. It's Maris.

Mike barely reacts, looking up from Robbie only momentarily before giving him his attention again. He starts telling Robbie about how he should look out for me because I do things like make people lose their job, but he does it in a Mickey Mouse voice this time.

"Cómo podría usted, hijo mío?" Maris pleads from behind me.

Mike pays her no mind, and my eyes are on him and Robbie. Robbie is enraptured with Mike's performance, which has now changed to a rendition of the ABC's as Kermit the Frog. Robbie utters a deep, low sound ending in a hiccup, but it is definitely a laugh. It echoes in the open kitchen, and it's so enticing that I stand up, hoping I can watch his face if he does it again.

"Oh my gosh!" says Kaylen, hovering closer to Mike as well. "That's his very first laugh!"

"Really?" I say, looking from Kaylen's delighted face to Robbie, who grins widely as long, low syllables push their way out of his mouth. It sounds like he's not sure how to string them together. "He saved it for me!"

"Kid never had a good *reason* to laugh before now," Ezra says. "Pretty much *nothing* was funny while you were gone. Except for that time last week I was on the phone with Kaylen and Gabe walked in and I pretended it was you I was talking to instead." Ezra guffaws. "Gabe's reaction was freakin' priceless."

"That was so mean, Ezra," Kaylen chides. "You were such a jerk to him."

"Mean, shmean," Ezra rolls his eyes. "Got him to admit the truth, didn't I?"

"What was that?" I ask.

"That he really did love you. Seriously. He was begging you to come back. Kaylen totally played along."

"I did not!" Kaylen says, crossing her arms. "I was totally silent. I didn't know what else to do!" Her cheeks and eyes are turning red.

Mike laughs. "I like how your brother thinks, Whitley. Good job, little bro." He holds up a hand and they high-five.

I cross my arms and frown at Ezra. "That was mean, Ezra. To Gabriel *and* Kaylen."

"Mijo!" Maris demands, this time too loudly for anyone to ignore. "You speak to me this minute!"

"And say what, Mamá?" Mike says tiredly, handing Robbie back to me.

"Tell me where I failed you," she says, though it sounds more like an accusation than a genuine question.

Mike didn't miss the tone either. He ignores her and heads the opposite direction, only to meet Dan, who begins speaking to him in a low voice. I can't make out what he's saying, but Mike's head is bowed.

Maris, on the other hand, looks like someone slapped her. But she's upstaged by Letty, who bounds into the kitchen. "Ezra, what up little homie!" She gives him a head-to-toe. "You sure are filling out nicely." She punches his arm.

"Letty?" Ezra says. "How—?" He looks at me and back at her, shakes his head. "So you come back with the guy that kidnapped you. And your best friend from like four years ago." He puts his hands on his hips. "This plot must have taken a weird twist."

At that moment, Carl appears from the garage behind Ezra, followed by Robert.

"Dad?" Kaylen breathes.

Ezra whips around. "Dang, Wen. *And* you bring back Carl? What soap opera have I walked into?"

"Mina and Selena!" Letty quips.

"Goth Queens of Bad Mother Shut-Yo-Mouthery!" I laugh.

"Duhhh-dudut-duhhh, dutdut-duhh!" Letty sings.

Ezra looks between us, stunned, before settling his amazement on me. "Who *are* you?"

"Was that the A-Team?" Mike says, having removed himself from whatever conversation his parents were trying to have with him to join our little reunion.

"Little Mickey knows the A-Team!" Letty squeals. She grabs on to his arm and flutters her eyelashes at him. "Let's get married. It's written in the Gummy Bears."

"Violeta…" he croons, caressing her cheek. "Querida… Are you telling me that you love green as much as I do? Mis sueños se han hecho realidad…"

She gives him a look of disgust and shoves him away. "Never!" she screams. "Die, you orange-hating scum!"

"Oh. M'gosh," Ezra says, scratching his head with a finger. "What is *happening*?"

"My brother, indulging in his usual la dolce vita," Gabriel says dryly, leaning against the fridge. I didn't see him come in.

"I have no idea what that means, but it rocks," Ezra says. Then to me he says, "Next time you're out getting kidnapped again, bring back more of this:" He points to Letty and Mike. "And less of *that*:" He points at Carl. "And take this one with you." He points at Gabriel.

I stand up and swat his hand away. "Isn't it your bedtime yet?"

"I believe it's *everyone's* bedtime," Robert says. "It's been a trying day."

"Whaaat?" Ezra whines. "They just got back! And I thought they were being chased and there was gonna be a big throwdown! And now everyone is going to *bed*? This is the worst episode of Mina and Selena *ever*!"

"No signs of them?" Mike asks Mark who has joined us.

Mark shakes his head. "Total silence out there. But from what I hear the riots are getting worse, so..."

"I don't like this," Mike says, uneasy. "The riots have to be their doing. And if they're getting worse, that means they're inflating this distraction because they're about to raise hell."

"We're going to run heavy shifts tonight. If they show, we'll be ready."

"I don't like this," Mike says again, shaking his head. "We need to get out of here. Somewhere they'll have to expose themselves."

"No," I say firmly. "Uncle Moby says we make our stand here, so we stay here."

Mike throws his hands up and looks at Robert. "Why am I here again?" The way he says it sounds like he and Robert have already had a talk. He doesn't wait for an answer. He pushes past his mom and dad, headed for the stairs.

Everyone else disperses, and I look down to find that Robbie has fallen asleep in my arms.

"A moment, Wendy?" Robert says.

"I'll take him," Gabriel says, easing Robbie out of my arms. "I'll see you upstairs."

When it's just Robert and me, he puts his hands on my shoulders and gives me a mild smile, looks down at the floor. I think he's finding words. He looks up, examines my face. "It's good to see you unabashedly embracing life again, Wendy. I know you've been going all day, that Gabe and Robbie could benefit from your company, but would you mind… sitting up with me upstairs in the atrium?"

"Sure, what is it?" I ask, unsure if I should be looking forward to what my uncle has to say. I'm not sure how to translate his behavior.

He shakes his head. "Just sitting. I… have a lot on my mind that unfortunately has to stay there. And I… believe I could benefit from your strength nearby. And I believe you could benefit from the time to gather your thoughts, perhaps?"

"Of course," I say, knowing that if Uncle Moby is asking for me to put his request above others, he must truly need it.

When I find Gabriel to let him know where I'll be, I expect him to be bothered that I'm leaving him alone again, especially when we've just been reunited, but instead he says, "By all means. The man never asks for a personal favor from anyone, all while giving them in spades." He looks toward the window, thoughtful. "I need to apologize to him. For now, I'm pleased to acquiesce to any request he may have." He looks at me. "He's been protecting and watching over you far better in the last two years than I ever have."

"Don't do that, Gabriel," I say, touching the side of his face.

"I'm not. I'm merely expressing gratitude that he's been such a huge part of your life. I've jealously guarded you, selfishly wanting to be your everything. But life has proven that I can't be. You have aspirations and goals, people that count on you, that influence you and help you in ways I've failed. I'm finally starting to accept that you've grown wings, but I still want to be relevant in your life."

I put my other hand on his face, cradling him. "Oh… Gabriel," I say softly, looking into his eyes. "*You* are the reason I ever believed wings were possible. You will *always* be relevant. The *most* relevant. Other people come and go, but you are the one I always want to stay."

"Thank you for saying so," he says, "but I didn't intend my words as a complaint. I'm just letting you know where I am, what I'm working on. I want to always be better. I want that to be the thing that sets me apart—that I always strive to be better for you today than I was yesterday."

I laugh softly and kiss him. "You have plenty that sets you apart already, Gabriel. You are… a force unto yourself."

Forty-eight

I wake up at sunrise because the Atrium lets in so much light, both overhead and on two sides. But it looks like Robert beat me because I find myself alone with the plants here, staring up at the sky through the glass. Last night went exactly as Robert said. We sat, Robert in a recliner on the other side of the coffee table and me on the couch. I tried to talk to him a few times, but he was more inclined to silent ponderings in the moonlight that spilled into the room. When I stopped wondering if Robert needed to talk, I found myself grateful for the opportunity to decompress everything I've built up in the past few weeks, just as Uncle Moby said.

I ended up thinking about Mike. I thought about what he sacrificed in order to make sure I tasted freedom again. I replayed the time I've spent with him. I remembered the woman he mentioned leaving behind, and I wondered about her, what qualities she must possess to capture the interest of someone as complex as Mike. A realization came to me slowly and unassumingly as I pondered it: I care deeply for Mike. I want to say I love him, but it's hard to wrap my head around because such things are always painted scandalously. What I feel for Mike doesn't seem outrageous to me, only natural and logical. So it's hard to place my feelings for him in a light that would generally earn a hefty dose of judgment. Because of course, I am married to Gabriel. I have no plans to change that, but I need to tell him. Ironically I think it will help our relationship. The longer I thought about Gabriel and his struggles, the more sense it made to assume that Gabriel already *knew* about my feelings. He often intuits things about me before I'm consciously aware of them. And maybe he has been so hard to reason with because he worries I've been hiding it from him. I haven't, but I can see how it would appear that way.

Letty rushes in just then, wearing pajamas, her face red and her eyes wide. "Holy Mother, Wen!" she says. "I was downstairs getting breakfast and a bunch of dudes claiming to be homeland security just showed up to search the house! They have dogs!"

I jump up. "What!" I say. "Seriously? For what?"

"They're taking your uncle in, they said. For breaking the no-fly thing. He's going to be questioned about the riots."

"That's bull!" I exclaim, heading for the stairs with her.

"Be careful, Wen. It's like, super serious down there."

After two flights, I run right into Mike, who catches me before I fall. "Stay here," he hisses, blocking my way.

"Mike, they can't take Robert!" I say, trying to push past him. "You know what this is really about!"

"I know," he says in a low voice, putting his hands on my shoulders like Robert did last night. "It's an excuse to sniff around and take down the surveillance system if they can and confiscate weapons legitimately. Chances are only a couple of them are actually Guild, but once they're done we'll be defenseless."

"What about Robert? We can't let them take him!"

Mike crosses his arms. "You're the one who said he knew what he was doing. But either way, *you* can't put up a stink and give them a reason to take *you*, too."

"That's what I was about to say," Letty chimes in.

"What is going on in here?" Gabriel says from behind me.

Letty whips around and breaks into a rapid-speed explanation before anyone can reply.

Gabriel's brow furrows. "Where's Farlen?" Then, to Kaylen who walks up behind him, bleary-eyed, he says, "Kaylee, go get Robbie, please. And Ezra."

"Farlen is the tall dude with the dark hair?" Letty says. "He's talking to the homeland security people. They confiscated everyone's weapons, and that dude looks like he's gonna jump someone any second."

"And we're sure that this is, in fact, *actually* a homeland agency?" Gabriel says, moving closer to me and taking my hand.

"We actually have no idea," I say. "But Mike says at least some of them have to be Guild."

"No time for speculation. If we're going to act, we have to do it fast," Mike says.

I hear the front door open from the base of the stairs and the hustle and bustle of people coming through. Several of them ascend the stairs where we are, suited and flashing badges. They start barking at us to remain still and hand over any weapons. Mike is the only one to hand anything over, and they search each of us for good measure. They find the gun I forgot I had strapped to my ankle—I never did change out of my street clothes last night. Kaylen and Ezra with Robbie, along with Gabriel's parents and Carl have joined us by the time the suits order us downstairs. There we find Robert's men standing against the wall in the grand foyer. I take Robbie from Kaylen and back into Gabriel, who puts his arms around me protectively. Robbie must pick up on the tension because he starts crying, adding an extra note of frenzy to the atmosphere.

They question us about the weapons that have already been confiscated and what we know about Robert's involvement in the riots.

"No one in this room has anything to say to you. Direct all your questions to Robert's lawyer." It's Mark. I don't see Farlen. Or Robert.

But one of the suits gets in my face anyway, asking if the gun they took from me is registered.

"Are you deaf? I believe Mark told you to talk to my uncle's lawyer," I say nastily.

"Then we'll be taking you in for questioning as well," he says. He gives an order and someone starts pulling me toward the door.

"No!" Gabriel booms, pushing his way through the men that have surrounded me. "You take her, you take me, too."

"Gabriel," I say. "Please. One of us has to stay with Robbie." But I actually think *none* of us should be separated. We need to put a stop to this. *Right now*. But how?

The tension in the air can be cut with a knife, and I wonder how many of us are thinking the same thing. Mike cracks first when someone takes a hold of him. He performs an easy twist of the man's arm and slams him face-first into a wall. The boom echoes in the high-ceilinged room.

Sport coats rustle. Gun safeties click off. Holsters shift. The room is full of these sounds as our captors assemble in a formation and some fifteen guns aim at us lined up along the walls. At least three weapons are pointed at Mike.

"Release him!" one of the suits yells.

Mike doesn't move, but his shoulders are heaving. A quick turn of his arm will crack the man's neck and take his life. I can't see much of Mike's face, but I'm terrified for him. I'm terrified for all of us. But if Mike doesn't release the man, he *will* die. With probably ten bullet holes to the back.

"Let him go!" another voice commands. "Hands up!"

From somewhere to my right, Maris says something desperately in Spanish, but Mike remains rooted.

"Bloody hell, man," Gabriel says. "You're going to get all of us killed."

My eyes sting with tears. "Mike," I say softly, wanting to take a step toward him but being afraid to move with so many guns ready to shoot. "Please. Let him go."

"This isn't homeland," Mike growls. "I know half these guys."

"I get it. But people are going to get hurt."

"Of course they will," he snaps.

"Not this way," I beg.

Still he doesn't budge.

My eyes dart around the room. He's got to stop. But what will Mike listen to?

"*I* say when to jump, Mike," I say sternly, hoping it works.

Mike releases the man, takes two steps back, hands in the air. Two men pile onto him, throwing him into the floor and cuffing him. He doesn't fight back.

A sliver of my anxiety eases, but a new fear takes its place. If anyone *could* have gotten us out of this, Mike could have. And now he's down. Why did he have to attack that guy right off the bat? He's ruined any chance of overpowering these people. Now, if anyone tries, we're all going to be dead.

I grip Robbie like a lifeline, breath held, eyes bulging at the line of gun barrels aimed at us. Frightened that a massacre will occur from the sheer concentration of unspent adrenaline building in the room, I turn toward the wall to protect Robbie. But someone screams at me, "Turn around! Face forward!"

A faint but high-pitched hum emanates from all around us suddenly. The Guild-homeland people all cower at the sound, gripping their heads and yanking out earpieces. I think it's coming from their communicators.

Robert's people, unaffected by the sound—and maybe expecting it—react immediately. They leap into the foray; fists and feet, grunts and yelps fill the room. Mike has regained his feet. Hands still bound, he cuts a foot across someone's face and follows it up by ramming them with his head. Gabriel has wrapped me and Robbie in both arms, plastering us against the wall as Robert's people disarm every single one of our captors like a well-trained unit. They put them to the floor, hog tied and gagged. And just like that, we have the upper hand.

Rooted to my spot, I scan the bodies littering the floor. I'm having trouble believing what we just did. Maybe I should have grasped the seriousness of the Guild's threat in any of the times I've dealt with them, but it's now no longer just Mike and me on the run. It's about fifteen of Robert's guys. It's Gabriel and Letty and Dan and Maris. It's also Carl—he's removing weapons from some of the tied-up men. This war now has sides. And I'm certain this is only the beginning.

"Darren and Floyd. Get the ones outside before they recover." Mark steps over the body of his victim, hands on his hips. "Wendy, they'll be sending more. Your orders?"

"What just happened—with the sound?" I stutter. Even Robbie has stopped screaming, squirming in my arms to see the mess around us—toppled lamps and tables and off-kilter frames on the walls. Some of the men on the floor have blood coming from their ears. They're alive, but I have no idea what kind of damage has been done.

Mark winks. "The best damn anti-surveillance tech in action. Don't worry. Just some busted eardrums. A few knocked out. They'll be okay."

"That was sick," Mike says, kicking a couple of stray guns out of reach of their owners. "You hacked their frequency? I don't get how that's possible even though I just saw it."

"*Counter*-hack, Dumas," Mark says, waving a hand. "You manage to disable a Qual-Soft system, you still get a nice little parting gift for your effort." He turns to me again. "It's in our best interest to decide a strategy immediately. This isn't over. Our surveillance is down now, so we're running a bit blind. I have backup radios and Robert keeps a vault of weapons in the front room."

"Wait, why are you asking *me*? Where's Robert?" I say.

"They've taken him in already. Farlen is with him."

"*In where*?" I demand.

Mark shrugs. "My orders are to follow *your* orders."

"But… it's not government that has him. It's *them*." I turn to Mike. "The Guild. Will they hurt him to get to me?"

"They don't torture people for ransom, Whitley," Mike says patronizingly. "They go by rules of engagement."

"Rules of engagement! Oh thank heavens!" Gabriel mocks. "Their immorality has an ambiguous set of rules!"

"Cherubic girls with mind-altering abilities are scary as hell, Mike, and are definitely a form of torture," I retort as I watch Mark and two of his guys push the massive coffee table out from in front of the couch in the next room over.

"Yep. So let's hope this is the Guild making an assault and not Andre unsupervised," Mike says.

With the rug rolled out of the way, Mark lifts a trap door in the floor in the front room.

Mike's already beside them, and his head falls to the side as he peers around it. "Oh my damn."

The door is in my way so I come around to see. "Whoa," I say in a hushed voice, staring at a five foot, yawning concrete hole in the floor filled with shelves of weapons, which begin to ascend to our level. "Uncle Moby's a prepper? Crap, are those rocket launchers?"

"RPGs," Mark says.

"Oh *shoot*," Ezra says, coming up beside me. "Uncle Rob's batman. He's all suave in business, but he's got this whole other life where he's building an ass-kicking empire. –Hey, are there any batarangs in there?"

Mark is already distributing weapons. "Wendy, still waiting on what you want us to do."

Instinctively I take a step back, rethinking this idea. But we're already in. The fifteen guys tied up in the entryway are evidence of that. The Guild needs to hurt. If we get out of this, they need to think twice about coming at us again. I refuse to spend my life running. I'll figure this natural disaster thing out, dammit, if they'll leave me alone a second to actually *do* that. What ever happened to knocking on someone's freaking door and asking for a favor?

The whole thing makes me mad, mad enough that I think we can do this. I think we *should* do this.

I look to Mike for his opinion, but he's examining the tiny earpiece in his hand. "These are slick. One piece, but not custom? Do they stay in?"

"They'll expand to fit your ear once you insert them," Mark says. "They have an insane range. These are prototypes, aka, the super-secret, not-for-sale stuff."

"How do you initiate transmission?" Mike says.

"Two ways," Mark replies. "Either tap the ear first. Or say, 'Transmit' before speaking."

"Rob has the goods," Mike says, tucking the piece in his left ear. "I'm with Ezra though. We need batarangs."

"You are so ridiculous," Gabriel says, turning a gun over in his hands before holstering it. "If this is how you treat life and death situations, it's no wonder you got confused about right and wrong."

"This is *not* life and death, Gabe," Mike says, slinging a rifle over his shoulder. "This is my job and I enjoy it. I finally get to take Andre down, and I am *not* losing."

"He's kinda right about that," I say, giving Gabriel a chagrinned smile. "I'm glad he's on *our* side finally."

"That has yet to be determined," Gabriel says, holstering a second pistol at his ankle. He looks at me. "If you're thinking we should make a stand, I'm with you. This cat and mouse game needs to end. Time to show them we're lions."

"Wendy? Make a stand? With a gun?" Mike scoffs. "She's all about clean hands and consciences. Peaceful *negotiation.*"

I glare at him as I hand Robbie to Kaylen. I choose a gun and holster it.

"Shut your face, Little Mickey," Letty says, testing several different guns in her hand. "You are forgetting our assault outside the hotel when Wen punched bullet holes in everything that moved. We saved your ass—which is mighty fine by the way."

"Why thank you," Mike says, his only response to Letty. "They have *families*, Whitley," he goads. "What if you kill someone's daddy?"

I jerk the straps on my Kevlar vest tighter. "They attacked *us*. They brought their guns first. They could actually choose to talk, and they don't," I say matter-of-factly. "I might be able to get past that. But then they took my Uncle Moby. They *will* give him back."

"Aw naw, she ain't playin' anymore," Mike says. "That's my girl. Don't forget what I told you about keeping your gun up between shots. I saw you getting sloppy at the hotel."

Looks like Mike's happy to be in his element. Gabriel sighs next to me. "I'm afraid I have no idea what you're capable of anymore," he says softly near my ear, "but I would entreat you not to be reckless. Please, be safe."

I give him a peck on the lips. "I will be." I look up. "Kaylen, you and Ezra are going to take Robbie and hide out in this hole with

Maris." I snap a finger at Ezra whose mouth is already open to protest. "No argument," I say. "You don't know how to use a gun, and you're too young."

"What about you?" Ezra whines. "You're the one they want. *You* should be in here with us."

I shake my head, fastening a second holster to my waist. "I'm also the safest one in this group because the Guild doesn't want me dead." I look at Letty. "You don't have to be up here. You can look out for Ezra and—"

"Hells to the no!" Letty says, adhering the final strip of Velcro to her vest. "Dad didn't teach me to shoot so I could hide in a hole."

I grin and fist bump her, wishing I'd involved Letty in my life sooner. But I didn't know how much I'd affected her, and the loyalty that brought with it.

I look at Carl, who has been standing silently apart from the group. "You in?"

Darren comes in through the front door. "The outside is clear. Robert and Farlen are gone. Floyd's on the roof."

Mark hands him new communicators and glances at me before saying, "Looks like Wendy wants to take a defensive strategy. Take your team to the back. I'll take the front. Levi will go up to the roof with Floyd."

"They'll take out your eyes up above as soon as they can," Mike warns. "Watch for snipers. Lots of nearby roofs for them to set up shop and I'm betting they've already cleared the neighborhood."

"I'm taking the roof in that case," I say loudly.

"Don't be ridiculous," Mike says. "You don't know what you're doing. We need eyes on all sides from up there. We need a team. Not one girl with a gun and no experience."

"I'll go with her," Carl says, stepping forward.

"Fantastic," Mike drawls. "It's capture the flag, where everyone can see it. There's even a bonus flag in the exact same place! This is going to be a bloodbath. They're going to surround the property like ants, take out the perimeter with sheer numbers. While everyone's distracted with trying to, I don't know, *live* through the onslaught; they'll drop in with a helicopter and pluck you right off the roof with a stun-gun."

I picture exactly what Mike's threatening. He's right that they can easily outnumber us if they want to. It's going to give them confidence and they probably won't hesitate to converge on us with those numbers.

"Do they have any weapons technology we need to know about beforehand?" I ask, thinking we might be able to exploit their confidence.

"The Guild is not militaristic," Mike says. "Their intellectual resources have been almost entirely devoted to Prime Human development and keeping a lid on these natural disasters."

"Yet here we are... about to be assaulted by these people. Again," Ezra says. "*That* never happens."

"Andre's off his leash. Anything's possible."

"So that's a no to crazy weapons," I say. "Perfect. Then what we're going to do is draw them in. I want them to think they can take us down with their numbers. I want every single Gordy boot banging at the gates. Then, we take out their fleet with these rocket launchers."

The room is silent. Mark seems to be considering it. Mike is flabbergasted that I would suggest such a thing.

Gabriel sighs heavily from behind me. He's been awfully quiet so I turn to him. "What do *you* think?"

"Your logic is sound, and I like the plan. But you need someone with you who is trained. You've never fired an RPG before—to my knowledge."

Encouraged by his confidence, I say, "I'll take Mike then."

Mike's eyes are wide, and he looks around and then back at me. "Oh wait, you're totally serious?" He looks at Gabriel. "You're cool with this? Your wife a sitting duck on the roof with a grenade launcher?"

Gabriel spreads his feet and puts his hands on his hips. "Wendy has an excellent point, which is that she is valuable *alive*. She is a capable woman, and formidable when she decides to do something. Furthermore, I'm not her father. I don't tell her what to do. Robert put her in charge, and I've spent several weeks fighting the two of them and their plans. I'm done with that." He simpers at Mike—an unusual expression for Gabriel. "It's part of this new me that just *goes* with things."

Mike holds his hands up. "Alright. I'll accompany the bait—I mean Whitley—to the roof and let her order me around."

"Her *name* is Wendy, you bloody traitor," Gabriel says calmly. "If you feel you must refer to her by her last name, it is Dumas. Shouldn't be hard to remember, since you share it."

"Sure thing, Gabe," Mike says brightly as Mark leads a group of men out. "I forget because it's hard to believe she actually married you. Still haven't wrapped my brain around it."

Gabriel emits a low growl, and I put a hand on his arm, which calms him immediately. "Shut the hell up and behave yourself, Mike," I say. "Or I'll stick you in the hole with Kaylen and Ezra… and your mom." Maris, I notice, is not in the room at the moment. Ezra went to get snacks out of the kitchen for their sojourn in the weapon room—always the practical kid, thinking of potato chips when life is upended.

"Yes, Ma'am," Mike says, saluting me.

"Let's go," I say, kissing Robbie on the forehead.

Gabriel touches my arm before I can leave. He puts his hand on my cheek, and just like that it's only him and me in the room. "May I kiss you, Wendy?" he whispers.

"Thought you'd never ask," I reply, standing on tip-toes to meet my lips to his and closing my eyes. I touch his face with my fingertips, relishing the softness of his hand on my neck and the way his lips explore mine, lingering, asking, receiving. The conversation of our lips ebbs and flows. No words pass between us, but the communication is clear. The sweetness of the moment is the gentleness I have been craving from him since I got back. I hope this is the beginning of the end of the rough edges he has acquired the last few weeks.

Gabriel and I squeeze hands one last time before I lead Carl and Mike up to the roof. On the way, with the taste of Gabriel on my mouth, I relive the kiss, realizing rather suddenly that it was the most natural kiss I have experienced since I lost my abilities. Never once did I long for something else. I was just… speaking to him in a different language. And I finally didn't worry that he'd misunderstand.

Confidence, I decide. That's what's really been lacking all this time. With emodar and somatosense, I never had to wonder about his feelings—or anyone else's. But then the training wheels got yanked off, and I realized I didn't know how to ride a bike. I got thrown into the race and had to figure out how to balance on my own really quickly. I finally figured it out. I finally know what I'm doing.

Well, except for firing a rocket launcher. I don't know how to do that. But I figured out how to be a regular person, limited in perception and confined to my own head for the first time in my whole life. I can handle a rocket launcher.

Forty-nine

It's like this house was built for defense... roof balcony, natural places for cover all over the yard..." Mike comments when we reach the third floor, where I spent the night on the couch to keep Uncle Moby company. Mike's right. The atrium has a set of stairs leading up to a roof balcony, one that will hugely maximize visibility of the surroundings. Like the neighbors' homes and the street out front.

"Knowing Rob, it *was*," Carl says, following me up to the balcony. We can see Robert's guys fanning out into the front and back yards. Gabriel is in the back yard near Letty. A couple Guild vehicles are out on the street, but with no activity around them. What are they waiting for?

"I say we take out the neighbors' roofs," Mike says. "Preemptively. I don't want to wait until they start shooting. From up there, they can have pretty accurate sights on our men."

I hesitate to destroy peoples' property, but Mike's right. The last thing I want is a sniper taking out our people.

I tap my ear. "Can we confirm the neighboring homes are empty?"

"Darren, verify that," I hear Mark say.

"Help me get the rocket launchers," I tell Mike, who is on one knee, scanning the perimeter through a pair of fancy binoculars we found in the weapons room. "You can show me how to set them up here."

"That hill makes it hard to see them coming from far away. They could be right at the base of it, building forces and we'd have no idea." Mike stands at the same time I hear a dull shot. He grunts and falls back to his knees, propping himself with a free hand, his other hand gripping his stomach.

"Mike!" I say, crawling over to him, looking around us for the source of the shot but see nothing. Panicked, I can't look away from Mike's bloody T-shirt. I don't know what to do with my hands.

"Shit," Mike says, looking at his stomach; his face turns a shade lighter.

"Lay down," I tell him, pushing gently.

"Roof team," Mark's saying in my ear. "I heard a shot. Are you okay up there?"

Carl is at my side suddenly, lifting Mike's hand from the bloody spot in his stomach to see. "Slow bleed," Carl says. "We'll need to keep pressure on it. And you need to lie flat."

Voices are yelling in my ear, namely Gabriel demanding to know what's going on.

I look up to find a stream of vehicles headed down the street toward Robert's house from the exact place Mike called. Guys are also running in on foot.

"Mike took a hit to the gut," I say into my communicator. "He's okay for the moment. But we can't move him. Everyone stay hidden. There's a sniper up high. Plus, they're coming up the road. They're here. I hope you're ready down there."

"Can you give me a count?" Mark says.

I look up to see.

"Take out the roofs," Mike says between grunts. "That's more important."

"Right," I say. "I got this. Carl, you keep pressure." I hop up to go downstairs, but hesitate, turning around again.

"I can also keep my eye on the roads headed this way," Carl says calmly, wrongly translating my hesitation. "I'll keep Mark abreast."

"Fire a couple shots that way with your pistol," Mike says, pointing at a nearby roof. "That's where the shot came from. We need to scare them a little so you have time to set up."

I pull my gun out, scan the roof for where they might be hiding. There's a chimney; I bet that's where they are…

I hold the gun with both hands, keeping my eyes open while I fire, like Mike taught me. I shoot at the chimney four times. I have no idea how much time that will buy me, whether a few randomly aimed shots will do anything but make them laugh, but that's actually exactly what I want.

I crouch back down. "I can't use the RPG yet. They need to think all we have up here is a handgun. If I use the grenade launcher, they'll be careful about gathering around the perimeter. I want them in a cluster."

"Dammit, if we don't take out the roofs, they'll have clear sights on our guys below," Mike says. "I get your plan, but my brother is down there."

"And *my* husband," I say firmly. "But like you said, the yard's full of trees and stuff. There's cover." I tap my ear. "I'm going to keep them distracted by shooting at the neighboring roofs, but you guys need to watch your overhead cover. I'll keep them as busy as I can until we're ready to activate the bug bomb."

"Bug bomb?" Mike laughs, only to have the laughter turn into audible groans of pain.

"Yeah, it's my code name for the operation," I say, sticking my tongue out at him.

"Funny, funny Wendy," he rolls his eyes. "Just tell me you're going to bust a cap in someone's ass with your piece and my life will be complete."

Hey, look. Mr. Niceguy is back. All it took was a bullet to the gut. Idiot…

I stand up, and send a couple more shots to the suspect roof. I do the same for the other neighbors. The one to the backside is pretty far away, so I doubt I hit the actual roof.

My head turns on a swivel for the next several minutes. I spot movement on one roof, so I send two shots that direction. Meanwhile I keep my eye on the scene below, let Mark know where they're moving. Mark is good at what he does. He's firing just enough to keep the Gordies hesitant about crossing the wall. Mark's guys fan out more, but keep close to the wall's perimeter as well as the gate that crosses the driveway.

The Gordies are doing exactly what I hoped: slowly congregating right outside the walls. There are definitely a *lot* of them. We are easily outnumbered. I catch sight of a helicopter approaching from the distance. For a second I worry that Mike was right and they're going to fly over me. I also dislike that I can see our guys. If I can see them, so can others.

The helicopter moves closer.

"Wendy, get off the roof," Gabriel's voice says in my ear.

"Is that a helicopter?" Mike asks, twisting his head around to see. Instinctively, I lean over him, worried they've actually come to take another shot at him.

But Mike isn't lying helpless. He jumps to his feet, putting his arms around me at the same time and lunging for the stairs. Carl is close behind us. But I watch over his shoulder, dumbstruck when the helicopter comes no closer. It remains hovering over the yard.

The cold realization of what they're actually doing falls over me. "Noooo!" I scream, fruitlessly reaching out.

Mike turns slightly. He sees exactly what I do:

They're going to fire on the grounds from above.

On all the people in the front yard…

Helplessness leaves me barren and empty, but it's quickly filled with the lead weight of dread. It makes my whole body hard to maneuver. My hand weighs ten pounds as I lift it to tap my ear. "Look out below!" I yell into my communicator as Mike puts me down none too carefully. "Take cover! Take cover!"

Mark is shouting orders to his men in my ear. What can I do? What can I do?

Nothing. I'm on top of a three story building with Carl and now the Guild knows everyone below is expendable. Could I have made this extraction any easier?

So I watch in dumb horror, frozen in place, knowing my world is about to burn. I watch the deadly beam stream from the helicopter, aimed at the center of the front yard.

Reflexively, I shield my eyes with my arm, but I feel and hear the blast of it. The acrid heat singes my nose. I step back instinctively, blinking my eyes to see past the smoke and debris in the air. Did that really happen?

We're in a neighborhood. In America. And someone just shot a missile into our yard, leaving a funnel of dirt and smoke and blackened earth. Two trees are on fire. I step toward the railing, looking for bodies, but don't see any. I don't know if that's good or bad.

The helicopter is still hovering, about fifty yards away from my position. I cough and put my hands over my mouth, my eyes tearing up not only from the smoke but from helplessness. From shock and fury.

I need to do something.

They need to burn.

I turn my head away and catch sight of Mike. He's holding a rocket launcher and several other guns I saw him bring up from the weapons room. I'd forgotten about those… Maybe if we fire on their fleet outside the gates, they'll at least pause their aerial assault long enough for everyone to clear out of the grounds.

Mike doesn't take the RPG though. He grabs something that looks a little like an assault rifle but with a shorter and wider barrel. Legs spread, he puts the butt of the gun against his shoulder.

"Get down. Turn around," he says to me. "This is much closer range than their shot."

Confused what he means, I get down on my knees, turn around, but watch over my shoulder.

He fires. The sound is quiet, a dull, metallic pop.

I don't get a chance to see the effect, because Mike has thrown himself over me, pinning me underneath him just as an explosion sounds close by, like it could be right here on the roof. It's followed by a second explosion, this one much louder. The house shakes. I hear debris hitting the roof around us. More smoke. And scorching heat.

After a few seconds, Mike releases me and stands up. I do the same, shielding my eyes a little to keep the dust out. I finally catch sight of it: the helicopter, a tangled, flaming mess on the ground almost exactly in the blackened hole it created only moments ago. Mike took down the helicopter?

Why didn't I think of that?

Mike has already gone to work though, grabbing the actual RPG and loading it with a grenade. His shirt is now more red than white. Blood is dripping from the hem of it. I glance around for Carl, and it looks like he made out okay. He's staring at the war zone below, just as I am.

And then, a second gunshot.

I whip my head around.

Mike drops to his knees. He has so much blood on his shirt already that I can't tell if he's taken a second hit. But he wouldn't be acting like that if he hadn't…

"Oh no," I say, breath knocked out of me that I didn't know I had. I barely make it to his side, so afraid I think my heart is giving out. That's when I see that the shot made it into his thigh.

He grips his leg, groaning.

"Carl!" I shout, but Carl is already here when I look over my shoulder.

He puts his hands, already covered in Mike's blood, on the new wound. "Bullet didn't go all the way through," he says with ridiculous calm, testing the leg wound with his fingers, eliciting a litany of curses from Mike. The leg seems to be bleeding more than the abdomen, pooling between Carl's fingers. But it may be the copious amounts of blood everywhere that makes it look that way. "I think it nicked an artery."

My face is cold and my hands are shaking. I realize I'm gripping Mike's hand in one of mine. My other is maintaining pressure on his abdomen, but it feels like a losing battle as red streams between my fingers. Hot tears come to my eyes as he heaves in agony. "Idiot," I say, biting my lip, trying to control my fear. "No vest? *Why?*"

"A vest wouldn't have covered my leg," Mike growls. His face is truly turning white now.

I glare at him, because being irritated is more manageable than my terror for his life beneath it all.

"I'm too badass for Kevlar," he gasps, answering my look.

"Don't do this," I quaver hoarsely, my hands growing slippery.

"Do what? Die? I didn't know you cared so much, Whitley," he says, and I think he's growing delirious. "You have black smudges on your face." He licks his thumb and reaches up and rubs my cheek with it. "Oh snap," he says, looking at his thumb. "I got blood on your face."

"Stop it, Mike!" I yell. Oh God. He's delirious. He's going to die.

My tone rouses him, and his eyes grow wild. "Wendy, you need to use that RPG on their fleet! You're wasting time." He lets go of my hand and pushes me off of him.

I look up and around at the thick smoke in the air, and it's only then that I really hear all of the shouting in my ear and the gunshots coming from below. Everything is in chaos. No one knows what to do. I'm supposed to be in charge and I'm totally sucking at it. I count seven vehicles at the front. Five near the house to the rear. Countless men converging on our property. I need to do this before they scale the wall.

"Pull back from the wall," I say into my communicator, walking over to pick up the RPG Mike dropped. I repeat the command over and over to break through the chaos of commands in my ear until they quiet and I have everyone's attention. Carl hovers over Mike, one hand on each of the holes in his body.

The line quiets as Mike instructs me how to use the launcher.

It's pretty simple, but Mike warns me that it's much louder than the mini-grenade launcher he used on the helicopter, with a much more powerful kickback. He has me set up the tripod and lay on the ground on my stomach, the barrel held steady by the railing on the roof.

"Eyes open, Whitley," he says, his voice growing more faint. "Don't let it get away from you."

"Anyone not clear of the wall?" I say into my communicator.

"All clear," Mark says.

I blow out through pursed lips, double and triple-checking my aim.

I hold my grip on the launcher as tightly as I can, using every bit of my strength, and pull the trigger.

I must have exploded. But I'm still aware, so I must be wrong. I hear a second explosion, this one further away. I blink until my vision comes into focus. There's a fireball burning at a now-demolished portion of the wall.

"Reload," Mike says hoarsely. "Don't waste time."

I do as he asks, but not as quickly as I need to. I feel a little dizzy. I reach for another grenade, mindlessly following Mike's instructions and avoiding looking at all the blood covering him.

I lie down and take aim again. When I look through the sights, I finally see that I took out a huge portion of the front wall. This time I want to go a little farther and hit right in the middle of all their vehicles.

I line the sights up a second time, grip the launcher firmly, and pull the trigger, this time prepared for the sound. But it still shakes me head to toe. I've probably eliminated what little hearing I have left. But at least I recover more quickly, looking to see that my hit was a little further right than I intended, but three vehicles took the damage anyway.

I hear Mike say, "Reload," but I don't need prompting. I grab another grenade, load up, position the barrel against the railing. I take a lot less time aiming, and I steel myself against the sound. It hits the place I wanted to the first time, throwing an SUV into the air and crashing it satisfyingly into another one.

I grab another grenade. Reload. Position. Aim. Hold tight. Fire.

It's a hot mess down there. Men are scrambling, running every which way, looking for cover.

And then I remember the roof next door. I don't know if they're up there still, but I'm going to knock them off if I can. So I reload, walk over to that side of the balcony. I lie down, aim, hold on, and fire at the chimney where I think our friend has been hiding.

I hit it, dead-on. Debris blocks my view, and I don't waste time looking. I have a second grenade in my hand, so I go to face the back yard.

"Everyone clear of the back yard?" I ask as I set up my tripod.

"Wendy!" says a voice beside me. It's Gabriel. Dirty, pale, but not bloody. "Mike? Where is he?"

I point to the other side of the balcony and then turn back around to reload, robotic, determined as I take aim at a cluster of men scrambling in retreat over the back wall.

Lying down on my stomach, I realize this shot is further away than I've yet attempted. But I'm nothing but confident as I take aim for the rear neighbor's driveway where they've parked three SUVs. I watch doors open and close as they pile in. But I'm not letting them get away only to attack us later.

They're going down.

I fire.

Direct hit right at the head of the driveway. Flying black cars. Flaming trees. Perfect.

I stand up. Go back to the front. Reload.

This time I aim for the street where I can see them organizing their retreat.

I fire. Another hit. More cars rolling over like soccer balls. Five or more this time. Flames ascend into the sky. Smoke. Crumbled cement and asphalt.

I work quickly, reloading and firing with the two remaining grenades I have on the roof, barely stopping to assess the damage between.

When I'm out of ammo, I stand and watch the mayhem. It looks like every single one of their legion of vehicles is either toppled or exploded.

By contrast, the sky is cloudless blue. The surrounding area is green and alive. But in front of me is a twisted mass of smoking chaos. The handiwork of the barrel I hold in my hand like a walking stick. I look at it, feeling a camaraderie with it, like it's become an extension of myself. I feel powerful. Capable.

I catch movement out of the corner of my eye and I look back to the madness my hands have wrought.

They're running.

But bodies are everywhere.

And I feel nothing.

Fifty

"*Aaaaagh!*" a voice yells in agony from behind me.

I whip around. Gabriel is holding Mike's shoulders down, and Carl's sitting on his lower legs. They're both having a heck of a time. Mike's a lot stronger than both of them together. Carl's holding a small, bloody pocket knife.

"He's moving too much," Carl says, wiping his brow. "I'm going to hit the artery and we'll be worse off. Where is that damn kit I asked for?"

I tap my ear as I run over to them. "Mark, Darren, anyone, I need a first aid kit on the roof right *now*."

"We're on it," Mark says in my ear. "Corben is already headed up to you."

I come to Mike's side. "The bullet?" I ask, noticing that Carl's got his belt strapped around the top of Mike's thigh and his pants cut way open to expose the wound, a fleshy mess I'm surprised Carl can make sense of.

Someone bursts up from the stairs with a large, grey satchel.

"Thank God," Carl says, grabbing the bag and digging through it. He lifts out several items and sets them aside.

"Gahhh!" Mike says, panting, his head lolling back and forth. "Dammit."

Gabriel, I finally notice, has been silent, staring down at Mike with pale horror.

"Mike," I say, gripping his hand to get his attention. "You've got to hold still. We're trying to help you."

"Like hell," he says. "You want me to die, too, don't you?"

I grip both his hands. "Of course not. We've got to get the bullet out. We're four stories up and you'll bleed out before we get you to a hospital if we can't stop it first. You need to hold still so Carl can work."

"He's cutting my fucking leg off!" Mike yells at me, a frenzied look in his eyes.

"Wendy, we need him absolutely still," Carl says. "Corben will sit on his legs with me, but he gets away from Gabe every time and goes for me. Can you help him? Maybe the four of us can hold him down. I've got some actual tools now, so I should be able to work more quickly."

I put my knees on either side of his waist, straddling him, careful to keep the weight on my knees and not on his abdomen. I place my hands next to Gabriel's white-knuckled grip.

"AAAARGH!" Mike roars, lifting the entire weight of me and Gabriel.

I put an arm across his collar bone and force all of my weight there. "Shhhhh," I tell him, putting a hand on his cheek.

"Dammit, why can't he pass out already?" Carl grumbles. "He's flexing his whole leg. It's like digging a bullet out of a steel beam."

"Hold on a second," I say, repositioning myself. I grip both sides of Mike's face in my hands. "Mike," I say, looking into his vacant eyes, searching for recognition. "Mike," I say more loudly, my face only inches from his.

He looks up and down, side-to-side.

"Mike!" I shout. "Look at me!"

His eyes finally settle on my face.

"Wendy?" he says. "What the hell are you doing? Where's Gabe?"

"Right here," I say, reaching up and grabbing the back of Gabriel's neck to bring his face next to mine. "We're both here."

"Did you get them?" Mike asks.

"Blew them all to hell. Right now we're trying to save your life."

His brow furrows slightly. "Why?" he asks.

"Why?" I say, confused. "Why what?"

"Why are you trying to save me? I wanna go out with a bang!"

"Don't be stupid," I say. "Gabriel and I both need you."

"Gabe hates me. And you... you're just going to ruin my life if I have one."

I nudge Gabriel. He hasn't said a word, but rather looks as pale as Mike. And he's sweating.

"Wendy, I need to get this bullet out ASAP," Carl says from behind me.

"Gabriel doesn't hate you," I say, glancing at Gabriel, wishing he'd open his mouth that is never short of words.

"I'm—I'm sorry," Gabriel croaks finally. "I'm—I don't feel well." I see tears in his eyes.

Confused and irritated, I look back at Mike. "He's in shock. Mike, he doesn't hate you. If he hated you, he wouldn't be up here trying to save you. And I'm not going to ruin your life. I'm going to save it. If you'll let me."

He gives me a look I can't translate. "Every time I look at you…" he hesitates, looking down and then back up to my face. "I hate looking at you."

"Why?" I whisper, his words tugging my insides. "I want to help you. Why won't you let me?"

He looks at Gabriel, stares at him.

I look from Gabriel's expression to his. And it's like watching a silent communication. I swear they know what each other is saying. It is the first time I have seen the two and felt that they share something truly special, something that has been clouded over by Mike's constant belligerence and Gabriel's indifference. It stirs something in me, kind of like awe. There is this Mike-shaped piece of Gabriel I have never seen before now. A vulnerability between the two. A connection that has been hidden from me. How have I never noticed before?

Mike must get the answer to whatever he was asking his brother, because finally, while still staring at Gabriel, Mike says, "Because looking at you makes me want to never look at anything or anyone ever again."

I'm rendered speechless, but for only a moment. Weeks of frustration that have been banging at the inside of my head are finally released in a wave of fluid understanding. And happiness. Compassion overwhelms me. I look at Gabriel, whose head is bowed low and whose eyes are closed. I was right that Gabriel has known something. He is not surprised by Mike's admission, and I bet he wouldn't be surprised by mine either. Every action by the two of them that has confused me the past few weeks finally makes blessed sense. Mike makes sense. Gabriel's jealous rampage while I was gone makes sense.

I already went over this last night with myself—my feelings for Mike. But I only fleetingly wondered if Mike felt the same because of the woman he mentioned. Only now I know that woman is me. I kind of want to laugh triumphantly that Mike is the person I always imagined he was. And I want to smack him and tell him he's an idiot. How much trouble he could have saved himself all this time if he'd just said his true feelings instead of always searching for new methods of emotional defense. He's *so* stupid. And transparent. I *knew* the person he showed me wasn't the real him.

Something instantly soothing spills into me, like gulping air after suffocating.

"Just let me die," Mike says, looking away now. "It will be easier for everyone."

"Oh shut up," I say. "You're as dramatic as Gabriel. What do you want? Everyone to tell you what a beautiful asset you are to our lives and how much we need you to live? That's a total lie. You're a pain in everyone's ass. You're a jerk. You can't make a right decision to save your life... Literally." I gesture at him. "But you know what? Somehow I've come to love you, because underneath it all you haven't been able to hide yourself completely. Why else would I have put up with your abuse? So it's out there now and nobody imploded. Nobody's world crashed. And you're not going to stupidly kill yourself over unrequited love. Because I love you. Believe it or not but I really do want you around if only to keep my patience limber. So summon all your badassery, and hold your leg still like all our lives depend on it. Because Gabriel and I need you. I know it's hard to feel what you do, to keep it all inside, so don't and I promise it will be okay. Just trust me. Because I have *always* trusted you." I kiss his cheek and cradle his face in my hands.

Mike shudders a little violently at first, stilling gradually until he has relaxed beneath me. "That was the crappiest appeal to live that I've ever heard," he says quietly, but mostly due to the effort. "If you weren't straddling me right now, I probably would have decided to just die. But fortunately for you, I'm helpless when hot women hold me down. I'll subject myself to medieval torture if that's what you want. Gabe's gonna kick my ass after this, but it's totally worth it."

"I think your living would be beneficial for both of us," Gabriel says finally, though he still sounds labored.

"Just be still. And don't leave us," I say as I lay gingerly against his chest, worried by how pale he's becoming. I reach for one of Gabriel's hands, gripping it in assurance while I embrace Mike in hopes of erasing his frustration and strife, if only for a moment so we can save him. I told Mike it was going to be okay, and although I don't know how exactly, I know it will.

What I feel for him is not a threat to Gabriel. I know this for certain now. It's not the jittery, breath-stealing, in-love feeling you get when you meet someone. That's not really love. That's some kind of uncontrollable, biological response that's coupled with meeting someone you click with that inevitably wears off. But I *love* Mike. For real. Because like Gabriel said not too many months ago, love is an action, not a feeling. Mike has been showing his love since he kidnapped me, looking out for me, reassuring me when I truly needed it. And I've been loving him by sticking with him and not letting him become a person I know he doesn't want to be. We push each other to be better. That's what happens when people love each other with action and not with just feelings. And that's why I'm not afraid of what I feel for him.

"Got it," Carl says finally. "A few stitches and then we can get him downstairs and into a car for the hospital."

I sit up, climbing off of Mike to reveal the blood still seeping from the gunshot wound at his stomach. He frowns. "What? He's not done yet and you're better than Morphine."

Carl clears his throat. "Actually, that *is* Morphine. Thanks to my brother for having a fully-stocked emergency kit. Found it at the bottom a few minutes ago."

I laugh when Mike wrinkles his nose. "My powers are limited, Mike." And then I remember Robert, now that Carl has mentioned his preparation—which has never failed.

"What is it?" Mike says, seeing my expression change.

"Robert," Gabriel answers. "We don't know where he is."

I look up at Gabriel and smile. He knows me so well. I squeeze his hand again.

"I've got a solution for that," Mike says confidently.

I tilt my chin questioningly.

"You remember our bargaining chips?"

The Grid spokes... "Oh gosh, you're right!" I say excitedly. "You think they'll go for a trade?"

"Oh yeah," Mike says. "In fact, getting the grid back is probably another reason why they took him in the first place."

"Perfect!" I say, grinning.

"First things first, kids," Carl says, busy stitching, his hands, which are now gloved, covered in blood. "It might *seem* like he's out of the woods, but that's probably the Morphine talking. This is a scary pool of blood. I'm surprised he's still alert. Let's get him to the hospital before we start ransom trades."

"Wendy," Mark says, not in my ear this time.

I look up, heaviness settling over me at Mark's solemn expression. "How many?" I ask, remembering the blackened spot in the front yard. That begs the question how we'll get out of here with the injured. The road is a pockmarked mess of pits and flaming cars.

"Three," Mark says. "Four more injured. I called for an ambulance. But no land lines or cell phones going out. They've put some kind of dampener in this area."

"Then we take all of them ourselves. Is there a way out? I saw everyone scatter," I say. I scan the perimeter, which is bizarrely free of law enforcement. We've just had a war and no one thought explosions in a gated community was odd. The Guild must have some serious influence.

"All done," Carl says. "Let me take a look at that other wound."

"Wendy, I don't think it's a good idea for you to go to the hospital," Mark says as I scoot out of Carl's way. "They've cleared out, but you just shot military-grade weaponry from the rooftop. We have, possibly, actual members of a homeland security agency bound up downstairs. The entire neighborhood looks like it was in the middle of a serious guerilla war. And not a single cop. I don't know what's going on, but it feels like a scene from Enemy of the State."

"I am with *you*," Mike says, pointing a finger at Mark like a gun and pulling the proverbial 'trigger,' sounding a little too happy-go-lucky. "But what you see right here? This is the Guild's scope." He laughs, a little too bubbly to not be drug-influenced. "And Andre just took it and ran with it. He's finally gonna get it…" He turns his head to look at me. "You," he says, looking me straight in the eye. "That. Was. Epic. Andre bit off way more than he could chew, messin' with *you*."

I look at Mark. "Suggestions?"

"I'm going with my brother to the hospital," Gabriel says.

"Uh oh. I'm in trouble," Mike says. "Wendy… don't leave me with him. He's going to finish me off…"

I roll my eyes at Mike. "I'm going with you," I say to Gabriel. "I'm not going to be separated again. I can't do it."

"Someone needs to be with Robbie and Kaylen and Ezra," Gabriel says, and I can't really make out his expression. But he looks unwell, pale and overly tired. "And most of all, you need protection."

"Just give me a gun. I'll be fine… Gabriel, are you okay?"

He puts his hands over his neck. "Wendy, I'm not telling you you're incapable. But I physically cannot leave Mike. And I cannot stand the idea of exposing you further. Yes, I'm okay. Just worried." His voice is strained.

"What do you mean, you can't *physically* leave him?" I say.

"I… I mean exactly that."

"Well that's a new one," Mike says. "Is it 'cuz I'm dying?"

"Or incredibly close to death. Feels like tugging on stitches, but all over," Gabriel says. "Gah!" he exclaims, shuddering.

"That's fucked up," Mike says. "I never felt that when *you* were dying. And why are you feeling *anything*?"

"I was never quite this close. And stop using that word. You sound like more of an imbecile than you already are."

"What are you two talking about?" I demand.

"I'm bleeding out slowly. And I'm drugged up. I have a perfectly good excuse. In fact, so do you. Let it loose. Just this once. You know you want to. Your wife just told me she loves me. Don't tell me that doesn't have your head constipated with ripe phrases dying to punch a hole through your mouth."

"It has far less power than you imagine," Gabriel replies. "But I can tell you wish it were otherwise. You never could lose gracefully."

"Because I never lost."

I open my mouth to ask what exactly he expected, but Carl says, "I'm going to have to interject here. I've done what I can do on this one. The bullet is too deep. Let's transport him. Everyone goes. No splitting up. We have manpower and money on our side, so let's not be timid."

"I agree," I say, standing. I am *definitely* going to get to the bottom of this conversation, but not right now. "I'm taking my rocket launcher though. And my gun."

"See that?" Mike says to Gabe as Mark and a few other men get Mike loaded onto a stretcher. "That's all me. Your wife is now officially a gun-toting badass."

"Mmm," Gabriel says as we head for the stairs. "You're after credit, are you? I have a laundry list. Would you like me to recite it?"

"You're supposed to tell me how much you want me to live. Not tell me everything I've done wrong. I'm dying, after all."

"For now, you're not."

"How do you know?"

Gabriel sighs. "I just know."

"Son of a bitch," Mike says.

"It's really a shame that I can't influence your language," Gabriel says.

"Why do you think I use it? Makes me feel… like me."

"The past seven years of keeping your real career a secret from me and living a secret life didn't do that?"

"For a few years, yeah. But then you married *her*. I spent a lot of time in your head, under the guise of my job. But, I'm… well I'm a fuck up. I did a lot of things I'm not proud of."

"Don't use that word again."

Mike tries to make a derisive sound, but he can't get it out so it turns into a cough. "O'course, 'cuz proper language solves everything."

"Controlling your mouth is the beginning of controlling everything else. You could use some self-control."

"Don't preach to me about self-control. I just spent like a month with your wife and I never once laid a hand on her—well not *that* way. Except that one time… But that was more like opportunistic. And it served a purpose."

Gabriel, who is walking ahead of me, just behind Mike's stretcher, groans. "I don't want to know. I don't want to know…"

"Aw, you know you do. 'Course, if I were you I'd be more worried about that pharmacist she lured in like a trained escort. Twisting his poor little pharmacist mind with body language manipulation. 'Oh I'm sorry I touched your arm! I'm a hugger and I was just so grateful!'" Mike says, his voice now high-pitched and mocking. "All it took was givin' her a big ol' smackaroo on the mouth!" Then he gurgles a laugh, and I face-palm behind Gabriel.

In the last week I've shot people with an actual gun, crawled through air vents, rappelled down the side of a building, vandalized property, stolen cars, used a grenade launcher on actual people and property, and told my husband's brother that I love him.

My gosh, I haven't felt so alive and capable since I possessed supernatural abilities.

Fifty-one

*H*ow worried should I be?" Gabriel asks, breaking the meditative silence we've been sharing in the plastic chairs just outside the operating room where Mike is. I don't know what time it is. Evening?

"I think he'll be okay," I say, twirling Robbie's downy hair into a swirl on the top of his head as he sleeps. He's lying on top of a hospital gown I put on over my shirt that's covered in dried blood. I feel antsy. No one has an interest in interrogating us about why we came in with five men with gunshot and shrapnel wounds. So either someone has been bribed to look the other way where we're concerned and the Guild is mounting another attack, or it might be that a large part of the staff was sent to LA and San Francisco to deal with the relief efforts, leaving no one to care. Meanwhile, I've asked Mark to see if he can't get the Guild's attention to propose a trade.

Gabriel has been silent, but when I glance at him, his face is screwed in frustration. He sees me watching him and says, "I meant… about your feelings for Mike."

I look down at the floor. Finally. Gabriel has been unreachable since we left Robert's Redland's house. I didn't press him because I feel so… drained. I don't want an argument right now. But I expected him to want to talk about it anyway. "Why would you worry?"

"Why *wouldn't* I worry?" he repeats back to me. "My wife is in love with my brother and I shouldn't *worry*?"

"Whoa, whoa, whoa," I say, holding up a hand. "Do I *look* like a googly-eyed school-girl? I never said I was in love with him. I said I loved him."

"There's a difference?" He looks at his hands, only just now noticing the blood he's yet to wash off.

"Of course. One is this flighty, fluttery thing where you're all but drunk when the other person is around. You can't think straight and all you want to do is be around them all the time. Let's just think about that for a second. Are you saying I *lied* to you when I told you Mike drove me batty the whole time I was with him?"

"Well… no, but love and hate are often mistaken for each other. And the fact remains that you *do* love him, which is, if I understand you, on a level reserved for what you and I share within our marriage." Gabriel begins working at getting every speck of blood off his hands using the edge of his T-shirt.

"Love isn't reserved for marriage. I can love anyone I want. I love plenty of people other than you."

He gives me a look of disbelief. "You know what I'm saying, Wendy." More vigorous hand scrubbing.

"Oh yeah. I know what you're saying. But you haven't thought it through. All that talk we had right before Robbie was born about what it meant to love each other, and you think that my love for you is different from my love for anyone else?"

He pauses but doesn't look at me. "So I'm not special to you."

I restrain the urge to roll my eyes. "I'm married to you. I almost died with you. I bore your child. Of course you're special. But love is love. It doesn't have variations."

He sits back and crosses his arms, observing me with a critical eye. "You seem to have spent some time thinking about this. How long have you known?"

"What? That Mike cared about me?"

"Wendy," Gabriel says patronizingly, "Mike *loves* you. Don't water it down to some sort of familial concern."

I huff. "I say it that way because I think I've always known he *cared* about me. But only on the roof did I realize how *much*. And yes, I've been thinking about it. Since last night when I was sitting with Uncle Moby and realized I loved Mike. And then of course you clammed up after we left the roof and we've had nothing but waiting to do. So I've spent it thinking."

"And what led you to believe that this situation is as harmless as you make it sound?"

"When I saw Quinn a few days ago, I had this conversation with Mike afterward about how Quinn would always be a part of me because he had a hand in who I am. Mike accused me of still having feelings for Quinn and I didn't deny it. In fact, every time I see Quinn he becomes less and less of this enigma of my past. He was a big force in my life. He's finally maturing, coming to terms with decisions he made. He has my mark on him. And I have his mark on me. I can't undo that. But given how far I've come and what he did to get me here, how can I want to?"

I adjust my weight, careful not to jostle Robbie. "So then Mike asked about my relationship with you before I touched you. He made a really good argument for the fact that what we had back then was a committed friendship because there wasn't a physical aspect. The only difference was the commitment we made at the alter. And I couldn't deny that either. Take away the physical part and what are we really, at a basic level? Best friends. Confidants. We have chosen to do life together rather than apart, to share as much of ourselves with one another as we're capable. Love is a byproduct. It's the benefit of sticking by each other. I love you more and more. I appreciate you more and more. I just spent over a month with Mike, discovering things about him, facing danger beside him and watching him agonize over his own morality. I've watched him do things for me that he didn't want to admit he did out of kindness or affection. So yeah, I've grown to love him. He's so gentle beneath his giant mask of fake. He's so wounded and lost. It's not just his job. It's you, your parents, me... His whole life is a mess."

"And you telling him that you love him isn't going to confuse it further?" Gabriel says. I can hear genuine questioning in his voice.

I shake my head. "Mike's secrets have destroyed him. He desperately needs to be given opportunities to be himself. He's been hiding all these years from everyone, including you. I know who I am. I'm confident enough in my relationship with you to say I love Mike and still remain as committed as ever to you. I can do that for Mike, so why shouldn't I?"

Gabriel rubs the back of his neck, stretches his legs out. "I'm struggling because when you left, you and I were *not* on solid ground. So when you say you're confident in our relationship, that's news to me."

"You thought I left you for him, didn't you?" I say.

He tilts his head just so, and in that tiny motion I can tell I'm right.

"Why would you think that? After everything we've been through?" I say. "Rocky ground or not, I have never wanted anyone else beside me."

He hangs his head, reaches for me. "Hold my hand," he whispers. He clears his throat. "Wendy, I wish it were as simple as you describe."

"Why can't it be?"

"Because my relationship with Mike is anything but typical," he says. "And I had foolishly hoped to spare you the madness of it."

I wait for him to continue, containing my impatience, still twirling the curly wisps of Robbie's hair with my finger. When Gabriel spends excessive time agonizing over his next words, I turn to him and say, "Gabriel. Be straight with me. Life is too crazy right now to let stuff like this fester."

"You're right," Gabriel says, though it almost sounds like he's saying it to himself. He shifts his feet. Crosses his arms. Uncrosses them. "Mike shares my experiences if we are near and shadows of them when we are apart. It's a limited mirror-touch synesthesia."

"Synesthesia?" I say. "Ezra has that."

"Ah, he automatically associates numbers with certain colors I presume?" Gabriel says.

I nod. "He says colors help him come up with equations. Wrong colors together mean the wrong equation or something like that. Mom had the same thing. So what's mirror-touch?"

"Similar to somatosense," he says.

"Like when we could share physical experiences in the colorworld?"

"Yes, but it doesn't require physical contact for Mike. He feels what I do physically and emotionally. And it's only one-way. I often feel an intangible connection with Mike, but not like Mike does with me."

I'm dumbstruck as I grasp the implications. "How?" I ask, disbelieving that such a thing could be real outside of a life force ability. "Why have you never told me this?"

"To the first question, I don't know. To the second, false hope. Self-deception. Lack of understanding... all the reasons a person might choose to lie to themselves about something so bizarre. I've never known how to deal with it, Wendy. Except to run. Because my brother always falls for the same woman as me. Always, without fail, every time. And she has always developed like feelings for both of us. Given our connection, it makes sense. But it has been the hardest part to deal with. The typical scenario would go like this: I meet a woman. Date her. Start to like her. She meets Mike, who spares no flirtation, and she becomes confused about her feelings. And then either she washes her hands of both of us, or she drops me for Mike, the less demanding, more approachable and down-to-earth brother. Yet still she would remain, stuck in limbo between us. I'd pester and poke until she decided both of us were too much of a hassle. I grew up, but never got over the constant rejection. I was always slated to be the less-preferable one. When I went to college, we found some reprieve. Distance helped. But only so long as that distance remained. For as soon as we came together again, it was as if we never parted. Such is this particular instance."

My head is spinning, not settling on anything. I don't know how to take that. What does it mean? *What does it mean?* And why didn't he tell me? Ever?

"So you... married me because... you wanted to make some kind of stupid *claim* before *he* could?" A few tears come to my eyes. The Gabriel I know isn't capable of this kind of deception. I turn slightly to face him, keeping Robbie sprawled against my chest. "And the whole death-touch thing... you jumped at being with me because you figured it was your best chance at keeping your brother disinterested." I narrow my eyes. "Isn't it? You thought he wouldn't want me like that. You decided you'd pick the most undesirable girl you could imagine and it would give you a better chance of 'winning,' huh?"

"No," he whispers, shaking his head. "That's not how it was."

"Then how *was* it, Gabriel?" I say, gritting my teeth.

"Wendy, you were there," he says, scrambling. "You were in my head. You know how I felt about you. It wasn't fake. It wasn't 'settling.' Did my relationship with my brother increase my urgency? Maybe. Such urgency has been ingrained in me since puberty. But tell me what I should have done? You were already one step away from running even after we got married. I wanted so badly for a chance to build something with you before you spent time with him. Do you think I was obligated to tell you, 'hey, I need you to meet my brother to make sure you don't want him instead?' What should I have *done*?"

I turn away from him, gulping air, but all I taste is confusion. I don't know why I'm getting so upset. I only know I am. Thank goodness Robbie's here to keep me from yelling. Something about this is so outside the Gabriel I know that it feels like betrayal. I don't suppose he was obligated to do as he's suggesting. And I have no idea how I would have reacted. I was such a mess then, coming to terms with the new supernatural forces in my life. And what if I *had* met Mike and become attracted to him? I didn't have the same understanding or maturity about relationships that I do now. I can't say what I would have done.

But there have been plenty of times since that he could have told me. Why didn't he?

"*Wendy*," Gabriel entreats. "I was so desperate I lied to myself. You met him the day of the wedding and I watched your reaction and saw nothing there. And Mike was just… angry. At me, I assumed. About the compound. But I *welcomed* it. I wanted his indifference so badly that I didn't once question him. I… I pretended our history did not exist."

I can hear Gabriel's voice cracking, but I can't look at him or I'll cry even more than I am already.

Oh God. Mike was right…

"That was the end of it for me," Gabriel says. "I refused to entertain any other possibility but that his antagonism toward you was a sign of freedom from him. I can see the self-deception now, but at the time I bought into it so well it was hidden from even me. It lasted through our separation, our illness, and Robbie's birth. It wasn't until I learned he had taken you that it all came crashing down on me, the implications of the lie I lived. And all the things I should have done to prevent it tore at me day after day."

The ensuing silence pounds in my ears as the Gabriel I once knew becomes someone else. But who, I can't say. Everything feels uncertain, even the ground beneath my feet. Pieces of me are crumbling and I hold very still to keep them from blowing away.

"We were always bound. But we were always at war," he says finally. "Straining apart and clinging together. We could never find balance. I always met them, and Mike always drove them away. And he was gleeful about it. To him it was… a validation that he was separate from me. And when they left he'd tell me he was saving me from myself, that the right one wouldn't leave. But Mike never cared about something long-term. He liked that hold over me because he hated the hold I had over him. It was a vicious cycle that neither of us could escape."

I swallow, still unable to think. Robbie turns his head to lay on his other cheek and I gaze at his sleeping face, willing myself to become lost in the sight. But his own predicament rears its ugly head and my heart breaks all over again. I need Gabriel. I need him so badly right now. But I don't know who *this* Gabriel is.

"Wendy…" he pleads again.

Mark appears from around the corner at that moment. "They've accepted the request for a trade."

I sit up. "Robert and Farlen?"

He nods. "Their Grid technology for both of them."

"When?"

"Tomorrow. Noon."

"Where?"

"Where you've hidden the spokes. They said they'll track you and arrive on site with Robert."

"How do I know they'll hand Robert over once they know where the spokes are? And how do I know they won't immediately come after *me*?"

"I don't know, Wendy," Mark says, his expression as uncertain as mine.

I slump in my chair. I need Uncle Moby. I need him more than ever. I don't care about their dumb Grid spokes. I just want Robert.

"We'll take the chance," I say. "If they don't follow through… well, I've got a grenade launcher, and Mike knows where their hidey-holes are."

Fifty-two

Wendy, I don't push back on your decisions often, but this time, I'd really like you to listen to me and not go," Mark says. "It's unnecessary exposure. We can absolutely handle this without your involvement. Robert made it clear that your security is our number one priority, even over his own."

My shoulders slump. My only argument is that I'm the only one that knows what the shack where the Grid spokes are hidden actually looks like even though Mark has a pretty good idea. He helped me scan a satellite image using what I could remember about my route with Mike through the central valley. We found what looks like the shack from above. I'm ninety-nine percent sure that's it, but I'm worried about what will happen if it's not the right place.

"Keep me posted," I say. "I want to know as *soon* as you have Robert and Farlen."

Mark and I walk through the first set of double doors to exit the hospital and he puts an arm in front of me. "You need to stay indoors. Keep an eye on my men. And when was the last time you ate or really slept? It's going to take us a few hours to get there. You might as well get a nap in the meantime. We don't need a farewell."

"I don't know that that's possible," I say as one of our SUVs parks in front of the glass to pick up Mark. "But I'll try."

Mark turns to go, but I stop him and throw my arms around him. "You know you guys are part of my family, too."

Mark chortles. "You have your weapon?"

"Yes, Mark."

"Is your communicator on?"

I tap my ear. "Checking in. Everyone doing okay out there?"

I hear a chorus of all clears in my ear. I nod at Mark.

"What's the protocol if you get ambushed here?"

"Switch on live feed surveillance. Catch the bastards red-handed on camera," I reply.

"Perfect. Darren's your point man, okay?"

"I *know*, Mark." I shoo my hand at him.

He turns to go, but stops and says in a low voice over his shoulder. "Just in case, grenade launcher is in my car, parked out back." He winks at me and I watch him go through the glass doors.

I grin and wave as he gets in the SUV, and then I stick my tongue out as they accelerate into the pre-dawn light.

I watch two more SUVs fall in line behind Mark's, mouthing a silent prayer that they all come back in one piece with Robert and Farlen.

I wrap my arms around myself, about to turn back to Mike's room when a pair of headlights turning into the parking lot at top speed catch my attention. Must be someone in need of medical attention ASAP. It materializes as a van and jerks to a stop right up to the front doors where I am. I put my hand to my gun as the van door slides open and two bodies are thrown before I really grasp what's going on.

I leap for the door as the van squeals away.

My eyes rest on the body closest to me. I lean forward to see only to immediately stagger backward. *Oh my God*.

"Robert!" I scream, half leaping and half falling to where Robert's battered body lies on the asphalt. I roll him over to find that his face is gaunt. I comprehend crusted blood and bruises and dirt, but the emptiness in his face is the only thing I really see.

I don't think he's breathing.

With shaking fingers I search for a pulse.

He's cold.

This can't be.

My fingers search his neck over and over. I must be doing this wrong. But my eyes are blurring and I can only feel my way around his neck. I give up, putting my cheek to his chest, begging. *Heartbeat, heartbeat, heartbeat… Please. Oh God, please.*

I am met with silence.

And cold.

I can't *see*.

I dig my palms into my eyes to clear away the tears, but everything is blurry. I catch a glimpse. His skin is grayer than I expect. I look away, allowing my eyes to well up again.

"No," I say firmly, putting my hands on his cheeks. I didn't just see that. If I rewind… pretend I didn't see the absence, then a miracle can happen. Uncle Moby can come back.

His skin is cool.

I'm delirious. I'm sleepwalking. Imagining all of this.

"Come back," I cry.

Wait. I'm at a hospital! They can resuscitate him.

"Help!" I yell, looking up finally. "I need a doctor!"

I don't see doctor's scrubs. Or nurses. But I see Mark. He falls to his knees beside me. I don't comprehend his expression. But he puts a hand on Robert's neck.

I look from Robert's face to Mark's. Back and forth.

Mark shakes his head. Doesn't move. Only stares.

"He… he…" I gulp. I look back to my Uncle Moby's face before falling to his chest again. I cling to him. "Come back!" I cry out. "Bring him back! You bring him back right now!"

No heartbeat.

Not real. Not real…

But it is real. They just threw his body out of the side of a van. He was dead before he ever arrived.

Rage fills my chest like hot oil. It burns through me and I let it. I want it to burn me up. I want to disappear into nothing.

I'm going, too. You're not leaving me here alone.

I inhale fury and the flames burn hotter. The pressure of the heat presses down on me like gravity. I don't resist. I squeeze him harder, trying to make myself smaller, wanting the black hole to squeeze me into nothing. I want to be nothing.

My body convulses in rebellion against me, and I gasp for the air I've been resisting. As my lungs expand, I can't hang on to anger. It cracks like hot glass in cold water. It shatters into hundreds of pieces that fall through my grasp.

The emptiness of sorrow takes its place. And the tears come to fill up the spaces of my shattered soul. It feels like drowning. Parts of me are carried away. Possibilities that once were. Moments that might have been. Until I am left desolate. My throat aches and my eyes burn. My hands ache. And my heart… It has come out of my chest to be hammered by the elements.

I can't. I can't. Not without you.

"I can't." I hear the sound of my own voice break forth. I can't what?

I can't anything. I can't move. I can't think. I cannot move forward. Not without him.

"Don't take him," I sob. "Please, don't take him!"

And then the endless, useless chorus of whys.

No answer.

No answer.

Silence.

Alone.

And I'm out of tears.

I lift my head. Look around. People. I remember seeing the other body thrown from the van. I remember the shape of it.

Farlen.

"Where's Farlen?" I demand.

Mark's face appears. "He's pretty beat up. But alive. He's getting taken care of."

I look down at my Uncle Moby's face again. Really see it finally. Bruises everywhere. His jaw looks out of line. Cut lips. Crusted blood. His clothes are ripped.

"He's been beaten to death," I say, scanning his body for a gunshot wound or otherwise. I see no indication of one.

"It appears that way," Mark says softly from beside me.

"Why?" I whisper. I shake my head, sickened at the thought of my Uncle Moby being subjected to beatings.

Bile rises in my throat and I swallow, struggling to keep it down. I reach for Uncle Moby's lifeless hand. He has welts on his wrists. Images of him being tied up and beaten fill my head and I sob once. Struggle to keep it together. Push the images away. But this is unconscionable. I didn't think the Guild had this in them. I really didn't.

I also truly don't think I can do this without Uncle Moby.

My eyes well up again and I wipe them, sniffing. My hands are shaking. I feel small and abandoned. My mom lost track of me once at Disneyland. I remember what it felt like to imagine I would never be with her again, that I would wander forever. As a child it seemed like a true possibility. But now… now the certainty of living the rest of my life without my Uncle Moby, my rock, my guide, my shelter in insecurity… It's just as terrifying.

"I love you, Uncle Moby," I whisper, wondering, hoping, and choosing to believe that his life force is still nearby. "How can I do this without you?"

I can't bear to look at him anymore—the evidence of his painful death. It should never, ever happen to someone as good and kind as my uncle.

I rest his hand gently over his middle and scoot away, wrapping my hands around my knees, thinking, *What now? What next? Where do I go? What do I do?* I rock back and forth, utterly lost. I'm so lost. And the pressure is building in my head again. I want to die. I want to die right now.

"Wendy," a familiar voice says, and arms wrap around me from behind. "I'm here."

I turn into Gabriel's chest, let him lift me off of the ground and lead me inside.

But I barely make it. I fall into a chair just inside, collapsing against Gabriel, who grips me tightly, holding my arms as I flail and pound his chest in anguish. This sorrow has finality. This time it's not 'come back.' This time it's 'goodbye.' And now, every time I think beyond this moment, all I can see is Uncle Moby's absence.

Fifty-three

Carl backs up until he hits the wall behind him. "No," he whispers. "Wendy, no."

Kaylen has her hands over her mouth, her eyes glistening. She shakes her head vigorously.

Dammit. My eyes are starting to well up again. I paste my lips together, keeping it together.

"This can't be," Carl says, looking as lost as I feel.

Ezra's face is rigid. He stands stock-still, hands clenched. Behind him is Letty, arms crossed, head bowed. And Gabriel's parents in the corner, Dan's arm around Maris.

The rest of the room, consisting of the ten of Robert's men who were uninjured, stand around us, taking in the news that most already know since they were on watch, and some are hearing for the first time. Gabriel is behind me, Mark next to me. Robbie is in the next room sleeping in a bassinet the hospital loaned me.

I wrap my arms around myself. I swore I was going to keep it together when I told them. Dear God, I don't have emodar, but I swear I can still perceive the room being sucked of energy as the news of Robert's death punches each of them in the gut. I swayed on my feet right after the words came out of my mouth moments ago, *Robert was beaten to death and tossed on the ground in front of me like garbage.*

It doesn't sound real even though I saw it. Robert encompasses all that is good and right and worthy in this world. Where I saw chaos, Robert saw the beautiful connectedness of humanity. Where I saw weakness, Robert saw fertile ground for the seeds of true power. His force, though quiet and unassuming, reached further than I ever knew. I didn't *have* to know what Robert knew. In fact, most days

I was glad I didn't know. And while all of this would be enough to intimidate any regular person, the best part of Robert was that when I saw sorrow, he did, too.

Kaylen has erupted into sobs and Ezra is hanging on to her, stupidly trying to keep his own tears from making an exit. Carl is weeping now, and Letty has her hand on his back.

"Wendy," Mark says, "we'll remain on site and on alert, but we'd request a day of mourning before you brief us on your next move."

"Next move?" I say. "I'm not in charge here."

Someone behind me clears their throat, and I turn to find a short black man stepping forward. I recognize him as one of Robert's personal assistants. I'm pretty sure his name is Dwight, and though he's not part of Robert's muscle, he is always somewhere nearby. He was always at the ready when Robert needed something done.

"Mrs. Dumas, actually, you are," Dwight says in his gentle African lilt. "Robert bequeathed the entirety of his assets to you in the event of his death."

I blink at the man, stunned. "Why the hell would he do that?" I blurt, now terrified for a new reason. As if I wasn't already feeling inadequate... I get *more* responsibility?

Dwight looks perplexed at my outburst, which has drawn the attention of everyone in the room.

"I, uh, sorry." I shake my head. "I'm just overwhelmed. I didn't expect that." I look around at the eyes now on me. "I don't have a next move. I don't want a day of mourning. I want a month. I want to be done with this, and I'm—" I catch the sob forcing its way upward. I take a couple steps backward, away from their expectations. I'm twenty-one. Other than Kaylen and Ezra I'm probably younger than all of these people by at least a few years.

Instinctively, and for just a moment, I search for my uncle among the faces of the room, needing the encouraging twinkle of his eye, the tilt of his head, the lift of his chin. I catch myself and almost lose it again. I close my eyes, wishing more than anything that I could smell the scent of ginger tea right now.

Oh God, how do I do this? Help me do this.

A hand rests on the small of my back. "Robert would say vulnerability is a sign of strength," Gabriel whispers softly in my ear. "They are mourning as well. So mourn with them."

I search for the words to express the feelings of my soul. I force my hands behind my back, but unable to handle the sadness on their faces, I look above and past them all. "Uncle Moby was my light post. He always encouraged me to find my own way. And I did because no matter where I was, I could always look for my light post… And now… now the light post is gone and I didn't realize how much his mere presence affected… everything. How even from miles away, his light made the unknown less scary. Uncle Moby and I didn't have a whole lot of actual conversations. But I also remember that in the times we did talk, so much was said, even when the word count was low. I felt… I knew he was always looking out for me… I always knew that. In my darkest hours, it gave me strength to just know he was there. Even when he allowed stuff to happen to me that he might have had the power to prevent, I trusted him. I trusted that he was helping me on the path of least resistance."

Tears spill onto my cheeks and I take a pause. "*I trusted him. And now that he's gone, I'm trying to trust him again. I'm trying to trust… the things he saw in me. I'm trying to trust the things he taught me. So… bear with me while I do all of that without my light post.*"

My own words bring to mind exactly how much Robert esteemed me. I feel so unworthy of that confidence. I'm a child. I've barely learned to walk and I'm being asked to perform on a balance beam.

Suddenly I don't know why I'm here at all. Robert made a mistake. I take another step back, running into Gabriel.

"I've never told a soul this before, but Robert found me next to a dumpster in Queens," says a voice. I turn to see one of Robert's guys, who has been sitting in the rear, stand up. I recognize his weathered face for the friendly wrinkles at the corners of his eyes. I know his name is Paul. "He asked me, 'Do you want a second chance?' I thought he must be some kind of angel. How did he know I'd prayed for a second chance every day like a mantra? I'd done some things that weren't nice. I'd been living at the bottom for so long that I forgot the life I'd lived before. There was just… survival. I answered, 'Yeah, I do. But guys like me don't get real second chances.' And Robert said, 'Today they do. Come with me.' And I've been working for him ever since, just following his light. So I know what you mean. He saw things in us that we didn't, gave us things we didn't deserve. Mrs. Dumas, you and your family were important to Robert for reasons beyond just relation. He always knew more than the rest of us and saw more. He was dead set on protecting you and what you knew. It's what he gave his life for. And if it was that important to him, it's that important to me. Because I'm still chasing his light and I will until the day I die. I'm with you." Then Paul sits down.

My mouth parts, but as I try to conjure a response, another guy stands. I cannot remember his name. Louis maybe? "Baseball game, outside a bathroom," he says. "Somehow Robert knew what I was planning the next day. Had revenge on my mind, actually. But Robert befriended me. And we talked, and the whole time I got this feeling from the questions he'd ask that he knew what I was planning. And I thought it must be God talking to me, trying to get my attention so I'd change my mind." The guy smiles, lost in memory. "Well now I'm sure that God really was, only he was using Robert to do it. And Robert and me, we've been friends ever since. That's what all of us will tell you. Robert was our friend above all. And God was always in his ear and that's why I've stuck by him *and* his family. I'm with you, Mrs. Dumas," he says, looking at me with a smile. He sits.

Darren stands and says, "Robert watched me win three million at a casino. I was a little drunk and really on top of the world when he said to me, 'Tomorrow you're going to lose every bit of that money and also your entire savings. And then you're going to think really strongly about killing yourself, but when you do, I want you to call this number. Someone worth living for will answer.' He tucked a card with just a phone number written on it in my coat pocket and he said, 'And then I'll see you in this exact spot in three days.' And then he walked away. Of course I thought he was crazy. Turns out that was exactly what happened. Exactly. And the number I called..." Darren sniffs back a few tears and his jaw goes rigid. "It was my ex-wife's number, only I didn't recognize it because I hadn't spoken to her in forever. But it wasn't her that answered. It was my six-year old daughter."

Darren pauses and clears the tears from his throat, his eyes glassy and his face red. "I will *never* forget the sound of my daughter's voice that night. It was like being called back to life by angels themselves and I knew I wasn't done. So I waited for Robert three days later like he told me to. You don't ignore it when someone like that crosses your path. So I didn't. And he's been like a father to me ever since. I'd follow him into death, into war, into hell. And I still will. It's clear to me that he knew something about you, Mrs. Dumas. So I'm with you, too."

Man after man stands then. Some only say where Robert found them and don't give the full account. Others give the most fantastic stories I have ever heard. In my head I name them: The Robert Chronicles. Because they need to be in a book somewhere. People need to read about my uncle, this amazing person who truly was some kind of angel incarnate. And from their stories it's also clear that Robert's ability was something he had truly mastered for good. Even though I thought I grasped Robert's scope, to hear how he placed himself in these people's lives like he did adds a whole new level of understanding, and I'm awestruck. I think everyone is. I suspect this may be the first time they've realized how much they all share in common. Just listening to them... they aren't the kind of stories anyone else would believe. But all of us do because we all knew Robert. And it binds us all.

Each person that stands finishes by declaring allegiance to me in some way. I started off about six inches tall, but by the end of it, my confidence has grown. Robert was an angel among us. And when an angel calls you up, as Robert has me, you start to wonder if there's something about yourself you've missed. By God, I'm going to find it. I'm not going to let that man's memory down. *I owe him.*

Dwight goes last, the quietly efficient African man. "Robert and I have been friends for around thirty years. I knew him before the man he became. And I saw the tragedy that turned him into the man you all know. The change in him after his wife died was so sudden that I felt sure it was some kind of divine intervention that must have changed his attitudes so much." Dwight chuckles. "Whether he told us or not, we all knew he had a special talent. But it was more than the supernatural that made him who he was. His wisdom and insight into what motivated people was unparalleled. I believe a genie could have come down and granted me any wish I could imagine and it would not be nearly as incredible as the miracles I've seen wrought by Robert Haricott's hands. What kept me by his side? The addiction of seeing him do it over and over again but for different people each time. And everyone here is correct: Robert believed in what Mrs. Dumas was doing for reasons that I doubt any of us truly understood. But he did call us together and say in no uncertain terms that of all the jobs he'd ever had us do, he wanted to make it clear that Mrs. Dumas and her family were the most important ones. It's obvious to me that this message was loud and clear." Dwight turns to me. "Robert was with you and Mr. Dumas, and so are we."

I feel a kinship with everyone here. They are my family. We all followed a great man. "Thank you for your stories," I say as I look at the faces around the room. "I know they are… special to each of you. Sacred. I have tried to live a lot of the things my uncle taught me, tried to remember them all. The truth is that most of the time the power of the things he said and did would hit me later. Like now. As I've listened to your stories, I realize that my uncle sought each of you out. It wasn't this happenstance thing. There were possibly hundreds, maybe thousands of people he could have helped just as he did you—and maybe he did. But he chose each of you specifically to work for him. Whatever he knew about me, he chose you for this task."

The truth of my words spurns me forward. "Look, I started out not having a clue how I was going to do this without him. But as usual, I'm probably underestimating my uncle. Before I knew him, Robert was setting things in motion in my life. And after I met him, I quickly learned that he was always in the details of things that were going on. He'd put me on a path and I didn't realize it until later. He taught me things without me realizing it was him until after the fact. I also know my uncle had a rule: Don't mess with life and death. Let them fall how they may. I believe he would keep that rule even for himself. I believe my uncle was not ignorant of his fate tonight. He knew it and he faced it with courage. But he also set things in motion. He didn't just leave. He planned. He prepared. He checked and rechecked variables. And though I'm flying blind again, I trust that he left me on a path he'd prepared. We all are. You say you're with me. But I'm also with you. And Robert is with all of us. We're going to take a day, and I'm going to come up with a plan. And then we're going to fix what's gone wrong. And one last thing, I'm Wendy. Not Mrs. Dumas. We're family."

I look to Mark, who takes it as his cue to start passing orders for protection shifts. My men and one woman pat me on the back as they leave, and I recite their names as they leave. Now that I know Robert chose them all for me, I'm ashamed I haven't gotten to know each of them better. I vow to do that. And I vow to be the person Robert always believed that I am.

Fifty-four

With the waiting room mostly clear, Gabriel, Ezra, Kaylen, Carl, Letty, and I take up a circle of chairs. I don't want to think about this right now. I want to take care of our wounded and mourn my uncle. I want to cuddle with Robbie and have a late night talk with Gabriel. Nobody, with maybe the exception of Letty, looks like they want to do this either. But things need to be decided once and for all. We need a plan. Quickly.

"First of all, does anyone besides Carl *not* think that these natural disasters need to be addressed in the colorworld?" I say to the group.

"Could I say something?" Carl holds a hand up.

"No," Ezra scoffs. Balancing his chair on its back legs he says to the rest of us, "Why is he here?"

"Because Carl can see the colorworld," I say. I turn to Carl. "If you have something to say *other* than that the disasters are a product of geological evolution, sure, you can say something."

Ezra lets his chair hit the floor and gives Carl a look of disgust. "Are you kidding? He's got to be lying."

"He's not," I say. "And I really don't want to spend any more time on disbelief and snide remarks, Ezra."

"Then why can't *he* check in with Mother Nature in the colorworld?" he says, crossing his arms.

"Because he can't see squat and he can't hear or smell it like I can," I say, flustered. "Can we get back on track? Carl, you have the floor."

"Are we sure this is advisable?" Gabriel says. "Involving Carl in sensitive topics having to do with the makeup of the colorworld?"

I stand up, hands on hips. "Listen up, people. Carl is here because Carl is freaking smart. He's been thinking about life forces for a long time, longer than we've been alive. I know you guys have no personal proof of his recovery, but I do. I've seen it. If you all trust what we know about the colorworld, then you know what getting your ability back like that means. I'm not saying he's Mother Theresa, but I'm saying he's turned over a new leaf. Carl also hates the Guild and if he left our protection that's exactly where he'd end up now that he's not in hiding. He's basically at our mercy at this point, and we need him. Robert knew it, too. That's why he helped me find Carl. So enough of this should we/shouldn't we trust him. We share what we need to and nothing more. The end." I sit down. "Carl?"

Carl clears his throat, stands, and walks to the middle of the circle. "Just wanted to say... I'm sorry." He wipes his face. He puts his hands on his hips, looks down at the floor. I see his arms shaking just barely. I recognize it as a depth of sorrow so strong that it's forcing its way outward even if he won't let himself express it. He manages to calm down though. "I'm going to honor my brother, best I can. And your mother. Both of them. Yeah, I wish you'd stay far away from anything to do with the Guild, but I'm with you—whatever you decide on."

I watch Carl adjusting to the moment of vulnerability and I feel a little pride. Given his past of murder, lies, and manipulation, it's mind-blowing to imagine he's come this far this quickly. Until now he has been someone I have always worked to disassociate myself from. But now I have such compassion for him and his obstacles ahead.

Before he can walk back to his chair, I leap up and over to him. I wrap my arms around my father gently. "I forgive you," I whisper, and how true it is. I forgave Carl a long time ago.

At first he stands ramrod straight. But then I feel a pressure on my right, and a familiar cry: Kaylen's. "I forgive you, too," she says.

He trembles and puts his arms around both of us. Then something unexpected happens. My heart, which has been subdued since my most recent cry over Robert's death, opens. Gentle warmth pours in. After so much acrimony and then indifference toward him, I feel something for Carl I never expected: affection.

He releases us awkwardly and sinks into a chair. Kaylen sits next to him, resting her cheek on his shoulder.

I'm not sure how exactly it happened, but I suddenly feel stronger than I did before. I'm in control and the sting of sorrow isn't quite as pronounced. I have new hope for us, a band of renegades with extremely flawed histories and complicated relationships. If

Mike were here that picture would be complete. I miss him... I think he belongs here. Gabriel and Ezra's expressions reveal that they are skeptical of Carl still, but it only adds to our dynamic.

Letty fits in perfectly with our group. She and I catch each others' eyes and she smiles and winks.

I clap my hands. "Everyone, back on topic. Natural disasters. Colorworld. Go."

"Detective work," Ezra says. "Comb all hypno-touch records to account for anyone born a Prime. Narrow it down. There's your guy."

I shake my head, cross my arms. "The Guild has been at this for years, doing exactly that."

"I get that they'd keep track of all their own creations, but have they accounted for all of Carl's victims?" Ezra says.

I look to Carl.

"Most likely not," Carl replies. He clears his throat. "There is a much longer story, but suffice it to say, my goal has always been to increase the number of Primes outside of those the Guild controls. I knew life force abilities were the future, but I didn't want the Guild to have a monopoly on them. The problem was I didn't have the same resources. Where the Guild could do hypno-touch and harvest reproductive cells from the dying, I was dependent on hypno-touch and good old-fashioned reproduction. My method was much slower, so I was always searching for a way to do hypno-touch more safely and have a wider selection of possible candidates, which is why Wendy was so important. And Alma... her ability in conjunction with mine held so much promise. You told me Rob guided you to Alma's grave and ultimately her son, Mike, and I'm more convinced that I was on the right track with that."

Gabriel, elbows on knees, face pensive, says, "Yes, Wendy said you were trying to show her something about Mike in the colorworld. What was it?"

"Alma could move her life force," Carl says.

"Move it?" I ask, leaning forward, intrigued.

"Alma's life force ability was unclear for so long," Carl explains. "She could... plant ideas. We called her the subliminal messenger because that was the best way we knew to articulate it."

Just like Mike...

"But then I watched her in the energy world once," Carl says. "Being unable to see much detail I don't know how exactly it happened, but part of her life force bulged out from her. It touched that of the person she was speaking to and then returned to her. I had no idea what she was doing, whether she *knew* what she was doing. But I watched her quite often after that. Through a series of experiments, we discovered it was a manifestation of her ability. When she was influencing someone, either purposely or unintentionally, she would touch them with her life force. What happened when she touched them this way, I can't say, but later, when I was searching for a way to fix the life forces that were damaged, Alma's ability was one I felt had the best potential to do that."

"Hey that sounds kinda like what you did, Wen," Ezra says.

Perplexed, I lean back in my chair again. As Ezra pointed out, I could move my life force once. That's how I saved myself from death by leukemia. Did it operate the same way Alma's did? And can Mike do the same thing?

"You… Could you…?" Carl shifts in his seat, and I can tell he wants to grill me, but is struggling not to. "Is that how you saved them?"

I shake my head, not sure Carl needs to know details on that, but I look at Gabriel, lift my eyebrows. He must be thinking what I am, which is that Carl is probably right about Alma. Kaylen could move life forces telekinetically but never knew it until she actually *saw* them and *tried*. So if Alma could have *seen* what she was doing, she might have been able to find the control. If she could have, then it's likely Mike can.

"You know what doesn't make sense?" Ezra says, crossing his arms and glaring at Carl. "If you knew about Primes—about the Guild—why the hell did you do hypno-touch on my sister when she was tiny?"

"I never did," he admits, his shoulders slumping.

I sit up. "But… Why would you tell me that? Why would you tell *Leena* that? That's the whole reason she took me away!"

"Because I didn't want you to know about the Guild, about Primes. They are so… idealistic, their message so attractive. In the beginning of my hypno-touch career, I lost my clients to them. I faced pressure and death-threats for what I'd done. That's what prompted me to fake my own death. When I came back to work, I hid the identity of my clients, worked in secret. When it came to you I didn't want you to know about the world of Primes for as long as possible. I needed you focused on a hypno-touch, on finding a better way to do it. I needed you to have urgency, so I let you believe a lot of things to motivate you."

"But the diabetes... the nut allergy?"

He closes his eyes and nods. "You have to remember that back then I didn't know much about Primes, and I was desperate after realizing what would happen to Gina. I was blindly scrambling. From what I could tell after you were born, you were an empath like your mother and nothing else. So I needed to have a backup plan. I believe Leena saw me experimenting with you once, trying to determine if you had any energy world sharing ability. I had you in a trance, seeing if I could get you to push yourself into the energy world. It looked like hypno-touch, and she didn't ask questions. She just took you."

"But... If she didn't have hypno-touch until Pneumatikon, why did she get sick so quickly?" Ezra says, referring to the company owned by Louise that gave me a death-touch.

"Adult Primes are more sensitive to hypno-touch," Carl sighs. "When she came out of it, remember her touch moved from completely innocuous to lethal. Her senses improved dramatically, not like typical subjects."

"Kaylen's been having it her whole life," I point out. "She's a Prime but she never got sick."

Carl tilts his head quizzically. "Why would you assume she's a Prime?"

"Because of her ratio," I say.

"And because her telekinesis ain't no joke," Ezra says. "Regular hypno-touch doesn't make Jean Grey prodigies like her."

"Her ratio?" Carl says.

"Don't concern yourself with it," Gabriel says. "The point is Kaylen must be a Prime. Do you deny that?"

Carl slumps. "I can't help but be enthralled with how much you know about life force science. It's my instinct to barter information... old habits." He rubs his face again, looks at Kaylen, then me. "Kaylen was a Prime case study, an attempt to understand how Prime abilities were different, how hypno-touch affected them. The only explanation I have for why she didn't get sick sooner was because Prime children are a whole different animal. Their abilities don't develop all at once or with any consistent pattern. They are, at times, extra sensitive to environmental factors, while other times exceptionally resistant. It depends on the child and the ability. Kaylen did not seem to respond to hypno-touch until she was around nine years old, and even then

I can't say whether it was simply her Prime ability maturing or the hypno-touch itself that caused the change. Or both. Plus, Kaylen wasn't very cooperative when we were testing her. The Guild could probably give you more definite statistics on Prime child development. Adults, on the other hand... well you can see how quickly Wendy responded to one session."

I cross my arms and my ankles, thinking. Somehow all of this needs to link back to Mike. He's important. Robert *pointed* me to him. If what Carl believed about Alma's ability is correct, then Mike may be able to duplicate Kaylen's precision. But that may not be enough. He would still need to be able to tell *which* strands need to be pulled and reinsert strands where they need to go. We tried before to learn if there was a difference between head strands and chest strands, but none of us could tell. And with only Carl's sight, we won't be able to make out individual strands, let alone tell the difference between them. We'd need to see more...

I pause on an idea. If Mike's light is the same kind of light as the rest of us, I can only imagine what more Carl could see if he was linked up to it. But by the same token, I'm not entirely sure Carl would be safe touching Mike with that kind of wattage. Gabriel once referred to my death-touch as 'frying the motherboard.' Can it work in reverse? Would Mike fry *Carl's* motherboard?

"Do you think Carl would be safe touching Mike?" I say.

All eyes turn to me. Gabriel's mouth opens. "You want to... enhance Carl's ability? To see more?"

"That much light might kill him!" Kaylen says.

"Channeling light..." Carl muses. "That's how it works then?"

"I'm leery," Gabriel says. "It's very likely that he'd die."

"Then the only choice is for me to have hypno-touch. Once I can see, *I'll* touch Mike."

"*That* is a stupid idea," Ezra says. "I am not on board with you scrambling your life force again."

"I don't like it either," Kaylen says. "We don't know enough. And you have a responsibility to Robbie, Wendy. To be around for him. Those Guild people have a lot of resources. You're telling me they can't come up with something to find whoever is causing the problem? What exactly are they expecting you to do? Sniff out energy trails? This isn't Star-Trek."

I lean away in surprise. Not only is Kaylen being more forceful and forward than I'm used to, but she made a geek reference. My lip quirks. "Valid points," I say, trying to keep from laughing so she doesn't think I'm making light of her concerns.

"Gabe says the assumption is that we put strands back in the wrong place," Ezra says. "I buy that. But do you want me to give you the probability of pulling those same strands out? It's a long ass number with a bunch of zeroes in the front. So many zeroes you might as well call it zero."

I nod. "I believe you."

"Then why are you proposing it?" Gabriel says, exasperated.

"Because it's the right thing to do. I can feel it."

"That's not a valid reason. You're being reckless."

"Says you. But I bet those strands that are in the wrong place are probably going to come out a lot easier than any of the others. Remember when we inserted them? We had to have faith that they had some kind of intelligence, and they did. They threaded themselves once they were inserted. This is no different. I obviously still have my ability, and if we think of strands as like, say, electrical wires, I'd guess things are wired wrong, shorting out my ability. Electrical current has to do with magnetism, right? I bet it's a much weaker force that's holding the strands that are in the wrong place."

"That's a compelling idea. But the other issue is that channeling is not part of your natural ability," Gabriel says.

"Right. But I got *that* ability from something even more imprecise: hypno-touch. So we pull out extra strands. Remember how all of the hypno-touch people lost their abilities gradually? That's because hypno-touch abilities aren't dependent on specific strands. They're dependent on *number* of strands pulled. And Carl just said Primes are more susceptible anyway."

Gabriel frowns and I can tell I've at least made him think.

Ezra rolls his eyes. "Even if you are right, (and that's a big FAT if), why are you so sure Mike's light—which I hear is like a thousand suns—is not going to kill you?"

I shrug. "Because there's no reason to believe otherwise. The only people that *actually* died from my ability were people who were so far gone that their life forces didn't know how to *hold* light."

"You don't know what Dina's *or* Derek's life forces looked like when you touched them," Gabriel says. "Or Don's."

"I've got it!" Ezra says, sitting up straight and throwing a finger in the air. "Only people whose names start with the letter 'D' are susceptible to light overload. So she's totally safe!"

"Louise starts with an 'L,'" Kaylen says.

He waves his hand. "Three out of four. Louise was batshit crazy. She doesn't count."

"Ezra…" I say, hanging on to my patience.

"Oh you think that's a stupid way to analyze data, huh?" He leans forward. "Well that's exactly what you sound like, going on about strands *wanting* to come out and hypno-touch being *imprecise* as a reason you're going to be able to channel your ability. And oh, you've only seen *one* of the people you killed actually *in* the colorworld, so you actually have no *clue* what a life force has to look like to be susceptible to light overload. But nobody panic, 'cuz Wen's got a *feeling* it's all going to work out!"

Ezra crosses his arms and glowers at me. "Bullshit. You're just jumping at the chance to put yourself in the line of fire. Trying to play the hero because it makes you feel alive when the truth is that you want to have your stupid ass ability back so you don't have to think about how boring and miserable your *normal* life is. You don't think about how the shit you do affects anyone else. I'm over it. I don't even know why the hell you have me in here if you'd already decided what you were going to do anyway. What you really wanted was for all of us to agree with you so you could feel better about something you *know* is a stupid idea. So go do whatever the hell you want. That's always what you do anyway." He stands up and storms out of the room.

With everyone looking at me—anxiously I might add—I expect to feel censured or defensive. I expect to feel upset. But instead I feel absolved because I *don't* experience any of those things. I have compassion for Ezra because I get how scary what I'm proposing is. He's also just lost Robert, so the possibility of losing someone else is not something he can stomach right now. He's thinking of numerical probability and nothing else. But sometimes it doesn't matter how logical your arguments are. Fear skews logic. He's afraid. And I'm not.

"I get how this looks," I say. "Ezra has good points. I've been unsatisfied ninety percent of the time since I lost my abilities so of course you should question my motives. And yeah, I already knew what I wanted to do before I called this meeting. But I wasn't looking for you to agree with me. I'm not stupid or naïve enough to believe that *any* of you would be on board with my idea. I wanted you to push back so I could be sure of my own motives, so I could hammer out the details. This is what I'm doing. It's going to be okay."

No response. Just stares.

"I'm going to find a shower now." I stand up. "And find a bed. Then tomorrow we're going to do something to turn the tide." I walk out of the room, hoping I looked as confident as I felt, and that when I see them all again, they'll be ready to stop fighting me and instead fight the real problem. I know I am.

Fifty-five

Gabriel insists on talking through the hypno-touch plan before Carl starts. He's stalling but I resolve to be patient. His face has been in thinking mode for several minutes when he finally says, "Number one: you did not retain any of your ability when we put your strands back. We take that to mean that we mixed up where some of the strands were supposed to go. That means that for a natural ability to work, there is a very specific configuration. Number two: Kaylen's ability all but disappeared as soon as she put a small bundle into her chest. What we saw after she did that was what Kaylen's ability would have been if it were merely hypno-touch driven. My theory about that is that head strands have no bearing on either hypno-touch *or* a natural-born ability. *But*, if even one strand is out of place in the chest, a natural ability does not work at all. What *that* then implies is that we need to get every single misplaced strand out of your chest in order to activate your natural ability. Carl, did you ever have success with hypno-touch centered over the head?"

I look at Carl.

"No," Carl replies. "Hypno-touch near the head never appeared to have any benefit. And I concur with your observations about head strands having no bearing on an ability. But it sounds like strands managed to get displaced from there anyway?"

"Just not nearly so many as the chest," I say, tapping my chin.

"It doesn't appear to matter if some of those chest strands end up in the head," Gabriel says. "You just can't have head strands in the chest."

"So we focus on the chest," I say.

"We focus on the chest," Gabriel says, and he and I look each other in the eye for a moment.

"Could you give us a moment, Carl?" I say.

Carl gets up without a word, leaves the room.

I reach up to touch Gabriel's cheek and he holds my hand there, sighs. Then he tugs me to his chest.

"Thank you for always standing behind me," I say, tucking my face against him and inhaling his scent. "I mean it. I love you so much for always supporting me."

I know Gabriel is only going along with this because I asked him to. Like every other time he's been on my side when he didn't agree. Kaylen and Ezra have made themselves scarce. Letty has been hanging with Robert's men, taking up protection shifts. Mike, if he were awake, would be casting his opinion with everyone else and telling me what an idiot I am.

And here is Gabriel. With me. Behind me. Helping me. Ignoring his own feelings in order to validate mine. I hug him harder, tears coming to my eyes, overflowing with the love I have for him. I'm looking forward to being able to share my feelings with him more perfectly.

"I love you, too," he says, but I hear questioning at the end of it. He grips me harder.

"Gabriel, it's going to be okay," I say.

He doesn't reply, but kisses the top of my head.

"Talk to me," I say, trying to pull away to see him, but he holds me close.

"I can't…" he chokes.

"Why not?"

"You won't like what I say."

"Just tell me. Get it off your chest. If this goes well, I'm about to read your mind anyway."

"Bloody hell, Wendy. I can't make sense of my own mind right now."

I put my arms around his waist. "You're mad at me. Because I'm risking my life?"

"It's not just you. It's everything."

"What can I do?"

Silence passes between us for a while before Gabriel says, "I don't know, Wendy. But I feel like you're drifting away from me and there's nothing I can do to stop it."

I lean away to look at his face. "I know I've changed, but I'm not going anywhere, Gabriel. *I'm not going anywhere*. Please, believe me. I want you more than ever. I need you more than ever."

His only reply is to kiss my forehead, letting his lips linger. "Thank you. I'm going to do my best to hang on to that. Are you ready?"

"Only if you are."

He looks at me. "I'll never be ready to gamble with your life. Right now, I'm only ready to follow your lead."

I smile gently. "Good enough."

I go to the door to get Carl and then lie down on the cot. Carl stands over me and starts to regulate his respirations to relax while Gabriel sits nearby, arms crossed, head bowed. I have to admit that what he said about me drifting away feels more like the opposite; *he's* the one drifting. I've never felt Gabriel so distant. It's not just a lack of emodar. In the months I spent withdrawing after losing my abilities, I always felt him reaching. I guess it's my turn to do that.

Now *I'm* starting to get stressed out, so I close my eyes and start my own controlled breathing, the kind I would do if I were going into the colorworld. I've got to help Carl in any way I can. Maybe I can influence my own strands to do what we need.

"Here we go," Carl says softly.

I don't open my eyes. I have to admit the mere *thought* of what strand-pulling sounds like has me cringing even though I can't hear it.

After a while, maybe thirty minutes in, sound bombards me suddenly, like someone has yanked cotton out of my ears. I put my hands up instinctively and gasp. I'm working to contain the sounds when several other sensations overtake me. My nerves have activated in synchrony. Everything looks and feels lit up. I snap my eyes shut and shudder several times. My muscles twitch and I want to hop up and do several laps around the hospital to equalize the sensation. But I force myself to lie still, puffing deliberately through my lips. As the tension leaves my limbs, a whisper of perception comes to my attention, growing steadily stronger as I calm. It's familiar, funneling excitement into my core.

It's Gabriel. His driving inquisitiveness is unmistakable.

I allow it to wrap me up from the inside until it feels like an embrace. I sigh, but it catches in my throat. I can only cry tears of happiness and relief as the hollows of loneliness I've been carrying around slowly fill until I'm whole again. Holding a sob of joy, I start sputtering as I smile and cry all at once. I have been isolated for so long, and it's only in having Gabriel in there with me again that I remember how truly devastating it was to lose my ability all those months ago. The relief is more profound than any I have ever experienced.

"Are you okay?" Carl's voice asks.

I nod vigorously. I open my eyes to find Gabriel. The details of his features jump out at me. I'm finally *seeing* him again. I reach for him, letting him pull me into his arms.

I'm speechless as I bury my face into his neck. The touch of his skin has begun to build a definite magnetism between us that conjures many forgotten physical sensations that I used to enjoy with Gabriel. So much of him has been hidden from me… It's like being separated from someone for a year, only communicating via video and voice, and then one day they're in front of you and you realize all the parts of them that you missed but couldn't articulate.

Gabriel, meanwhile, has relaxed in the most exquisite relief. He has obviously translated my reaction accurately. He hugs me tightly and sighs. "Thank heavens… But that was quick!"

He's right. It *was* quick, but I am too consumed with rediscovering the weightlessness of connection. The worry and stress of the past nine months dissolve away and I want nothing more than to fuse my emotions with his. I channel myself into the colorworld then, pleased at how easy it is. I guess it's like riding a bike. '*Gabriel,*' I think to him. '*I can't believe I forgot how wonderful it is to have you with me whenever you are in the room. I can't believe… so much of you I've been without. I can't even put words to it. That's it. That is definitely the part I missed the most.*'

'*Oh my,*' Gabriel replies, stunned into immobility with the sensations of the colorworld and the abilities I share with him so suddenly. '*That is possibly more than full-strength? Wendy, I feel as if you are melded to me in every way.*' He takes heaving breaths, holding me ever tighter, and we are both simply overcome with each other's presence.

"It worked, I take it?" Carl asks.

"Completely," I say, lost in the delicious detail around me. Even if it is a hospital room, it is the most dazzling room I've seen in a long time. "And Gabriel is right. That was *really* fast. I can't believe you managed to get them all out that quickly."

"Indeed," Gabriel says, struggling to get his mind to engage, but it's clear that both of us are preoccupied with reacquainting ourselves with each other. "Well, Love, this moment will be made perfect if you can demonstrate that you can move your strands and reverse what we've just done at a moment's notice."

I had completely forgotten about that... but I couldn't agree more, so I concentrate, searching for the sensation I felt that day when I realized I could move my own strands.

But nothing happens.

Fifty-six

Eighty-two thousand, two hundred thirty-eight," Gabriel says in astonishment as his eyes dart back and forth across my displaced strands that are splayed around me in the small hospital pool. I'm not surprised by the number. I've seen enough mussed life forces in the water to tell that I am missing a lot less than the usual number. What's more, we looked at my chest swirl in the mirror and determined that while it is slightly off, it's not quite as disorderly as a typical hypno-touch victim.

I force myself to shut off the world and think. It's obvious that between Gabriel and me, I am the most rational, and I need to maintain that confidence so Gabriel doesn't lose it. Thank goodness it's only him and Carl. With my emodar in full effect, I'm already battling their worry. It's making me faint.

My personal calm is going to wear thin. I can't control my strands or perceive them. If we can't move my strands, we can't fix them…

Stop it, Wen! You were gung ho about how this was the right thing only half an hour ago. It still is. Stop freaking out so you can think.

"Do you think we need to get more out?" I ask.

Gabriel's worry grows like a monolith and he's fighting for an explanation. "I don't think that's it," he says weakly. "Your ability came back suddenly, telling us that we got all your head strands out of your chest. Why would your strand control ability not appear *with* it? What's more, I can tell your ability is just as powerful as before, maybe more so. I don't want to displace more strands and possibly make things worse when it's not necessary."

I let go of Gabriel's skin then because I want to look at the brightness of his life force compared to mine, to see if I've gotten dimmer. I spent most of the last year sulking over my lost ability and then being angry about Robbie's diagnosis. Pretty much nothing positive.

But it's immediately obvious that's not the case. Gabriel and I are too close in brightness to spot a difference.

Why can't I feel my strands?

I want to tell Carl to keep working, but that's more likely a panicked gut-reaction. Eighty thousand is a lot even if it's less than a third of what I had displaced before. And this is my second go-round. Who knows how quickly I'll get sick?

Gabriel's expression is hard and focused. His intellect is speeding a mile a minute and I become distracted by it for a moment. Carl is just staring at us, waiting for… a demonstration of our skill with life force science maybe.

Gabriel shakes his head. "I have no clue why you can't feel your strands."

That is possibly the worst thing he could say. For Gabriel to not even have a *theory* is unheard of. Does that mean Mike's purpose is moving strands around and not for light? I'm tempted to go see him right now to find out. He woke up a few hours ago, but he was groggy and bad-tempered. I wasn't there, but it sounds like he's not quite cognizant enough to do life force ability experiments.

I lift myself up onto the edge of the pool. I'm going to hear it from Kaylen and Ezra if I don't figure this out soon. They don't yet know, but I can only keep this from them for so long. I rub my hands from the top of my head down to my face. Gabriel's worry is overpowering.

"We need to tell Kaylen and Ezra," Gabriel says. "We need more insight."

"Just… hang on a second," I say before he can go. "I don't need more than one person in the room hating me right now. I need the space to think."

Gabriel sinks into a nearby chair, chin in hands. "Nobody hates you. We just don't… well it's hard to accept this new fearless you, one who seems to know everything."

"I don't know everything," I say, letting my hands fall into the water with a splash. "And what I know and what I need to know are spread by a wider gap than ever. But the last month has told me this is what I'm supposed to do, that I'm on the right track. You just have to… trust me."

"I realize that. You've been acquainting yourself with this new mission for a lot longer than us, though. We've been spending the time trying to get you back, not plotting how we're going to subdue natural disasters. Bear that in mind."

"You say you were able to move your individual strands before?" Carl says.

"That's how I saved Kaylen and then myself."

"That... I'm having a hard time understanding why your ability would evolve that way in the first place," Carl says.

"You're not alone in that lack," Gabriel says. "While I'm certain it has a logical explanation, its sudden appearance at precisely the last minute is baffling."

"I think we need to understand how it appeared suddenly in the first place before we get upset about it not coming back like we expected," I point out. *In other words, stop freaking out.*

"I've been thinking about it on and off since it happened," Gabriel says. "I thought it must be connected to your other abilities in a more logical way than I gave it credit for. But that's obviously not the case. Now I have no clue."

Carl sits back, crosses his legs and arms. "Only because having it occur outside of her other abilities is something you didn't consider before. Be patient. I believe you'll figure it out. And you have some time. You were obviously expecting this as a fool-proof backup plan. And having it not go exactly that way is going to make you feel lost. Give your intellect some time to catch up and your shock some time to dissipate."

"I agree," I say, thankful for Carl's confidence in the room. "I don't have an answer at this exact moment, Gabriel. But I still know this was the right move."

Gabriel rubs his face. "Trusting you is the name of the game an awful lot lately."

Isn't that the truth. God, please let me not be mistaken about this whole plan.

ℸ

"Wendy, I have phone call for you," a voice says behind me.

I let go of Farlen's inert hand and leave the colorworld at the same time. I've been trying to reach Farlen telepathically, but so far I've gotten no response from him.

Mike is slowly waking up, and I'm hoping I'll be able to hold a conversation with him tomorrow. I would have touched him already, to take advantage of his light so I can get a jump on figuring out the problem, but it feels wrong to do it without talking to Mike about it first. The light belongs to him. I can't just *take* it. I turn around to see Dwight framed in the doorway. "Who is it?"

"I'm not positive. They would only speak to you, but they claim to be from the Guild."

Gabriel and I look at each other, wide-eyed. "I suppose you ought to take it," he says when I don't move.

I watch the ventilator inflate Farlen's lungs twice before I hold my hand out to Dwight. He puts a phone in it.

"This is Wendy."

"Hello, Wendy. My name is Ohr, and I was chosen as your liaison to the Guild Council. I hope you'll give me a moment of your time to explain some things."

For a second I think this is a prank call. This guy, Ohr, sounds so nice and normal. His cadence so natural and his tone non-confrontational, like he's about to explain a recipe rather than why his organization made an assault on my uncle's home and then dropped his dead body and Farlen's almost-dead body off at my feet.

"You have my attention," I manage to say, putting him on speakerphone.

"First and foremost," Ohr says, "I want to extend my deepest and most heartfelt apology for how things have been handled." He sighs heavily. "Andre's actions weren't sanctioned. He has gone rogue and taken several of our members with him. I'm unsure what his goals are, but he has proven that he goes by a different set of rules. We're making every effort to find him, but for right now he's out there, and he's a threat to us as well as to you and your family. You have the regrets of the entire Guild for allowing him to take things as far as he did. Robert Haricott's loss… it can't really be summated. But the world as a whole will feel it."

It takes me a minute to process what he's said. "What you're saying—essentially—is that killing my uncle and his men wasn't really your fault, and you're hoping I'll only hate you a little bit instead of a lot. You want to tell me this because…? *Why* are you telling me this?"

"Because I want to offer you protection. Andre is after something or he would not have had a reason to brutalize your uncle and his bodyguard. I have not only an interest but an obligation in keeping you safe from him until I can detain him."

"I *have* protection. Besides, why would I accept it from *you*? After everything you've done to me?"

"I'd like you to entertain the possibility that everything you think you know about the Guild is skewed. The perception you have was created by individuals who desired to defame us. Andre and his lackeys. Your father, Carl. Louise. I'm asking for a second chance, an opportunity to prove who we are—an organization interested in bettering humanity."

"I have *zero* interest in giving you another chance," I say tartly. "I have zero reason to extend trust to you in any way, shape, or form."

"Do you not have your freedom intact?" Ohr says. "I have the resources to come down on you ten more times over. But I haven't because that's not who *we* are. You think a hospital gives you protection because it's a public place? You haven't been taken because I haven't ordered it."

"Is that a threat?"

"No," he says, showing the first signs of losing patience. "I want your cooperation. I need it. *We* need it. The *world* needs it."

"Well, when you put it that way… *no*. Ohr, whoever you are, let me explain how this will go: my team and I—whom I actually trust—will figure out your problem. If I need something, I'll let you know. In the meantime, you can demonstrate your congeniality by not trying to kidnap me or anyone else in my family." Then I add snottily, "It really slows my progress having to run from you idiot people all the time."

"I have no intention of abducting you," Ohr says, almost offended. "One more item of business before you make your plans. Andre was right about one thing: we *can* help your son."

"Showing your true colors sure didn't take long, did it?" I snarl. "Don't you worry. Andre did you justice. Holding my son's life over my head is so classy and bighearted. Know what? How about this: you guys find ten kids out there with my son's same condition and help *them* first. Prove you can actually do something with all your fancy science without demanding something in return. Then we'll talk."

"Very well, Mrs. Dumas," Ohr replies, somewhat more jovially than I expected. "Have it your way. You have my word, we will not plague your efforts. But please be wary. Andre *is* a threat. I truly don't want to see any more awful things happen to you and yours."

"Sure thing."

"In the meantime, any chance you'd be willing to return our Grid technology? It saves lives you know."

"Fat chance."

He sighs.

"I'll return it when I'm no longer convinced you're going to use it against me."

"Those are ambiguous terms. I don't have time to meet undefined goals. I'll search the entire central valley before you're sufficiently satisfied."

"Knock yourself out," I say.

"Or I could wait until you need something. That's bound to happen soon."

"Whatever."

"Mrs. Dumas, before I go, one more thing."

"What's that?"

"Things are *not* getting better. Work quickly."

The call ends, and I hand the phone to Dwight. "Thank you," I tell him, Ohr's last words reverberating in my head. "I will not plague your efforts…" I mock under my breath. "Unless of course Andre conveniently does it for me…" I huff, irritated that I have been left confused about the Guild rather than more sure.

"How much of what he said do you trust?" Gabriel asks.

I shake my head. "The last part for sure. But he's probably right about not coming after us, at least not right away. They could have taken us here. Things are getting bad enough, quickly enough out there to justify overt action. So I think we're secure for the most part. At least for now. I'll ask Mike when he perks up." I look at Dwight. "We should still be on our toes though. Will you let Mark know?"

"Absolutely, Mrs. Dumas," the small man says. "Will there be anything else? Preparations for travel?"

"Not right now. We need some recovery first. And I need to think about what to do next. But I feel safe enough that we should book some rooms at the hotel next door so people can sleep in beds finally."

Dwight nods once and leaves.

I look at Farlen's face, wondering what he will tell us if he manages to wake up, whether he will remember anything about the people that did this to him. I wasn't quite honest with Dwight and Gabriel: I feel a *lot* more secure after that phone call. Ohr's story jives with what Mike has told me. That's not to say Mike hasn't been fooled, and maybe I *need* to feel secure badly enough that I'm willing to accept Ohr's explanation. But I've been going with my gut a lot these days. And it's worked out.

I may not yet know how to fix my life force should I need to in a pinch, but after the initial upset, I'm calm. The answer will come. And Gabriel has done exactly what I asked, which was to trust me. He's been worried alright, but about everything in general. He opted not to immediately tell Ezra and Kaylen about my hypno-touch. I think he doesn't want their negativity either.

"A hotel room is an excellent idea," Gabriel says. "I'm absolutely beat. I feel like I haven't really slept in weeks."

"Then let's go," I say, taking him by the arm. "I'm going to need you back in top form. We've got stuff to figure out."

"You sure are raring to go," he says as we stroll into the hall. "I have to say, your exuberance has me anticipating our next undertaking. You're a force, my love."

I almost pause in my step. That's how I always thought of Robert. Joy infuses my being because Gabriel has validated the courage I've felt growing by the day. I miss Robert terribly, but I trust myself. Probably more than I ever have before.

Fifty-seven

Hey there, sunshine," I say when Mike turns his head toward me and blinks his eyes blearily. I was told he argued with Maris last night about something, which means he's feeling better, so I came over first thing in the morning. I'm ready to work. And I know what I need to do first.

He groans from under his oxygen mask.

I smile at him and lean in. "What? You love seeing my face. Remember?"

He rolls his eyes.

"Your fake face loses its effectiveness when your feelings don't match," I say, determined to be as up front with him as possible.

He gives me a calculating look while I analyze the rhythm of his emotions. They're similar to Gabriel's, like having a familiar, comforting scent intertwined with a new arrangement.

He reaches up and pulls his oxygen mask down. "Say you didn't."

"I did."

"You're an idiot."

I prop my chin in my hand and rest my elbow on the railing next to him. "I'm totally stoked to see you awake."

"I hate you."

"Your racing heart and bliss say otherwise."

He scowls. "Why are you doing that?"

"Making you admit to what you feel? Because I am not going to let things get awkward between us."

"How is that *not* awkward?"

"Awkwardness comes from nobody acknowledging the elephant in the room."

"No. Awkwardness is part of the territory when you're cursed to mirror your brother's feelings for his wife. Nothing is going to make that situation less shitty. I seriously thought better of you. You don't get to call my feelings out just because you know they're there. It's vindictive and it's insensitive. To both me *and* Gabe."

"Oh right. You're such an expert on sensitivity," I snap. "You make a sport out of jerking my feelings around. And I let you, because I know you're just hiding. So screw you. I'm not going to let *my* feelings get buried under a veil of secrecy and shame. I'm not going to drive a wedge in my marriage by pretending something that's not true. Gabriel knows where I stand. And now so do you. My conscience is clear. You, on the other hand, are going to be burdened under your own emotions if you keep burying them—which you can't do anymore, by the way. You wanna prolong your misery? Go ahead. I may love you, and I may love Gabriel, but I'm not taking responsibility for how either of you handle it."

He glowers at me. "You've got it all figured out, huh? You got your little mind-reading skills back and now you're feeling confident again. You've got everyone under your thumb. You may know how I *feel* but that has nothing to do with what I *want*. And what I *want* is to erase them so I don't have to fight against myself twenty-four-seven. Or in the very least, sleep through it. Why the hell am I awake anyway?"

I shift in my seat, hard-pressed *not* to be pricked by his words. But the reality is that lashing out at me inflicted him as much as it did me, maybe more so, and I have to hold myself back from reaching out to put my hand on his.

He turns his face away from me.

I sigh, letting his belligerence flow through me like water. I wish he would be on the outside what I know he is on the inside. Why can't he see how much he's harming himself?

"Love isn't a feeling, Mike," I say. "Love is a force we make. Those *feelings* you're having are just one way it manifests. Even if you erased them, you wouldn't erase the cause."

He looks at me again. "Maybe you're right. Maybe I *don't* love you. Maybe I'm confused because I feel what Gabe does."

I shake my head. "Even if it started as merely *feelings*, it's become more."

"How would you know that?"

"Two reasons. The first is that I sense a connection with you that I do with Gabriel. A bond that's sort of… ingrained. The more I acknowledge it, the clearer it becomes. The second reason is because I understand emotions. You can see them in the colorworld. And they change the structure of whatever they touch. So what you feel becomes part of you in a real way. Everything you think does."

He tries to cross his arms and then cringes and puts his hands back at his sides. "Well I *think* I hate you. That counts for something according to you."

I roll my eyes. "Mike, you are welcome to live in denial all you want. But you're not going to do anything but torment yourself and everyone else in the process."

"Is that why you're here? To get me to admit to my feelings aloud to you? Not gonna happen. You might as well leave."

I chuckle quietly. "Oh Mike. I don't need you to admit your feelings to *me*. You're the one that needs to hear yourself say them aloud. And no, that's not why I came here originally. It was just a necessary caveat because you chose to be a jerk right off the bat."

He rubs his temples wearily. "Then *why* are you here?"

"To touch you. I've been thinking about it all night."

He balks. "Excuse me?"

"Can I touch your hand?" I say.

"No. Why?"

"*Because*, Michael, you have some serious life force wattage, and I want to tap into it so I can see more with my ability. Maybe solve the natural disaster problem?"

He thinks for a moment. "Are you shittin' me?"

I give him a look. "I just mucked up my life force so I could fix your Prime Human problem. I'd think you'd want to help me out with that."

He grows suspicious. "Where is Gabe?"

I shrug. "Sleeping probably. He was wiped last night and it's like seven A.M."

He tilts his head. "What day is it? Wait, I totally forgot. Did you do the exchange like I told you?"

I steel myself. "We tried to. But they—" My throat catches. I look up, holding tears that I thought were a lot further away than they apparently are.

"What is it?" Mike says, sitting up, but then he curses and flops back down.

I try to not hear my words as they leave my mouth, "Mark was about to leave for the exchange, but a van pulled up in front of the hospital and dumped Farlen and my uncle out and drove off."

Mike does a double-take, tries to sit up again. Curses again.

"They were both beaten. Only Farlen survived. He's in a coma and on a ventilator."

Mike's eyes are wide.

I bring my knees up into my chair. "It was a message, right?"

"I—" Mike shakes his head vigorously. "I don't—That's not them—" His eyes narrow suddenly. "*Andre*," he growls.

That's what Ohr said, too. I bite my lip for several seconds. Is Mike just blind to who the Guild really is or is he right? "You're going to have to convince me," I say. "Because in my head, the Guild and Andre are the same thing."

"They are *not*," he insists. "Look, the Guild has grown by leaps and bounds the last five years. Since the outset, they've micromanaged everything through the Guild Council. Ten years ago they realized they were going to have to delegate or collapse. That meant trusting people to handle things outside of the Council. When you trust, you're going to get burned. It's the nature of the beast. They combat this with what they call dyads. Teams of two, totally different personality types, a checks and balances system. Reassignment doesn't happen except in extreme cases. You make your dyad work. There's no such thing as not dealing with your differences. The end. No ifs, ands, or buts. Andre is the other half of my dyad. Has been from day one of my activation. I know everything about him. I know stuff about that guy that gives me nightmares still."

I give him a look of disbelief. "For real? You sure acted like Andre was your boss. 'Sir' and all that."

He snorts. "We had a complicated arrangement about how to deal with you. I won't get into it. But Andre wanted you to believe that he was the one calling all the shots, that I didn't get a say so that you would be more afraid of him and less afraid of me. I was supposed to play good cop earning your trust in case Andre's tactics didn't work." Mike sniggers. "Let's just say I took liberties. Played my part a little too well so that in no way would Andre win. I wanted him to go down, and I wanted it on tape. When that was done, I'd get a new dyad partner and deal with you for real."

"What's Andre's ability?"

"Enhancing the abilities of others."

"So the Yes-ish got a little bump from time to time?" I joke.

"No idea. When Andre was a tolerable human being, I was too much of a dunce with my talent to notice an improvement. When I got better with it, Andre and I stopped playing together nicely. He never offered a bump."

"Is it only temporary? The bump?" I ask, curious.

"Only if Andre wills it so," Mike says dryly. "Andre giveth and Andre taketh away."

"What are the limits? Can he improve abilities indefinitely?"

Mike shakes his head. "He'd have to recharge. How long would vary. Sometimes days. Sometimes weeks. So he was selective about when he used it. He'd save it up."

I prop my chin in my hand as an idea takes shape. It takes on additional dimensions and makes so much sense of things I almost leap out of my chair. "Your light!" I exclaim, hands gripping Mike's bed rail. "Holy crap! I just freaking figured out why you shine like the sun!"

"Because I'm amazing," he says matter-of-factly.

"You wish," I huff and then wave my hand impatiently. "If we go with what we know about life force abilities—that they improve as light increases—then what Andre does is give people light. That's how you improve abilities. If you've been Andre's dyad partner for seven years or whatever, he could have been feeding you light all these years. I mean, I have no idea where he gets the actual light from, but if you weren't demonstrating improvement, why would he bother taking the light away? So you've been accumulating light because of Andre." I sit back, stunned by my own epiphany.

Mike is grimacing though. "That sounds horrible. I don't want a thing from that sick bastard."

I cross my arms, still grasping all the implications of this realization. "But I don't get why you don't have your own army already or something. With your light from Andre and your ability, you should be unstoppable. You should have tagged me years ago." I look at Mike for an answer. "Unless you're *still* a dunce with your ability."

He shrugs. "This is your idea. I have no clue. Plus, I thought you said evil people lose their abilities."

"He probably has. Which would definitely make it impossible for him to take back the light he gave you—maybe that's why you still have it. Do you at least know what Andre wants? Ultimately? What did he want from Robert?"

Mike turns solemn and hesitant, but when I stare at him, he says, "To eliminate Robert as a player and to break you."

My breaths come quickly, and the gash in my heart rips open again. I turn away from Mike to gain my composure again, but it looks like I'm going to have to release some tears first.

How could anyone look at what Robert had done with his life and want him gone? It's evil. Pure evil. My face is wet and I keep wiping it, but more tears come. I begin to feel materially drawn toward Mike though, the magnetism I feel between my skin and others' at times. Mike must be softening toward me, because the magnetism has always come and gone with how aligned I am with another person emotionally. When we are at odds, it disappears. Ironically, it is this connection that builds between us that calms me and not his hand I notice has come to rest on my back.

I don't turn around though, afraid that this softer side of Mike will disappear as soon as my face is in his view.

"I'm sorry about your uncle," he says.

"Thanks," I sniffle.

"The good news is Andre no longer has Guild resources. The assault in Redlands and then Robert... it's completely in the open now. He'll be stripped of rank and kicked out. Although my guess is he knows this and just left. Probably to start a cult or something."

I turn back toward him, but lock my eyes on silent television across the room showing an advertisement for a car dealership. Who in their right mind is thinking about their next car purchase at a time like this? Vandalism fires have ripped through downtown LA and the national guard has been called in to enforce a curfew and keep the peace. "Someone named Ohr called," I say. "Said it was all Andre, too. I was after your honest gut-reaction."

"Ohr?!" Mike says. "You're kidding!"

"I take it you know him."

"I know *of* him. He's first chair on the Guild *Council*. You can't get any more big shot than him. He *called*? What did he want?"

"To blame Andre. To send protection against Andre. To work with me. I told him to shove it."

"You…? Holy Mierda." Mike looks up at the ceiling, in shock.

"He said he won't come after us. Was he telling the truth?"

"My opinion is yes."

"Your opinion? I thought it was always 'thus sayeth Mike' when it came to the Guild."

He gives me a sidelong glance. He reaches up over his head, grips the railing in either hand. I can tell it hurts him, but that's probably the point.

Come out, Mike, I think longingly to his fortified mental wall. *Come out.* I put my chin in my hands and wait.

"Stop that," he says.

I just sigh. I'm going to wait him out until me being here next to him no longer takes so much mental effort on his part.

Minutes pass in silence. Maris comes in. Her eyes stray to me only briefly, but she says, "Hola! Wendy, you're up early. Have you eaten?"

I scrutinize her emotions. Is she trying to get rid of me? I have no idea how much she knows about… well, anything. "Not hungry. I heard Mike was awake and I need to talk to him."

"Didn't sound like much talking was going on to me," she says, pushing aside the curtains of the window. The room itself is quite small, and three people is a crowd. Especially emotionally. "Michael needs his rest," she says, removing one of Mike's pillows from under his head and shaking it out expertly. "And your family needs you."

I watch her busy herself with Mike's bedding, reading the message loud and clear. Looks like I'm about to have a clash of wills with my mother-in-law.

"I'm not leaving," I say, leaning back in my chair and propping my feet on the railing of Mike's bed.

Mike, meanwhile, is still staring at the ceiling.

She turns around, hands on her hips. We assess one another. Aggravation mounts within her like a pot about to boil over. She's definitely not planning on backing down easily. "Michael is not your concern. Gabriel is."

I see… She thinks I'm making a play for Mike. So she knows something after all. Not as much as she thinks she does…

"Maris, relax. I've been alone with Mike for weeks. I pulled a staple out of his rear while he was unconscious. He's flaunted his bare chest up and down the west coast and from here to Chicago with me a mere foot away. We've slept next to each other in cars. Shoot, he even tried to shove his tongue down my throat that one time, yet I still managed to resist such charm." I simper at Mike's look of protest.

Maris' mouth has dropped open.

"Don't let her fool you," Mike says. "She took her time with that staple after she had diligently searched every inch of my chest. And she enjoyed the kiss more than she lets on."

I smile evilly at him. I shrug innocently at Maris. "I might have spent some extra time with his behind, but I was just taking back the power he stole from me when he straddled me on his apartment floor and tied me up. He made me feel violated and dirty."

"The great thing about Wendy is that when she feels dirty, she takes a shower," Mike comes back smoothly. "Like that one time she took her clothes off and made me hold the water hose up so she could not feel dirty anymore."

"Seriously?!" I mouth to him, hardly able to contain my laughter now. Maris is about to lose her marbles. I manage to keep a straight face though when I look at Maris again and throw my hands up. "He'd saved my life like five times! He deserved a reward!"

Maris is at a complete loss. "You!" she shouts, followed by rapid-fire Spanish. Then she shouts, "Out!" while shooing me with her hands, getting in my face.

"Shhhh!" I say, putting my hands on hers. "We're kidding, okay?"

"Don't trust her, Mamá," Mike says. "That girl needs a chaperone when she's around me."

I glare at him, and then I stand and put my hands on my hips. "Take it easy, Maris. I'm positive I can keep my hands to myself while he's got two bullet holes in him, smells like he hasn't showered in days, and has morning breath that could kill a kitten."

"That was low," Mike scowls at me.

Maris throws her hands up. "Santa Maria! I give up!" she shouts before mumbling in Spanish and clipping briskly out of the room.

I fall back in my chair and Mike and I burst out laughing.

"That was amazing," I say. "She's going to think twice before sticking her nose where it doesn't belong."

"Probably. But now she thinks you're an unfaithful hussy. She said as much. A curse on the family… all that."

"Ugh, seriously?"

He nods. "You just lost your sainthood. I hope the fun was worth it."

I purse my lips. "I think it was…"

"I think you're right."

I catch him smiling at me before he resumes a frown. I'm going to have to start over with waiting him out, but after only a moment he says, "If the only thing I had to admit was the feelings I have for you, I would have done it already. You think that saying that out loud is going to give me freedom to finally be me. But the problem is I don't *know* who I am. Never have. My whole adult life has been spent trying to figure it out. I've loved Gabe and lost myself. I've hated him and it did nothing but transferred back to me."

"I know who you are."

"Shut up. You only think that 'cuz I've kept all the really shitty shit to myself. But I'm sick of you pitying me, making me your project like I'm a troubled adolescent that needs kid gloves. Everything I've done, I own. I knew what I was doing when I did it. I wasn't lying to myself. Every bit of the crap you've been through is my doing. Everything. You never would have ended up at the compound if it weren't for me seeking you out with my ability for years. Neither would Gabe. You never would have left Gabe without my whispering in your ear that he was a sorry bastard who wanted to control you. Letty never would have gotten into the summer internship in Monterey and then shown up at your uncle's house and delivered the news from Gabe about your uncle's meeting with Carl. The seeds of suspicion… all me. The fertility drug… Your doubt in yourself, in Gabe, the past nine months. I infiltrated your thoughts every spare moment I had. I have been focused on tearing you down. I made you want to give up. And I instigated and watched it all from afar like a devil bent on your destruction. I wanted to devastate you. I wanted to see you bleed. I wanted you stripped down to nothing but a life force ability that the Guild could use. Robbie's illness—I brought you that fertility drug without hesitation. And your uncle? He'd still be alive if it weren't for all of that. I've done my best to destroy everything you love. And I've just about succeeded."

I shudder as the coldness of his words burrows into me. He's numb finally. Empty.

"The only person here who isn't being honest with themselves is you," Mike finishes.

The ensuing silence weighs a thousand pounds. He has closed his eyes to me, but rage has moved to span his indifference.

What am I? Angry? Sad? How is it that I can both see and experience the throes of his hatred toward me and cannot find a reaction? I believe what he said, about his need to dehumanize me because then it might mean that he wouldn't have to carry around the thing he believes is more burdensome: love.

Idiot. On an angry whim, and intent on making him face his emotions once and for all, I snatch up his bare hand.

Fifty-eight

Heaven help me but I forgot about Mike's light and the way it might feel pouring into me full-blast like this. I was only trying to share my mind with him. But I've grabbed a power line. I can't let go as the electricity pulses through my arm and out into my chest and other extremities. Although the more I think about it, the less it's like electricity per se. It's like getting stitches, a weird pulling sensation on my skin, except the tugging is intensified and spread throughout my whole body, as if thousands of threads are being pulled through me at once to tie all my parts together. It's a connectedness that feels good to the point of being sensual.

As this sensation becomes less present and violent, a roar in my ears grabs my attention. The volume of everything around me has increased, but more remarkable is the clarity of those sounds. Nothing is muffled. Nothing is unclear. Everything is sharp and defined and unbelievably easy to discern. Controlling the sounds used to take practice, but the individuality of each sound makes it nearly effortless. I don't have to pick them out and file them away, because to my enhanced ears they are each so unique. Their vibrations are more than an audible perception. They're feel and taste and sensations of color dancing through my mind. Picking them apart is as easy as telling a baby's cry from a steamboat horn. The swish of someone's lab coat down the hallway is drastically different from the nurse several rooms away tucking new sheets around a freshly stripped bed. The sounds themselves are so lush that I can almost see their sources in my mind. *My ears can see.*

I wonder, if I kept my eyes closed as they are now, would I be able to walk down the hall as unhindered as I would with my eyes open?

"Wendy?" Mike interrupts worriedly. His voice is unbelievably nuanced, laced with an edge of fear, the quickness of uncertainty, and the softness of affection. Like the other sounds, Mike's voice carries color and taste. I want him to keep talking so I can further experience the sound. I shiver with pleasure and sigh with contentment.

"Damn, woman. You're freaking me out." He tries to pull his hand from mine, but I yank it back with both of mine, only now realizing that I'm resting my forehead on the railing of Mike's bed.

"I'm fine," I say, not quite ready to open my eyes. I hear an echo after I speak, and I test it again, "I'm fine... Fine... Fine..." My voice comes back to me altered slightly, and an image of the dimensions of the room flashes into my mind.

"I got it. You're fine," Mike grumbles. "I'd say it's more like you're high. You've got a goofy smile on your face and you're hugging my arm like it's your stuffed animal. What are you *doing*?"

"Listening to you talk," I say. The sound of my voice echoes back to me and I sense the wall five feet away, obscured by something with a bulky instrument on it. This is a little like echolocation, but it comes with not only shapes, but colors, too. An aged beige and black and brown.

"You've lost your mind. Did you steal someone's meds?"

"Mike, did you know your voice sounds like what's in your head? The gravelly rumble gets a liiiittle bit louder when you're deflecting me. And you draw out the letter 'i' a tad when you're happy. Your 'd' sounds sharper when you're afraid. You're trying not to enjoy the fact that I'm touching you and you're afraid because you don't know what's going on right now. I didn't have to read your emotions for that... Your voice is incredibly musical."

"Huh? My voice is *musical*? Seriously woman. Get a grip. And get off me."

I sigh. "No. I'm not done. I still haven't opened my eyes yet."

"Can you at least tell me what you're doing? *Other* than listening to my mesmerizing voice?"

"Your light has enhanced my senses, just like I told you it would. It has connected them. Like my emodar is actually part of my hearing now, and smell..." I sniff a few times. "I hadn't noticed that part until now. Your smell sort of belongs with everything else. You *smell* like fear and happiness and rejection. Man, this is so *weird*!"

"Yeah. Weird. From my end, that's an understatement," he huffs.

"It's okay to like having me close."

"What?" he says, startled.

"Yes, I just picked the question out of your brain."

"Question?"

"Yes, I'm reading your mind." Actually, it's more like I'm reading his internal dialogue, a fragmented and distracted collection of words spaced and punctuated with emotions. I didn't know I could until I focused on consciously reading his emotions. I guess my emodar has graduated to telepathy, and my senses have graduated to empathy.

"Stop that!" he says.

"Don't be afraid. I already know how you feel. But it looks like you haven't actually acknowledged it."

He tries to pull his hand from mine, but I hold fast. Of course, if Mike *actually* wanted to get his hand away from me, he absolutely could. Gosh, his continual denial is ridiculous. Like adamantly declaring that you're wearing a yellow shirt when it's obvious to everyone that it's blue.

"What's the worst that could happen, Mike?" I say when his fear takes over coherency.

Since I asked the question, he can't help processing it and automatically answering it internally.

"Rejection," I whisper as I translate the images and feelings that cross his mind automatically. "But I told you I loved you. That's not rejection. And it doesn't require anything of you."

His reply flashes to life in words and images. A woman I don't recognize in the cradle of Mike's arms. Laughing with yet another woman in a restaurant. Gabriel bowed over, his face hidden. And then his face twisted in anger and then helplessness. *Robbie*. Mike's parents shaking their heads in disappointment. Flash after flash. Confusion. They are the images of a family torn apart by two brothers irrevocably bound by something deeper than family ties.

"You are afraid of me choosing you and breaking Gabriel's heart. Like everyone in the past."

Twangs of loneliness. Empty spaces. Invisibility. But all the while the unseen presence of Gabriel at his shoulder... And my face bringing the struggle to the forefront over and over.

"You're afraid you'll never be your own person, separate, capable of loving someone else and being happy."

"Stop it," Mike says weakly, yet his hand remains attached to mine.

I perceive a draw for Gabriel then, a longing to be near him but pushing away at the same time. He fears being lost.

"You're afraid you'll always be a slave to him," I say as Mike's story takes on momentum, pouring forth. He no longer tries to stop it. "Because he's more driven, more in control of what he feels and thinks and wants. He will always be the guiding force, and you will always be… an auxiliary. That's why you joined the Guild, why you did everything you did, even hurting me and him and your parents. You thought you could rip yourself away from him, sever the bond."

"Shut up," Mike says tremulously.

But I'm speechless now anyway. I wish I could unknow what I just learned. The depth of sorrow is awful. Mike is enslaved by Gabriel's force of will. And Gabriel does not have the power to free him.

I want to push myself away, to keep my distance, while at the same time wanting to cling to him and take his hurts away.

"What can I do?" I ask, opening my eyes finally to see his face. But what I am confronted with is a world of textures so intricate that I can hardly tear my eyes away from the fibrous structure of the threads of Mike's gown. I keep trying to see more, stunned that I actually can; it's like using a microscope. The threads take on yet another texture—scaled like human hair. And transparent. The sensation of seeing something so microscopic freaks me out a little and I retreat my eyes, bringing the front of Mike's hospital gown back into my view, and then Mike himself.

He's staring at me, his face stricken and confused.

"Holy moley," I say, gaping at him. And then I remember what he just confessed and I regret getting distracted so easily. But then… that was insane what I did with my eyes just now.

I clear my throat. We stare at each other some more. And then his eyes dart up and away. He pulls his hand from mine before I know what's happening.

The world goes dark.

All I can see are shapes and shadows at first. It's like pressing on your eyes for several moments and then letting go and everything being black for a few seconds before your eyes start working again. Mine do this before returning the world to normal and the details of only moments ago fade into memory.

"You need to leave," Mike says, staring at the wall again.

"Why?"

"Because now you know there isn't jack squat to be gained by me being up front about feelings I never asked for. I saw your expression and it confirmed exactly that. So now you have no good reason to be in here irritating me except to make my life hell as payback."

"You're such an idiot," I frown at him. "Yeah, my heart bleeds for you. Yeah, I understand the problem now. But if you'd spend less time guarding yourself it would leave more time to think about possibility. Mike, I'm trying to figure out the cause of natural disasters around the *world* and it didn't occur to you that I might actually be able to help you with your problem? Something like what you've got going on with Gabriel has to have a manifestation in the colorworld."

He snaps his head my direction, electrified by the possibility. "You really think so? And you might be able to like… fix it?"

I shrug. "If anyone can help you, I can."

"Help him do what?" says Gabriel's voice from behind me.

I turn to find him standing in the doorway. It looks like he found a shower and a fresh pair of jeans. And a suspicious frown again. "Hey!" I say, determined to be upbeat around Gabriel's jealousy if it kills me. "So guess what? I can endure Mike's light."

Gabriel's mouth opens. "You didn't, Wendy."

I nod enthusiastically. "I'm pretty sure I just saw a molecule with my own eyes. And my hearing was so good that I was able to see the room with my eyes closed. Crazy, right?"

"I can't believe you did that without telling me," Gabriel says, hands on hips.

"I didn't want to waste time arguing. Like we're doing right now. We could already be looking in the colorworld, but you'd rather berate me over something I was going to do anyway."

He rubs his face.

Mike laughs. "She has an agenda, no regard for other peoples' feelings, and an argument for everything. She's becoming you, so if you're bugged by it, you only have yourself to blame."

Gabriel's eyes shift from me to Mike and back again, caught between amusement and dread. "Let's get this bloody hell over with then." He strides over to the bed, dragging a stool behind him.

"Hey look. A real expression of frustration finally." Mike looks at me. "You've done it now. He's got a potty mouth. Oh hell, are you two switching places?"

"Pretty sure you're going to want to close your eyes," I say to Mike, ignoring his comment. "Because you'll share my abilities and the sound alone will probably overwhelm you because you aren't used to it." I look at Gabriel. "You'll pretty much be able to read our minds, and it can get distracting. Just a warning."

Gabriel locks fingers with me and sits up straight. "I have zero interest in being in my brother's twisted mind, so I doubt I'll be exploring it."

"Payback time, brother," Mike says. "I've been stuck in your head our whole lives."

I roll my eyes. They are being so juvenile. It's not the most mature response, but I'm feeling unapologetic so I snatch up Mike's hand and yank us into the colorworld in practically the same breath. That should shut them both up.

Fifty-nine

The transition is like a punch in the gut. It's like turning on the radio and not realizing the volume was left in the maxed-out position. The burst of sound rocks my whole body. And Mike's power pours into me at the same time. I'm immobile for a time.

When I recover, I hear Mike spewing a litany of curses. I feel him, too, jolted and astonished and confused over the experience that he hasn't quite put words to—other than words of profanity.

Gabriel, meanwhile, has strictly ignored Mike, meditating to center himself with the focus only he possesses.

I keep my eyes closed at first to get used to one sensory experience at a time. This particular one—the experience of colorworld sounds—has captured me like a moving musical composition, pulsing with emotion. When I first experienced the colorworld, the notes generated by life forces moving against one another was the most dynamic auditory experience there. It wasn't until several visits later that I noticed what sounded like voices in the background. Gabriel said it was in a language he'd never heard and couldn't translate.

But Mike makes the difference this time. Just as his voice carried emotion when my senses were enhanced, the colorworld voices do, too. Not only can I pick out one, I can feel it, and I am sure it has a consciousness behind it, wherever it's coming from. And I would call all of the consciousness' I hear childlike in their purity and brevity. Without a context, I am clueless about their precise message. I can only experience them, just as I would a piece of music without lyrics.

"The voices…" I say to Gabriel, squeezing his hand. "Have you listened?"

"Indeed," he says quietly. "They're aware of us."

"Really?" I breathe. "How do you know?"

He shrugs mentally. "Emotional currents and inflections."

Gabriel picked up more than I did. I wonder if he could actually translate the language?

"It would take quite a bit of time," Gabriel answers, reminding me that he can read my mind if he chooses, although I'm surprised that he's paying attention with everything else going on. But then, Gabriel has always had exceptional skill with handling the colorworld, no matter how overwhelming it has been to me and everyone else.

"It's a matter of practiced mental control," he says, answering me yet again. "Remember I spent a lot of time inside my own head growing up. It was the only part of me I could exercise."

"Are you going to survive, Mike?" I say, squeezing his hand now.

The only reply is a series of grunts and mental profanity.

"His heart rate is elevating," Gabriel says. "It's going to bring the nurse in."

I look for Mike mentally, only to realize he's not readily accessible. Mike is so scattered from all of the sensory input that it's hard to locate him amid the din.

'*Mike*,' I say to him mentally. I repeat his name several times until his attention is on me. '*Focus on me and nothing else*.'

"Oh sure, piece of cake," Mike replies sarcastically, but his attention comes together slowly anyway.

'*Have you looked yet?*' I ask *Gabriel.*

'*A bit. It's quite something.*'

'*I bet that's an understatement*,' I think right before I open my eyes.

One would think that the wall in front of me would be a nice simple surface to look at first in this new colorworld. But simple is not the word I'd use. It does carry the usual qualities of objects in the colorworld: a hue far removed from its natural color that shifts with my perspective, as well as the sensation of movement within the object. But now I can see deeper into the wall than ever before as my vision magnifies it without much effort. The perception of movement I have always felt about objects in the colorworld is finally explained. It reminds me of the card stunts performed by a stadium of people. Moving and changing images are created with choreographed use of colored cards or fabric or t-shirts. The structure of the wall is like this, where crystalline facets shift based on some invisible force, changing the overall structure, one that appears to have unlimited possibilities.

The shifts are also directional, like dominoes. They move across the wall from all different directions, like converging waves, but it's never chaotic. And I'm not sure if it's just me, but that wall structure appears to be changing more quickly as I watch, almost as if the act of me watching affects it.

I could sit here and contemplate the wall all day. After a while I remember I can zoom out. When I do, watching the colorworld inside this hospital room in more 'normal' proportions, an ever more astounding picture holds me spellbound. I have to fight against my own barriers of comprehension to process the smallest part of it

Moving. Alive. Color. Busy. Those aren't quite right. *Woven. Tapestry. Connected. Interaction.*

'*Harmony*,' Gabriel thinks, having listened to my internal monologue.

'*Yeah!*' I reply, thinking there is no other more accurate term. '*Hey! Have you ever seen Bee Movie?*'

'*You're talking about the part where the two bees, Barry and his friend Adam, just had their job orientation and Barry complains about the unfairness of having to choose one job that they'll have for the rest of their life. Adam chastises him for questioning the system because bees have the most perfectly functioning society on earth. Barry says, "You ever think maybe things work a little too well around here?" All the while, they're standing directly in the middle of bumper to bumper traffic that's travelling at highway speeds without a hiccup, and Barry and Adam don't realize how seamless it is? No, I've never seen it.*'

My mouth is open in surprise and before I can ask the question, Gabriel thinks, '*I saw the scene in your head as you remembered it. It does seem like a perfect example to illustrate in a small way what we're looking at.*'

'*Your sudden skill with reading my mind is unsettling*,' I reply. '*The scene flashed in my head for less than a second.*'

'*Hmm. Seemed slower than that to me.*'

'*Everyone's mind seems slow compared to yours,*' Mike comments, surprising me that not only has he been listening but he's also figured out how to speak mentally.

'*Right, well anyway, that scene is exactly what this is like,*' I think. '*Except way bigger. Like a million interconnected freeways in this room alone, all with free-flowing traffic that never pauses, with new freeways being made and eliminated all the time.*'

'*It's many times more than a million*,' Gabriel thinks.

'*Whatever it is, I can only look at a small piece at a time without my head spinning and my eyes blurring from the strain*,' I think, trying to comprehend more of these interacting freeways of movement at once. But the reality is that matter is all around me in the colorworld, the molecules of air, the walls, bedding, the dust... All these elements are seamlessly interacting with one another while at the same time interacting with a thousand other things at the exact same time, yet it's precise no matter where I look.

As I attempt to place myself in the context of so much busy movement, a kind of inertia pulls at me, like I am totally out of sync with it all. I feel *off*.

'*Oh my, that is frightening*,' Gabriel thinks, resonating with my thoughts.

Meanwhile, I simply stare. And stare. And stare. The sight is changing me internally. I feel different, like reality is no longer a mystery. The world itself is held together by paths of movement that weave together. Individually those paths look fragile, easily influenced—such as me merely watching one. But the millions of lines of movement acting together create an overall system as strong as iron by comparison.

It's reality. I'm looking at the fabric of reality...

'*Everything is affected by the things around it*,' Gabriel remarks. '*Remember the energy vapor we often saw in the colorworld, usually in concentrated amounts surrounding people?*'

'*Yes!*' I think. '*We're seeing that energy vapor effect in more detail. It's not a vapor at all. It's just...a flow of movement transferring from one thing to the next. It's actually coming from everything here though...Does that mean the movement is that much crazier around people and that's why we are able to see it without the aid of Mike's extra light? I haven't even looked at a life force yet. I'm a little afraid it's going to turn my head inside out.*'

'*Yes. I believe the energy vapor was, previous to now, the only visual manifestation of the continuous interaction going on between life forces and objects*,' Gabriel explains. '*Everything is connected. Everything moves and interacts with everything else harmoniously. Thinking together. One thing. The whole of everything is functioning as a single entity. It's the only way to explain the seamlessness of it. The same is true no matter how microscopic or macroscopic you get.*'

You can see how things are connected on every level because of how everything is moving in comparison to everything else.'

'*Now that I'm thinking about it,*' I offer, '*the colors... They make sense now. Like... like... They feel right...*' I wrinkle my nose, disliking how vague that sounds. '*Argh!*'

'*I know. Remember, I can feel what you do. I even feel it myself. What you're trying to articulate is that resonance and wavelengths align. Let's call the pathways of movement—the energy vapor—change events. The speed of these change events surrounding a particular object is synchronous with the wavelength of that object's corresponding electromagnetic radiation.*'

'*Uhh...*' I reply.

'*Dude,*' Mike thinks impatiently. '*What the hell?*'

Gabriel sighs. '*The speed of movement determines the color we see. It's absolutely fascinating, actually. Wendy, this shows us that your colorworld sight is, in effect, a highly evolved form of chromesthesia.*'

'*More words I don't know...*' I think.

'*It's seeing colors when you hear sound*s,' Mike explains. '*Lots of people have it. Some just see the colors in their mind. Others actually see the colors around them, like a projection. That's you.*'

'*Yes,*' Gabriel agrees. '*Think of light waves—colors—as vibrations. And different speeds of vibration mean different sounds. Consequently, for someone with chromesthesia, those varying vibrations also mean seeing different colors. You perceive the vibration of movement of change events surrounding an object, and that projects a particular color.*'

'*Whoa... So like, there's a rhyme and reason to the colors then,*' I marvel.

'*Yes,*' Gabriel replies.

At that moment, someone walks in. A quick check with my regular vision shows that it's Dwight. "Wendy, I have some papers for you to sign... Do you have a moment?" he says.

"Could you hold on one moment right there, Dwight?" Gabriel says.

"I'm sorry," Dwight says, taking a step backward. "I can come back later if this isn't a good time."

"No, no. I need a subject for observation," Gabriel says. "Stand right where you are if you would."

"All right..." Dwight says.

I've barely heard their interaction because I'm finally looking at a life force in this new and improved colorworld for the first time. And it's breathtaking. Dwight's life force strands are exquisitely crystalline in structure. But each one is completely different— yet always changing, their makeup cycling through innumerable geometric patterns.

'*Like snowflakes*,' Gabriel observes.

"Snowflakes really are all unique?" I ask.

'*Oh yes. It's a great mystery. They have the same molecular makeup, yet no two snowflakes have ever been found to be identical.*'

'*Then that's the perfect analogy*,' I agree, finally allowing my eyes to zoom in more closely as they've been begging me to. While in the natural world eyes become strained by trying to see small things, the opposite is true here. My eyes are strained when I attempt to process the bigger picture due to taking in so much at once.

What I see on a deeper level is a lot like I have seen in the rest of the room—a continuously shifting world driven by paths of change—the change events Gabriel described that move through reality. The difference is that here it is happening *much* more quickly, almost in a blur.

"Wen, everyone says I have to ask you about ordering food—" Ezra stops abruptly and I zoom back out to see that Ezra's life force has joined Dwight's. "You!" he says accusatorially. "Couldn't even give yourself and all of us a few days to recover before you went jumping into danger? You didn't even tell us! And you're touching *him*?!"

I can already feel how upset Ezra is, but after what I've seen, I have no regrets. The exceptionally ordered and interwoven nature of reality has me balanced and profoundly peaceful. "Relax, Ezra," I say, smiling at him. "I'm alive. We're figuring stuff out. It's going to be okay."

"Yes, and stand right where you are, please, Ezra," Gabriel says, and I can feel and hear the slightly higher pitch to his voice, indicating his excitement over something new.

Ezra's eyes narrow and he slumps against the door jamb. "Great. I'll stand here and starve then," he grumbles.

I revert my vision back into the colorworld, and make a quick scan of Ezra's life force, knowing that's what's got Gabriel so excited, though with the insane level of detail to analyze, I have no idea what part of it has got Gabriel's interest. It's *all* fascinating. I should be able to pick it out of Gabriel's brain, but all I'm getting from him are the wheels of his insanely quick intellect. It spins faster and faster, and like centrifugal motion it captures me and steals my ability to shift focus. It forces my eyes shut.

He continues to spin, winding my brain up tighter and tighter, the tension becoming more and more uncomfortable. As I'm looking for my voice to yell at him to stop, his consciousness suddenly releases mine, like cutting the strings and lending the sensation that my brain has been set adrift in a space without gravity. I feel floaty and disconnected for a moment until the voices of the colorworld steal my attention once more and ground me.

I perceive Gabriel's hand still in mine, but I can't seem to locate his consciousness except to sense that he is still mentally here. Mike is with me though, and I think toward him, '*Did you feel that?*'

'*Assuming you mean Gabe's brain trying to yank mine out, yeah. Gabe, what the hell was that about?*'

But Gabriel doesn't reply. I open my eyes and move the colorworld out of focus to see Gabriel's face. His eyes are open and he appears to be staring at Dwight and Ezra. His lips twitch and he sits ramrod straight next to me.

"Are you okay, Gabriel?" I ask, growing worried that… that…

"That he broke his brain?" Mike finishes.

"I can't feel him," I say. "It's like that one time when he was in a coma."

"What do we do?"

"Push him out of the colorworld," Ezra suggests.

"I'm not sure…" I say, although I tentatively try to release his hand.

Gabriel suddenly grips mine solidly. '*Wait,*' he thinks clearly.

"He says wait," I tell everyone.

"There's a surprise," Ezra says. "So, before we all have our minds blown by whatever the Brain comes up with, I have a question."

"What?" I say.

"Now that you're running the Haricott empire, can I *please* get funding to develop a batarang?"

"Whaaat?" I say, not expecting *that* request out of the hundred more likely possibilities.

"That is an *excellent* question," Mike says, and I notice he figured out how to push the colorworld out of his sight. "In a situation like this, batarangs are a must-have. I'm thinking different variations. Explosive ones, gas-filled, heat-seeking…"

I snort.

"Yeah! Like Green Arrow's quiver!" Ezra says.

"We're discovering the secrets of the universe and you two are excited over… batarangs?" I say.

"Correction," Ezra says. "*Gabe* is discovering the secrets of the universe. The rest of us have to think about practical things, like secret organizations coming after us with advanced technology. What's *your* plan? Rocket launchers for everyone?"

"You know Wendy doesn't like people getting hurt," Mike says. "She's got a new line of tie-dyed colorworld team shirts in the works and we're all going to shave our heads in solidarity. Going to hypnotize the masses with rainbow swirly colors and chanting."

I jar Mike with my elbow, but Ezra guffaws.

"We'll make her a batarang that explodes in rainbow confetti then," Ezra says.

"We're going to have to come up with a line of non-lethal ones," Mike says, tapping his chin with his free hand. "I want one that makes a fart sound and smell when you throw it. It'll be a great diversion—everyone looking around to figure out whodunit."

"Awesome!" Ezra says, gesturing excitedly with his hands. "I'm writing that one down."

"Oh my gosh…" I roll my eyes.

"Good Gad," Gabriel interrupts at long last. "I just counted to Octodecillion."

Ezra rolls his eyes. "Everyone hold on to your IQ. The Brain is back."

"That's a number?" I say.

"Oh yes. I have a thing for numbers, as you might imagine. So I know the number scale all the way to centillion. I've always wanted to test myself to see how high I can count. Nothing observable on earth goes up that high in count. But this presented quite an opportunity."

"What did you count?"

"Dwight and Ezra's… what shall I call them?" Gabriel ponders. "I counted the pieces that make up the crystalline structure of their strands—as far down as I can see."

I am rendered speechless for a minute. I know what he's talking about. The individual pieces that shift one-by-one in a domino effect. To count all of them? I cannot comprehend how that's possible. But I keep *trying*.

"My head is going to explode if I think about that," I say. "Hey… how did you manage to count that if he isn't in a pool with the life force strands spread out?"

"Because now I can differentiate strands—helps me keep track. The particles are also unique. It is much easier to keep track of things that look different versus things that look the same. And the strands are shifting enough on the outside of the body in enough places that they all make themselves visible for long enough to count them."

"But… what about the strands *inside* the body?" I say.

"Oh I can't count those because I can't see them. But managing what I *can* see is quite invigorating!"

My mouth is open. "But the particles are always *changing* at that level. How do you keep track of things that are changing all the time? Come on. You just estimated, right? Do you have an exact number?"

"Of course. I wouldn't have said I counted to it if I'd guessed. That's ridiculous. The number is seven octodecillion, four hundred fourty-eight septendecillion, five—"

"Stop!"

"What?"

"Gabriel!" I shout. "You act like all you did was count a pile of oranges. You just accomplished a feat the rest of us can't even fathom. How do you hold that much in your brain? And furthermore, the structure of a strand changes. How do you count something whose number is always changing?"

"The basic elements of the strands change in a predictable way across the entire strand, allowing me to use that prediction to count accurately. And you're right, the number is probably different now than what it was a few moments ago. As for how I hold it together, it's more of an awareness rather than some kind of nuts and bolts counting. I'm aware of what I see in a way that allows me to count it as if it's intuited rather than using the number system. Obviously, if I actually had to mentally count one, two, three, and so on, I would be a lot slower. The numbers… well they kind of come to me in the same way you can look at a domino and know the number of dots without actually counting them. It's intuited from seeing the quantity before and then I compound those numbers as I work. Understand?"

"Okay, okay. You can count. Got it." I shudder, having worked myself up. "What's part two? I can tell there's something else."

"Yes. You observed the kinetic movement between particles on a microscopic scale, did you not?"

"It's the only way to really get what's going on," I say. "You try to see too much at once and it's a blur."

"Indeed. I spent some time watching their life forces cycle through change events. They appear to change from the inside out, meaning a life force strand changes starting at the end that is inserted inside the body and the shift moves outward to the end that attaches to the skin *outside* the body. Never does a strand start changing from the middle. Secondly, I noticed that Dwight's life force does this more quickly than Ezra's. In essence, this means that Ezra's life force is changing more slowly than Dwight's. I don't know what this means, whether every life force changes at such a noticeably different pace. But it's noteworthy. I'd need to see a number of other subjects to make any definitive deductions."

"Well I have a question," Ezra says, crossing his arms.

"Is it related or are you going to ask for a utility belt next?" I say.

He opens his mouth like he hadn't considered that, but then says, "Can you guys actually see Mike's life force now? Assuming that you're siphoning his light to see all of this, you guys should all be the same brightness. Can you see what his life force is doing that's making it so bright?"

I almost explain that I have a theory about that, but I'd like to see his life force anyway. I turn my attention to Mike—who is definitely easier to see now that his light has equalized among us. "What theory with Andre?" Gabriel says just as I notice that something seems off about Mike's life force. It takes me a minute to figure out what because my eyes naturally zoom in on him when I need to look at his life force as a whole. When I finally have it, I practice looking from him to Ezra and Dwight across the way.

Mike's seems… smaller? More compact? Tighter?

"Condensed is the term I would initially use, however I believe that's inaccurate," Gabriel says in response to my internal ponderings. "One moment."

He starts counting, but to avoid losing myself like I did the last time, I detach from his mental processes before I can get sucked in. He doesn't take nearly as long as the last time, maybe a couple minutes before resurfacing. As soon as he does, he lets go of me, props his chin in his hand, and I can tell he's worried and he's trying to keep it from blowing out of proportion.

"What?" I say, letting go of Mike finally. His colorworld is pretty hard to endure. So much sensory input and not enough brain capability to process it all is nerve-racking after a while. Though my own vision is pretty flat compared to using Mike's light, I know how to use it because I came by it on my own—not from borrowed light. Relieved as well, Mike exhales and rubs his face several times after I let go of him.

"Ezra," Gabriel says calmly—too calmly. "His total count is eleven billion, one hundred forty million, six hundred eighty-five thousand, eight hundred and forty-four."

"He has less strands…" Ezra says. "*Way* less." He pushes off the door jamb, his hands come to his sides. "That's like… *oh damn*."

I catch on more slowly. Eleven billion. People have a number much closer to thirty billion. "Oh my gosh," I whisper. I can't say it out loud. Mike's missing around nineteen billion strands. Gabriel has about nineteen billion strands *more* than he should. I put my hand over my mouth.

Gabriel nods. "I have nineteen billion of Mike's strands."

Sixty

What other explanation is there?

Mike *cured* Gabriel years ago when Gabriel was dying of Spinal Muscular Atrophy at age six by giving him nineteen billion of his own strands. *Because he can move them.* Having extra strands cured Gabriel's body. It makes sense because the strands have a profound effect on a body's health. That also explains the bizarre connection between the two. It explains... well, everything.

"I need some air," Gabriel says, standing abruptly and heading for the door.

I vacillate between going after him and giving him space, settling on the latter because I'm not sure what I think about the whole thing, let alone what to say to Gabriel about it. I've seen and learned so much in the last hour that I can't put any of it into context right now. I'm going to need a long night's sleep first.

Ezra has pulled up one of the rolling stools and crossed his arms over the bed tray table, looking mystified as well. His eyes go distant when he says, "Like... how is Mike even *alive* missing that many strands?"

I shake my head slowly. "I... I'm not sure." I look at Mike, who is caught up in some kind of revelatory moment. His face is brightening as I watch him—so opposite to my own roiling confusion. "You're... Why are you grinning like you won the lottery?"

Mike's eyes shift to me immediately. "This is the happiest day of my life." He grabs my arm and shakes it, eyes frenzied and excited, but the sensation of his energy passing into me has me frozen in place and I hiss as I struggle to equalize.

"Oh, sorry!" he says, letting go of me. "I am so giddy I want to like... pick you up and spin you around right now. Damn hospital bed. 'Course, you're probably picking up all that. Wen! You were right. You were *right*!"

"Right about what?" Gosh, Mike feels as high as a kite.

"That you'd figure it out—be able to help me. I feel fantastic!"

"But..." I say, unsure of what he means. I *feel* what he means, but I don't understand the whys. Unless... Oh God. He doesn't think I can fix this, does he? Move his strands back to him? Actually, we probably could if we thought about it long enough, but where would that leave Gabriel? I don't think he can survive without those extra strands. But does it mean Mike's life will be cut way short? Other than his gunshot wounds, he's been the picture of health... I put my face in my hands. What a mess...

"Hey," Mike says gently, careful to touch my shoulder this time so as not to come in contact with my skin. "What's wrong?"

I look up at him, elbows on the railing of his bed, unsure of how to put this.

"Dude, if we get your strands back to you, chances are pretty good that Gabe would die," Ezra says bluntly, saving my butt of course. "But none of us are gonna tell you what to do with your own life force. That'd be rude. Or presumptuous at least."

"What?" Mike says. "You seriously thought I was going to ask you to put them back? Hell no. I can put two and two together. That's not even a possibility."

Relief floods into me, but confusion remains. "Why are you so over the moon then?"

Mike laughs, rubs my head like I'm a little kid. Every time his skin meets mine it's like the melding of magnets and an electrical current, at least on my side. But I'm more bewildered at how buoyant he is. This kind of cheeriness is *not* something I *ever* associated with Mike. I didn't know the guy was *capable* of being so happy.

He watches my expression, shaking his head and laughing. "Wen, it's like you said that one day. Sometimes you suddenly realize something about yourself that makes a bunch of confusing shit in your past make undeniable sense."

"Yeah... *Oh*."

Mike nods emphatically at my expression. "You got me. Now imagine that instead of figuring out a few things about yourself, your *whole life* makes sense now. Like... who you are is no longer this weird, confusing mix of stuff." Mike looks heavenward, starts babbling in Spanish and throwing his hands around emphatically.

"Dude, are you *praying*?" Ezra says.

Mike ignores him, a smile permanently plastered to his face. Suddenly though, he sits up, obviously ignoring the discomfort with little effort, grabs my face in both hands, and kisses me right on the cheek with a loud smack before falling back into his pillows. "Thank you... Man, that sounds so lame for how I feel right now. But I will never, *ever* be able to thank you enough for this."

"Well, ah, I'm picking it up from you so... You're welcome," I say, stunned by his reaction still.

"Welp!" Ezra says, slapping his knees and standing. "I got a lot more than I bargained for coming in here. I am still hungry, so I'm off to do real life stuff. Like ask the nurses where to get good takeout—which, by the way, you need to give me *permission* to order." Ezra rolls his eyes, looking back at Dwight who has been waiting patiently in the doorway.

"Yeah, yeah, it's fine," I say to Dwight. "And thank you for letting us borrow you for a bit. Oh yeah, you had something to talk to me about, right?"

"Just your signature on a couple things," Dwight says. "More to come. But this will get you started and able to use your assets should the immediate need arise."

"Right..." I say, steeling myself. Ezra makes an abrupt exit.

Dwight places a small stack of papers in my lap, already marked with neon sticky tabs. He hands me a pen and offers an encouraging smile. "Robert made quite a few preparations for this ahead of time to make the process relatively painless. A lot went into rearranging the executive organization of Qual-Soft so that it could continue without his involvement. But you have complete veto power in any situation. Everything he owned is solely yours. No contingencies. Most of it was actually already signed over to you prior to his death—you just were not made aware."

I look at Dwight. "He *did* know. That he was going to die, didn't he? That's why all this was prepared ahead of time."

Dwight gives a slight shrug. "As Robert would say, we all know we are going to die. It's what we spend our whole lives preparing for."

"He *would* say that, wouldn't he?" I say, glancing over the paper before putting my signature to it. I sign a few more places and hand the collection back to Dwight.

I watch his back retreat, thinking about Mike, who has barely paused to breathe during his lengthy epiphany.

I look at Mike. "So you don't… you aren't *bothered* by the fact that you're missing over half of your life force strands?"

"They're not missing. They're *in use*," Mike says. "Sure, I guess it's a little weird. But…" He becomes slightly apprehensive and he looks from the door to me. "Can I confess something?"

I cross my arms. "No, you may not. I know I was in your head and everything, but now you're taking this too far."

Mike gives me a look, unsure.

"I'm kidding, Mike," I say, rolling my eyes.

"How should I know that? You're the mind reader," he says. "Anyway, what I was going to say was that I've always been jealous of Gabe. You know, with all his talents. He's so damn smart and people are drawn to him. They like him and he does it all so naturally. If I'm being honest, that's the main reason I started focusing on my physical fitness. I figured I was never going to beat him in the brains department. Knowing that Gabe's carrying around part of me, well it has me sort of at peace with that, because some of that's gotta be me, you know?"

I pause, trying to wrap my head around that without the whole idea becoming too bizarre to stomach. I'm not sure I succeed. I kind of wish again that I didn't know what I know now. But when I let myself experience Mike's emotions fully, it's hard not be grateful for bringing it to light. I love Mike, and I have seen him battling himself enough times that I know he needs this. How can I not be ecstatic for him?

"It's going to take me some time to get used to the idea, but I'm happy for you, Mike," I say. "Really."

He smiles at me. Again. "You're the one that said having everything on the table would make awkward stuff way easier to deal with."

"Yeah… I did say that, didn't I?"

"Yep. And I totally believe it now. Which brings me to my next confession."

"Oh boy," I say playfully, but I'm more anxious than I'd like to admit.

"Years ago," Mike says, "I met a girl named Gemma Rossi."

Sixty-one

Fear strikes my heart. In the light of everything going on, I have blessedly forgotten about my alter ego and Mike's reaction to it. But now *he's* bringing it up. Finally. But I'm not equipped to deal with what is surely going to twist yet another aspect of the Gabriel-Mike-Wendy triangle of freakishness. *Uuuugh.*

"I don't think I can do this right now," I say in a small voice, standing.

"Wendy, don't go!" Mike says to my back.

I stop and look heavenward. I close my eyes. "Mike. I— It's too much right now."

"Please," he begs. "I need to—I have to say this. I need you to know. *I need you to know.*" I hear his voice catch. Mike is crying?

I bow my head and sigh. After all the time I've spent digging Mike out of his pit of misery, to make him face his feelings, I can't abandon him when he's made himself this vulnerable. I turn around. His eyes are red, and when he sees my reluctance he feels rejection and begins to reel in the emotions he has put on the line.

I rush to his side, take his hand, and shake my head as I close my eyes and wait for the rush of energy to equalize. "I'm sorry," I croak as soon as I can get the words out. "I'm just afraid. That's all. I want to be here for you, but I'm scared that what you'll say will… change things in a way I can't handle."

"Afraid? Please. You shot a rocket launcher like eighteen times," he says.

"That's getting really pissed and pulling a trigger. That's easy."

He thinks about it. "Yeah, okay. This is totally different. But just trust me, okay? You can handle this."

"Trust you? Are you using my line?"

"Yep. Is it working?"

I roll my eyes and smile. "Anything for you, Mike. Go ahead. Implode my world."

"What do you remember about the night you went to the Detritus Art Benefit?" he asks.

I sit back in my chair, prop my feet on the lower bed railing. "Faceless crowds. Fumbling through the night. Misery. Anger. I wanted to die. Kind of surprised I didn't try. I woke up in the morning in a wooden crate in the back not remembering how I got there. Figured I must have gotten my hands on some alcohol. Or maybe some drugs. I don't know. Either way I didn't remember how I got there. If I hadn't been so broken up over my daughter, I probably would have been more freaked out about the missing hours."

Mike shakes his head slowly, mystified. "The crate... that's where I met you. We had a conversation. But you never told me your name and never showed your face."

I snap my head up. "You... How...?"

"At that point in my career I was trying a lot of different avenues," he explains. "We figured you might be artistic because of Gina. We knew you had diabetes. We knew you might be going by Wendy. We knew you were sixteen. We had an age-progressed image we were working with. Going to art museums and exhibitions was my latest tactic. My ability is often a numbers game. I figured if you were into art, you would likely feel moved to go to at least one of the many events I had scheduled to be at. Gabe showed up at my apartment unannounced like he often did. Wanted to know what I was up to that night. I told him and added the excuse that I was going to be looking for a birthday gift for mom. I didn't really want him with me, especially since he has a dampening effect on what I can do. But he insisted on coming because that's just what he does, and getting together on a whim was just what *we* did. I figured, 'What the hell. If this girl is going to show up, she has probably already decided it.' So I took him with me."

"I never showed my face? That's a little... odd."

"You're getting ahead of the story."

I wave a hand. "Fine. Continue."

"We saw your piece. The cloud. It was the perfect thing for Mom. The placard didn't say who the artist was, and Gabe made it a point to find out. I was glad to have something to keep him occupied while I scouted the place to see if you'd show up. While I was walking around, Andre called and started riding me about bringing my brother on Guild business. It got a little heated and Gabe was nearby, so I let myself through the closest door so he didn't catch up to me while I was having a verbal throw-down. I didn't need him asking questions."

"Okay. And where do I come in?"

"Ended up being a door to the back room. I heard someone crying. So I went to check it out. Heard it come from this giant crate. I tried to move the top off, but you yelled at me."

"Was I drunk?"

"I would have bet money you weren't. If Gabe could remember he'd agree."

"I met him, too?"

"He showed up not long after that because asking around wasn't cutting it. And Gabe and I can always find each other. He thought I was snooping around the back to find the name of the anonymous sculptor who made the cloud and wanted in."

"Ugh. That is such bad etiquette. When an artist wants to remain anonymous, it's for good reason. It's rude to push like that… but then, the word 'private' is a button Gabriel always feels driven to push." I sigh. "I do love him for that though…"

"Well you have to understand… The cloud…" Mike shakes his head, lost in nostalgia. "I don't give two shakes about art usually. That was the first and only time art 'spoke' to me as they say. It was more like yelled."

"So what did we talk about?"

"You were pretty guarded. Obviously something big and awful had happened, but you wouldn't go into specifics. Only said art was bullshit and you were quitting. I asked on a whim if the piece was yours. You reacted exactly the same as you did just now. Specifically I believe you said, 'Anonymous means it's none of your business, idiot.'" He gives me a sidelong glance. "You do love to call me that a lot."

I shrug. "It's true. I say it in my head at least five times a day about you. Looks like you haven't changed much." I grin at him.

He gives me a disgruntled look. "Or you're just mean. Anyway, you seemed relieved to talk even if it was about everything but what was bugging you. Found out you had loved rain, which is why you made the cloud. But art had ruined everything. I didn't read you as a teenager, and I also never would have guessed Detritus would be selling art from their students. All of this is to say I never once imagined you might be who I was looking for."

"That is so bizarre."

"Yeah. What on earth led you to crawl into a crate anyway? They have bathrooms for crying."

I roll my eyes. "That part is *not* weird. Walls and boxes always gave me security. At home it was my bathtub. The weird part is that I had a conversation with two dudes and I don't remember any of it."

"It gets weirder."

I throw my hands up. "Of course it does. I should stop using the word 'weird.' My life has normalized it."

"When the conversation kind of wound down, you said, 'I can't believe I told you guys all that. Especially because you're both trying to get my number… and even after I tell you my art career is over. Guys are such asswipes. Go back to the party and find another girl to fall for it.'"

"Go me," I laugh. I can totally see that coming out of my mouth. Although sadly, this event may have been the start of my less than impressive year of debauchery.

"It was brilliant. Gabe was falling all over his words, trying to 'win your esteem' as he put it." Mike rolls his eyes.

"And you?" I ask.

Mike gives me a mischievous look. "Told you that you were full of yourself. We went back and forth, me goading you, saying you weren't brave enough to make those accusations in the open. You just kept coming at me about my ego, and I ate it up. Gabe, on the other hand, was at a total loss because you ignored everything he said. At one point, you told him gushing that much was a creeper red flag." Mike laughs.

"And neither of us remembers…" I muse, mystified by that. "Any clue why Gabriel doesn't remember?"

Mike blows through pursed lips. "When Gabe and I left, he was predictably in a bad mood. Of course, neither of us went home with a number, but I had faith in my resources. You were obviously dealing with some stuff, so I'd find you when the time was right. But the bottom fell out for Gabe when I was driving him home. Biggest fight we've ever had. I still remember what he said that started it: 'I realize the purpose of your life is the unending pursuit of sexual acquisitions, but I'd like to ask a personal favor that at least this once you will refrain from adding that young woman's name—whatever it may be—to your list of mountains conquered.'"

"Unending pursuit of sexual acquisitions, eh?" I say. "That sounds like quite the job description."

Mike frowns. "Gabe has always liked to imagine me as some kind of man whore who jumps from one bed to the next. I think it made him feel better about himself since he couldn't hang on to a woman to save his life. Whatever Gabe has told you about me, it's his distorted perception of the truth."

"So Gabriel pled for my virtue and you what? Insulted his brain?"

"I told him he was a desperate lapdog with zero standards, and he told me I treated women like disposables. And those were the nice things we said. Oh man did we get into it... the things that came out of our mouths... It became about everything and nothing all at the same time." Mike shakes his head, a bit awed, a bit disgusted. "When we got to his apartment building, we had a brawl, fists and all. But it was basically like punching myself, the way I felt what he did." Mike's eyes go distant. "You'd think that would have stopped me. But I got more furious, more desperate to somehow... rip apart whatever it was that bound us together. God, I hated him. But we were like rubber bands. We pulled apart further and further each time, but we only snapped back harder. And I think when I kind of got how fruitless it was, I figured I'd use him to destroy myself instead." He looks at me finally. "That fight... the mindlessness...the loss of control... Even that makes sense now." He shudders.

Spellbound by the story and Mike's quiet disgust and then relief, I remain silent. I wonder about Gabriel, how it is I've never suspected anything abnormally amiss between them. Maybe Gabriel is more unaffected because he is wholly himself plus Mike, while Mike is half of himself with his other half attached to Gabriel? Ugh. My mind is in knots.

"I knocked Gabe out, and that's when I came to, saw what we were doing," Mike continues. "We were both a bloody, bruised mess. My shoulder was dislocated, and I broke some fingers and a couple ribs. I drove Gabe to the ER where he woke up and didn't remember a thing from the entire night. The doctor said it was a concussion, that the amnesia would wear off. But it never did."

"What did you tell Gabriel?"

"I told him about buying the cloud piece for mom, and about the argument that escalated in the car. Not about the 'box girl' as I thought of you until I learned your name—at least the one I *thought* was yours. Gabe didn't really ask questions for once in his life. But he got it. We had always walked a precarious line between the tightest of friends and the gravest of enemies. It wasn't exactly hard to expect that we would have a knock-down-drag-out if one of us disrupted the balance. We both kind of figured one day it would happen."

"Sounds that way," I say, though I have to admit the idea of Gabriel being involved in something so… primal sounds unlike him.

"Now the awkward part," Mike sighs. "It was pretty easy to find out your name was Gemma Rossi from the art community, so in the years following, I was looking for Wendy the energy world medium for my job, and I was looking for Gemma Rossi for myself. The fact that Gabe had forgotten—even if it was a concussion—felt like a sign that Gemma was going to change things, that for once she wasn't going to be someone I stole from Gabe. That agreement about whoever got the girl won… it was Neanderthal bullshit. I hated it. But we could never be *separate* so it was necessary if we wanted to keep our relationship. So in my mind, Gemma represented hope. But of course, finding you was not nearly as easy as I thought. I couldn't find a picture of you anywhere."

"Yeah… It was part of my 'artist persona' to be as anonymous as possible." I roll my eyes. "At least that's what my mom said. But I know now it was her sneaky way of protecting my identity."

"I told you she was a really smart woman," Mike says. "But for me it was this… quest. I romanticized the whole thing in my head. Sometimes I wondered if I'd had a hallucination because of the fight trauma. After all, I was the only witness. But I was happy to cling to the delusion. It kept me sane. Especially when I met you, Wendy the energy world medium, and the feelings I expected would come because of Gabe became too much to ignore. I kept hanging on to the hope that one day I'd find Gemma and it would erase all the confusion surrounding you and Gabe. Gemma was going to save me from *you*."

"And then you found out me and Gemma were the same person… Oh Mike…" I say, hollow from Mike's devastation.

Mike nods solemnly. "Felt like God was pissing in my cornflakes."

"Sorry," I say meekly, feeling immediately stupid and embarrassed for such a trivial expression of compassion.

"It's not your fault." Mike laughs mirthlessly. "None of it is." He looks at me. "I'm sorry for being an SOB all this time. You didn't deserve it."

I open my mouth several times, but the words I intend to say each time sound empty in my head. An expression of sympathy is in order, but I don't truly know what it's been like for Mike. How dare I pretend I do for the sake of filling the silence?

Mike's melancholy lifts as quickly as it came though and his eyes comb over me. "I just realized… I was right after all… Wendy, I—" His eyes search mine. "Damn," he breathes, examining my face like he's never seen it before. "Gemma Rossi… She's even more than I hoped she'd be. I just didn't expect… I was so blind…"

He tilts his head the other way, as if to gain another angle to see me. The attention would have me really uncomfortable—perhaps a little worried about his intentions, but being an empath, I know his words are genuine expressions, not veiled inferences. He's just trying to articulate his insights.

"When you yelled at me at Carl's house, I was like, Dang, this girl *owns* me." He laughs to himself. "I keep inventing new ways to get her to hate me and she just won't! In fact, she gets better every day at shoving my face in my own feelings and totally confusing me by the stuff that comes out of her mouth. She's got an answer for everything, but it's like, stuff I've never heard, stuff I don't understand. 'I may not trust Andre. But I trust you,' she says. How? I kidnap her, tie her up, throw her in a prison, and she trusts *me*? What the hell is wrong with this girl? And her backward ideas about relationships… committed friendship? Almond trees? Crap is more important than the end-point? And don't get me started on the stuff she intuits and I have no idea how. Like finding her father when the Guild has poured millions into locating him and come up empty. She's like an oracle, because when she says things and I think she's mental, turns out later she was right. All this time I've written it off, but when I look at the timeline of her life—and I know her biography—she gets shit done. Only she's crazy and I can't figure out how she believes the things she does, acts like it's the God-honest truth of the universe, and it works for her… How the hell does it work for her so well? I see her flying. But by God I can't see any wings. She's defying gravity. She's defying everything I thought I had figured out."

He looks at me. "And the only conclusion I came to is that you knew something I didn't. I figured if I stuck around I could figure it out. But what do I get from you? 'I know I'm married to your brother, Mike, but admit you love me, and I swear it'll all turn out fine!'" Mike shakes his head. "One of the dumbest things I ever heard you say, and I thought, this time… this time she's wrong. But here we are. And it *is* fine. I'm sitting here, reciting my life story, but seeing it totally differently than I ever conceived of. Like, how many times have I gone over that night at Detritus in my head? And only *now* when I tell *you* do I realize that I needed Gemma as much as I imagined. She brought understanding all right. It was just… a different kind."

I blink several times, realizing my eyes are wet. I reach up to wipe them.

"Wendy," he says quietly. "I don't know if it matters to you, if you need to hear it, but I love you. Legitimately. I didn't want to say it before because I had always thought of my feelings for you as not mine. I've been mirroring Gabe's emotions for so long that I don't ever trust what I feel, but I do now."

He touches my shoulder again and looks me in the eye as he says, "I want you to know that, *and* this: I know you love Gabe, that you chose Gabe. I know how much he loves you. I *feel* it. All the time you were apart from him and over the distance I felt how he changed, how he felt believing you'd left him for me on purpose. That's a big part of the decisions I made, trying to get you back to him. I couldn't take his emotions even though they were faint and far away. It was torture feeling his heartbreak. I will never, ever do anything to purposely jeopardize what you two have. I want you to be able to trust me not just with your life, but in the way I trust *you*. I may be slated to experience every blip of emotion that Gabe does for you, but you've given me hope back that one day I can find someone, and loving you at the same time won't get in the way. Because like you said, we'll always be a part of each other. And that's okay."

I blink away tears, poignantly humbled by Mike's confession. "Wow," I whisper. "That's like… the nicest thing anyone has ever said to me." I tilt my head, baffled. "How is it you're capable of saying both the most terrible and the most wonderful things to me? Extreme much?"

He smirks, but he's exultant inside. "Don't know what to do with that, do ya? I'm actually a nice guy most of the time. So I guess you better figure it out."

I smile at him, recognizing Mike's epiphany as all too familiar. I'm struck with how unorthodox our exchange would sound to most people. Mike's telling me about the depth of his feelings for me, his brother's wife. Convention says it's wrong. But how can I feel his festering wounds healing as he speaks and think this moment anything but beautiful?

It has me wondering about a lot of things. Like what my marriage to Gabriel *means*. I want him. I *need* him. But I never promised to never feel emotionally connected to anyone else, and the whole idea of marriage being a death sentence to one's freedom to love others seems backward to me. The boundaries of love are a lot fuzzier now. Beyond physical fidelity, what exactly is monogamy? Mike and Gabriel's life force connection aside, how much exclusivity in my feelings and actions belong to Gabriel?

And Gabriel... How will *he* see this? A life force dependency on Mike is not going to sit well with him...

"I appreciate you respecting my relationship with Gabriel," I say. "But what you've had to go through just to keep Gabriel alive... It's a lot to ask of someone. I think Gabriel's going to have a really hard time accepting it."

"Oh I know. I feel him, remember? But look, I may not know how, and I may not remember it, but I made this sacrifice for Gabe." He shrugs. "And I'd do it again. No question."

"He probably knows that. But I'm not sure how to help him... be okay with it. I don't exactly have experience with something like this."

"Wendy..." Mike says, growing somewhat frustrated, "I don't mean to sound insensitive, but there's no kinder way to put it. Gabe's going to have to get over it. And he has you. He has Robbie. He has a hell of a lot to be grateful for. Stuff I've only dreamed of. If I can accept this, he sure as hell can. He'd better find peace with it. Or he's going to lose everything. He's going to end up like me—the old me before today."

Sixty-two

*H*ey you," I say, coming up behind Gabriel and putting my arms around him. I've found him sitting on a bench outside the hotel we're staying at.

He reaches up to touch my hands, holding them there against his chest. A great shudder escapes him. He's on an emotional precipice, the possibility of taking just one step forward into destruction all too real. It scares me. I need to remind him that the ground is still solid, but I'm lost for the right words.

"Walk with me," I whisper in his ear, pulling at his hands.

He follows, exhaustion weighing down his steps.

"I'm not going anywhere," I tell him, keeping my arm wrapped around his.

He stops, turns to me, searches my face.

"I'm *not* going anywhere," I tell him again.

"Are you telling yourself or me?" he asks.

I tilt my head. "You, Gabriel. I'm telling *you*."

"Have you asked yourself though? Whether you *want* to go?"

"*No*," I say firmly. "Why would I do that?"

"It's important to flush out things you don't want to admit."

"Things I don't want to admit?" I say, outrage coloring my tone. "*Gabriel*! We went over this already. I chose you when I married you. I choose you now. I choose you tomorrow. There is no question!"

He waves a hand. "I asked whether you *wanted* to, not whether you were *going* to."

"What I *want*? I *want* for you to stop being so insecure and trust me!"

"This isn't about trust. This isn't about my insecurity," he says, far too calmly. "This is about you and how you feel about the situation."

I stare at him, dumfounded. What do I say to that? "It's screwy…" I try. "It's messed up. But it's not insurmountable."

That doesn't seem to be the response he was looking for. He sighs and starts walking again.

I jog after him. "I think *you're* the one that needs to talk," I say, coming up beside him. "Your emotions are all over the place and you just found out you're alive because Mike donated some strands. I'm trying to give you assurance that this doesn't affect my commitment to you, to give you some stability, and you're interrogating me like you want to find a chink."

"Maybe you're right. But I'd feel better if I knew you were being one hundred percent honest about your feelings."

"I have been! Remember on the roof? When I told Mike I loved him? Remember in the hospital when I elaborated? Gabriel! What is this really about?"

He rakes his hands over his eyes, an edge of his internal composure cracking. "I don't know… I don't know. My head is everywhere and nowhere. Up is down. Down is up. I'm pushing you about it because… because I want to feel something other than numb. I want you to scream at me so I can react, and then maybe I can yank myself out of this…this…limbo."

I put my arms around him, realizing that the odd blur of emotions I'm getting from him is shock. It's got to wear off before he's going to be able to talk coherently about it. All I can do is be here when he's ready. "We're going to get through this," I reassure him. "You're going to make sense of it and you're going to manage beautifully, extraordinarily. That's who you are."

"But… I can't see a single solution that's acceptable. Not one. It's all black. So many questions. The ones that have answers I can't think about without becoming nauseated by the prospects. This is… perverse. I shouldn't… I should not be alive!" His last words come out in a sob and I hold him tighter.

"I don't know the answers," I say. "But I will. *We* will. Just like always. I felt exactly like this after I came away from Pneumatikon with a death touch. It's just how you *feel*. It's not reality."

He fidgets and heaves. "Tell me something."

I'm not sure what he means, but it *feels* like he wants to believe me. "Nothing has changed, Gabriel," I say. "You are the same person I married. I still love you as much as ever. We have a son that needs us as much today as he did yesterday. We have a family. The world is in the same place. The *only* difference is what we know. We haven't lost our ability to choose what to do with tomorrow. You haven't lost your ability to choose what to do with your life. Those things should give you comfort."

"But what I know is exactly why I do the things I do."

"Then until you know how to integrate the knowledge, you keep doing what you're doing."

He considers it.

"I believe in you," I say.

"Well, you shouldn't. I know nothing."

"But I do. You have never failed me."

"Yes I have. When I left you to force you to do what I wanted."

"It sucked, but you didn't fail me. We wouldn't be here right now if it weren't for you."

"You *want* to be here? Four good men are dead. Farlen is in a coma and may not wake up. Robert is dead. Our son is slowly dying... *Here* is pretty awful."

"That's only because it's the middle. The middle is terrible. The middle is where people give up. But it's also where the *wrong* solutions fall away and the *right* ones are revealed. A little longer, Gabriel. Hold on."

"*How* long?" he entreats. "How much can I possibly take? I'm losing everything around me. My identity... Even you! You're dying as you stand here because we don't have the knowledge to fix your life force. I need one thing to go right! An ounce of understanding. A moment of clarity. And then maybe I can do what you ask and hang on to the belief that things will get better, that I won't be in this place of no understanding, of utter confusion forever."

I hold his face firmly in both of my hands. "You're not lost. I know exactly where you are, Gabriel. I know this darkness so, so well. Nine months of it. *But this is not reality.* Don't trust it. Don't trust darkness. It wants you to think that the world you once knew is gone. But it's not. Just reach out." I grab his hands, put them on my face. "Trust the shapes you find. They might look like shadows of their former selves, but trust them. Follow them. Eventually your heart and your mind will make up the difference. They'll fill in the dark areas and you'll see the light again. And then the colors."

Gabriel has his eyes closed, his hands on my face, and I can feel him trying. So I channel us into the colorworld to help him, letting him experience *me* to give him something to grab onto. I marvel at the abyss he's dug in his mind, and without feeling it now it would be hard to remember precisely what it felt like when I was in his place. The devastation and fury... The sense of betrayal yanks me back to the moment I realized that saving Kaylen wouldn't happen. I believed I'd been abandoned in my moment of greatest need. The sorrow of having my faith in the order of the universe let me down... An unparalleled helplessness.

But then I remember the quiet compulsion I felt. To reach out and save myself. The miracle of moving my strands... Was it reserved for just that moment? I don't know... But it saved me. And Kaylen. It also saved Robbie. *Three* people were saved that day.

Was it Mike, perhaps? From afar? We need to experiment with him, see if he can move his strands like Alma could, but do it at will. I wonder if his ability is limited because of his strand count? Can Gabriel do the same thing since he has a portion of Mike's strands? Maybe it was Gabriel who saved me somehow. He was touching me that day and maybe his ability transferred to—"

"Oh my God!" I cry, my eyes popping open to the brilliant lights of the colorworld.

Gabriel, shaken by my outburst, looks at me with demanding inquisition. "What—?"

"Robbie!" I say. "It was Robbie!"

"Robbie?" he says, confused but hard-pressed to be anything but hopeful at my emotions.

"Where's Robbie?" I demand, turning this way and that like maybe I've forgotten he's out here with us. He's not, but my excitement is running away from coherency.

"With Kaylen. Or my mother," Gabriel replies. "Wendy—"

"I was pregnant that day," I say, forcing my enthusiasm to take a back seat for a second. "When I moved my strands. Robbie is a *Prime*. He must have a life force ability. Maybe more than one. What if he's a channel, Gabriel? Like me? He can share his abilities. And what if one of them is like Mike's ability—to move his strands? That's what he shared with me that day while he was in the womb! That's why I could move them then but not now!"

Gabriel is floored, his eyes as wide as saucers as he goes over the logic.

"Good Gad," he exclaims when his intellect winds to a close. "Wendy, I do believe you are one hundred percent right!"

"We need to test it!"

Both of us take off at a run back into the hotel. We're on the first floor, so we don't have to go far. We bang on Kaylen's door first. She opens it and we find Ezra with her. Neither of them look happy, but we're not stopping to find out why. "Robbie here?" I blurt.

Kaylen shakes her head, and both her and Ezra's expression change to curiosity when they see our energy. We leave them at the door and head three doors down to Maris and Dan's room and pound on the door.

Gabriel and I have also drawn the attention of Mark and the three other guys on duty. "Is everything okay?" Mark asks just as Maris opens the door, Robbie in her arms.

She scolds us in Spanish and then in English, "Trying to put him down for his morning nap and you two come banging down the door. Since you're here, you can do it so I can go check on Michael." She glares at me. "See what damage has been done."

I don't want to rudely snatch Robbie from her, but Gabriel has no such consideration. He plucks Robbie right out of her arms without explanation and hands him to me.

"Okay, Robbie, we're going to see some pretty colors," I say, as he reaches for my face with one hand. I take his hand in mine and kiss him on the forehead as I close my eyes. After five deep breaths, I let myself fall into the colorworld once more. And then I search out my strands.

And there they are. Perceiving them is as easy as feeling my leg. I locate all of the free ends, bringing them out in front of me. Thousands of tiny fingers, awaiting my command.

"It works. I can move them," I breathe, sinking to the floor because adrenaline and suspense have left me spent.

"Usted tenía razón," Gabriel whispers, having lowered to the floor with me. "Robbie saved us all."

Gabriel and I look at one another, overcome at the same time. At first, I am awestruck. Then, the humbling realization of what this means washes over me in ever-growing waves. If I hadn't been given the fertility drug, I never would have gotten pregnant. If I hadn't gotten pregnant with Robbie, I'd be dead. And Kaylen, too. And if I'm truly the person who can fix what's going on with the world, then Robbie saved the world, too.

I look down at Robbie, now shrouded in his life force before my eyes. It's all violet sparkles with dancing rainbows as the light bounces off the facets of his strands. And it's bound with mine like we are one. I wonder if life forces grow like the body. He's not burdened with an extra bulk of strands. They seem to fit him.

I brush Robbie's soul lightly with mine. He smells faintly like new cotton and clay mixed together. It reminds me of fresh plaster, of the experience of fresco paints ready in my hands. It is a sensation which I have not felt in many years but now flashes to mind as solidly as if I had experienced it yesterday. He also smells a bit like Gabriel: curious and seeking.

"He smells like you, Love," Gabriel says then. "Like humidity. It always made me think of the high right after a good workout."

I laugh. "I was thinking he smelled like *you*. A workout, huh? You never told me I smelled like a sweaty mess."

Gabriel rolls his eyes. "I didn't say you smelled *like* a workout. I said you smelled like the *feeling* after a workout."

"Well I don't care *what* he smells like. That kid is a miracle-worker," Ezra says, having smartly assumed what's going on.

"It was Robbie that let you move them?" Kaylen says. "That's... that's incredible."

"Saved by a four month-old," says Ezra. "That sounds about right for our big, happy, freak-show family. Back from the dead dad who once dabbled in energy hoodoo and killed people, mom who lived on the run like she was in witness protection and had superhero brains, uncle who saw the future, sister who can see psychedelic colors and shoots missiles from residential rooftops, nephew that can control his life force, and sister's husband who counts like Rain-man and doesn't speak English but whose brother once worked for secret superhero organization and kidnapped sister. And then there's the fact that half of us were adopted so we're not even related. I'm pretty sure I missed something though. Man, I need to start writing this crap down." He looks at Kaylen. "You're the resident organizer around here. Think you can come up with a family glossary? Hey! I got an idea. We'll do family trading cards with power stats."

High from the moment, I can't help laughing. "We do have a complex family tree."

"Complex?" Ezra scoffs. "It's like Days of our Lives, Superhero Edition."

"Do you think he has any miracles left?" Kaylen asks, somewhat hesitantly. "Like maybe one to save himself?"

My heart aches at the tentative hope behind her words. But it's compassion for her, not for Robbie. In fact, until this very moment

I haven't stopped to consider what my own newly reacquired ability can do for Robbie. I've been thinking about how I would fix the problem going on in the world and how I can help Mike. How did that happen?

Did I forget about Robbie? Do I somehow care for him less?

I hold him against me and pat his back, demanding of myself that I find the answer to that, but I feel placid. So I draw up the image of Robbie older, confined to a wheelchair.

But I can't make it out clearly. It keeps getting away from me. The picture is inaccurate, silly even. Robbie's emotions, however, are far more interesting. His consciousness is much quieter than the four other people near me. But if I really focus on him, the most obvious difference is a lack of any conflict, any push or pull. Rather, he's probably what I would call obliviously happy. And gently fluctuating. He changes with the winds of experience as easily as changing clothes. They are the emotions of a child: innocent, simple, lacking in the complexity of thought that usually governs adult emotions.

Robbie takes for granted his mortality. It's kind of like how people don't question gravity until someone tells them it exists. I guess I'd call it childlike acceptance. It's light and airy. But one day he's going to face his mortality. He's going to face his limitations. He's going to look around and see all that he can't do that he *should* be able to.

A moment of clarity washes over me suddenly and my eyes water. I cling to Robbie, hoping that he retains the fierce confidence I am feeling at this very moment.

"Who are we to say his life will not be enough?" I say.

I look around me at the confused faces.

"Enough what?" I ask them, looking from one pair of eyes to another. "Enough walking? Enough talking? Enough sights and sounds and new experiences? We don't get to simultaneously pity and encourage him. We only get to choose one. We can only *do* one."

"But we don't pity him," Kaylen says.

"Yes we do," I say. "We feel sorry for him because he won't have the same things we do. Because we don't want him to be different. We want him to have the same as us. We want him to *be* the same as us. But what makes our limited lives more valuable than what he'll have anyway? If we all lived in wheelchairs without the ability to talk none of us would know any different either. If I hadn't lived with the colorworld at my fingertips I would never have had those nine months of misery afterward. Because I wouldn't know any better. And if I had never lost my ability in the first place I wouldn't have learned how life could be just as full without it. I didn't learn less because of the lack. I actually learned more. I learned about listening and watching and being patient. I learned how to live with uncertainty and how to trust people and how to be let down by them without losing parts of myself. And most of all I learned to be confident in myself, no matter how many senses I did or did not have."

I stand up, holding Robbie on my hip, getting more incensed by the moment. I look down at Robbie. "I'm sorry I wasted so much time hating your circumstances. You will have an amazing life, no matter how long it is, and while I am around, I'll show you exactly that."

I look around me at the others who appear to be experiencing varying emotions. Then my eyes rest on Gabriel, who is pensive. "*You* are the most capable man I have ever known by a landslide. You have the mental discipline of a legion of warriors. You have the determination of a thousand men. The endurance of an entire race of marathon runners. You speak more languages than I could ever hope to learn in my lifetime. You're a genius. You're so brilliant, while still so compassionate. How so much power and humility can reside at the same time in one person is still hard for me to believe. That's not dumb luck, Gabriel. That's the result of being cornered in your own mind for years and *thriving* there. Without your limitations as a child I am *positive* you would never have gained the godlike skills you have. If Robbie can gain what you have, it will be worth every mile he never walked and every year he lost. He's so lucky, Gabriel…" My eyes spill over. "He's so lucky to have you as an example of what he can do."

I look down at Robbie again. "People always say that you never know how long you have. But sometimes you do. Sometimes you are a little boy born with muscular dystrophy and you know already how much time you *won't* have. So why should we be angry that we know the future? What is it we *actually* want for him?"

Speechless stares meet my question.

"We want him to be happy, right?" I say. "Well, happiness isn't manufactured. It doesn't come just because you did XYZ. A healthy body and a long life don't make happiness. It comes when we stop fighting our circumstances, when instead we use what we have to accomplish our goals. Then when we recognize how capable we actually are… when we finally see some part of ourselves clearly, it's like figuring out how to open the shades to let the light in. Everyone has to learn how to open the shades. You don't get to sail toward happiness no matter how capable, or healthy, or privileged you are. And you aren't kept from it no matter how limited your body is."

Gabriel rests a hand on Robbie's head and looks at him thoughtfully.

"Well then," Ezra says. "That was a *speech*."

"Wen knows her stuff," Letty says, saluting me. "Get it, girl."

I don't remember when she came into the hall, but I smile at her. "I'm trying."

Letty waves a hand. "I don't see trying. Only doing."

"That's exactly what you have to do when you're in the middle," I say, looking at Gabriel.

"So I've been told," Gabriel says. "I just wish middles didn't always have to feel like the end."

I reach over and squeeze his hand. "All good middles feel like the end."

Epilogue

The airport in Missoula changed their mind," Mark says. "They want a list of firearms on board." He shoves a bag in an overhead bin and turns to me for instructions.

We're about to take off for the first place we'll attempt to track change events from localized disasters in the colorworld—Star Trek stuff, as Kaylen said once. The most recent disaster was a cluster of tornadoes that hit western Montana earlier today. We're going to go see what we can see. "And?" I say to Mark, tossing my bag on my seat so I can sign the paper Dwight has put in front of me. I scan it. "A house in Wyoming?"

"A ranch," Dwight replies. "Robert had been shopping for one for a year. He signed the purchase agreement before he died, but their attorney insisted on a new one with your signature."

I give him a questioning look. Why would Robert want a ranch in Wyoming?

"We can either give them the list and risk them not letting us land there or we can find an alternative landing strip," Mark says.

"Find an alternative," I reply. I catch Jessie's arm as she passes me. "Did you find anything on board?"

Jessie is the person in charge of all surveillance sweeps, every time we come and go, no matter where it is. She shakes her head. "Squeaky clean."

"The hospital cameras... they've been scrubbed?"

She nods. "No problem."

"Thanks." I turn my attention back to Dwight. "Any idea why Robert was buying the ranch?"

"He said it was a good idea."

I give him a mischievous smile. That's what he always says any time I ask why Robert did this or that thing that boggles me. I've enjoyed getting Robert's past instructions through Dwight. It's almost like he's still here, whispering cryptic things in my ear and expecting me to trust him with little to no information—which I'm happy to do. Robert's truly monolithic empire requires so many decisions that I'm glad to have a few things I can trust that Robert put in motion specifically for my benefit. "I guess I better take his advice," I say, initialing the pages Dwight indicates and signing the last page.

I hand the pen to Dwight, about to sit down next to Gabriel, who is holding Robbie asleep on his shoulder, when Darren bounds into the plane and makes a beeline for me.

"Kaylen is unaccounted for," Darren says, red-faced.

"What do you mean?"

"We can't find her."

"I know the definition, Darren. I'm asking the status, where you've looked, when she went missing, whether you've tried calling her…"

"Sorry," Darren says, and I immediately feel bad for being short with him. "I'm just pissed that I've managed to lose someone. Her phone goes straight to voicemail. And I was coming on board to see if anyone remembers riding over from the hotel with her."

"Has anyone seen Kaylen?" I yell down the length of the plane.

"Bathroom?" Ezra offers, hopping to his feet to check.

"I saw her at breakfast last," Carl says. "Did she make the convoy out here from the hospital?"

Lots of mumbling, but it doesn't sound like anyone remembers seeing her in one of the five vehicles that transported everyone—including an awake and mentally functioning Farlen—out to the airport.

I look at Mark next to me, but he's already dialing the hospital.

"Great," I grumble, looking at the time on my phone. I call Kaylen. It goes straight to voicemail just like Darren said. We're cleared for takeoff in thirty minutes. It's not like Kaylen's a toddler who wandered off. Where could she be?

"Not in the bathroom," Ezra says, bounding back into the main cabin.

I look at Mark. He's still on the phone, but he shakes his head.

"Someone needs to go back to the hospital and look for her," I say.

"I'm on it," Darren says.

"Thanks," I say. "Dwight, can we get a new time slot for takeoff?"

"On my way," he says, filing past me to the exit.

"Are we sure she wasn't taken?" Gabriel asks quietly from my elbow so as not to wake Robbie.

I squat down beside him, disturbed that this possibility hadn't occurred to me. But once it does, an anvil drops in my stomach as a flash of Robert and Farlen being tossed from a van passes in front of my mind's eye. Farlen can't talk yet, so I still have no idea what transpired with Robert and him. I put my hand over my mouth. "Oh no, Gabriel. Do you really think someone took her?"

Gabriel gives a worried sigh. "Where else could she be? She would have realized by now that she missed us and called."

I whip out my phone and stand up. I thumb through my contacts and choose the first most likely suspect.

He picks up after three rings. "Mrs. Dumas, to what do I owe the pleasure?"

"Did you take Kaylen?" I demand, putting my phone on speaker.

"No. I gave you my word," Ohr, my Guild *liaison*, replies patiently.

"Shoot," I mumble, looking down at my feet.

"Has Andre made any demands?" Ohr asks when I don't say anything further.

"No. I take it you haven't located him? How is that? You found me like twice when I was on the run. You have all these people with Prime Human skills and you can't pinpoint where he is?"

"Andre is invisible."

"Nobody is invisible."

"I was referring to Andre's life force ability."

I'm confused. Does Andre have another skill outside of enhancing others' life force abilities? I look at Gabriel, who shakes his head.

Ohr laughs heartily for several seconds. This is the fourth time I've spoken to him, and every time I do he speaks to me like we've known each other a long time, like kidnapping me is water under the bridge and we're making a second go of our relationship. I think I might be letting him.

"Nobody has the ability to be invisible," Ohr says finally. "Not like you're thinking."

"Then what are you *talking* about?" I snap impatiently.

"I'm sorry, Mrs. Dumas. That was a test. I was interested in what you would deduce from my statement." He clears his throat. "Invisibility is a term we use for individuals who have lost their life force abilities. For reasons that perhaps only you know, once someone has lost their ability, they are difficult if not impossible to be detected or affected by the life force abilities of others. They are, essentially, invisible to the forces that move among us."

"But my skin kills those people."

"That's not your actual skill," Ohr says. "Your skill is *sharing* what you see, to which they are blind, as I understand."

"They die, Ohr."

"A side-effect of blindness."

"But my emodar worked on both Louise *and* Carl."

"Really? In that case, how on earth did Louise ever lead you to believe she had benevolent intentions?"

"She was... well, she was a psychopath. You know, no emotions?"

Ohr chuckles. "Whether Louise *actually* had no emotions, or whether you were just unable to accurately read them, both cases prove my point. However it happens, she was Invisible. As for your father, I said it was difficult to read Invisibles, not always impossible. He was related to you, carried your 'emotional range' as it were. We can speak to specifics all day; I'm speaking in generalities. As a general rule, the Invisible are untouchable by our Prime Human abilities. Sure, we may use more practical means, but Andre knows our system, our methods, our people working on the outside. No one can stay out of our sights better than him. And your newest team member, Mike Dumas, of course."

I sigh. This is just awful.

"A question you may want to ask, Mrs. Dumas, is how it is your protection detail failed to do their job. Are you sure you don't want to rethink the staff I offered to help you?"

"Shut up, Ohr. Don't act like you don't have people keeping a wide perimeter around us all the time anyway. I don't need your people any closer, thank you. You already have cronies waiting in Missoula, I assume?"

"Kalispell, actually. You can't land in Missoula with all of those weapons."

Seriously? How does the guy know where I'm landing before I do? "That's just creepy," I say.

He chuckles. "Always a pleasure, Mrs. Dumas. Is there anything else I can do for you then?"

"Since you asked, have pizzas delivered to my plane for all my people since we're grounded until we can find Kaylen," I say snarkily.

"And milkshakes!" Ezra yells.

Ohr laughs again right as I hang up the phone.

"I believe you actually enjoy talking to that man," Gabriel points out.

I shrug and plop in my seat to await word from Darren when he reaches the hotel. "Keep your enemies close, right?"

Ezra scoots into a seat in front of us. "I've been worried about her," he says quietly. "Kaylen. She's been really distant lately. Man, I hope she's okay..."

"We've all been dealing with Robert's loss," I say. "Kaylen's not really in your face about her feelings."

"Not with you," Ezra says. "She loves to whine to me about everything though."

"Really?" I say. Whining is not the Kaylen I know.

"*Ehh*, you're more like her idol," he replies. "She's not gonna complain to her idol."

I wave a hand. "Whatever. Either way, if she's not at that hotel, Andre took her. And if Andre took her, we need to change our plans. We know what Andre is capable of. Finding Kaylen comes first."

Carl appears then, leaning against the headrest of Ezra's chair. "Unless it wasn't Andre. She confessed to me the other day that she didn't understand why you weren't accepting the Guild's help to treat Robbie's illness. She's not someone afraid to take matters into her own hands."

"What matters? You're saying she ran away? To do what?"

"I'm not saying anything definitively," Carl holds his hands up. "But if Kaylen believes she could exchange something for the Guild's help, she wouldn't be afraid to do it. She has as much information about the colorworld as you do, does she not? She has bargaining power. She knows it. She was raised by me."

"But she knows Ohr is a liar and can't be trusted!" I say.

"Wendy, you just had a civil conversation with Ohr and even made jokes," Carl says. "The impression you've given all of us over the past week and a half is that he is a reasonable human being who can be negotiated with and perhaps molded. Dangerous Prime Human Overlord is not the vibe you've been sending."

My phone rings.

"Darren, what's the word?" I say after I put it on speaker.

"She's not here. But I have an envelope. It was left for you anonymously at the front desk," he says.

"Open it, please."

I hear the rip of an envelope. "A letter," Darren says. "Signed by Kaylen."

"What does it say?"

"Dear Family, I think I know where to find Andre. Don't look for me. I'll find you when the time is right. I have something to do. I hope you don't mind, I took a big chunk of the spare cash. Give Robbie a kiss for me every night, and tell my Dad to stick close by you all. I don't want him falling off the wagon. I love you all so much. Kaylen."

I sit back in my seat. I can read between the lines. Kaylen's gone to get revenge on Andre. And she's probably going to get herself killed in the process.

"We have to find her," Ezra says, fear in his eyes.

"How?" I say.

"She says she knows where Andre is," Gabriel says. "If we can figure out what she apparently did, we can track her."

"Her phone was left in her room," Darren says. "It shows she's been receiving phone calls from an unknown number for the last couple days. Calls last anywhere from one to fifteen minutes."

"Can we track those?" I ask.

"Not after the fact," Jessie says over my shoulder. "Not on *her* phone. Yours and Gabe's are the ones that are constantly monitored, always recording."

"Dammit." I draw my knees up. "Okay, thanks, Darren. You guys take a look around for any other clues and then head back. We need to talk about what to do."

"I can't believe she did this," Ezra says after I hang up. "I mean, we talked about that bastard getting what he deserved, but I didn't think she was going to do something this crazy."

"You and Kaylen talked about revenge?" I say. "Ezra…"

"Gawd, Wen. Don't lecture me. It was right after it happened. We were all in total shock, horrified that anyone would do twisted crap like that to anyone, let alone Uncle Rob. What did you expect us to talk about? Having faith that Karma would do its job?"

"You're right, Ezra," Gabriel says. "We all pondered revenge, if only for a moment."

"But Kaylen obviously wasn't just talking," I say.

"At this point we need to determine our next move," Gabriel says.

"We do exactly what she said to do," Mike's voice says, and I look up to see him leaning heavily on a crutch. He groans and puts a hand to his injured side.

"You keep tottering around on that one crutch and it's never going to heal," Gabriel says.

Mike lowers himself gingerly into a seat across the aisle without a comeback. He's been awfully docile around Gabriel. It's like the two have exchanged places. Mike is more at peace, more in control, and Gabriel is always the one grumbling and making caustic remarks toward Mike. Gabriel's troubled still, but I haven't had a moment to address it. The Haricott empire calls. And Ohr calls. And the world calls. And now Kaylen has made her independence known at the worst possible time.

"Kaylen can handle herself," Mike continues.

"But she's only—oh wait. She's eighteen now," I say.

"So technically she's an adult," Mike says. "She made a choice. You can't chase her down and make her come home."

"She's going to get herself killed going after Andre," I protest.

"Again. Adult. And she's also ballsy when it counts. I saw the footage from the mall in Monterey. She's a lamb and a lion. A lot less… ethically torn about protecting her own than, say, you."

I scowl at Mike.

"I wish she'd have taken me with her at least. So she wouldn't be alone," Ezra says. "What are we going to do?"

That is definitely the question of the day. We've got an extensive agenda, and though I'm scared for Kaylen, tracking her down and begging her to come back isn't necessarily the best course of action. I close my eyes, bite my lip, suppress overprotective Wendy and embrace grown-up Wendy who has some years of experience, who has done things other people saw as irresponsible or perilous. I came out okay. Kaylen is allowed to choose and learn from her own path. That sounds like something Robert would say, actually. And it makes me smile to know he rubbed off on me enough that I'm starting to think like him.

"We're going to do what Kaylen asked us to do," I say. "She'll find her way back."

I look at Ezra, knowing he will likely be the most torn about that decision.

"She needs this," Ezra says with a lot more conviction than I would have guessed. "She—well let's just say she's been having a hard time feeling needed. She's smart. But still cautious. And Mike's right. She's not afraid to…" He looks at me with a slight grimace. "Do what needs to be done," he finishes.

I'm just grateful I don't have to fight with Ezra. I nod at him and stand, look around for Mark. "Kalispell, I'm guessing?"

"Yes," Mark says. "Darren just arrived. We can be in the air in ten."

"Perfect," I say, sitting back down.

Gabriel chuckles. "I do love watching you work, Love."

"If you ever want to jump in, order a few people around, make some decisions, I would not be offended," I reply. I say it lightheartedly, but I mean it honestly, maybe a little pleadingly.

Sitting on the sidelines is not something Gabriel does, and he's been doing it nonstop since I got back. After Robert's death, when so many decisions started falling in my lap, I'd ask his opinion, and he'd say, "You're the show, Love. Robert rightfully trusted your judgment and so do I." Gabriel felt so confident when he'd tell me that, so I've had to believe he meant it. I'm allowing him the space to grow, to change into whatever is going to allow him to be at peace with his connection to Mike, but I miss his powerful, purposeful presence at my side.

His response this time is to reach over and squeeze my hand.

I look over at him. "I love you," I say. I touch Robbie's sleeping head. "I love both of you."

"We're lucky men," he says, but I catch an edge of sorrow behind the words.

I'm about to ask him to talk to me, but Darren bounds onto the plane, hands laden with pizza boxes, Louis behind him carrying trays of full Styrofoam cups.

I look questioningly at Mark. Did he order pizza? He always okays things like that with me first.

"Where did that come from?" Mark says, stepping toward Darren.

Darren stops short. "You didn't order pizza?"

I come to my feet. "Are those milkshakes?" I say disbelievingly. Louis glances from the cups to my face and I know I'm right.

"Ohr sent them," I say, crossing my arms and shaking my head. "Put them on the table, Darren."

"Is it okay to eat, do you think?" Mark says under his breath to me.

I shrug. "Probably. But someone can be the guinea pig if you want. If he spiked them, I doubt it's with something lethal."

"Oh man, Ohr knows good pizza," Ezra says.

I look over to see him shoveling down a slice.

"There's your guinea pig," Mark mumbles to me.

"Ezra!" I protest. "We get pizza from the enemy and you don't even pause before dumping it down the hatch?"

"Oh please," Ezra garbles through a full mouth, selecting one of the milkshakes. "Enemies don't give out trade secrets…"

"Trade secrets? About the Invisibles?" I say. "Ohr had to give me a good reason why he hasn't found Andre. I don't know if he was telling the truth."

"They don't send you one of their special neurologists to wake up one of your bodyguards from a coma…" Ezra fires back.

"I traded his stupid Grid spokes for helping Farlen," I reply. "What else was I going to do with them?"

"They don't send you pizza and milkshakes…" Ezra says.

"And they don't send you the cure to your diabetes," Mike says, staring down into one of the pizza boxes.

"What!?" I leap to my feet, coming next to Mike to find three vials and syringes packed securely in one of the pizza boxes. Instructions included. "Dang…" I whisper, touching one of the vials.

Carl sighs. "You're giving him what he wants, Wendy. He wants to make sure you keep it up. You work for him and you don't even know it."

"Old crusades never really die, do they, old man?" Ezra says. "Give it up."

I look to Mike for his opinion.

"What're you asking me for?" he says.

"Because you're from the Guild."

"Not anymore, bonita," he says, patting the top of my head. "I'm retired."

"Miiike!" I whine. "You're my intel guy!"

He grabs a slice of pizza. "Fine. My opinion is that he definitely is trying to win you over. Who cares what for? If you keep your head, you can play it smart. You have the ear of the most powerful man in the world. Use it."

"Absolute power corrupts…" Carl says quietly in the background.

"Sage advice, brother," Gabriel says, taking a slice of his own. He looks at me now. "Let Ohr think you're working on his behalf. Slowly lead him where you want him."

"Well, well," I say, "who am I to differ with something the two of you actually agree on?"

Gabriel and Mike glance at one another and then back at me simultaneously. It kind of freaks me out how synchronous it is. Gabriel breaks it with, "Mike and I have always been formidable at tasks we choose to undertake together."

"We have," Mike agrees. "If only we could choose the same task more often."

"We do have the same task currently," Gabriel says, holding Mike's plate so he can limp to a seat with his crutch. "We both love Wendy. We want her to succeed at this mission."

The plane goes nearly silent.

"Awwwkward…" Ezra says.

After only a pause though, Mike laughs, "Elephants have a really hard time hiding in this family, don't they?"

"Psshh," Ezra says. "Our elephants are all colors of the rainbow and they always jump around and shout at people."

"In that case," Mike says, "I'm only sticking around this travelling circus because I owe Wendy. The rest of you can suck eggs."

"The truth is out!" Ezra says, throwing up a dramatic hand. "The anticipated season premier of Days of our Lives, Superhero Edition! Mike, life force donor to his brother, Gabe, will declare his love and his loyalties. Kaylen, trusted sister and friend, will seek revenge. And Wendy, new heiress to the Kingdom of Haricott, will nurture the trust of Ohr, the rivaling Prime Human big cheese. Can this band of outcasts come together for the cause of humanity? Be sure to tune in for this unforgettable episode!"

LOOK FOR BOOK 5 IN THE COLORWORLD SERIES:

DREAMWORLD

Visit the official site:

ColorworldBooks.com

To the Team:

Colorworld is an extraordinary story not just within the pages but outside of them as well. We're doing something that hasn't been done before, and that's literally traversing the United States and Canada to tell everyone we encounter about it while gathering a team of people with varying talents to help us. I did a quick count and came up with approximately 40 people that have been and are involved in casting their various talents directly into the Colorworld pot so that the story and message can be told in other dimensions. This is not how creatives (especially artists) generally work, in case you were wondering. It's against the grain. It defies the solitary nature of the creator.

But some guy dreamed this up (Not me, I'm one of those solitary creators), because he thought this story needed a lot more legs than just mine. That person is my husband. And interestingly, it was the rough draft of *Shadoworld* I was writing in early 2012 when my husband challenged me to set a date for publishing the very first book in this series, *Colorworld*.

Shadoworld found its feet, however, while being carried all over the midwest, east coast states, and Canada this year. It's been whispering to me in the cold, the hot, the hungry, the destitute, and through every single broken moment on this Colorworld Book Tour (#CWBT). I've wanted to quit. I really, really have. But as life would have it, I've had a lot of people out there watching me. They've fed my family. They've housed me when I can't take one more night in my RV. They've let me do laundry at their homes. They've paid for my gas. They've bought my books. They've bought this travelling circus breakfast, lunch, dinner, and snacks—and other random things to make my life easier while living full-time in an RV. You don't know how absolutely loved I've felt. You have no idea how many times I said to myself, "You can't quit. These people are counting on you. They're watching. Show them what can be done when you don't give up. You owe them every last ounce of yourself."

So thank you, my Fans. My friends. My friends that have become fans and my fans that have become friends. I'm not quitting. This tour belongs to you.

Thanks to Elissa Glover, for without her hospitality, Shadoworld would have grossly missed its deadline. Like, hideously.

And then there are the artists. Did you all know that most of our tour is paid for by other artists? Well it is. I can't say enough about them. I can't really express the humility that brings me to tears when I think of them and what they have done to feed my family, and to help the Colorworld story is extend to the far reaches of North America.

My copy editors, as always, deserve a big shout out:

Marie Zimmerly

Kristin Scadden South

Tiffany Thornton

The Colorworld Books Social Media Team brings the Colorworld story-behind-the-story to you on every social media outlet we get our hands on. They own this project too:

Kristin Scadden South

Angela Breeland

Bradley Kelly

Speaking of social media, I want to thank all of the people and organizations who have interviewed us over the past nine months. Social media doesn't work its magic without people to spread the word!

Finally, thank you to my husband. Work is the legacy of our romance. Maybe that seems precisely not romantic, but work is who we are individually, as people. So it's fitting that it would be the thing we want to share most with one another. We met at work. We've been in various businesses together ever since. We are and have always been our best married selves when we are working side-by-side as much as humanly possible. The Colorworld Book Tour works because Brad and I work. We thrive on being together, twenty-four hours a day, seven days a week. I'm absolutely convinced Brad loves me better than any man in history has ever loved a woman. He's my guy. He's *the* guy. When the rubber hits the road, Brad is the accelerator. Everything that is most beautiful about this series was inspired by the beauty of my own love story with this man. And that's not fiction.

64129942R00281

Made in the USA
Lexington, KY
29 May 2017